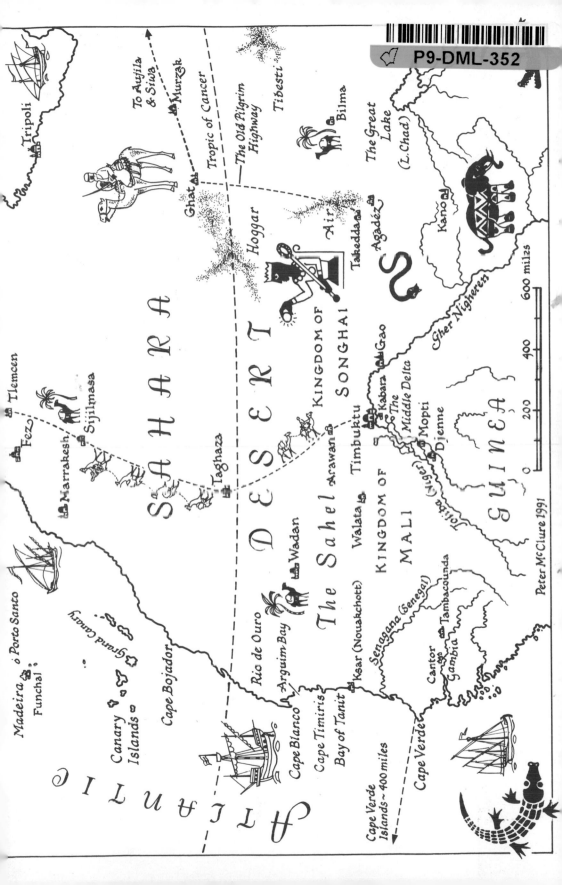

ATLANTIC

Tripoli

To Aujila & Siwa
Murzak
Tibesti
Bilma

Tropic of Cancer
The Old Pilgrim Highway
The Great Lake
(L. Chad)

Ghat
Hoggar
Air
Agadez
Takedda
Kano

SAHARA DESERT

Tlemcen
Fez
Marrakesh
Sijilmasa
Taghaza

KINGDOM OF SONGHAI

Arawan
Timbuktu
Kabara Gao
The Middle Delta
Mopti
Djenne

The Sahel

Wadan
Walata
KINGDOM OF MALI

Rio de Ouro
Arguim Bay
Ksar (Nouakchott)

Cape Blanco
Cape Timiris
Bay of Tanit

Senagana (Senegal)
Cantor
Gambia
Tambacounda

GUINEA

Madeira ó Porto Santo
Funchal
Canary Islands
Grand Canary

Cape Bojador

Cape Verde
Cape Verde Islands ~ 400 miles

Joliba (Niger)
Gher Nigheres

0   200   400   600 miles

Peter McClure 1991

F
DUN
Dunnett, Dorothy

Scales of gold

48258

$23.50

ALSO BY DOROTHY DUNNETT

The Game of Kings
Queens' Play
The Disorderly Knights
Pawn in Frankincense
The Ringed Castle
Checkmate
King Hereafter

Dolly and the Singing Bird (Rum Affair)
Dolly and the Cookie Bird
Dolly and the Doctor Bird
Dolly and the Starry Bird
Dolly and the Nanny Bird
Dolly and the Bird of Paradise (Tropical Issue)
Moroccan Traffic

Niccolò Rising
The Spring of the Ram
Race of Scorpions

The Scottish Highlands
(in collaboration with Alastair Dunnett)

The House of Niccolò

Scales of Gold

Dorothy Dunnett

ALFRED A. KNOPF *New York* 1992

THIS IS A BORZOI BOOK
PUBLISHED BY ALFRED A. KNOPF, INC.

Copyright © 1992 by Dorothy Dunnett
All rights reserved under International and Pan-American Copyright Conventions.
Published in the United States by Alfred A. Knopf, Inc., New York.
Distributed by Random House, Inc., New York.

Library of Congress Cataloging-in-Publication Data
Dunnett, Dorothy.
Scales of gold / Dorothy Dunnett. — 1st American ed.
p.   cm. — (The House of Niccolò)
ISBN 0-394-58627-1
1. Fifteenth century—Fiction.   2. Belgium—
History—To 1555—Fiction.   I. Title.   II. Series:
Dunnett, Dorothy.   House of Niccolò.
PR6054.U56S33   1992
823'.914—dc20   91-58554
CIP

Manufactured in the United States of America
First American Edition

Characters

May, 1464 – July, 1468
(Those marked * are recorded in history)

Rulers
*Flanders: Duke Philip of Burgundy; Duke Charles, his son
*Venice: Doge Cristoforo Moro
*England. King Edward IV, House of York (Henry VI, House of Lancaster, imprisoned)
*Scotland: King James III
*France: King Louis XI
*Popes: Pius II, Paul II
*Milan: Duke Francesco Sforza; Galeazzo Sforza, his son
*Cyprus: King James de Lusignan (Zacco)
*Portugal: King Alfonso V, nephew of Henry the Navigator
*Ottoman Empire: Sultan Mehmet II
*Aragon, Spain: King John II, uncle of Ferrante of Naples
*Castile, Spain: King Henry
*Ethiopia: Emperor Zara Ya'qob

House of Niccolò:
IN VENICE AND BRUGES:
Nicholas vander Poele (Niccolò), son of the first wife of Simon de St Pol
Gregorio of Asti, lawyer
Margot, Gregorio's mistress
Father Godscalc of Cologne, chaplain and apothecary
Loppe (Lopez), former Guinea slave
Julius of Bologna, notary
Cristoffels, manager, seconded to the Charetty company
John (Jannekin) Bonkle, bastard of Edward Bonkle of Edinburgh

UNDER CONTRACT ABROAD:
Tobias Beventini of Grado, physician
Astorre (Syrus de Astariis), mercenary commander
Thomas, English captain, in Cyprus
John le Grant, engineer and shipmaster, in Cyprus

SEAMEN, THE GUINEA VOYAGES:
Jorge da Silves, Portuguese master of the *San Niccolò*
Vicente, first mate of the *San Niccolò*
Melchiorre Cataneo, ex *Ciaretti*, second mate of the *San Niccolò*
Estêvão, helmsman of the *San Niccolò*
Fernão, helmsman of the *San Niccolò*
Luis, seaman on the *San Niccolò*

Filipe, boy on the *San Niccolò*
Lázaro, boy on the *San Niccolò*
Vito, ex *Ciaretti*, seaman-carpenter on the *San Niccolò*
Manoli, ex *Ciaretti*, seaman on the *San Niccolò*
Triadano of Ragusa, master of the *Ciaretti*
Ochoa de Marchena, Spanish master of the *Ghost/Doria*

Flanders and the Duchy of Burgundy:
THE CHARETTY COMPANY:
Mathilde (Tilde) de Charetty, daughter of Marian, late first wife of Nicholas
Catherine, her younger sister
Henninc, dyeworks manager in Bruges

OTHER FAMILIES IN FLANDERS AND BURGUNDY:
*Henry van Borselen, seigneur of Veere
Florence van Borselen, half-brother of Henry
Gelis van Borselen, younger daughter of Florence
Henry (Arigho) de St Pol, child of the late Katelina, sister of Gelis
*Wolfaert van Borselen, son of Henry van Borselen
*Mary his wife, aunt of James III of Scotland
*Alexander, Duke of Albany, her nephew, brother of James III
*Paul van Borselen, bastard son of Wolfaert
*Louis de Gruuthuse, merchant nobleman
*Marguerite van Borselen, his wife
*Tommaso Portinari, manager, Medici company in Bruges
*Benedetto Dei, Medici agent and merchant
*Antony of Bourbon, bastard of Duke Philip
*Baudouin, his half-brother
*Sir Simon de Lalaing, seigneur of Santes
*Ernoul de Lalaing, his son
*Anselm Adorne of the Hôtel Jerusalem
*Margriet van der Banck, his wife
*Anselm Sersanders, his nephew
*Jehan Metteneye, host to the Scots merchants
*Colard Mansion, scribe and illustrator
*Bartolomeo Giorgio (Zorzi), merchant of Pera and Cyprus

Republic of Venice:
*Marietta Barovier, glassmaker of Murano
*Alvise da Ca' da Mosto, merchant explorer
*Antonio da Ca' da Mosto, his brother
*Marco Corner, merchant, sugar-grower in Cyprus
*Fiorenza of Naxos, his wife
*Catherine, his daughter
*Giovanni (Vanni) Loredano, deputy Bailie in Cyprus
*Valenza of Naxos, his wife
*Caterino Zeno, merchant
*Violante of Naxos, his wife
*Paul Erizzo, Venetian Bailie in Cyprus
*Anne, his daughter
*Piero Bembo, merchant
*Bessarion (John) of Trebizond, Cardinal Patriarch of Constantinople
*Alessandro di Niccolò Martelli, Medici company
*Alvise Duodo, galley commander and merchant

The families of St Pol (Scots) and Vasquez (Portuguese):
Jordan de St Pol, vicomte de Ribérac
Simon de St Pol of Kilmirren, his son
Lucia, sister of Simon and widow of Tristão Vasquez
Matten, her maid
Isobella (Bel) of Cuthilgurdy, her Scots companion
Diniz, son of Lucia and the late Tristão Vasquez
*Sir João Vasquez, secretary to the Duchess of Burgundy and "uncle" to Diniz
Jaime, factor of the St Pol estate at Ponta do Sol
Inêz, his wife

Republic of Florence:
*Cosimo di Giovanni de' Medici
*Piero de' Medici, his son and successor
*Alessandra Macinghi negli Strozzi, widow
*Lorenzo di Matteo Strozzi of Naples, her son

The Vatachino Company and Associates (Genoese):
*David de Salmeton, broker, merchant and agent
Martin, broker, merchant and agent
Raffaelo Doria, commander of the *Fortado*
Tati, his servant girl
Michael Crackbene, ex *Doria*, sailing-master of the *Fortado*
*Urbano Lomellini, Genoese plantation owner, Madeira
*Baptista Lomellini, his brother
*Gilles Lomellini, host to Genoese merchants in Bruges
*Prosper Schiatfino de Camulio de' Medici, former envoy of Milan

Kingdom of Portugal:
*Diogo Gomes, former sea captain, Treasurer of Palace of Sintra
*Zarco, Captain of the Funchal region of Madeira

Princes of Guinea:
*Zughalin, Jalofo King of the Senagana
*Gnumi Mansa, under-King in the Gambia
*Bati Mansa, under-King in the Gambia

Muslims of Guinea:
Saloum ibn Hani, marabout, freed Mandingua interpreter
Ahmad al-Qali, freed captive and guide
*Muhammed ben Idir, prince and Timbuktu-Koy
*Umar, his son and successor
*Akil ag Malwal, Maghsharen Tuareg commander
*And-Agh-Muhammed al-Kabir, Qadi and scholar
*al-Mukhtar, Muhammed and Ahmed, scholars, his sons
*Muhammed Aqit, judge and scholar
*Katib Musa, of the imamate of Sankore
Abderrahman ibn Said, merchant of Timbuktu
Jilali and Mustapha, his brothers
(Umar ibn Muhammad al-Kaburi)
Zuhra, his wife

The House of Niccolò

Nicholas vander Poele q.v. — 2) 1460 ≈ Marian 1441 1) Cornelis de Charetty
1420~1461 — 1400~1458
(b.1410)

1465-4 ≈ 2) Primaflora (origin unknown)

Michelle 1441 ≈ 2) Thibault 1) 1411 ≈ Josine
— Vicomte de Fleury of Dijon — b.1398
(b.1393)

Jordan de St.Pol Vicomte de Ribérac 1424 ≈ Alice Shaw
(b.1407)

Alan de St.Pol Kt. Lord of Kilmirren 1405~1460

Elizabeth de St.Pol 1410~1431

Esota ≈ Jaak de Fleury d.s.p. 1466 1409~1460

Adelina b.1442

Sophie 1912~1947 1440 ≈ 1) Simon de St.Pol ≈ 2) 1460 Katelina van Borselen 1440~1464
(b.1425)

Gelis van Borselen St.Pol (b.1430)

Lucia de Vasquez 1420~1463 1445 ≈ Tristão

(b.1445)

Diniz Vasquez b.1446

Henry 'de St.Pol' b.1461

Felix 1442~1460 — Mathilde (Tilde) b.1447 — Catherine b.1448

Nicholas vander Poele b.1440

Marian de Charetty 1) q.v. 1463-4 2) ≈ Primaflora q.v. 1460 ≈ Nicholas vander Poele b.1440

Henry 'de St.Pol' q.v. (assumed heir of Simon de St.Pol)

Chapter 1

To those who remembered him, it was typical that Nicholas should sail into Venice just as the latest news reached the Rialto, causing the ducat to fall below fifty groats and dip against the écu. Instead of leading the welcome party, Gregorio sent Cristoffels to St Mark's Basin instead, with a group of senior officials who didn't know Nicholas. He hoped Cristoffels remembered what his employer looked like.

The word, of course, had spread to the Exchange that vander Poele's ship had passed the bar and was on its way to the anchorage. In the midst of the flurry – affirming deals, sending off couriers with drafts and remittances – Gregorio suffered snatches of good-humoured banter. For more than two years he had run the Bank of Niccolò in place of its founder, and his fellow lawyers and brokers liked to claim he lived in dread of the coming accounting. It might have been funnier if it hadn't, in its way, been correct.

He had posted a couple of runners between St Mark's and the Rialto. When the cry came from the Bridge, he was reasonably ready to leave. It meant only that the ship's boat from the *Adorno* had reached the Foscari bend, and he could still achieve the Bank building before it. The Grand Canal was a long, busy waterway lined with palaces; and the roundship's crew, long at sea, would scarcely speed with a heavy craft laden with luggage.

Nevertheless, Gregorio went immediately to the Bridge, throwing instructions to a scurrying junior. It was too hot for his doublet and gown, even considering the occasion; even considering what Margot thought about it. He let his servant, trotting, button him into his pourpoint and shed his clerk at the steps, although he turned to call after him: '*And remember, purchase at usance!*' Then he fought to the rail at the top of the drawbridge and paused for a sight of the Grand Canal stretching before him.

The sun, admitted tax-free between the palaces of two of his clients, struck the water and blinded him. He pulled down the brim of his hat until it met his unhandsome nose, and trained his middle-aged eyes, which were thirty-two like the rest of him, on the confusion of intermeshed oars belonging to passenger skiffs, heavy barges and lighters, vessels laden with fish and with vegetables passing up and down and across on their daily purposes. A two-pole gondola came towards him, gilded and tasselled and managed by liveried Negroes wearing the badge of the family Loredano. It slid under the Bridge, making way for a jolting boatful of overnight revellers in carnival mantles and masks. They passed, screaming into the dazzle.

Beyond them stood his Bank, a third of the way between the Bridge and the bend. His Bank, his office, his warehouse, his home. The Casa di Niccolò, all now to reside in the hands of a man whose script on the outside of a letter-packet made him feel faint.

He should hurry. Clattering down the far side of the Bridge, Gregorio turned right and set off quickly along his own bank, striding up and down bridges and passing between the rocking gondolas and noble façades of the richest side of the richest highway in Venice. Glancing from time to time at the canal, he saw some altercation had jammed it. He had seldom seen its traffic so thick or so sluggish. He slackened his pace. Nothing was going to row very fast at this rate.

Now he could see the jutting edge of his Bank, its red and white patterned wall washed over with light from the side-canal and a crowd grouped on the Grand Canal frontage before it. His household and clerks, out to catch a first glimpse of their master.

Margot wouldn't be there, she would be watching upstairs on the balcony. Margot, to whom he was not married and whom he would trust before anyone, had read the last reports written by Nicholas before sailing to Venice from Cyprus. In these Nicholas had set down, for the eye of his lawyer alone, his private reasons for leaving the island. They had been brief, and contained neither excuse nor apology. Nor had he indicated what he intended to do once he reached Venice. Gregorio, much disturbed, didn't know what to expect of this meeting.

He did intend, however, to arrive first at the Bank. It looked as if he would. The mooring posts before the double doors of the Ca' Niccolò were still empty; he had had his freight vessels moved round to the side. He had also sent a few extra men to the Basin. Robbers were not very likely, but Nicholas had achieved notorious success for himself and his Bank while in Cyprus. In business, Nicholas was unerring, and merciless, if not caught in time.

And now he was here. The great boat from the roundship was

suddenly visible: an ugly, well-painted vessel, low in the water with coffers and men, and lying athwart the crowded canal as it waited to cross to its mooring. The rowers were the *Adorno*'s own marines, dressed in caps and clean tunics. Packed among them were the Bank's envoys, and servants.

Distinguishable from them all were the two principal passengers, seated aft and robed as for the elaborate charade of their landing. One he knew at once by his colour and size: *Loppe*, by God! Lopez, the gifted African who managed what could be managed in Nicholas's aberrant life, including his sugar estates.

And the other, his equal in towering brawn, was Nicholas vander Poele, Flemish merchant, shading his eyes as he scanned the congestion. The sun flashed on a ring at his knuckle.

He had made some concessions to heat: his short coat was of silk, and his twisted headgear, concealing all but some tufts of brown hair, was stitched from the thinnest of linen. His face below it was baked brown and smooth as a biscuit and his eyes, grossly large, gave his concentrated gaze an aspect of innocence which the curve of his lips contradicted. Gregorio, standing in shade, thought to call and then didn't. Lopez sat, looking about him and once, Gregorio noticed, leaned to murmur to Nicholas, who glanced briefly upwards.

The oars idled, unable to progress. Watermen shouted. The cause of the blockage, abruptly revealed, proved to be a single craft ineptly managed upstream, its passage marked by the drumming of timber and a chorus of curses accompanied by outbursts of bibulous laughter. A boatload, it appeared, of shouting, carolling revellers, its sides furrowed and scraped, its oars scarred, its bow and blades gouging for it a battering passage. As it rampaged through the water, the sun glinted on a handful of fur and a mask.

It was the carnival boat he had noticed. The situation of the ducat in relation to the groat and the mark abandoned its place in Gregorio's consciousness.

The *Adorno*'s boat, in midstream, waited with whatever patience men had, within sight of the end of a voyage. Nicholas looked about him, listening to Lopez, and stooping to grope for some possession or other beneath him. The festive boat blundered closer, and those endangered hastened, with shouts, to move further off. With professional competence, the *Adorno*'s rowers dug in their oars and swung their great boat aside from its passage.

Now the party-goers were plain: the wide-brimmed black hats of the oarsmen, the painted chins and lurid masks of the twelve burly men they were carrying. The leader stood cloaked in the prow, one foot on the gunwale, one flamboyant fist cocked on its knee. On his

head was the mask of a goose and below the cloak his other hand,
like those of his comrades, was hidden.

It could not have been by chance that, this time, the carnival
craft suddenly found the application and skill to avoid every boat
in its path. It was not by chance that, instead of stumbling from
vessel to vessel, it adroitly slipped through each watery space until,
conducted smoothly and well, it came shooting suddenly forward,
the ramming prow aimed straight for the laden ship's boat from
Cyprus.

Gregorio's shout was one of a chorus of warning. The mariners
dug in their oars, changing angle to lessen the impact. The expected
crash didn't come. Just before the two boats collided, the pursuing
oarsmen feathered their blades. The masked figure bent down,
and, lifting something heavy and small, threw it hard. It fell within
the ship's boat, clicked and held. It was a grappling iron. As the
two boats whipped together, the man in the goose mask threw
himself from his own boat to the other, and his companions followed.

Gregorio saw the mariners half rise and stagger; saw Cristoffels
and the rest use their fists, saw the flood of revellers pour down the
big vessel, fending off blows, to where the coffers were piled. The
boat rocked. At the farthest end, Lopez sprang to his feet. Nicholas
gathered what he was holding and rose, his right arm drawing
painfully back. In his grasp was a bow, short and ornate and
powerful, its arrow trained on the leader.

He said, 'Turn back your cloaks, and drop your weapons into
the water.'

The man in the goose mask cried out. He screamed, 'Monseigneur,
don't shoot! Wait! Have mercy! My lords, we beg for our lives!' With
frantic hands he unfastened his cloak, his gaze piteous. Hastily he cast
off the garment and lifting the object he bore, extended it trembling to
Nicholas. Then, with a whistle of devilish laughter, he tossed it aloft.

It hung, with the eyes of everyone on it: a carnival wand made of
paper, with a grotesque, gilded head at one end. Then it began to
descend in a spiral of unravelling ribbon. Someone started to
laugh. Squealing, cackling and booing, the men in motley joined in
the hilarity and, thrusting their hands from their cloaks, each
produced an identical baton, brightly ribboned, with fantastic
knobs of goblins and dragons with which they set about slapping
their victims. They carried no weapons at all.

Around the two boats, a chuckle arose. On the other side of the
canal, people thrust forward to see what was happening, and faces
appeared at grand windows. On the open gallery of the Palazzo
Barzizza, directly opposite, there was a sudden, short movement.

Lopez said, 'Ser Niccolò.'

It was so brief and so quiet that Gregorio wouldn't have caught it except that all his attention was on them. The revellers continued to caper. Nicholas turned, the strung bow swinging through ninety degrees with him. The man in the goose mask had let down his points and was preparing a final, copious gesture.

The Negro stretched across Nicholas, and, seizing the man like a dribbling sack, lifted and set him down standing before them. The man, surprised, gave a howl. The floating audience, now on its feet, grasped one another and laughed, even when the man howled again. Then the laughter started to die as those closest saw his falling arms swing at the elbows, and blood cascade frothing and red from the slackening mouth under the mask. Driven hard through his chest was an arrow.

Lopez dropped to one knee, holding the body and pulling it free of Nicholas. The boarders stopped. In the moment's silence that followed the shock, Nicholas adjusted his aim, his gaze never leaving the highest, splendid tiered gallery of the merchant's house opposite. Then he released his fingers and shot.

Far across the canal someone screamed, the sound speaking from wall to wall of the palaces. The man who had been on the balcony opposite was there no longer, but his body, jerking forwards, was hurtling into the canal. There it sank, the shards of a bow floating upwards.

Then the air was filled with cries, from men and women and seagulls.

On the boat, the revellers dumbly recoiled and turning, scrambled back to the craft they had come from. The grapple jerked free and, seizing their looms, the oarsmen threw their boat sideways and into reverse, setting course for the basin and the wider waters of the lagoon, and leaving their leader behind them.

The boats which half-heartedly started to follow fell back. A ring of craft formed about Nicholas and, across the canal, a group of watermen sought about to retrieve the dead bowman. As the *Adorno*'s boat came to the bank, Gregorio saw the face of the unarmed reveller, bare of its mask. It was no one he knew. Nor, if they caught them, would the drunken boatload of boarders admit to anything, he supposed. They had carried no weapons. They had been decoys, that was all.

Something was bruising Gregorio's arm: Margot's fingers. 'I saw it,' she said. 'The man on the gallery was aiming at Nicholas.'

'I think so,' he said. 'Lopez had noticed him. Nicholas and he were both on guard; they expected it. But for that, no one would have known where, in the confusion, the arrow had come from.'

'Expected it?' Margot said. She was pale, from shock and from running. 'Expected an attack on his life? On his homecoming?'

Gregorio didn't answer. She had read that letter from Cyprus, as he had. They should have realised what it meant. He watched the big boat coming near and said, 'Lopez. He will stay here. It must be made perfectly clear to the household –'

'It will be,' Margot said.

The boat berthed. Nicholas stepped ashore and smiled at them all. He said, 'Welcome home. I thought I should perhaps say it for you. Gentlemen, I do beg your pardon. If you'll give me leave to settle affairs with the Magistrate – Goro, will you come with me? – then I shall be delighted to come back at leisure and meet you. Don't, on any account, delay your dinner.'

The water was still full of boats, and people exclaiming. Across the canal, men and vessels were clustered beneath the Palazzo Barzizza. A dead man lay in the boat at his feet. Gregorio could see the official craft approaching between them. He said, 'Your clothes . . .'

'Blood, I know,' Nicholas said. 'I paid a lot for this coat. I wanted to make an impression.'

A cursory dent appeared in one cheek and then vanished. It was meant perhaps to signal distress, masked by a kind of grim humour. Without an accompanying glance, it looked merely indifferent.

Under the coat, his doublet turned out to be clean. He threw the stained garment to his servant and turned, adjusting his expression, to deal with the Magistrate. Gregorio said, 'Do you know who it was?'

'Oh, I should think so,' Nicholas said. 'But I shan't say if you don't.'

Later, returning with Nicholas to the Bank, Gregorio thought to count his blessings, which amounted after consideration to one. There would be no prosecution.

Nicholas, who could always act, had acted with awful aplomb. Who wished for his death? He feared – the enemies of the Venetian Republic. There were those who, whatever their oaths, hesitated to join the Serenissima in her crusade against the infidel Turk. He laid no personal blame on the Duke of Burgundy or on France, although today's news must shake the credit of every bank, and not only his own. Neither would he point to the city of Genoa, which might resent a soldier and merchant whose deeds served the nobler Republic. Indeed, he saw here no Christian crime. The name of Niccolò vander Poele was well known to be cursed by the Infidel.

Gregorio, at this point, had swallowed. The Magistrate, on the other hand, had exclaimed, 'He used a Mameluke bow, the assassin!'

'Even here!' Nicholas said. He said it after a moment.

'. . . But of course he is unknown. He entered the Palazzo unseen. Nevertheless, you are right. Whatever his colour, the Egyptians have paid him. Didn't your army in Cyprus annihilate the entire Mameluke force in that island?'

'They died, certainly,' Nicholas said.

'And their leader, in single combat with yourself?'

'I did fight the Mameluke emir, it is true. I have his rather fine bow.'

'And you killed him?' The Magistrate was entranced.

'The King killed him. I cut off his arm. He had no further need of his bow as a consequence,' said Nicholas helpfully.

At this point, the Magistrate got up and insisted on shaking his hand. So did his secretary and one or two clerks. Something kindly was said about permits for weapons, and Nicholas was full of contrition. He had hesitated to apply. The Signory might consider he overvalued his services, to think himself endangered because of them. The Magistrate shook both hands, reassuring him.

Gregorio, who was feeling queasy, sat mute. He hardly opened his mouth for the rest of the interview. He might have found himself pointing out that nothing Nicholas had ever done had been intended for the profit of Venice. Venice had simply been lucky.

Returning in the official boat, Nicholas broke without hesitation into Flemish. 'You're all right? I can see Margot is. And the soul of discretion as usual. I thought you were about to explode.'

'Two deaths were enough,' Gregorio said. 'So what was really behind it? Not that farrago about the Genoese or the Burgundians or the French? Anyway, what do you know about the news from Burgundy?'

Escorting Nicholas were two armed men with the Lion of St Mark on their breastplates. The Magistrate had decided that Nicholas ought to be protected. He said, 'Come on, the dockyard always knows more than the Loggia. I heard as soon as I landed that the Duke had sent to beg off the papal crusade, and so the groat was bound to improve. Trading must have been at its wildest: I'm sorry.'

'It rose three on the ducat,' Gregorio said. 'I sent a courier to your newest office in Bruges. It's been quite inconvenient, your arrival. So who paid your assassin? Not the Sultan of Cairo, for God's sake?'

'Well, not for God's sake,' Nicholas said. 'I might be on his list, but Mamelukes prefer quieter quieti; it would be a stab or some poison. I rather favour a madman from Bruges, although I hear Simon isn't in Venice. Still, one of them could always have bribed some old loyal retainer. And of course, there are rival brokers. Has anyone tried to kill you of late?'

'I suffer from overwork and neglect,' Gregorio said, 'but apart from that, no. Our one vicious rival is presently confining itself to killing the business, or trying to. You had a taste of the Vatachino in Cyprus. Would they murder?'

'Their man in Cyprus wouldn't,' Nicholas said. 'Or not yet. They don't just want to get rid of us; they want to run rings round us beforehand. I'm not asking you what I want to ask you.'

'I noticed,' Gregorio said. 'I propose to make you wait until we are private. My – your staff are good men. They saw you. What are you going to tell them?'

'What do you think? Goro, they've been aching to have your life threatened. They long to be menaced. They want nothing more than to be the most hated Bank in Western Europe. I shall tell them that such is their power, the Signory's own men have been sent to protect them. To make their wills, and pray, and prepare to become a legend in their own lifetimes. I think we have arrived.'

They had. Gregorio disembarked, and slipped the boatmen some coins, and turned to do something about the Signory's bodyguard, such as send them down to the kitchens. He realized he was happy, and ravenous. He turned and found Nicholas on the wharf, gazing up at the face of his Bank, with its handsome balcony and tall Gothic windows.

It was the briefest of surveys, but it called to mind that Nicholas had barely seen the mansion before, and never in occupation. He had created the business and left. Whatever his homecoming had spoiled, it hadn't been the return to a home. He had none that Gregorio knew of, unless you counted an estate office in Cyprus. This building belonged to the Signory. And the house he had called home in Bruges had belonged to his wife, who was dead. It meant, as it turned out, that he could make himself at home instantly, anywhere.

It took him an hour to assimilate the Bank, from the entrance hall where Margot and Cristoffels received him to the third storey, where all the seniors but himself had their lodgings. Along with the geography of the Bank, he absorbed the people, from the clerks in the mezzanine counting-house to the men in the storerooms and warehouses, the boatmen at the wharves; the household servants indoors and out in the courtyard. He greeted many by name, and most with some obvious grasp of their duties.

It was not the magic it seemed: by every packet from Cyprus he had commanded this detail. The result, as he had foreseen, was to transform him at once from a symbol into a person. They were not going to like or respect him immediately, but the seeds had been sown; the easy manner barely touched with authority was perfectly judged. And, as he had divined, the events of the morning had done nothing to diminish his stature. He made light of his share, but hinted at the burdens borne by great institutions, whose success could shape kingdoms. They liked that.

It was the same in the counting-house after dinner when, alone with Cristoffels and Lopez, he and Gregorio went over the ledgers. It wasn't the tête-à-tête Gregorio had either hoped for or dreaded. At the end, Nicholas closed the last cover and said, 'Eighty thousand. We're still low on capital, aren't we? Because, I know, you've got the rest all out working. But the Republic isn't going to ease up on war taxes, and we're near the top of the list for her loans. You know I've been called to the Collegio tomorrow?'

'I wrote to you that they wanted a loan,' Gregorio said.

'So the Crusade is still going on?' Nicholas said. 'Without France or Burgundy, with the Pope at death's door?'

'You sailed past Ancona,' said Gregorio. 'The papal fleet's there, and the Pope is on his way to lead it. Every town is crammed full of soldiers waiting to join him. You must have seen them in Venice today. Spanish, Flemings, Germans, Sc –'

'Scots, of course,' Nicholas said. His face, across the short, laden table was shadowed, and the scar Jordan de Ribérac had given him sank into mild hollows. 'And if the Crusade doesn't happen? If the Pope dies, then Venice unaided has to sweep her own doorstep. In other words, find the means to keep her colonies free of the Turks. So what will she ask for? Ten thousand? Twenty? What can we stand?'

'You see what we have,' Gregorio said. 'What can you add to it?'

'Now I've stupidly walked out of Cyprus? Quite a lot,' Nicholas said. 'Ten thousand ducats a year from Loppe's sugar, and a quarter of that from other trading, courtesy of the new agents we've established in Alexandria and Damascus. You know about that. And let's say five thousand a year from half the army under Thomas and John, although that depends on the King, and on Cairo. Unfortunately, it all rather depends on the King's whim and Cairo, but I think we could count on two years of it.'

'Half the army?' said Gregorio. One of their successes had been a highly trained mercenary troop, born from Marian de Charetty's travelling bodyguard.

'Yes. Captain Astorre has the other half, and the doctor's gone with him. He was going to take a job here in Venice, until he heard who the commander-in-chief was. I thought I told you? You did get my last letter? I thought from your manner you must have.'

'Yes. Yes, I did,' Gregorio said.

'Well, I didn't mean you to forget *all* of it,' Nicholas said. 'So on top of what you expect, there's perhaps a net fifteen thousand in prospect from me plus, of course, what I've brought on the ship. I got cullet. You did lease the island, and the Strozzis sent in their man?'

'He's there,' Gregorio said. 'In a booth near the Baroviers'. And there's something else that will help. You asked about the ship that you lost.'

'The ship I had stolen,' Nicholas said. His face lightened. 'The Vatachino have paid the insurance?'

'In full. To the penny. For the loss of the ship and its rigging. For the loss of the contract you had with the King, and the trade it would have brought you. For the cargo it carried . . . Did it carry a cargo?'

'I'm sure it did,' Nicholas said. 'And they paid it? You have all the money?'

'All of it, although they tried very hard to avoid it. So they didn't run rings round you this time. In fact, the money's worth more than the roundship.'

'It would be nice to have both,' Nicholas said. 'Meantime, thank God, we do have a galley. You haven't told me where the *Ciaretti* is.' He waited. 'Goro? If she's sunk, I'll sink you with her.'

'She's in Ancona,' Gregorio said. 'Requisitioned for the Crusade. What do you think I could do to prevent it? It's lucky you've got the *Adorno* you came with.'

'Well, Great Jesus it would be, if she didn't need a full repair and refit,' Nicholas said. 'She got blown up in Cyprus, and we had to patch her with oakum and horse-glue. You mean we haven't a ship? I have to wait for the *Adorno* or hire one?'

Gregorio stared at him, sobered. He said, 'Does it matter? The Flanders galleys can take on your cargo.'

Nicholas gazed back at him, saying nothing. It came to Gregorio that, with Cristoffels there, there were matters they hadn't discussed, and that he had taken too much, it now seemed, for granted. He said slowly, 'You do mean to stay? You have come back to stay with the Bank?'

Like a ghost from the past, one dimple appeared, and then vanished. 'After what happened today?' Nicholas replied. 'I don't know. I'll tell you when I do. In a month's time, perhaps. I want you to take me to Murano tomorrow. Will Julius have arrived?'

'Julius?' Gregorio said. He recovered. 'You heard about that as well.'

'Didn't you want me to? Someone came on board who said there was a Bruges party on its way south. He remembered Julius from years ago. Why is he coming?'

When in doubt, tell the truth. Gregorio said, 'To see you, very likely. And, of course, business. I don't suppose he'll be here all that soon.'

Julius was the notary of the Charetty company of Bruges, which had once employed all of them. Julius would have few qualms about relating the gossip of Bruges to his former companions whom – even yet – he could hardly bring himself to take seriously. Julius could be a curse, or a blessing.

Gregorio hesitated. He said, 'You don't – you really don't know your ultimate plans?'

'My *ultimate* plans!' Nicholas said. 'Of course I know my *ultimate* plans. To become the richest man in the world; and fart in the face of the devil. Be sure to tell Julius, if you happen to see him before I do.'

Later, sitting alone with Gregorio, Cristoffels said, 'He is not the same as his letters. As clever, but not the same.'

'He has been travelling,' Gregorio said. 'You are remembering him as he was. He is older.'

He saw Cristoffels glance at him, and then smile. He had to smile back. Age was relative. Nicholas was twenty-three.

Chapter 2

JULIUS OF BRUGES, thumping into the Ca' Niccolò next day, pounded up the stairs to the private office and banged Gregorio on the back. Gregorio's quill split, and he got up. He said, 'You came. I didn't expect you so . . . Good.'

'You think I had any choice?' Julius said. He often envied Gregorio, getting his own way for two and a half years. But, of course, that had come to an end. He looked about. 'And very nice too. So what's going on? Where is he?'

'Nicholas went out early this morning,' Gregorio said. 'But Lopez is about; I'll get someone to call him. You look very fresh. Did you have a good journey? Who came with you?' Noticeably, he didn't say what was going on. He looked, Julius thought, a little distraught. Julius was amused but of course, didn't show it. He felt playful.

He said, 'I brought along Tilde de Charetty. She's sitting upstairs in your grand room with Margot. Your mistress and mine.' It was a joke. Mathilde de Charetty, having inherited the Charetty company from her mother, was the employer of Julius. She was seventeen years old and no one's mistress, as yet, in the other sense.

'So how does she feel about Nicholas?' Gregorio said, getting up and putting his doublet on. He called to someone as he opened the door. He looked really unhealthy. With Nicholas around, Julius wasn't surprised. It had been Gregorio's choice to leave the Charetty company and join Nicholas. The last time Nicholas had been in Bruges, Tilde and her sister had had him arrested.

Julius said, 'I told her she damned well had to be polite, but you'll never get her to trust him. All right, you came to Bruges and convinced her you could set up a branch without harming her. But now here's Nicholas back, with a reputation that would sicken a weasel. Can we rely on him to respect an agreement?'

'Yes,' said Gregorio.

'Well, that's reassuring,' said Julius tartly. He'd expected some help from Gregorio. They were of an age, and both lawyers. They had both been working for Tilde's mother's dyeworks in Bruges when Tilde's mother took a fancy to one of her apprentices and married him. And now the apprentice occupied his own three-storey well-furnished Bank on the Grand Canal by the Rialto. Here.

Gregorio said, 'I really can't tell you more: he only came back yesterday morning, and we've talked nothing but business. But Tilde and Catherine, after all, are his step-daughters. I'm sure he won't let them down.'

'Tell that to Tilde,' Julius said.

They went to tell it to Tilde. On the way, in between pricing the furniture, Julius learned that Nicholas had left before dawn for a series of meetings which (he gathered) might well last until nightfall. Nicholas would be compelled to see to his cargo, to report to the Signory, and to spend some time at the yard where his damaged roundship was being placed in dry dock. He had also (Gregorio said) sent to arrange several personal visits.

'I can guess where,' Julius said, though he couldn't. When Nicholas was a boy, the whole of Bruges always knew where to look for him, give or take a hayloft or two. Of course, he was out of the kitchen league now. Ruminating, not without some nostalgia, Julius climbed the staircase and found himself confronting Loppe, planted foursquare at the top like a tombstone. Julius seized and shook his hand, while Loppe's teeth and eyes shone. Until joining the Charetty company, Julius had never expected to find himself on any sort of terms with a Negro; but Loppe, of course, was unique. He hoped to God, again, that Tilde would behave herself. Gregorio opened the doors of the salon.

Both the women were there. Margot got up and came forward. No one had ever worked out how a man like Gregorio, with his pedantic style and scrag-end face and abysmal swordsmanship, could attract and keep a handsome woman like Margot. Julius, like everyone else, had tried to fathom why the two didn't marry, and had even asked two or three times, but without receiving much satisfaction. He could imagine several possible reasons. Julius himself, as it happened, was the result of an embarrassing slip by a celibate. He didn't know where Margot came from.

Mind you, youth counted for something and, even beside Margot, Tilde de Charetty didn't come off too badly. She had missed her mother's strong chestnut hair and high colour, but she was rounded all right where she should be, and her solemn expression suited the shape of her face, although her brow, like her temper, wrinkled too easily.

After Marian's death, Tilde had gone about in old-fashioned thick-folded robes, with her brown hair in tightly coiled plaits. As her manager, Julius had found it depressing. Recently, however, she had seemed to take stock, and sent her mother's costlier clothes to be remade. Today her hair rippled loose from a caul, and she had on an exceptional pendant and an overdress grand enough to be bridal. She had behaved remarkably well, too, on the journey: six weeks from beginning to end, with all the roads crowded, and snow and mud over the Alps.

Of course, she had travelled here from Flanders before, escorted that time by Gregorio. Now, she jumped up flushing as soon as the lawyer entered the room, and her expression changed to a smile. She had expected Nicholas, Julius saw. She had always blamed Nicholas for inducing her mother to marry him, and had a good deal more to blame him for now. That was why she was here. Concern for her trade was the least of it.

Gregorio looked pleased to see her as well. He took her hand in his old-fashioned way and said, 'Demoiselle, welcome to Venice. You look charming. We are all so happy to see you.' He didn't release her. He said, 'You remember Loppe? Now factor for all the Bank's sugar estates.'

The flush and the smile had been for the man who was kind to her when her mother died. Loppe was the slave elevated by her mother's apprentice. 'I remember him, of course,' Tilde de Charetty said. 'That old broker at Sluys had him before we did. It must be useful, being able to swim.'

Fortunately, in all the years Julius had known him, Loppe had never taken offence. He said, in his accentless Flemish, 'Buoyancy, demoiselle, is always an asset.' He had had command of five languages even when he first came to Bruges. He waited, and sat when Tilde did.

Tilde looked at Gregorio. 'Margot says you don't mind our coming?'

'No, of course not, although you've missed Nicholas. He'll call on you as soon as he can, that I promise. Where are you staying? With the Medici bankers again?'

'Yes. Margot seemed to think,' Tilde went on, 'that we might see Claes today. In a few minutes. When he steps in on his way to Murano. Perhaps we might go to Murano along with him?'

She had called Nicholas by his dyeyard name, and you could see Gregorio didn't much like it. Or perhaps it was the suggestion about Murano he didn't like. Julius found his interest sharpening.

Murano was an island one mile north of Venice. Why was Nicholas going there? He said venturesomely, 'A voyage? In this heat, what could be better? Unless, of course, we should be intruding?'

'Perhaps he has a wife there,' said Tilde de Charetty. 'Another wife. He seems very carnal by nature.' She sat, her hands in her lap and her eyes modestly on them.

Julius nearly laughed. Instead, he said hastily, 'We kept hearing gossip.'

'There was something, a matter of form,' said Gregorio. 'Nicholas has no ties at present. I don't really see why you shouldn't come with us to Murano. Nicholas and I have an appointment, but you could pass the time viewing the island. And you can exchange all your news on the way.'

'He's not in prison then?' said Tilde de Charetty.

Gregorio, rising to summon a servant, turned and stood still. 'No. Why should he be?'

'We heard about yesterday's killings. Didn't he kill someone yesterday? And these stories of what happened in Cyprus. You know. That's why we're here.'

Gregorio came back. He said, 'I thought you were here to make sure he respected your dyerights in Bruges.'

He's worried, Julius thought. He's not sure of Nicholas. But now he rather likes the idea of our meeting him. Why?

Tilde said, 'Tommaso Portinari says vander Poele has turned into a soldier and got a taste for killing, the way some people do.'

Like an extremely deep bell, the soft voice of Loppe contradicted her. 'I should not say so, demoiselle, and I was in Cyprus.'

Tilde turned her head. 'I thought you were on the sugar estates.'

'Then perhaps,' Loppe said, 'let me say that I was in the boat yesterday when the two men were killed. One was an assassin, and the other his hireling. Meester Nicholas shot one of them only, to preserve his own life.'

'And that is true,' Gregorio said. 'If you want to know more, Nicholas will tell you, I'm sure, when he comes. Meanwhile, I should much rather hear your adventures. Let me send for some wine, and perhaps something to eat.' He went again to the door.

'Well, thank you,' said Julius. 'But to return to the shooting. Who paid the assassin? Do you know?'

A servant appeared. Gregorio spoke to him before he replied. Then he said, 'It seems to have been an Egyptian. Someone from Cairo with a grudge against Nicholas.'

'Because of the massacre of the Mamelukes in Cyprus. We heard about it in Bruges,' said Tilde de Charetty. 'Claes. I couldn't believe it. Tommaso Portinari —'

'You heard in *Bruges?*' Gregorio said.

She looked at him in the way Julius knew all too well. She said, 'I told you, that's why we came. Because of the letters from Cyprus to everyone. I don't really think Nicholas will want to keep his Bruges bureau open now, do you?'

'Letters to whom?' Gregorio said. He came back and sat down.

'To virtually everyone. She's right,' Julius said. 'The Scots, the Portuguese, the van Borselen family. I'm not surprised Nicholas is afraid for his life. I'm only surprised a Mameluke got there first. I hope he's well guarded.'

Gregorio looked from Julius to Tilde. He said, 'And that really is why you're here, I suppose? If Nicholas dies, you'd like to know our contingency plans for the Bank?'

He sounded brusque. More interestingly, he hadn't asked who sent those informative letters from Cyprus to Flanders and Portugal. He didn't need to, Julius supposed. Everyone, including the insurers, knew who had stolen from Cyprus with the *Doria*, the Bank's missing roundship. Everyone knew that the letter-writer was the same person. 'It's nothing to do with us,' said Julius in a mollifying way, shaking his head several times in Tilde's direction.

Tilde said, 'But the Bank is rich, isn't it? If they kill Nicholas, Meester Gregorio, will you get all the money?'

There was the kind of pause that often followed Tilde's interventions. Then Gregorio said, 'All the founding members of the Bank possess shares. Those of Nicholas would go to his heirs. The names of these are his own concern, surely. And as it happens, he's quite well protected. I think you might even count on his survival.'

It was unlike Gregorio to be caustic with Tilde, but Julius couldn't blame him. The brat had come here, for sure, chiefly to witness the denunciation and downfall of Nicholas. But there was more to it than that. If Nicholas died without contriving to marry again, Tilde and her sister might have a very good claim to inherit.

Nicholas arrived half an hour later, bringing with him the heat of the May afternoon and, Julius supposed, an excellent briefing from Loppe, who had excused himself earlier. The doors opened. Tilde half rose and sat down. Julius got up and walked forward and found a reminiscent smile sliding on to his face. He said, 'You bastard, you look just the same.'

'How disappointing of me,' Nicholas said. 'Thriving on money, I suppose. How are you? And Tilde? You've caught me, I'm afraid, in a crisis. Would tomorrow be better? Or do you really want to come with me to Murano?' Julius stopped smiling.

Quite apart from that discouraging greeting, Nicholas did not, in fact, look quite the same. The stupendous brocade must have impressed the shipyard, if not the Palace. His hair had been brushed straight and compelled to stay that way under an expensive hat of fine straw. Below it, his face had the stretched look that comes after long travelling and dubious food. Julius, recently consulting his mirror, had noticed that he looked almost the same way himself.

It accounted also, Julius hoped, for the present attitude of high-handed detachment: not something Nicholas had ever been guilty of in the past. Half the time, in the old days, he appeared to be sitting inside your mind. Today, he showed no desire to come closer than spitting distance, even when he turned his attention to Tilde. His gaze, mild enough, reached her face by way of the stuff of her gown and her pendant. And Tilde, sustaining the survey, tilted her head and returned him a smile that made Julius wince.

Nicholas gave no sign at all that he noticed it. He said, 'It sets you off, as is perfectly fitting. I don't want to quarrel. We shan't do you any harm with our branch. I have nothing to do with dyes now.'

'I know. You lost the royal dyeworks in Cyprus, didn't you?' Tilde remarked. 'To the Vatachino. Julius says the Vatachino are going to be the big new power in trade.' If you looked closely, you could see she was breathless.

'Everyone in business has a frightening story about the Vatachino,' Julius said quickly. 'They've got a foothold in Bruges, and they're into every damned thing.'

'Especially dyes. Perhaps you ought to be watching them instead of me,' Nicholas observed, still very mildly.

'Julius isn't refining sugar like you are,' Tilde said. 'Julius thinks we should stick to our business. The Vatachino must have cost you quite a bit, this last year or two.'

'It's kind of you to be worried,' said Nicholas. 'But I have tried to hold my own. Would you forgive me? I must get out of this rig before going.'

Julius always appreciated it when Nicholas made a mistake. He said, 'Yes, we heard how you were holding your own. You tricked the Vatachino into insuring our old friend the *Doria* before the old man sailed it out of Cyprus with Crackbene. I hope to God you're not going to Portugal after it? Or maybe you don't need to. Did the grasping devils pay up?'

'They paid up,' said Nicholas. 'Margot, will Tilde need some sort of head covering? It's not a long way, but we've a barge to tow with us. Suppose we leave as soon as we can?'

'. . . Because you know who is waiting in Portugal,' Julius continued, cheerfully unrelenting. 'The old man sent letters about you. The widow's there, and her son. The girl's family are going, from Bruges. I've got a letter for you from her husband.'

He fumbled for it in his purse, while trying not to miss any reaction. He could never understand how Nicholas hid what he was thinking. My God, he must have come all the way from Cyprus knowing that Simon was the first person he'd hear from. He found the packet and handed it over, expecting Nicholas to open it, or walk off to read it. Instead he said, 'Why not tell me what's in it? You know already, I'm sure.'

'Well, you can imagine,' Julius said. Gregorio was glaring at him, and that pretty woman didn't look very pleased. He cleared his throat. 'Not knowing any different, they do blame you for everything. They say they will deal with you here if they have to –'

'Deal with me?'

'Kill you. They will come to Venice if need be, but they would prefer you to come west and face them.'

'They?'

'The bereaved families,' Julius said.

'Oh. One by one or all together?' Nicholas asked. He glanced at the hour-glass.

Julius said, 'The old man likes to lay his own traps. His son is the lad who'll come after you. Really, you'd better explain. Whatever you tell them, we'll back you.'

'So Simon has challenged me,' Nicholas said. He still held the letter unopened.

'You killed his wife,' Tilde de Charetty said. 'You killed his sister's husband. You imprisoned his father and nephew, and you would have killed them as well if they hadn't escaped.' Margot got up and put an arm round her shoulders. The girl trembled.

'On the Bank's very own ship. Well, they got their own back,' Nicholas said. 'I take it you don't want to come to Murano? I'm enjoying the talk, but it is getting late.'

'You're not answering?' the girl blurted out. Margot's hand tightened.

'You didn't ask me anything,' Nicholas said.

'She was wrong to ask you,' said Julius. 'But –'

'She was wrong to ask me,' Nicholas said. 'This is my house, and this is something I will not at present discuss. I should have thought the reasons were obvious. If you think you can talk about something else, I shall be delighted to have your company. Excuse me, if you will, while you think about it.'

In the end they went to Murano, largely because Tilde, although shaken, was determined, and nothing, really, would have stopped Julius. Waiting while Nicholas changed, and Margot took Tilde to her chamber, Julius strolled with Gregorio to the landing-stage. He said, 'Do *you* know what happened?'

'In Cyprus? I know what happened, but not why it happened. I don't know why he won't explain either, but he always has reasons: I'm not going to push him.'

'Perhaps you don't want to know,' Julius said. He waited, and then said, 'It affects the Bank. Rumours.'

Gregorio said, 'Of course he knows that. Otherwise he wouldn't have written to me. He's said he'll decide in four weeks if he's leaving. I'm willing to wait until then.'

Julius said, 'I hear a whisper that he's taken an island.' He didn't say how he knew.

'It doesn't mean he's going to stay,' Gregorio said. 'He has a factor and two fiefs in Cyprus. He's free to go anywhere.' He paused. He said, 'Would it be breaking a confidence to tell me what was in the letter from de Ribérac's son?'

'Breaking a confidence!' Julius said. 'He wanted me to read it aloud as he wrote it, and make copies for Catherine and Tilde. That letter was written in sulphur.' He fell silent a moment, remembering.

Gregorio said, 'It was his wife who died. The worst thing that could possibly happen. Nicholas and this violent man, at war with each other for years. And now this.'

Julius said, 'If Nicholas told me he had nothing to do with the death of Simon de St Pol's wife, I think I should believe him. So why doesn't he? The wretched man is convinced it was part of some great murderous scheme to leave him a widower, and that his only child will be the next victim. The grandfather thinks so as well. They've even sent the boy off to some hiding place.'

'They don't usually agree, Simon and Jordan de Ribérac,' said Gregorio absently.

'This time, they do,' Julius said. 'By God, they do. Although it was apparently all the old man could manage to prevent Simon from coming straight here to turn our wealthy young friend into pigfood. Instead, they've sent him this letter.'

'Which says what?' Gregorio said.

'Wouldn't you prefer to read it?' said Nicholas, appearing briskly. He tossed the paper, open, towards Gregorio, who caught it just before it reached the canal.

Nicholas said, 'It's not very newsy. It gives me two options. I can remain here and die a bankrupt poltroon, killer of women and gentlefolk. Or, if I wish to call myself a man, I am invited to pursue my lord Simon in his various homes and places of business and be prepared to meet my match in both areas. It doesn't sound very enticing.'

He had paraphrased the letter which was, as he said, very short. He had omitted the third accusation made against him. Julius saw Gregorio, reading, halt at the relevant passage. Nicholas, he realised, was watching him. Loppe, who had also arrived, plainly dressed, had walked to the wharf. Julius said, in some discomfort, 'You see, death isn't enough. He wants to ruin you. He says you set out to subvert his company.'

'Well, of course,' Nicholas said. 'He sent his entire family to dismantle mine. Isn't that the whole object of being in business?' Gregorio folded the letter and Nicholas took it back, displaying a smile and both dimples.

'So what are you going to do?' Julius said.

'Go to Murano,' Nicholas said. 'I haven't got a ship that can go anywhere else. Julius, get the girl, will you? I haven't time to wait about till it's dark.'

They embarked as soon as Tilde came, studiously composed. Reared in Bruges, she was accustomed to water. She stepped down beside Julius into the Bank's big lagoon boat, while Nicholas and Loppe took their seats. Gregorio, jumping down, spoke to the oarsmen, who wore the Bank's livery. Beside them were two men-at-arms bearing the Lion of St Mark on their breastplates.

It occurred to Julius that it might have been wiser to take Tilde straight back to the Martelli-Medici palazzo. On the other hand, he liked being active. It had been dull in some ways, in Bruges. It had been dull, to be candid, without Nicholas. He liked pitting his wits against Nicholas. He felt pleased, among all these Italian manipulators, to have a good Flemish card up his sleeve.

Chapter 3

OOL AND PLACID, home to waterfowl and the drifting vessels of fishermen, the lagoon of Venice filled the shallow, sandy miles between the city and the head of the gulf on which it lay. Of all the green islands on its milky surface, only one was nearer to Venice than the five slips of land that made up Murano. Which was a pity, because even an hour away over the water, the air was still filled with the din of a city going to war and, in the morning, the sea was as busy as the Grand Canal with boats going to market, bearing their fish and their produce to feed the overstuffed, overwrought Serenissima.

Now the traffic was thin, although the soldiers stayed alert, and Loppe's vigilance, Gregorio noted, never flagged. Tilde, remembered as a girl of some fortitude, had nevertheless moved close to Julius. Nicholas, his gaze on the sea, paid no attention to anyone.

It had been foolish of Julius to let the girl come, and wrong of Nicholas to encourage it. Julius, in Gregorio's view, was a competent Bologna-trained notary with a cast of mind which led him too often into pointless adventure. He had been, no doubt, an excellent and comradely mentor to the Charetty young, including Nicholas in his subservient youth. He still entertained, Gregorio thought, a delusion of ascendancy over Nicholas which Nicholas had either failed or chosen not to dispel, although, Gregorio supposed, he had some means, in crisis, of making sure that Julius respected his wishes.

Compared with Julius, Gregorio had little shared background with Nicholas: had seen none of his boyhood; had never fought with him; had never taken part in his bizarre escapades overseas. But he had looked after the Charetty business in Bruges when Nicholas was abroad, and his wife still alive, with young daughters. For over two years, he had run his Bank in Venice, and had been forced to receive for that period a torrential correspondence he would not have foregone.

Gregorio, not a vain man, recognised that it was a common experience to imagine one understood Nicholas vander Poele; and to harbour an impulse to help and protect him. He reminded himself that the subject of such a humane interest did not always remain innocent, or worthy of it. One must not be beguiled.

Gregorio sat, his face remote; and his fingers of their own volition caressed the place on his shoulder where once, for upholding Nicholas, he had received a sword-thrust from the lord Simon of St Pol who had written that chilling letter. The letter with the accusation which Nicholas had not repeated in full. *Killer of women and gentlefolk*, it had said. *And despoiler of boys*, it had added. Gregorio felt cold, and then amazingly hot.

'It's getting hotter,' Tilde de Charetty said. She sat up. The holy island, the one nearest to Venice, had fallen behind. Ahead in the distance lay the sunlit snows of the blue mainland mountains. By contrast, the land which now seemed so close to their bows was green and populous, scattered with red and cream buildings and the towers of churches. By some trick of the sun, the composition appeared to be sparkling, like the effect of dew on a garden. 'Why is it getting warmer?' she said.

'Because this is Murano,' said Gregorio, emerging from his thoughts and wiping his brow. 'It's hot because of the glasshouses. This is where all the glass of Venice is made.'

The island's sultriness eddied about them, carrying odours of baked clay and charred wood and metal. 'Glass!' said Tilde. 'You didn't tell me!'

She was looking at Julius who was far too interested in gazing elsewhere. Nicholas, in laconic Italian, was directing the oarsmen towards the entrance to the nearest and narrowest of the canals that wound through the island. As it began to open to view, you could see the mooring posts with their boats on either side, and the piles of boxes and barrels and sacks on the working-space between the water and the irregular line of crooked brick buildings. It was the Rio di Santo Stefano, where all the workshops were. Gregorio hoped to God Nicholas knew what he was doing.

Julius said to the girl, 'I thought you'd enjoy the surprise.' He chopped Nicholas on the arm. 'I knew it. You've bought your way into glass, haven't you?'

'It would be hard to deny it,' said Nicholas. For Tilde's sake, he had switched back to Flemish. 'It's a pretty place, Murano, I'm told, away from the furnaces. Gardens, vineyards, hospices where you would be welcome. You and Tilde may want to walk, or the

boat will take you wherever you fancy. We shall meet you back
here in two hours.'

Tilde said, 'I should like to see inside a glass workshop.'

'I thought you might,' Nicholas said. 'Gregorio says this is one
of the best, and they will make you welcome. You will excuse us?'

Gregorio had made no such pronouncement, but Nicholas, it
was clear, had received advice from someone: the berth to which he
directed the boat belonged to a luminary of the Glassmakers'
Guild who was already emerging to greet them. Tilde disembarked,
aided by Julius and Lopez. Nicholas and Gregorio landed, made
the necessary introductions, and stood aside as Julius and the girl
entered the building.

Nicholas called after them, 'In two hours' time, then, at this
place!' and, taking Gregorio's elbow, began to walk smartly along
the canal path. Lopez followed, and behind him the two soldiers
came running. Turning, Gregorio saw Julius step out of the
glassworker's house and look after them with a displeased expression. Then the Magistrate emerged and led him in again. 'Good,'
said Nicholas. 'So where is the Barovier workshop?'

'He'll try to find you,' Gregorio said. 'Julius. As soon as he's
free.'

'No, he won't,' Nicholas said. 'He had a good look at the barge.
It's full of glassmaking stuff: alum and cullet and cobalt. He's
found out I've been acquiring an island. He'll pay the boatmen to
take him there. It'll take him two hours and a half to get back.'

'It shouldn't,' said Gregorio. It was a silly remark, and he wasn't
surprised when Nicholas didn't trouble to answer. At the same
time, he wondered if Nicholas realised that they, too, would have
time on their hands. Their business wouldn't take long, and they
wouldn't be encouraged to linger. He couldn't imagine Nicholas
strolling among the parks and gardens and vineyards. He caught
himself wondering if he should ask about brothels. Nicholas, to his
Bank, was an enigma as well as a responsibility.

They left their escort by the canal, outside the arcaded ground
floor of the handsome brick house they were to visit. Only the wall
that stretched on either side indicated the amount of ground
which, sprawling behind, contained the wide yards, the warehouses,
the wells, the furnace areas, the painting-sheds, the tool-making
offices, the towers of broken glass and the towers of sand and the
sacks and sacks of soda ash that comprised the multiple operations
of the finest glasshouse in the world.

Then its owner came to the entrance to meet them, and took a
dislike to Nicholas on the spot.

Marietta Barovier was late-born but not all that young: her

father had died four years previously after forty years at the top of
his profession. Yet her hair under its grimy cloth was thick and
black, and her olive skin slick as chamois with perpetual sweat. Her
eyes, large and heavy-lidded, were piercingly dark, and her body
sturdy and short in a stained canvas smock that hung calf-length.
Below that, she wore thonged leather shoes grey with scorching.
She said, '*This* is not the head of your Bank?'

Nicholas considered her. 'Signor Gregorio tells me what to do,'
he said. He waited, and gave a brief smile. 'In fact, madonna, he
and I are partners. But he has had the privilege, which I have not,
of seeing your glasshouse.'

'You would like to see it?' she said. 'Then come this way.' She
frowned at Gregorio, and he recognised, with a start, that she was
displeased to a degree that might lose them the contract. She said,
'You may leave your servant here.'

Nicholas produced his lethal dimples again. 'He is not my
servant,' he said, 'he is my factor. His name is Lopez. I should like
him to come.'

'Very well,' said Marietta Barovier, and striding through the
house, led the way into open air, and towards the shimmering heat
within which lay the ribbed beehive shapes of the kilns.

Gregorio had seen it before: the scarred, glistening bodies,
clothed from the waist in stained drawers; the frieze of spidery
tools; the long metal rods with their glowing tips; the bloody glare
of the kiln-vents, within which the mounded shapes of the glass
stood insubstantial in the extreme light. And, like dancers, musicians, the maestri with their tongs, tweaking, shaping and rolling
the yard-long rods with their drooping vermilion phalli; or seated
on stools, the slender tube caressed between palms. They made
soundless music, playing the rod like a pipe while the glimmering
end-jewel inflated, paused, and inflated to become, cooling, a
weightless circle of nothing.

A man, hastening from the furnace, brought a molten lump that,
swung, became a rope of sugar, a handle. A rod whirled in a
glistening arc until the globe at its end lengthened into a neck. The
men worked in near-silence, their arms powerful as those of a
bowman, or a man used to a sword, or a stave. But they were
handling glass.

Gregorio turned to look at the founder of the Banco di Niccolò
and then remained looking, surprised, for Nicholas stood as if
mesmerised. He moved slowly, when called. He followed mutely as
Marietta Barovier led them impatiently through the rest of the
process and back through the storerooms to the house. There,
among the finished pieces, he wakened, and peered at the shelves.

Gregorio watched. The woman stood by the door, her hands on her hips, her lips pursed. Rambling round the brilliant display, Nicholas examined the bottles and tumblers, the jugs and the cups and the beakers, the hanging lamps and the phials, stopping sometimes to lift one and study it. Gregorio's mind was actually worrying over the terms of the contract when Nicholas tilted a gorgeous glass to the light, and then, opening his fingers, allowed it to drop spectacularly to the ground. It lay as frost in the dust, with only shells to show what it once was.

Marietta Barovier, daughter of the greatest glassmaker in the world, said, 'You will pay the cost of that, to the last ducat. And then leave. This contract is cancelled.'

Nicholas smiled at her. His skin glistened. Beneath the ridiculous cap he now wore, his curls dripped; his eyelashes were beaded. 'It would deserve to be,' Nicholas said, 'if you set a master's price on that glass, and I paid it. I don't mean to insult you, but I should like you to treat me, too, with respect. Those are the shelves of your rejects. You keep them, perhaps, for tuition. You do not sell them, I am perfectly sure.'

She stared at him. Her black eyes were ringed with brown. She said, 'How was it flawed?'

'How? The blue trailing was perfect, but the flowing of the enamels had failed. A mishap in the annealing-chamber. My friends from Damascus tell me they have the same trouble at times.'

She looked at him, then she turned her head and nodded abruptly. A man, bowing low, began to sweep the glass from her feet. She said, 'It was plain glass your manager spoke of.'

'It is plain glass I want,' Nicholas said. 'But there is profit, and joy, in the making of all things. I cannot teach you or your workmen, but if you care, I can bring a man here, a Syrian. He works my sugar now, in exile in Cyprus. He would come. Signor Lopez here could arrange it.'

'Come into my office,' she said. And entering and offering seats, she said, 'You know something of glass.'

'Something,' Nicholas said. 'But at second hand only. I brought you a gift.'

Gregorio had no idea what he meant. To the quick glance the woman threw him, he could only reply with a smile. What Nicholas drew from his satchel was a mosque lamp. He said, 'They have lost the means, now, to make them. Soon, they will have to buy from the West. Could you copy this?'

She took it from him. Briefly, Gregorio saw it: an oblong, enamelled and gilded. 'Of course,' she said. 'But Venice is at war with Constantinople.'

'I have an agent in Alexandria,' he said. 'There is a good potential market, even in war. I have brought carpets to copy, and other things. But I knew you could make the glass if you had an example. Accept it, please. It comes with no obligations. If you decide to make them, you can use other merchants.'

She sat with the lamp in her hands, and looked at him. She said, 'Perhaps, after all, you are the head of a Bank. I shall look at this. I shall tell you something. I have been impressed by the quality of the goods you have sent me. I learn that you have brought another bargeload today. The yard is full of broken glass. I have no more warehouse space to keep it.'

'You have enough, then?' Nicholas said. He was almost smiling.

She opened her lips in a genuine smile, showing blackened teeth, and a sweetness beneath all the weariness. 'You must know, one never has enough. I have considered what Signor Gregorio has proposed. I am satisfied with the bargain and so, I take it, are the Council.'

'We spoke of it this morning,' Nicholas said. 'Madonna?'

She raised her brows.

Nicholas sat, muscular knees planted apart, wide brow wrinkled. He reached up and scratched under his cap which tilted back, allowing a frenzy of hair to escape. One dimple appeared. He said, 'I shouldn't have done that. The trouble is, when you're new, people don't take you seriously. Your father must have been a good *padrone di fornace.*'

'He was,' she said.

'Because they follow you, all those men out there. They know you, and in any case, you are a maestra. It is harder for me.'

'Signor Gregorio spoke well of you,' she said.

Nicholas said, 'My friend Lopez would have been harsher. Madonna, if we agree, there are papers to sign. After that, if I may, we should like to visit our friend the Florentine. He is no trouble? You are not unhappy to have him so close?'

'The booth was too small for any purpose of ours,' she said. 'He sleeps there and buys his food from us. He passes for a worker in gold, and the dogs protect him as well as our stock.'

'During the day?' Nicholas asked.

'During the day, of course, they are tied up.' She followed his gaze to the window. 'Why? You saw one of the dogs? They are fierce.'

'No,' Nicholas said. He rose and crossed the room. Beneath the sleeveless pourpoint, his shirt was soaked and his hose might have been dye on the skin: Gregorio saw the woman's eyes follow him. Nicholas said, 'I thought I saw someone. Could he have heard us?'

'There was nothing to hear,' said Marietta Barovier.

'Only that there was something to hide,' Nicholas said. He opened the door to the yard, looking first about, and then down, where the rough ground was sprinkled with ash. Already, Gregorio could see, the house-shadow had lengthened: the long storeroom outside lay half in darkness. Then Nicholas said, 'Yes. This way!' and flung himself outside. Over his shoulder he said, 'Fetch the soldiers!'

Lopez was already beside him, and Marietta Barovier, following quickly, stood in the doorway looking after them. In the yard, men turned and looked up. Gregorio wheeled and raced through the house, heedless of rattling shelves. The soldiers were in the front where they had left them, and came running as he threw them explanations. Then he was back in the yard, which was crowded.

The main gathering seemed to be round the storehouse. Lopez, appearing, said, 'It was a man. Meester Nicholas cut off his escape, and he was forced to run back. They think he is hiding in there.'

'A spy?' Gregorio said. 'Or another marksman?'

'He doesn't seem to be armed,' said the Negro. Gregorio looked at him, and ran on.

Approaching the barn, he could hear the voice of one of the soldiers demanding in harsh Italian that the man inside give himself up. Nicholas was standing beside him, breathing quickly. The woman Barovier was moving about her workers, talking. The barn seemed to be filled with straw, and clay pots and channels, and sacks of barillo, stamped with the name of the Strozzi of Alicante. When no one came out, the two soldiers moved in, followed by a number of burly yardmen in aprons, bars in their hands. Within moments, someone screamed.

Nicholas was still standing outside. Gregorio walked up to him. He said, 'Who is it? Do you know?'

'No,' Nicholas said. They were dragging out the intruder by the arms. His face was covered with blood and his booted feet trailed. He was a small man, pallid of limb and dressed as a labourer. One of the soldiers came over to Nicholas. Under his helmet, his face was lit with delight. 'We have him, my lord. We'll find his weapon, and we'll find out who hired him.'

'Well done,' Nicholas said. He seemed to be studying the captive, who at that moment looked up. Instead of speaking, Nicholas turned back to the soldier. He said, 'Search for a weapon, but I don't think you should interrogate him here. Can you keep him under lock and key until the boat comes to take us back to the city? Then he can be restrained under proper conditions.'

'Proper conditions?' said the man-at-arms. 'My lord, the wretch tried to kill you.'

The man spoke, through bleeding lips. 'I didn't! My lord, believe me! I was only –'

'I think,' Nicholas said, 'you should bandage his lips. They seem to be bleeding. And he sounds as if he is going to be tiresome. Madonna, forgive me. But since we are here, might I ask you to show us the booth you were speaking of? I meant to pay it a visit.'

It seemed odd, after all that had happened. Gregorio saw that again, the woman was taken aback. But, after all, that was why he was here. There was no reason to abandon his purpose. After a moment she nodded, and pointed the way.

The booth lay against one distant wall, and consisted of a long, low building of brick, safely tiled. It had once held a small furnace, but now only contained the Florentine and his possessions, and his workshop.

The Florentine was nervous of Nicholas but he gained confidence as soon as he was asked to present what he was doing, and would have kept them longer if Nicholas had not brought the short interview to a close. Gregorio thought again how little he missed and how quickly, when it suited him, he could establish himself with almost anyone. He had also seen, which was obvious, that the relationship between the man and the Barovier woman was good enough.

By the time they had all returned to the house, the crowd had dispersed and the miscreant had been tied up in the dyeshed, with one soldier beside him, and another outside the door. It was proposed that they should remain there. The presence of another assassin on Murano seemed altogether unlikely.

In the office, during the signing of documents, Marietta Barovier asked the questions Gregorio hadn't asked. 'I understood you thought this man a spy, but in reality, it seems you feared an assassin? Why? Why have the Signory given you bodyguards?'

It was Lopez who replied. 'Excuse me, madonna: perhaps you may not have heard. There was an attempt to kill Messer Niccolò yesterday at the moment of his arrival. It is because of his services in Cyprus. The King has many enemies.'

Then she looked up, as the signing was finished, and said, 'So you are a powerful young man, to cause such offence. What have I to fear from you?'

Nicholas smiled. 'That I shall beat you down in the price of the goblet I am about to buy from you,' he said; and smoothly completed his business, and smoothly took his departure, his doublet over his shoulder, followed by Gregorio and Lopez.

Outside, Lopez said, 'It is late.'

In one sense it was true. As the sun set, the waterside had filled with people: with women seated sewing on stools, and children running, and dogs leaping and barking. Skerries poled their way up and down with a ripple of water, and floating straw lurched and settled again. Gregorio said, 'We have an hour and a half to put off. If you would like a pitcher of wine and some fine fish, there is a tavern I know.'

'I should like to do it,' Nicholas said, 'but Lopez and I have a private visit to pay. Where can I hire a light boat he and I can row without help?'

'I know someone,' Gregorio said. 'You would prefer me to stay behind? Am I meant to pretend you are still on the island?'

'Especially if Julius comes,' Nicholas said.

'And that is why you sent him off with Tilde? Not because of the Florentine?'

'Because of both,' Nicholas said.

There was a pause. Then Gregorio said, 'You can't trust those men with the fellow you caught. They'll try to beat something out of him.'

'I've told them I'll report them if they do. I can't do more, Goro. He mustn't be freed, you know that. I need a charge that will keep him in a prison cell for a month; and spying's no good.'

It was not what Gregorio had meant. It was the first time, to his recollection, that Nicholas had failed to read the inner sense of a message. Gregorio turned his gaze from Nicholas to Lopez, and found Lopez looking away.

Rather than say too much, Gregorio said nothing, and occupied himself with negotiating a boat that would suit. He watched them set off from a deserted spot on the shore, and saw they were pulling for the south-west, not the north, although the haze of evening prevented him from following their course precisely. In any case, his task was to turn back and find a tavern-keeper who would swear, if it came to it, that they had all three passed the time on his premises. He picked his way there, deeply anxious.

In the boat, Loppe spoke, as Nicholas knew he would. 'Why didn't you tell him?'

'After today,' Nicholas said. He was hot, with the strings of his shirt neatly tied and his doublet fast buttoned. The boat skimmed beneath them: they were two powerful men. Behind them, the holy island, the island of San Michele, was already close. He hoped that Bessarion had kept his promise, and the monks were ready for him, and the man he was hoping to meet.

Loppe said, 'Messer Gregorio was right. They will beat the man.'

They had reached the landing-stage. Above them, the new bell-tower caught the last of the light; below, the red brick walls of the monastery were in darkness. Nicholas drew the boat in and, releasing his oars, took the mooring rope and jumped out. He said, 'Perhaps I should have left you there with him? Perhaps you would like to go back?'

Loppe didn't answer. After a moment, Nicholas said, 'I don't expect to be long,' and walked towards the gates, where he saw someone coming to meet him. He held down his breathing, and sought in his memory for all he had picked up of Latin. Then he went forward smiling. One made a plan, and one held to it.

Above him, a bell started to toll, and the din of the Arsenal floated over the water.

Chapter 4

THROUGH THE CENTURIES, many men of religion had found retreat in one or other of the islands of the lagoon, but the monks of the Camaldolite monastery of San Michele tilled their plots and walked their cloisters and sang and prayed in their church within shouting distance of the mercantile heart of the world. They made a virtue of it. When the time came, the great Cardinal Bessarion would leave his priceless Greek books to St Mark's and not to them; but they in their turn had found their own source of spiritual and secular riches; had identified a channel into which the streams of their learning might be turned to the benefit of both mankind and God. They drew maps.

The room to which they took Nicholas was the one where their cartographers worked; where until his death five years before the greatest of them all had drawn together, from manuscripts, from old and new sailing charts, from stories brought him by travellers, all that was known of the world, and used it to make his great planisphere.

The original of the map was here, now; and the abbot, waiting beside it to greet him. And beside the abbot, the Venetian trader who had sailed into Bruges on the Flanders galleys when Nicholas was a boy of fourteen, and who had since found out more about some parts of the world than Fra Mauro had ever been able to put in his map.

The abbot said, 'My lord Niccolò. I have the Cardinal Patriarch's word that you go on God's work, but in secrecy. We also know and trust the Patriarch of Antioch, Ludovico da Bologna your friend, who has laboured for God between the four points of the compass. Because of them, we have received you here so that you may have some sense of the precious map we possess, and may make yourself known to our guest. He has agreed to talk with you briefly. It is for him to say whether or not you may look for more than that.

Meanwhile, speak your minds to each other. Learn. And put it to such work that you will be blessed.'

He left. The Venetian merchant looked after him, and then turned back to Nicholas. He said, 'They are good people.'

'It is true,' Nicholas said. 'Such men may be too confiding. But the map was sponsored by Portugal. The King has been sent an exact copy. I shall do no less for the Church than Portugal did. Or yourself.' He made a small pause. 'Today, at severe cost to my Bank, I have also agreed to grant the Republic a loan which may well ease the lot of her citizens.'

'My father would thank you,' said Signor Alvise da Ca' da Mosto. 'But the journey you contemplate is not, I trust, one of necessity. There is no guaranteed outcome, material or other, in such a venture.'

'It would be folly, certainly, to go unprepared,' Nicholas said. 'I am told that only here on this map may one inspect the interior of Ethiopia in detail, whether one means to travel from the east or the west.'

'I can tell you nothing about Ethiopia,' the nobleman said. 'Prince Henry did not go there.'

'Tell me where he went,' Nicholas said. 'The abbot is right. I have a great deal to learn.'

What he did not have was time. Fra Mauro had elected to draw his planisphere upside down, with Ethiopia at the top and England at the bottom. Nicholas scanned the map while he was listening, reading the cramped Italian legends and committing the place names to memory. He asked few questions. What he wanted, and worked to receive, was an undertaking to meet again. He had just obtained it when the abbot re-entered the room, and the interview ended.

Escorting him to the door the abbot was remarkably affable. Outside the chamber, he turned. 'My son, you have thanked me enough. The land of Prester John attracts many who profess religion, but have other reasons for seeking it. I am glad you are not of their number. The good Cardinal who sent you has said so. Your confessor affirms it, who longs to serve God at your side.'

'My confessor?' said Nicholas.

'You had no idea he was here? He passed the afternoon with us in prayer, and will be glad to share your journey back to the Rialto. I place him in your care.'

'My *confessor*?' said Nicholas.

A burly man of middle years was walking towards them, dressed in a priest's black cap and gown, and with his unblinking brown eyes fixed on Nicholas.

'Father Godscalc,' Nicholas said.

'My son,' Godscalc said. The softness of his voice would have been of itself a bad enough sign. 'Is it not the hand of the Almighty that brought us two together on sacred ground, and myself in need of succour? You have a boat?'

'No. Yes,' Nicholas said.

'I had a word with Lopez outside,' the priest said. 'I thought it unlikely he was waiting for anyone else. You were in a hurry, the good abbot said.'

'Yes,' said Nicholas. 'Yes, of course. Come along.' He reverted to Latin for his farewells to the abbot. Godscalc's Latin was better than his German or his Flemish. Walking through the cloisters, the priest took his arm. It felt like being arrested. The priest said, 'I heard you were coming here, when making my humble call on Cardinal Bessarion.'

'You came with Julius from Bruges,' Nicholas said. 'He didn't tell me.'

'Perhaps he didn't have time,' Godscalc said. 'I hear you are in haste this evening yourself. We can talk of your plans in the boat.'

They had reached the gate to the sea. Nicholas released himself and stopped. He said, 'I can't take you anywhere. I have to go across to Murano.'

'So I gather,' said Godscalc. 'Julius and young Tilde are there, and you don't want them to know where you've been.'

Nicholas stared at what he could see of him. He said, 'Loppe told you? Of course, you noticed Loppe.'

'The porters had noticed him before I did. How could you bring him here?' Godscalc said. 'How could you subject another human being to that humiliation? Or don't you know how a black man is regarded in Venice? I want to talk to you. Get into the boat.'

He had begun to walk down the jetty. Loppe, a dim figure against the distant lights of Murano, was already waiting, the rope in his hand. Nicholas couldn't see his expression and controlled the flood of anger he himself felt. For Loppe, for Julius, for Godscalc.

He faced the priest and said, 'Of course, you'll tell Julius about this?'

'About what?' said the chaplain of the Charetty company. 'That you are pretending a spiritual mission to the mythical king of a land no one can get into? That you've had a ghostly summons to abandon your Bank to rally the Christian natives of Africa? I am afraid,' said Father Godscalc, 'that Julius will merely find it amusing, which is more than I do. In any case, he will find out about it for himself, the moment he calls on the Cardinal.'

Loppe said, 'Father, you had better get into the boat. Voices carry.'

Nicholas said, 'I don't want him to know yet. I didn't want anyone to know. Why the . . . Why are you here?' He followed Godscalc into the boat and tramped across it and sat down, still staring at Godscalc as Loppe cast off and jumped in. Loppe took up his oars, and after a moment Nicholas got hold of his and dug them in, pulling the craft away from the island with two or three strokes and then stopping. He had lost track of time. However expertly delayed, Julius must be on Murano by now. Loppe, watching him, also put up his oars. They drifted.

Godscalc said, 'I am not your chaplain now, Nicholas, as you know. I saved your face for you because Cardinal Bessarion gave you credence, and I would do nothing to hurt him. But unless you satisfy me, I shall tell Bessarion to have nothing to do with you, and the abbot to see that you are given no help. I am sorry, Loppe.'

'Loppe knows all there is to know,' Nicholas said. It was a lie, but this was a night for mendacity. The boat rocked up and down, and Loppe brushed the water with his blades to keep her from drifting.

'Then I want the truth,' Godscalc said.

'Of course,' Nicholas said. 'You have the means to make me tell it.' The last glow in the west had long gone, and the lights of Venice lay on the water. They were not strong enough to show the hurt he hoped he had caused.

Godscalc said, 'You have some scheme to go to Africa?'

'Ask Gregorio how many schemes I have. This is one. A contingency plan. It may never be needed.'

'And if you go, it will not be by way of Egypt?'

'I could trade with Egypt. As things are, I couldn't go there myself just yet,' Nicholas said. He was supposed to be telling the truth. That was true. He would be killed, for what he had done in Cyprus.

'So you mean to approach it from another direction. From Barbary, or beyond the Pillars of Hercules?'

'From some such place. It was to learn more that I asked to come here today,' Nicholas said. That was also true, so far as it went. He knew, without seeing Godscalc's face, that it didn't go far enough.

Godscalc said, 'Let me repeat. You intend to reach Ethiopia by travelling south of the Sahara desert. That is where da Mosto has been.'

'Yes,' Nicholas said.

'And by sea. That is why you are awaiting the repair of your boat.'

'I couldn't go without it,' said Nicholas. It sounded true, but it wasn't.

'But you mean to travel to Ethiopia,' Godscalc said. He had said it before. Loppe, dissatisfied with the angle of the boat, initiated two or three thoughtful strokes. After a moment, Nicholas joined him. He continued rowing without making much effort.

Nicholas said, 'I don't know what I mean to do. It's a possibility. I'm exploring it. Am I a criminal?'

'You are a very good liar,' Godscalc said. 'You have always been. Did you kill Katelina van Borselen?'

He should have expected it. Spray fell into the boat. He leaned forward to take the next stroke, this time keeping it even. Loppe, as ever, followed him. He said, 'The rumours in Bruges? I should only lie to you.'

'You are asking me for my silence. I am asking you about a young, misguided woman whose child –'

'No!' said Nicholas. The boat rocked, and then started to settle. He said, 'If you try to compel me that way, you'll be sorry.'

'Why?' said Godscalc. 'I have nothing to lose but my life. It hasn't escaped you. From here, I couldn't swim back. Who killed Simon's wife?'

There seemed no way to avoid answering, although he tried to think of one. He said eventually, 'She died in the siege of Famagusta. She was there because of me, but I didn't kill her.'

'And the father of Diniz?' said Godscalc. He had no right. It was pointless. One could tell the truth or make up any story.

'No,' said Nicholas. 'He was Simon's partner and hence my rival in business. He died because I was there, but I didn't kill him.'

'So your conscience is free,' Godscalc said. 'And in Ethiopia, or on the way to Ethiopia? Who will be there because of you; who will perish?'

'I have no idea,' Nicholas said. 'But I understand you long to serve God at my side. If I go, why not come along and restrain me? Africa may emerge unscathed from the ordeal.'

They had come too far. Loppe had stopped rowing. Nicholas lifted the blades, but kept his hands steady on the shafts. It was the only thing that kept his hands steady. Water lapped. Godscalc said, 'Can it be that you believe all the legends? About the great race of priest-kings known from antiquity; about the Christian warrior-prince named Prester John who, if summoned, will rise to smite the unfaithful?'

'You've forgotten,' Nicholas said. 'I met one of his envoys when we were in Fiesole four years ago. There was a Coptic priory in Nicosia. I've spent more time than I like to remember with

Ludovico da Bologna, our eminent Patriarch of Antioch, who has made it his life's mission to shuttle between the Christian princes of the West and the East, each begging the other for armies. And even if Zara Ya'qob isn't Prester John, someone certainly sent envoys to the Council of Florence who knew what Ethiopia was really like: it's all in the map I've just seen.'

'Why are you angry?' said Godscalc.

Nicholas didn't reply. Godscalc waited and then said, 'Perhaps I prefer it when you are angry. The Christian role of that country is not in any doubt. But there is every reason to doubt that you care for it. What has attracted you is the myth. The myth of Prester John, descendant of Sheba and Solomon. The tales of the miraculous mirror and the Fountain of Youth and the rivers of jewels. The country where there is gold in such abundance that men prefer to barter in shells. Oh, you are greedy,' said Father Godscalc.

Silence fell. Loppe, stirring the water, kept the boat where it was. Nicholas said, 'You are quick to judge. If I were to go, my Bank would have to underwrite both the trip and my absence. I should owe it some profit. That is not incompatible with what Cardinal Bessarion wants. I should become a legate, like Antioch, bringing an isolated church within the grasp of the West. We are all greedy for something.'

It made Godscalc pause. Then he said, 'But you would prefer Julius to learn all this later. Why? What are you waiting for?'

His hands were steady now, for he could deal with this, and make the answer convincing. He said, 'To see if the Crusade will be launched. If the Pope and Bessarion sail from Ancona, I am unlikely to be encouraged to sail in the opposite direction. You know Julius, and Tilde. I prefer not to agitate them over an expedition that may never happen.'

The air was fresher now, but tempered still by the drifts of warmth from Murano. Seated with his back to those dim, distant fires, Nicholas watched his shadow swinging before him. Godscalc said, 'What else happened on Cyprus that was so unspeakably terrible?'

He was calm enough even for that one. 'The weather,' Nicholas said, 'on occasion. The rest was delightful. I have a moderate amount of land here and there. Some day, you should come and see it.'

'When you are so free with your invitations,' Godscalc said, 'I have a feeling that you expect shortly to find yourself elsewhere. Very well. I am out of order. Let us return to the matter at hand. Have you been candid? You have not. Have you convinced me?

Only that an impetuous young man like Julius should not hear of something that may not occur. Should it happen at all? I doubt it. But on the other hand, you cannot depart overnight, and by the time your plans are in better order, I shall know more about you and about them. You have my silence meantime.'

'Do I thank you?' said Nicholas.

'You think it's none of my business?' said Godscalc. 'There are heathens in worse places than Africa. So how are you going to deliver me home without coming face to face with my notary and your step-daughter?'

Compared with what had just taken place, it was not difficult. They brought the boat back to its owner, and secured another, with oarsmen, to take Father Godscalc alone to the city.

Lit by the landing-stage flares, his rough-hewn face with its heavy nose and black brows looked grim. He nodded, but made no move to touch them, far less give them his blessing. It was hardly surprising. There had been a moment during that journey when he knew, and Nicholas knew, he had been close to being manhandled into the water. Or more likely, they would both have arrived there. He was a strong man, Father Godscalc.

Nicholas stood for a moment and watched his black bulk in the stern of the boat as it moved across the lagoon. He didn't turn to look back. Loppe said, 'We should hurry. Meester Gregorio will have told lies enough.'

'Meester Gregorio,' Nicholas said, 'as you know, is only a beginner. Did the porters give you trouble?'

Loppe laughed, a rare thing. He said, 'Don't you think I am used to it?'

They passed the Bank's boat on the way to the tavern. It lay tied up at the main landing-stage, with a watchman beside it. Julius and Tilde had arrived. Without running, which would have been conspicuous, Nicholas led the way to the tavern.

Now there were fewer people about, and all the boats on the Rio di Santo Stefano were tied up and empty. The evening social life of the town was taking place elsewhere. Here, in the working-quarter, squares of flickering light fell on the water from the upper storeys that leaned over the path, and there was an eavesdrip of continuous domestic noise, of chatter and laughter and argument and the wailing of children, and the clatter of dishes and spoons.

All Nicholas had eaten today had been some bread and cheese, brought to him when the financial negotiation with the boatyard owner had reached its spectacular apogee. Before that, he had spent some time at the customs building, where the officers had agreed to normal rates for everything but the shells. Then the war tax, of course, went on top. He had found his own clerks checking the sugar and salt, and waited until they had turned over and labelled the damasks. Then, business done, he had taken them all off to the tavern for some wine, customs searchers included, but hadn't offered them food.

From there, he had gone to the Palace, in order freely to beggar himself. And after the boatyard, of course, had come his call on the Cardinal. It had been a grinding sort of day. It was a slight want of food which had spoiled his handling of Godscalc, on top of the voyage from Cyprus. Cyprus, island of love and prostitution and unforgettable misery.

In Cyprus now, the river-beds would be parched and the flowers ghosts of themselves. The lemons would hang in their leaves. And the sheets of his bed would smell of spice and incense and the warm flesh of orange, and woman.

He said, 'I really must find something to eat,' and then laughed and said, 'No, I mustn't.' There was his little spy to collect, and Julius and Tilde waiting for him, being fed anxious untruths by Gregorio.

Loppe said, 'Here's the tavern. Five minutes won't matter.'

It was the place where they had left Gregorio. Though it was now crowded, they were offered wine and meat, which they ate outside. Gregorio was not there, but had left them a message. Nicholas read it aloud.

'He says he met Julius and the girl on the landing-stage and told them we'd gone to visit the Bishop of Torcello, who has a mansion here. The Bishop of . . .?'

'Julius couldn't disprove it,' said Loppe. With Nicholas, he didn't use titles.

'All right. While we're supposed to be at the Bishop's, Gregorio will take the other two to the Santa Maria gardens – where are they? – and entertain them until we manage to come. He suggests that before we arrive, we collect the man that we captured and send him under proper authority back to the Rialto. Either that, or to the Podestà here. Signed Gregorio, lawyer. He's annoyed.'

'It isn't surprising,' Loppe said. 'What will you do? What he suggests is no good. You don't want this fellow telling his story.'

'He won't. He'll go back with us, and by the time he tells it, it won't matter. We'll go to the Baroviers' now and transfer him and his guards to the boat. What in the name of the devil did they put in that meat?'

'Brimstone?' said Loppe. It was curt. Nicholas usually had a respect for Loppe's warnings. On the other hand, if everybody felt like being offended tonight, it was nothing to him.

In the short time they had been indoors, true night had fallen. This time the lamps at the mooring posts shone yellow and bright and there were blundering moths in the air, along with the odours of food and wet timber and weed. Below them, the water was pink from the fires that still burned in the yards behind the occasional house. Roof-tops and chimneys stood black against the low glare; and above, there hung the exquisite counterfeit of a sunset, cloud-packed, released each night freshly blown from the kilns.

His gaze on the heavens, Nicholas crashed into a solid, unmoving object which made no effort to get out of his way.

'So here you are,' Julius said. 'How very strange. The Bishop of Torcello had never heard of you.'

Chapter 5

FROM ONE'S EARLIEST recollection, from boyhood, Julius had looked the same: bright-eyed and stalwart and inquisitive.

The Barovier house was just beside them. Nicholas drew a long breath and said, 'You came to look for us?'

'Taking the air,' Julius said. 'I left Tilde and Gregorio at the gardens. Gregorio thought it might be quite dangerous for me to go for a walk on my own, but I reminded him that you had a bodyguard. I don't see them, by the way.'

Nicholas had the impression, he didn't know why, that Loppe wanted to laugh. Nicholas said, 'Gregorio wouldn't want Tilde to be worried. Someone tried to make a target of me again, but we caught him. He's locked in one of the glassmakers' sheds until you came back with the boat.'

'That's just happened?' Julius said.

'You've just missed it. I had to go to the Podestà, that was all. Will Tilde mind sharing the boat? It'll be safe. The two soldiers are with him.'

'Who is he? Where is he?' said Julius.

'We don't know who he is. Here,' said Nicholas, indicating the Barovier house. He had begun to feel that he had invented the entire day, playing all the parts himself.

To Marietta Barovier, emerging immediately, he introduced a startled Julius. She barely looked at him. She said, 'You will remove these men, I demand it. If you had stayed away very much longer, I would have gone myself to the Magistrate. They are animals.'

Loppe, behind him, was standing very still. Nicholas said, 'Who? The soldiers? The prisoner?'

'You wanted to know who had paid him,' said the woman. She marched through the house and flung open the door to the yard. Heat burst upon them, and a chiaroscuro of black and red, laced with points of swaying yellow. The red glittered in her eyes, and in those of Julius.

Julius said, 'You work at night?'

'We are the Barovier,' the woman said. 'We work at night. We, alone of all makers of glass, work in winter. You know why? Because we make what no one else does, pure *cristallo*. Pure, colourless glass, of the kind your Florentine needs, Venice needs. I made a contract for that. I did not make a contract to imprison a man to be beaten until he screams. Your soldiers are animals.'

'They belong to the Serenissima,' Nicholas said. 'The Republic pays them to protect me. But it is not right that they should take the law into their own hands. Let me remove them.'

There was no screaming, now, from the store where they had locked the man he had caught. The soldiers, both sitting outside, scrambled to their feet when they saw him. The leader started to speak. Nicholas said, 'Be silent. I gave you orders. What were they?'

The man looked sulky. He said, 'You wished to know the name of your enemy.'

'My orders,' said Nicholas, 'were to leave your prisoner untouched, or I would report you to your captain. Have you done this?'

'He needed only a little persuasion,' the second man said.

'That is not what I hear,' Nicholas said. 'Show me the man.'

The key hung outside the shed door. The principal bodyguard took it. Nicholas saw Julius brace himself, and the second man place himself ready, his sword in one hand. Marietta Barovier didn't move. Behind her, the yard began to fall silent as men lifted their tools and drew near. The key turned, and the door was flung open.

No one rushed out. The short man Nicholas had chased from the window lay inside on the dirt floor, his face bruised and bloodied, his tunic blotched, his arm twisted beneath him. He didn't move.

Nicholas walked in. He said, 'Why not kill him outright at the beginning? Where is the use of the law if a man doesn't live to be tried? What can we believe of his story if he is no longer alive to be questioned?' He came out. They were all staring at him, except Loppe. He said, 'Leave him. He is not the one who is going to be dealt with.'

The soldier said, 'Monseigneur . . .'

'Get to the boat,' Nicholas said. 'For every word you speak I shall see you lose a week's wages.'

They turned. They were halfway into the house when the scream came from behind, and then a confusion of shouting. Nicholas swung about. The cry had come from the woman, kneeling on the dirt by the body. But now there was no body, but a man with a broken face and a tunic drenched in blood who staggered out of the shed and began to cross the yard at a stumbling run, towards the glowing kilns and torchlit benches. And the woman, having screamed, fell.

Surprise at first held them all fast. Then every man in the yard began to run whooping after him.

Nicholas, kneeling, lifted Marietta Barovier in his arms. Almost immediately, she began to stir, and raised her fingers to the mark of the blow on her temple. Then she opened her eyes, and shaking free said, 'Stop it. Go and stop it.' And as he helped her to her feet, she held the door and shouted over the yard to her workers.

Some of them heard, and hesitated and turned, but most were beyond earshot, and beyond heeding. A cage of dogs, somewhere unseen, began to set up a frenzy of barking. Nicholas stood, rigidly holding Donna Barovier's arm. He heard Julius declare, 'No!' in an angry voice, and then begin to run after the crowd.

Loppe waited a moment. He said, 'He won't get away?' in a questioning voice; and then began to run after Julius. He was a good runner. Nicholas dropped the woman's arm and, using all his weight, shouldered his way after the others.

Shadows streamed over the ground. Against the red light, the vermilion eyes of the kilns, the bodies of men flickered and danced, their arms upraised, brandishing, hurling. Shovels flailed. Iron bars glimmered like lances, some with the live glowing gather still alight at the tip. Like cabalistic signs, pincers burned in the air, and burning stuff arched and sizzled.

You could see from the rush and swing of the crowd how their quarry was trying to evade them, dashing from shelter to shelter; trying to gain enough ground to reach the distant wall and climb over. Suddenly animated, Nicholas thrust ahead, flinging bodies aside, wrenching weapons away, shouting commands. Men fought, resisting him. He found Loppe at his side, and then Julius. Julius cried, 'The bastards! One man!'

It was human nature, Nicholas knew well enough. While he had lain on the ground, the victim of heartless authority, they had been sorry for that small, incompetent man. By running, he had turned himself into a sport. Now they were combining to herd him, attempting to corner him by one of the kilns. Some of those nearest were thrusting their rods into the fire, renewing their heat. They advanced towards the cowering figure, one swinging the red glistening glass into a noose, another whirling a burning globe at the end of a gut of twisting, glittering red.

Their victim screamed and began running. Such was his desperation and speed that he broke through the far ring of the crowd. Beyond was the waste ground, the heaps of sand, the piles of barrels, the wall at the end that might lead to freedom, were it not ten feet in height.

The fugitive ran for his life, and Nicholas, pelting after him, at last took the lead. He heard the voice of Julius, furiously calling in the clamour behind him. He heard, ahead, the pounding of feet on the dirt, trying this way and that as the man sought to shake him off.

Nicholas reduced his speed, and drew in his considerable breath, and said, 'Don't run. You won't be harmed.' Julius came to his right side, and Loppe to his left. The crowd also slowed. He said over his shoulder, 'Stand still. He can't get away.'

'Not from us, he won't,' a voice said, and a missile came flying over the shoulder of Nicholas to land in the darkness in front. It was followed by others. The feet ahead, which had hesitated, began running again, their sound altered to an irregular crunch. The footsteps became more deliberate, and took another direction, and became part of another pattern of noise, coarse and grumbling, overlaid by an intermittent silvery torrent, as from a glacier in thaw.

Beside Nicholas, somebody cheered. Somebody said, 'The silly fool's trying to climb up to the wall through the cullet.'

Cullet was broken glass. He had brought the donna Marietta so much, she had piled it against the far wall of the yard in a ridge twenty feet wide, stacked beyond a man's height and unstable. A bridge to the wall, perhaps, to a man in extremity. But not to a man with one undamaged arm who, trying to balance and climb, would have to clutch at whatever he could as the mass shifted and spilled. A man who might or might not have shoes on his feet.

Nicholas stepped forward, sinking and sliding on glass. He called again. 'Come down. We shan't harm you.' Not surprisingly, the dim, scrambling figure didn't stop.

No one was running now. They had all come to a halt, blocking the light so that the wall of crumbling glass gave back only sound; the continuing punch and slide of the footsteps, the cadenza of an uneven fall. Julius said, 'We'll have to go in and get him.'

Perhaps he was overheard. At that moment, the crowd shifted and parted, and a shaft of diluted red light fell on the glass, turning it into a cliff of rock amethyst. Near the top, a black figure stood, its white face made rosy. From behind, someone lifted a brick, and took aim, and threw.

It struck its target. The man threw his arms up and fell. As he thudded into the glass, its hoarse chatter turned into a roar as it rushed over and round him. Even then, you could see the mound heave, the rattle of still-falling glass by turns cushioned and brittle as the buried man tried to move, tried to push the mass off with his hands, to jerk free his limbs, to twist his face and find air among the split blocks and knuckles and shards that pressed down on him.

They had started forward with their shovels when the final fall came, and they jumped back, choking and coughing in the abrasive white dust. This time it lasted a while; a complete collapse of the stack, loud and continuing and final. And after that, there was no movement at all.

Once they had dug it out, they put the body on canvas, and took it back to the shed it had come from. The soldiers, silent now, helped. After that, Nicholas sent them back to the boat, with a message to collect Messer Gregorio and the lady. Julius and Loppe he dispatched to the office to find water and a brush for their clothes; they went without speaking. He himself stayed in the yard.

His mind, by that time, had all the options assembled. He would have to remain, to deal with the officers and the paperwork with which, as from yesterday, he was familiar. It would be most convenient if the boat left without him, and Loppe and Julius with it. He could hire another and follow, when he had dealt with the two other matters.

One of them was already to hand, in the person of Marietta Barovier, standing before him in the wavering light. There was no shouting now, and even the dogs had ceased barking. Round about them the men, low-voiced, were closing down all their work for the night. On the maestra's orders, the cullet had been left until daylight. She had said other things to them too, which they wouldn't soon forget. Her face, tired before, was now haggard.

He didn't know what she would say to him. But for him, and the Florentine, the intruder would never have come; she would never have had to keep him; her good, skilled workforce would never have escaped her authority.

Nicholas said, 'The blame for all that was mine. I shall report the death as an accident. He was an assassin; he escaped, and ran into the glass.'

In the lights that remained, he could see her eyes, and the bruise on her brow. She said, 'He escaped because your bodyguard thrashed him.'

'They will be punished,' Nicholas said. It was one of the smaller lies of the evening. He had made a very precise bargain with the two soldiers of the Serenissima.

He continued in the same subdued voice. 'Men act in such a way when they are excited. Even your father could not have quelled them, any more than we could, or the soldiers. They are not bad men, your people. They will feel shame tomorrow, and be easy to manage. But still, it should not have happened. If you want, we shall tear up the contract.'

'He wanted to kill you?' she said. 'And someone else, yesterday? Why?'

'I told you,' said Nicholas. 'I have come to success very young. I make mistakes. I am resented. I can only say, it will never happen again.' He stopped. 'If you want, I shall ask the Florentine to pack up and leave. I should see him, in any case.'

'Oh, see him,' she said. As the shock left her, some colour had returned to her face. She said, 'The fault was that of the soldiers. I do not see how you could have prevented it. You tried to help.'

He waited. She said, 'Your hands are cut. Go and see to the welfare of your man, and then come to the office. I see no reason to disturb our arrangement.' He watched her turn and walk off. She had not waited for thanks. After a few paces he heard her say to someone, 'He is there. But be quick about it. It is nearly time to let loose the dogs.' He saw she was speaking to Julius.

Since he saw no point in returning to the house, and did not want to go to the booth, the conflict took place where he stood, in the darkening yard with its streams of hot and cold air, and its kernels of dull, glowing fire. Julius simply walked up and said, 'The man you killed. He was a spy, not an assassin.'

'The man I killed?'

'You let him loose. You knew he was a spy. You guessed who paid him. You wanted to stop him confessing.'

'Why should I want to do that?' Nicholas said. He cast his mind back. During the chase, Julius must have questioned the soldiers. He hoped Julius was the only person they'd told.

Julius said, 'Because you didn't want his employers to guess what you were up to. Because you're damned well afraid of his employers, as we all are, and have picked your own dirty way of dealing with them. That man is dead meat, and all the rest of him flayed into ribbons and wrapped round that foul stack of glassware, because he confessed to something you didn't want known. You do know who employed him?'

'Yes,' said Nicholas.

'Well, so do I,' Julius said. 'He told the soldiers as soon as they touched him. He was paid by the nasty company you tricked into insuring your ship. The Vatachino told him to follow you.'

Nicholas didn't reply.

Julius said, 'So what was the secret you would go to those lengths to protect? Who is the Florentine?'

Sometimes, if you let Julius blow off enough steam, you could divert him. Nicholas said, 'He's a man working with glass. You know my plans for the island. They could still be upset, and the Signory won't release a glassworking permit for anywhere else. I want to keep it quiet for a time, and it was worth holding the spy for a while on a more serious charge. Then it would have been dropped, and he would have gone free. That is all.'

'You let him escape,' Julius repeated.

'I thought he was dead,' Nicholas said. 'Damn it, why should I let him escape and tell the Vatachino all he knew, when he was already as good as in prison? Look, do you think we could go in? I've got depositions to deal with, and I don't want to be here when they let the dogs out. Even if you think it would be appropriate.'

'Where is the Florentine?' Julius said. It had been inevitable.

'It's a business secret,' said Nicholas austerely.

Even in the dark, he could see Julius flush. Julius said, 'I have shares in your God-damned Bank.'

'Have you? Well,' Nicholas said, 'all right; but don't tell the Charetty company.' And he led Julius, expectant and softened, to the booth by the wall.

He wished that, sometimes, fate would settle for drama or comedy. He wished that the more difficult events of his life were not always in terrible juxtaposition to the ludicrous. He had fading hopes that, one day, he would wake up and find that he was firmly in one successful mode, and about to stay there. He reached the low booth and rapped on the closed shutters.

If he had been nervous of Nicholas before, the man inside was now frankly terrified. When he was persuaded at length to open the door, it was necessary to spend quite some time explaining the running about and the shouting. To make it worse, as they were speaking the dogs began barking again.

'She promised,' the fellow kept saying. 'Monna Alessandra Macinghi negli Strozzi. She promised I should be protected. I shouldn't be in Murano. I should be under guard in a city. I want to go back to the Strozzi in Florence.'

'Of course,' Nicholas said. He avoided looking at Julius. 'You may go where you please. But only here can you work with *cristallo*. I understood this was your greatest ambition?'

'It is true,' the man said. ('*Monna Alessandra?*' Julius murmured.)

'And you are having success? It is providing the results that you hoped for?' ('*And her son Lorenzo*,' Nicholas murmured back.)

'Beyond my wildest dreams,' said the Florentine, looking from one to the other. 'It is true. It is unsurpassable.'

'May we see?' Nicholas said 'It is new and wonderful to us all.'

He watched the man rise and disappear. Julius said, 'What have the Strozzi to do with it?'

'They supply barillo, salt-marsh weed, for the soda ash. They know the market. Monna Alessandra wants to make a lot of money almost as much as I do.'

He watched the Florentine coming back with the flat-lidded box in his hands. They had been discussing these boxes, he and Gregorio. He didn't think they were as good as they should be. He saw Julius frown as the thing was set down. It was perhaps a foot square, and all of three inches deep. The Florentine opened the lid.

Artists always wanted to draw Julius, although he rarely had the patience to let them. His face would have looked well in marble; the blunt symmetry of the cheekbones and the straight, classical nose were enlivened by the slanting, archaic eyes with which he examined his fellows. Trained on the box, they were blank.

'You're staggered, I knew it,' said Nicholas. 'So many sets! You've never seen so many, and look at the binding. It's leather. And the box. Two long double wells, and look how every piece lies without touching. Near vision on this side, and long sight on the other. Try one. Tilde'll love it.'

And before Julius could move, he lifted one of the Florentine's artefacts out of the box, clipped it on to the other man's nose, and sat back on his heels, gazing at him. 'Now that,' said Nicholas, 'is what I call a miracle. You look like Catullus. Or Vitruvius, maybe. Or you would, if they ever wore spectacles.'

'Spectacles?' Julius said. He moved his chin carefully up and down. Behind thick circles of glass, his eyes looked like ships' biscuits. The upturned V on his nose gave him an air of fearful surprise which was not entirely misleading.

'*Rodoli da ogli* precisely,' Nicholas said. 'Never before ground quite like this. Never before created from the special pure glass that only the Barovier know how to make. That lot, once the permit comes through, is destined for the Duke of Milan. After that, the King of Naples. Then Rome. Then Flanders. Then France, Spain, Germany, England. Every court will want to have them.'

'They're all blind?' Julius said. He pulled the lenses off, with some difficulty. His face had gone red. 'It's a wonder they manage to win so many wars.'

'Scholars need them,' Nicholas said. He put a pair on his own nose and peered about in a bemused way. 'Painters, teachers, men of the church, men of the law. Ordinary people as well, but they can't afford them. Courtiers? They seldom need them, of course, but they're not going to refuse if their short-sighted prince suggests that there is nothing more dashing than a bit of glass on the nose. They're a mark of nobility.'

'You hope to make them one,' Julius contradicted. His eyes were beginning to sparkle.

'No, they are. The Strozzi family have been acting as dealers for years, but their glasses are not very good. The market is there. We just have to step in and capture it.'

Julius was staring at him. He said, 'I see what makes people want to put you quietly out of the way. Who will this make you popular with? Apart from your better-known enemies?'

Nicholas considered. 'I don't think the Medici will like it very much,' he said. 'But I don't think they would bother to kill for it. Sir, my colleague is in ecstasies over your lenses.'

'He is?' said the Florentine. He looked pleased. He added, 'I get little company. Perhaps you would both stay and share a flask of wine?'

'We must go. But,' Nicholas said, delving into his purse, 'you will permit us to come back, and drink our health meantime? There is so much to ask and to see. That is, if you feel you could bring yourself to stay? I must tell you, such genius should not be wasted in Florence.'

'You are kind. You are kind. Yes,' said the Florentine. 'Under such patronage as yours, an artist must flourish. Monna Alessandra said so herself.'

'I'll wager she did,' Julius said, as they bowed themselves out of the door. 'What percentage is she to get? How much did you leave him just now?'

'Mind your own business,' said Nicholas. 'It's very noisy. Why is it so noisy? Oh, great God, they've let out the dogs.'

He walked with Julius to the landing-stage to see him board the Bank's boat and leave with everyone else to return to the city. On the way, recollections of the early part of the evening returned, naturally enough, to chafe Julius, but to a milder degree.

Nicholas was able to explain that the bodyguard, from unsolicited good feeling, would support their story that the dead man had been a would-be assassin. Gregorio knew he was not, but affirmed that accusing the Vatachino would do more harm than good. Julius, applied to, agreed that something should be done about the Vatachino company; brokers, dyers, sugar refiners and malign opponents.

'They're devils in Bruges,' Julius said. 'A man called Martin, making deals where he shouldn't. It's damaging everyone's business – Simon's as well as ours.'

'A man called Martin?' Nicholas repeated.

'Yes. Was that the man who poached your dyeworks in Cyprus?'

'No. That was a man called David,' Nicholas said. 'Two men in the field, therefore. Who else?'

'That's all I know of,' said Julius. 'And the man or men who operate them. But I've no idea who they are.'

'Then perhaps we ought to find out,' said Nicholas.

Within sight of the boat, Tilde jumped out and ran towards them. She looked frightened. Nicholas said, "Tell her about the spectacles. That'll cheer her up. Gregorio knows.'

'I'm surprised,' Julius said. 'I thought you did everything on your own nowadays.' He smiled at Tilde, who had abruptly arrived, and, flicking her cheek, turned her to walk with them back to the boat. She held his arm. She had heard the story of the glassworks assassin. She was close to alarmed tears.

Gregorio, watching all three approach, didn't rise, Nicholas noticed, and appeared dry-eyed to a degree. Here and there in the lawyer's schooled face were traces of a number of unhelpful entrenchments that needed to be thought about. Loppe, seated beside him, said nothing, which sometimes made Nicholas angry.

Nicholas said, 'And what a day of good cheer it has been. Have you had a merry time, friends? So did we. Blood, carnage and sack, and now, although less exciting, the Magistracy of Murano in its pomp. But be not disturbed. He that is greatest in office is but a statue of glass.'

'When are you coming?' said Gregorio. He spoke in Italian.

Nicholas switched to Tuscan and made it quite loud. 'Who can tell? Go to bed. We have a fricassé to bury.'

'You're frightening Tilde,' said Julius impatiently, getting into the boat.

'No, I'm not. Her Italian isn't good enough. I'll call on you. In a week.'

'Don't be a fool,' Julius said. 'I'll be round tomorrow with Godscalc. I forgot to tell you. Father Godscalc is here.'

'*Is* he?' said Gregorio.

'Is he?' said Nicholas. 'We must try to keep him in business.'

He waved them off and walked back to the glasshouse rather slowly. Undeniably, Julius had had the last word.

Chapter 6

URING THE DAYS that followed, the act of watching Nicholas vander Poele became a popular Venetian pastime. Among the watchers, no doubt, were those who wished him no particular good. The remainder were divided among those who were captivated by his energy, his person, or his habit of making himself the centre of a welter of bloodshed.

He gave them plenty to look at, even though he was equally skilled (as his colleagues discovered) at evaporating when he wanted no witnesses. They saw him (he had his own two-oar *barchetta* by now) being swept along this canal or that, usually with his manager or some other colleague beside him. They saw him cross St Mark's Square at noon with a column of retainers and emerge from the Palace having, so rumour said, paid for his Venetian privileges, including his house, with a loan which would give the captain-general a few peaceful nights.

They saw him on foot, always accompanied, running up and down bridges and along footpaths in many different quarters: by the quays, or among the network of workshops where the weavers were, and the craftsmen in carpentry. He was seen coming out of a rope-walk, and going into a sugar refinery. He was interested, it seemed, in rare books.

And people, of course, visited the Ca' Niccolò. It was said that he had brought strange things from Cyprus – weaves of silk and patterns of carpets of a kind rarely seen – and was investing money in having them copied. It was said that, in between selling his cargo, he was buying many things, of which the cheapest was hemp seed. It was said (but the Collegio didn't confirm) that he had acquired an island north of Murano, and imported all that was necessary to erect on it the world's finest glasshouse. It was said that he was spending ducats in the style of a prince, and much of it on entertaining. This last, Gregorio could endorse.

He had been half-prepared for this phenomenon: the correspondence from Cyprus had foreshadowed it. Translated into physical
terms, the shock of one man's vitality had brought the building to
life. Now, as well as the crammed hours of talk and travel, he
found himself executing the role of a banquet-manager.

He and Margot, of course, had entertained, although not on this
scale. It was his job, as well as his pleasure. His weakness was
poetry, but he was fond also of music, and had found himself a
master who would teach him the finer points of the fiddle and
psaltery. They were acquainted with painters and writers and had a
circle of friends with whom they played cards and took wine, as
well as the grander circle of clients who would come, now and
then, to sit in their courtyard and listen to some new composition,
and whom they would attend on some formal, slight occasion in
return.

He knew, of course, that many of those same noblemen had land
and interests in Cyprus, and that their higher involvement was or
had been with Nicholas. This was borne out by the frequency with
which Nicholas disappeared into their homes. Most of them lived
near the Rialto, having the money and the mercantile interests to
justify it. The social life of the Bank lost Nicholas periodically to
the Loredani and the Corner and the Bembi, to the Contarini and
the Zeno. Sometimes Gregorio and Margot were commanded to
accompany Nicholas, even though it was not entirely sure that they
had been invited.

The homes so treated generally belonged to merchants with
young, lively wives, and especially those living in matrimony with
the three princesses of Naxos, one of whom had been at Trebizond
and two on Cyprus at the same time as Nicholas. Gregorio never
discussed this interesting aspect of life at the Ca' Niccolò with
Julius, although Julius frequently asked.

The personal life of Nicholas engaged Julius a great deal. When
calling to chat to Gregorio, which he did remarkably often, he
always brought the conversation round to where Nicholas spent his
nights. It was, of course, a recognised courtesy that well-run
houses should be made known to a newcomer, pending his choice
of more exclusive companionship. Nicholas would receive no lack
of advice and no lack of offers for the latter, Gregorio thought, as
each host showed himself eager to help. He was surprised, himself,
at the quality and good looks of the candidates, until he
remembered the existence of Primaflora. On Cyprus, Nicholas had
not only chosen a courtesan, he had married her.

To Julius, Gregorio always said, 'I don't know what he does, it's
up to him. But after the last two, I don't see him rushing to

marry.' There were times when he regretted summoning Julius. He was filled with foreboding by the presence of Tilde and her accusations and acrimony.

He was relieved, consequently, when the situation between Tilde and Nicholas seemed, with time, to be easing. Whereas Julius always seemed to find Nicholas absent, Tilde's occasional visits to Margot often led to a passing encounter, and once to a trip to his office, where Nicholas showed no objection to Tilde seating herself by his table and asking a number of pointed questions about mercantile matters.

He answered her, Gregorio noticed, with remarkable candour, taking for granted – which was true – that she had long known the basics of business, having helped to run her own since her mother died. As the conversation developed they sounded like cronies, each taking turns to ask and to comment. Then Nicholas, having apparently judged her capacity, launched into a proper description of the joint agency he was planting in Alexandria, quoting harbour dues, custom taxes, bribery scales, fondaco charges, storage costs, range of goods per season, and percentage profit after freight and insurance, all mixed with examples and anecdotes, and suffused with a kind of dream-like enthusiasm that was, Gregorio thought, only half manufactured.

It worked with hardened merchants and clerks; it didn't fail to bewitch an aggressive, plain girl of seventeen with a good grasp of business. When at the end Margot came to take her away, her colour was heightened and her flattened nose shining. She hadn't asked any more questions about whom he'd killed lately, or who would run the Bank when he was dead. Gregorio thought she would probably cool down outside, and then wish she had. He made to leave, but Nicholas called him back to his seat. Nicholas said, 'They're not doing well.'

To an experienced ear, it had been obvious. Gregorio said, 'I don't think it's the Charetty's fault. The Duke's sick; trading's slipped; all the money's going on the French quarrel; the Scots are threatening to take their business from Bruges, and Florence isn't being helpful with loans. A temporary rise in the groat isn't going to do very much. And any good business that's left is being threatened by the Vatachino.' He paused and said crossly, 'You really ought to stay and see Julius.'

'That isn't what he wants to see me about,' Nicholas said. 'No. It *is* partly their fault. I left them with the core of a good escort and courier business, and Julius should have stopped Tilde from wreck-ing it. He can run a straightforward business better than most when he wants to. In any case, you have to hope, don't you, that the downturn is mostly his fault? Otherwise you've opened a branch in a pretty stupid place.'

'On your orders,' Gregorio said.

'Well, of course my orders,' said Nicholas. 'I sent them from Cyprus and you went to Bruges to implement them. If you found them imprudent or fatuous, don't you suppose it was your job to tell me?'

It was difficult, sometimes, to keep your temper with Nicholas.

Of all the visitors to the Ca' Niccolò at this time, the most welcome was Father Godscalc, the Charetty company chaplain. Not that Gregorio knew him well, even though they had joined the Widow Charetty almost together. As priest, makeshift physician and scribe, Godscalc had spent most of his early service abroad with the Charetty army and Nicholas. Even so, Gregorio's memory of the man was quite clear; the bulk, the dark, uneven complexion, and the profusion of curling black hair over brown eyes translucent as resin. On Gregorio's one subsequent trip to Bruges (now discounted) the priest had been away, reportedly conducting some business in Germany. Gregorio wondered what Godscalc would make now of the Widow's widower.

Nicholas had been missing on the occasion of Godscalc's first visit to the Ca' Niccolò, but since the priest came with Julius, it was not perhaps unexpected. The next time, arriving alone and finding himself no more successful, Godscalc sighed. 'Ah, the coward.' Like many Germans, he had studied at Fulda, and still had a touch of Irish about him.

They sat in Gregorio's sanctum on the mezzanine floor, its low windows open on the Grand Canal. Noise floated inwards, and a little air. Gregorio said, 'You should see him when threatened with Julius.'

'Is that so?' said the priest. 'In that case, I should be sorry for Julius. I hear another man tried to make his mark on our friend in Murano. May I?' He picked a book from Gregorio's shelves and opened it up. He said, 'It's quite a good copy.'

'I know,' Gregorio said. 'The man at Murano wasn't an assassin, he was a spy.'

The priest replaced the book and took down another. He said, 'Was that all? In that case, I am truly sorry for Julius. Does he pose a terrible threat? I'm surprised. I even thought – I may be wrong – that you summoned him.'

Gregorio said, 'Nicholas had been away a long time. Catherine and Tilde are his step-daughters.'

The priest said, 'You didn't send for Catherine or Tilde.'

'He knows Nicholas,' Gregorio said.

'Now that makes sense,' the priest said. 'You were disturbed about Nicholas. Why?'

Despite everything, Gregorio felt an obligation to his senior partner. 'He sent me a letter from Cyprus. He told me he was coming back, because Simon's wife and his sister's husband had died, and he would be blamed for it. Also he had kept a boy of the same family as his prisoner.'

'Diniz,' said the priest thoughtfully. 'His grandfather rescued him.'

'Nicholas had already freed him,' Gregorio said. 'His grandfather stole the roundship *Doria* and got Crackbene its master to sail him home with the boy.'

'Did the boy want to go?' Godscalc said.

It was the kind of question Julius asked. It was followed, as a rule, by allusions to Zacco, King of Cyprus, who was young and unmarried. Gregorio said, 'Nicholas hasn't said.'

'No, he wouldn't,' said Godscalc. 'Now that is an edition worth having. You and I will have a talk about that. Meantime what does Loppe think about it?'

'About the book?' Gregorio said curtly. It was recognised that Lopez knew a great deal about Nicholas, but he still disliked the question in this particular context. It also reminded him of a recent excursion from Murano from which he had been excluded.

Godscalc closed the book and laid his broad hands on it. He said, 'You were concerned enough to invite Julius, who has many qualities, but is not the most discreet of men. There are some ambiguities therefore that you have already weighed and dismissed. For those that remain, I am a willing listener, and a silent one, and one who has more experience, maybe, than either of you. So what is Loppe's view of the boy Diniz?'

Gregorio said, 'I thought we were talking of printing. Lopez says that Jordan de Ribérac took the boy from Nicholas against the boy's will. He says the boy fears his grandfather.'

'Do you tell me?' said the priest. 'As for printing, it is my own fault for opening a book. You would hear that Nicholas took himself to Germany a year or two back, and I was in Cologne myself recently. I was sorry to miss you in Bruges. I wanted to talk to you then about Nicholas.'

He scratched his chin and spoke slowly, giving Gregorio this time all his attention. 'So he would be shocked, you would suppose, when the young lad he'd freed was snatched away from the island by de Ribérac. Are you not surprised that he didn't take ship and try to stop them? And wouldn't you expect an innocent man to rush to disabuse the minds of all those poor wretches who think they've been wronged? Apart, indeed, from saving himself from their arrows? But I hear the insurance claim was happily met. That done, it might be felt that there was no call to waste time on a voyage.'

'Nicholas couldn't leave Cyprus,' Gregorio said. 'He had no ship. And by the time he had settled his affairs, Diniz had been with the old man for weeks; they were both home, and the tales had been spread.'

'But even so, he came here,' the priest said. 'Was it the wife, now, that held him up? That was a marriage soon begun and soon ended. What has Loppe to say of that?'

'Nothing,' Gregorio said. 'Or the barest facts, which bring their own warning. Nicholas married the woman on Rhodes, and the annulment was effected on Cyprus.'

Father Godscalc looked surprised. 'So fast? They have powerful lawyers on Cyprus.'

'A King can usually get what he wants,' Gregorio said.

'Ah,' said the priest. He was silent. Then he said, 'But Zacco has not married the girl?'

'Of course not,' said Gregorio.

'Ah, dear Lord,' said the priest. He lifted his fist and struck a blow at the table that made Gregorio flinch. He said, 'This is a wicked mess and, man of experience that I've made myself out to be, I do not know what to do about it. Tell me something. Does Nicholas know where Jordan de Ribérac is?'

Gregorio supposed he should answer. He said, 'He knows where everyone is, by my guess. Diniz, Simon, his father. The van Borselen, even. Couriers pass all the time with that sort of news. I don't know about the ship, though; or Crackbene.'

'I see,' said the priest, and sat a moment, gripping his knees. He looked up. 'You're a sensible man. What do you think we've got here? Is he hell-bent on revenge?'

'Nicholas?' Gregorio said. 'He wants to be the richest man in the world, or so he says. Certainly, it's a financial empire that he is building.'

'What for? Palaces? Possessions? Country estates? Rare food and wine and costly women and the admiration of Bruges? Or if not, what? You don't need money to kill.'

'You do, to humiliate,' Gregorio said. 'And to protect yourself while you're doing it. The spy whom Nicholas got rid of on Murano had been put on his track by the Vatachino. And the Vatachino, Julius thinks, are Genoese.'

'Is that important?' said the priest.

'It could be, to Nicholas. You'll notice that wherever they are,

the Vatachino seem to strike at Venetian trade. Hence they and we
are direct rivals. Nicholas advanced Venetian interests in Trebizond
and in Cyprus. It was his work at Famagusta that starved the
Genoese out of the city and gave Zacco the throne. Even his ship is
a Genoese prize: it was the capture of the *Adorno* that forced the
Genoese to surrender. If the Vatachino are Genoese, their first
ambition must be to pay him out, one way or another.'

'Whether they are Genoese or not,' Godscalc said. 'That is what
I came to tell you. There is a man called Martin in Bruges who is
one of their two prime officials. I saw him in Venice today.'

As soon as Nicholas returned, Gregorio, talking, followed him to
his room. 'Martin. A man of about forty, red-haired and built like
a wrestler, with iron hooks in his mind. That's Father Godscalc's
description. I've never heard of the man. All our dealings here
have been with David de Salmeton.'

'And mine,' Nicholas said. 'Also with iron hooks in his mind,
but pretty. What else did Godscalc tell you?'

'Martin doesn't matter?' Gregorio said.

'I didn't say that. I wondered if Godscalc wanted to say
something particular about the Charetty company.'

'He's worried,' said Gregorio. 'Not for himself, of course, but
about Tilde and Catherine. He said that, in any case, it was time
Tilde got married, and to someone as rich as possible; except that
the estate would have trouble producing a dowry. He was joking,
of course.'

'Of course,' Nicholas said. Soaked with the heat of the city he
had already pulled open his shirt and walked to the window. They
were alone. He said, 'Don't you ever feel hot? No, you never go
out. Does Cristoffels ever talk about the old days in Bruges?'

Gregorio looked at his back, which was immense. He said, 'He
liked it well enough.' He added carefully, 'He's learned a lot since
he came here.'

Nicholas turned. He said, 'I'd better see Julius, and find out
how they're really placed. If it's a temporary problem, then Cristoffels and Henninc might manage well enough on Tilde's behalf,
releasing Julius to use his talents elsewhere. You haven't really had
a chance to assess him?'

'Julius?' Gregorio said. He felt as if walking a path laid with
snares. He said, 'I've been in touch by letter often enough. I
should say he makes good decisions.'

'Trained in Bologna,' Nicholas said. 'You really ought to get out
more.'

There was a long pause. 'Yes,' said Gregorio. After a moment he added, 'By the way, I mentioned the loan. I told Father Godscalc about the Bank's extended offer to the Signory. But you should speak to him yourself.'

'Yes, I shall,' Nicholas said. 'Although it sounds to me as if you have each said all there is to say.'

There was some business to discuss. As he left, Gregorio turned at the door. 'Martin. Should you have extra protection?'

'Perhaps, but not against the Vatachino,' Nicholas said. 'I think we should give a reception.'

'And invite them?' said Gregorio.

'It would be a small reception in that case. No, I was thinking of something rather larger than usual. Where would you put four hundred people?'

Gregorio looked at him. 'Not here. One would borrow, or hire.'

'Then hire. A place on the Canal, with the largest possible public rooms, and a garden. We do have money for that?'

'Yes,' said Gregorio. 'When?'

'In two weeks' time. Will people come at short notice? Yes, they will, I am sure. And it gives us two weeks to plan.'

'Plan what?' Gregorio said.

'The future,' said Nicholas.

Reclining scented upon her lagoon, Venice was a city of festivals, a city of water-parties and music, of masquerades and stately processions, of entertainments of the circus and entertainments of a more intimate kind, behind silken curtains.

In time of war, it was still there, although muted, this civilised deployment of leisure. What had to be judged, for those who proposed to be hosts, was the invisible place on the scale, the vibration between one quarter-tone and the next which it was proper for them to occupy.

After months of living in Venice, Margot had acquired such a sense. From God knew where, Nicholas had it as well. Hence the Palazzo where he received his guests on the appointed night was graceful but not of ducal dimensions. The servants were many, but only his own wore the Bank's livery. The garlands were exquisite, but didn't clothe every pillar or staircase; the food was well-served and plentiful but did not include ostrich eggs, or a fanciful relish of parrot tongues. In a conversation to which Margot had not been privy, Lopez had received the duty of remaining to safeguard the affairs of the Bank.

If there were no pretensions, there were some surprises: a portative organ; a lutenist composer and some chamber players known to Gregorio. In due course, some of those couples present elected

to dance, swaying round the room in grave, weaving columns, the
women slowly spinning, slowly sinking to curtsey, and later resting
on cushions, while fruit was brought, and more wine, and a few
acrobats in sparkling costumes somersaulted before them. The
doors to the lamplit gardens stood open and men and women stood
by the fountain or strolled, their scent mixed with that of the
flowers. To Gregorio, Margot said, 'What is wrong?'

'Nothing,' he said.

By arrangement, Margot was not the hostess on this, the Bank's
grand reception. When Nicholas asked, she had been happy to
agree that the honour should go to Tilde, and thought it no
hardship to help with her robing and grooming. Mathilde de
Charetty, walking at her step-father's side in rustling damask with
pearls in her shining brown hair, showed, for once, her mother's
bright blood in her cheeks, and her shadowed eyes shone. And
Nicholas treated her as he had treated her mother.

Margot, moving about and speaking to those women she knew,
listened to the undertone of the conversation, and was satisfied.
Some of these people were strangers: clients of the Bank briefly
met; noblemen and their wives representing one authority or
another, and a group from the Council, who owed the House of
Niccolò more than that courtesy. Some, merchants and bankers
met on the Rialto, she had come to know very well. There was, of
course, the Charetty party: Julius, and Godscalc the priest, and
Alessandro Martelli of the Medici Bank in Venice, with whom they
were staying.

Alessandro, elderly and inquisitive, was connected by marriage
to the Strozzi family and (Margot saw with amusement) was not
above quizzing Nicholas about young Lorenzo. Courteously
baulked, he shifted the subject to the Strozzi in Bruges.

'You know our old man, Cosimo de' Medici, is dying? When it
comes, who knows what will happen to all those heavily borrowed
companies? The Strozzi? Zorzi? You know, of course, your old
friend Zorzi of the Cyprus dyeworks has opened business in
Bruges? Trade! Trade! Who would enter trade,' said Martelli,
'when he could be his own man, sitting in his one chair at night,
being read to?'

She saw Nicholas smile, his face obedient to his mind, as it
always was. Merchants' gossip. Merchants' gossip and lawyers'
gossip: she had had her fair share. Unless . . . She caught again that
look on Gregorio's face and saw Nicholas, glancing past Martelli,
notice it also and, waiting, meet Gregorio's eyes. Then Nicholas
ended his conversation and moved to yet other guests – a Duodo,
one of the captains of the Flemish galleys, and then Paul Erizzo

and his daughter, who had been on Cyprus with him, as had so many others. As, it sometimes seemed, had been everyone in the room.

The first person he had greeted, when Tilde was still on his arm, had been Marco Corner, whose family had drawn its wealth for generations from Cyprus sugar. And with Corner had been Giovanni Loredano, also of Cyprus, and Caterino Zeno, whose business was alum, not sugar, and who was in that particular group because all three men had married sisters.

Margot knew about the princesses of Naxos. She saw each exquisite consort approach, regard Nicholas and then, smiling, offer her cheek. She saw each in turn consider his step-daughter, smile, and give her, also, a loving kiss. She heard the one called Fiorenza say to Nicholas, 'We were so sad. So truly sad. The sweet lady Katelina, to suffer so. And you, you lost so much. We feel for you.'

He looked at her, and the half-dimpled smile he was using tonight was quite absent. He said, 'Thank you. It is good of you to be concerned.' Then he touched Tilde's arm, and moved on.

Later, when the girl, tiring, had found refuge with the womenfolk of the Martelli family, the priest Godscalc joined Margot where she stood with Julius in the grand salon, waiting for the trumpets to send their call to gather the guests for the last entertainment. Godscalc said, 'It has been a success, has it not? Although I miss the Nicholas I once knew.'

Julius pulled a face. 'The ostrich? The waterworks? All those beatings? No one would believe it of him now. Solemn and rich, and soon to be fat.'

Godscalc said, 'Perhaps he carries more burdens now. The responsibility of a Bank must be heavy. I thought Gregorio, too, looked oppressed. Demoiselle Margot? Is Gregorio well?'

'He's probably heard what Corner had to say,' Julius said. 'About King Zacco and the Egyptians. Nicholas knows.'

'What about them?' said Godscalc.

'Someone's tried to kill Zacco in Cyprus. The Sultan of Cairo is exacting triple tribute in restitution for the Mameluke slaughter, and there are rumours of Venetian merchants being arrested in Syria. King Zacco owes Corner thousands of ducats and has nothing to pay him with. Nothing to pay anyone with. He's sitting on all the rent incomes and sugar money, and what army he has is living on promises. Will that affect Nicholas? The lapse of the Bank's income from Cyprus?'

'It will affect the Bank's standing here, once it's known,' Godscalc said. 'Corner should not speak of these things so freely.'

'He was discreet enough,' Julius said. 'I have a feeling other
is going about, but I can't put my finger on it. Ah, the
ts. I must say, he's arranged things very well. You must
a great help to him.'

k you,' said Margot. She understood, from Gregorio, that
was a shrewd man of business, and had been taking a close
rest recently in the workings of the Bank. It struck her that a
ttle feminine training wouldn't do him any harm. She began to
move away, to encourage people to gather where Nicholas wanted.
She saw him come in, and look for her, and smile. Then he walked
over to Tilde.

It had not occurred to her until then that what Julius said was
true. The Claes of Bruges had gone. Or perhaps, translated to a
wider arena, the charming attributes were now more clearly seen
for what they had always been. Then the trumpets blew, and the
tree full of birds was wheeled on, drawn by child-cherubs.

She and Gregorio had seen it prepared. There had been no time
for a great artefact, one of the hand-carved witty devices which had
absorbed Nicholas in Bruges and even in Trebizond, she had
heard. It was simply a tree, with its branches laden with sparkling
birds of every variety, made of feathers and plaster and paper. Set
down, it began to revolve on its base, emitting sweet, trilling
music. Speckled light, bright as ducats, swept over the coffered
ceiling and the splendid doorways and the smooth painted faces of
the women, rousing the facets from their jewels. They began,
politely, to applaud even before they noticed its cause. Every bird
on the tree wore an eyeglass.

Nicholas clapped his hands, and stepped forward, smiling.
Tilde's face, looking at him, was glowing and young. Primaflora,
thought Margot suddenly. The way he knows how to hold himself,
how to choose the fine hose, the tunic, the shirt that became him;
the way he uses his voice. Of course he knew how to judge what
was called for this evening. He married a courtesan. All her arts are
his, now.

He spoke for no more than a moment: enough to thank them for
their presence, and for all they had done to make him welcome in
Venice. He hoped, in token of it, that they would accept a frivolity,
and if the design was not wholly pleasing, that they would bring
the lenses to the Casa Barovier at Murano, where there were as
many again to exchange them with. That the glasses served any
practical purpose went wholly unmentioned.

The musicians, who had been silent, began to play. Cherubs
tripped through the room, bearing ribboned trays spangled with
spectacles. Ringed hands hovered, and dipped. The guests, their

hands to their faces, ducked their heads up and down and moving, bumped into one another and laughed. They peered at objects and, detaching the lenses, held them at arm's length to look through. They exchanged sets, and gathered round Nicholas, amused, asking questions. Godscalc stood silent, watching. Julius stood, his mouth slightly open, and then turned to Gregorio. 'What it'll have cost him!'

'Seed corn,' Gregorio said. 'They will all come to Murano, and buy.' Without the lappets, his face looked naked and drawn beneath a hat with a roll.

Margot said, 'Who is that?'

A red-haired man, powerfully built, had appeared in the doorway, with other men dressed in black standing behind him. He looked about, taking his time, until his gaze fell on Nicholas. Then, signalling the others to stay, he began to shoulder his way through the room.

He was noticed. The guests were too well-mannered to turn, or to fall silent, but few missed his journey to where Nicholas stood, and although those beside Nicholas moved accommodatingly to one side, they were not out of earshot. The man said, 'Vander Poele? Nicholas vander Poele of the House of Niccolò? Your Negro didn't seem to know where you were.'

Chapter 7

BESIDE MARGOT, Gregorio started to move. The priest Godscalc also began to walk quickly over to Nicholas. For a moment, Nicholas looked down at the man without speaking. Then he said, 'I am Niccolò vander Poele. As you see, I am not precisely in hiding although not, I'm afraid, with leisure to talk to you. They should have told you so at the door.'

It was true. There had been no message from below; no outcry even. At the doors of this chamber there were no servants to be seen, only the companions of the man who was speaking, dressed in the black robes of lawyers.

The man said, 'One makes one's arrangements. In cases of fraud, there is a temptation, perhaps excusable, for those accused to try to abscond. My name is Martin, and I speak on behalf of the firm of Vatachino, merchants and brokers. The charge against you is a serious one. We can discuss it here, or in private.'

'I have a choice?' Nicholas said. 'How courteous. In that case, I shall join you in the *bottega* below, but not immediately. I promise not to abscond: indeed my partner Signor Gregorio will go with you, and stay till I come.'

'We are not, I am afraid, empowered to deal with Signor Gregorio,' said the man Martin. Despite the red hair and blue eyes, his Italian had a tinge in it of Catalan, and his face was Latin rather than northern in style, its nose long, its jowls heavy. 'It is here and now, with yourself, or below.'

He was not, so far, speaking loudly, although it was clear enough from where Margot was standing. In the further parts of the room, the event might be passing unnoticed. Music played; the polite conversation continued, though muted. Nicholas said, 'I rather think I *shall* throw you out.' His own servants were moving towards him.

The red-haired man looked at them. 'Trained in your army?

Even so, I might be heard to make a point or two before they knock me down.'

'And I should be heard to make an answering point or two after you had gone. Or we could debate the points below, in the *bottega*, when I am ready. I am sure that is what you prefer. Gregorio, go with them.'

Gregorio looked at him. The red-haired man stood still. Godscalc's face was watchful and heavy but Julius beside him was bright of eye. Tilde looked frightened. For a moment, anything could have happened. Then the man Martin snapped his fingers.

One of his clerks, holding a document, hurried forward. Martin took the paper and extended it to Nicholas. 'Our claim for twenty-five thousand ducats,' he said. 'There is nothing to discuss, but since it seems to alarm you, I shall wait for you below.'

His bow included not only Nicholas but all those within earshot. He retired, Gregorio leading the way. He and his men had gained the head of the stairs when Nicholas, following swiftly, said, 'Wait!'

The man turned, one foot on the step. Nicholas said, 'It seemed to me that your view of the world could be bettered. Allow me.'

His hands, touching the man Martin's face, drew back and busied themselves with the back of his head. He stepped aside. Martin, frowning, his fists bunched, jerked himself violently free and switched his gaze to the salon he'd left. His eyes flashed.

Margot saw she had made a mistake about the man Martin. His eyes didn't flash. His eyes, greatly diminished, looked like fish eggs. The glare came, Margot saw, from a pair of eyeglasses fixed to his nose and securely tied to the back of his hat in such a way that dislodgement was virtually impossible.

Whatever view of the world he had held, it hadn't improved it. He groped with one hand. With the other, he tried to prise off the lenses. He staggered and began to fall down the steps.

Gregorio made some effort to catch him, but Nicholas stood and watched him crash between the wall and the balustrade and finally slither full length to a landing. For a moment he lay, and for a moment Nicholas looked down at him. Then Gregorio brushed past and ran to drop on his knees by the fellow, while Nicholas returned to the salon.

The doorway was crowded, and there was a good deal of laughter. Someone slapped Nicholas on the back. He said, 'He's broken them. I regard that as an insult. I shall deduct the price from the twenty-five thousand ducats.'

The gentle laughter increased, and a passage opened to allow him to re-enter and move about, as before. There had been no

point in concealing the crux of the encounter. They all knew what
had happened by now, although no one there would be so ill-bred
as to mention it.

The Cyprus income had gone. The Signory had swept out half
his reserves with a loan. And now he was being brought to law on
some charge which, if proved, would convict him of fraud and cost
the Bank the equal of a year of its profit.

No one showed impoliteness, but at the same time, no one
stayed long after that. As, group by group, the gathering thinned,
Margot saw Julius quieten, and the stiffness of the smile on
Cristoffels' face. Godscalc, with a priest's self-command, showed
no alteration. Tilde she found she had lost.

Searching, a little concerned, she found the girl outside the
grand room, in the cooler air of the long gallery, looking down at
the strung lamps and the glittering water and the swirl of gondolas
departing from the garlanded jetty. Nicholas had been there for the
final ten minutes; smiling, self-possessed, exchanging civilities as
his guests settled back within their gilded silk canopies, visible in
the dark only as jewel-sparkle, and teeth, and packs of bodiless
lenses, withdrawing in silence, like wolves.

Tilde was crying. She said, 'He's going to lose me my business.
Mother meant him to help. Now, when we need him, he's useless.
He's only an apprentice, you know.'

'You don't need him,' said Margot. She put her arm round the
girl and drew her close. 'I think he will help you, for love of you
and your mother. But you don't need him. You are going to be all
your mother was. Don't be afraid.'

'It is not the end of the Bank of Niccolò,' Gregorio said. 'It is close
to it.'

Dawn was near. They sat, supporting themselves in their various
ways on the stools in the counting-house of the Casa Niccolò:
Gregorio and Cristoffels; Julius and Godscalc; Nicholas and Lopez,
who had admitted them. Tilde had been induced to go home by
the Martelli, and Margot in her wisdom had retired.

Nicholas said, 'Tell me what happened again.' He sat at
Gregorio's table, and before him were the ledgers Gregorio had
given him as soon as they had come in, and sheets of paper on
which he had already begun, as he spoke, to scribble columns of
figures.

He was not penitent, Godscalc saw. He was concerned with the
Bank's position, and nothing else. He also wanted to know why the
man Martin had not waited to see him; what he had said to
Gregorio; what he meant to do next.

Gregorio said, 'Of course he couldn't stay after that. He was quite badly bruised. He'd been laughed at. He made very little effort to elaborate on the paper he'd given you, but, if you read it, I'll tell you what his demands are. Why did you do it? He'd given in once. You could have talked him round somehow.'

His voice died. Nicholas, making notes, skimming his way through the document, paid no attention. Godscalc, drawing on what he knew of him, saw that everyone here was irrelevant; that the mechanism in that twenty-three-year-old felicitous mind was performing its accustomed ritual and, like one of his own ingenious artefacts, would eventually present what it had wrought. He saw that Julius was watching Nicholas eagerly, and that Lopez was watching Julius.

The silence lasted no more than a moment. Then Nicholas threw down his pen and, pushing the papers away, flung out his arms, easing his shoulders. He yawned, shuddering, and re-opened his eyes. They were enormously bright.

'Well?' said Julius.

'The Vatachino want twenty-five thousand ducats. If we pay, it *is* the end of the Bank of Niccolò. And, of course, the Charetty company, if you can't manage without us.'

'That isn't possible,' Julius said. He looked sallow.

'You want the actual figures?' Nicholas said. 'Eighty thousand ducats in stock and capital, less the Vatachino's twenty-five thousand. Less twenty thousand we've loaned to the Signory, less ten thousand Bonkle has loaned out in Bruges – that was the news Gregorio was looking sick about – less two to three thousand for the investments we've begun in hemp and printing and weaving, which we can't now go on with, and a forfeit of at least five hundred from withdrawing from the lease of the island, and a loss of three thousand if we aren't allowed to.

'On the income side, a loss of up to eighteen thousand ducats a year if the Cypriot trade has been throttled – that's the news I was looking sick about. Leaving a reserve of nineteen thousand ducats: too small to meet any major withdrawals, never mind pay for fresh business. Income from deals already completed might, added to that, keep this building and its staff for a year. Any run on our funds before that would leave us bankrupt. And of course there will be a run on our funds.'

'By the Vatachino,' said Gregorio slowly.

'By people who owe them a favour, at least. Take time to admire them, Goro. They are superb; they are artists. Everything came together tonight, even the news from Bruges and Cyprus, where the disasters were only partly their doing. And last of all, this crushing demand for restitution for fraud.'

From sallow, Julius had become red. He said, 'But you're talking of paying it. So you've given them some sort of case. What have you done? If we have to close, it's not going to be the Vatachino's fault, is it? It wasn't the Vatachino who got the Muslims slaughtered in Cyprus. You weren't helping the Bank very much when you flung the superb and artistic Martin down the stairs.'

'No, but it did me a lot of good,' said Nicholas mildly. 'Now do you want to hear the good bits?'

Father Godscalc heard himself sigh. Looking round, he saw that none of them knew what Nicholas meant. That most of them, although loyally backing him, had felt a fraction, at least, of what Julius had just expressed. All except Lopez, in whom he discerned a curious tension.

Nicholas said, 'It all rests, as Julius says, on the fraud claim, which will have to be paid. The Vatachino are taking us to law for exacting insurance for a ship which was not our property. The sum they ask, which is extortionate, refers to the amount they paid us for the loss of the ship, its apparel and tackle and cargo, as insured *omni risicum, periculum et fortunam Dei, maris et gentium.* It demands the forfeit of the premium, which was eighteen per cent, and a further forfeit for the loss of interest on the moneys wrongly paid us, and for the fraud to which they were exposed.

'The ship, as you may have guessed, was the *Doria*, which was stolen from me in Cyprus and which I had insured with the Vatachino, but under a pseudonym. Its original name was the *Ribérac*.'

'Owned by Simon's father,' Julius said. Despite himself, Godscalc supposed, his eyes rested on the scar Jordan de Ribérac had once inflicted.

'Owned by the vicomte de Ribérac, stolen by Simon his son, and given me as a prize by the Emperor David of Trebizond. The Emperor is dead, and Simon will hardly admit to a crime, so the rights of the case will take some time to prove. In the meantime, the Vatachino has obtained a court ruling that the money must be returned. The Signory, to whom we have been generous recently, have been unable to reverse the decision, but have advised that it would be sufficient if the Bank supplies material assets to the value demanded. What Martin gave us tonight was a list of such assets.'

'Which are?' Julius said.

Gregorio answered. 'The house we occupy, which is worth six thousand ducats. The island we have leased for the making of glass, and all the raw materials we have deposited on it. The business we have established for the making of eyeglasses on Murano, and all the stocks connected with it. And lastly, the roundship *Adorno*, which brought Nicholas from Cyprus, with her cargo, as at present in store at the Basin.' He stopped. 'The good news, Nicholas?'

It was Cristoffels who said, 'But this house isn't ours. It was a gift from the Serenissima.'

'Therefore,' Nicholas said, 'the Vatachino cannot possess it. Likewise, the making of eyeglasses is based on the premises of the Barovier, heavily financed by the Signory and upon whose reputation the export of Venetian glasses depends. In return for housing the Florentine, I supply the Barovier with extremely cheap sand, barillo and cullet, not to mention some very good alum. The Signory have ruled that the work of the Florentine is unassailably connected with the Bank, and must not be transferred.'

Julius said, 'But can you keep up those cheap supplies without the Levant? What about the barillo?'

Nicholas smiled at him, using both dimples. 'From Spain. Courtesy of the Strozzi.'

Godscalc said, 'So your eyeglasses are safe, and your house. But the island?'

'Oh, I've lost the island,' Nicholas said. 'And everything for glassmaking that is on it. The Vatachino are willing to take it in lieu of part of the debt. They seemed to know all about it already.'

'Well, everyone knew,' Julius said. 'Didn't they?'

'No,' said Nicholas.

'Nicholas?' Gregorio said.

Julius said, 'I didn't know it was a secret.'

'*Nicholas?*' Gregorio said again.

Nicholas said, 'Gregorio wants me to tell you that I was quite glad that you went there, because I was rather hoping the Vatachino would buy out our lease. I never meant to make glass. The Signory were quite happy for me to specialise in my lenses. They would prefer the glassmaking shops concentrated on Murano. In fact, I don't think they will allow a glassmaking licence to anyone else.'

Godscalc got to his feet rather suddenly. He said, 'I am beginning to feel uncomfortable. You used Julius to draw attention to the island. The Vatachino bought the lease, and it's useless?'

The large, bright eyes were watchful, but neither defiant nor remorseful. 'Yes,' said Nicholas. 'But of course, if you consider the ship, the balance is entirely redressed. I understand they have already taken possession of the *Adorno* where she sits being refitted. And the cargo has been sealed in the warehouse. It means we have no roundship, but only eight thousand ducats to pay. And, of course, we shall argue the case and may eventually win it.'

'And the loans will mature,' Julius said.

'In five years,' Nicholas said. 'Oh, we shall have money. But we have to live through the years that are coming before that. So I have a plan.'

He had had a plan for a long time, Godscalc realised. He had admired the Vatachino, as he had said, for the quality of their strategy. He had matched it himself, trying to forecast, step by step, what they might do. He had seen, perhaps, only some of the campaign against him, but knew enough of their gifts, and their flamboyance, to guess that some sort of climax was planned. And so he had elected to hold a reception, and thereby chosen, himself, the date of his own downfall.

Godscalc sat. Nicholas said, 'I am leaving tomorrow night on a venture which should bring us all the money we need. I hope to do so unseen. The day will be full of formalities: it will be seen that we are paying, and that we are not evading our obligations. It will shortly be obvious that the Bank's prospects have never been better. You will have one year during which you must exert caution, but after that, all should be well. Since I shall be taking the risk as well as the opprobrium, I have a favour to ask, of him, of you and of Margot. I want Gregorio with me.'

Cristoffels had flushed. Godscalc said, 'You have no right. You excluded Gregorio from your confidence. You are committing him to something he knows nothing of, and cannot understand.'

'But you are here,' Nicholas said. 'You will tell him. You will direct him to refuse. You will refuse yourself, no doubt.' His eyes were on Gregorio.

Gregorio said, 'This is something Lopez knows? The night –'

'The night Loppe rowed me to San Michele,' Nicholas said. 'I went to speak to da Mosto about his discoveries. I have spoken to others. In time of war, princes need money, and ships. In a war of religion, a ruler who cannot storm Constantinople himself will support an exploit with a Christian objective, which will cost him nothing and might bring him fame. I want to sail down the west coast of Africa as far as da Mosto has gone; and land; and find a way, if it can be found, to Ethiopia.'

'You're crazy,' said Julius.

'You have no ship,' Gregorio said. The lath of his nose, in the lamplight, looked white, and his cheekbones had sharpened.

Nicholas kept his gaze on him. He said, 'The papal commander has freed our galley at Ancona for this one purpose. Half the cargo I brought from Cyprus has also gone to Ancona, where the Vatachino can't touch it. I have a master, and the crew is being hired. As soon as I join her, we sail . . . Father?'

Godscalc realised he had closed his eyes. He opened them. He said, 'Go on. I do not want to be included in any part of what you are saying.' He waited, and Nicholas looked away.

Cristoffels said, 'But . . .'

'But what?' said Julius. 'He's demented.'

'. . . but would you take a galley south past the Pillars of Hercules? Out of the Middle Sea and *south*? It would need a caravel, or a roundship.'

'We have a roundship,' Nicholas said.

They took a long time, Godscalc thought, to see what he was driving at. The craft, the contrivance, the devices that had brought them all here to this room, listening to the obvious, inevitable solution to all their difficulties. Then Julius said, 'The *Doria*? Nicholas, you incredible bastard. You've hit on the idea of recovering the *Doria*? Where is she?'

'Portugal,' Nicholas said. 'We've repaid the insurance. I feel we may as well have the use of her until the courts decide in our favour. She shouldn't be too hard to take.'

'Well, that makes sense,' Julius said. 'But after that, why not bring her back? You don't really want to battle down to Madeira and the Senagana and fight your way across Africa, do you? Anyway, you'd find yourself face to face with . . .' His voice trailed away.

'All those who invited him there,' Gregorio finished. 'You brought the letter. Portugal is where Jordan de Ribérac went with the *Doria*, and Diniz his grandson. Portugal is where Simon has gone, and where all his business interests are – Portugal and Madeira and Africa. Portugal is where the van Borselen family went, to recover their grandchild. Simon issued the challenge, and Nicholas all along meant to take it up, and has made it impossible for us or anyone else to prevent him. Stop him, and the Bank fails.'

As once before, it was Cristoffels who stirred uneasily. 'But . . .' he began.

'Go on,' said Godscalc gently.

The young factor cleared his throat. 'But with such competition, what cargo could he bring back that would save the Bank in a year? With respect?'

Then Father Godscalc chose to intervene at last, and Nicholas, who had laid his arms on the table, drew them back and sat upright, his head poised, his eyes level.

Godscalc said, 'If he were going to Ethiopia, I doubt if he would bring back his life, and certainly not the magic mirror and jewelled sands of the legend. But of course, he is going somewhere rather nearer and much more rewarding; although, it is true, few merchants have managed to find it. But not every merchant has Loppe, do they, Nicholas? In Loppe you have a guide and an interpreter as well as a friend; someone who will follow you anywhere, whom you can expose to any trial and who will not complain. You are taking Loppe to the Guinea coast that he came from, and you expect to bring back all you desire: what will baulk the Vatachino and frustrate Simon's prospects; restore the Bank and establish you as the wealthy man you now want to be. You know what is drawing him? He is going to the market no white men attend. He is going to sail up the River of Gold.'

He knew it was useless. He knew, no matter how clearly or how bitterly he spoke, that few of them would see the iniquity of it. Julius appeared transfixed, even translated. On the face of Cristoffels was a growing, confused admiration. Only in Gregorio and Loppe did he see something different. On Gregorio's face a sort of resignation; and in Loppe's face, uncharacteristically, anger.

The anger was for him. Loppe said, 'I think, Father, that I look like a man. Do I seem to you to have the brain of a child? Do I seem to you like a girl, running after a protector?'

Godscalc was silent. Then he said, 'No. I insulted your intelligence, and your manhood. It has been a long night. I am sorry.'

'Perhaps,' said Loppe, 'we have all said enough.' His eyes were on Nicholas.

Rose-coloured light filled the low windows, and a seagull wailed. Nicholas said, 'Yes. We can leave the rest till tomorrow. There is a bed for Father Godscalc?'

'I shall show him,' said Loppe.

Outside, although the stairway was dark, there were sounds of distant bustling, and the muted clatter of kitchen activity. Loppe said, 'There is a place next to Cristoffels.' On the top floor, he stopped at a door.

Godscalc said, 'I didn't mean to belittle your friendship. I am concerned for him, too.'

Loppe turned. He said, 'He will go, no matter what.'

'I realise that,' the priest said. He paused. He said, 'In the boat, his answers – half his answers – were meant to mislead. I wish I knew the truth of the other half.'

In the dark, he could see nothing of the other man's face. Then Loppe said, 'The man Tristão Vasquez died as he said. He had stolen vine cuttings for Madeira. The plan was that the lady Katelina should also die, as in the outcome she did. Those who arranged it were the Queen and the lady Primaflora.'

'His *wife*?' the priest said.

'Nicholas didn't know. He thought he had purchased the demoiselle's safety. Instead, both she and Diniz ended in Famagusta, where she died.'

'Which Nicholas was besieging,' Godscalc said. Loppe was silent. Godscalc said, 'And the boy Diniz. Nicholas had freed him, but his grandfather went to extraordinary lengths to take him away?'

Loppe said, 'You don't understand, do you? The family may never admit it, but Nicholas and Diniz are cousins. Nicholas knows it. Diniz, I think, knows it is possible. On Cyprus, Nicholas and the boy built a friendship. After years of hatred, the demoiselle Katelina also learned to know him, and understand. Nicholas stayed with the demoiselle till her death. He saw Jordan de Ribérac denounce the boy's trust as unnatural and snatch him away. That is why Nicholas couldn't race after him. It would only have made matters worse.'

Nothing stirred. 'Oh, Lord of Mercy,' Godscalc said. Then: 'She died in the siege?'

'Of wounds and starvation. Diniz starved with her, but lived. Nicholas shared their last weeks in the city. He will never speak of it. Many things happened on Cyprus,' said Loppe. 'Tobie, John, all of us know them, or guess them. But that was the most terrible.'

A boat rocking, in darkness. And something unsaid which even Loppe knew nothing about. 'He will have to speak about Cyprus,' the priest said, 'if he goes where I think he is going. He wants to make his peace with Simon, with Jordan, with Tristão's widow? He will never do it. And there is the sister.'

'The sister?' Loppe said.

'Don't you remember, the only sister of Katelina van Borselen? Her mother is dead, her father ailing, her sister killed, she thinks, in the feud between Simon and Nicholas, and Katelina's child left a half-orphan far from Flanders. There is a family crushed, and no one but Gelis to speak for it. She left for the south as we came here. She will be in Portugal now, with the Vasquez. And there is tragedy brewing, for Gelis van Borselen holds only one man to blame.'

Loppe said, 'You speak as if Nicholas didn't know it. Do you think he planned all this without planning that too? He will deal with his family, and the Vatachino, and finding the gold that he needs for the Bank and the Charetty.'

'He will try. He may succeed,' Godscalc said. 'Intrigue is his life, as we saw today, as you saw on Cyprus. Intrigue, and danger, and a taste for what he transforms, often enough, into high adventure. But whether he means it or not, people die.'

'It is a hazard,' said Loppe, and gave a wry smile. 'He told me, long ago, not to trust him. It is good advice. One does not leave him, however.'

Even where they stood, it was now light. Godscalc said, 'I

remember. I remember what was said in the boat. And yes, I shall go with you.'

He went to his room then, and prayed, and realised that all through his prayers he had been thinking of a tap on the door which had come, once, in Trebizond. But of course men grew, and changed, and tonight the tap did not come.

Chapter 8

As accurately reported by Godscalc, the demoiselle Gelis van Borselen, accompanied by a small but cowed bodyguard, had left Flanders for Portugal and had arrived, full of purpose, at the Algarve home of her dead sister's husband. The demoiselle Gelis had found Simon absent, his child and father invisible, and her sister's killer hourly expected to descend on a household of twittering women of whom the most agitated, by far, was Simon de St Pol's sister Lucia, who begged her sister-in-law, sobbing, to stay.

She remained, since that had been her intention, but found it remarkably wearing. The name of Nicholas vander Poele could hardly be mentioned: even so late as today, an incautious word could provoke an outburst. 'I hate him!' had screamed Lucia de St Pol e Vasquez, throwing herself on the floor which was of marble, although furnished with cushions. She was Scottish, and perhaps used to rushes.

'We all hate him,' said Gelis, wincing a little.

'He is a murderer. We shall die here, with no one to mourn us. He is a classical monster, a Crocus.'

It was an interesting thought, so far as it went. 'Chronos, perhaps?' Gelis said. 'The father who ate all his children?' There were two members of the Vasquez household in the room, who gratefully left when she nodded. She wondered what other guests usually did.

Lucia lifted her head. She said, 'My father Jordan devours all his children. That is why he is so fat.' Then she began laughing and crying together. She had fallen, as always, without disarranging a strand of her bright yellow hair.

Gelis sat, looking out at the sea. The wind was in the wrong direction. After a while, the widow said with a touch of petulance, 'He hates Simon and me. He wants this brute vander Poele to come and kill me.'

She was probably right. Gelis reflected that the same might even be true of the woman's son Diniz, who was about the same age as herself and who had not stayed, either, to defend his dam from the brute vander Poele or his grandfather. Then she thought she might be maligning the youth. He had gone to join the Christian fleet. He hadn't even known, very likely, that Claes was on his way to the Algarve. Claes, or Nicholas. He didn't use his servant's name now.

Since she had arrived on this interminable visit, Gelis observed that they had all been given adequate notice of vander Poele's westward itinerary. Merchants in four Spanish ports had been notified, and dispatches relayed as far to the north-west as Lisbon. You would think he wished to advise all his enemies. Indeed, he had. Simon, having issued his challenge, was absent.

She wondered if Claes could know that Lucia was here, unprotected. She wondered if Claes had learned that her own father was dead, and that if he dared to come he would certainly find her here, preparing for retribution. She assumed that he did. With Claes, you left nothing to chance.

Lucia's sobs were fading. In a moment, if nothing happened, they would be renewed. Gelis van Borselen rose. She said, 'You must be brave. Remember the letters from Katelina. She didn't blame Nicholas. We may all have misjudged him.' She stooped and gave the woman her hand.

The woman said, 'You're treating me as a child. Your sister wrote them when she was dying. You said so yourself. She would put whatever he told her. He turned my boy Diniz against me. He is trying to destroy every friend Simon has. He's a fiend in disguise.' She struggled to her feet, and allowed herself to be placed on a settle. She exclaimed, 'How could he leave me, my father! He should be here, defending his Lucia!'

'I don't know,' said Gelis. 'I shall do what I can in his place.'

She kept all the hatred out of her voice; otherwise the poor woman would lose what few wits she had.

She sat and thought about a broker called David de Salmeton.

The wind was in the wrong direction, which irritated Nicholas, although it was not always possible to detect it.

Gregorio of Asti didn't mind in the least. 'I really ought to get out more!' he shouted to anyone who would listen. 'That's what Nicholas said!'

He had proclaimed it before, when the first euphoria of sailing out of Ancona had struck him; and had repeated it since, against various states of the wind. A deskbound man all his life; a man whose only travels for years had been by horse or by mule from one inkwell to another, Gregorio had suddenly received the sea and the sky, and the absence of Margot was his only regret.

From the moment of their departure, the purpose of their voyage had been made clear to all on board the *Ciaretti*, from her new Ragusan captain Triadano to her mariners and her benches of oarsmen. Whatever their owner's ultimate mission, their first purpose was trade: to land and sell on the Spanish and Portuguese coasts the goods entrusted to them by merchants, and to buy in return what they could bring back and sell for profit. Then, with or without their owner, they would return.

It was known, of course, that having reached as far west as a galley could naturally sail, vander Poele meant to transfer to some other ship for a venture that had to do with evangelising rather than trade. Only the three men travelling with him – Gregorio, Godscalc and Loppe – suspected what ship he intended to use. And when the ports of call were selected – four in Spain and one at Lagos in Portugal – only these three knew, or assumed they knew, that the call at Lagos was the only one of the five that really mattered. Which was not strictly correct.

The truth was, in any case, that the sea swept such problems away; swept away all the conventions and burdens of normal life. The big, crowded ship became home. Whether under magnificent sail or propelled by brown, chanting oarsmen, she throbbed with noise and vigour and movement, with laughter and argument, with an apparent disorder which, on the blare of a trumpet, could resolve itself into a tattoo of running feet; a display of speed and precision which turned Gregorio dumb.

Then later, under the stars, there would be singing and good food and gambling, and talk. But the talk was about ports, or weather, or women, or fights; or if Nicholas were there, a competition to do with some game, or verse, or story he had just invented. It was not about why they were here.

For Godscalc, the tap on the door had never come. He hadn't interfered with the last visit Nicholas had paid to Cardinal Bessarion and his household of expatriate Greeks. He had even agreed to be present at that final encounter, and received with him the Cardinal's blessing, and the letters which would release their ship and smooth their path at the end of the voyage.

He saw, with shamed anger, the faith these churchmen placed in them all. This young man was to open a new way to Prester John's kingdom, isolated by the Mameluke wars. Ethiopia new-found would march side by side with her Christian fellows against the forces of evil and ignorance: the churches of East and West would emerge triumphant as one glorious whole.

Afterwards, he had said to Nicholas, 'I will make you hold to that. I warn you. I will not be forsworn.'

'I hear you,' said Nicholas. 'I heard you the last time.'

On that last, frantic day, the priest had found it in him to set his hand to whatever was needed. He had taken his share in the talks which persuaded Cristoffels to exchange Venice for Bruges, where he would manage Tilde's business, while Julius gave up Bruges for Venice in order to take Gregorio's place at the Bank. The way had been adroitly prepared, and Nicholas had unhurriedly presented his case and unhurriedly obtained their agreement. The priest watched the flush with which Julius concealed his pleasure, and the war in Gregorio's face as love and anxiety fought with the longing for change. Nicholas had judged it well.

With Tilde, it had been different. Julius, left to coax agreement from the youthful head of the Charetty company, had met with plain fury. Tilde, storming from the Martelli Palazzo to the Casa di Noccolò, had begun to accuse Nicholas of plotting to ruin her business and ended in Margot's room, unkindly betrayed by her nerves and her stomach.

Godscalc, called to her bedside, had let her tell him everything she wished she had said. He said nothing against it. Instead, at the end, he had taken a considerable breath and proceeded to give her a succinct account of what, as he understood it, had happened to Nicholas on Cyprus. Long before he finished, she was lying quite still. She said crossly, 'But Lopez would say anything.'

The priest said, 'Perhaps. But this time, it must be said, there are quite a few witnesses who could bear him out, not least the Venetians. In any event, I don't think Nicholas has the destruction of the Charetty company in the forefront of his mind after that, and indeed you shouldn't complain. If he makes a profit at all, you will certainly benefit. As for the changes: they're reasonable. They have to be made. Think them through. Let him know you endorse them. You may not like him, but we all depend on him.'

He hoped he had struck the right note but couldn't be sure. Later, Margot had come down and said, 'She's agreed. It was just a little too sudden, losing Julius and Nicholas both. Did you know Nicholas once sent her a *farmuk*?'

'A what?' Godscalc said, and then remembered. A small Turkish toy. He said, 'She must have been very young.'

'Yes,' Margot said. 'She asked me how dangerous this voyage would be. She is afraid.'

'There is no need for either of you to be afraid,' Godscalc had said. 'Nicholas means to come back, and bring us all with him.' It was what he believed.

Once at sea, it was usually Gregorio who, as purser and notary, accompanied Nicholas on his business ashore where the sales, he noted, were made in cash, whereas the purchases were not. On the island of Mallorca, he saw for the first time sacks and boxes brought directly from Africa: Barbary wool and Bougie leather and gum arabic. He went with Nicholas and Triadano of Ragusa to look at a collection of charts and brought back on board a Jew Nicholas seemed to have heard of, who stayed a long time and talked Hebrew with Loppe. They met a man who had traded with the Charetty at Bruges, and Gregorio nearly got drunk with him.

On the main Spanish coast at Valencia, everyone knew of the Strozzi and quite a few had heard what Nicholas and his army had done for their King's nephew Ferrante in Italy. They were given some extremely sporting concessions. After trading, Nicholas found his way innocently to a large, well-run sugar-mill, originally founded by Germans. Now, the manager confided, it was owned by a firm called Vatachino. Their man Martin sometimes called, or a younger lord, David. Neither was in the city at present.

Father Godscalc, attending Mass with his ears open, reported hearty Genoese complaints about Portuguese interference in North Africa. In the days of King John, Portuguese troops had seized the city of Ceuta, opposite the Pillars of Hercules, and bought themselves and their garrison fifty years of permanent trouble, for no visible profit. 'They say,' Godscalc said, 'that the Arabs are trying to retake the town yet again, and a Portuguese fleet has sailed to help with reinforcements from Flanders.'

'So someone told me,' Nicholas had said.

'Did they?' said Godscalc. And receiving no response, had added tartly, 'We shall learn more further south, I suppose.'

Further south, the port of Málaga, which belonged to the Kingdom of Granada, had more Genoese in it than Moorish caftans and turbans, and the sight of the loggias, the banks and the benches full of doublets and hats was almost as amazing as the view of the markets and warehouses heaped with ripe Moorish fruit and bright silk, as well as Portuguese sugar and dyestuffs. Nicholas moved from office to office, examining goods, discussing deals, and picking up gossip in both Italian and Arabic.

Here, whatever he got had to be paid for, including the gossip. From Trebizond to Famagusta, the Genoese had little to thank Nicholas for; and the Vatachino had interests everywhere. On shore, six seamen from the *Ciaretti* accompanied Nicholas and Gregorio wherever they went.

Wherever they went, Gregorio had also come to realise, Nicholas asked the same two questions, one concerning a man, and the other concerning a ship. Mallorca and Valencia had not supplied the answers.

Málaga gave the answer to a different question. Nicholas, returning on board with the scent of Africa clinging still to his clothes, joined Gregorio and Godscalc and Loppe in the great cabin, sat, and spoke. 'Father Godscalc? Remember the rumour about Ceuta being protected by Flanders? Would you like to hear the truth of it?' He looked incandescent.

'If it wouldn't shock me,' said Godscalc.

'What in God's name would ever shock you? Gregorio: remember that day in Venice when Duke Philip of Burgundy sent to say he couldn't join the crusade until next year?'

'And the groat improved,' said Gregorio decorously.

'Well, listen. He's dying. He thinks he's dying. He hasn't fulfilled his knightly vow. So, dear brethren, he has decided to send a fleet anyway, with two or three thousand men under two of his sons.'

'Illegitimate sons?' said Gregorio dryly.

'Illegitimate half-brothers,' said Nicholas. 'Antony and Baudouin, in fact. And since they were coming by sea, they called in at Portugal where the King is a nephew of the Duchess of Burgundy, and therefore by marriage their half – half – half . . .'

'Never mind,' said Gregorio. 'What happened?'

'The King asked them a favour, since they were passing. On their way to the big crusade at Ancona, to drop into his little crusade on the Barbary coast, and help to free a besieged Portuguese garrison. So, after picking up a few extra ships –'

'Extra ships?' the priest said quickly.

'– one of these being French, it seems that the Burgundians have landed at Ceuta, accompanied among others by eighty-two volunteers from the city of Ghent dressed in black with silver Gs on their backs, which I hope the Barbary pirates can read. Reports say they look like staying for ever, but the Moors don't seem to mind, and it's probably cheaper than going to Ancona, and nicely positioned if either the Pope or Duke Philip expires.'

'Nicholas,' Godscalc said automatically. 'A *French* ship?' he added.

Nicholas smiled. 'A roundship called the *Ribérac*,' he said. 'Found at Lagos, and commandeered for a year's service from its owner, who had just brought a cargo from Cyprus. The owner being –'

'Jordan de Ribérac!' Loppe exclaimed. 'You've discovered the *Doria*? He restored her original name? There's no doubt it's the roundship he took from you?'

'No,' Nicholas said.

'But she's now anchored off Ceuta?'

'Awkward,' Nicholas said. 'But not without possibilities. The honourable vicomte himself has been called back to France.'

'So who is with the ship?' said Loppe softly. 'Crackbene? He was employed to bring her from Cyprus; he might stay to sail her for Portugal?'

No one spoke. At every port, Nicholas had asked about a ship, and a man. Now the ship had been found. Godscalc said, 'I have no knowledge at all of the roundship; but a sailing-master called Michael Crackbene has been for some weeks in prison for debt at Sanlúcar de Barrameda. Debt, and drink, and a killing. He is unlikely to get out.'

'I wondered if you knew,' Nicholas said.

'And if I hadn't?' the priest said. 'It is our next port of call. Or was to have been.'

'It still is,' Nicholas said. 'Unless you want to buy all the cargo yourself.'

At Zibelterra, the strait that separated Spain from Barbary was so narrow that Gregorio, sailing past, thought that but for the mist he might have glimpsed the masts of the Portuguese fleet below Ceuta, and the high sides of the *Doria* among them.

The *Doria*, or the *Ribérac*, for which Nicholas had just forfeited twenty-five thousand ducats, or its equivalent. Small wonder he meant to have the ship back. Small wonder he was hunting Mick Crackbene, who had left his employment without notice on Cyprus, and, taking contract with Jordan de Ribérac, had sailed the old man and his grandson and the boat out of everyone's reach. Or so he had thought.

Sanlúcar de Barrameda, the port of Seville, lay in the colder, unfriendly ocean west of Cádiz, and close to the point where the Spanish frontier met that of Portugal and trading galleys bound for London or Flanders would prepare for the long journey north, past Biscay and the wine ports of Gascony. From here, galleys only went north, or turned back eastwards.

Because the journey upriver to Seville was slow, the *Ciaretti* lay in Sanlúcar to unload and load, denying her passengers a glimpse of the effete and gorgeous kingdom of Castile, whose court preferred Saracen customs. Sanlúcar, like all seaports, was full of taverns and warehouses and whores, as well as the grander houses and persons of the officials and merchants. Its jetties were covered with fish scales.

This time, Father Godscalc insisted on landing with Nicholas and Gregorio. They went on shore together, escorted as always, but found a strange absence of the usual officials, and the doors on which they knocked remained shut against them, as well as the afternoon heat. Further into the town, the narrow streets were filled with people who should have been working, and a sprinkling of well-dressed men and women in silks, most of them riding. There was an air of festivity.

'It isn't a Saint's Day,' said Gregorio, returning to report. 'It's the Genoese consul's daughter's wedding, and they're treating the town: plenty to drink and everyone invited, but no business today.' He looked about him. 'Where's Nicholas?'

Father Godscalc looked about too, and then clapped a hand to his face. Behind it, Gregorio felt, was a large, stifled curse. Eventually he removed it and said, 'Where he meant to be, I should guess. At the prison. Without a bodyguard. I swore I wouldn't let him do this.'

'You couldn't help it,' Gregorio said. 'Not with these crowds. What do you want to do?'

'Find the prison,' the priest said. 'I'll take two of the men. Stay here with the others. If I don't join you, come looking.'

But for his anxiety, Gregorio would have enjoyed standing where he was, at the edge of the marketplace, with children clinging to his legs and their parents slapping him on the back, or offering him a gulp of wine from a flask, or a sugared pastry out of a napkin. His escort, though watchful, didn't fuss. He carried no money. He wasn't the primary target.

Girls tried to slip their arms in his, and burly men attempted to explain what was going to happen in a form of Spanish thicker than the kind he was used to in Bruges. He was going to witness mock fighting, it seemed; some on foot, some on horseback and some between animals of various kinds. Oxen were going to play some sort of part. Gregorio, who had missed all the exotica of Cyprus and Trebizond, wished that Nicholas were less of a handful, and hadn't managed to ruin a really promising afternoon. By insisting on hounding Crackbene, Nicholas had put himself in jeopardy, and the rest of them to some trouble. He really deserved all he got.

At the same time, Godscalc had been away for ten minutes, and that was ten minutes too long. Grimly, Gregorio collected his men, asked the way to the prison and, followed by curious stares, set off towards it.

Halfway there, he caught sight of Godscalc pushing his way towards him. Beside him were the two men-at-arms and an unknown gentleman in a red velvet hat and a doublet with elaborate gold buttons. Godscalc said, 'Ah, there you are. Let me introduce you. This officer is from the Genoese casa, and brings an invitation for you and me to watch the entertainment from the balcony of his house. The running of the bulls.'

'The . . .?' Gregorio said. 'What about . . .?'

'That,' the priest said, 'has all been taken care of. There is absolutely nothing to worry about. Do you have your rosary, now?'

'No,' said Gregorio blankly.

'Ah, well,' said the priest. 'I have a good bit of credit, and I hope He remembers it.' And, returning to his place by the Genoese, he resumed striding forward. Gregorio and the bodyguard followed.

The Genoese house had a gallery round two of its sides from which the marketplace was in full view, as well as the streets leading to it. The Genoese casa was full of men called Centurione, or Lomellini or Giustiniani or Spinola, all of whom had cousins working in Bruges who knew the Charetty company. Nobody mentioned the House of Niccolò, and Father Godscalc frowned whenever Gregorio opened his mouth. It meant either that Nicholas was safe, or that his situation, whatever it was, was past mending.

So, in a distracted fashion, the lawyer found himself following the entertainment below: the grand procession, the dances, the acrobats, the races, the mock battles between mounted teams in different colours, using light shields and spears. The crowds behind the barriers cheered, and the flags fluttered against the blue sky, and serving-girls brought in bread and olives and grapes and filled his cup with Andalusian wine. The shadows grew longer, and the air became milk-warm and pleasant. He began to laugh at two mummers on horseback.

He realised he had seen them before, on opposing sides in the battles, one in red and one in yellow with casques made of buckram and satin. Now they had feathers as well, and light lances of which they never let go, but which they used to threaten and prick at each other as they jumped in and out of the saddle, and knelt, and ran, and achieved fearsome misses and occasional spectacular hits.

The horses were jennets, trained for dancing round the young bulls to enable the picador to plant his *garrocha*. They had seen some of that already, but these two had not taken part. Now, you would say they were playing double roles: each the beast and the picador also. And the young bull in yellow was Nicholas.

As the idea entered his head, Gregorio realised it was preposterous: suggested by some similarity of height, a width of shoulder, a type of inventiveness. Then he saw the expression on the priest's face beside him; and turned back to the arena in horror. It *was* Nicholas.

Of the two, he had the better seat on the horse. Or that was not exactly true: what he possessed was a bodily control of his mount which he must have learned in the East; a trick from Persia,

Turkey, Byzantium, where men played games on light horses like this. It left his arms free for whatever he chose. And what he chose was pure comedy at the expense of his opponent.

There could be no doubt, now, who his fellow mummer in scarlet must be. One couldn't imagine how the prison governor could have been persuaded to let him out to be mocked at, or how he could have brought himself to agree. But the other man, there was no doubt, was Michael Crackbene.

They had been told, presumably, to entertain, and this they did. But Nicholas, wielding his spear, was also wielding his anger, and knew very well how to make a strike hurt. And Crackbene, though more at home on the sea than in the saddle, was none the less an athletic man, with the blood of Vikings in him, and determination, and anger. Vaulting, running, whirling his spear, he fended Nicholas off, and sometimes managed a strike, upon which Nicholas flung his arms open and bellowed. When hit, Crackbene also, clowning, lamented. The spectators cackled and cheered, while Gregorio saw the spots of blood on the yellow, and the spots of black on the red, and knew it wasn't all mime. Then the thunder of hooves drowned the laughter.

A running of oxen. The burly man had tried to explain, in the bright afternoon when the sun was high and hot. Now it was low and yellow, and the arena was half in black shadow, and the drumming of hooves came from behind the Genoese casa and then from the paved street beside it, from which boys and men, running in comical terror, debouched screaming into the marketplace. After them poured a torrent of animals.

Oxen was the word they had used: an innocuous word to do with watermeadows and ploughs and slow, lethargic beasts which had no connection – no possible link – with a herd of gleaming, terrified, frothing young bulls being forced through the streets of Sanlúcar and finding themselves now in an open space, surrounded by crowds and occupied by two vulnerable men on two vulnerable horses.

It seemed to Gregorio that Nicholas shouted something to his opponent. Certainly, ramming his spear into its slot, he galloped across, and, seizing the other man's reins, attempted to race with him from the arena. He was halfway there when the beasts were upon them, muzzles dripping, horns ducking and goring. Crackbene's horse staggered and fell. The herd crowded about it. Exclaiming, the crowds beyond the barriers parted.

Crackbene stood for a moment, bleeding and buffeted, and then, twisting about, slammed his hands on a bull's neck and vaulted. He landed, thighs spread, on its rump, and reaching forward, seized a horn in each fist. The bull bucked and threw up its hooves. Nicholas, moving behind, pulled out his spear and, controlling his plunging, white-eyed horse, pierced the bull again and again on the rump. The bull, bellowing, forced its way to the fence and burst through. The jennet followed. Its sides scored and bleeding, the second horse reached the vacated barrier and jumped.

The herd was attempting to follow when, almost too late, a band of Sanlúcar worthies blocked their way, riding up with their whips and their lances. The stamping, dust-covered animals faltered, backed and began to seek another way out. Towards the sea, over the heads of the crowds, the stampeding bull and the jennet had merged into the distance. Gregorio, on his feet, found the priest on his feet also beside him. The Genoese in the red cap said, 'They will both be killed,' and crossed himself soberly.

Somewhere in the pronouncement was a thread of satisfaction. Gregorio realised that, whatever bargain had been struck, the Genoese had always hoped that both would be killed. He said, 'If God is good, no.'

'God is good,' said the priest distinctly. Walking back to the barrier was the jennet, its gait stumbling and slow and blood on its muzzle. On its back was the mummer in yellow. The Genoese said, 'Ah. We have, it seems, to mourn the death of our prisoner. A sprightly man, but short of temper in drink. It was to be expected, and there will be no recriminations. The entertainment was all.'

'Of course,' the priest said. 'We are privileged, who have taken part in it. And now, if you will permit, it seems that Signor Niccolò might well appreciate our company back to the ship. We shall see you tomorrow, no doubt?'

'No doubt,' said the Genoese. 'I have seldom laughed so much. Your young master is a natural jester. Give him a hump and bells, and he would be immortal.'

They returned to the ship without crossing the market, their men-at-arms with them, and Nicholas in their midst, silent and stripped of his finery. Even so, half the men they met in the street recognised him, and wanted to hail him and laugh. He returned their sallies, showing his dimples, and explaining his gashes as love-bites. At the jetty he stopped.

The smaller ship's boat was there, with its oarsmen and Loppe. Loppe said, 'Yes. It's all right.'

'What a pity,' Nicholas said. And when Godscalc made to say something, turned on him a look of stark fury that made the priest stop. On board, he walked to his cabin and turned at the entrance. The blood, running together, made strange damascened shapes on his doublet. He said, 'You had better come in.' And they followed him, Loppe drawing the curtain behind.

Inside, Michael Crackbene rose to his feet in his red mummer's costume, blotched also with blood. Without the casque, his broad, blond face showed pale and repressed; his chest heaved. He opened his lips.

'If you speak,' Nicholas said, 'I shall probably kill you. Our next call is Portugal. You will disembark there, and I hope never to see you again. In the meanwhile, Loppe will show you where to lie so that none of us will be required to set eyes on you. Get out.'

'I will speak,' the sailing-master said. 'Even if you kill me. I meant you no harm. I fulfilled my contract. I was free. All men operate so. One day Piccinino fights for Milan, the next day against him. It is all by contract.'

'And Diniz?' Nicholas said. 'Get out of my sight.'

'You saved my life,' Crackbene said. His voice was puzzled. But when Nicholas looked at him, he turned and left, followed by Loppe. A moment later Gregorio, too, left.

The galley rocked. The heavy curtain, blocking the light, reduced the great cabin to dimness. It smelt of damp wood, and salt, and the metal of the weapons hung on the wall, and the faint odours of cooking, and humanity, and fresh blood. The priest said, 'Now? Or shall we come back when the lamps are lit?'

'Oh, now,' Nicholas said. 'Sit down. Our next call is Lagos, and we ought to have matters straight before then. He thought I was going to forgive him.'

'Surely not,' the priest said, and then fell silent as Nicholas looked at him.

Nicholas said, 'You've wanted to know my state of mind ever since I came back from Cyprus, so let me make you really happy and tell you. I'm sorry, of course, about the deaths of Katelina and Tristão Vasquez, but they're over. Simon can do what he likes about Katelina's child; I'm not going to hunt down a baby; it's up to Simon to rear him. I'm angry that Jordan took away Tristão's son, but Diniz is eighteen or more. If he wants to get away from his grandfather, he can presumably do it himself.'

'Can he?' said Godscalc. 'Leaving his mother and her business to fend for themselves? From this moment on, you will be directly competing with St Pol & Vasquez on their own ground. What, in this storm of decision-making, are you going to do about that?'

'What do you think?' Nicholas said. 'Withdraw from the contest and let the Bank fail? You know very well I've always kept my hands off Simon and his father, but their business has nothing sacred about it. And if the competition ranges Diniz against me, everyone ought to be pleased.'

It was too dark now to see his face. Godscalc said, 'He may

range against you and starve. Nicholas, they are blood of your blood, even though they repudiate you. You must take the first step. You must meet Simon at Lagos and make him see that there is no need to pursue this vendetta. If you were to combine your two businesses, there would be no one stronger to fight the Vatachino. Won't you do that? I should come, if you wanted me. Simon would listen.'

In the darkness, Nicholas gave a soft laugh. 'What do you wager? I don't mind trying, provided I'm wearing my cuirass. But if they won't be convinced, I'm not going to coy them for ever, or spare them the less gentlemanly aspects of common trade.'

'Oh, I shouldn't place any wagers on what might happen,' said Father Godscalc. 'Simon de St Pol is nearly your equal in stubbornness. But at least you would have tried, and I should be relieved of the black thought I have that you are truly the nameless child Simon thinks you are, and your mother a harlot.'

The vessel creaked. Below the curtain, a line of light showed where the lamps on deck had been lit, and there was a distant sound of men's voices, and of the footsteps of crewmen in the leisurely tempo of harbour. Nicholas said, 'That doesn't draw blood any more.'

Doesn't it? Godscalc thought.

He said, 'I notice, sure enough, you are becoming an impervious man. So, Simon is ruined, his sister made destitute and the boy's future put back in your hands. After that, you cannot claim any kinship.'

'I wasn't planning to,' Nicholas said. He was speaking a little more slowly than usual. 'I'm saying what Crackbene was saying, except that I'm giving due warning. That contract is finished. It was valid, but I've chosen to finish it. Now I've started another.'

'Balderdash,' Godscalc said. 'Crackbene was talking of filling his purse. You speak of denying family ties – ties that you persuaded me, you persuaded *Marian* you would give your heart's blood to have recognised. If this is the truth, you've made fools of us. And that isn't all. How dare you dismiss Katelina like that, or the death of Lucia's husband, or the fate of the lad Diniz? I can understand, heaven knows, why you leave Katelina's child in Simon's hands; it would never live otherwise. If he has wronged you, don't you remember how he has been wronged?'

'Only he doesn't know it,' Nicholas said.

'That is despicable,' Godscalc said. He found he had risen to his feet. He said, 'You had a great gift: you could withstand almost anything because you tried to understand the other man's mind. It would be a sad thing if the child Claes could accept blows, but the man Nicholas cannot.'

'I have been accepting them for the last ten minutes,' Nicholas said. 'I understand perfectly. I disagree, that is all. Do you want to leave me?'

'Yes,' Godscalc said sadly. 'But I dare not.'

He stayed aboard the following day, when Nicholas went ashore with Gregorio to accomplish their trading. The day after that, the *Ciaretti* raised anchor and sailed north-west to Portuguese waters, and journey's end; and journey's beginning.

Chapter 9

THE MOORS, OF COURSE, had named the Al Gharb, the southernmost province of Portugal, which meant *Western Land*. Fear had named its most south-westerly point *The End of the World*. Less than thirty miles short of the End of the World stood Lagos, the Roman Lacobriga, capital of the Algarve, and the harbour from which the small ships sent out by Prince Henry of Portugal had ventured south, to discover whether the ocean ended beyond Cape Bojador in the Sea of Obscurity; whether there were heathens to convert or Christians to trade and ally with.

The *Ciaretti* dropped anchor at night, and by dawn, the Governor's boat stood below, with a summons.

This time, neither Godscalc nor Gregorio went with Nicholas. This time, they knew it was not a matter of trade, but the discussion of a complex proposition already tabled by courier, to which they were not so far privy.

Father Godscalc, early risen, remained in his quarters. Gregorio, disturbed, watched Nicholas leave, elaborately dressed and attended, and also watched the small boat that soon after put ashore Michael Crackbene.

Somewhere up that steep castled hill, or on the river-bank with its markets and palaces, or on the tall headland that enclosed the western harbour, was the house built for João Vasquez, secretary to the Duchess of Burgundy, and shared by his kinsman Tristão's widow and family. Lucia de St Pol was living there, and possibly Diniz her son, and probably Simon her brother. And perhaps, if Godscalc was right, Gelis van Borselen, whose sister had died on Cyprus. But for the moment, in the Governor's charge, Nicholas was surely protected.

A long time later, the Governor's boat returned, and Nicholas and his retinue came aboard, accompanied by a man with the dark,

bitten face of a seaman. The retinue bowed and dispersed, all but
their interpreter Loppe, and Gregorio and Godscalc found
themselves summoned to the great cabin.

The stranger, introduced as Jorge da Silves, was a short, lean
Portuguese of taciturn disposition. After a little wine and some
surly exchanges, it emerged that he spoke and understood Catalan.
A little later, Gregorio gathered that he was a sea captain of note,
who had taken ships down the west coast of Africa. Much later,
Gregorio guessed that he knew both Ca' da Mosto and the Jew in
Mallorca, and that Nicholas wanted his services.

If it was for Nicholas, it was for the Bank. Gregorio, accustomed
to Catalan, did his best to please, and was glad to see the fellow, as
he thought, responding a little. The priest added his professional
skills, and Nicholas all his specialised charm. The man, accompanied by Loppe, left the boat a little flushed, and not far from
smiling. Godscalc said, 'All right. Who was that?'

'You will get to know him very well,' Nicholas said. 'He is the
captain who is going to take us up the African arm of the Nile.'

'On a raft?' Godscalc said. Ever since Sanlúcar, Godscalc had
been sarcastic with Nicholas.

'In a caravel,' Nicholas said. 'The kind of little lateen-rigged
three-master that Prince Henry developed for Africa. The only
ship that can sail close to the wind coming home.'

'You haven't got one,' said Gregorio. 'And don't tell me Senhor
da Silves has a thousand crowns invested in anything.'

'I have one,' Nicholas said. 'Nearly finished, and lying there in
the shipyard. Leased to me by the Portuguese King, provided I fit
her out and load her cargo myself, and pay him a quarter of my
eventual profit, together with all the charts I can make of my
journey. In return, the King will be renowned as the man who
opened the way to Ethiopia.'

'You've got her for *nothing*?' said Godscalc.

'Does it seem so? said Nicholas. 'I had the impression I took
some trouble to lay all the ground work. Tomorrow we view her
and complete all the documentation. Today, I thought I should
visit the home of the Vasquez. You said you felt you ought to be
present.'

It seemed to Gregorio that Godscalc's face became heavy, like
dough. The priest said, 'Who is there? You do know?'

'Oh, yes,' Nicholas said. 'It's going to be very dangerous. There
is no one there but Simon's sister and Gelis van Borselen.'

He spoke to Godscalc, and curtly, with none of the relief that
would have seemed natural. Godscalc's face in turn darkened
again. He said, 'Simon has gone? Jordan is still away?'

'Apparently,' Nicholas said. 'So I have only the ladies to charm.'

'They won't let you in,' Gregorio said.

'I thought of taking a squadron of soldiers,' Nicholas said. 'Or keeping the porter in talk while I send a party round the back wall with high ladders. Or hiding some men in a cart, and driving it into their courtyard, dressed as a wife from the *campo* selling chickens.'

Godscalc said, 'Stop trifling. You'd lose your caravel if you did any of that.'

'It does no harm to dream. In real dreary life, the Governor has sent to ask the Widow Vasquez to receive the lord Niccolò vander Poele, her old Flemish friend and commander of the next Portuguese voyage to Guinea. His Excellency's chamberlain will supply and accompany an escort, and the Palace has loaned us some horses. There they are, on the quay with their groom. You may come of course, or not, as you wish. There will not, I am afraid, be any bloodshed. Now that Tristão is dead, the Portuguese could easily remove Simon's licence to trade and ask him to go back to Scotland. Lucia daren't offend them.'

'Have you ever met her?' said Gregorio. 'Simon's sister?'

'Not to my knowledge,' Nicholas said. 'But I remember Gelis.'

Gregorio said nothing at all. Whatever the Governor believed, Nicholas was here neither as an old friend of the Vasquez, nor as the leader of the next voyage to Guinea. He was here to explain how Tristão Vasquez and Katelina van Borselen had met their deaths. Gregorio was mortally glad he was not going to be there to listen.

The house occupied by the two Vasquez families was large and built high on the hill, although outside the wall of the castle. Glancing back, as the small cavalcade began to approach it, Nicholas could see the masts of the *Ciaretti* as she lay, her hatch covers off, discharging that part of the cargo destined for immediate warehousing.

She was the only boat in the bay, apart from fishing vessels and a caravel recently in, which lay being careened in the busy yards of the estuary. The town was full of her seamen. It wouldn't be difficult to make up a crew, when he needed one. Her cargo was also warehoused, but in a different quarter, being alive. The double line of black slaves was already ashore before he dropped anchor and, inspected and valued, would soon be brought to market. It was where Loppe had been bought by his first master, who taught him Portuguese and trained him to produce sugar. The chamberlain riding beside him said something, and Godscalc replied. Soon, they would arrive at the house.

Some time ago, Nicholas had begun to realise that Jordan de Ribérac had not chosen to wait for him here. It was not hard to find out that Louis of France, deprived for too long of his foremost financial adviser, had compelled the vicomte de Ribérac to return forthwith to Court.

On the other hand, had Jordan de Ribérac really wished it, he could have found means to remain. If he had gone, it was because he planned a different, slower revenge. Nicholas assumed an execution was planned. The scar on his cheek, given long ago, had been a token of intent, often renewed.

What else would Jordan do? He would send the child somewhere safe; and this he had done. No messenger had been able to trace the three-year-old heir born to Katelina. One might have thought Henry de St Pol dead, except that the boy's nurses had also vanished from view, and the word from Katelina's kinsmen in Bruges conveyed no impression of dreadful despair; only the angry hurt of a family parted from its daughter's sole child.

And the boy was not in Simon's erratic grasp: Simon until recently had been here, in Portugal, waiting for Nicholas. Then he had gone, the Governor said, to take ship from Lisbon since the Barbary war had left Lagos empty of vessels. Ship for where, he didn't know. Scotland, perhaps. Or Madeira, now that the company's plantations needed a master. But his lady sister, the Senhora Lucia, would tell Senhor Niccolò all about that.

Would she? Married at fifteen, Lucia de St Pol was still young; not much more than a decade older than he was. But through Nicholas, it would seem, she had lost the partner in a long, happy marriage, and also lost, in another way, her delightful son Diniz.

Brought from Cyprus to part him from Nicholas, Diniz would continue, surely, to be kept out of reach. The boy might rebel; but he had his mother's business to run. And a scandal, it would surely be put to him, would harm Nicholas as much as himself. Jordan was clever.

Which left Gelis van Borselen, who would be eighteen or nineteen and a woman, instead of the short, strident child who had been jealous of Katelina her sister. Wilful Katelina, who had given herself out of pique to an apprentice, and died as a result, broken and starved in Famagusta.

Godscalc said, 'Nicholas, we have arrived.'

The residence, now he saw it, was surprisingly like his own estate house in Kouklia: a walled yard approached by an archway and surrounded on all sides by buildings, of which the principal was a long red-tiled house of two storeys. Downhill, the town hummed like a beehive, and the hammer-blows and cries of the shipyards sounded distant and festive as firecrackers.

The double doors of the archway were already open. The porter, bowing, ushered them through to the yard where they dismounted, leaving their escort. Led by a steward, the chamberlain mounted the steps to the doors of Tristão's home, Godscalc and Nicholas following. At the top was a long, open balcony, and within, another door which gave access, it proved, to an anteroom, and then to a further, larger chamber within which the steward hurried alone. Nicholas could hear his voice, and a woman's. Then he returned and nodded, and stood aside as the Palace official entered, and then signalled that the gentlemen from the *Ciaretti* should follow him.

Godscalc said, 'After you. Remember? You are beginning an entirely new contract.'

It was to be expected that Simon's sister would have his yellow hair and blue eyes, but not that she would be tall, as tall, Nicholas conjectured, surprised, as Diniz her son, who was not of course here. The only other person here was a maid, who had also risen, a piece of sewing in her hands. Simon's sister came forward.

In fact, her hair was not the butter-yellow of Simon's, but something nearer to the colour of oats, and her brows and lashes were brown. Her facial bones, too, although marked, lacked the symmetry that made Simon's face beautiful, and all his conquests so easy.

Watching her give her hand to the Governor's chamberlain, Nicholas thought he saw none the less a hint of the same jouster's freedom of carriage; and ran an assessing eye, before he could stop himself, over the black, high-seamed day gown of mourning which affirmed, clearly enough, the shape and proportions of the body beneath it. There, he had no need to guess, all Lucia's real excellence lay.

Then he realised how he knew, and it was like being slammed in the stomach. Of course, this wasn't Lucia.

He waited. His breath came back, parcel by parcel, although the pain remained in his throat. The chamberlain introduced him. 'My lord, you know, of course, the lady Gelis van Borselen.'

'I believe,' she said, 'he thought I was my hostess. The lady Lucia, I am sorry to say, is unwell. And Father Godscalc? Now I know the mission you speak of is serious.' Her blue eyes, unwinking, stared into those of the priest.

You could see, if you knew him, that Godscalc's colour had risen. He said, 'We are not here to speak of our mission. They tell me your father died on the way here. You have lost both parents now to the grave, as well as a sister. We who knew them, mourn with you.'

'Thank you,' said Gelis van Borselen. 'I have my own confessor.'

'He is with you?' Godscalc said. She had seated herself, and waved to them all to take seats. A manservant carried in wine.

'No,' she said. She might have been made out of driftwood. Behind, her attendant sat on her stool, her sewing clutched in both hands, her black eyes glaring.

Nicholas said, 'But I remember your maid. That is Matten, surely?'

A Lenten carnival, when he was an apprentice and Gelis a spoilt child in Bruges, evading Matten's busy care. Waves of hatred reached him from the corner. He could feel them.

'I am surprised,' Gelis said. 'I thought it was only Katelina you knew. Please take some wine. It is harmless.'

He said, the wine in his hand, 'It is alone in that property. I came to speak to you about Katelina. Later, perhaps, if the others will forgive us.'

'Ah,' said Gelis. Unfolding her hands, she raised a kerchief to the corner of each dry, still unwinking blue eye. She said, 'One day, it would – it will – give me unspeakable comfort. But not just yet. The agitation is more than I can bear. The chamberlain will understand.'

'Of course, of course,' said that aristocrat, who meant well, and was enjoying his wine. 'The effect on Senhora Lucia has been tragic. That I know.'

'In what way?' said Father Godscalc. His knuckles showed white, Nicholas noticed, the way they did when he was apprehensive in battle.

'Oh, anger,' said Katelina's sister. 'It is usual, I think. Anger against anyone and everyone; even against the husband who died.'

'As perhaps you feel anger against Katelina?' said the priest.

She placed her chin on one hand and looked at him. 'For being dead, yes. As a competitor, no. That was what you meant?'

'Forgive me,' Godscalc said. 'Each pair of sisters is different. I am glad you are here, at least, with the demoiselle Lucia. And I hope her son is bringing her solace. To know what actually happened, from one who was there, is of great moment.'

To himself, Nicholas groaned. The girl merely opened her eyes and said, 'You were there? On Rhodes? In Famagusta?'

'Surely,' said the priest, 'you believe Diniz?' For the sake of the official, he smiled. 'A boy of transparent honesty, I am told. Unless, impaired in health, he made a bad journey? We have heard nothing of him.'

'Neither have we,' said the girl. 'But let us speak of –'

'The young senhor?' said the chamberlain. 'There is no news, of course, but we know where he is. So gallant! So determined, despite the terrible siege, to forgo the comfort of home, and strike another blow against Satan! The young man is with the armies in Ceuta.'

Nicholas found, too late, that he was on his feet. The girl's brows had lifted. He turned, and walked to look from the window. Crackbene had probably known it, but hadn't told him. Hadn't, rather, been given a chance. Godscalc said, 'Why?' His voice was rough.

The chamberlain said, 'It is not for me to say. One knows, of course, that it was not the wish of my lord his grandfather, but who would deflect a Christian soul so impelled?'

Not the wish of my lord his grandfather. Behind him, Nicholas heard Godscalc draw breath, and turned. Godscalc said, 'By what means – That is, when did the boy go?'

'When the Burgundians came,' said the chamberlain. 'Was it not? When the fleet came from Bruges with the Bastard of Burgundy? That was when.'

'Naturally, his kinsmen are proud,' the girl said. 'What are material considerations when a young warrior leaves on crusade? You, too, have answered the summons, and, whatever the cost, your names will be written in letters of gold. And now, being so recently bereaved, I fear I must ask you to forgive me.'

Nicholas turned. The chamberlain was already rising. Nicholas said, 'We have hardly eased your mourning. Perhaps I could, before going. Or at least, speak to the senhora.'

It was, by now, only a matter of form; a matter of letting her know that he did not propose to give up. As he expected, she refused, sadly and employing the kerchief. The woman Matten had already jerked open the door. The chamberlain, taking his leave, said, 'We have overtired you,' a little anxiously.

'I hope we have,' Nicholas said, facing her. He spoke very softly. 'I mean you to think about this. Enough lives have been wrecked. How did Jordan get Simon to leave? Did he pay him?'

Faint as powder on ice, points of colour appeared on her skin. 'Of course,' she said. 'As much as was needed. It was not expensive.'

He turned then, and let Godscalc walk with him out of the room. He let them bring his horse, too, and actually joined the cavalcade out of the gates and a short way down the hill before he stopped the chamberlain and made his excuses to leave them. Godscalc, looking suddenly grim, took his horse and stared down at him thoughtfully. He said, 'You will risk yourself unattended?'

'There is no risk, padre,' said Nicholas. The chamberlain smiled, and set his horse in motion again. It was assumed, naturally, that he had in mind some feminine company. Which, of course, he had.

He waited until they were all out of sight, while children played, and men and women with their burdens thrust past him. His head felt hollow. A boy climbed up to his level, a basket of live conger eels on his head. The leathery heap passed by his shoulder, the sun rousing the smell. Nicholas crossed the alley and went into a tavern where it was dark and cooler, and a plump, olive-skinned woman brought a flask of wine for him, and a cup, and he tried out his very average Portuguese on her. She helped him finish the flask, and then he emerged and climbed uphill, back to the house of the Vasquez.

He had misled Godscalc only slightly. It had been politic to have the formal interview first: to be received by them all without protest. After that, he planned a less orthodox entry. He thought he might manage to make one, despite his piquant encounter with Crackbene and his more recent duel, in which different barbs had showered upon him. And the physical shock of – the shock.

He had expected nothing like that. He had expected tears, and sullen silence, and whispered abuse and perhaps threats from them both. He hadn't known, either, that Diniz the idiot, the *idiot*, was fighting in Ceuta. He might already be dead.

Circling the walls, he found a place with a window he could reach, and enough footholds to get himself up to the sill and unlatch the shutters, and begin to ease them open a fraction. The room from the outside looked small, and he had counted on finding it empty. At worst, one or other of the women would be there and he could say what he had come to say. They must be satisfied by now that he couldn't afford to do them an injury.

Unfortunately, he was wrong on every count. The room was not only occupied, it was a bedchamber; and the woman lying in bed was the last person to welcome a man looming between opening shutters. She screamed, and continued to scream.

A distant woman's voice spoke. 'The dolt's come in the wrong window.'

Another woman's voice answered. 'Don't you fret; I'll get the brute. Holy Mother of God, have you blown out my match?'

He might have closed the shutters, scrambled down the wall he had climbed, and got himself safely away. The option didn't even enter his mind, any more than it would have when he was eighteen in Bruges. Nicholas lifted both hands and, punching the shutters aside, vaulted over a dressing-chest and crashed with its toiletries into the chamber.

The floor was covered with shards. Above him was the bed of the screaming woman, who was sitting up, a warming-brick grasped in both hands. The doors flew apart. A second woman jumped in:

a squat, grey-haired person on the operating side of what looked like a fully-primed handgun. It was trained in his direction. He noticed, with sorrow, that no one had blown out the match. It glowed in the fingers of Gelis van Borselen, standing behind the grey-haired markswoman and preparing to use it. He started to laugh, and got hiccoughs.

He was trying to make a placatory joke in three languages when everything exploded at once.

It couldn't have been the hackbut, because he was still alive, with a headache.

He was in the room he had been entertained in hours earlier, except that he was lying stretched on the floor with a circle of women sitting around him. One of them still held a hackbut, but at an unusual angle. She was asleep.

Next to her was a flushed woman with deep yellow hair and eyes the dense blue of cornflowers. Lucia, widow of Tristão and sister to Simon; the lady who had screamed in the bed.

Next to her was Gelis van Borselen. She said, 'Basil the Bulgar-slayer. We assumed you would have noticed the window next door, with a balcony. It was a much easier climb.'

Nicholas sat up. The room swung. Nothing had been done either to him or for him; he was not bound, and was still fully dressed, if dishevelled. His clothes felt abused, as if penetrated by many ill-wishing eyes through to his skeleton. There was blood in his hair, which was uncovered. He said, 'Why didn't you ask me to stay? It would have been simpler.' He used Flemish, as she had.

'Then we couldn't have hit you with a brick.'

'You could have killed me,' Nicholas said. It was a suggestion, not a complaint. 'As an intruder.'

'Not as of the moment,' said Gelis van Borselen. 'We are confined to a small-injury tariff. Push the carpet away. You will stain it.'

'I'm sorry,' Nicholas said. He pushed the carpet away and found a handkerchief to apply to his head, which was throbbing. He then made to get up. The yellow-haired woman screamed, and the person with the gun abruptly opened her eyes and levelled it.

Gelis van Borselen said, 'I think you should stay where you are. Bel has been up all night watching for you. Lucia, if you scream again, the servants will hear you. Say what you have to say.'

'Me?' Nicholas said. He remembered having a lot to drink in a tavern.

'Yes. That is Lucia Vasquez. You have to tell her you didn't kill Tristão her husband, or enslave her son in a dyeyard and then attempt to seduce him.'

'*Gelis!*' said the yellow-haired woman. She was perfectly beautiful. She was only ten years older than he was. She started to sob.

Nicholas said, 'Look, slow down, will you? I'll tell her, but that's no way to do it.'

'You don't even need to tell her,' said the young woman. 'We have Katelina's own letter. Tristão died by mistake, and you employed Diniz for his own good, and he disliked you so much he took an axe to you. She even says you had nothing to do with the way she was dying. Lucia thinks you dictated the letter, but I'm prepared to believe anything.'

Lucia, widow of Tristão Vasquez, raised her face. Even weeping, she still looked remarkable. 'But for Claes vander Poele, Katelina would never have gone to Cyprus.'

The broad woman with the hackbut laid it down and, crossing, sat down and took Lucia's hand. She said, 'My God, she would have had to go somewhere; ask anyone. This last two year and more, Simon never bounced on the same buttocks twice.'

Nicholas choked. Katelina's sister said, 'You understand Scots? Bel of Cuthilgurdy, Lucia's companion. There's a lot of truth in what she says. What else did you want to tell us?'

Nicholas rested on the rather cold tiles and stared at her. He said, 'I haven't told you anything yet.'

'That's true,' she said. 'I rather thought you'd be quicker. So the Bank isn't doing too well, and you'd like to talk of a merger?'

He sat cross-kneed like a gnome, and covered his face with his hands. He spread his fingers and looked at her. 'You think Simon would agree?'

'No,' she said. 'We don't even know where he is. Anyway, he's had other offers.'

'The fool!' Lucia said. 'We're going to be homeless!' She dragged her hand away and hugged herself, rocking. The woman Bel patted her back.

'What offers?' Nicholas said. His head was hot, and his bottom was cold. Someone scratched on the door and the woman Bel got up and answered. The steward came in, glancing at Nicholas, and then at his mistress, who was currently speechless.

Gelis van Borselen, who was not, spoke to him kindly. 'Senhor vander Poele was attacked and came back to ask help. You want the senhora?'

'Yes?' said Lucia, making a feeble recovery.

The steward said, 'The gentleman has come back.'

Nicholas got to his feet. The girl gave him a quick, annoyed glance, but nobody screamed. The steward said, 'The gentleman who called before. Senhor David de Salmeton.'

'*His* offer?' Nicholas said. They all looked at him. There were no stools within reach. He sat down on the floor again, his toes pointing upwards. They were scuffed. The orange side of his hose displayed dirt on the knee. His head swam. There was a conversation, and the steward went out. And in came David de Salmeton, *mignon*, perfect, composed as in those last days in Cyprus when Zacco . . . when the King had deliberately brought him to Court. David de Salmeton, agent of the Vatachino company to whom Nicholas had just paid twenty-five thousand ducats – or its equivalent – for the *Doria*.

Nicholas said, 'I was just passing through. I do want you to meet Gelis van Borselen. Or no. You have met already?'

The lustrous eyes dwelled on him, widened a little in the cleft-chinned delicate face, and then moved to the lady of the house. David de Salmeton bowed to Lucia, inclined his head to her companion and bowed again to Gelis van Borselen, at whom he raised his perfect, arched brows.

'He was just passing through,' the demoiselle said, switching to French. They both looked down at Nicholas and the servant, after waiting a moment, left the room. The stout woman picked up the hackbut and sat down.

A small red stain appeared on the rug and Nicholas picked up his kerchief again and put it on top of his head, pushing the carpet away. 'Sorry,' he said.

'Monsieur Nikko?' said David de Salmeton. 'Or is the name personal between yourself and the King? I should not wish to intrude on past felicity.'

He didn't smile, but conveyed musical courtesy. He hadn't smiled in Zacco's palace. *When the time comes*, David de Salmeton had remarked on that occasion, *we shall offer you a reasonable price for your business.* That was what the concerted financial attack in Venice had been about. And if Martin's colleague was here, it was because the Vatachino had business in Spain and Portugal, in Madeira and Africa, and wanted no competition.

Nicholas said, 'I don't mind what you call me. I would suggest you came and sat on the rug, but it might soil the skirt of your doublet. I thought you were going to Africa?'

'Excuse me,' said Gelis van Borselen. They both looked at her. She said, 'Perhaps, gentlemen, you should retire to a tavern? Unless, of course, you came here to say something?'

Laughter, unwanted, began to well up again. Nicholas said, 'I think we've both come to say the same thing.'

'Have you?' said Gelis. 'Monsieur de Salmeton? You wish to assure us as well that you have no carnal longing for Madame Lucia's son?'

'*Gelis!*' the blonde woman exploded.

The grey-haired woman thumped the hackbut on the floor. A dribble of powder spilled out. The young exquisite was gazing back at the Borselen girl, a gleam in his eyes. He didn't look shocked.

Of course he didn't: he'd been here before. That was how the Borselen girl had known the Bank was in trouble. And since Simon was not Portuguese, and Diniz Vasquez was away fighting Moors at a singularly inopportune moment – naturally, the Vatachino were here. 'You want to buy St Pol & Vasquez. Toss you for them,' Nicholas offered.

Sober, he would never have said it. Simon's sister sprang to her feet, her face the only creased object between her immaculate yellow hair and her immaculate brocade bedgown. The woman called Bel picked up the hackbut and cradled it to her bosom. The girl Gelis van Borselen sat where she was. 'You can't afford us,' she said.

'Us?' Nicholas said.

For the second time, her skin showed a pricking of colour. She said, 'Katelina's husband and his sister. What were you going to offer for their business?'

'Promises,' said David de Salmeton. 'Part of what he hopes to bring back from Africa. He will give you, in a moment, a promissory note of some size. I, on the other hand, will match his offer in gold ducats now.'

Since there was no seat, the man had found a book-lectern and leaned on it, one aristocratic hand displayed on its edge. His shirt and pale doublet were embroidered, and he wore slippers, not boots. Nicholas, looking at him attentively, couldn't see where he could be carrying more than a handkerchief. He frowned, and carried the frown, elevated, to Gelis van Borselen. She said, 'It doesn't arise. The company has received other offers.'

'You haven't heard mine,' Nicholas said. It was only to see what she would say.

'And we don't want to!' said Simon's sister. 'Do you think we should dream of selling the business to you?'

'Yes, if it was failing,' Nicholas said. He shifted on the cold floor. For one reason or another, he was going to have to leave soon.

'And you would still buy it?' Gelis van Borselen said.

'Yes. Up till now,' Nicholas said, 'it hasn't had me to run it.' He sat, clasping his bloodstained kerchief round his dirt-encased knees, and let his smile spread and dimple under his matted hair.

'It is a powerful argument,' said Gelis van Borselen. 'Very well.

Submit your offers in writing, and declare when and how you would settle. Madame will communicate in due course. You are both going to Africa?'

Nicholas looked at the prie-dieu, and the dark, liquid eyes returned the look. 'Not together,' Nicholas said.

'Ah!' said David de Salmeton. 'I had hoped . . . That is, surely you planned, like myself, to call on the way at Madeira? The plantations of St Pol & Vasquez are there. I hoped your new caravel might offer me passage at, of course, the right price.'

'Free,' Nicholas said. 'Provided I am the new owner of St Pol & Vasquez. Otherwise the ship will be full, I much fear, of inedible merchandise. Demoiselles, I must leave.' He got up.

'A cool drink?' said Gelis van Borselen. 'There is no hurry, surely.'

There was not so much hurry that he couldn't make them all an extremely elaborate bow. He said to David de Salmeton, 'Perhaps we shall meet in Madeira. Or elsewhere.'

'I'm sure of it,' the agent said. 'There are Negroes enough for us all, although I envy you that young Guinea fellow you've tamed. He'll take you straight to the pick of the bunch. I'm told the piccaninnies are charming.'

'I'll send you one,' Nicholas said; and got himself outside quite adequately, he was so angry.

The plump, friendly woman was still in the tavern when he eventually called on his way back, and so was Father Godscalc, sitting in a settled way before a small, half-empty flask.

Nicholas paused. The woman had her foot on the steps. Godscalc said, 'If you want them, the chamberlain has given me the addresses of three proper houses. You have one bastard too many already.' Then he looked again and said, 'Who did that to you?'

'Simon's sister,' Nicholas said, 'hit me on the head with a brick.' He sat down, overwhelmed by the humour of it. He said, 'The Vatachino were there.'

Godscalc said nothing.

Nicholas said, 'And Gelis. Gelis van –'

Godscalc said, 'So what of it? You knew what to expect.' He waited and then said not unkindly, 'And they are not alike. You would hardly think they were sisters.'

'No,' said Nicholas.

He heard Godscalc throw a coin on the table and get up. Godscalc said, 'Come. I have a horse. Time you were back on board ship.'

Chapter 10

STRANDED WITH THREE thousand Portuguese and two thousand Burgundians on one of the Pillars of Hercules, Diniz Vasquez was far too stubborn to admit that he had made a mistake in coming to Africa.

From the hill-top fort to which he had been posted, he looked across fourteen miles of water to the opposite Pillar, named Jabal Tariq by the Moors who had occupied the rock until practically yesterday. To his right was the Middle Sea. To his left was the Ocean Sea of the West. Behind him on its narrow peninsula lay the Christian city he had come to relieve, called Septem Fratres by the Romans, and Ceuta today.

The name referred to seven hills and not to any visible record for brotherhood. In seizing it fifty years ago, the King of Portugal had proclaimed a number of charitable aims, such as gaining access to the desert beyond, and hence to the savage blacks of the south whose souls required to be rescued. He wished to stop Barbary pirates from preying on Christian shipping. He wanted to sap Muslim confidence. He had his eye on all the other Moorish garrisons on the coastal strip (which, once dislodged, would have no use for their hinterland cornfields). And he also wanted to remove from unworthy hands the greatest African mart in the West.

All the riches of Africa and the Indies came to Ceuta, brought by caravan up through the Sahara. The Turks might throttle trade in the east, but to Ceuta on thousands of camels came the goods that the Genoese, too, saw and coveted; the rice and the salt, the silks and peppers and ginger, the elephants' teeth. The slaves. And the gold.

The theory was excellent. In practice, Portugal managed to conquer little but Ceuta. In the outcome, ringed by enemies, they found it impossible to penetrate the Sahara. And the Moors of Ceuta regretfully shifted their caravan terminal a shade to the east, leaving twenty-four thousand stalls crumbling and vacant.

In the years that followed, the displaced Moors returned quite a lot, often with shiploads of friends from Granada, and had to be beaten off once again, with many fine feats of arms. A German knight errant dispatched a Saracen champion here in single combat, during the wave of Christian feeling that followed the fall of Constantinople.

That was when the Duke of Burgundy held his great feast in Lille, where a giant dressed as a Saracen had brought in a weeping damsel, representing Holy Church lamenting oppression, and mounted upon a plaster elephant. Upon which everyone present, including the Duke's illegitimate sons, had sworn to perform high deeds of arms and wash their hands in the blood of the Infidel. Eleven years ago, that had been.

That was why two of the bastards were here, and not before time: the older would never see forty again. All the commanders were old, and famous for jousting, and anxious about their immortal souls. The knight Simon de Lalaing was probably sixty, and his two sons were no chickens: Ernoul was close by Diniz now.

Ernoul's cousin had been one of the most famous knights of all time. Ernoul's father and cousin had jousted in Scotland when Diniz was two, and Ernoul assumed Diniz had heard all about it. Ernoul was bountifully scathing on the subject of skulking Islamic dogs who abandoned their siege the moment the relieving force landed and, instead of offering battle like men, lured soldiers out through the gates and then fell on them.

Skirmishing parties returned with half their numbers or not at all. Guides were few and irresolute. And although heralds emerged and challenges were read out in all the customary language of chivalry, even ordinary decency seemed to have gone. No one replied. Ernoul, who was destined for the Church, had received in a matter of weeks all the reinforcement his faith might have needed. He hated the Saracens.

Diniz Vasquez, who for personal reasons had learned to hate at least one man of Muslim persuasion, began, on the contrary, to find his convictions diminish. He had come because of what had happened on Cyprus, and to escape the clutches of grandfather Jordan. But in defying Jordan, he had left his mother unchampioned, and her livelihood in the hands of an agent.

He had thought – he still thought – that her brother Simon should take care of it all, but of late he had had doubts about the warlike, brilliant Simon. He had had doubts about beauty, in men and in women. He was eighteen years old, and a passionate virgin.

Doubts about beauty, and doubts about faith. Ernoul of Burgundy said, 'You realise His Holiness might even be dead, and

the Crusade called off before we can join it? Men are living in
Paradise who helped fight for Constantinople, and I haven't killed
a Moor since I came here.'

'Join the next foraging party,' said Diniz; and then regretted it.
The fault was hardly Ernoul's. Ernoul begged daily to lead the
next sally into the hills. Charging, drums beating, into oblivion
seemed more proper for a man of birth, a future prince of the
Church, than messing about bringing in fodder and unloading
storeships. Hoisting in stores was routine: the food supply of Ceuta
had never really been interrupted. Diniz had not, after all, come to
the relief of a citadel that was in extremis.

He had begun to doubt, even, if he had come to kill Moors. The
Portuguese, the Ghenters, the Burgundians fought for the greater
glory of God, Christ against Antichrist, as well as for personal
redemption. Diniz, son of a trader, had been reared to believe the
division less arbitrary. Before coming here, he had fuelled his
hatred with the deeds of one Egyptian Mameluke. Now he
remembered a great Arab doctor, serving the Christian sick in the
horror of Famagusta, with Nicholas at his side. And how in
Trebizond, he had been told, Nicholas had taken arms against
Turks, but the Turcoman Uzum Hasan had been his ally.

His unseeing eyes found they were watching a galley making
heavy weather of crossing the narrows. The Spanish port of
Algeciras lay behind her and, once past the Rock, the wind and the
current were pushing her east. From the efforts she made to adjust,
he saw that she was trying to come into Ceuta.

Afterwards, he remembered asking Ernoul if they were expecting
a victualling ship, and being told that they were. It meant casks of
arrows, and supplies of powder at least for the bombards, and
pikes and bows and crates for the smiths and the armourers. And,
usually, a nice selection of fresh fish and meat and some fruit. He
helped unload if he had to. It made him feel sick.

Today, being on duty elsewhere, he didn't have to; and by the
time the galley arrived and found a place to drop anchor, Diniz was
free and on his way down to the sea-moat and the isthmus,
threading past the old souks and crumbling palaces in order to eat
and play dice at the castle with a couple of bowmen from Lisbon.
The galley's captain went by, on his way up the stairs to the
governor, followed by his clerk with his inkhorn and papers. The
captain, he'd heard, was a Ragusan. The scribe was double the size
that scribes usually were, and what his cap left uncovered was
obscured by the whorls of two grandiloquent eyeglasses. They
glinted at Diniz.

Diniz had to get up at midnight to take his turn at the watch on the walls. He had been there an hour when he became aware that the ship's clerk was standing beside him. The starlight glimmered on glass, and a voice he had missed for six months addressed him in almost inaudible French. 'How much did you lose? The man you had on your left is notorious in twenty-five cities.'

Diniz turned, his throat closed. 'Ah no,' Nicholas said, and laid a large, calm hand over his. 'Don't give me away. Or, if you remember, we shall both be arrested for sodomy.'

He always went to the heart of the trouble. Diniz produced a sound which began as a laugh. He said, 'It was awful. They made me. I wouldn't have left you.'

'I know,' Nicholas said. 'Master Michael Crackbene and I have had a conversation about that. Did your grandfather make you come here?'

This time, he managed a proper laugh, although quietly. 'It was the last thing he wanted.' And then, with sudden anxiety, 'They wouldn't believe me. Have you seen them?'

'Your grandfather and Simon? No. They've both gone. I've seen your mother. And Gelis van Borselen is at Lagos.' The calming grip loosened, and Nicholas, taking off the affair on his nose, settled his arms on the parapet, holding the glass in one hand. A bird cried in the night. He said, 'So you've found your vocation? You are taking the Cross?'

Taking the Cross. It was the sort of thing the Lalaing brothers were in the habit of saying. Diniz said, 'Why are you here?'

'Not because your mother sent me,' Nicholas said. 'She seemed . . . seemed to think I was lying as well. No. I had a call to make anyway. And I wondered if you knew that David de Salmeton was at Lagos? The Vatachino want to buy out your company.'

Doubts about beauty, and doubts about faith. David de Salmeton of the silken hair and feminine hands, annexing the dyeyard in Cyprus. Diniz said, 'She wouldn't sell!'

'She will, to someone,' Nicholas said. 'She has at least two other offers. One of them from me.'

Along the wall, someone spoke. Against the deep blue of the night and the black rounded chain of the hills, nothing moved. Nicholas added tranquilly, 'It wasn't serious. I couldn't afford it. It was only to slow matters down. But for some reason Simon has left, and she has the decision to make.'

Diniz said, 'You think I should go back.'

And Nicholas said, 'I think Jordan thinks you should go back. He paid Simon, I'm told, to get out of Portugal. And that leaves only you.'

'I won't be coerced,' Diniz said.

'No,' said Nicholas.

Silence fell. Instead of the irritations and tedium of the campaign, Diniz found his mind invaded again by the fear his grandfather inspired; the angry pity for Lucia his mother; his disillusionment with Simon, that flower of chivalry her brother. He knew he ought to go back, and that he wouldn't. Not even for Nicholas, who had searched him out to tell him. Searched him out, incongruously dressed as a ship's clerk from a galley. *I had a call to make anyway.*

Diniz said, for the second time, and much more abruptly, 'Why are you here?'

Then Nicholas stirred. He wrinkled his nose like a dog and sat the eyeglasses on it again. 'Guess,' he said.

Further along the walls, out of sight, someone was whistling. Below in the town, a donkey brayed, and a dog began to bark, and broke off with a squeal. A scent of incense floated up from the mosques turned into churches, together with the smells of humanity and of the sea. In the bay, the lanterns of the fleet that had brought the Burgundians festooned the darkness and, by their interrupted reflections, gave substance to the host of small boats that also littered the water.

Nicholas had sailed in the supply ship that had come in from Lagos today; a great galley of Florentine build that had seen long and hard service. He knew what ships Nicholas had. This one fitted all he knew of the *Ciaretti*, which had stayed with the Bank all the time that Nicholas had been in Cyprus.

He had watched her come in, flying the Portuguese flag. He had watched the fuss she made, seeking a berth, before settling next to one of the troopships. Diniz had paid little attention. Otherwise he would have realised sooner that he recognised the roundship beside her, because he had sailed in that same ship from Cyprus. She was the *Doria*, the vessel which Jordan and Crackbene had stolen. Diniz said, without explanation or context, 'You can't!' His breath caught.

He felt Nicholas move. Nicholas said, 'I hope the garrison can manage without it. Wouldn't you think so?'

Diniz boiled with frustration. 'You can't. How can you?'

He heard, rather than saw, Nicholas give a smile. Nicholas said, 'It wasn't hard to arrange. There's only a watchman aboard, and a roundship doesn't need much of a crew. We'll transfer twenty-five mariners, and they'll take her over to Spain before daylight.'

'And then where?' Diniz said. 'Jordan leased her to Portugal for a year.'

'She wasn't Jordan's to lease,' Nicholas said. 'You don't mind? By the time she lifts anchor, you won't be on watch.'

He had thought of everything. Diniz said, 'You're going with her?'

'Great God no,' Nicholas said. 'Triadano and I have to stay behind, expressing sympathy and completing our business.'

'Of course,' Diniz said. 'And then to Venice, picking up the rescued roundship on the way.' It was neat, and successful, and brilliant. He said, his eyes damp, 'I don't suppose you need an able dyeworks apprentice?' Then he said, 'It's all right. I didn't mean it.'

Nicholas said, 'I know you didn't. I asked you if you were taking the Cross?'

Diniz' head ached. He said with sudden conviction, 'No. I don't belong here.' He stopped. He said, 'I suppose I should go back to Lagos.'

'Only you can decide,' Nicholas said. 'But if you want, I can carry you. I have to take the *Ciaretti* back to load cargo. She does sail back to Venice, but I have to stay and make money. The Bank and the Charetty company are in need of funds. I told you, I think, that I couldn't really afford to bid for your company.'

He didn't believe it. He said, 'How? What has happened?'

'The Vatachino,' Nicholas said. 'Among other things. So I'm taking Ludovico da Bologna's advice, and launching my own private crusade into the African interior. That's why I need the *Doria*. She'll load at Sanlúcar, and meet me off the African coast at Madeira.'

'How will you get there?' said Diniz.

'By caravel, licensed by Portugal. I shall have to pay for it.'

'With African gold,' Diniz said.

'I have to redeem the Bank,' Nicholas said. It was all he said. He wasn't like Jordan. He didn't coerce. He presented the facts, and then waited.

Diniz said, 'When does my mother decide? About selling the business?'

'Why?' said Nicholas.

'Because surely she should inspect the plantations first? See her managers?'

'What are you asking?' Nicholas said.

Diniz said, 'Take us both to Madeira. I'll come with you to Lagos and persuade her.'

'She may have sold,' Nicholas said. 'I told you who was there.'

'Yes,' Diniz said. 'Gelis van Borselen.'

Nicholas said, 'I won't involve her. Neither should you.'

'She is involved,' said Diniz. 'She drives my mother wild, but she listens to her. I think she won't let her sell. I think she might persuade my mother to go to Madeira.'

'On my ship?' Nicholas said. 'After the death of your father? Don't expect it. She may be troubled enough that you turned back from Ceuta.'

The sharpness of the words cut, and a deeper anguish welled up. 'They weren't starving,' said Diniz.

'It isn't a sin,' Nicholas said.

It was not, perhaps, quite as easy as Nicholas had made out to man Jordan's roundship and sail it out of harbour, and when it was finally done, she had to deceive the fast ships Ceuta sent off to locate her. But she had a good start, and when daylight came they were still casting about. By the time they got as far as Sanlúcar the *Doria* was drawn up in dock draped with matting and her name had been changed. She had been there for two weeks, said the Spanish authorities. The Venetian consul in Seville was Antonio da Ca' da Mosto.

Behind in Ceuta, there was an eruption of charge, counter-charge and horror over the purloining of the roundship *Doria*, but the blame, it was finally concluded, lay with pirates and renegades who, stealing through in the night, had manned and taken her for their own illicit purposes. The officer in charge of the watch was, fortuitously, of such a high degree that no punishment could be inflicted.

A letter of explanation was dictated to be sent to His Sacred Majesty, and another to the lord vicomte de Ribérac, who had leased the ship to Portugal for the highest of motives. Both letters stressed the hardships being suffered in Ceuta, the loss of gallant young lives, and the consequent exhaustion of the rest of the garrison. The governor also mentioned that his pay was eighteen months in arrears, and the amount of supplies just unloaded had been rather less than he asked for.

This was true, since a third of it lay safely locked in Sanlúcar. The rest, however, exactly matched the bill of lading handed over (and written) by the clerk of the *Ciaretti*. The *Ciaretti* also, naturally, carried both letters back to Lagos, along with young Senhor Vasquez, who had been recalled to deal with his widowed mother's affairs.

His release had not been hard to procure. Autumn was here. The Moorish offensive against Ceuta was over. If the Bastard of Burgundy were to fulfil his vow in a greater arena, he should be proceeding immediately to the Pope's side. Or at the worst, wintering in some port in Europe where he could be reached from his father's bier or bedside in Brussels.

Throughout it all, the young Senhor Diniz saw nothing of

Nicholas in Ceuta, and very little on the voyage to Lagos, on a ship encumbered with returning officials. Nicholas, on the other hand, saw rather more of him than Diniz knew. Landed at Lagos, he let the passengers go ashore, and then had Diniz brought to his cabin. He took his eyeglasses off.

Physically, the boy had matured. The hollow-cheeked, bloodless youngster of Famagusta was a man of middle height who would never be broad, but who now had the shoulders, the neck and the forearms of a soldier. He looked his father's son, except for the shape of his eyes and something about the set of his back, which came from his half-Scottish blood. Nicholas said, 'Are you sorry?'

'No,' said Diniz. His eyes were bright. He said, 'You'll come to the house with me?'

'I think that would be a remarkably bad idea,' Nicholas said. 'No. It's your own affair, what you and your people decide. Anyway, I'm supposed to be out of town. Send and tell me tomorrow what happened.'

Diniz said, 'I thought I'd tell them . . .'

Nicholas rose. He said, 'Diniz, I don't want to know. You've had time to think. It's your business. If your mother wants, I'll take her to Madeira. But I shan't take you without her.'

The boy's skin darkened. Then he said, 'Of course not,' and left.

Nicholas went ashore in disguise, and passed the hours until sunset in the house Gregorio had taken, for ostensibly he had spent the last days in Lisbon, not Ceuta, and was not due to return until evening. He used the time to talk to his companions in residence, among them Jorge da Silves, now installed to supervise the commissioning of the vessel whose master he would be.

Time now was precious. Heat and rain were the enemy: every voyage to and from the African coast had to be made between September and May. In three weeks the ship had to be ready, to the last detail of equipment, provisions and crew. On this, the first day of his return, Nicholas mastered the reports, read the lists, and discussed the last fitting-out of the caravel. It had a name.

'The *what!*' Nicholas said.

'The *San Niccolò,*' Gregorio said. 'We had to call the ship something. What are you going to use for the other one? The *Doria,* the *Ribérac,* or just *Future Trouble?* Stolen, unlicensed, and trading where anyone can blow her out of the water? Who's going to sail her?'

'No one reputable, you may be sure,' Nicholas said. He didn't want to upset anyone, yet. He didn't particularly want a ship named after himself either, but knew well enough when to recognise a gesture. He said, 'I wonder whom Jordan insured her with?'

By the time he went to bed that night he had seen over his completed ship, now afloat. After the *Ciaretti*, the caravel felt like a fishing-boat. Half the length, three-masted, beamy, she answered to twenty-five mariners, as the slender *Ciaretti* answered to two hundred or more, and had room in her stout pinewood belly for food and water and cargo; and a rig and a rudder to take her anywhere her captain had heart to go. Still warm from the sun, she was so new she smelt like a banquet, and shone in the lamplight like satin. The pain he felt this time, unwisely, was joy.

Next day, he was arguing over some drawings of collapsable boats when Bel of Cuthilgurdy was announced, and for a moment he couldn't recall who she was. Then she came in, upholstered from neck to floor like a tent and wearing a linen towel on her head, bunched heavily over each ear. She was not carrying a hackbut. She said, 'Aye. And are ye sober today?'

Simon's sister's companion. He said, 'You need to come very early for that,' and smiled at her, and got rid of the others who fortunately didn't speak Scots. He found her a cushioned stool and some wine. When she sat, all the stool and part of the floor disappeared. He sat down opposite. 'Now, about sodomy,' she began.

'. . . Yes?' said Nicholas.

'Oh, ye can cackle,' said the woman. Her eyes were brown as two coppers. 'But spoil that laddie's good name, and I'll have ye cold as a chine of boiled mutton. He's for going to Madoora.'

'Madeira,' Nicholas said. 'With his mother?'

'Ye know Mistress Lucia?' the woman said. 'Well, you've cause to. She got three good dunts on ye afore we pulled her away.'

'You had a hackbut,' said Nicholas.

'But I didna use it. No. Ye don't want Mistress Lucia on Madoora.'

'Worse than sodomy?' Nicholas said.

'You're a cheeky young bastard,' she said.

'So I'm told,' Nicholas said. He lost his inclination to laugh.

She said, 'Aye. That's you, then. Now listen. My wee lady doesna want to go to Madoora: she's feared. But she's just as feared the boy will escape her again. She's not the one to stand up to bullying, Mistress Lucia. She's seen ower muckle.'

She paused. He didn't say anything. She went on, her voice dry. 'There's no doubt, my fine Master Niccolò, that she will lose her grip of the business if someone doesna go out to Madoora and fight for it. The boy's willing. He's better than naebody.'

'He's a good deal better than that,' Nicholas said.

'I'll take your word for it,' said the woman. 'His mother – you'll

allow – is inordinate light in her humours, poor lass, and not sort-
able.'

Nicholas said, 'He would be on my ship for three days. Presumably you have a good factor at Funchal? Or does he practise
sodomy too?'

'Oh, aye, you're a clever hoor,' said Bel of Cuthilgurdy, 'and
would lay that tongue of yours against anybody. But there's never
been cause to complain about Jaime, and the lad will be safe in his
hands. Forbye, the girl will go, and me with her.'

'The girl?' But of course he remembered.

'Gelis. Sister to Simon's sorry young wife. The boy says ye
tended the lass Katelina in Cyprus.'

'Her sister doesn't think so,' said Nicholas.

'Then the two of us, I take it, won't be let go. And Diniz can't
go. And hence the company falls into your pooch? Supple tricks,
Master Niccolò.' Her consonants could have cut tin.

Gregorio opened the door, said, 'Oh. Forgive me,' and closed it.
The hour-glass was empty. Nicholas stretched out his hand and
reversed it. The drawings he had disputed so violently had rolled
themselves up. They weren't so bad: with one major change, they
would give him the adjustable, the portable boats which were
going to make all the difference. He had meant to ride to Sagres
today, but it was getting late now to go visiting. He said, 'Does
Simon pay you? Or Jordan?'

She must be between forty and fifty. Her features were floury
and blunt as a pastryskin over a pudding. She said, 'Seek your
excuse somewhere else. Mistress Lucia pays me, when I'm paid.
My gash is my own.'

Nicholas rose, looking at her. He went to the door and, opening
it, called. Father Godscalc came in.

'This,' Nicholas said, 'is Mistress Bel, companion to the lady
mother of Diniz. She says Diniz may sail with us to Madeira,
provided she and Gelis van Borselen come also. Otherwise, since
his mother can't go, he can't either.'

Godscalc looked from him to the woman. 'You're the priest?'
she said. 'Gelis said ye were nimble.'

'Demoiselle,' Godscalc said. He stood, looming darkly and
thoughtfully over her. He said, 'You would leave your bereaved
mistress here?'

'That's the idea,' said Bel of Cuthilgurdy. 'When the King goes
abroad, the sleekit jackmen are made to go with him.'

'Gelis van Borselen?' Godscalc said.

'I think,' Nicholas said, 'she means the delectable David. He
said he was going to Madeira.'

'He's gone,' said the woman. 'If it's the bonny wee broker ye mean. Got a berth on a Portuguese ship for Porto Santo as soon as your own ship went off. He can cross to Funchal easy from there.'

'Without first making his offer?' said Nicholas. 'Or was it turned down?'

She sat, her hands folded in front of her, smiling. 'Let's say he has other competitors.'

'On the island? Another firm? Who?' Nicholas said.

So far as he could read her look, it was pitying. 'Now, what would an auld carline ken? To find out the rights of that, ye'd need to go to Madoora.'

'Madeira,' Godscalc said, and Nicholas let him. She knew what she was saying. She knew what she had come to demand of him. And he knew, and she knew, that she was going to get it.

Chapter 11

'**Y**OU'RE NOT PLEASED,' Godscalc said, at the hurried supper they took, the four of them, after she'd gone. 'You should be. Diniz will protect you against Simon.'

'The ladies won't,' Nicholas said. 'You think Simon is going to be on Madeira?'

'They said he might be,' Gregorio said. 'He can't safeguard his business from Scotland. And he sent you that letter.'

He and the padre often supported each other, Nicholas noticed, since Venice. Since Venice Gregorio, always agile-minded and effective, had developed in range, in curiosity, in confidence. Now he might find it less easy to slip into the quiet ways of the past, playing music or cards, or talking dreamily under the starlight. And Godscalc, pursuing his own dogged course, had encouraged him. The harshness Nicholas had met in San Michele had hardened into something to be watched. Only once, in the tavern, had Godscalc allowed him a measure of the protective friendship he had had as a boy. But that was all right. No one owed anything to a banker; and vice versa, of course.

Gregorio continued to talk. 'Of course, there's no law that says you've got to take up Simon's challenge. You can land the ladies and Diniz and sail.'

'Leaving Simon free to sell to whom he pleases,' Godscalc commented. His knife, upright in his fist, had two sardines on it. 'Something Nicholas had expected to prevent, I deduce, given three days with the volatile Lucia.'

'There is that,' Nicholas said. As it happened, he had wished himself alone from pure impulse: a desire to board his virgin ship free of memories, and threatened only by the violence of Nature.

'Am I wrong?' Godscalc said. There was no escape: his expression was heavy and mutinous.

'And you a priest?' Nicholas said. 'But assuming I do want St

Pol & Vasquez, wouldn't it make better sense to let Simon and Lucia sell, if they want to, and take the company over myself once I have money enough? On the whole, I'd rather fight the Vatachino than Simon.'

'Perhaps the Vatachino won't succeed in getting it,' Gregorio said.

Nicholas said, 'You've met David de Salmeton. He'll do what I'd do. Buy from Lucia on her own. Or allow Simon to sell, and then buy from the buyer. Don't you know yet what we're dealing with? Did you never wonder why the Vatachino haven't interfered with us, or the *Ciaretti*, since Venice?'

'You've been too well protected,' said Loppe.

'And at Ceuta, you covered your tracks,' said the priest. 'They're not miracle men. De Salmeton didn't know you were on the *Ciaretti*, and she sailed without warning. They always do, for fear of corsairs.'

'Oh, come,' Nicholas said. 'The *Ciaretti* leaves, and I disappear? It would take four days to discover I wasn't in Lisbon, and no time at all to find out what her cargo was, and therefore where she must be going. Diniz and the *Doria* were both in Ceuta: it was a reasonable guess that I was going to try for them both. But de Salmeton didn't send to warn either Governor, or try to stop either ship.'

'Perhaps he had other ideas,' Gregorio said. 'If he knows where she is, the *Doria* may not be at Sanlúcar very much longer.'

'I'll be surprised,' Nicholas said. 'She's extraordinarily well protected, and he can have very few men at his command.'

'Perhaps that's why he didn't stop you?' said Gregorio. 'Suppose all he's really concerned with is taking over St Pol & Vasquez, and your absence gave him the chance to slip off to Madeira and do it?'

'Then why not have me caught and imprisoned?' Nicholas said. 'Why not send a warning to Ceuta?'

He was watching Loppe, who suddenly answered. 'Because he has made up his mind that you will take Diniz to Africa.' It was not what Nicholas had expected.

'No, surely,' said Godscalc.

'I wonder,' said Nicholas. 'I wonder if that's what he is counting on.' He had stopped looking at Loppe.

'Why?' said Gregorio.

Loppe was silent. Godscalc drew an angry breath. Nicholas said, 'On the chance that we'd both find the source of the gold. Get to Ethiopia, even. Then on the way back, something would happen to me, and to Diniz, if it hadn't happened already. Then he'd salvage the ships and the gold and end up with St Pol & Vasquez. I told you. They're exquisite adversaries.'

'You like them,' said Godscalc.

'I admire them. Different thing,' Nicholas said. He thought Godscalc would corner him afterwards and deliver a lecture, but he didn't. He remembered, belatedly, that he had drawn up his projection without even thinking of Godscalc.

He went to Sagres next day, a ride of fifteen miles, accompanied by a short retinue of followers, and Jorge da Silves, and Loppe.

Loppe, in the sleeveless robe and light cap they all wore, would not find his standing misunderstood here, where of all spots in the world the navigator, the interpreter, the man of special talents was valued.

From here, the most south-westerly corner of Europe, the late Henry, Prince of Portugal, Governor of Ceuta, Governor of the Algarve, Grand Master of the Order of Christ, had launched the expeditions of trade and discovery through which men like Alvise da Ca' da Mosto had found their way down the African coast.

The ships might have sailed from Lagos, but to Sagres and the prince's farm at Raposeira had come the Jews and the Arabs, the Catalans and the Germans, the Venetians and the Genoese whose combined knowledge of charts, of navigation, of ship design had made the voyages possible, and the courtiers and captains who sailed on them.

Some of these, in retirement, had returned to their lands, or to Lisbon. Some had married and kept fine estate among the orchards of Lagos. Others had settled near this, the ultimate headland; precipitous, bare, and scoured by north-westerly tempests from unknowable oceans. Standing at Sagres, or on the single Cape that lay westward, one looked down sheer sandstone cliffs twenty times the height of a man with the white of dashed foam at their feet; and abroad at the flat, shoreless ocean, upon which laboured the flecks that were vessels and the infinitesimal specks that were souls, witness to man's perseverance, his greed and his courage.

Before leaving for Ceuta, Nicholas had begun to seek out and comb the minds of these men, and found in Jorge da Silves a willing mentor and escort. He was discovering – with some difficulty, for the Portuguese was a singularly reticent man – that pride itself could take second place to obsession. Da Silves had served great commanders; he had tested his courage in terrible waters, and longed to return to them. 'Beware,' the Jew of Mallorca had said, smiling. 'Jorge da Silves will take you further than you conceivably wish to go.'

The man they were visiting today had been the companion of Prince Henry's last years, as well as one of the most eminent of his captains; yet he lived simply when away from his post at the Palace at Sintra, and his house was blockish and plain, although with well-tended stables and bakehouse and mews set among the tousled palms bent askew in the courtyard. Nicholas, riding in with da Silves and his servants, noticed two horses unsaddled and steaming, and a horse-cloth whose blazon he recognised.

So, it seemed, did Jorge da Silves. He stood, his boots astride, his whip in his hand, and said, 'Diniz Vasquez? Why is he here?'

Loppe's head turned. Nicholas said, 'I don't know. Although, as I told you, we are taking Senhor Diniz and two of the ladies to Madeira.' The news, he remembered, had been coolly received. He wondered if he now understood why. Then the door opened and a man emerged smiling; a lean grey fellow with a moustache and a stick, informal in chemise and slippers and hose with yesterday's beard pricking his chin: Diogo Gomes, who had been to the Gambia and beyond. With him, hurrying forward, was the boy Diniz.

'Jorge!'

'And so you are home!' said Jorge da Silves, and received the boy, smiling. Then he stepped back.

Diniz, eyes glowing, was still holding his arm. 'You are to sail the new caravel! I've just heard. And I shall be on it.' He looked over at Nicholas. 'I called at your house, and they told me you were going to the headland, then here. You must listen! There is so much Senhor Diogo has to tell you!'

'This boy!' said the man with the stick affectionately. 'What, child, can I tell that you haven't already got from me, or Aires or João since you were in swaddling clothes?'

The boy coloured. The face of the Portuguese had turned cold. Nicholas said, 'Perhaps I ought to have consulted Diniz instead of you, senhor. But he is only travelling as far as Madeira, and with his mother's consent. If, Diniz, I am right? Your mother has agreed that you and the ladies should go?'

'Gelis has decided,' said Diniz; but his eyes, shifting away, had fallen on Loppe. He walked over and held out his hand. 'This is better than Cyprus.'

'It is different,' Loppe said. And their host, walking over, held out his hand also to Loppe and said, 'I have heard of you. Senhor vander Poele is fortunate to have such a guide. Come in, all of you, and let us talk about this hell-hole you are determined to visit.'

The words were light enough. They covered the same trace of defensiveness Nicholas had observed among all this brotherhood of solitary voyagers; even among those with crooked limbs and warped yellow skin and heads that nodded and trembled, who would never travel again.

They spoke of marvels, of course: of the monstrous horse-fishes and lizards; of the tattooed women with gold-burdened ears, or stretched lips, or pendulous breasts, or of the kings with thirty wives each. That had to be listened to. But the advice Nicholas wanted was harder to come by, even from Diogo Gomes.

Africa? Jorge there knew all that he did. The Moors lived in the north – Diniz knew that, he'd fought them at Ceuta, good lad. But walk out of the back door of Ceuta, and there was the Sahara desert before you, stretching south for fifty-two days to the Sahel. And what was the Sahel? A belt of scrubland with rivers and grazing and trees, that divided the sands of the north from your tropical Land of the Blacks, a place of heat and rain and forest not even a madman could penetrate.

'So that's your interior,' said Diogo Gomes, drinking up his cup of sweet wine. 'That's the way the caravans go, north to south, taking silk and silver and salt down through the desert to these damned tricky marts of the Sahel and then plodding back north, your camels bow-legged with gold.

'That is, not *your* camels. Christians are barred from that route. But being brighter than most, we found we could sail round the edge of the desert and, landing from time to time, entice some of the gold to the coast. All right so far as it goes. But why not go further, you ask, and cut into the north-to-south traffic?'

'Ca' da Mosto tried it,' said Nicholas. 'He said it couldn't be done.'

'And you didn't believe him,' said Gomes. 'Well, I'll show you. Where's the map?' And he put his cup down and, leaning over, stabbed a scarred finger.

'There. There is Ceuta. There's your north African shore in the Middle Sea. Follow me west through the Straits to the Ocean. Watch the African coast, how it bends to the south and the west – still green, still full of unchristian peasants, the devils. These are fishing villages. And now, see?'

He shifted his cup, and Diniz caught the map as it began to roll up. The commander flattened it with a broad hand, drinking absently. 'Now look at the coast. Flat and pale, the sign of a damned, waterless land fit for no one but nomads, for you're sailing down the edge of the Sahara with a steady north-easterly pushing you, and the sea with more sand than water in it, as your lead-line'll tell you. There's Cape Bojador, which men thought couldn't be passed. A hundred miles south of the Grand Canary, that's all it is, but nasty with rocks, keep well clear. Keep off the whole God-damned coast, watch out for rips, and don't flatter yourself there's a place safe to anchor.'

'The current is south-west,' said Jorge da Silves.

'You want me to show you where it isn't? You wait,' said Diogo Gomes. He was red, but only partly from wine. 'But now, you want to keep going south, and there's the Rio de Ouro which you ought to know is a gulf, not a river, and leading straight into the desert, where the only gold is already on camel backs. Correct? And so go on until you've made three hundred miles since Bojador, and you're coming to the good white stone of Cape Blanco and within it, the gulf we are speaking of; the first place for a thousand miles that will give you quiet nights and fresh water, for all it's as bleak as a legless man's toe.'

'Arguim,' said Nicholas. 'Where Ca da' Mosto went inland by camel.'

Diogo Gomes looked up. 'You met him; you know what he found out. The gold travelling north passes through a market called Wadan that lies six days inland from Arguim; and six days beyond that, there's another, better market called Taghaza. But that's twelve days into the desert, in a land without water and full of robbers and nomads. You set up a trading-post there, and you have to set up some means of providing it with water and food and enough men and arms to protect it. You think you could do that?'

'No,' said Nicholas.

'No. If you want to tap the real wealth, sure enough that's where some of it is. But meanwhile we have to content ourselves with what the dealers fetch to the coast. The Tawny Moors bring the stuff from Wadan to Arguim and sell to Christian ships with a Portuguese licence, and to nobody else. Pirates are hanged. Traders who sell arms to the Muslims are burned for heresy. Business isn't quite what it was – in the Prince's time you'd find the warehouses full, and fifteen caravels would load every year. Soon, it may be like that again; but meantime you'll still find the odd ship in the anchorage, and you should get enough gold to make it worth your while, and the King's. Gold and whatever else you may be after.'

Diniz said, 'Could you reach Prester John from Wadan?'

The map rolled up with a smack. Diogo Gomes sat back and looked from him to Nicholas. He said, 'Did King Alfonso require it?'

Nicholas paused. Diniz said, 'No, but the Pope did. The Pope freed a galley, and asked the King to give Senhor Niccolò all his assistance to reach Ethiopia.'

'I see,' said the commander. His eyes in the unshaven face were watchful and narrowed. 'So now what will you do? That is, you've heard, I assume?'

'No,' Nicholas said. He laid a hand on Diniz' arm. 'The Pope?'

'The Holy Father, God rest him, is dead,' said Diogo Gomes. 'And the Crusade from Ancona is halted. The fleets and the armies have gone.'

'But,' said Diniz, 'the threat from the Turk still exists.' Nicholas took his hand away.

Diogo Gomes said, 'Naturally.' He recovered, and repeated himself, rather slowly. 'Naturally, to link hands with Prester John and his Christian armies is still Holy Church's great desire. Any man who did so . . . You have this in mind, Senhor Niccolò? This? If so, you would have to sail much further south than Arguim. You would have to penetrate the interior from the Sahel.'

'The land my lord Diogo knows better than anyone,' said Jorge da Silves, his hands laced hard together. 'Where the rivers begin. The rivers outlandishly named, any one of which may be the great Nile, and the highway we are seeking.'

Diogo Gomes took the flask in his hands and held it ready to pour, his face scanning them all. 'Is that what you want?' said the commander. 'Then I shall tell you what I found out, and willingly. I believed you had your eyes set on the gold mart at Wadan.'

Nicholas smiled. 'The Franciscans have drilled me too well. But I won't hide from you that I need to find gold if I go to the Sahel. I have funds to replace.'

'The marts are there,' Gomes said. 'As I told you. It is where the northern caravans come to unload. They might sell to you, if you are circumspect, and if you reach there. There are many dangers; curiosity being the greatest.'

Nicholas said, 'You travelled further inland than Ca' da Mosto ever did. Two hundred miles?'

'And turned back,' said Diogo Gomes. 'Men become frightened, and sicken, and die. There must be enough to man your ship home. Men ask incautious questions.'

'About Wangara?' Nicholas said.

The seaman's eyes rose to his. 'You know the name?'

'Many people know the name,' Nicholas said.

'Then forget it again,' said Diogo Gomes. 'Unless your friend Lopez here is going to betray it. Is that why you have brought him?'

It was Loppe who answered, unruffled as ever, dignified as ever. He said, 'My lord, if I knew it, I should not tell that secret to my worst enemy. I sail as an interpreter, nothing else. Senhor Niccolò seeks a way across the Sahel to the land of Prester John, and he has come to you for the kind of help which I cannot give him.'

The hand on the map slackened, and for a moment it seemed that the scroll would be allowed, for the last time, to close. Jorge da

Silves suddenly spoke. 'But this is so. The King has confided a new caravel to the venture, and his trust. I, as sailing-master, would fear to lead it so far without his Treasurer's wisdom.'

Pride against obsession. Better than anyone, Jorge da Silves knew how loyalty and instinct could compete. For a moment, no one said anything. Then Diogo Gomes heaved a sigh. He said, 'Why not. It is what the Prince would have wished. Only, you understand, in his day he chose the captains. We knew them.'

'You know me,' said Jorge da Silves.

He had flushed. He didn't say, as he might have said, that some of those same captains had been robbers and murderers. Gomes made no apology. He only said, 'Well. Let us pass round the flask, and I shall tell you what I can, and you must ask what you will. For it is a far land, and a dangerous one, and you will have little armour but your intelligence.'

It was late when they left, and Diniz rode with them for some time in silence. After a while he said, 'The old man. He wished he were going to sea again.'

Nicholas didn't look round. He said, 'This sea is for fit men who will leave no grief behind them.'

'You expect to return,' Diniz said.

'I leave men behind me,' said Nicholas.

'My mother has Simon,' said Diniz. 'My uncle Simon may be in Madeira.'

'Your uncle Simon is not Portuguese,' Nicholas said. 'You are your mother's man. You and no other.'

There was a long pause. Diniz said, 'What is Wangara?'

Loppe said nothing, and the captain was silent. Nicholas said, 'The source of the gold.'

'Where is it?' said Diniz. This time, Loppe looked at him sharply.

Nicholas said, 'No one knows. Those who try to find out are killed. That is another reason why you are not going to Guinea.' And the boy said nothing more.

It was a relief when they came to the place in Lagos where their roads parted and Diniz, turning abruptly, rode up the steep hill to his home. In the ten days that were left, Nicholas doubted if he would see him again, and was annoyed and sorry together. But he had undertaken to convey him to his parents' house in Madeira, with the baleful Gelis, and Bel of Cuthilgurdy, their coffers and servants. He had promised nothing else.

Before supper that night Father Godscalc strode in to confront Nicholas and Loppe in their parlour, a thick scroll riding under his arm. There was ink on his thumb, and a great blotch of it under his chin. He said, 'I've reached a conclusion. You don't go to Madeira.'

It had been a long day, but that should never matter. Nicholas remained with his expensive hose stretched before him, and his elbows hung behind over the only chair in the room with a back. He said, 'Because of Simon, because of Diniz, because of Gelis, because of David de Salmeton, or because of St Pol & Vasquez? I can't afford to agree with you.'

'Yes, you can,' Godscalc said. The map had flattened under his arm. He drew it out and threw it warm on a table and then sat down, his feet splayed, his two large toes braced in their leathers like bombards.

He said, 'Tell Diniz you can't take him to Madeira. Leave the Borselen girl. They won't sell to David de Salmeton; you can persuade them. In any case, miss out Madeira. I thought Simon might see sense and join with you, but now I doubt it. I will not have you confront him, the boy at your side. Go straight to Guinea, or call at the Grand Canary if you have to. But, Nicholas, go past Madeira.'

'I can't,' Nicholas said. 'I have to meet the *Ghost* from Sanlúcar, and she's already halfway there.' He waited.

Godscalc said, 'The old *Doria* you got out of Ceuta. You've renamed her?'

'It seemed advisable. And not so old. Built in 1460 for Jordan de Ribérac, from whom his son Simon purloined her. The Vatachino thought her worth a great deal of money.'

'I see,' said Godscalc. 'And will a new name stop Simon from recognising her in Madeira?'

'Perhaps, if she anchors far enough out,' Nicholas said. 'In any case, she's got a good spread of sail and few to chase her. We need her. In Prince Henry's time, the *San Niccolò* would have been sailing in convoy.'

Godscalc sat as still as a monk in a psalter, a large hand on each knee of his gown. He said, 'The old *Doria*. She's a big ship for an escort. With a big cargo space. Fifty times as large as the *Niccolò*. What have you loaded her with?'

'Horses,' Nicholas said. 'And a few things intended for Ceuta. She also has a new master: Ochoa de Marchena.' Nicholas picked up the thick scroll and pinched it judiciously. It produced an ample sound, like a pea pod many times magnified. Inside was a chart of the Canary Islands. He sat down and looked at it. He needed Godscalc, that was the trouble.

'Ochoa de Marchena is a pirate,' Godscalc said.

Nicholas said, 'Do you think I'd risk an honest man's skin in an ownerless ship? Although he is honest, I'm told, in his way.'

'As Mick Crackbene?' Godscalc said. 'I'm surprised you didn't ask him.'

'Are you indeed,' Nicholas said. 'So is that all?'

'Yes,' said Godscalc. 'Provided you agree to leave the girl and Diniz in Lagos, and pick up the *Ghost* in Madeira without going on shore. And provided that you tell me what you're going to bring back in her hold, seeing that you can't sail a roundship across Africa.'

Nicholas inflated his lungs. He unhooked his arms and, assembling his feet under his knees, leaned forward and clasped his hands gently. He looked up. 'You're telling me that you've heard the Pope's dead.'

'You must be glad,' Godscalc said. 'Your vows are void. You don't need to locate any Christians.'

'I don't need to,' Nicholas said. 'But I'm told that if I go upriver from the Sahel, I may come across them. I'm also told I'll find baptisable heathens. I thought that was why you were here.'

'Oh, yes. To baptise them for what?' Godscalc said.

He had waited so long for the question that, now it came, he let his exasperation show. 'As you mentioned,' Nicholas said, 'the roundship has plenty of cargo space. They wouldn't be crowded.'

Loppe jerked up his head, and then said nothing. Nicholas outstared the priest. Godscalc said, 'Nicholas, I am sorry, but I can't follow your mind any longer. I hope I'm mistaken. But for Loppe's sake, the question has to be asked. Are you trading in slaves?'

Nicholas said, 'Prince Henry engaged in it. The Vatachino will, if they can buy their way in.'

'What are you saying?' said Godscalc. His hands, sliding upwards, gripped his powerful thighs till his fingers were barred pink and white. 'That it will continue, so why not take part in it? That there are degrees, within which some sort of purchase might be palatable? That there are savages who, out of despair and starvation, would already be willing to come, and others, gifted like Loppe, who would come gladly, but that they have no idea what good fortune awaits them? What are you saying?'

I am saying, go away and don't meddle. Except that he couldn't, aloud. Nicholas said, 'That neither Loppe nor I can give you an answer. Either the consoling answer you'd like, or the other you don't want to think about. Why do you think Loppe wants to go back?'

'To join his family,' Godscalc said. His gaze, painfully fierce, moved between Nicholas and the African, where it rested.

Loppe returned the look with composure, his eyes the colour of egg-white and ink; his skin smooth and black within his Venetian clothes. He said, 'I have no family, Father. I was taken at Taghaza, and batch-sold in Tangier for Lagos. I have no one to support. If I went back, all I could bring of value is what I have learned, and I don't know what I have learned, for I only know half of it. I have to see the rest for myself. There is slavery and there is service. I have worked beside men far from home, who are nevertheless contented.'

Godscalc didn't at once respond. The silence was one of compassion. Then he turned to Nicholas. 'Go on with this, if you want him to hate you.'

Nicholas smiled and Loppe, catching it, smiled in return. Nicholas said, 'I'll take a chance. Persuade him out of it, of course, if you like. Persuade Diniz, too, while you're at it. I don't quite know how you'll stop him going to Madeira, short of tying him up.'

'You won't do what I ask?' Godscalc said.

Nicholas stood. 'No. But now, you don't need to come.'

He thought the priest would answer at once; but he just rose to his feet, and stood in silence a moment. Then he stretched out his hand for the roll and, collecting it, walked from the room.

Loppe said, 'Ah, Nicholas.'

Nicholas said, 'He is better away.'

He looked up at the silence. Loppe said, 'But he isn't away. He has to come now. You have compelled him.'

Chapter 12

IN THE THIRD WEEK of October, the Governor came to the wharf with his gentlemen to bid Godspeed to the Venetian merchant and banker who, by His Christian Majesty's grace, was about to take the word of the Lord to the heathen, and bring back from the converts many comforts.

The Governor had hopes of this expedition. He had exerted himself, the previous night, to hold a banquet of some splendour for the near-gentlemen who were to lead it, and this morning, despite the hour and the rain, felt confident he would not regret it. Nicholas kissed his hand and embarked, glittering, on one of the *San Niccolò*'s boats.

With him were Gregorio his purser, Loppe his steward and the self-contained figure of Father Godscalc, his apothecary and chaplain. Already on board was the determined group of his Madeira-bound passengers. Father Godscalc, if he had tried, had not dissuaded Diniz Vasquez from coming, or Gelis van Borselen and Bel her companion. Neither had the priest gone back to Venice, although he had stood long at the quay and watched the *Ciaretti* turn home, fully laden. He had left then, in silence, to prepare for this, his unhappy voyage as the pedagogue, the conscience of Nicholas.

The ship rode in deep water, her masts rocking, her passengers out of the way as she made ready to sail. They had practised this, the formal routine of departure, and Nicholas knew it by heart. He took his place on the high vestibule of the poop, watching without seeming to watch as the orders passed from captain to mate, and from mate to the helm and the mariners. The bare feet thudded on deck: stowing the companionway; hooking the tackle and hoisting the ship's boats inboard.

A whistle blew and was followed by jerks of racketing noise: the anchor-chain coming in, bringing the new, two-hundred-pound anchor strewn with weed and sand that would be unlike the weed and sand of its next bedding. Then a rush and a chanting of voices and the ship trembled as the triangular foresail rose and broke out, followed by the great racking heave as the mainsail began to ride up.

The helm stirred. The caravel moved, the sea bathing her flank. The smell of paint struck Nicholas for the last time, and the odours of sawn wood and resin and pristine white hemp, and the great flaxen draught of new canvas as the mainsail shook out its folds and was pulled in and bellied, and the mizzen sail followed.

Then the wind found her and nudged, and for the first time the *San Niccolò* heeled, dipping her gleaming black flank in the sea, and all the limp smells of earth were blown through her and vanished. The second mate, gripping a trumpet, came up the ladder and stood, his gaze switching from the captain to the six handgunners dodging across to the rail, match in hand. Nicholas turned his eyes to the shore, slowly receding.

The wharf was crowded, and the rough beach, and the path along the edge of the estuary. Not only the King's representatives but the whole of Lagos had come to watch the *San Niccolò* leave; for those who had not built her had equipped and provisioned her, and those who had done none of these had stood on the shore waving off other ships bound for Bilad Ghana, the Country of Wealth, and had seen them return as, God willing, this pretty caravel would, laden with parrots and feathers and ostrich eggs, and Negroes, and gold.

On board, the trumpeter's fanfare rang out: a strong one, for he had good lungs, and did it for pleasure. Then, gay as fireworks, there came a crackle of fire from the red-capped *schioppettieri* on deck, hazed in smoke and coughing and panting from their stint at the yards. Behind them, stamping into rough line, stood those seamen who could be spared.

On shore, the Governor lifted his hand. A grey posy of smoke showed itself on the wall of the fort, heralding the thunder of its number one culverin, followed by the second and third, up to six. The noise knocked from end to end of the bay, sending up screaming birds and punctuating the roar from hundreds of throats as, bonnets in hand, the town of Lagos bade them Godspeed.

On board, Gelis van Borselen stood, her hood back, her wheaten hair wet and her emotionless gaze upon Nicholas. 'You must be happy,' she said.

Three days at sea is not long, except when the ship is new and untried, and there is no comfortable coast to apply to. If there is, indeed, no land within sight at all, so that landfall must be worked for. Then three days can seem as exhausting as six, and also as useful as six. A new ship and a new crew and their master are on trial together, and it is the master who must bring them under his hand.

But for Gelis, it would have brought Nicholas as close to happiness as he expected to come. He already knew half his seamen: there were only seventeen, of which two had come from the *Ciaretti*, as had Melchiorre Cataneo, the *sottocomito*, or second mate, with the trumpet. The mate himself was da Silves' excellent man, and the three helmsmen his choice. As for the rest, the seamen themselves provided the cooks and carpenters, the sailmakers and bowmen and gunners, and expected and got double money for double jobs. Gelis said, 'You have a very small crew.'

He had anticipated, and got, Diniz on deck. He had hoped, once at sea, that the women would keep to their cabin. Instead, they both climbed to the poop; Gelis with her boat-cloak folded firmly about her and her footing sure as a goat's. With her trussed hair and her fixed blue eyes and her skin wet and unevenly coloured she was absolutely unlike her dead sister except, of course, in build, and in the shape of her brows which, skilfully trimmed, still suggested the strong, natural shape of her family. Bel was circular.

Bel said, 'I wouldn't say small. Look at yon one.' They were both speaking Scots, and so did Nicholas.

Nicholas said, 'I bought twenty, and they threw in the big one. You're quite safe. Lateen rigging needs very few seamen.'

'And it leaves more room for cargo,' said Gelis.

'And for passengers,' Nicholas said. He saw Diniz approaching. He added, 'You don't mind the movement?'

'No, what a pity,' she said. 'It was Katelina who used to be sick. Did your first wife travel well?'

Diniz said, 'You make her sound like a cask of Madeira,' and then swallowed and blushed, caught between euphoria and uncertainty.

Nicholas said, 'The Charetty didn't have a ship then. My second wife rather enjoyed it.'

'I expect,' said Gelis, 'you had a much larger crew. Diniz likes sailing, don't you, Diniz? Claes sailed with you and your father, and threw his plants overboard.'

'I have these impulses,' Nicholas said. Since they wouldn't go away, he excused himself and joined Gregorio in the hold. It was a problem of stowage, and infinitely preferable. When Diniz tried to join him presently he was in genuine conference with Jorge and the sailmaker, and later there were half a dozen minor emergencies which meant he ate bread and cheese on his hunkers while the rest were supping above. He hoped Godscalc was keeping them happy and retained Loppe, when he could, by the helm. Then the dark came, and thick cloud, and the real navigational problems began, followed by others. Jorge didn't go to bed, and neither did he.

When day broke, grey and squally, he was not in the mood for badinage, and more than a little preoccupied with a fierce and unpredictable wind which had usurped the promised north-easterly and was knocking spume off the waves. Mast, stays and cordage were all in his thoughts, and the broad beam of the ship made movement on deck highly uncomfortable. When Bel the Scots-woman appeared, he asked her fairly politely to stay in her cabin.

Beneath a powerful shawl, the round brown eyes inspected him narrowly. The wind howled and the mizzen suddenly flapped. There was a rush of wet feet on the deck. Bel said, 'Oh, never fear, we're good sailors. Where are we?'

'At sea,' said Gelis, arriving. 'What a murky night. How dead is your reckoning?'

He said, 'I'm sorry. We have to keep the deck clear for sailing.'

'We could hold a rope for ye,' said Bel. Her eyes ranged round the grey tossing ocean. She said, 'We thought we might see some land. If we're pointing at the Pillars of Hercules, then I owe her two ducats, or she'll take it in doppias. She's a great one for a wager.'

'We're sailing south-west,' Nicholas said.

'Are we?' said Gelis. They happened, because of work on a spar, to be sailing south-east at the time, but there was no one within earshot to contradict him.

He said, 'If you doubt me, there might be land to be seen from the crow's-nest.' It leaned against streaming cloud, at the top of the mainmast. He saw Gelis, her head back, consider it.

Bel said, 'There should be a wager in that.' Her expression was wicked.

Temptation seized him, and then he remembered what he was doing. Nicholas said, 'No, there isn't. Below, please.'

They obeyed him but only, he fully realised, because they had sufficiently amused themselves.

That night, he joined them for supper, along with those seniors not already on duty. It was not because he had nothing else to do. In the least of the day's incidents, a seaman fuddled with illicit drink had caught one of the two young *grumetes* with his hand in his pouch, and had beaten him senseless.

Nicholas had dealt with it. It wasn't unusual. It was the sort of thing to be expected from a new-gathered crew at the outset of a ticklish voyage and hardly worth mentioning.

Gelis was of another opinion. Attacking her see-sawing soup, she looked up as soon as Nicholas, stooping, came to the table. 'Don't tell me!' she said. 'You waited to sew the boy into his shroud. Or was it the seaman?' Godscalc stiffened.

'Not my job,' Nicholas said. 'You're enjoying the soup? There is plenty.'

'So I suppose,' she said. 'The crew diminishes daily.'

'But not the passengers,' Nicholas said, sitting down with deliberation. Gelis van Borselen was mourning her sister in the only way that she knew, and she didn't want him to be passive. That he realised.

Diniz was there. Diniz had had plenty of sleep, and was anxious to please. He said, 'You have to keep discipline.'

'I'm glad to hear it. I understand the man thrashed a child,' Gelis said.

Nicholas ate.

Gelis said, 'Did you hear me?'

'I'm sorry?' said Nicholas.

Diniz said, 'He was drunk. The seaman was drunk and Nicholas had him thrashed in his turn. It's over,' he said.

'And the boy? Filipe?' Gelis said.

'Sewed in his shroud,' Nicholas said.

Diniz said, 'No. You let him off. Bel's looking after him.'

'Bel says it isn't his fault,' Gelis said. 'She says the other boy, Lázaro, put him up to it.'

The fat woman was, of course, right. Lázaro was a natural bully. Nicholas ate, his mind on the pins of the rudder. Diniz said, 'You should get rid of the thief and the man.'

Nicholas said, 'Oh, the boy of course goes. We'll see what becomes of the man.'

He winced at the bang as Gelis laid down her knife. 'The child is dismissed, and the drunkard who beat him can stay?'

'Yes, if he sobers,' said Nicholas. 'He's said to be a good mariner, Luis. Every sea-going man makes that mistake once.'

'How sad,' said Gelis, 'for any children they meet. And the enterprising Lázaro also keeps his position?'

'It sounds,' Nicholas said, 'as if Lázaro might be handier than Filipe in a tight corner. A voyage like this needs survivors.'

'Your priest is remarkably quiet,' Gelis said.

'That's because he's a survivor,' Nicholas said. He waited, on edge, for Godscalc to speak, and then felt let down when he didn't.

Gelis said, 'How will he earn his living ashore?'

'He prays over people,' said Nicholas.

'Filipe. On Madeira.'

'Diniz will give him work on the Vasquez estate.'

'A thief?' Diniz said. He looked taken aback.

'You wanted me to get rid of him,' Nicholas said.

Diniz said, 'As a matter of discipline.'

'But not of philanthropy.' He heard his own voice. He had not intended to do this. He wasn't sure why he was doing this to Diniz and not to Gelis, except that he was tired of the boy's dumb supplication. Or just tired. His ship moved beneath him, her sails full, her men settling, her course apparently true. Nicholas said, 'So shall we talk about oranges?'

And Diniz went white.

No one moved. Father Godscalc's heavy face flattened. Diniz said, 'You invited us.' He spoke very calmly.

Nicholas said, 'Of course. I couldn't dismiss you.'

'You have hundreds!' said Diniz. 'Isn't it insulting to compare these two things?'

'I have hundreds less six,' Nicholas said. 'You were asked to respect some supplies, but you didn't. Since you were leaving, I wouldn't have mentioned it. If you'd been staying, I should. Lázaro and Filipe also broke rules. Lázaro can be made to behave. Filipe is too soft to take discipline. He'll cause trouble again, and they'll kill him. Sending him ashore is a kindness to everybody.'

Diniz had turned even paler. 'You must be glad I am going. Or if I stayed, would you treat me like Lázaro?

'Oh,' said Gelis, 'be quiet. His ship is falling apart, and he's ashamed of it. Mother of Jesus, all this fuss about *oranges*? How else have we sinned? Have we taken a walnut too many, or breathed too much of your air?'

It occurred to Nicholas that he had been rather successful. He rose, projecting, he hoped, faint impatience. 'Please,' he said, 'feel free to breathe. The use you make of your breath is another matter.'

Diniz also rose, and stood as if about to be hanged. He said, 'I was wrong. I apologise. I hardly thought the crime was worth airing in public. But I can't allow your comparison. As a gentleman, you ought to withdraw it.'

'As a gentleman?' Gelis said. 'Holy Virgin, show me a peasant.'

'That's easy,' said Bel of Cuthilgurdy, opening the door. 'There's one lying sick in his cot, and crying to know what he'll do on Madeira. I'm told to tell ye the rudder's just sprung.'

Unguardedly, Nicholas laughed. He straightened his face. He said, 'Then I must go. But it is a very fair question. I think you should decide between you what you will do with the boy in Madeira, while I go and ensure that he gets there.'

The next day, towards noon, the horizon offered a cluster of misty blue slopes. 'The Pillars of Hercules?' Gelis said hopefully.

'Na, na,' said the fat woman Bel. 'What could that be but a great island? A steep, woody devil topped by a rain-cloud, which means fast rivers for milling, and good soil to swell out your canes, and warm-weather flowers to turn into beeswax, and grapes twelve inches long in the bunch for your wine. That's the Isle of Madeira, and ye can pey me twa ducats. Yes, Master Gregorio?'

Gregorio smiled. He said, 'We have a good navigator. You should have saved your two ducats.'

'It kept hope alive,' Gelis said. 'But are we sure? Master vander Poele, where are you?'

He was within earshot, and better rested. He said, 'I don't know. How much money was it again?'

'Two ducats it's Madeira,' said Gregorio helpfully.

'The dear Lord forgive me,' said Nicholas. 'I meant to get to Madeira. But I'm afraid those are the Pillars of Hercules.'

He was delighted, walking away, to see that for a single brief moment they believed him.

A true landfall. Despite the winds, despite the mishaps, the ship was on perfect course for a land which had been found within living memory, lying elusive and quiet at the edge of the Green Sea of Shades, where, even yet, the straying ship might not find her.

Nicholas had seen it all for himself, shinning barefoot early that morning to the peak of the yardarm, watched by the narrowed eyes of da Silves. Below him, the ship leaned away from the light, the long shadows sliding in rhythm as she shouldered the waves running under her. She had come through her trials: the trials that, but for his haste, should have been conducted off Lagos, with a whole repairyard of craftsmen to support him.

As it was, they had set her to rights as they went. She would sail into the harbour of Funchal with her spars and rudder in order, her sails easy, her trim well-judged, and her crew at the beginning of making a vigorous, if somewhat opinionated team. He wanted her to look well, for he didn't know what awaited him.

They neared the anchorage just before dusk. For the last hour or two, among all the bustle of refurbishing ship, they all took time to stand on deck beneath the soft, blustering wind from the sails and watch the island appear; the biggest of the archipelago, thirty-five miles in length: a wild, mountainous, uninhabited place less than fifty years since, and now growing to wealth under the rule of its Portuguese captains.

The bay of the southern capital opened up. Nicholas saw a sprinkling of low painted houses on the volcanic slopes behind it, and the white of a chapel, and a large house, higher up, above which he thought he caught sight of a flagstaff. Low by the shingle he could see the rectangle of a stone customs house from which a boat was putting off, no doubt to lead them to their anchorage.

Jorge da Silves was ready. As the boat threaded towards him, he began to guide the *San Niccolò* to the edge of the swaying flock of fisher-vessels and barges and row-boats that occupied the inner part of the bay, while Nicholas watched.

These were not what interested him. From a long way off, he had seen the masts of two much larger ships, one a roundship and one a caravel like his own. The roundship, for all her peculiarities of shape and her unnatural colour, was one so well known to him that he identified her from her outline alone. The caravel, painted blue, was a stranger, and in spite of the uncertain gusts in the bay, the *San Niccolò* edged past at close enough quarters for him to see the name on her side: the *Fortado*.

'Have you heard of her?' It was Godscalc, surprisingly, standing beside him.

Nicholas said, 'Yes. She's Portuguese owned, and does a trade in yew bowstaves and sugar. I suspect she brought David de Salmeton from Porto Santo to Funchal.' The caravel, in the poor light, showed some activity. The roundship, on the other hand, looked almost deserted, as if most of her crew were on shore. Occasionally she gave a small shiver, accompanied by a hollow drumming that carried fitfully over the water. Her topsides were scarlet.

The harbour boat, arriving and amiable, allowed them to drop anchor a judicious distance away from both the roundship and caravel. Godscalc watched the manoeuvre without pleasure. He said, 'And that, I suppose, is your *Ghost*, with her horses. You still think her reincarnation will pass muster? David de Salmeton must know her as well as Simon – Who is that going ashore?'

'Diniz,' Nicholas said. The boy jumped into the harbour boat as he spoke and looked up, his face set in the lamplight. 'He wished to leave first. . . . What were you asking? Would de Salmeton recognise the *Ghost* as the *Doria*? Not for sure. He didn't see her on Cyprus, and has no proof, although he'll suspect her, of course.'

'And Simon?' said Godscalc.

'If he were to board her, perhaps. But I remind you. Ochoa de Marchena is a pirate. If threatened with boarding, he'll sail. Are you going below? It is customary to give a supper on deck, and they'll wish to put up the awnings.'

'A supper?' said Godscalc.

'To celebrate our arrival. And say farewell, of course, to the ladies, whose magnificence we ought to try to match.' The awnings lay on deck already, and were being untied with the greatest alacrity.

'The ladies are going this evening?' said Godscalc.

'To stay with the Captain of Funchal. Diniz has gone to arrange it, and then will take horse to his family estate, where they will join him tomorrow. Ponta do Sol, twenty-five miles round the coast to the west.'

'So he has gone,' Godscalc said. Nicholas said nothing. He had met the same guarded surprise from Jorge da Silves. Godscalc said, 'Whom will he find there?'

'The factor's family,' Nicholas said. 'And perhaps his uncle Simon de St Pol of Kilmirren. In which case anything really might happen.'

Godscalc said, 'Simon might be in Funchal already.'

'Yes,' said Nicholas.

'And come out forthwith to see you.'

'Yes,' said Nicholas. He had stopped at the top of the ladder, because Godscalc had stopped at the bottom.

Godscalc said, 'You say the *Ghost* can take to her heels. Can the *Niccolò*, if she isn't provisioned?'

'Not before I've seen Simon,' said Nicholas. 'Afterwards – yes, if we have to. That was why I was mean about oranges.'

Whatever else she had on her mind, Gelis van Borselen knew what was required of the guests of honour at a homecoming feast, and especially if the guests were on shipboard, and ladies. Her gowns were all drab, out of mourning for her parents and sister, but she fished out the costliest, and enlivened it with a cat's cradle of ribbons in her salt-whitened hair and a necklace of corals. Bel of Cuthilgurdy, taking her place at the trestles, was remarkably grand in creased velvet and Filipe, in attendance, was neat and comely if pale. He had already, under Bel's eye, been marched to make his peace with the big seaman Luis, who tweaked him by the ear and told him he bore him no grudges, while the boy's eyelids flickered.

By now they knew every man by his name and the men knew well enough how to behave in superior company, although, like effervescence, the success of their landfall kept manifesting itself in raised voices and bursts of quick laughter. The lamps shone on the meat, four days old and still fresh: duck and mutton and pork, and platters of peppered fish steaks, and baskets piled high with soft bread. And when their first hunger had died, the tambourer lifted his drum, and the fifer his pipe, and Gregorio, slipping below, brought his fiddle out, and tuned it, and led into the choruses he had already heard all the way from Ancona. And Nicholas, astride

this bench and that, perched on a table, his arm wound round a
shroud, shared sea-going gossip and sea-going jokes while the wine
went round without stint under awnings spread like butterfly
wings in the bay, frazzled with the glow of ships' lanterns and
within a bowshot of the black mountainous shore, with its powder
of lights and the distant sound, like a hush, of its torrents.

He had not parted with Diniz light-heartedly. Their discussion
had been hurried and curt – no more than was necessary to
establish that, should Simon be found at Ponta do Sol, the *San
Niccolò* would wait for his coming.

'He may not be there,' Diniz had said. 'Or want to come.'

'Then send me word. I can't wait more than two or three days.
And you'll be busy enough, settling your mother's affairs. Your
uncle will help you.'

You could help me, said the expression on the boy's face, but he
didn't say it aloud. Neither did Nicholas reiterate all the things
that, under other circumstances, he would have said. 'Study your
property. Analyse the books the way you learned in Nicosia. Weigh
up whether you and your uncle can manage. Consider what offers
you may get. Remember, the Vatachino are your uncle's rivals
elsewhere; to sell to them would be dangerous. Nevertheless, refuse
nothing outright. You want to keep other growers in hope; you
don't want them to join the Vatachino against you.'

As if against his will, Diniz said, 'What if we can't run the
business ourselves?'

'You and your uncle? Of course you can,' Nicholas said.

'I could have sold it to you,' Diniz said. 'But for my grandfather
and Simon.'

'When I'm tired of life,' Nicholas said, 'I'll remember the offer.
Don't sell St Pol & Vasquez to anyone. That would be my advice.'

Diniz had stood, at last, as if unwilling to go. He said, 'If I were
free . . .'

And Nicholas said, 'If you owned only the clothes that you stood
in, the answer would still be no.'

Lamps ablaze, banners fluttering, noisy with music and laughter,
for an hour the *San Niccolò* rocked in the bay, the centre of all
attention. Nicholas, clowning his way through some doggerel, saw
the knots of men at the rails of the other ships in the harbour;
heard the splash of oars as boats returning from shore circled the
caravel en route to their mother ships; was aware that other dark
boats came and lingered and went. So far, no one had challenged
him. He had set a man aloft, just in case.

The chirrup of sound, when it came, was just enough to warn
those below who were listening. Nicholas rose, hardly noticed, and

slipped aft. Clear of the hubbub and laughter, he could hear the splash of muffled oars and the half-felt bump that meant a boat had lodged at the base of the ladder. By then, four of his men were at the caravel's side, their swords drawn. Nicholas joined them, and looked down.

There was no great barge at his feet filled with cuirasses; no coats of arms, or threatening crossbows or hackbuts, and the face he dreaded to see was not present. A ship's boat lay below him, manned by two pairs of half-naked oarsmen, and rising from its midst was a fellow in a great floating hat, bound to his cranium by hanks of gay ribbons. The head tipped back, revealing the bristled chin, the formless face, the violent bonhomie of a man he had met once before, in strict secrecy, in a room of the villa at Lagos. A man who, of all men, he did not want to see at this moment. Ochoa de Marchena, pirate; Spaniard; master of the resurrected round-ship, the *Ghost*, floating somewhere behind in the darkness.

Nicholas said, very sweetly, 'Go away.'

The unshaven jaw hoisted a red, dismayed lip. 'Oh, I am disliked. I kill myself. Your signal is read, and my crew is aboard, but I kill myself. Why does Señor Niccolò frown? His guests are surely ashore?'

'One of them is,' Nicholas said. 'Can't you count? The rest are still here.'

The toothless face lengthened like wax. 'No food, no wine, no kiss for Ochoa?'

'It depends,' Nicholas said. 'Why don't you keep watching the flags?'

'Tonight?' the man said.

'Perhaps,' said Nicholas.

'Of course,' said the man. A bubble winked inside his gums. He said, 'The woman is pretty.'

'She saw you?' said Nicholas.

The face below, ploughed by pox-marks and scars, displayed horror. 'I waved to her. It was only civil. She is of the enemy party? I have exposed myself? Execute me!' Ochoa de Marchena flung his arms wide, letting go the sides of the ladder and falling backwards through the empty air towards his boat. Two of his crew silently caught him and set him upright in a practised way in the well. 'What can I do?' he added, peering from under his hat. He was dressed, Nicholas noticed, in scarlet satin.

'Go away,' said Nicholas equably; and watched them do just that. Returned to his feast, he was prepared for questions, but none came. He had to remark at large to the company: 'The roundship master, presenting his compliments. He wouldn't come aboard; they have sickness. No sign of the barge for the ladies?'

'Perhaps,' said Gelis van Borselen, 'we should think twice about disembarking. If the *Ghost* has sickness on board, she must have infected all Funchal by now. All her crew were on shore till she recalled them.'

'I didn't know –' Nicholas began, his voice easy.

'I recognised signals? You should live on a hillside with an excitable widow and nothing to read except the ships in the harbour. You told the *Ghost* to recall them.'

Nicholas smiled. 'I wish I had that kind of power. I did put up a lantern for water.'

'They must have very good eyesight,' she said. 'I'd have sent that kind of order by Diniz. Jordan de Ribérac leased a roundship called the *Doria* to Portugal. I heard it was stolen from Ceuta.'

'Was it?' said Nicholas.

'While you were away.'

'In Lisbon,' said Nicholas.

'I heard you once claimed it was yours. Is that the same ship?'

'No, of course not,' said Nicholas. 'This is the *Ghost* out of Seville, with a Spanish master who likes ogling ladies. I said you were busy, but if you wish I could ask him back over.'

'I think you should,' said Gelis van Borselen. He was trying to think what to say when the whistle blew again. Blew, not chirruped. He drew a deep breath.

Gelis van Borselen continued to view him. He wondered how she kept her eyes from watering. 'Simon,' she said. 'He knows ships. He knows his father's ship. Let him tell us.'

Chapter 13

THIS TIME, THERE WAS no concealing that something was going to happen. The music died, and the laughter. Nicholas stood, collecting the attention of Gregorio and Father Godscalc and Loppe, all of whom got to their feet and came quietly to join him. One of his men ran towards him. He was smiling.

'Signor, the viceregal barge for the demoiselle and her attendants. They are loading the boxes. Captain Zarco has sent a gentleman to attend them. Here he is.'

Nicholas had time to feel enormous relief, and astonishment that he had forgotten, and time even to register that whatever he might like to believe, his meeting with Simon was something that occupied most of his thoughts. Then – 'Here I am,' said David de Salmeton, walking softly from the head of the ladder and resting his dark, long-lashed gaze on Nicholas. 'I do believe you'd forgotten me.'

The brilliant light flamed on the jewels that buttoned his doublet, that weighted his fingers, that clasped the cunning drape of his hat below which his hair hung warmly curling, like Zacco's.

Nicholas didn't know why now, and not in Lagos, he should be put in mind so suddenly of Cyprus and its King. Compared with the power of Zacco, David de Salmeton was a sinister toy: an ivory figurine possessing the same comeliness but without the fierce, immature courage. Perhaps David de Salmeton had courage. Perhaps maturity *was* courage, but it didn't wring the heart, as the King's did. On the other hand, David de Salmeton didn't come with a mace in his grasp, or a leopard, or a sword with which to cut off a Mameluke's head for a friend. Or with a lure for a hawk, or a woman.

David de Salmeton said softly, 'You *have* forgotten me,' and Nicholas turned, and brought him into the company.

The feast was over. The agent seated himself, wine in hand, between Nicholas and Gelis van Borselen, while boxes appeared and were hoisted below to the barge. The agent smiled. 'Now do tell me. Voices carry so. You were speaking about the *Doria*?'

'Never heard of it,' Nicholas said. 'Have you dined? There is a good piece of beef and some puddings left.' He spoke French, as de Salmeton had. He recognised, with sorrow, that the man would understand Flemish and Scots. The girl's face, as he watched, became animated.

'You heard me speak of the *Doria*,' Gelis said. 'The *Ghost* seems her very double, although Monsieur Niccolò doesn't agree. And perhaps he should know, since her master has privately called on him.'

'They tell me her lines are the same,' David de Salmeton remarked. 'But, they say, she is painted a different colour.'

'And, I am sure, would be very different within,' Nicholas said. 'You came in the *Fortado*?'

'And sailed past the *Ghost*, spar to spar. Some of our crew had seen Monsieur de Ribérac's vessel in Lagos, and wanted to swear the two ships were the same. But who could tell, except one who had sailed in her?' He moved his grave, liquid gaze. 'Perhaps one may be found to examine her, less busy than Monsieur Nikko?'

'I dare say,' Nicholas said. 'Why not ask Diniz Vasquez, who sailed in her from Cyprus? Where is he?'

'Or his Uncle Simon?' the young woman said. 'Son of Jordan de Ribérac? Where is he?'

A manicured eyebrow rose by a whisker. The agent said, 'I fear almost to answer you both. The boy has sped, so I hear, to his father's *quinta* at Ponta do Sol. The lord Simon is not on the island, having gone home, his business completed. So, if the *Ghost* is to be identified, other experts must do it. They should be easily found.'

He appeared to be assessing his wine cup. Beyond the vacated benches around them, Nicholas saw Gregorio's face, and that of the priest. Near at hand Gelis, too, was looking at him. Gelis said, 'Am I to do all the work?'

'It's your family,' Nicholas said.

'No, it isn't,' she said. 'Any day of the week, you may have St Pol Simon with pleasure. So?' She turned to the agent. 'What business has the lord Simon completed, apart from digesting his meals? His sister assumed there would be none until Diniz arrived with her authority.'

'The lady Lucia? Exquisite creature,' said the broker. 'But with her husband deceased, and Diniz, forgive me, a child, the lord

Simon had to act in his own interests. He decided to sell what he could get out.'

'*What he could!*' Gelis said. 'He owned half . . . The great booby's *sold half the business?*'

'Lend you a brick,' Nicholas said automatically. The woman Bel glared at him. He was thinking.

David de Salmeton seemed unaffected. He raised his free hand by a half-inch. 'Simon is not of Portuguese birth. His permit to trade was subject to the whim of the Portuguese government, with whom his stock is not high, and he had a youth and a widow as partners. The St Pol plantations were his to sell, and the investments to realise.'

'He sold them to you?' said Nicholas suddenly. He wouldn't have thought so, but for something he imagined he read in the other man's face. It might have been irony.

'Why, no,' said David de Salmeton. 'I was unable to tempt him. He was afraid, it seems, to add to our strength as his rival elsewhere.'

'Well, he had some sense,' said Gelis. 'But that seems to be the extent of it. He should have sold to young Diniz. At the very least, he should have waited to talk to him.'

'He had an unmatchable offer,' said the agent. 'Conditional on immediate acceptance. I regard his decision as sensible.' His eyes had moved to Nicholas, with the same amused shadow behind them.

'Any man would,' Nicholas said. 'To whom did he sell?' To himself, his voice sounded over-clear, but that was because the tables were empty, and the sounds of hilarity no longer to be competed against. He thought, anyway, he guessed the answer.

It came in the musical voice that was of a piece with the face and ringed hands, and at odds with the neat muscularity of the frame. 'He chose the Lomellini of Genoa. You know them.'

Nicholas knew them. He knew the Lomellini from Cyprus and Rhodes. He knew them from Bruges, where they engaged in trade for the Duchess of Burgundy. The Lomellini bought alum, and sent laden supply ships to Ceuta. Members of the Lomellini in Lisbon controlled the entire Portuguese exports of cork and cane sugar: their methods had forced the Vasquez lands out of profit until the Duchess's secretary, a Vasquez, complained. Through intermarriage with Portuguese ladies of birth, the Lomellini had obtained naturalisation. Here on Madeira, the brothers Urbano and Baptista cultivated great estates, and sold wine and sugar and honey in Europe. They also sent vessels to Africa.

Through its favour at court, St Pol & Vasquez had been able to hold its own among the two hundred families permitted to exploit Madeira. Even now Tristão was dead, his son might have done as well, with the help of his factor, and the support of his partner and uncle. Now, without the St Pol money and assets, Diniz was left with a broken-backed heritage.

For a moment, Nicholas looked out to sea. Simon had sent him an ultimatum and he had come west to meet it, not knowing if he would escape with his life; or if, in saving his Bank, there would come a time when he had to choose between that and the family his mother had married into.

Simon had issued a challenge. Simon had come and, wittingly or not, had destroyed the livelihood of his sister and nephew. And then he had gone, without waiting for Nicholas. Simon the athlete; the jouster finer than he would ever be. Simon, who had won every fight they had ever had in the past and who had, but didn't know it, the ultimate reason to kill him. So why wasn't he here?

The flash of a cup warned him, but half its wine still struck his shoulder; then Gelis tossed the pewter on to the board. She said, 'Oh good, Claes, I have your attention. Of course, you and the Vatachino planned this between you.'

He let the wine drip while, thinking, he looked at her. Surprise flashed across de Salmeton's face and softened into something else. The agent said, 'I can see, to be sure, it might seem so. We both benefit. I have to say, however, that the outcome was an accident. My instructions were to buy St Pol & Vasquez for the Vatachino. The lord Simon refused me; a pity. An even greater pity, I thought, should the company fall to some arriviste Venetian Bank. Urbano Lomellini agreed with me. He made a winning offer, and showed himself glad of my counsel. My dear Monsieur Nikko, your doublet is ruined.'

'I have another,' Nicholas said. The barge was ready. The tramping had ceased and Bel of Cuthilgurdy was standing at her mistress's shoulder, with the boy Filipe lurking behind.

Gelis spoke to her without turning. 'Simon has sold his share of the company. For how big a nest egg, I wonder? Enough, I suppose, to farm out his son, and keep himself in comfort in Scotland. How thoughtful you've been, Monsieur de Salmeton. How much did you advise he should get?'

'You would have to ask Urbano Lomellini,' said de Salmeton. 'One regrets.'

'One will regret when I have reversed the agreement,' Gelis van Borselen said. She rose, her gaze sharpening on Nicholas. She said, 'No collusion? Prove it, then. Come with me and help me cancel the bargain.'

Tardily, David de Salmeton rose to his complete, charming, miniature height. 'My dear demoiselle! The transaction is over. Simon has already removed all the sum that was owed him. And even if he had not, you should beware of asking Monsieur Nikko to help you. He covets your dead sister's business.'

Nicholas moved, but Gelis spoke immediately. 'Simon has *taken* his money? In specie?'

'In gold,' the broker said. 'And in venture shares. They may well attract a fine return. There may be money to spare for his sister.'

'Venture shares?' said Nicholas gently.

'An investment in the *Fortado* which brought me,' said David de Salmeton. 'She sails under licence for Africa. What profit she makes, the Lomellini will share with my lord Simon.'

Nicholas gazed at him, unseeing. That, then, was what Simon intended. Here was the threat to the Bank, to his fortunes, to his future, and the Lomellini – the Genoese; the Genoese cynically advised by the Vatachino – to carry it out. All that was missing was Simon's own presence. 'She may be unlucky,' said Nicholas.

'Perhaps,' de Salmeton said. 'Is that the barge calling? Perhaps. But in the African trade, the *Fortado* has a sure market, and no competitor but yourselves. And who knows when you may leave, with the history of the *Ghost* now in question? Demoiselle? The Captain expects you on shore.'

She was on her feet as he spoke. 'Yes. My small coffer. Bel, help me find it.'

She brushed past and went aft, the plump woman following. Loppe's voice greeted them and then faded along with their steps. David de Salmeton put down his cup and rose, smoothing the silk of his sleeves with his fingertips. 'A tiresome young lady, but handsome. She might be worth some attention.' He tilted his head towards Nicholas. 'I, too, miss the rough comforts of Cyprus. Funchal has somewhat less to offer. Nevertheless, the Captain sent you his most civil greetings. Indeed, he suggested I bring you a wench.'

'You didn't bring one?' Nicholas said, still seated.

'I hesitated to commit you to the sex. Apropos of which subject' – a light hand came to lie at his shoulder – 'the boy's remaining share of the plantation would not, in my opinion, be in any way viable on its own, even were you to be free to pursue it. The *Ghost* is, of course, the *Doria*, and will be proved so tomorrow.'

'I must set my soul in order,' said Nicholas. 'Unless there is any way to prevent this calamity?'

The hand remained a moment longer. Then, 'How melancholy,' said David de Salmeton, withdrawing his fingers and glancing at them. 'You are still very damp. How unfortunate that I must go ashore. No, I can find little hope. I see the barge is ready and the ladies are waiting. I must join them.'

In the faces of the ladies, one tall, one short, nothing could be read as they waited. It was perfectly extraordinary therefore how, joining them at the head of the ladder, Monsieur David de Salmeton lost his footing and actually fell into the water, striking his head several times on the platform, the ladder and the strakes of the boat so that when they fished him up (which the crew of the boat did immediately) he was quite unconscious.

There followed, on deck, a period of somewhat heavy-handed resuscitation. Nicholas, who had taken his share, looked up at last from the still, breathing face and said, 'What shall we do? He's concussed.'

Bel Cuthilgurdy, immobile as a pyramid on her shins, said, 'Christ fend us!' It sounded like *Crivens!* She added, 'See, I'll help take him below, with his man. Filipe, go on down and make up a pallet.'

'Bel?' said Gelis van Borselen.

Her companion, now standing, looked round. 'You get into the boat. I'll bring the puir soul when he's better. And since there's room, why for not take the lawyer? There's a man might untangle a contract.'

'Master Gregorio's fees,' Nicholas said, 'are extortionate.' He felt as if he had had twice as much wine as he had.

'I expect I could pay them,' said Gelis van Borselen. 'I have just observed that the *Ghost* is not the *Doria*. I should swear to it anywhere.'

Now he knew he was drunk. 'Have I missed something?' Nicholas said.

She turned, her coffer under her arm. 'It seems your habit,' she said. 'Except for what is thrown at you. Ask yourself why David de Salmeton should help the Lomellini to buy? Was it only to spite you?'

'A fee was mentioned,' said Nicholas. 'The sale, one assumes, wasn't preventable.' He knew now, though, that he was cold sober.

'The fee was to delude us and Simon,' she said. 'The truth is that the Vatachino and the Lomellini are secret associates. It made no difference which bought St Pol & Vasquez. The *Fortado* sailing for Africa is funded by both.'

'Along with a large stake from the deluded Simon,' said Nicholas. 'Poor bastard.'

'Is it funny?' she said.

'No,' said Nicholas. 'Not if it's true. You must think it is. You nearly killed him.'

'I did my best,' said Gelis van Borselen. 'It's true. Your Negro told me just now. He knew the Lomellini men in the barge from his slave days.'

'Loppe?' he said.

She said, 'The wife of Urbano Lomellini is a Lopez. She keeps her slaves, who respect her. I believe your man, despite his motive for telling me. I also spoke to one of his friends, who confirmed it. Since Simon left, the two companies paid less attention to secrecy.'

'Why keep it secret?' he said. 'Why not boast of it just now?'

'That is why I asked for your lawyer,' she said. 'Monsieur de Salmeton said the sale couldn't be broken, but he would guess that you would spare no effort to break it, if you knew the Vatachino were part of it. It offers some hope.'

'Yes. Take Gregorio. I'll stay with Mistress Bel and nurse poor Monsieur David,' said Nicholas.

She frowned. 'You can't detain him. He must go ashore when he wants.'

'I don't want to keep him,' said Nicholas. 'Especially since we all know that the *Ghost* isn't the *Doria*.'

He wondered if she would smile, but she didn't. She nodded briefly and left. Gregorio, looking startled, went after her. Nicholas watched the barge pull away. Now everything had changed, and everything had to be done quickly.

The *Ghost* must leave: she was waiting; he had sent her the order. Sooner than that, he must leave himself, before de Salmeton roused. And lastly, the *San Niccolò* must be made ready to sail, but unobtrusively, so that when David de Salmeton wakened he would see a ship asleep for the night, but prepared, as would be prudent, to leave her anchorage in the morning.

Recovered, he would be allowed to take boat for shore. He would certainly notice, in daylight, the absence of the *Ghost*, and hence the loss of his chance to delay Nicholas. As soon as he physically could, he would order the *Fortado* to sea. But by then, Nicholas hoped, the *San Niccolò* herself would be away.

He had come to African waters apprehensive of many things. He had not expected a race.

It went smoothly. He spoke aside to the master, and went below to see Bel and her patient, and held a conversation with Loppe. He found Father Godscalc and told him most of his plans, and advised him to sleep while he could. By then his boat was ready, on the lee side. He waited until Godscalc had gone, and then ran down the side and got in. A wave passed under his keel, and all the little boats rocked at their moorings. It came from the *Ghost*, her masts moving silently in the dark as she slipped her cable, and was towed out of harbour.

He knew, on shore, where to hire a horse, and they found him a guide very quickly. It was only twenty-five miles to Ponta do Sol on a path that went clear down the coast, but he couldn't risk missing his way. Diniz would be at Ponta do Sol, and he must reach him soon. Before, distraught at the news of his uncle, the boy thought of taking horse east, and attempting to reboard the caravel.

If I were free, he had said. Well, he was now.

Even without the guide, Nicholas would have known he was approaching the estate of Tristão Vasquez by the smells beaten into the grindstones: the dense vinous breath of the presses, and the aroma he could never forget, the herbal sweetness that still steamed, he hoped, from his copper vats by the temple at Kouklia.

It had not been a talkative journey. The track was only the width of a wagon, and soft and pitted with use: another aspect of the moist balmy climate that produced the tropical profusion of flower and foliage he could only sense, and the darting, bustling life of the undergrowth. His guide possessed a flambeau, but had not needed to light it. The night had cleared, and the starlight and the strange reflected light of the sea on his left-hand side were enough. He rode, for the moment enveloped again in the tranquil detachment he had gained, and then lost, in the solitary months after Marian's death, and had found again only in Cyprus, on his way to and from Kouklia.

He met no one on the road: no frantic boy spurring back, bereaved, adrift and now pauperised by the golden uncle whom his father, out of generosity, had made his partner in a fine, growing business. He was going to be in time.

Before the guide spoke, the rush of the stream told him he was coming towards Diniz' patrimony. The limits of the tilled land were not easy to define in the darkness, but he saw a bridge and a mill and a collection of cabins, and further off a stockade within which appeared a number of roofs, mostly thatched, and all of them illuminated by the glowing lamps in the windows of a much larger residence whose upper storey he could discern.

The gates to the stockade stood open, sign of perturbation enough, and as he and the guide dismounted and went in, a brace of dogs began to bark wildly, causing a baby somewhere to cry. A man's voice shouted an enquiry, and Nicholas stopped in a pool of light.

The central house of two storeys was lit along its full length, the windows neither shuttered nor covered with muslin, and its walls thick with vines. A man, fully clothed, came out on the balcony, and Nicholas took off his hat to show his face. He said, 'Nicholas vander Poele of Venice. I hoped to see Senhor Diniz.' It was halfway through the night.

'Wait,' said the man. Against the light he was broad-built but not young, and his voice had a ring of authority. He could be no one but the factor.

Nicholas waited, hearing a confused sound of voices through the open window. Then almost immediately the door below burst open and Diniz came out and stopped. The slanting light sharpened the hollows of cheekbone and eye and his hair, uncovered, hung in rough strands. There was no trace left of the tight-lipped hauteur of his leaving. He said, 'I knew you would come.'

'I'm sorry,' said Nicholas.

'Yes. So am I,' Diniz said. 'We're not – You must be tired. Come upstairs.' The man from the balcony came out at his back, inclined his head and, walking past Nicholas, went to speak to his guide. Diniz said, 'He's my father's . . . he's the Vasquez factor, Jaime, who lives here. He has seven children.'

The implications of the news, then, had already made themselves apparent. Nicholas said, 'We'll talk about it inside.' Following the boy up to the first floor, he saw how pale he was, and dirty, as if he had forgotten to wash after his journey. In the white-walled family room, there were moths round every lamp but no one present, although he noticed a wooden hobbyhorse lying, and a woman's sewing thrown on a chair. Diniz stopped in the middle and turned.

'They say the transaction can't be reversed. Jaime was forced to supply all the figures and documents, and although my father's notary went to Funchal and objected, it seemed my uncle was free to dispose of his share. The notary said there were more lawyers for the Lomellini than he knew ever existed. He begged St Pol to wait, but he wouldn't.'

'Did he give a reason?' Nicholas said.

Tonight, stunned by the enormity of his idol's conduct, Diniz had lost all constraint. He said, 'My uncle told them I was weak, and under your influence, and would give you anything that you wanted once you got here. That was why it had to be drawn up so quickly.'

The factor had entered the room and was standing quietly by the door. Something about the way he stood reminded Nicholas of Jorge da Silves. Diniz said, 'You have to let me come with you.'

The factor spoke, his voice lighter than might have been expected. 'That would not be wise.'

Nicholas said, 'It might be very wise, if you were an impediment to your family. Since you're not, stay and fight.'

'What with?' Diniz said. 'You have no money, you told me. Otherwise you could take my share now.'

'Thank you,' Nicholas said. 'All I need is a loss-making venture. Senhor Jaime, I have ridden a long way, but not to rob you or Diniz. Might we sit? I have a proposal to make.'

They hesitated, but they sat. He took the cushioned box that remained and, setting his hands on either side, looked from one to the other. The factor's face, broad and parched as a fig, returned the look with a steady attention. Nicholas said, 'I have no money to offer, but I have a man of exceptional skills, who has managed my Bank in Venice for almost three years and who could tell you, in a matter of weeks, whether this estate could be made to support you. He is in Funchal at the moment If you and your lawyer approved, I could lend him to you, at no cost at all to yourselves.'

'But he would expect a share in the business?' said the factor.

'No,' said Nicholas. 'If I bring back Guinea gold, we may talk. Even then, there is no obligation. And as well as Gregorio, you would have Gelis van Borselen to help you. There might be more hope than you think.'

The factor pondered. Protruding from his rolled sleeves were arms scarred and knotted with labour, and his face at this moment worked to produce a deeply ruminative sniff. Then he said, 'I will get my wife. Senhor Diniz should eat. I must think of this.'

'Of course,' Nicholas said. 'Now is not the time. But I shall leave you the name of the man, and a note for him. And I am sorry – I have already eaten. I didn't mean to delay your own supper.'

The boy fell asleep before the food came, comforted by the promise of help and by the sound of earnest voices in congress. The factor's wife, arriving with soup, curtseyed to Nicholas and poured him a bowl, but laid another by the boy's side without waking him. She murmured, 'Fatherless child!' She had been in bed, and wore a rough mantle bundled about her and her hair thrust somehow into a cloth. Nicholas reflected, without envy, that he was only five or six years older than Diniz but was more used to suspicion than compassion. And was not fatherless. That was the trouble.

He sighed, and ate the soup, and some bread, and continued his low conversation with Senhor Jaime. A good man, he suspected, doing the work of two people out of the fondness he had had for Senhor Tristão.

What he learned was not encouraging, although he didn't say so. The little estate, shorn of its other half, could provide a living perhaps for a year. Until he came back. If he didn't, it would be Gregorio's problem. Along with the Bank and the Charetty.

The boy slept. Nicholas said, 'I must leave him a letter. And write one for you to give to Gregorio, if you have a desk I might use. I have to go fairly soon.'

The man looked up. His wife said, 'There's a bed. I've put sheets on it.'

'I hope you ask me again,' Nicholas said. 'And offer me soup. But I have to go, and it would be best before he wakes and asks questions.'

They made no more effort to stop him. The factor led him to a small writing room, its walls covered with bits of string and spiked papers and hasty reminders in charcoal, and accommodating a stool, a box and a counter. There was a pot of quills, and an inkwell and a knife, and the factor got him some paper and wax. He had his own seal, the sight of which would alarm Gregorio immediately. He knew Gregorio would never forgive him.

He was heating the wax for the letter when he lifted his head, hearing the thud of distant hooves over the murmur and pop of his lamp. He let the wax drop and, pressing his seal in the blister, rose quickly, the letter with its superscription laid on the desk. It was to be expected that a fit man like de Salmeton would quickly recover, and further to be expected that, once on shore, he would make all the trouble he could, even to commanding a string of the Captain's best horsemen. But at least the *Ghost* would have gone.

The dogs began barking as he blew out the lamp and began to pick his way through the house to find some lesser exit that would serve him. His horse was in the stable. He would have to saddle it, too, unless he managed to get hold of one of those coming in, however blown. He only needed to cover twelve miles. He heard the horses clatter over the bridge — not so many of them — and thought he smelled fresh air from a passage. Then as he turned a corner, the brilliant light of a lamp came to blind him, carried by the factor with Diniz stumbling sleepily after him. Diniz said, 'Who is it?' and saw him.

Until Diniz seized his arm, he still thought he might escape. After that, there was nothing he could immediately do but appear not to be dragged to the portal. Standing within the crowded front door, he saw a small troop had ridden into the courtyard. It was led by a person he knew; whose name, indeed, he had just finished writing. Behind it was a cloaked figure mounted side-saddle. It was not David de Salmeton. For a violent moment, he wished that it were. Then Gregorio, dismounting, was saying, in a voice hoarse with tiredness, 'The *quinta* of the family Vasquez? *Nicholas, are you here?*'

And after Gregorio's, there spoke a familiar feminine voice. 'We know he is here. It is what he is doing here that rivets us.'

Gelis van Borselen, how? Through some tell-tale spy on shore, he deduced, or the man who had hired him his hackney. She was here, with Gregorio.

Diniz dropped his grasp and ran into the yard. Gregorio waited for him, looking uneasy. Gelis, standing beside him, was the epitome of a fine, pale malevolence. In a matter of seconds, she would notice him. Nicholas backed into the shadows, turned, and sprinted.

He found, at speed, the side exit. He raced amid some unwanted yapping and braying to the stables. He found and saddled his horse, all the time hearing the voice of Diniz, now angry, and the cold voice of Gelis, and the weary mutter of Gregorio. A drowsy Portuguese voice at his elbow said, 'My lord returns? Allow his servant.' The guide had been asleep in the straw.

'Go back to sleep,' Nicholas said. 'I have no need of you.' He mounted.

'My lord!' said the guide. 'It is dark! One may stumble or drown!'

'I have no need of you,' Nicholas repeated. He remembered, with sorrow, how very highly he had rewarded the fellow.

'My lord!' said the man; and ran out after him.

'There he is!' Gelis cried.

They caught him just over the bridge, and he had time to wish that he had waited, in a dignified fashion. Diniz said, 'You were leaving!'

'I have to go,' Nicholas said.

'After what?' said Gelis van Borselen. Apart from the circles under her eyes, she was quite unaltered. 'What have you got him to promise you?'

'Diniz? Nothing,' said Nicholas. 'I have to go.'

'Where?'

He paused. 'Funchal,' he said warily.

'And why?' said Gelis van Borselen.

Gregorio said, 'Nicholas. The *San Niccolò* has sailed out of harbour.'

'With David de Salmeton?' said Nicholas recklessly.

'No. As soon as he left. So what are you doing here?'

'Leaving,' said Nicholas. 'I'm expected by friends. Gregorio, I've left you a letter. Senhor Jaime, I have to thank you and your lady. Diniz, goodbye.'

It was Gregorio who held his reins and bodily stopped him: Gregorio, who, he would have thought, even more than the girl or the factor would have wanted him parted from Diniz. Gregorio said, 'Where are you going? You owe it to us to tell us.'

Nicholas said, 'I'm going to Câmara de Lobos. Help them. It's all in the letter, for Christ's sake.'

'I am going with you,' said Diniz.

'No, you are not,' said the girl, and brought her foot hard down on his, while snapping over her shoulder, 'Let him *go*, damn you.'

'What?' said Gregorio. He slackened his grip. Nicholas tore his reins free and dug his spurs into his horse. It jibbed resentfully, then bounded as he collected the reins and did it again. He heard stumbling footsteps beside him, and then a sudden, desperate drag on his saddle and girth. Diniz was mounting behind him.

The horse faltered. Clawing, the boy got into place and once there, grasped Nicholas in both hands. He was sobbing for breath. He said, 'Go. For my father's sake.' Nicholas lifted his whip. Gelis van Borselen, on her own horse, appeared suddenly at his side. She said, 'It is your father's name, Diniz.'

The boy raised a fist and hammered on Nicholas's back. Nicholas reined in his horse, and the other horse stopped. Nicholas said, 'Do you want me to whip him to the ground? Talk to him if you want. I don't care either way, but I must go.' He could hardly breathe, with the grip Diniz had on him.

The girl said, 'If you won't throw him off, then I will.' He saw her lean from her mount. Diniz growled. Then, lifting his hand, he delivered such a slap to the rump he was sitting on that the horse bolted. Nicholas bellowed. He fought it all the way out of the gates before he got control out on the road. The horse, shuddering, stopped. The girl, mounting fast, had raced after him. She stopped at his side, and sat panting. He caught a glimpse of surprise on her face.

Nicholas spoke to the boy clinging behind him. 'Use your head, Diniz. Whatever you want, this is no way to do things; without planning, without speaking to Jaime. Get down and go into the house. Listen and make up your mind. No one will force you either way. I'll wait fifteen minutes, then go.'

The girl said nothing, which he hadn't expected. He waited. The arms clenched about him slowly slackened. Diniz said, 'You won't wait.'

'Now I think,' Nicholas said, 'you *are* insulting me.' He met the girl's eyes, then saw them shift behind him. Diniz dismounted and looked at him. The girl dismounted as well and stood quietly holding her reins. Then Diniz turned, and they walked over the yard to the house, leaving Nicholas waiting.

Gregorio joined him. 'What are you doing?' He was weary.

'Giving him a semblance of choice. He must elect to stay, not be forced to it.'

'And if he won't?' Gregorio said.

'Then he's too young as yet to help anyone. He'll come back as a man,' Nicholas said, 'and take proper possession, if there's anything left that belongs to him. I take it you couldn't cancel the sale?'

'No,' said Gregorio. 'The part owned by St Pol has quite gone.'

'So Diniz needs you,' Nicholas said. He sat and waited.

'I don't want this,' Gregorio said.

'I know,' said Nicholas. 'Instead of garnering gold, you get to settle the bill for my sins. Do what you can. Don't forget them if you have to go back to Venice. Julius is a good man, but if the *Fortado* is better than I think she is, you may have to carry a great weight between you.'

'The *Fortado*?' Gregorio said. 'She's really sailing for Africa? With de Salmeton?'

'I think that's unlikely. The Vatachino couldn't spare him. But yes, she's sailing. And the Vatachino are financing her, and the Lomellini, and Simon; Gelis will have told you. We're going to have to fight for our gold.'

'And if Diniz wants to fight beside you, you'll take him?'

'You were willing,' Nicholas said. It was necessary.

Gregorio said, 'But you need swordsmen. I understand.'

He had walked halfway back to the house, his shadow behind him, when the front door opened again and the factor Jaime came out and spoke to him, and then called for his grooms. Five minutes passed; then Diniz rode out to Nicholas, a bag strapped at his back and his eyes unusually bright.

Behind him, cloaked and mounted, was Gelis van Borselen. Nicholas said, 'Where are you going?'

'To a nunnery,' she said. 'Oh, how your face cleared! I go wherever you go with Diniz. We have made a bargain.'

'Not with me,' Nicholas said.

'You said you didn't care either way,' said Gelis van Borselen. 'If he comes, I come. I thought you were in a hurry?'

'Diniz,' Nicholas said. 'We are going to Africa.'

'I can't stop her,' he said. 'I don't care. I need the gold for my mother.'

He looked driven. Nicholas turned on the girl. 'You're doing this for Lucia too? Well, why not. I'm sure she thinks you can manage. But I'd mind out for the brick if young Diniz gets buggered despite you.'

Diniz went patchily red. Gelis said, 'Shouldn't we ride? I heard you'd gone. I guessed the *San Niccolò* would creep out and pick you up somewhere. I told Bel to slip back on board and come with her.'

'Along with your luggage?' said Nicholas. All she had slung on her horse was her coffer.

'I left quite a lot in my cabin. I shan't miss my luggage,' she said.

'Good,' said Nicholas. 'Then we might as well ride.'

He had never seen Câmara de Lobos in daylight. Asleep under the stars, it was a pretty village, huddled among wattle fences and great skeins of fishing nets drying. The village boats rocked in the bay, surrounding a single great vessel, quietly at anchor where the water was deeper. She was a roundship.

Two men rose when he rode down to the beach, and spoke to him softly, and held the horses as all three dismounted. Far out, a light boat began to move from the mother ship, which had put up a lantern. Diniz said, 'That isn't the *Niccolò*.'

'No,' said Nicholas. 'That is the *Ghost*, our allotted transport to Africa. Full of pirates, but deficient in clothing and women. I don't recommend it; not on one coffer.'

'Where is the *Niccolò*?' Gelis asked. For the first time, she looked disconcerted.

'Speeding to Arguim,' he said. 'Bearing Bel of Cuthilgurdy, it seems, and your wardrobe. I assume you'll see sense now and stay on Madeira. I can't protect a woman out there.'

'I never thought you could,' said Gelis van Borselen. 'It isn't your forte.'

She didn't see sense. He could have detained her by force, but he didn't. Partly, perhaps, because the solitary Bel was now on the *Niccolò* somewhere ahead of them. Partly because, denied his conclusion with Simon, he felt compelled to confront and to master his demon in some other form. Partly, then, to chastise himself.

He thought how pleased Father Godscalc ought to be.

Chapter 14

IT WAS NO SURPRISE to Ochoa de Marchena to send his caique to Câmara de Lobos and find it return with a youth of eighteen and a young lady of nineteen, as well as his owner. As well, that is, as the man who had signed him on as master. Who owned the *Ghost* didn't concern him. He was quite surprised, however, when the girl was allotted the wainscoted cabin, and the owner and the boy joined the mate and himself in the big one.

The council of war, too, was unexpectedly brisk. Instead of sailing in convoy, the *San Niccolò* in all her legitimacy had fled the harbour at Funchal and was now making straight for the African coast, pausing to take on fresh stores in the Canary Islands. The *Ghost*, with her great spread of canvas, was to make all haste to catch and protect her. Preferably in Grand Canary itself. The *Ghost* of Seville, full of horses, had no permission to sell them in Portuguese Africa.

Ochoa de Marchena didn't need it spelled out. He had treated them to one of his soft, toothless grins. 'You heard the *Fortado*'s been licensed for Guinea as well? You don't want her to clean out your market before you.'

'I'd quite like to get to Arguim first,' his patron had remarked. He looked livelier than you'd expect, though unshaven. 'She'll have left Funchal by now. She knows, I'm sure, where you're going. What do you think she will do?'

Ochoa always liked a man who asked his opinion. He said, 'Take the same route as us; she can't avoid it. The quickest way to raise Arguim is to sail by the Canaries until their peaks are hull down, and then cross to the coast above Blanco. Her advantage is that she's fully provisioned. So she won't stop. She'll go straight over to Guinea.'

'Is she well manned?'

'She's got a well-practised crew. I don't know what master; she

changed command when she got her new orders. She was diverted
from Ceuta: the crusade came to a halt, and the *Fortado* had a load
of grain and gear she'd no use for. That's what she'll be selling at
Arguim.'

'Diniz?' the patron had said unexpectedly.

And the boy, asleep on his feet, had said, 'That's right. It was a
regular run. I can tell you what she carried.'

'Can you? Good. And being a caravel, her sailing speed will be
much like the *Niccolò*'s? Other things being equal?'

Ochoa had laughed. 'You asking about Jorge da Silves? I'll tell
you. He wants a knighthood in the Order of Christ.'

'So?'

'So he'll burn water for you, if he thinks he'll get a name for it.
He'll get to Arguim first. But what about your next port? You'll
have the *Fortado* after you, empty and angry. And she's licensed.'

'I wasn't asking you to sink her,' vander Poele said. He had a
mild way of speaking.

Ochoa had laughed again. 'No, you weren't. But she might fall
off the end of the world. No one could blame me for that.'

'Not if you brought absolute proof. So we call at Grand Canary?'

'Why?' said the young lady. She wasn't asleep. Her face was
familiar.

She was the one he'd been told not to wave to. Ochoa said, 'Do I
answer?'

'You might as well,' vander Poele said. 'She doesn't like the
Fortado either.'

'She was a guest of the Captain at Funchal,' said Ochoa.

'Then if she swims ashore to complain, we'll be sorry. We call at
the Grand Canary because we require a receipt for having offloaded
horses. Also, the *San Niccolò* will have arrived, and I'm joining
her.'

She said, 'I won't be put on shore.'

Ochoa, pleased, left the patron to answer. The patron said, 'Who
would dare? Diniz, however, had best come with me. Father
Godscalc might worry.'

Later, when the girl had retired, Ochoa thumped into his cot by
the others. 'So the young lady stays with Ochoa?'

The *Ghost* was in the full ocean by then, her course set for south
by south-east, her square sails bellying, her round starboard flank
seething and dipping. The first of an uneasy dawn lit her mast-top.
The patron stirred, and delivered an answer. Its import was nega-
tive. Its nature – its *poetic* nature – was such that Ochoa de
Marchena was awed. Seized with joy, he leaned over his owner and
kissed him.

In the event, circumstances saw to it that nothing disembarked at Grand Canary four days later but twenty-five mythical horses: mythical only to the inhabitants of the island, that was. They were real enough on the *Ghost*, where it seemed likely that they would stove in the planks between decks. And there was no question of transferring to the *Niccolò*, because the *Niccolò* had gone straight past La Palma without stopping (so the port officer cheerfully informed them) and down the east coast of the Canary as if the devil himself were coming after her. 'And let us hope,' he said, 'that she has her supplies well aboard, because she'll find little but water at Arguim.'

The port officer was Castilian, and he approved the brave Castilian flag the *Ghost* was flying, as well as being well acquainted with Ochoa de Marchena. Nicholas, fretfully ashore and plied with heavy Andalusian wine, enquired whether the captain was sure it was the caravel he had witnessed.

'No doubt!' he said. 'New, and black-painted as you describe. Not but what I thought her a roundship at first, with a square-cut sail instead of a lateen.'

All at once, the Andalusian wine tasted magnificent. Nicholas said, 'That should send her bowling along, once she picks up the north-easterly wind.'

'She was in a hurry, that is so. Very few go to such trouble. Although I saw another, not two hours behind, which had used the very same trick,' said the officer. 'Older. Blue. Portuguese shipmates, no doubt, with gold in their eye and a fast turn-round in mind.'

'Oh, my dear,' said Ochoa de Marchena. 'How you have made his wine bitter! We execrate the little blue boat, and were praying for every kind of misadventure. When did she pass?'

'Why, at nona, or thereabouts,' said the port officer. 'And handled by a seaman, that I can tell you. But a caravel hasn't your spread of sail. Go to it, Ochoa. You'll catch her before sunset, if you want to.'

The wine of Jerez had never been so quickly abandoned. The sails were drawing and the lead-line armed before the commissary had properly packed down their stores: the cheeses and biscuit and meat the *San Niccolò* would be in sore need of, and a few handy parcels of orchella and some dragon's blood that Nicholas had thrown into the boat as a bargain.

Watching from the great cabin, Gelis – still perforce on board – was triumphant, and Diniz excited. 'What has happened?'

Nicholas joined them with reluctance. Since Funchal he had seen much of Diniz, by turns anxious and elated to find himself

liberated on his grandfather's roundship. For Nicholas, the return
to the former *Doria*, haunted by Primaflora, by the recollection of
Pagano Doria, had been unwelcome. He found it hard to deal with
Gelis and had been thankful that, until now, she had learned to
keep to her cabin. Ochoa's crew of exuberant cut-throats were a
different matter from the *San Niccolò*'s seamen.

But now, the lizard stare on her face, she seemed stimulated as
well as amused by what he was telling them. 'You say the *Niccolò*
should get to Arguim first. But if the *Fortado* follows her in, she
will certainly warn the fort that a third, unauthorised vessel is
coming, and the Portuguese factor will prevent you from trading.
Surely he would stop you in any case?'

'Maybe,' Nicholas said. 'Maybe not. He likes horses.'

'I see,' she said. There was contempt in her voice. 'And that is
the only peril?'

'The *Fortado* knows we may be the *Doria* and will report that.
She also knows, I suppose, that I am here, and not on my own
licensed caravel, which would certainly give the Portuguese authorities grounds for searching us.'

'And finding all of us, and the horses, on a stolen ship run by
Castilian pirates. End of venture,' said Diniz.

'She doesn't know,' said Gelis van Borselen.

'What?' said Diniz. She didn't look at him.

'David de Salmeton didn't know you had left the *San Niccolò*. It
didn't occur to him that you would, and I didn't tell him. So the
Fortado thinks you're still on board your own caravel, and that I
am still in Madeira, staying with Diniz. It is what I told them at
Funchal.'

Nicholas gazed at her. The strength of her hatred unnerved him.
He should have been sorry for the Vatachino, had he not been
quite apprehensive for himself. Diniz said eagerly, 'So now you
can blow her out of the water.'

Slowly, Nicholas removed his gaze from the girl's. She had lifted
an eyebrow.

'That's so,' he said. 'Mind you, we'd have to sink her and leave no
survivors, or the *Ghost* would be as ardently sought as the *Doria*. And
we have to catch her up first. The coast is less than sixty miles off.'

The prospect of drowning or slaughtering thirty compatriots
serving the Lomellini, the Vatachino and Simon did not, it was
clear, preoccupy Diniz. He said, 'The *African* coast?' with some
pleasure, and then added, 'But it's a bad lee shore, according to
Diogo. Ships don't immediately cross: they take a late diagonal
west to Cape Blanco. That gives you four or five hundred miles to
catch up with her. A good three days at seven knots.'

The wind was pranking about from the south-west and gusting. 'We're doing five knots,' Nicholas said. 'We shan't do better until we catch the right weather, and the caravels will manage three and a half if they're lucky. I wonder.'

'What?' said Diniz.

'What guns the *Fortado* carries,' said Nicholas. 'Ochoa will know.'

Diniz grinned, but Gelis, he was pleased to see, didn't.

He resisted telling Diniz his plans, and Gelis, retired to her cabin, didn't ask. Just before sunset the ragged clouds cleared, and Ochoa dressed a spar to the mast and went up himself to the peak, a wolfskin cap on his head with its upper jaw over one ear. He slid down almost immediately. 'The *Fortado* is in sight. Now we know her course and shall soon know her speed; she has no suspicion. All we have to do is hold back until dark. And there is plenty to do. The wind is coming.'

By the time Diniz came up from his supper to discover the cause of the banging and rolling, the wind was dead astern and the *Ghost* had changed her shape yet again. The forecastle and poop both seemed higher; the boats were differently stowed and the rail of the quarter-deck altered; while her mizzen-sail, which had been a triangular lateen, was now square, although at present reefed in order to slow her. Lastly, the mysterious chests which had lain on her deck were now dismantled, disclosing six bombards and four breechloading swivel-guns. In the waist, neatly folded, lay a quantity of old thin sailcloth.

'What are you doing?' Diniz said. 'They've put out our lamps.'

'My lamp has been taken away,' said the angry voice of Gelis almost immediately.

'That is right, my treasured ones,' said Ochoa de Marchena. 'See, pick your way to the binnacle. *Per gratia di Dio et del beato messer Sante Niccholò*, as they say in the Levant. We show no lights while we catch up with the *Fortado*, for there is no moon and the stars are cloud-covered. And just recently we have come into the path of the north-easterly, which will propel us all the way to Arguim, once our business is finished.'

'You *are* going to blow her out of the water!' said Diniz exultantly.

'Nonsense,' said Nicholas, his face suspended diabolically in the same binnacle light. 'We intend to put her to a small inconvenience before the night is quite over, but it won't be for some hours yet, and there is no need for the lady to lose sleep or her lamp. I shall have it put back, demoiselle, so long as you have no objection to having your doorway made fast. One gleam from that, and it might be the *Fortado* which blows us out of the water.'

'Then I'd rather be on deck when she did it,' Gelis said. 'Keep your lantern.'

She was not on deck, however, when they caught up with the *Fortado*, for Ochoa, a cape over the glory of his stolen cuirass and sword, had dispatched her below, together with the three or four whores from the forecastle and the groom for the horses.

Up on deck, the big stern lantern was cold, and every other light was extinguished except for the two binnacles, secure in their boxes. The sailcloth had gone, but beside the guns the faintest glow showed where the slow-matches burned in their barrels and men moved about on bare feet, speaking softly. Diniz said, 'Where is she? The *Fortado*? Has she seen us?'

'There,' said Nicholas, pointing ahead and to the right. Having no armour, he had borrowed for himself and Diniz from the seamen's stock of leather tunics and helms. 'No. She's darkened, as we are. When we reach the top of the swell, you can just see the green of her wake. We want to get between her and the wind on the same tack, so that she loses way and may even brouch-to. Then we fire as we pass her.'

'The cannon?' said Diniz. He sounded breathless. 'You said —'

'I said we'd mind our manners. The cannon are only there in case she doesn't mind hers.' As he spoke, the rigging shuddered under his hand, although the sky was so dark he could see no one. He said, 'We're going to slow her, that's all. We can do it with handguns.'

'I can use one,' said Diniz. 'Where are they?'

He told him, and let Ochoa give him his orders. The others already had theirs. The best three marksmen to fire first; shattering the rudder as they came up. Then, as they came abreast, as many balls as they could let off against the concave cloth, the sheets and braces of the temporary squaresail.

'For, see, my angels, my little mice,' said Ochoa de Marchena. 'Her mizzen-sail cannot be set in this wind, for it would steal the wind from the rest; and she has her foresail held flat as a board until the wind settles, much though she would like to fly after your poor *San Niccolò*, labouring ahead in the dark (although you may be calm, Jorge will not risk his life until he has his honour). So we must wrest from her the squaresail, which I will take my oath is the only one that she has, and is of light flax of the kind that might even rip free from its sheets and yard and take to the sky like a bird, like an expensive bird never to be captured. And even if it is not, she may turn round to the wind and be caught aback, and then what will happen? Delay, delay, my children. Delay and mortification.'

A small inconvenience, nothing more. The Vatachino and Simon were not on board; this was a matter of trade, not of war. If she still had her cannon from her Ceuta days (and Ochoa had seen no sign of them), the *Fortado* was unlikely to test them against the gleaming power of the roundship's armoury, trained on her flank.

Any crew worth the name could repair small-arms damage; could replace a main with a lateen sail, patch canvas and splice rope and rig up jury spars. The beauty of it was that it took time, and the *Fortado*'s sailing thereafter would be sluggish – sluggish enough to let the little *San Niccolò* fly ahead to the market at Arguim, and for himself to follow briskly and do his business there, and transfer to the *San Niccolò* before anyone stopped him, such as Father Godscalc.

It was a reasonable plan, and it began well enough, for the watch on the *Fortado* was evidently poor and no warning cries, or whistles, or drumbeats floated back to the *Ghost*, although her bow wave must now have been visible. Admired by Nicholas from Ochoa's side, the roundship spread her canvas, presented her gleaming red quarter to the formidable wind and began to cut through the heaving sea and up towards the weather side of the other ship's stern.

Ochoa, a burning slow-match over each ear, stood gripping the rail of the poop, his eyes on the just-discernible dark shape ahead and her seething green wake off his beam. The helmsman and his mate waited, rigid and ghostly in the compass light. And throughout the dark and silent roundship, points of dusky red flame glimmered along the deck, in the waist, on the forecastle, above in the rigging where the hackbutters waited, Diniz among them, their guns primed and their matches ready to touch.

Then they were within range of the *Fortado*'s sternpost, and Ochoa gave the order to fire.

The noise and flame from the handguns followed instantly, but only one of the balls struck the rudder, for even as they fired, the *Fortado* started to turn by the lee. At the same instant, the stern lantern of the caravel sprang to life, flinging a great yellow beam over the water, and followed by other lamps at masthead and rigging and poop, so that the *Ghost*, looming to windward, became brilliant.

They had been tricked. The *Fortado*, fully manned and alert, had seen them and was waiting, prepared for them. The light showed her stern and waist busy with men, their voices now ringing out. And although her squaresail had spilled air, it could be seen that the caravel's mainbraces were manned, and a moment later the foresail broke out and, catching the wind not yet masked by the *Ghost*, began to assist her to swing.

Ochoa screamed orders. The vessel shook as her sails were reset and she rolled, her pace slackening. The caravel continued to turn. The *Ghost*'s hackbutters, hardly hesitating, kept up their deliberate fire, and with the rudder much less accessible, transferred their attentions to the retreating mainsail and rigging. In the lamplight, the activity on the *Fortado* was quite clear, and also the immobile figure of a knight in full armour, plumed helmet and all, standing exposed on the poop deck. Another, in worn helm and cuirass, bellowed orders below him.

The knight was unknown, but Nicholas recognised the helm and the voice of the master. They belonged to Mick Crackbene, the man he had fought and got rid of at Lagos. Got rid of for ever, he'd hoped. Nicholas started to run.

Seized and dragged into darkness, Diniz was swinging the stock of his handgun before he saw his assailant. 'Get down,' Nicholas said. 'Or cover your face. Crackbene's there. Crackbene's sailing that ship. He mustn't see us.' He pulled his own neckerchief from his jerkin and held it out. The boy jerked to his knees.

The deck swayed. Ochoa's voice and the mate's shouted hoarsely. Diniz glared at the *Fortado*. Ignoring the kerchief and Nicholas, he lurched to his feet with his weapon, paused, and launched himself directly into the light. It wasn't surprising. Prisoner of his grand-father, Diniz had been wrested from Cyprus on the same roundship on whose deck he now stood, and Michael Crackbene had been his gaoler.

Nicholas scrambled after. The *Fortado* was already slanting away, her mainsail adapting, her blue starboard flank beginning to lift as she was set to veer west and north. Something glittered along the line of her rail. The man in armour still stood at the stern, but the other had changed his position. Judging Diniz just within reach, Nicholas obeyed a roll of the ship and flung himself on him. As the boy crashed, collapsing beneath him, Nicholas realised what he had seen: a line of swivelling cannon, hitherto covered. Then he understood what Ochoa was shouting, and heard the *comito* repeat the command, and saw that in the moments he had missed, the three great bombards and two breechloaders along the *Ghost*'s starboard rail were all standing ready and manned, the matches ready to touch.

He thought afterwards that he shouted an order, but if so, it had no effect. In explosion after thundering explosion, the *Ghost*'s leeside bombards fired one by one at each heave of the ship; fired at the Portuguese caravel *Fortado*, licensed by her monarch to trade off the Guinea coast. The first three-hundred-pound ball shredded her mainsail. The second raked her from rail to rail just above the well of the deck, so that two of her cannon sprang into the sea. The third pierced the pavilion of the poop, and went on to break her mizzen in half.

There was no fourth, for Nicholas had got to the swivel-gunner by then, and knocked him back from his post. The man rounded on him; others loomed; the mate leaped forward, his hand on his sword, and Nicholas whipped out his blade. High on the poop deck Ochoa held back at first and said nothing. Then he shrieked a command, and then another, in his mumbling, furious voice. The men stood panting, their fists doubled, but on the second invitation they jumped as if he had flayed them and, abandoning the guns, scampered to set their hands to the toil of getting the ship on her way.

Even so, the ship's lash came out before the sails were drawing to Ochoa's satisfaction, for it was plain that his men had no relish for running off from a prize, and especially one that had been all set, by God, to tempt them round and rake them with a broadside. But Ochoa, for all his fancy clothes, had a rude way, Nicholas suspected, with dissidents. At least, before Diniz was fully recovered the sails had filled, the helm returned to its course and, picking up speed, the *Ghost* abandoned her victim and, flying before the steady, violent wind, resumed her passage to Arguim.

Searching for Diniz, Nicholas found him sitting clutching his broken head in the great cabin, with the lamp lit and Gelis van Borselen busy with water and linen beside him. Nicholas hesitated, seeing the light; and then said nothing. At present the *Fortado* was in no state to follow, and although she might try to fire, they must be at the extreme range of her guns or passing beyond it. He stood, therefore, one hand pressed above to the deckhead against the tilting and rolling beneath him, and said, 'Is it bad? Diniz, I'm sorry. The rascals were turning to give us a broadside.'

He didn't know what to expect. In fact Diniz jerked up his head on hearing his voice, sending the bowl of pink water surging over the cabin and splashing the girl with its contents. Diniz exclaimed, 'She says we fired first, and I missed it! She says the mizzenmast broke, and the poop was wrecked. He must be dead. You must have killed half of them.'

'I didn't mean to kill any of them,' Nicholas said. 'It was Ochoa's idea.'

He turned his eyes from the flushed face of Diniz to the girl. Her hair ruffled, her hood fallen back, she looked as composed as a tall marble caryatid, undisturbed by battle or gunfire, far less her recent feminine company. She said, 'From what you say, it was just as well he conceived it. There was a man on the *Fortado* who knew you both?'

'He may not have seen us,' said Nicholas. 'In any case –'

'He's probably dead,' Diniz repeated. The bandage-end, not yet neatened, hung rakishly over one cheek in a style reminiscent of one of Ochoa de Marchena's confections.

Nicholas said, 'In the name of hell, what has come over you? You were excessively lofty about the Lalaing brothers calling out Arabs in Ceuta, but you don't seem to have many qualms about Christians.'

Diniz said, 'I suppose the Genoese in Famagusta weren't Christians!' Then he sucked in his breath.

Nicholas swore. Gelis said, 'How exciting. I can't remember when I last debated religion. I think Diniz is right.'

Diniz said, 'I shouldn't have spoken.'

'Why not?' said Gelis van Borselen. 'We mustn't lose sight of the wider issues. Involuntary martyrdom of its nature is sad, but consider the souls you will proceed to encounter and save, now this man and his friends can't denounce you.'

'They can't anyway,' Nicholas said. 'Even if they speak from their coffins. There is no way they can get to Arguim before us. Can I finish that for you?'

She had begun to tie the end of the bandage, forcing Diniz' glowering face down. She turned her head from left to right slowly. Diniz said, 'If we hadn't fired first, they'd have killed us.'

He wasn't speaking to Gelis. 'Ah,' said Gelis none the less. 'Ah, but they might have fired over our heads. I'm sure that's what Nicholas has in mind. You don't mind if I call you Nicholas, Claes? Or Nikko, perhaps?'

'You needn't call me anything,' Nicholas said, 'after Arguim. May I tell you both what is going to happen there? We three transfer by boat from the *Ghost* to the *Niccolò*, so that it appears we've been there all the time. The *Ghost* has no permit to sell, but the Portuguese factor is greedy for horses. The *Niccolò* will even offer to help with the paperwork. Meanwhile the demoiselle packs, takes her companion and lands. The trading-post is quite large, and the factor's wife will be happy to entertain two charming ladies and set them aboard the next ship for Madeira.' He finished on a reasonable note. In fact, he didn't care how he finished.

Gelis had completed her task. The circlet of linen was tied in a chic lovers' knot. She picked up the bowl and held it on her splashed skirts. 'Oh dear,' she said. 'I mustn't kill anybody? And Diniz has to go back as well?'

Diniz said, 'No, of course I'm going on. But he's right. You must go, and Bel. It's far too dangerous.'

'What a discovery,' Gelis said. 'You made a promise at Ponta do Sol. You don't go unless I come with you.'

She raised her brows at the boy. The boy glanced at Nicholas who, steadied by the negligent arm over his head, continued to sway with his eyes almost shut. Diniz said, 'Then I take it back. I don't need protecting from him. I thought you'd have seen that by now. And I thought he'd get rid of you, anyway.'

'You thought he could get rid of me?' Gelis said. 'May God in His mercy give me patience. He can barely get his ship to obey him, never mind anything else. Of course I shan't go. And Bel had better stay on board, we may need her. Tell me, Nikko . . .'

'No,' said Nicholas.

'Claes? Tell me, Claes, how you expect to go on? Certainly, you will beat the *Fortado* to Arguim, but since she has not unhappily sunk, she will surely hunt this ship south and impeach her?'

'Impeach the *Ghost*?' Nicholas said. 'You haven't seen what we've done. Come and look at her.' He was far from at ease in her company, but his arm had grown numb, and the bench she occupied was his bed.

She made no demur. They walked, leaving Diniz, the length of the deck. The lamps had been lit. The false erections were already half down, and the guns cleaned, cooled and covered. Fulfilling his hopes, the men sniggered and called as she passed, saying nothing. The bawds were all out of sight.

He took her to the side – the side which, throughout, had faced the *Fortado*. Firmly pegged and smoothed from long practice, a length of sailcloth covered her strakes from bow to stern and down to the waterline. Seen at night; seen even over the water by lamplight, the roundship appeared painted white; appeared to be without flag or name, and with few of the characteristics of either the *Ghost* or her shell the *Doria*.

Rolling with the ship, the master approached them. Nicholas said, 'That's why Ochoa couldn't turn fully and follow. There was only enough cloth for one side. Just as well, you ravening jackal. You might have ruined the game.'

Manifest in clean lilac taffeta, Ochoa gave an agreeable wink. 'So whatever the mischief, demoiselle, the *Fortado* cannot say it was the fault of our splendid red *Ghost*.'

'Can't they?' Gelis said.

'She means,' Nicholas said, 'that whoever the caravel thought had attacked her, she would still blame the *Ghost*.'

Ochoa de Marchena leaned over and patted the demoiselle's sleeve. 'There is acumen. But we, too, have our genius. Yes, the *Ghost* will be accused. Our enemy's crew will be instructed to report their attacker as red, and of our style and even our name. But a man paid to lie can be paid more to come out with the truth.

And if two such poor men, taken separately, confide to the Portuguese agent that the marauder was really white, and had no name and no flag, and was shaped thus and thus – will the truth not prevail?'

'The truth?' said Gelis.

'In a manner of speaking,' said Nicholas. 'Do you know, I think I might go to bed.'

Chapter 15

THE DAY AFTER THAT, the cry of '*Tier-ra!*' came from the masthead, and Nicholas, already on deck, stayed to watch the line between sea and sky darken.

Land. The edge of the desert.

The selfsame cry heard off Madeira had brought him a shock of delight stronger than all his cares at that moment. Off Grand Canary the call, no less thankful, had seemed to promise reunion at last with his caravel, and separation, at last, from his penance.

In both he had been disappointed. The girl was still in his life, like an ulcer.

The dispute had hung in the air for three days, during which Diniz and Gelis van Borselen had to put up with one another at table, and with Nicholas rather less often, since he spent most of his time on the poop deck.

The *Fortado* lay crippled somewhere behind. Somewhere ahead, sailing at a caravel's speed, was the *San Niccolò*. It would be pleasant to raise her.

Ochoa was soothing. The caravel had had four hours' start; she had spent more time in easier waters; Jorge was experienced in choosing a course and would not, like the *Ghost*, have had to stop or to deviate. Moreover, the *Niccolò* would be in urgent need of provisions, having loaded nothing since Lagos but some hurried barrels of water at Funchal. They would meet her at Arguim.

Detecting a note of anxiety, Nicholas didn't argue. The round-ship, lunging and hissing, was close to her maximum speed. More canvas would put her bows under.

He had had his blazing row with Ochoa, and had hammered it into his head that so long as he, the patron, was on board, no cannon would fire without his permission. It was not a popular edict. The crew were Ochoa's, and unused to an employer who meddled. When a man showed too bold a resentment, Ochoa put him promptly in chains, which was even less popular. The little mice might comply, but in the long run a divided command would impair Ochoa's authority. It would be as well for Ochoa, also, to get to Arguim quickly.

Nicholas was well aware of the dangers. As the sun increased its heat and the ship, running free, fell into the routine of fair-weather sailing, he kept a light touch in his relations with the upper seamen of the poop, and showed no disposition to check the rough games, the bloody contests, the obscene entertainments the men chose to indulge in. He also kept an unobtrusive eye on his passengers.

The horses were Diniz' salvation. Cooped up sweating below on a daily diet of hay and a hundred buckets of sorely grudged water, the *Ghost*'s twenty-five valuable Berbers were no longer the fire-eaters who had embarked at Sanlúcar. Their condition was closer to that of the pigs, the goats and the poultry which had also, in logic, become the groom's charge until eaten. Forking hay and shovelling dung-laden straw, the man was first shocked and then pleased to find the young Portuguese happy to help him.

It suited Diniz, who had been reared on the land. His headache waned; he found the labour undemanding and restful; he began to think the smell of fresh air quite peculiar. Also the man took to him readily, and he was not entirely shunned by the crew, who knew he had been in Ceuta and who had assessed and approved of his shooting. He appeared in the cabin for food, although Gelis recoiled and Nicholas and Ochoa did all the talking. He also liked to stand by himself at the rail, watching the pallid crust of the coast sliding past, separated from him by the heaving blue ocean, so weighty, so endless, so deep.

Diniz was not afraid. He and his father had lived on Madeira. Madeira was on the same ponderous sea. Over there was Cape Bojador, *caput finis Africae*, the spume of whose reefs, seething and flashing with fish, had made mariners think that the sea boiled; that magnetic rocks would dismantle their vessels; that ahead was the brink: the terrible cataract at the end of the world. The man who ventured his life in these waters was clearly deranged, the wise men of the Koran had thought.

Men knew better now. Diniz had seen fishing-boats. There were porpoises in the water and birds he knew in the air. Certainly, as Ochoa set a course nearer land, he saw the sea flush, as if stained by pus or by blood, but this was merely sand, Ochoa explained, spilled and tumbled from the long, clinging, crumbling cliffs. And that very day a haze of light rosy sand brushed the roundship, sifting over the deck and sliding into the folds of men's shirts, patching their glistening faces and bodies like fawnskins. It lay as dust on the sea, except where the ship smoothed it clean with her sides, and her wake trailed a gloss in the water. There was no mystery in it.

The best tales, at this time, came from Ochoa, and especially if Gelis were there. He wanted her to remember the great island peak he had steered by; twelve thousand feet high, and named after the fire on its summit. Had they landed there, instead of on Grand Canary, he would have shown her naked savages painted with goat fat and coloured red and yellow and green like a carpet. And merry they were on that island: dancing, laughing and singing all day; for there was fruit to be had for no labour, and every man could fill a field with his wives. 'And you have never wanted to stay?' Gelis said.

Diniz thought her unwise in some of the things she said and did now to amuse herself. She would even linger on deck while the men took their ease in the bows, and once, when they were laying coins on the flight of two birds, she joined in, and carried the prize. When she made gift of it back to the common purse they said no direct word to thank her, but made no objection, either, when she wanted to try the next wager.

That time she lost, and soon after left, though still smiling. The next day she did it again, over a match between two fighting crickets. She remained for half a turn of the glass, and took some tentative chaffing, and went. She had only one gown, but kept it neat; and covered her head and shoulders and neck with fresh linen. She was tall, and spoke like a man, but she wasn't one. There was only one day to Arguim, and if for no other reason, Diniz knew he had to talk somehow to Nicholas.

The chance came that night after supper, when Gelis left table early, and the master and mate were already on deck, having eaten. The sails were being reduced. Forty miles, Ochoa reckoned, lay between the *Ghost* and Cape Blanco that evening, and he had no wish to come across it in darkness; already, he was as close to the shore as was prudent. No, he wanted to raise Blanco by first light. Behind Blanco was the greatest gulf on the coast, twenty miles of it. And ten miles beyond that was Arguim.

Alone with Nicholas at the table, Diniz played with his cloying Madeira, and wondered how to begin. He said, 'The *Fortado* didn't catch up.'

'Did you suppose she would?' Nicholas said, without looking up. He had come late, and was cutting up meat with precision. Despite an enviable deposit of garments, he inhabited nothing grander on board than hose and shirt and a loose sleeveless pourpoint, although the tags and cords were apt to be gold. His complexion, merely mellowed by sunlight, was saved from daintiness by the scar on one cheek, in the same way that his size was offset by his bearing, and his unthreatening mien by the range of his voice.

His thatch, tousled with salt, would scarcely bed the round cap he crammed on it and ought to have been cut. It was not cut, Diniz conjectured, because tomorrow in truly commonplace guise Nicholas had to smuggle the three of them aboard the *San Niccolò*, where they were supposed to have been ever since Funchal.

Diniz said, pursuing his point, 'Ochoa says the *Fortado* should be a whole day behind us.' He paused, without really expecting any grateful acknowledgement. 'He says you must expect a few dead in that sort of skirmish. The men wouldn't have stood for being fired on. It's true. I've been talking to some of them. I tried to explain how you thought.'

'I heard,' Nicholas said. 'Even the horses have become versed in polemics. I notice that Gelis, too, thought we were on the brink of a mutiny.'

'Is *that* why she did it?' said Diniz.

The door opened. 'I thought I might be missing a council of war. Did what?' said Gelis, sitting down.

'Raised the crew's hopes,' Nicholas said. 'It made me feel very nervous. If you take up soliciting, it makes me expendable.'

'Why else do you think I did it?' she said.

She had annoyed Diniz, interrupting. Diniz said, 'Don't be silly. Ochoa won't harm him. At the very least, Ochoa needs him at Arguim. Someone's got to negotiate for the horses.'

'Still?' said Gelis. 'I thought we were keeping the horses as pets?'

Diniz was not ashamed to speak for the horses. He said, 'We must land them at Arguim. They can hardly go further and give you a return for their keep.' He heard Gelis sigh.

'That,' said Nicholas, 'is exactly the point I was hoping to put to you both. It is true you've been easy to transport – no kicking, no grooming, no mucking-out – but I have told you before: seriously, this is where it all ends. We should arrive at Arguim about noon, and you should start to pack now. I'm not taking you further.'

Diniz found that Gelis, having sighed, had left him to speak. He said, 'We argued this out before. The ladies go on shore, but I stay with you on the *Niccolò*.' Nicholas sat, his elbows set on the table, and his hands clasped in non-supplication. Over them, his gaze was direct. Diniz added stiffly, 'That is to say, it's your ship.'

'I'm glad someone remembered,' Nicholas said. 'Come or not as you please; you've been warned. You damage your family name, if you do. And you leave the women endangered.'

'My family name?' Diniz said. 'My family head got the damage. I don't know who could imagine a friendship between you and me now. As for Gelis, she is a wolf pack in one person. And Bel is as bad.'

'Thank you,' said Gelis. She tightened her lips.

Nicholas said, over his undisturbed hands, 'Then Diniz comes. And the demoiselle and her friend leave at Arguim.'

Gelis smiled at him. When she smiled like that, her eyes seemed to stretch to her ears. She said, 'Perhaps I should warn you. If you try to put me on shore, I shall tell the trading-post everything. The proper name of the *Ghost*, and who hired her, and what exactly happened to the *Fortado*.'

She was the most relentless person Diniz had ever met. He stared at her in amazement.

Nicholas considered her too. He said, 'Ruining yourself and Diniz as well? Hardly.'

'Try it,' she said.

'You interrupted me. Hardly the vengeance Katelina would have wanted. Diniz helped nurse her when he was starving himself.'

'Starving,' she said, 'from your blockade.' Her face was quite calm.

Diniz drew breath and then stopped, for his arm was being gripped. Nicholas said, 'All right, I have a better idea.' A dimple appeared, and deepened slowly in either cheek. Diniz, unfamiliar with the sight, kept quiet. Nicholas said, 'Here it is. I set *Diniz* on shore; and you're bound by your promise to stay with him.'

She said, 'So you will send Diniz away?'

'If he agrees to go,' Nicholas said. 'Otherwise you'll have to tell all, as you say. Including how he shot up the *Fortado* with his handgun. Or if you like, I'll tell that bit.'

'Diniz?' Gelis van Borselen said. She was inviting him to come. She was prepared to do anything, it seemed, to part him from Nicholas.

Diniz said, 'I'm staying. I don't care what happens.'

'That's obvious,' Nicholas said. 'Well, I do believe in democracy. You've both had your say, not that it makes any difference. You all go on shore, but not till we're sailing. Then tell what tales you like. Both ships will be gone; the *Ghost*, when next seen, will be, I expect, quite unrecognisable. As for me, the success of my mission should make up for my errors.'

Gelis said, 'In other words, you hope to bribe the King of Portugal into forgiving you. There is such a thing as justice.'

'Are you dealing in justice?' Nicholas said. 'Let me congratulate you, when I recover my breath. Me, I'm in the business of finding gold and converting the heathen and bringing Ethiopia into a war, if I can find it. Portugal yearns; the Throne of St Peter is eager. What can be closer to justice than religion and gold? How could you expect justice without them?'

Diniz felt himself flush. Gelis sat, swayed by the ship, and fleetingly her eyes were intent. She said, 'But what is this? We heard no cries of distaste over the terms of your service in Cyprus.'

'I couldn't afford them,' Nicholas said. 'I can't afford them now. I doubt if I shall ever be able to afford them, or even want to. Look at Ochoa. A happy man.'

'He would be the better,' she said, 'of some teeth.' Diniz saw that her eyes and those of Nicholas had engaged. His face, normally a conjurer's bag of expressions, had turned still. Hers, below the folded linen that dressed her pale hair, remained thoughtful, but her gaze was brighter and sharper. She said, 'What is the *Ghost* taking on board, when she unloads her horses?'

Nicholas smiled. The conjurer, unpacking his box, produced the dimples, the under-lines of habitual laughter, the immense light eyes, lakes of deception. He said, 'Whatever the *Niccolò* leaves. Gold and gum, pepper and cotton and feathers. Anything.'

'In all this space?' Gelis said.

Diniz drew in his breath and Nicholas, who had long ago removed his hand, glanced at him and at the girl. He was still smiling. He said, 'You mean, am I buying slaves? Yes, I am. I would have told you before, except that it was none of your business. It still isn't. But it should reconcile you at least to going home, healthily disgusted.'

'We use slaves,' Diniz volunteered. 'In Ponta do Sol. We've black servants in Lagos. They're happy. They're free, most of them.' He spoke tentatively, but he did speak. It was true. His father had bought them.

'I expect they are,' Gelis said. 'But that isn't the point, is it?'

'And they were baptised,' Diniz said. There was some justification. He was angry that Nicholas wasn't helping him; the more so that he understood very well what Gelis meant. Because people would pay for good help, the blacks were worth money to traders. They didn't volunteer to become happy servants; they were trapped and beaten and marched to the markets where their employers bought them. And before the evolution of such civilised practices, they were simply plucked by ships' crews from the beaches: fathers fled; women rushed to drown in the sea; mothers hid their children under the mud.

It was not the case now. He wanted to put his father's point of view, but Nicholas wouldn't allow it; stopped him speaking, and asked Gelis to go to her cabin.

She didn't refuse. He was a large man, standing beside her. He could quite well have marched her below. As it was, she rose, and balanced, and walked, pausing to turn as she passed him. 'Religion and gold,' Gelis said. 'You were right, weren't you, Claes? They have nothing in common with justice.'

The horses, heavy and drowsy below, were the best comfort Diniz could find. He would miss them. Tomorrow they, too, would step on unknown shores and labour for unknown masters. Tomorrow, men and women and children would occupy the same straw. Horses and slaves, to a merchant, were merchandise. It wasn't right. It wasn't right, unless the end justified it.

He spent some time below. Then he spread his blanket in the great cabin and pretended, when the other men came, to be already asleep.

He wakened to daylight and shouting, and came on deck to find the ship floating like the spectre she was in a suspension of fine ruddy sand.

It was far more dense than before. However thinned by the draught of her passing, it hung in impassive red veils beyond, giving Diniz a shadowy glimpse of the jut of Cape Blanco, its long white plateau no more than two miles behind. Of the deep bay the ship was traversing, there was no sign at all. The *Ghost* occupying her circle of sea seemed like a dog on a treadmill, always sailing but never progressing; and every now and then, as the breeze brought it, sand would enter the ship in soft flurries, striking the canvas with a hoarse and echoing wheeze, while rendering noiseless all human activity. Ochoa de Marchena said, 'It happens. It will wear off through the morning.' And later: 'We hailed a boat in the night. It's good news. See how our young man is happy! The *San Niccolò* is anchored in Arguim, and has been there for two days.'

Two days. Diniz couldn't see Nicholas, and wondered how anyone could refer to him as young. He wondered, too, at the speed Jorge da Silves had made with the caravel, even given his familiarity with the coast. Lastly, he wondered how the same Jorge would go about conducting his business in his patron's name without his patron on board, and what excuse he was making to linger. He could hardly say that he had a stolen roundship to wait for.

Ochoa, who knew the coast almost as well as Jorge, came to cheer him from time to time, a piece of bread or a chicken leg in his hand. Ochoa pointed out the sudden glare in the water that screamed a warning of rocks, but was caused by the little sardine fish in its thousands. He described the great fighting tunny: on a clear day, Senhor Diniz would see the fishing-boats and the huts of their owners edging the sands and mudflats of this very bay, to which they brought back their catch to salt and sell later through Arguim. 'For whose protection, of course,' Ochoa said, 'they pay a small toll. Indeed, a rather large toll. But it gives them sole rights, and that is always expensive.'

The fog of sand lingered all morning; the food Diniz found in the cabin was gritty. Gelis didn't appear. He took time to pack, since he was certainly leaving – for the *San Niccolò*, he hoped, despite everything. He saw that Nicholas, too, had stowed and strapped all his belongings. He came in once, lowering a flask from his lips, and said, 'You're ready, good. Better still if the sand doesn't clear: we can slip quietly across to the *Niccolò*.' He smiled. There was no gold today on his shirt. He said, 'Would you like some of this? There's no mud in it.'

It was Madeira wine. Diniz drank and wiped and corked the flask as Nicholas had done, handing it back. He said, 'Will they start trading without you?'

'They may. We made an arrangement. If Jorge doubts that we're coming, the second mate will pass himself off as me. We'll know soon. The Cape of Arguim is just ahead: we're reducing sail until the tide makes. It's tricky. I've asked the demoiselle to stay below, not to be seen. There's no harm in your coming up, if you want to.'

'How is she?' said Diniz as they walked.

'Charming,' said Nicholas.

Diniz saw Cape Arguim from the deck, although it was very low and surrounded by dunes, and slips of sand licked by foam stood all about it. The sky was suddenly brighter. It was two hours to high water, and the wind had changed at last to blow from the north-east. 'Damnation,' said Nicholas.

The haze of sand thinned. Beyond the Cape, a socket-like gulf, stark and treeless, seemed to run sharply north, a stony mass in its depths, its beaches glimmering. The entrance was patched and streaked with sandy shoals and snarled with cross-currents. The *Ghost* made no effort to enter. She rattled on to the voice of the leadsman until she had passed two-thirds of the entrance. Only then did Ochoa call strongly. There was a rush of feet; the ship trembled and Diniz half lost his footing as the *Ghost* abruptly changed course and swung pitching into the bay.

The wind was just strong enough to bring her round. She moved as if on ratchets, bumping over the troublesome water, but she continued to swing until she lay to the opposite tack, eluding the sand bar and slipping into the calm of the channel, itself dulled with sand. Water sifted along her lee side. The ship fell into silence except for the rapid clear voice repeating the soundings, and Ochoa's commands, and the calls of the mate and the helmsman. The sun, long obscured, glowed overhead suddenly, lurid and coarse as an orange.

With equal suddenness, a ship appeared on the far side of the gulf, carrying a great deal of sail. Carrying too much sail, you would say, to navigate in such difficult waters, even though she was coming out of the gulf and not entering, and turning south and away with the wind. Then he recognised her. The ship was the *San Niccolò*.

She was too far off to hail. Neither vessel could sail across to the other. The caravel made no change to her sails. For a moment, Diniz even wondered if the *Ghost* had been seen, forgetting that every man on the *Niccolò* must be looking for her. He heard Ochoa curse, his face caught between anger and puzzlement. Nicholas spoke to him, but Diniz couldn't hear what he said. The two ships continued to move, the roundship sailing cautiously inwards; the caravel crowding sail to get out. She looked as splendid as she had leaving Lagos: glittering black with her snowy new sails, and her Portuguese flag uncurling over her. She had another one, too.

She was flying two Portuguese flags. Diniz peered at them. A puff-ball appeared on her flank. There was a flash, and a bang travelled over the water. The helmsman shouted. Ochoa opened his mouth, and Nicholas rammed a fist on his shoulder. Ochoa's mouth closed. A second white puff appeared, and another harmless explosion took place.

The *San Niccolò* had fired two warning guns. Then, without waiting, she held her course southwards. 'What is it?' said Diniz, reaching Nicholas.

He was gazing into the gulf. The sun burned. The veils, lifting, began to reveal the white beaches, the green and blue water. The stony mass shifted apart to become a group of two small shaly islands and a larger one to the right which rose to a modest height from the sea, and then tumbled down to flat sand at its southern end. There were buildings on that, both on the shore and crowning the high ground behind it. The ground was not quite high enough to conceal the masts of a ship, flying the flag of the royal house of Portugal.

Nicholas for a moment said nothing. It was Ochoa who suddenly giggled. 'Did you suppose our *Fortado* had transposed herself? No. This is another danger, or your friends would not have warned you with guns. We see a Portuguese patrol ship, I think.'

'Waiting for us?' Nicholas said. The deck tilted beneath them: the helmsman, in the absence of orders, was holding the *Ghost* to her course. He could do little else; the stream gave him no room to turn.

'Expecting us? No. But waiting for us now, to find out why we are here. What do you wish, Senhor Niccolò, my dear? We can kedge ourselves backwards, but it will be slow. We can advance close to the island and then turn and come out by the western channel the *San Niccolò* used – but that would bring us under our royal friend's guns. Or we could go in and befool them.'

'Let's go in and befool them,' Nicholas said.

He and Ochoa went off. Sent below to the wainscoted cabin, Diniz talked and Gelis listened with patience. He ended, 'I don't know what Nicholas plans. He'll tell us. He's coming. We mustn't be seen. A boat has put off from the island already with armed soldiers in it.' He couldn't understand why she didn't show fear. From her face, you would think she was happy.

She *was* happy. She said, 'Have you unpacked yet? I have.' She tilted her head, looking at him with a kind of sympathetic affection. 'Hadn't you realised yet? Your poor horses. But of course – now nothing or no one can land.'

She wasn't quite accurate. Aboard the Portuguese crown caravel *Corpus Dei*, Ochoa de Marchena, wearing a deceased notary's mud-coloured doublet, made sure of that, in a glistening outfall of froth. Water, he explained, was all that he wanted. Half his casks had been broached, and he still had to sail down past Cape Verde to provision the isle of São Tiago. No mainland trading allowed or intended, although he wouldn't say no to some mutton. They were dead sick of tunny, his crewmen.

He didn't convince the royal captain immediately. The captain proposed to visit the *Ghost* (currently flying a Genoese flag), but the resident factor thought it unnecessary. The resident factor throughout had looked glum. Then Ochoa's trading had come under review, and he had to display the fine receipt for his horses. He thought it right, then, to mention the white roundship they'd seen, chasing after a Portuguese caravel. The *Fortado*, he thought she was called, but he couldn't go to her help, not with all that water to pump. But the casks were sound now. Repaired and sound and ready for water . . .

The explosion of a successful Ochoa returning on board was heard everywhere on the *Ghost*, including the wainscoted cabin. A few minutes later, Nicholas entered and, closing the door, sat down and looked from Diniz to the girl, whose smile was like the snap of a thumb in his face. Then he spoke.

'You know the *Niccolò*'s gone, so that I can't land you through her. I can't openly land you from the *Ghost*. I can, however, get you ashore in the boats we are sending for water. Once there, you'd have to hide until the *Corpus Dei* has decided to leave; then the Arguim factor would take care of you. He's been paid. He'd see you got to Madeira.'

'Are you talking to me?' Gelis said.

'Yes,' said Nicholas. 'But Diniz would have to go with you. I think I must be honest and say that I don't want him to go, but you need the protection. I must also be honest and say that I did once want you to stay, but not now. I can't see matters healing between us, and I don't think we should try. You have your own life to pick up. And truly, I cannot take you where we are going: I can't leave you alone on the *Ghost*; I can't send the *Niccolò* home with nothing accomplished; I can't take you into the interior. So I beg you, go ashore; and go home.'

The smile was still there, and unchanged. 'A speech,' she said.

'I have nothing to gain by it,' he said.

'You said you did,' Gelis said. 'But I don't mind at all if we upset one another. That's why I'm here.'

While they spoke, men ran about overhead; there was nervous shouting, and the creaking of tackle. The first boat was launched with a splash. From below came the rumble of barrels. Diniz stood. He said, 'Gelis. I have clothes that might fit. Push your hair in a cap. The factor's wife will give you a gown. Come while you can.'

She touched his chin with the tip of her finger. 'You would leave because of me? You are your father's son, Diniz.'

'And you are Katelina's sister,' he said. He had heard, in what Nicholas said, something he had not heard before. Diniz said, 'Give him a chance to forget.'

'Oh, for God's sake,' said Nicholas sharply. 'Let her make up her own mind.'

'No,' said Diniz. He found himself addressing her earnestly. 'We are all cursed with guilt, don't you see? For far more than my father, or Katelina. She understood.'

'You knew her well?' Gelis said. 'I don't think you did. I can't really care what you have on your conscience. This is between Claes and me.'

'But you are wrong about him,' Diniz said. He caught Nicholas by the shoulder, and, setting both hands to the neck of his shirt, ripped it down from its edge to its side-seam. Revealed between neck and shoulder was the deep raspberry cleft of an axe blow.

'I did that,' Diniz said. 'By mistake. I believed what you believe.'

Nicholas swore, pulling away and throwing together the cloth.

His eyes, startled and angry, shifted from Diniz to the door, beyond which they all heard footsteps approaching. Ochoa de Marchena appeared like a starfish.

'My children!' he said. 'You are not prepared! I am told I have two new oarsmen to take, and one of them is dressed like a nymph?'

Gelis stood. After a moment Nicholas rose, very quietly. Diniz said, 'I'll fetch her clothes. She'll be ready. I'll bring her.'

'Poor, pretty knave,' said Ochoa. 'Who is to keep the horses alive, now you are going? I have a great cargo, have I not? Twenty-five dying nags and some water.'

He held the door, wailing softly and crossly in Arabic. Diniz hurried towards it and turned, seeking Nicholas. Ochoa fluted and grumbled. 'And Jorge sleek in his caravel with the merchandise. He will say, of course, he feared we were lost. But whom will my little mice blame?'

'Come,' said Nicholas. He took Diniz impatiently by the arm.

Diniz, walking, called to Ochoa, 'The *San Niccolò* managed to fill her hold then? Gold, and pepper, and gum?'

'All of that,' Ochoa said. 'And forty slaves, the Portuguese devil, that should have been here in our straw, but that Jorge said he would take them, having a priest and a trustworthy Negro aboard. But!' said Ochoa, 'I tell my mice to be patient! More are waiting! Great broad stallions, and wriggling fillies, and curly-haired cupids, all to buy in the Gambia, if the horses hold out. Senhor Diniz, change your mind and the lady's: don't leave.'

Diniz stopped. Nicholas let go his arm.

Gelis said, 'Leave! With the horses so poorly? I shouldn't dream of it. Diniz wouldn't dream of it, either. And we want to make Messer vander Poele happy. You've changed our minds for us: we'll stay.'

Chapter 16

A s the *Ghost*, buzzing with discord, stood by to take on her water, the *San Niccolò* sailed south of Arguim with priestly mutiny breaking out on her decks.

Since the Isle of Arguim was found and claimed twenty years ago, hundreds of men had made their way there: seamen, merchants and craftsmen; the men who built the fort four years later; the masons who had planted the Portuguese arms carved in stone on each headland to replace the blackened crosses the explorers had left. Far fewer had sailed farther than that, to the Sahel, and the priests who went with them, if any, seldom made a loud stupid fuss about slaves.

Under the blistering sun of November, the *San Niccolò* travelled in a storm-cloud of anger. On her decks were forty black people and twenty-eight white, of whom twenty-four were the crew of Jorge da Silves. The remaining three, whose authority Jorge da Silves did not recognise, were Godscalc the chaplain, Loppe the Negro interpreter, and the young woman's companion who was there by mistake, and had a voice like a hinge on a codpiece.

All the way to Arguim, Bel of Cuthilgurdy had been Godscalc's anchor. She had not stayed at Funchal, although she had tenderly escorted the shaken David ashore. Her blunt, floury features, tied into the straw of her hat, had appeared soothingly at Godscalc's elbow immediately after he had heard, with disbelief, that Nicholas had left to find Diniz and that the *San Niccolò* was sailing without him. It was Bel who convinced him that Nicholas would re-embark from a bay down the coast; and likely Gregorio too, since the demoiselle and Gregorio had followed him. Nor had she been silenced for more than a moment when they sailed past the bay, and found out that it was the *Ghost*, not the *San Niccolò*, which was stopping there.

'The sailing-master's in a right stew,' advised Bel. 'The blue caravel's chasing behind, and we've to get to the markets afore it. That's why they're taking the triangles down and putting up tablecloths. And biscuit and salt beef again: we're not to stop and buy at the Canaries. I wanted to stop and buy at the Canaries.'

As Nicholas had learned to do, Godscalc listened. Biscuits and salt beef: they were short of food, then, but not of water. And the *Fortado* was coming. He knew, now, what the *Fortado* represented. On the surface, a Portuguese caravel on its way to Guinea with a licence to trade. In fact, a caravel propelled by the mercantile might of the Lomellini; the ill-will of the Vatachino; the single-minded venom of Simon, whose recent actions had lost him the goodwill of his sister-in-law.

Godscalc said, 'Mistress Bel? Why did you come back on board?'

'I've told you,' she said. 'I wanted to buy a canary. And of course, if the laddie Diniz gets himself on to the *Ghost*, so will Gelis. She doesna trust him with your Nicholas.'

'Do you?' Godscalc had said.

She was helping him at the time with the seaman-cook's blistered forearm. Since her excursion into the nursing of Filipe (on board again, and pallid, and sullen) she had been presented with a gashed hand, a broken toe and an aching tooth by a crew who preferred her cantankerous care to the chaplain's. She said, 'No, I wouldna trust anyone with your Nicholas, but she hasna had the chance to trip him up yet. First things first.'

'Meaning, first target the *Fortado*?' said Godscalc. The cook, departing, was blessing her. 'You stunned de Salmeton so that the *Ghost* could escape and find a way to impede the *Fortado*?'

'It would be handy,' said Bel. 'I'm sure Gelis thought it would be handy. And she didn't even know your Nicholas would be on the *Ghost* at the time.'

His anchor, but not an unmixed blessing.

Between Funchal and Arguim, by contrast, Father Godscalc saw little of the third member of his party. The adult crew, having found Loppe far from simple, had placed him in a familiar category: that of the able, trained Negro with whom they could be amiable without being intimate. The youngsters Lázaro and Filipe, once more confederates, thought it good sport to try and goad a black man wearing hose like a westerner. Godscalc, seeing that Loppe took it calmly, left him to himself. It took some restraint. Loppe would know if Nicholas intended to bring Diniz with him. Loppe, he noticed, scanned the ocean as intently as anyone, watching for following sails: a blue caravel, with a red roundship in pursuit of her. But the Negro volunteered nothing, and the padre refrained from testing his loyalty. In one respect, Godscalc was comforted. He had asked Jorge da Silves point blank if he intended to buy slaves at Arguim. And Jorge da Silves had said he did not.

When Arguim Bay began to appear, and still they were alone, with no sign of the *Ghost* or the *Fortado*, the prearranged plan came into effect. They were to enter and trade in the gulf, with Melchiorre, the second mate, acting as Nicholas.

It was hard not to feel fierce excitement, up until the moment they saw the patrol boat at anchor. They were about to set foot on strange shores; achieve the first stage of their mission; replenish their meagre provisions. In return for a thousand ducats of goods — cloth and carpets; alum and salt; shaving basins and pots — they would take whatever lay in the stone and mud warehouses they could see on the shore: precious white pepper and gold dust and ivory, brought in by the nomadic Tuareg traders and stockpiled in readiness. A ship like theirs, followed by a roundship as large as the *Ghost*, would probably empty the station.

The *Ghost*, of course, was not an authorised trader, but the factor was amenable, it seemed, to persuasion. It was not an issue that Godscalc felt entitled to worry about. He was not even greatly disturbed when Jorge da Silves pointed out that so long as the naval vessel remained, the outcast *Ghost*, when she arrived, could neither trade, nor should she come near the *Niccolò*. It seemed merely unfortunate that they were not to see Nicholas.

It would have eased Godscalc's mind, certainly, to wait for the *Ghost*'s safe arrival, but meanwhile he found intense interest in observing the passage of the caravel through the gulf's thready channel, and agreed with alacrity when the master proposed that he should accompany the first boats on shore. 'Because,' said Jorge da Silves, 'the nuisance of it is, that we shall have to carry the blacks.'

The word hung between them. It was a moment Godscalc would not forget; the moment that confirmed all his darkest fears of this voyage. From the day she had loaded her horses at Sanlúcar, the *Ghost* had meant to exchange them for slaves. Nicholas had not refuted it; only he, Godscalc, could not believe it of him. Jorge da Silves had denied it the other day with easy casuistry, knowing that it was the *Ghost* and not he who would handle them.

They had not meant to involve Godscalc himself. Perhaps they had hoped to load their living cargo in darkness . . . But no. Why should they trouble? It was a valid trade: they were not ashamed of it. And in any case, Loppe had to help them. That was why Loppe was here. That was the sin for which he, Godscalc, couldn't forgive Nicholas.

He, a priest, knew what slavery was. The Church had its own bondsmen; the law allowed a man to sell himself or others for debt. He understood that nations at war made slaves of their captives in place of slaughtering them. It had happened when the Turks had attacked Trebizond. Nicholas had come to him at Trebizond and placed his dilemma, and himself, in his hands.

His advice had been to leave. Nicholas had taken that advice, and knew what had followed. Was that why he was doing this? To flout, to punish him? But Byzantines – all Oriental nations – also used slaves: for the house, for the fields. The Crusaders had done, and the Jews. Christians had made slaves of barbarians, and the other way round. Many lived better, in the end, than at home. The Muslim world sold off their captives; the Church bought back what Christians it could. But the Muslim world also elevated them. Turks trained up alien children to become the elite of their army; captured children ruled Egypt as Mamelukes. Portugal, depleted by plague and by warfare, had welcomed the first frightened Negroes captured from Guinea; found them intelligent, biddable; had trained them, freed them, sent for more.

But now they were not acquired as prisoners of war. They were bought, seven hundred a year, as goods from middlemen who stole them from their villages. True, they would learn a civilised tongue; be baptised; earn their salvation. Their lives would not be hard. But what of the great, dark, barbarian land they came from? How could you bring a people to Christ while stealing their children?

So, thunderstruck on the deck of the *Niccolò*, Father Godscalc of Cologne seized the master of the ship by the collar and the arm, there before all his own men, and said, 'I will have no men purchased with coin and brought aboard this ship against their will. Swear that you will leave them.' And because rage gave him power, and he was a vigorous man accustomed to battlefields, he felt Jorge da Silves quiver before he stiffened and said, 'The sun has harmed you, padre. There are men all about.'

'But you and I are here,' said Father Godscalc. 'And I want a promise.'

Then Jorge da Silves took hold of himself and said, 'It is easily given, but it is not the promise you want. If I leave them, the next ship will carry them off. The *Fortado*, perhaps.' All who were not working the ship were watching, except Bel of Cuthilgurdy and Loppe.

Godscalc said quietly, 'Then take your coin and free them. If you fear to lose your profit, I shall try to make it up to you somehow.'

Jorge da Silves had regained his calm. He stood awkwardly as he was gripped and said, 'Padre, what good will it do to free them? They have been brought hundreds of miles from their homes; their captors rove the desert behind them. Do you expect the Tuareg to mount them on horseback and deliver them back to their huts, in whatever village they may have come from? They must be brought on board. I am glad they are coming on board, for they are your business.' And he straightened his neck, for Godscalc's clutch had become slack.

'My business?' he said.

'That is why you have this caravel,' said Jorge da Silves, and pulled himself free. 'To bring souls to Christ. To save the heathen. Speak to your Negro, to Lopez. Surely he has explained this?'

'I tried to explain it,' said Loppe, standing before him. Behind was Bel his anchor, his former anchor, who must have fetched him.

Loppe said, 'Father, let the master go. Let him bring them on board. Whatever happens to these people later, they will do better here than on the *Fortado*. Once they are on board, we shall listen to you. We were only afraid that, if you knew, you would abandon them.'

He had agreed, with a numbness amounting to despair, for he could see no alternative. He had gone to the island and, entering the warehouse where the captives lay, ill-fed and exhausted, young once-vigorous people of every shade from swarthy half-Berber to the dense, blue-black colour of Loppe, he had realised that, whatever their fate, it couldn't be worse than this. Only when brought into the light, and packed in boats, and finally taken on board one of the great birds of the sea, did their apathy break, and they fought, screaming, against being thrust into the hold, and clutched each other in terror as the seamen tried to bring the ship through the channel and, reaching the sea, to set the sails to run south once again.

No. If Nicholas was there, across the gulf in the red, shining roundship, Godscalc took no joy in the knowledge. He turned his back on the *Ghost*. He battled side by side with the rest until, somehow, the hoarse, desperate rabble had been induced to settle in some sort of order, and their groups and numbers identified, and the copper cauldron was set on the firebox. They were given bean soup and maize bread and water, and shown where to relieve themselves, for already the *San Niccolò* stank. Then all but the most violent slept, and Loppe, touching Father Godscalc on the shoulder, said, 'We should speak in the cabin. Mistress Bel is already there.'

Godscalc of Cologne walked with the step of an old man to the cabin. There, facing the Negro and the brooding figure of the woman from Scotland, he said, 'You have seen. Three are sick. There are only six, that I can find, who speak Arabic. The rest have almost no tongues in common. They appear to come from several tribes and no doubt many villages, to which neither we nor they know the way. I see you and Jorge are right. Once they have been brought to Arguim, they are already in irrevocable exile.'

'That is generally so,' said Loppe softly. There were hollows under his eyes.

Godscalc said, 'This therefore is an expedition to buy and sell slaves. You knew as much before you sailed, and so did Nicholas. If you held any discussions, I was not privy to them. I cannot excuse you.'

'I am sorry, Father,' said Loppe.

'Tush!' said Bel of Cuthilgurdy to no one in particular.

Father Godscalc rounded on her. 'And what does that mean? They cannot be helped, except by exchanging them for horses or money, as has been done, and taking them back to Portugal? So!' He swung back to Loppe. 'Why have you let Nicholas do this? Or did he compel you to accomplish it for him, select the best, the most promising? Was this his fee for sending you back to your family?'

'No,' said Loppe. He cleared his throat. Since leaving Arguim he had abandoned his pourpoint, and in his cap and collarless shirt might almost have been mistaken, Godscalc tried not to think, for one of the blackamoors lying on deck. Loppe said, 'Ser Niccolò meant to be here. If he had not told you the truth by now, then I should. He didn't expect to take slaves. It was I who persuaded him. It was the price of my help with the venture.'

Not the words of a blackamoor. Not the words, surely, of the man Godscalc had taken him to be. Godscalc said, 'I cannot believe you. Every soul that is purchased encourages the dealers to go and seize more.'

'No one is going to stop buying them,' Loppe said. 'Portugal needs Portuguese, and she doesn't mind if they are black and didn't wish to come in the first place. She has no qualms, for she is redeeming their souls. Jorge da Silves endorses that: he is a member of the Order of Christ. Prince Henry himself led the Order, and continued the trade to induce captains to sail further and further. One of his slaves is being reared as a priest by the Franciscans.'

'So,' said Godscalc, 'what is your excuse for selling your prisoners? To please the King of Portugal, who owns this fine caravel? To place your fellows in better homes than the Lomellini or the Vatachino might have offered? To disarm them by your example? This is what you have in mind?'

'Ser Niccolò did not ask me that,' Loppe said.

The grating voice of Bel of Cuthilgurdy spoke from her corner. 'Your Ser Niccolò knows you. Here's a good man doing his best. You need to help him.'

'I am sorry,' said Loppe. 'But I thought the padre knew us both.' He stopped, and seemed to make an effort. He said, 'I said in Lagos I wished to go back to Guinea to learn. I wanted you, a man of God, to come too; and Nicholas – and Ser Niccolò –'

'You think of him as Nicholas,' Godscalc said grimly. 'Why don't you call him so? You wanted us to see what was happening and act upon it? How?'

'I don't know,' said Loppe. The ship was moving fast now, tilting and plunging beneath them, the spray rattling her sides as her sailing-master sought for the speed that would keep her ahead of all rivals. You could hear seamen's voices, responding to the shrill of the whistle, and the tired, monotonous wail of a child, and sometimes a sudden cry, as fear broke through the exhaustion.

Loppe said, 'A long time from now, regulation may be possible. That is, once authority has established itself in this country, the rapine may be stopped, and dealers will become merely agents, who will convey to the coast those men and women who are willing to come. But before this can happen, men must agree that the object is worthy; and then that they must work towards it.'

Father Godscalc said, 'I think the object is worthy, and I am ready to be shown what you wish me to see, and to report on it. But in the short term, these poor wretches lie there, and I can see nothing that you or I may do except relieve some of their pains.'

'There is something,' Loppe said. His voice had warmed, just a little, from relief. He said, 'You spoke of irrevocable exile, and up till now that's been true. But a few of these people out there might be restored to the homes that they came from. Some are Sanhaja half-breeds: their villages are not far away, and they would have a good chance of reaching them from the shore. Some are from the coastal tribes of the Jalofos and could be landed in their own region, if they thought the risk of recapture worth while. The rest are from the territory of the Mandinguas, or from kingdoms lying beyond, in the south. Most of these do not know where they live. Their only chance would be a new life in Portugal.'

'You know all these tribes?' Godscalc said carefully.

'Some of them. I do not speak all the dialects.'

'Are you a son of one of these kings?' Godscalc asked; and was ashamed when Loppe smiled.

Loppe said, 'One of those with thirty wives? You know these are not kings as you speak of them; but rather the respected chiefs of their tribes. I cannot claim to be the son of such a leader, but I know some of the potentates who would give a holy man a fair hearing; and a few of the tribes whose men travel, and know of the tracks to the east. I can pay my fee.'

'I'm not one to contradict you,' said Bel of Cuthilgurdy. 'And you've pleased the Father, no doubt; but how will Jorge da Silves and the impecunious Nicholas see it? There's the *Ghost*, empty but for her travel-sore nags, and here's the *San Niccolò* piled high with slaves and their dinners instead of a full load of pepper. If you let half the slaves go, there's nothing left but heavenly credit, and not so much of that if you think of the converts you've lost. Added to which, the Order of Christ takes a religious interest in money. So excuse me if I ask: is that all the help you promised Jorge da Silves and Nicholas?'

Startled out of his bewilderment, Godscalc gazed at her. Loppe said, 'There is a box beside you, mistress. Lift the lid.'

It was the patron's chest, with a triple lock there had been no time to fasten. Bel of Cuthilgurdy leaned over, and heaved it open with her two sturdy arms. Godscalc rose and stood, the better to view it.

The box was full of gold. Between the fat bags of dust were piled collars and heavy gold bracelets. Loppe said, 'It doesn't take up much room. And there will be more, in the south.'

'How much is there?' Godscalc said.

'In weight? Over forty pounds, I should think. It should fetch about six thousand ducats, less the King's quarter at Lisbon. The price of forty horses, and seven hundred slaves.'

'How could you afford it?' said the woman. 'As well as buying the blacks?'

Loppe moved across, and closing the chest knelt to lock it. 'We sold all we had,' he said. 'The rest we paid for in cowrie shells. Ser – Nicholas brought them from Cyprus. They are the currency of the country, and light to carry when we move from the ships.'

'So the other gold marts are inland,' Godscalc said. 'And you will be taking us there. Or perhaps to the source of the gold?'

'No one knows the source of the gold,' Loppe said.

Far behind on the *Ghost*, the same questions were asked and answered; but not until well after Arguim, when Ochoa had completed his excursions on shore and the *Ghost*'s water barricoes were all full, and she had some food and some hay for her livestock. That she carried horses had not been discovered.

Even then, she had to be careful, easing out of the weedy lagoon under the threatening eye of the patrol boat and setting a course further west than she wanted. Fortunately, there was another flurry of sand; the veils dropped, and it became safe to turn southwards again. She put on her best speed. Ahead was the *San Niccolò* with her cargo, and Nicholas wanted to catch her before anyone else did.

It was night therefore before he called Diniz and the girl to sit with him in the great cabin, crammed with their gear. Fashioned of fur and straw, feathers and velvet and ribbon, Ochoa's hats yawed from their pegs as if grazing; suspended swords flashed; and from a wicker cage slung in a corner a dozen parrots screeched and fluttered and snapped.

No conversation on a ship could be private, but Nicholas had drawn the door-curtain back to deter eavesdroppers, and began by speaking in Flemish. He wondered what language Loppe had spoken in the inquisition he, too, must have faced across the twenty miles of dark sea that still separated them. Here, the boy was subdued, his eyes dark in the rolling swing of the lamplight. Gelis van Borselen looked a little drawn, perhaps with the heat. He knew the sea never made her unwell. She said, 'An apologia?'

Nicholas said, 'No. A school. You have made me your custodian. From time to time we shall meet like this, and I shall tell you my plans, and I shall also tell you the part I expect you to play in them. I shall listen if you object. I don't promise to accept your objection. Do you understand this?'

'On the principle of the oranges,' the girl said. The parrots squawked.

'On the principle, certainly, of a single command. Demoiselle?' Nicholas said, and turned to her fully. For the first time, he had forced himself to bring all his experience to this meeting with Gelis van Borselen. His relations with Diniz were simple, and could be made, he thought, painless or better. The opposite was the case with the girl. The hostility between them was dangerous, and now had to change. And the only way he could do it was by locking away all his past with Katelina – the past about which her younger sister had guessed a good deal, but not everything. If she had guessed everything, she would have told Simon.

So he said, 'Demoiselle. You want to punish me, even to loading me with the guilt of your very possible fate. It's a little hard on your friends. And at this rate, I might not think it a punishment.'

'You may die first,' she said. She spoke without humour, and for the first time directly. Diniz drew in his breath.

Nicholas said, 'But you haven't tried to bring it about?'

'I prefer a clear conscience,' she said. 'There are plenty of others less scrupulous.'

He said, with fleeting amusement, 'And that's a clear conscience? Well, maybe Father Godscalc would agree. He doesn't approve of my methods, as your Mistress Bel will no doubt shortly tell you. I expect he is raging up and down the *San Niccolò* at this moment, coming as near as he can to cursing Jorge da Silves and certainly me.'

'Over the slaves?' she said. 'Was he manacled when your sailing-master took them on board? He could have stopped it. He could have threatened to denounce you and the *Ghost* as I did.'

'He could,' Nicholas agreed. 'But no one would have believed him, would they? Can you see Father Godscalc condemning us all, including Diniz, to be hanged in public for piracy? Death to the crew. Confiscation of both the *Ghost* and the *Niccolò*. Disaster to my Bank and all those dependent on it and on Diniz. He may be pig-headed, the padre, but he's not blind deranged.'

Diniz was silent. The girl herself showed no change of expression, although the curious pricking of colour showed itself under her cheekbones. She said, 'You are upsetting the parrots. And you think Father Godscalc could save them by no other means, such as paying to free them himself? I imagine even Bel would have opened her purse for him, if he asked her. He is not a man of God. He is your minion.'

'I wish he were,' Nicholas said. 'In fact, someone else on board has given more thought to the care of these captives than you or me or Father Godscalc, and it is his suggestions which are going to be followed. Let me tell you what they are.'

He made it simple, the story of Loppe's design for the slaves the *San Niccolò* carried, and of his hopes for changing the trade in the future. As he spoke, the boy coloured up, but the girl sat like a stone, her lids tightened as if against glare. At the end she looked up. But it was Diniz who exclaimed, his eyes brilliant, 'I wish my father had heard you. And Lopez. But the blacks you already have, can it be done? Will the *Niccolò* put them off near their homes?'

'Those who wish it,' Nicholas said. 'I'm going to say now that I don't agree with Loppe over this. I think most of them will beg to leave, and will die.'

'I am sure,' the girl said, 'that enough will be kept to make a profit. And how is Loppe – Lopez? – to repay you?'

She was implacable, but he hadn't really expected a sunburst of charity. He wondered if Bel had asked the same question. He said, 'He will repay us as guide and interpreter. He speaks Mandingua and Jalofo and Arabic as well as Christian languages. He knows the Gambia and the lands to its east as do few other blacks whom you might pick up in Lagos or Madeira. Whomever the *Fortado* employs, it will be no one of that calibre, I can promise you. So, yes, you are right. We need Loppe, and he wouldn't have come without our support over the slaves. You know we are going to be together now for four months? We are committed?'

'I assumed so,' she said. She either felt nothing, or she could cover everything she was thinking. She added, 'I don't expect to stay on the ship when you leave her. I can ride. I can walk.'

'Among lions?' said Diniz in an annoyed voice. 'Among snakes? You'll have to stay on the ship. And what about Bel?'

Nicholas caught the edge of a glance from her, but chose to do nothing about it. She said, 'Bel is your mother's representative, Diniz, not mine. She makes up her own mind what she will do, and why.' And turning back to Nicholas, she said, 'She is your responsibility. All three of us are.'

He said, 'I should put it even wider than that. The two ships are my responsibility, and everyone in them. If I lead, and I suppose that I do, then private skirmishing could harm the whole expedition. Look, I don't expect you to change, or be generous. I do ask you to hold back your grievances meantime. After the spring, I don't care. It's open season.'

He ended a little more colourfully than he had meant. He had made her a speech once before. Because she wouldn't engage in discussion he had been driven to deliver a second one. Diniz said, 'She'll behave. I shall answer for her.'

There followed the kind of silence Nicholas had been punishing himself to avoid. The girl was watching him. Then she said, 'Shall I slap him for you?' And leaning over, she gave Diniz a tap on the cheek. 'My self-esteem is being usefully fostered. You are not supposed to undermine it.'

'You are not supposed to undermine his, either,' said Nicholas rather quickly. 'And I won't be tripped into discriminating between you. You both listen to what I have to say, and you both keep your prejudices out of it. Diniz, hand me the map.' It was time to tell them where they were going. They waited with the same air of intelligent attention he had seen worn by scholars at Louvain after a bout of professorial abuse. He had learned a lot at Louvain, including how people thought.

They were sailing, of course, to the Gambia, seven days to the south, and on the way they would make a call at the mouth of the Senagana. Diniz, brought up on the Algarve, had expected that. Both rivers traded in gold. At the Senagana, they could offload the horses. From the Gambia, they could strike upriver until the water ran out, and then continue on land. From there they might reach the Nile, Ethiopia. 'You still pretend that's where you're going?'

said Gelis van Borselen, and looked shocked when he almost
opened his mouth to the bait.

She, too, Nicholas thought, had made enquiries, but had
expected a voyage much longer. From Arguim to the Senagana
river was not above four hundred miles. 'So,' she said, 'I have only
three or four days in which to inflame the crew of the *Ghost*, and
watch you agonise over it. Then, I assume, we transfer to the
Niccolò? Or before?'

'As soon as we catch up with them,' Nicholas said. 'And I don't
think I have to tell you how to behave with the crew until then.'

'But you trust the master?' said Gelis van Borselen. 'As far as the
Gambia?' She had Baltic blue eyes shaped like almonds, and
outlined in brown lashes, not blonde. From her earliest years, she
had been clever.

'Ochoa?' said Diniz. 'Did you see what he did to the *Fortado*? Of
course we trust him.'

'With horses,' said the girl.

'I hired him. I trust him,' said Nicholas. 'At the moment, I'm
more concerned with what the *Fortado* may do.'

'Certainly, I hope your lookout is sharp-eyed,' Gelis said. 'Could
she possibly overtake us at night? And if she did, could she also
overtake the *San Niccolò* before the Senagana? I suppose she
could, if the *San Niccolò* lingers to put off her slaves. And if she
arrives ahead of both ships, you say there is a man on the *Fortado*
who knows the *Ghost* is stolen, and may have seen you aboard her.
But if he gets in first, whom would he warn? Diniz, who knows
everything, says there is no official factor on the Senagana so far.'

'There is now,' Nicholas said. 'That is what the patrol vessel was
doing. She's just returned from setting up a God-damned
Portuguese strong house.'

'Which would refuse to take the *Ghost*'s unlicensed horses,' said
Gelis thoughtfully. Diniz, champion of the horses, looked up.

'I think there might be a way around that,' Nicholas said.
'Meanwhile, I don't see how the *Fortado* could pass us, although
she may yet appear, towed by three thousand sea nymphs who
hope to go home and please Simon. If there's trouble, I'll warn
you. There are weapons here in the cabin.'

'Behind the hats and the parrots. The crossbow is too heavy,'
Gelis remarked, 'but if you could get me a light bow, I could use
it. Is the handgun as simple as it looks?'

Diniz opened his mouth. Nicholas said, 'It isn't difficult. You
need a reasonable eye. Would you like Diniz to teach you?'

'It might be wise,' the girl said. 'And anything else he thinks I
should know. I can sail. It might come in useful.'

'In case the blacks come chasing us in their war-canoes?' Diniz said. 'They stopped that ten years ago – more. They don't even shoot poisoned darts, except for their hunting. They've got Christians and Muslims among them. Some of them speak Portuguese.'

'I am quite sure,' said Gelis, 'that the tribes are models of civility. It was the vengeance of the *Fortado* I thought we were fleeing. Till tomorrow then? Unless we are fired on beforehand?'

They watched her leave. Diniz said, with gloom, 'She's worse when she's friendly.' He didn't seem to expect a reply.

Chapter 17

THE SECOND NIGHT out of Arguim, the *San Niccolò* ran aground off the Bay of Tanit, straining her planks and creating panic below, so that one of the black captives broke free and loosed eight others who burst on deck and dived into the water before they could be stopped. The caravel was a mile off shore at the time, and some of the swimmers got halfway there before the breakers or the spears of the fisher-boats stopped them.

It was all the more painful since precautions had been taken. Since losing the first four overboard north of Timiris it had been accepted that – as Jorge da Silves had always insisted – the slaves could not be permitted on deck. When seamen working between decks were attacked, it was found necessary to bow again to the master's experience, and put the adults under light restraint. There was then only one child left, the baby having been carried into the sea by its mother.

When, blazing in the dawn light behind them, the *Ghost* was perceived to be free of Arguim and about to join them at last, the *San Niccolò* was merely thankful, in its anguish, that its exhausted boat crews were about to receive aid to warp themselves free. Having seen or heard nothing of the *Fortado* since Funchal, the caravel gave its whole attention to its immediate difficulties. The two masters cried their enquiries and commands over the water; hawsers were thrown, and attached; and the seamen on both ships panted and strove, helped in silence by Godscalc and Loppe on one, and by Nicholas and Diniz rather more noisily on the other.

Bel of Cuthilgurdy stood by the stern lantern as soon as the roundship came close, and after some time the lamps on the *Ghost* glimmered on a darting, waving figure she thankfully recognised. Bel of Cuthilgurdy screamed, 'That's Gelis there, padre. And Lucia's lad, look – there's the boy Diniz. But I see none of your sleek chiel', Gregorio.'

Groaning and squealing, the caravel was beginning her slow slide off the sandbank. Godscalc, his heart sliding and sinking, said nothing. He had observed Nicholas striding about on the deck of the larger ship, and heard his voice – when had he developed such a voice? – uplifted in Spanish and Portuguese, mixed with indecencies from the Venetian patois of the Arsenal. Twice he had come to the rail to hold an impressively technical conversation with Jorge da Silves, who had responded with quite unnatural warmth, even allowing for a warrantable gratitude. A cordiality which, Godscalc suspected, would not extend to Ochoa de Marchena when, floating and in the anxious care of her carpenter, the *San Niccolò* prepared to welcome her owner on board once again with his party.

Godscalc, with the master and Bel at his side, watched the boat bringing the four of them from the *Ghost*.

The van Borselen girl looked the same. Her brow and cheekbones were browner perhaps, under the white of her kerchief, and her gown stained with the wear of two weeks, but there was no trace of distress in her bearing. The handsome youth beside her showed more emotion, his hands restless, his eyes constantly moving between the ship's decks and Nicholas. And Nicholas, a bonnet set on his hair and his working shirt under a doublet, sat riding the surge of the boat and holding some sort of low, profound discourse with a figure from carnival-time: a man whose hat bellied as big as a goatskin; whose hose climbed to his waist in eight colours, hardly fanned by the skirts of his doublet.

'Ochoa de Marchena,' said Jorge da Silves to the air. 'I wonder where lies the body tonight whose garments those are.'

'Wherever it is,' said Bel of Cuthilgurdy, 'it's looking nicer without them.'

First to board, Nicholas stood on the deck of his bright, virgin caravel, and looked past even Godscalc to Loppe. Then his gaze, softening, travelled over his seamen and returned to Bel of Cuthilgurdy, deepening into something that was not quite a smile, in response perhaps to something he saw in her face. 'Mistress Bel. And Father Godscalc.' There was no trace now of a smile. Nicholas said, 'I'm sorry I couldn't be here.'

'So am I,' Godscalc replied. The inspection had already passed beyond him.

'And the master. Well, Jorge. You kept in soundings all night.'

The master's head turned. 'By my orders,' Godscalc said. 'That is, the villages change place, and the dunes.' Beside him, Loppe stood perfectly still, his eyes only on Nicholas.

'Yes. There is a lot to discuss. As you see, Diniz has rejoined us, and the demoiselle. Perhaps Mistress Bel would like to hear her news while we talk. Jorge, the *Fortado* is probably following, if she hasn't cut in ahead of us. What damage do you have?'

'The report is coming. We shall sail, do not fear. We have wasted too much time as it is.'

Loppe said, 'We have one call to make.'

'No,' said Jorge da Silves. 'It is too late. And the surf begins before the Ksar, I have told you. We put off the rest at Senagana or nowhere.'

'What do I hear?' cried a voice from the ladder. Ochoa sprang on board. 'You do not want your magnificent savages? I shall take them, I. Beginning with that one. And your crew! Your crew! Compared with my mangy one-legged scum! Niccolino, where do you choose them?'

'You have heard me speak of Lopez,' said Nicholas pleasantly. He was impatient, Godscalc saw, but neither he nor Loppe showed offence. 'He is unfortunately attached to the expedition. But you know Señor Jorge da Silves of the Order of Christ?'

The lean, adamantine face of the Portuguese confronted, without evident pleasure, the formless Andalusian visage in the centre of which sagged a smile pink as offal. The Portuguese addressed it in the third person. 'Señor Ochoa may take what blacks he likes, provided that they are first baptised according to God's law. We have already lost precious souls to the devil.'

He shot a dark glance behind him. Godscalc stood, his arms folded, his balled fists meekly tucked in his sleeves. He said to Nicholas, 'The poop cabin is free.' Mistress Bel had taken the girl by the hand and disappeared. Diniz, unfortunately, was standing his ground. Nicholas said, 'Then we had better go there.'

He did, however, take longer than anyone else to reach the cabin, and both the sailing-masters and Diniz and Godscalc were seated before he came in, bringing Loppe; indeed, with his hand falling from Loppe's doublet shoulder. Godscalc was not surprised, although it did not greatly please either master. Five minutes with Loppe would have told Nicholas all he needed to know. Depending on one's viewpoint, Loppe was his most loyal friend, or his spy.

Nicholas said, 'We have a change of plan, so this must be quick. Jorge, what cargo do you have? Is there a paper?' There was, and he spoke as he read it. 'Gum – so many crates? Quintals of pepper . . . Orchella and dragon's blood – I have more, from Grand Canary. And gold, yes I see. And what slaves are there left?' He looked up. 'I know you have landed some, and others jumped overboard.'

'There are fifteen left,' Loppe said. 'They all understand what is happening. Most want to leave at the Senagana, or a fishing village just before it. Six are willing to come with us to the Gambia: two of these know how to reach their homes from there, and the rest will attempt to make their way, at any risk.' He paused. 'None wish to go with us to Portugal.'

'They thought you were going to eat them. Whoo! Whoo!' said Ochoa, merrily blowing out his candle-wax cheeks. 'And you *paid* for them, my chickens? I get a better return for my parrots, even though half are dead and a quarter pecked bald on the journey. Your magnificent Lopez must be a guide worth a fortune!'

'Ochoa?' said Nicholas. 'Do you see the water out there? The *Fortado* may appear any moment.'

'You have seen her?' said Jorge da Silves.

'Seen her!' said Ochoa, and flipped up his skirts with a finger. 'We shot –'

Nicholas said, 'We had an exchange in the dark. She has guns. She is certainly following. She knows the *Ghost* is the *Doria*, or will, as soon as she sees her in daylight. Also, there is now a Portuguese station at the Senagana, all of which means that the *Ghost* can neither appear there nor trade. Therefore we are now, at this moment, going to exchange our cargoes.'

Diniz sat up, his lips parting. Jorge da Silves said, 'You mean to put the gold and the rest on the *Ghost*?'

'And transfer the horses and the grain, dear hearts, to you,' said Ochoa. 'And you can keep your handsome Negroes, although I should have liked a little one for my cabin. Have I put it well?' He looked round at Nicholas.

'As you always do. You understand, Jorge, why we are doing this? You can sell: the *Ghost* can't. You'll have to redistribute ballast; think of food and water stocks, both of you. The *Niccolò* will keep any trading goods she still has, and the shells. There are fifteen people and twenty-five horses to carry for two days at least. And while we're trading, the *Ghost* will evaporate into some modest inlet where we hope the *Fortado* won't see her. But we have to make the main transfer now, and fast.'

'How?' said Diniz.

Ochoa gave him a simmering smile. 'Dear one! Did you not see the hoists already preparing? Go up on deck, and you will find the boat on its way with the first of your darlings. You will have two more days with your horses!'

They were all rising. Godscalc said, 'I don't understand. How does this other ship know you are the *Doria*?'

'Guess,' Nicholas said. 'No, there isn't time. Because Mick Crackbene has signed himself on as her sailing-master. What in hell is happening outside?'

They could heard the voice of Melchiorre upraised, protesting. Another voice joined it. Then the cabin curtain was wrenched to one side. 'You evil man,' said Gelis van Borselen to Nicholas. 'You knew this high-minded plan for the slaves was preposterous. You knew what was going to happen, and you let it.'

She stood, breathing deeply before him; her face sallow as if she had been poisoned. She said, 'They're dead, aren't they, most of them? Drowned; hacked to death by enemy tribesmen. They would have been taken to safety in Portugal, if you'd left them.'

A shudder ran through the ship. A boat had arrived. 'Please, not now,' Nicholas said.

'*Not now!*' she said. She lifted her voice until it rang through the cabin. She was shaking with rage. 'If they'd been bought by the worst trader in the world, this would never have happened. Would it? But because your pandering priest and your –'

'I meant, not now,' Nicholas said, and before Godscalc could cry out or help had pulled the girl forward and silenced her, one hand expertly over her lips, the other pinioning her with a kind of calm severity. He said over her head, 'Go on, all of you. Send the Scots woman. Tell me if the *Fortado* appears.'

The masters both left. Diniz hesitated and then made his way out, looking stricken. Only Godscalc and Loppe still remained, neither moving. For a moment the girl, looking at them, ceased her struggles. Then, her brow creased, she set herself to fight once again, and as the gagging hand tightened, she bit it.

Godscalc heard Nicholas hiss through his teeth. A rope of blood ran over his fingers and drops began to seep from under his palm. The shape of her eyes and her jaw altered again, but he kept his hand where it was, and reinforced the parody of an embrace with the other. The kind of stern but charitable embrace, Godscalc thought, a physician gives to a child in a fit. Yet her face was full of despair, and his, bent upon her, showed a compressed violence directed wholly inward. He had not looked towards Loppe since it started. Now he shook his head at her, and spoke.

'You're not thinking. We're in danger. Go to your cabin. Later. Later. Later, for this.' He let her lift her head free, turning her so that Godscalc could not see her face. Her hair, loosened, strayed down her back; his shirt and doublet were studded and trellised with blood. He released her as if unleashing a dog, and showed her a handkerchief, pushing it into her fists. 'Use it,' he said. 'Or they'll know for sure that we're cannibals. Bel is waiting.' He was not even thinking of what he was saying, Godscalc thought. He was listening.

She knew it too. She looked about her, and Godscalc met her

look, but thought that Loppe did not. She was a formidable girl, Godscalc thought, to have had so weak a sister. Formidable as the fiery mountain of the Canaries, and as abrasive.

She scrubbed her mouth across with the cloth, and then flung it down on the deck before Nicholas. His lacerated palm dripped on to it. 'At least,' she said, 'I have had a taste of power, and you another family memento.' She moved, putting her hand to the curtain, and spoke without looking round. 'Your ship,' she said. 'Your new ship. Your new ship stinks of death.' Then she went.

The sun blazed into the cabin. The deck outside shuddered as feet pounded and the bar of the boom-shadow swung. Tackle squealed and men roared and chanted. Nicholas turned, his back to the sun. Godscalc spoke, with unusual difficulty. 'Not just now, as you said. You must cover your hand.' He broke off. He began to say, 'You should have let her say it all.'

Nicholas looked at him, but not beyond him. 'It was better stopped,' he said. 'And it was bad for her, too. Can you come quickly? The horses are here.'

In the outcome, no slaves were landed on the beaches north of the Senagana, and the battle over their fate was deferred, if not forgotten. The caravel *Fortado* had appeared, finally, on the horizon.

Retiring exhausted that night, with the cargoes safely exchanged and the *Niccolò* sailing freely south with her consort at last, Godscalc woke to find everything changed. It was not only that the *Niccolò*, her spars extended, was breasting the waves like a gundog. The *Ghost*, after so belated and glorious a reunion, had abandoned them. That is, she had taken a course towards some islands so far to the west of Cape Verde that she was already hull down, making it apparent to anyone that she had no intention of trading in Guinea.

'She'll come back,' Nicholas explained, when found on the poop deck. 'During the night, or behind a clutter of fishing-boats. Then she'll hide herself a little away from the estuary and wait.'

'She has our cargo,' Diniz had remarked. He still looked sick. Only the crew appeared unaffected, if mildly mystified, by what had happened. It appalled Godscalc that Nicholas himself looked unchanged.

He was saying, 'She has a moderate amount, but not a full load. In any case, Ochoa is usually reliable, despite the rabble he chooses to work with. They'll wait. All we have to do is get to market before the *Fortado*.'

Godscalc already knew, from their voyage from Funchal and from their precipitous departure from Arguim, what Jorge da

Silves was capable of when he wanted to hurry. Once Jorge had the measure of the *Niccolò* he had tested her to the limit, putting off the boats with a peremptory rattle when the slaves came to be landed and thrusting on day and night past the low, featureless coast with its shifting dunes and treacherous sandbanks. He had crowded on sail even when forced by Godscalc to cling to the shallows rather than sail in deep water. That had been after the mother had flung herself into the sea, and Filipe and Lázaro had been beaten.

None of the slaves, dead or alive, had been baptised, which had been another bone of contention. He was not a witch doctor, saving souls with a sprinkle of water. There was more to baptism than that, whatever the Order of Christ might expect. Instead he gave them his care and his time, those who were left; and Loppe stayed with them if they would have him. Most of them distrusted Loppe, and had no use for a priest. The person they welcomed was Bel.

This morning she had spent in another place, with the girl. The uncharacteristic outburst of yesterday had proved to have a common physical reason, as Godscalc had privately suspected. Its immediate handling had also been physical. Faced with an overwrought girl, Nicholas, the best-served apprentice in Bruges, had known what to do better than Godscalc. Godscalc wondered how he had decided to exploit it.

He found out soon, for the girl came up before noon to see the *Fortado*. Everyone came from time to time; even Diniz, leaving his horses. Diniz was here, Godscalc now comprehended, partly because of Simon's treachery; partly to redeem his mother's fortune; and partly, there was no doubt, because of Nicholas, alternately friendly and alienating. Godscalc wished from the depths of his heart that Gregorio and not Diniz had been allowed to come on this voyage. He had no doubt at all that it had fallen out according to plan. Loppe, of course, had suspected. And the Vatachino had been sure.

Nicholas had not, however, expected Gelis van Borselen to persist. Godscalc would have wished her safe at home too; growing to womanhood, setting the fate of her sister behind her. As it was, her obsession fed on itself. She risked her life for no good except the one she least wanted: that she might unwittingly bring Nicholas to his senses.

It seemed unlikely she would. Loppe had been given a free rein in this terrible experiment for a reason. For all Nicholas might claim, this so-called Christian expedition to Ethiopia was concerned wholly with gold, and depended upon the advice of someone who knew about gold. And for all he further claimed, the gold was not for his Bank or for Diniz, but to salve his own pride and the scars of his dreadful and personal losses. His very real losses; of course one gave Nicholas that. One understood much about Nicholas, but one could not excuse.

Godscalc was silent therefore when Gelis climbed the steps to the deck, Bel behind her, and after a word with the master joined Diniz at the rail looking aft. She said, 'Is that the *Fortado*? The blue ship?'

'You can see it's blue?' Diniz said. 'No one could, early this morning. It got a better wind for a bit, and gained on us. You could see where the spar came down, if she was nearer. You could see where we shot right across her midships. Nicc— They say she must have carried out her own repairs. She can't have stayed long at Arguim; just for stores. She can't beat us, though.'

'Who says?' said Gelis.

'Nicc— Everyone does,' Diniz said. He had flushed. 'Are you feeling better?'

'Yes. Where is Nicc-everyone?' she asked.

'Behind you,' said Nicholas. 'Diniz is embarrassed, and so is his conscience. We are none of us particularly pleased with ourselves, if you'll believe it.'

Gelis said, 'My beliefs can't matter very much at the moment. I wished to say that however right I was, and am, I chose the wrong time and place to say it, and for that I apologise. I have said as much to Lopez.'

'Then you are braver than I am,' said Nicholas. 'But I'm glad you did it. You know we are putting off all but six at the Senagana? The Sanhaja have to find their way back up the coast, but speak Arabic, and will probably manage. Some of the blacks are Jalofos and swear they know where they're going. The rest seem to be saying the same, but we don't know their language. They may be killed. The alternative is to put them all in chains and take them to Portugal.'

'You would do that?' she said. She was wearing another gown. For a moment, her face looked different, too.

'No, I wouldn't,' said Nicholas. 'It would be cruel past bearing. But if they're still about when the *Fortado* arrives, some may be recaptured and auctioned by the Jalofos. Do we buy them in a second time, or do we let them go to the *Fortado* for a Christian employer in Portugal? I'll do whatever you say. There are three girls and an eight-year-old boy with no skin on. Lázaro thought he could rub the black off.'

'Nicholas,' Godscalc said.

'You don't have to stop him,' said Gelis. 'I tore his hand, and I haven't apologised. Nor am I going to. Yes. If they're recaptured, I think the *Fortado* should have them.'

'Diniz?' said Nicholas.

'She doesn't mean it. She's thinking it over,' said Diniz.

Godscalc looked at him, seeing to his surprise the soldier whom Nicholas had found, fighting at Ceuta. Perhaps Gelis van Borselen saw the same thing. There was a moment of stillness. Then she said, 'You're right. I don't mean it. It is too late for that.'

'It's for you to say,' Nicholas said. 'And for me to buy them, of course. You thought Mistress Bel might open her purse-strings.' It was impossible to tell whether he was surprised or annoyed or simply weary. All you could say was that he had been sufficiently moved to uproot the whole situation and throw it into their faces. Soon after that, the girl went below.

The remaining time was spent devising a plan. The *Fortado* sailed like a bird but, failing disaster, would reach the Senagana half a day after them. They nearly had a disaster: striking blind into a circus of dolphins driving a shoal of yellow mullet on shore. The rudder kicked and, heavy as she was, the caravel rocked before she fought her way through without damage. 'It happens here,' Jorge said. 'The mullet spawn: the heathens call in the dolphins to help them.'

'Call the dolphins?' said Bel. 'By name, or do they come in by numbers?'

'The fishermen smack the water with the flat of their paddles, and the dolphin respond. Let us hope the *Fortado* also has trouble,' Jorge said. He knew the coast. He had not ranged the seas in the manner of Ochoa, until his joints swelled and his gums released the stumps of his teeth; but he knew what to expect from the Senagana. Except at time of flood, nothing could traverse the bars of the great double estuary. The factor's mud house, reports said, had been hastily built on an island; the *Niccolò*, anchoring outside the river, a mile wide at its mouth, would send a party ashore and, according to the factor's advice, land their cargo and find their way to the market.

There were no warehouses as yet in Senagana. The trading was done away from the coast, as in Ca' da Mosta's time ten years before, at a village of the Jalofo King of the region. Nicholas and Jorge would lead, with the first mate and Godscalc and Loppe. And, naturally, the groom for the horses.

'And me,' said Diniz.

'If you wish, of course,' Nicholas said. 'But that would leave the ladies alone on the *Niccolò* when Mick Crackbene comes in. I thought you wanted to meet Mick Crackbene again. You might get yourself invited on board the *Fortado*.'

'So I might,' said Diniz slowly; and gave a laugh that caused Father Godscalc to look at Nicholas sharply. But Nicholas merely looked stupid.

Chapter 18

HALFWAY THROUGH the next morning, when the heat had driven everyone except the lookout under awnings, the Portuguese caravel *Fortado* furled her mainsail and bumped through the currents to drop anchor beside her pristine twin the *San Niccolò*, rocking sleepily off the African coast at the swampy mouth of the Senagana river. The surf-boats which had earlier surrounded the latter, obedient as dolphins, reappeared lurching over the breakers to greet the latest arrival with struggling chickens and baskets of pepper and catches of mullet, and armfuls of black and brown berries.

The oarsmen were of all races, from the half-naked blacks to the brown hazel-eyed Tuareg with their headcloths and skin shirts and breeches. And as the races were mixed, so the landscape showed a mingling of grass-covered dunes and low scrub and groves of coconut palms which was half Sahara and half something else. It was the edge of the Sahel, beyond which lay the interior, the green woodlands and grazings and bushes watered by the Senagana during its seeping, long-delayed summer flood, and giving life to bird and beast and to living communities. The dead, scorching breath of the desert had gone. Ripe smells, animal smells, reached out and seemed to sink heavily into the water. The smell of Africa, at long last.

The floating market was an immediate success with the *Fortado*, starved of proper provisioning since Funchal. Diniz, leaning languidly over the rail of the *Niccolò*, observed the summary nature of the transactions and deduced that the vendors were well aware that the factor had been absent since daybreak, while the buyers were not. This view was confirmed by a hail which presently reached him from across the water. Messer Raffaelo Doria presented his compliments, and would be honoured to speak to the gentleman Niccolò vander Poele, whom he believed to be on board. The language he used was Portuguese.

It had begun. Diniz, removing his gaze from a pleased scrutiny of certain patches and scars on the flanks of the neighbouring ship, peered at the speaker, who looked like a *comito*. 'The gentleman?' observed Diniz, after a while.

'Niccolò vander Poele. The Fleming.'

Gelis van Borselen, her crown heaped with sun-silvered ringlets, appeared beside Diniz and smiled dazzlingly over the water. The distant *comito* bowed. Diniz also sent him a smile. The *comito*, after a pause, repeated, 'The Fleming?'

'I am a Fleming,' said Gelis. 'And shall be happy to speak for my race. You have some matter to raise?'

'Yes. That is, no. That is, senhora, your servant. It is a gentleman I seek.'

Diniz threw back his shoulders. 'I am a gentleman,' he said. 'Is there some doubt?'

'A *Flemish* gentleman,' said the *comito*. 'Named Niccolò vander Poele.'

'There is no such gentleman,' said Diniz. 'You are misinformed.'

'But –' said the *comito*, his voice rising.

'That will do,' said another voice, the voice of authority. It was not, as Diniz had hoped, the voice of Michael Crackbene. It came from a well-built gentleman in a doublet and hat almost worthy of Ochoa de Marchena, except that as well as expensive, his clothing was tasteful. Also his accent was not Spanish but Genoese, and his language, when he took the other's place at the rail, was not Portuguese but Italian.

He said, 'I am Raffaelo Doria, commander of the *Fortado*. Do we misunderstand you? You must certainly have on board your licence-holder, a Flemish gentleman of the name you have heard. Or is the *San Niccolò* no longer trading?'

'Ah!' said the new, dulcet Gelis. 'But sir, as Senhor Vasquez tried to tell you, you have been misinformed. There is no gentleman here of that name. The former gentleman of that name is now a Knight of the Order of the Sword. He is properly Ser Niccolò at the very least.'

The commander, who had placed his gloved hands on the rail, now removed them. He said, 'I apologise for my mistake. I should like to speak to Ser Niccolò. Indeed, I am astonished that he has not heard our exchange, or our entry. We fired our cannon.'

'We took it,' said Gelis in surprise, 'that you wished to buy fish. Although, of course, all purchases should be made through the factor. Are you having a lucrative trip? Have you collected some very fine cargo?'

'Is he on board?' said her victim, flatly and finally.

Diniz considered. 'To tell the truth, no,' he said at length. 'Although we expect him quite soon. Indeed, I should invite you to come and await him, except that I have no authority.'

'You should invite them,' said Gelis suddenly and pettishly. 'I am tired of dull company.'

Diniz frowned at her. He repeated, 'I have no authority.'

'Then,' declaimed the masterful voice from over the water, 'perhaps the demoiselle would care to be the guest of the *Fortado* for an hour? When Messer – Ser Niccolò comes, he might join us.'

'Myself, alone?' said Gelis, stepping back. 'I am afraid not.'

'Of course, no. With Messer – Ser Vasquez, if he would do us the honour.'

'I am afraid,' said Gelis van Borselen, turning sideways, 'I go nowhere without female companionship. I shall stay with Mistress Bel.'

'But bring Mistress Bel!' cried the commander.

To the uninitiated, the deck of the *Fortado* appeared in good order: it was clean and trim, its awnings in decent repair, and the flask of wine produced for Diniz and the ladies was a good one, and very likely, thought Diniz, one of their last. He had a feeling the crew were below decks with a skin of Baobab juice. He wondered how many crew there still were. Raffaelo Doria said, 'You are interested, Senhor Vasquez, in our repairs?'

'You have had some damage, monseigneur?' said Diniz. 'We ran aground on a sandbank ourselves. It is easily done.'

'There's a tassel off their shades,' said Mistress Bel. 'When I'm more myself, I'd be pleased to bring over my needle.'

'Why, thank you,' said Raffaelo Doria. 'We are not in parade order, I fear. We were attacked – you didn't know? – and had to resort to some patching. Fortunately, we had a veteran of such matters aboard. You know him, I believe?' He waved his hand. A head appeared above the forward hatch and a big, thick-built man with fair hair emerged with composure and approached, rolling slightly with the tilt of the deck.

It was Michael Crackbene, once sailing-master to Nicholas, who had taken Jordan de Ribérac's money and helped Jordan bring Diniz from Cyprus. For nine months, Diniz had hated Michael Crackbene, but of course he was old enough, now, not to show it. He said, 'You found someone to give you a job.'

'Is it all kinds of repairs?' said Bel of Cuthilgurdy. 'There's a patch-stitch I'm fond of myself, but I'd rather not show you just now. I think it's the shellfish.'

'Master Nicholas isn't with you?' said Crackbene. He bowed to the company and, on Doria's instruction, found a seat. His eyes, discovering Gelis, rested on her with something like amazement.

'Happily not,' said Gelis van Borselen. 'Indeed, I think we too may have to relieve you of our company. From what Diniz tells me, I prefer not to stay in Master Crackbene's vicinity.'

'Why, I am sorry to hear that,' said Raffaelo Doria. 'Is it because of his appropriation of the *Doria*? You may not know that the ship belonged to Jordan de Ribérac in the first instance, and was annexed by your rash young knight Niccolò. After, I am sorry to say, causing the death of a distant cousin of mine, Pagano Doria. Am I right, Crackbene?'

'To the letter, my lord,' said Michael Crackbene. 'That was when she changed her name to *Doria* from *Ribérac*. And is now known as the *Ghost*.'

'There is a ship called the *Ghost* in these parts,' Gelis said. 'We saw her at Arguim. You mean that is the same ship as your *Doria*?'

'Well, hardly,' said Diniz. 'If you mean the red roundship that started at Funchal. She's nothing like the *Doria*, and I ought to know, I suppose.'

'I'm not so sure,' said Raffaelo Doria thoughtfully. 'Ships are easy to alter superficially. A look inside her would soon tell the truth.'

'I'm fairly sure it was the shellfish,' said his oldest guest. 'Maybe a drop more of your Madeira?'

Crackbene poured it. 'Certainly, a look inside would be interesting. I, for example, am convinced that it was the *Ghost* and her guns which attacked us.'

'You aren't sure?' Diniz said. 'Why, was it at night? Then it probably wasn't the *Ghost*. I told the agent at Arguim I saw a white roundship the previous day with some nasty armament on her.'

'Indeed, Senhor Diniz?' said Michael Crackbene. 'It makes you wonder where she was provisioning. My difficulty is that the ship which attacked us appeared – I may be wrong – appeared to carry not only Master Nicholas, but your good self. With a hackbut.'

'Crivens!' said Mistress Bel. 'Mind you, there's a lot of them about. I've shot them myself, in my time. Gelis, I'll need to excuse myself.'

There was a wave of suppressed embarrassment. Gelis said, 'I'll come with you,' and got up.

The commander rose also. He said, 'I am sorry. The lady feels herself unwell?'

'It was the shellfish,' said Gelis. 'I don't know where . . .'

'I shall get someone to take her,' said Raffaelo Doria. 'Hey, Tati! *Gahu!*'

The curtain of the poop cabin stirred, and a black Jalofo cherub in a white cotton chemise stood before them, hands modestly folded. Diniz, staring woodenly, identified it as a girl aged about twelve. The commander said, '*Dafa fun ope. Biir day metti.*' And to Gelis, 'Tati will take her below. There is no need for you to leave us.' And as the child led Bel away – 'But to return to what we were saying. Now I see you, I must confess that I would take you for the twin of the man who fired at our sails. Not knowing Ser Niccolò, I cannot say the same of him until I meet him. But Crackbene is amazingly sure.'

'Then he was mistaken,' said Gelis van Borselen, looking amused. 'I am afraid I must tell you that both Diniz and Ser Niccolò sailed with me all the way from Funchal.'

'On the *San Niccolò*?'

'What else?' said Gelis, transferring the smile to Mick Crackbene. She looked pretty. Diniz felt as thunderstruck as Michael Crackbene.

'And yet you and Mistress Bel went ashore at Funchal?' It was the commander again.

'How interested you have been in our movements. Yes, we went ashore. We followed Senhor Diniz to his plantation, and after he had talked to his factor, we rejoined the *San Niccolò* at Câmara de Lobos. Signor Doria, are you accusing us of something? I believed we were here as your guests.'

Raffaelo Doria smiled. He had square enamels sewn round the cuff of his hat, which matched the shape of his teeth and his fingertips; there were rings on his fingers. He said, 'How could I accuse any being so utterly captivating? In any case, I should require a little more proof. A personal tour, for example, of the *Ghost*, once the *Doria*.'

He spoke still to Gelis, and Diniz was happy to let him. If he thought Gelis the soft mark, all the better. Gelis said, 'I still don't see the relevance. I've told you she has nothing to do with us. So far as I'm concerned, you can search her all you like if you find her.'

'Oh, but we have found her,' Raffaelo Doria exclaimed. 'Did I not mention it? She is sitting sweetly just up the coast, under the impression, like the ostrich, that none can see her. And I would take a very large wager that our Ser Niccolò is with her at this moment, hiding also.'

'You're very sure,' Gelis said. She looked annoyed.

'More than sure,' said the commander cheerfully. He pulled off a ring. 'Sure enough to wager this ruby. Senhor Diniz, will you match me with a trinket?' Crackbene laughed.

Diniz said, 'I don't want your ring. In any case, don't mention gambling. You speak to Gelis van Borselen, the terror of Flanders.'

'Really? Demoiselle? Then you will accept my little wager?'

'If you insist.' She had pearls in her hair worth ten times the cost of his ring. She unwound them and her hair, pale as straw, fell to her shoulders. She said, 'I need a servant. Those against your little Tati.'

He laughed, 'Really, demoiselle!'

'Really,' she said. 'If you are right, you are running no danger.'

'Then of course I accept,' he said. But his eyes were not smiling, either then or when the child climbed back on deck, leading Bel of Cuthilgurdy, her arms laden.

'See what I've got!' shrieked Mistress Bel. 'Man, ye've a very large cargo: have ye not sold anything yet? Well, ye have now. And I paid for it, the lassie will tell ye. See, Gelis. Four great lengths of silk and wool cloth. A tin pan I was needing, and a wee puckle sugar. And look at what's inside this matting – what are your pearls doing off?'

Gelis looked up. 'They think Ser Niccolò is on the *Ghost*. I've told them he isn't,' she said.

Bel of Cuthilgurdy switched her gaze to Raffaelo Doria. It was reproachful. She said, 'Ye've never accepted a wager! She'll bankrupt you. Ye havena seen her between decks with the strokesmen. Is that someone coming out from the river?'

'Excuse me,' said the commander, and rose. The *comito*'s voice called from the rail. Fore and aft, the rails filled with seamen. Twenty-two, Diniz counted, including the officers, the commander and Crackbene. They had lost three, dead or wounded.

He understood the anxiety to meet Nicholas. He understood Crackbene, who had followed Doria. Diniz remembered the guttural accent, applied equally to Italian or French. The sailing-master had made no attempt to take Diniz aside, or excuse himself, or utter threats against Nicholas. Presumably there was no need. Diniz was of little consequence. The war was between Nicholas and Crackbene's masters, Jordan and Simon de St Pol.

The main deck was deserted. Diniz rose to join the rest at the side, and Gelis stayed only a moment, to settle Bel with her packets around her. Gelis said, 'Are you eased?' and touched her.

'Debonair, my wren,' said Bel of Cuthilgurdy. 'Debonair and of sweet cheer forbye. Go you and watch.' And Gelis, smiling again, crossed to Diniz.

Out of the shade, the sulphurous sun burned on the head and dazzled up from the water, thick with odours. Beside them the *San Niccolò* rolled in the swell: the spot they had chosen was too far out for perfect tranquillity. Since the last of the canoes had retreated, the estuary had filled with wildlife: flamingoes flew overhead, and pelicans stood on the sandbanks. The light glinted on the wings of familiar birds in the joy of their wintering, and the water was silver with fish. Sculling from between the marshy islands came a string of four boats, the first a pinnace full of armed men and flying the Portuguese flag.

'The factor,' said Raffaelo Doria. 'About to visit your masterless ship. How surprised he will be. And behind him – praise the Universal Creator! – a royal *almadia*, with two full barges behind her. Have you ever seen, demoiselle, a more imperial vessel? Ignore the fact that it is scooped from the trunk of a tree, and the oarsmen who propel it are close to naked. Observe the painted sides and the gilding. Look at the baldachin with its crimson silk awning, and the carved chair within, worthy you would say, of the Pope. And look at the great black King himself, his robes, the gold on his chest, the great belt round his waist, the . . .'

Silence fell. 'The spectacles on his nose?' Diniz enquired.

Raffaelo Doria gazed over the water. Gelis, leaning closer, laid a hand on his arm. 'And you are going to meet Nicholas after all,' she said. 'There he is, with the wives in the second boat. They all seem to be heading this way.'

Even a man made of iron (which Raffaelo Doria fortunately was) would have been depressed to see climbing aboard his fine caravel not only the Senagana representative of the Portuguese crown and his entourage but a coal-black Jalofo King of twenty stones' weight and six feet six inches in height from his bare feet to the feathers in his intricately-pleated black hair, the monarch being followed by six of his wives and eight pantalooned attendants, armed with spears and round shields and bearing his chair and a carpet.

The noise on the packed deck was tremendous, emanating largely but not entirely from the carpetful of delightful matrons, who were as black as the lord they surrounded, and wrapped from their armpits to their calves in brilliant Málaga silks, bright as parrots. Their necks, their arms and their ankles clacked with thick burnished gold and their teeth sparkled white as they exclaimed and chattered and shrieked.

It was true, Diniz saw, what was said. Of all the races known in these lands, the Jalofos were the most handsome, the most black and the most garrulous. The factor, attempting to make introductions, was overwhelmed by the mellow exuberance of his glittering guest who simply seized and embraced each white individual approaching the throne, and then passed him or her to his wives and officials in the manner of a parcel of food, to be stroked and pinched and laughed over.

Diniz, emerging giggling and breathless from the experience, sat on a hatchcover at the edge of the carpet and watched the scene with delight. You could see that Doria had endured it before and was almost able to hide his disgust. Crackbene made light of it, and so did Mistress Bel, who shrieked back with the best of them, and might never have heard the word shellfish. And Gelis van Borselen, the fastidious ice-maiden, approached the throne with her pale hair over her shoulders and intercepting the large, friendly hands, leaned forward and kissed the King's shoulder and then each of his palms before adroitly freeing herself with a smile. The King spoke, his face shining, and the factor said, 'He greets you, saying: *Do you have peace?* You should answer, *Nothing but peace.*'

'Is that all he said?' asked Gelis, the smile risen to her eyes. Curtseying in graceful retreat, she repeated his words in Jalofo and was pulled down among the circle of women next to Bel of Cuthilgurdy. The factor hesitated. 'I wouldna press the point,' said Mistress Bel. 'Or if you're dead keen, the wee lass Tati can tell ye the words in Italian. On the other hand, I hardly know the words in Italian myself, and I wouldna want to hear them while I was eating. You should hear what the wives want to do with Master Nicholas.'

'Where is he?' Diniz leaned forward.

Mistress Bel turned. 'Oh, you're there? Man, you'll be lucky to leave here with your clothes on. He's just coming aboard. Oh, dear, dear, dear. There he is, with the commander. Maybe they'll take to one another.' The girl Tati dumped a bowl of food on the carpet and stalked off to get more. The wives laughed and called after her in Jalofo, and she glanced at them scornfully. Diniz looked up at Nicholas.

He was alone. Diniz had already seen that Godscalc was not there, or Jorge da Silves, or the *comito*, or any of those who had left at dawn to accompany Nicholas and the factor to the home of the King. Moreover, the barges now tied up to the *Fortado* were not laden with gold. Diniz wondered, absently, what the wives of the King had wanted to do with Nicholas and, more to the point, what the commander would do, if he recognised him.

'We have not met,' said Raffaelo Doria, smiling with stony eyes at the Flemish Knight of the Sword. 'But you knew my cousin, I think.'

Nicholas looked rather hot, but not unhappy. Below the frenzied margin of hair, his eyes were as grotesque as the blackamoors' and his dimples rebellious. 'I have no doubt,' he said, 'that she was charming. Do you have many wives?'

'The usual number of one,' said the commander. 'There are different customs here.'

'That's it,' said Nicholas, with evident relief. 'The wives have brought him, you see. Representing the other three dozen. They want an aphrodisiac for him. I do hope you have something. Although I'm sure the King would like to trade on his own account. We left you some pepper.'

'You left –' said Doria. Visibly, he collected himself. 'You have already traded?'

'The factor guided us to the market,' Nicholas said. 'After all, none of us knew you were coming, and the King prefers to barter at home. It was really quite profitable. Three mule-loads of extremely fine gold.'

Diniz gasped. Three mule-loads was an impossible quantity. Three mule-loads represented all a depot could collect in six months. 'And the gold is already aboard?' Doria asked. His voice was not entirely natural.

'You haven't watched? You surprise me. No. Unlike you,' Nicholas said, 'we are not entirely committed to Mammon. Our priest wished to exercise his sacred calling. We have left him to come with the merchandise later. It was word of your arrival that spurred the King and the factor to leave . . . I see you have my young guests on board. And Michael Crackbene.'

Diniz saw Crackbene turn. He said, 'Monseigneur,' dryly to Nicholas.

'Surely not,' Nicholas said. 'A title better kept for the Vatachino, or the Lomellini, or the family St Pol. You have enough on your hands. Diniz, demoiselle, Mistress Bel: we should leave.'

Bel of Cuthilgurdy got to her feet, with the prodding help of two charming black wives. 'Oh dear,' she said. 'I've got all these packets. Ye wouldna credit the great bales of cloth that they've got in the hold.'

'The King will be delighted to hear it,' said Nicholas. 'As I said, we arranged to leave him some pepper to pay for it. It's down there in the barges.' One of the wives left Bel's side and, crossing to Nicholas, pointed to his bandaged hand. He smiled and let her take it.

'I can hardly believe it,' said Doria. 'You discharged your cargo at Arguim, and yet today you could buy the entire Senagana stockpile with the exception of some baskets of pepper? How could you pay for it?'

Nicholas smiled. The delightful Negress, finding the end of the bandage, had begun, giggling and chattering, to unwind it. 'Ye might well ask,' said Bel of Cuthilgurdy. Another of the wives was touching his doublet.

Nicholas said, 'We still had a few items to sell. Horses. A good load of wheat. Excuse me. If you untie the points ... Is there an interpreter?'

'Tati!' called Mistress Bel. 'Come and tell them. If they untie his points –' She broke off. 'She knows.'

'I suppose she does,' Diniz said. 'I rather think the wives know as well. What are they saying?'

'Excuse *me*,' said Raffaelo Doria. 'How could you possibly carry horses and all they require in addition to loading at – Ah! They were brought by the *Ghost!*'

'The what?' said Nicholas. 'Excuse me, my hand. Don't – What is she saying?'

'I think,' said the factor, coming over, 'that the ladies are concerned that some wild animal has attacked you, Senhor Niccolò, when perhaps you were feeding it. There is food in the palm of your left hand.'

Diniz choked. Nicholas said gravely, 'Tell her, Senhor, that it was more a case of *verba injuriosa* than wounds, and that I shall not feed the creature again. You agree, demoiselle?'

The girl lifted her eyes. 'Why, of course. There are far too many already eating out of your hand. How disgusting.'

'Bread and sheep's tallow,' said Nicholas. 'Mistress Bel's own private plaster. You were saying, my lord commander?'

'I was merely saying – to bring the factor into our conversation – that the *San Niccolò* must be severely overladen, and even potentially in debt, if she hopes to assume today's considerable cargo and also sail to trade in the Gambia. We, on the other hand, are well supplied with goods to barter, and intend to return to Lisbon forthwith. Why, then, do we not take care of your gold? Either as your carrier, or by buying it instead of you?' And he bared his square teeth in a grin.

Nicholas looked at the factor, who had become very red and was edging away from one of the ladies. The factor said, in a hurried way, 'It is a matter entirely between yourselves, senhores.' All the wives giggled, and the one who had embarrassed the factor made the same gesture and shouted at Nicholas. All the wives giggled again.

Bel said, 'They say the King can make ten children in two weeks and sometimes three in a night, and want to know if white men do better.' She stopped while Tati went on translating; and then added, 'And they ask whether the white will come off in the – in the act. Tati has told them it doesn't.'

'Bel!' said Gelis, shocked.

'Talking of ghosts –' said Raffaelo Doria, 'and in this country, they are sometimes closer at hand than you would think – you haven't answered my question. As the factor has said, he need not be involved. I am sure none of us wish to trouble him, even Crackbene. And I needn't mention my own experience with a revenant – yourself, my dear Messer Niccolò, who appear to have been in two places at once very recently. But we are mystifying everyone. Why don't we retire – the King is eating, and happy – and work it all out?'

'It's the shellfish,' said Bel of Cuthilgurdy. 'I knew the moment I saw ye. But that's a very good place down below, even though you've got all the bales sorted out just in front of it. That'll be the cloth that the King wanted kept for him?'

'Yes,' said Raffaelo Doria. Oddly isolated, Jalofo hilarity continued to ring through the caravel.

'Lovely stuff,' said Bel of Cuthilgurdy, poking busily among the heap of her packages and heaving out a long roll wrapped in a woven palm mat like a fish. 'Here's what I mean, if I open one end. Do you see it now, Gelis? I don't need to show ye, Signor Raffaelo. Lovely stuff for me and for you, but the wives wouldn't like it. The factor wouldn't like it. I don't know if even the King in Lisbon would like it. Master Nicholas?'

Clutching his points and his bandage, Nicholas peered. He said, 'What a pity. Is there a lot more of the same?'

'Bales and bales,' Mistress Bel said. 'All set out ready to lift.'

'May I see?' said the factor.

Nicholas blinked. 'It's for Signor Raffaelo to say.'

Raffaelo Doria began to speak and broke off. It was Michael Crackbene who placed his bulk between the article and the agent and responded heartily. 'And show the signor our buying mistakes? He would never trust us again.'

'But perhaps,' Nicholas said, 'there are other bales, elsewhere stored, which would prove to have cloth better chosen?' He raised the parcel and gave it to Diniz, who nearly dropped it.

'You insist?' said Raffaelo Doria.

'If you want the pepper,' said Nicholas. 'The King could hardly be expected to accept unwelcome goods in exchange. And one Portuguese ship would share the poor reputation of the other. Come. Have the cloth brought up on deck and give us all the pleasure of seeing it.' He paused. 'Unless there is anything else to discuss?'

The factor looked up from the lady who was trying to feed him a locust bean. 'You are not, then, transferring the gold to the *Fortado*?'

'No,' said Raffaelo Doria. 'No, we are not. Or not, at least, at the moment.'

*

Returned to the *San Niccolò* that evening, they wept.

'Doria's face!' Diniz cried.

'The King's face!' Mistress Bel moaned. 'When he found the bales full of cloth and no guns!'

'And we have one excellent new handgun inside the wicker,' said Nicholas. 'It was your doing, all of you. Diniz knew the *Fortado* was carrying arms when she was turned back from Ceuta. Mistress Bel –'

'Oh, Bel, laddie,' she said. 'Life's going to be too short for titles.'

'– Bel trampled over decorum and got herself down below, to verify they were there, and Doria was clearly going to sell them. Bel, you can unwind my points as well as my bandage any day. And the demoiselle –'

'Mistress Gelis,' said Gelis.

'That's daft,' said Bel shortly.

The mind of Diniz floated far above bickering. 'Gelis was wonderful,' Diniz said. 'The lies she told about the *Ghost*, and about Funchal, and how we all boarded the *Niccolò*. And she kissed the King.'

'It was rather hard to avoid it,' said Gelis. 'I also had an offer from two of the ladies. My favourite moment – my own favourite moment was when the King hove in sight. Were they real spectacles?'

'Do you mean it?' said Nicholas. 'How he managed ten inseminations in two years would be a mystery, unless you had seen what we've seen of his wives.'

Gelis said, 'I notice you didn't sell them any spectacles. Nicholas –'

'Claes,' he said. And then, 'Listen. That will be Jorge and Godscalc and Loppe.' And raising his voice, 'Melchiorre?'

The curtain drew back. 'They are coming,' said the second mate in Florentine Italian. 'Messer Niccolò, it is a triumph.'

'Perhaps,' Nicholas said. 'Shall we go and welcome them? Bel?'

The plump woman looked up at him. 'You evil-inclined man, what are you doing?'

'Welcoming my confessor,' said Nicholas; and went to the side.

Diniz followed. Now the sun sank low behind them, and its Oriental light lay on the water and the drowsing fowl and the wicker cabins that dotted the shore, and tinged the reedy islands with the colour of Persian brick. The *San Niccolò*'s boats, drawing behind them the rose-tinged arrows of their wake, made their way slowly towards the mother ship, bringing with them Godscalc and Loppe, the sailing-master and his mate, and the oarsmen who had set out with them that morning. What else the boats contained could not be seen.

Diniz said, 'Nicholas? A boat from the *Fortado*.'

'Of course,' Nicholas said; and waited.

Their own two boats arrived first, and disgorged their men, and were made secure while Nicholas stood at the head of the companionway and watched, hardly greeting his priest or his master or Loppe, except with a nod. Then, fast on their heels, came the pinnace from the *Fortado*, with Raffaelo Doria standing in it.

'Ser Niccolò vander Poele?' the commander called, and the rosy light beamed on his enamels, and his teeth, and the firm, jowelled, inimical face. 'A word with you, pray?'

The face of Nicholas, looking down, had no amusement left in it, but he laid his arms on the rail and clasped his hands gently. 'Monseigneur? It is late.'

'Late enough,' said Doria. 'No one can hear us. The factor has gone to the fort, and the King and his wives have gone home. It seems a good time to resume the little talk we had earlier. You will see that the men with me are armed. You will perhaps even notice that the cannon on the *Fortado* are prepared and pointing this way. I should not like to disturb the fort. But I must insist that you let me tow your boats to my ship with their purchases. It is for your own good. You are over your load-line.'

'I am? Then you are right,' Nicholas said. 'I had better sail. Unfortunately, I have need of the boats, even empty.'

'Why not? You may keep them,' said Doria. 'When I have emptied them.' He turned.

Behind, their painters loose, their crew paddling idly beside them, floated the *San Niccolò*'s two handsome boats, upside down. 'I thought I might as well empty them first,' Nicholas said. 'Then we can be on our way. Unless you still want them?'

Diniz said, 'Oh, my God.' Beside him, Gelis looked pale and even Bel had gone scarlet.

Doria said, 'You would do even this, to spite my owners?'

'I should do more than that,' Nicholas said. 'Perhaps the Vatachino know it better than you do. Let me wish you good night.'

'My lord!' came the cry over the water.

Nicholas, half withdrawn, stayed to watch, and the others stood on deck, listening.

'My lord!' It was not addressed to them, but to Doria, and it came from one of the *Fortado*'s own boats, speeding in from the ocean. 'My lord, the roundship has sailed!'

Raffaelo Doria looked up, and then across the water to the speaker. 'In what direction?'

'North!' came the bellow. 'North to north-west, and fully loaded!'

The *San Niccolò* rocked. The *Fortado*'s pinnace dipped in silence below. In the sea to the rear, a practised team was righting the *Niccolò*'s boats. The incoming vessel slackened its dash and, on a wave from Doria, turned and made doubtfully for the *Fortado*.

Raffaelo Doria looked up. He said, 'You had already loaded the gold? You had it carried overland to the roundship?'

'While you were entertaining the King and ourselves so very hospitably. As you recommended yourself,' Nicholas said, 'we elected to keep all our capacity for the Gambia. I'm afraid you left King Zughalin dissatisfied and less inclined to trust the Vatachino in the future – but at least you were not all hanged for arms running. And now I suppose you will leave. Do you have any particular plans?'

'Only one,' said Doria, 'for you personally. As for the rest – am I going north after the *Ghost*? It is tempting, but no. I think that, like you, I shall make my way south. It seems I have all this cloth, and there is no Portuguese factor, as yet, in that kingdom. We may even meet there.'

He bowed, leaving, and Nicholas turned from the rail. 'Well?' he said.

'Three mule-loads of gold?' Diniz said. 'Loaded on to the *Ghost*?'

'On its way to Madeira, and without the *Fortado* to dog it. It should get there,' Nicholas said. 'And Gregorio will know how to take care of it. And the Bank, I hope, will redeem itself all the more quickly, and Mistress Lucia's business. While, as it happens, we have done no more to messieurs Vatachino and Lomellini and St Pol than will deprive them of trade, and prevent them from replacing poison arrows with gunpowder, for what that is worth. Father? Do you feel less despairing?'

Godscalc stood, his face lined. He said, 'I have taken God's word today where it has not often been heard. That is all I can say.'

'Jorge?'

'It depends whom you trust,' said the shipmaster. 'But you could have done little else. And we are free to go to the Gambia.'

'Loppe?' said Nicholas.

'We are not all children,' said Loppe. 'Even those who came on board today. Do not be deceived.'

'You weren't there,' said Mistress Bel. 'They laughed at us, and had cause to. The demoiselle knows.'

'What?' said Loppe.

No one spoke. Diniz thought of the pearls, and the light silken hair, and the wager. Doria had believed Nicholas concealed on the

Ghost, and had been shown to be wrong. Gelis had won her stupid wager, and the child Tati was her reward. Except that the child Tati, freed of her bondage, had clung screaming to Doria her owner; had kissed Doria's feet weeping; and when finally wrested away, had tried to kill herself with his knife.

The white man was her lord. She was superior now to the Jalofos, who had sold her. She would not survive the shame of returning. And, perhaps, she had been taught to adore Raffaelo Doria as, rumour said, his kinsman Pagano Doria had made himself the first lover of another young girl. So they had left Tati with him.

Gelis van Borselen said to Loppe, 'You will hear the story from someone, no doubt. I apologised to you once before. This time, you will know that I mean it.'

Chapter 19

THROUGH THE HOT DAYS and cool nights of early December, the caravel *San Niccolò* sailed to her ultimate landfall in the great river belt of the Sahel, and all but the six slaves aboard her lay at night and dreamed of what might be still to come, for the way to the Fountain of Youth, to the River of Jewels, to the court of Sheba and Solomon was ahead, and open.

The *Fortado* had left the estuary first, and Nicholas had made no effort this time to forestall her for, he said, the race was won, and he was content. And that at least seemed true, whatever doubts some of them might harbour about the malice of Raffaelo Doria. Nicholas was content, and his caravel carried the glow of it, however fleeting, on the two hundred miles of its journey.

Of the twenty-five crew and six passengers, most could now expect to be wealthy, if they lived, and if the *Ghost* reached her destination in safety. Seventy kilos of gold three times over had been loaded into the *Ghost*, on top of what she carried already. She was a roundship, and hence would make no great speed sailing northwards, but Ochoa was a fine seaman, and a good fighter, and she carried a prime weight of ordnance.

As for the *Fortado*, said Nicholas, she was welcome to proceed south and buy whatever the Gambia traders had hauled to the mouth of the river. Then with any luck she would turn and go home, leaving the upper stream and its secrets to others.

What did he mean by its secrets? What else but finding out where it led? Did it join with the Senagana, as some said? Did it link with the east-flowing river men called the Joliba? And was the Joliba an arm of the Nile, flowing east to the heart of Ethiopia? Nicholas wished no harm to the *Fortado* going to Gambia, he said, but he would like to see the tip of her mast now and then, and the direction in which her guns might be currently pointing. And once she had got to the Gambia, he would very much like to see the back of her.

He was not altogether stupefied by good fortune.

There was, none the less, something fey about Nicholas – and his caravel. Since the departure of the *Ghost*, she had changed. When, on the first day of their sailing, Godscalc said, 'What has happened?' Bel of Cuthilgurdy smiled and looked up from her sewing.

'We've become mummers; barefaced maskers, my bodach. You and Lopez and Senhor Jorge did the serious work. The rest of us were thrown on our wits; made to jink our way into the *Fortado*; forced into cheatry; compelled to trust one another. I would tell you we gart Gelis laugh, if I thought you'd believe it. Hence what you might call a truce.'

'Including Gelis?' said the priest.

'That would be rash,' said Mistress Bel. 'But there's a reasonable understanding between her and Diniz. And she's less cocksure than she was with young Nicholas. Not that the waste of life we've seen could be forgotten, but he's managed to sweeten it.'

'Not for me; not for Loppe,' Godscalc said.

'Then he'll work on you both,' said Bel of Cuthilgurdy calmly. 'And despite your misdoubts, he has gone on to sail south. Can he be intent on more gold? Or is he a crusading son of the kirk after all?'

'I don't know,' Godscalc said. 'Perhaps gold makes men dizzy, like wine. The very ship seems to sing.'

'Do you say?' said Mistress Bel. 'Nothing vulgar, I hope.'

Through a day and a night, the *San Niccolò* danced her way south, and her light heart was not wholly due, Godscalc perceived, to the treasure. The ship had become a community: one already half formed before the disruptive advent of the slaves, and now welded close by their fortunes. Moving among the faces he and Bel and Loppe now knew so well Godscalc guessed that, laden with gold, they would have shown themselves readier to turn and go home than to go on. But they had regard for their master, and seemed to think that there might be other chances, now their lucky young patron was back. The slaves would have been kept to sell for good money if Niccolino'd been there, the word went. The name Ochoa had used in the Bay of Tanit had stuck.

Nicholas worked to make them his, too. He had the name and history of every man, and not only Melchiorre and Vito and Manoli who had sailed with him on his galley to Lagos. He cultivated the first mate, Jorge's lieutenant Vicente, and he took trouble with the boys: the active, insolent, well-beaten Lázaro, who was enough of a thug to be a natural seaman, and the causelessly insolent Filipe, who was not.

He had asked Bel, in Godscalc's hearing, not to protect Filipe when he was punished, but to let him deal with it himself, and Bel had agreed without arguing. Godscalc wondered if Nicholas had found out about the two boys and the blacks; he was bitterly unsure if it was right to conceal it. He dreamed of the baby rising to the rim of each wave like a butterfly.

Jorge, he supposed, had not really forgiven them for failing to keep their human merchandise. There were still six Negroes on board: all white-capped and shirted Mandinguas, and all free to rove the ship as they pleased, since they could understand what Loppe told them. Slighter in build and less talkative than the Jalofos, they were both quick and observant, as Godscalc found when he, too, tried to communicate with them. The natural leader, a tranquil man of about thirty-five with a fringe of a beard, knew Arabic and somewhere had picked up a few phrases of Portuguese, to which he was adding daily. In the absence of Loppe, it was Saloum who now helped to interpret. Their fellows who had leaped overboard had probably been as able and amiable as these, Godscalc thought, before they were captured. Only there had been no words to deal with their fear.

They had put the others ashore at the Senagana, but had said nothing of them to King Zughalin, for he would have set out to trap them again, and sell them cheerfully to the next comer. Godscalc had learned that tribes at war saw nothing wrong in seizing their rivals. Kings did little, either, to prevent parents within their own lands from selling the odd child, like Tati, although the loss of young, active boys would, he suspected, be frowned on. It was one of the hidden flaws in Loppe's programme. These people could not afford to lose the flower of their kindred; not unless they came back.

It had become the custom since Funchal for those who were not of the crew to gather just before noon at the *bitácula* on the poop deck, to see the pin set in the compass-card and to wait until the cry came that meant the shadow had moved to the fleur-de-lys point of the north. Then the binnacle's Venetian hour-glass would be lifted by Filipe or Lázaro and turned, as it was every half-hour, day and night, and the comparison made which would show how far east or west the ship might be sailing. At every stop they had made, the *balestilha* had been taken on shore – the cross-staff that ships carried in place of the heavy astrolabe used on land – and Godscalc had seen the creased charts and the worn tables written at Lagos with their lists of daily solar altitudes.

It did not surprise him that Nicholas was always present and active in matters of navigation. Numbers were his tools. It did surprise him to notice how much Gelis had mastered during a journey which had, after all, been made largely on the extraordinary roundship of Ochoa de Marchena. He had assumed, he saw wrongly, that a young woman of birth would have spent such a voyage modestly in her cabin below. It had already struck him to wonder what she had done during the engagement between the *Ghost* and the *Fortado*, but she had said nothing of it herself and Bel, consulted, had told him to mind his own business. That, at least, was what he thought that she said, and he always took Bel's advice concerning Gelis.

In any case, navigation mattered, whether they were out of sight of land, as they had been, or whether as now they were sailing down a treacherous coast invisible to them by night, and distorted through dust-clouds by day. The eighty feet of the *San Niccolò* pitched through the ocean, sailing wide, the set of her sails hardly altering, but the lead dipped and dipped from her side while the knots of the log told her speed.

From the poop deck, there was little to see. The coast they were passing was featureless still: a ribbon of low dunes and hillocks and bushes which became greener as the second day progressed, with a line of trees visible above the distant beaches, and the white of surf on low reefs, and a glimpse of mangrove islands, now seeming near and now far in the haze.

Early that morning they had passed the basalt cliff, fifty feet high, which marked, Jorge said, the western limit of Guinea, along with the green point called Cape Verde. After that, their course turned south-south-east, as did that of the *Fortado*, when she could be glimpsed. Having raised her, Jorge da Silves was quite content to keep his distance, hurrying when she hurried, but making no attempt to gain ground. Except in the matter of slaves, he seemed quite in accord with his patron's intentions.

Diniz, joining Godscalc under the pavilion of the poop, was happier trying to prove Nicholas wrong. 'What would you do if you were the *Fortado*, and having to report back to David de Salmeton? I'll tell you. You'd get to the Gambia quickly. You'd unload the arms as well as the legitimate cargo. You'd take on everything you can buy – including slaves, I shouldn't wonder. And then you'd arrange a warm welcome for the *Niccolò*.'

He sounded unaffectedly happy, visualising it. Also he smelt of horses again. Of the twenty-five they had brought, they had kept five for themselves. He added wisely, 'No one would know. We'd simply appear to have sunk with all hands in some accident. If I were Nicholas, I'd have hurried and wrecked the *Fortado* instead.'

'Did you mention this to Nicholas?' Godscalc said. He moved

away from the helm and the master, and leaned on the rail looking aft. Diniz followed him.

'He says the *Fortado* won't invite battle, because she wants to load and get her cargo home safely. He says she has nothing to gain since we're practically empty. I say that Crackbene and Doria can't afford to let him off. Think what he's done to them!' His dark, narrow face glowed.

'I suppose,' Godscalc said, 'it depends on how successful they are in the Gambia. The smiting of Nicholas might seem less compelling than a quick exit with a mountain of gold.'

'Except that they won't find much gold, according to Jorge,' Diniz said. 'Gum and pepper and cotton, perhaps. But when the Senagana has gold to sell, the Gambia doesn't.'

'You mean it comes from the same mines?' Godscalc said. 'But perhaps Doria knows how to obtain it at source.'

'No,' Diniz said. 'Even Diogo Gomes didn't know that. They keep it secret.'

'Who?'

'The heathens who mine it. They dig holes, and send their women down them with feathers.'

It sounded like a joke. Godscalc was in no mood for jokes. He said, 'Where did this nonsense come from?'

Diniz, as he usually did, kept his good manners. 'The classical writers spoke of it. All the navigators were told about it at Sagres. The Carthaginians came here for their gold: Herodotus wrote about it fifteen hundred years ago. The silent trade, it was called. No one ever saw who the miners were. No one knows, even yet.'

'Then how do they sell?' Godscalc said.

'You are telling him about the silent trade?' said Jorge da Silves, joining them unexpectedly. 'It has been done the same way for hundreds of years. The traders pile their goods on the banks of a river, each pile named for its owner, with a hollow of a certain size made beside it. Then they make a smoke signal, and go back to their boats. When they return, they find no people, but the hollows filled or part-filled with gold. If the gold is sufficient it is taken, and the salt – it is always salt – left for the miners. If not, they retreat again to their boats, upon which the amount of gold is increased. The trade depends on absolute honesty: this timid race, who are never seen, make no effort to make off with the salt until the gold has been removed.'

Diniz said, 'Of course, you know the story as well.'

'Of course,' said Jorge da Silves. 'And so, naturally, does Senhor Niccolò.'

'And the *Fortado*,' said Father Godscalc.

'Yes,' said Jorge da Silves. 'It is one reason why it is advisable to keep that vessel in sight. We trust she will do her business and turn, but the season is early. She may decide to linger, hoping for more. She may decide to find more for herself. And that is why it is better, Senhor Diniz, to have her ahead rather than following us.'

'I don't understand,' said Father Godscalc.

'Because, padre,' said Jorge da Silves, 'they may think that your Lopez has been persuaded to give up the secret.'

On shipboard, the second gathering of the day was at sunset – or perhaps the first, since that was when the new day was deemed to begin. Then the steam rose from the cooking-pots, and dishes of eggs would go round, and maize bread to dip in the stew, and a pail full of oysters, with all the usual hilarity directed at Bel who, in return, would explode like a good-humoured missile. After supper the air became cold and all but those serving the ship turn by turn through the night withdrew behind doors, or between decks, and soon slept.

Until that time, it was hard to find privacy, and what Godscalc wished to say to Nicholas was not for other ears – even those few who understood Flemish. He waited, therefore, until the ship was quiet and the after-deck empty but for Fernão standing stolidly at the helm with one of the boys in attendance.

Nicholas, in fact, elected to climb to the tiller before him, alarming Filipe and causing Loppe, who had been standing unseen in the shadows, to step into Godscalc's view. Godscalc hung back. He was therefore in the uncomfortable position of hearing Loppe move forward and address Nicholas by name from below.

Nicholas turned, his hair flickering in the light from the binnacle. Loppe said, 'You don't want me?' in Flemish. The helmsman and the boy were both watching.

Nicholas said, 'Come up.'

Loppe ran up the steps, his skin black on black, and only the vast leather jacket he wore dimly visible. He said, 'You think I am so easily influenced? There is no need to avoid me.' He smiled at the helmsman, who smiled back.

'I suppose not,' Nicholas said. 'You are all sons of Adam, as we are.'

Loppe laughed, the sound rumbling softly in his deep chest. He said, 'Oh, the bitterness! Very well. But I beg to share your apple as well as have you stung by my serpent. I shall not hold it against you if you smile.'

Nicholas stared at him. He said, 'Jesus son of David, I am preserving your sensibilities, you interfering bloman.'

'And when the time comes, I shall do whatever I choose. Does that annoy you as much as I hope?'

'Hosanna to thee, suffering Africa,' Nicholas said. 'I don't know why I listen to you. Especially as someone else seems to be listening too. Behind you. Oh. Father Godscalc?'

'As you unfortunately see,' Godscalc said. 'I was on my way to talk to you also. Probably on the same subject.'

There was a little silence. Then, 'Oh dear,' Nicholas said. 'The two ladies ought to be here; they are extremely adept at exploiting this vein. I assume it is the same vein? The Sun and I alone know the boy is beautiful?'

'Nicholas?' said Loppe. 'You won't divert him that way.'

'What do you want me to do, then?' Nicholas said.

'Why not tell me the truth?' Godscalc said. 'What has Loppe promised to do?'

Nicholas said very slowly, 'Loppe is not required to make promises. And I don't exact them.' In the bows of the ship, someone suddenly screamed.

Nicholas gripped the rail. A whistle blew. A man shouted, and then several others, and there came a pounding of feet and the voice of Vicente, yelling commands to the helmsman, to the mariners, to his deputy. The sheets of the mainsail flew free and the trumpet started to stutter and blare, summoning the full crew from below. Men ran forward, poles in their hands; the lead splashed and splashed in wider casts, and the mizzen also spilled its wind suddenly. A great shudder ran all through the ship, and a jolt that threw Godscalc to the deck, followed by another. He saw Jorge da Silves running towards him, and stagger as the ship lurched again. There came a squealing of timber.

'A reef,' Nicholas said. 'Not a sandbank, a reef. How could there be one in this place?'

The helmsman turned, livid with shock. The two boats, bobbing behind, had men and cable in them already, and the capstan was being rigged. The boy Filipe, staggering back, had flung an arm round the mizzenmast. He was whiter than the man, and was whimpering. Nicholas looked at him. Then he looked at the binnacle.

Loppe said, 'Nicholas, come. We must find out the damage.'

Nicholas said, 'You did that before.' He wasn't speaking to Loppe.

The boy whimpered again, but mixed with the whimper was a wild snigger.

Nicholas said, 'When she ran aground before. You did that.'

Godscalc picked himself up and strode forward. The whole deck was tilting. He could hardly hear himself speak for the uproar. Loppe, after waiting, had flung off to help with the anchor. Godscalc said, 'Filipe did this? What are you talking about?'

'Fornicator with blackamoors,' Filipe suddenly said. His voice was thin and breathless and girlish. 'Common scullion. My father would chain you to his . . .' His voice petered away. On his face, stiff and forgotten, was a defiant grin.

'I am talking about this,' Nicholas said; and delivered a blow that travelled straight from the shoulder.

Against the hubbub below, the boy's screams were hardly heard, except by Godscalc and the petrified helmsman and by Jorge da Silves who was stopped by them, while leaping up to the helm. Stopped by the screams, and by the crunch of fine breaking glass, and by the sight of the blood that welled black through the sobbing boy's shirt and under his arms as he hugged himself.

There was fresh blood, too, on the hand that Nicholas let drop to his side. He said nothing, but watched as reddened clots of sand slid to the deck from the boy's clothing. Jorge da Silves saw them too. His features, always grim, became waxlike. He drew back his arm, his knuckles stark, his eyes on the boy's twitching face.

Nicholas stopped him. 'Later. Padre, lock him below. And come back. I may need you to prevent me from doing anything stupid.'

It was a long night that followed, for the *San Niccolò* had hitched herself on her reef at slack water with the ebb still to come, and she had the choice, it first seemed, of sliding off with her holed bottom and sinking, or of staying stuck and breaking her back. In the end, the carpenters worked like bullocks down in the bilges and had her sufficiently sound to keep out the water by the time the boats had found a secure bed for their anchor.

Unfortunately, by then the ebb had reached such a state that it would have done the grounded ship as much damage again to warp her free. All they could do was haul up the contents of their wood store and make legs of it, to shore up their pretty new caravel until the flood came with the daylight. And even then their troubles were hardly over, for the day brought a fresh blowing of sand, and the men straining at the bars of the capstan could hardly open their mouths to chant, never mind give it their best effort. In the end, all that scudded along was the anchor, while the ship stayed firmly stuck until the next tide, when Jorge da Silves went out himself to seek better holding, and ended by manning both boats and succeeding in towing the *San Niccolò* backwards until she floated, scuffed and scarred and with some curious great patches below the waterline. Then, her sails set, she took up her journey south once again.

At the supper that followed, no one mentioned the *Fortado*, long since vanished. The crew, early fed, were asleep on deck but for the watch and so were the black passengers, who willy-nilly had worked their passage now towards the Gambia. The horses, exhausted by fright, drowsed below, all except one thrown by the collision, which had had to be dispatched with a hatchet. At the table, the master sat red-eyed and silent, and Diniz dozed beside Godscalc until sent to bed by Bel of Cuthilgurdy. The master excused himself, and then Loppe. Godscalc stayed, with the two women and Nicholas.

Godscalc said, 'So what about Filipe?'

'Ah,' said Nicholas. 'The court of enquiry.' His voice seemed rather flat, but he was not a man who needed much sleep, and he looked less fatigued in some ways than Bel or young Gelis who, besides the cook's work, had set their hands to a number of tasks not normally included in the education of well-bred ladies from Flanders and Scotland.

The thought reminded Godscalc of what Filipe had shouted last night. He had resented discipline, and feared it, and yet weakly invited it. Most of all, of proud Portuguese blood, he had resented discipline imposed by a dyeworks apprentice. Everyone who knew the St Pol family, Godscalc imagined, would have been told the origins of the lord Niccolò vander Poele, Knight of the Sword. Godscalc said, 'A personal enquiry: it is not for me to go further. How could Filipe run us aground?'

'Mechanically or morally?' Nicholas said. 'Morally, because he has very small scruples, and they haven't descended yet. Mechanically, because he was in charge of the hour-glass. The ship's course depends on its accuracy: if it isn't properly kept, you can't trust to your place on the chart. The glass can be made to lie by rough seas. Also, boys can speed the sand and shorten their watch by warming the glass in their shirts. The wind is cool and unpleasant these nights, and the helmsman gets sleepy. I should have noticed it sooner.'

'Did Filipe realise what might happen?' said Bel.

And Nicholas said, 'I think it unlikely,' which Godscalc conceived to be as good a lie as he had heard from him. From the lack of any following question, he guessed that Bel and even the girl guessed as much, too, and were impressed. He wished he didn't know that beneath everything Nicholas said and did there existed fathoms of labyrinthine calculation. Abruptly, he got up to leave, and with a little weariness found that Bel, normally welcome, had risen and was leaving along with him.

In the big, empty cabin Nicholas, too, made to move and then

changed his mind, since he and Gelis had been abandoned, he
assumed, for a purpose. They sat at opposite ends of the same
couchette with the uncovered lamp of palm oil glimmering on a
plate of bones and another of oyster shells: he had already wiped
his knife and put it away. At sea, and in this season, there were
very few insects.

She was consuming dates from a bowl in a meditative fashion.
He was aware that her hair was tightly coifed in linen as usual, and
that she wore one of her plain, shortened serge gowns powdered
as usual with dust. Since he rejoined the ship she had made no
effort, except on the *Fortado*, to appear feminine; and indeed he
got through most days without actually looking at her, since in that
way he was never taken unawares by some resemblance.

Most of the time, in any case, he was not thinking of her at all
but rather, as just now, of a number of things he had to do,
including visit Filipe in his cell and put the fear of God into him.
He already knew what he was going to do to settle the problem of
Filipe, which was to promote the appalling lout Lázaro to the rank
of mariner. He didn't deserve it, and it would take weeks to train
him, but it would part the two boys and send Filipe, with any luck,
looking for a new exemplar. Meanwhile, the quickest way with
Gelis van Borselen was sometimes the shortest one. Nicholas said,
'What are we supposed to be talking about?'

She tilted her head and, rounding her lips, spat a date stone clear
across the chamber to where Jorge's armour hung on the bulwark,
without hats or parrots. The article bounced, pinging melodiously,
from his Portuguese helm. She said, 'I thought you would know.
He's your priest. Can you do that?'

'Yes,' said Nicholas, without doing it. 'No. Whoever is in collusion with me at the moment, it is not Father Godscalc. So what
does Mistress Bel expect us to talk about?'

'Let me guess,' Gelis said. She took another date and held it
point upwards absently, as if about to work out a problem with
chalk. Then she said, 'I don't know,' and ate it. 'Unless you're
supposed to talk me out of travelling inland. Your man Lopez says
we are about to turn into the river-mouth and sail the caravel right
up the Gambia.' She spat. A cuirass complained briefly in alto.

'As far as it's navigable, yes.'

'For at least two hundred miles, Diniz says. Then you somehow
cross to the river Joliba, which is large, and flows east, and may
lead you to Ethiopia. If you intend to go to Ethiopia.'

'That's why Father Godscalc is here,' Nicholas said. He picked
up the pallid stones, looked at them, and dropped them into the
oyster dish. Gelis took a fresh date. She looked struck.

She said, 'Of course! It's Father Godscalc I'm supposed to be helping. All the time we were on the *Ghost*, Bel was warming him under her pinions. Father Godscalc has to return with his mission fulfilled, and Bel wants to know your intentions.'

'So tell her to ask me,' said Nicholas.

'You'd lie to her,' the girl said. She licked her fingers.

'I might,' he said. 'I might not. I think quite a lot of Mistress Bel.'

'Now that,' she said, 'is magnanimous. She and I think quite a lot of you; but perhaps in a different sense. We both think you are only here to seek out and establish control of the gold, and that you will abandon the mission party, or divert the mission party, almost immediately.'

'Have you a Bible?' said Nicholas. 'No? Jorge's crucifix there?' He enunciated carefully. 'I intend to stay with the caravel so long as she can navigate up the Gambia.'

'I expect you will,' Gelis said. 'Because the gold is further inland, isn't it? The mines can't be near the coast. Diniz says the silent trade must be further inland even than that. And the Sahara caravan terminus bringing the salt from the north for the silent trade must be farther east still – perhaps a very great distance from here. So what about Jorge's crucifix, and an undertaking that when you leave the caravel, you'll be taking the track for Ethiopia, and ignoring everything else?' She spat, and a greave buckle clicked. Her trajectory was moving all the time in his direction.

'That's all right,' he said. 'I did promise to tell you what our plans were, although not necessarily involving ratification by oath under threat of bombardment. If you hit the looking-glass, it will leave a most unpleasant mark.' He could tell, by the altered movement, that the ship had changed her course slightly, and wished he could go out and look. He kept his voice sweet and patient, to annoy her.

'I can tell you, and Godscalc knows, that the caravan terminus is thought to be somewhere along the course of the Joliba river, which is the way we propose to travel. If there's gold there, I shall buy it, because I shall probably need it. The terminus must be some weeks away, and the journey from there to our Black Magus might be as much again, and over mountainous land no one knows. We shan't get there by Epiphany.'

'Or at all? You haven't begun, and you're saying that the mission is hopeless?'

'I thought Bel wanted me to discourage you. In fact, we'll try. If we get there, they'll canonise Godscalc. If we don't, we'll bring back maps to help others. And on the way there are settlements he can visit. I'm told the local rulers convert fairly easily, given a pair of falcons and a consignment of handguns. The Holy Father should have hired the *Fortado*.'

'You despise Godscalc,' she said. 'And these black people. And Lopez.'

'I can't help my humble childhood,' Nicholas said. 'And as for Godscalc, I don't see any harm in paying a modicum for your beliefs and at least buying a hearing. After that, the message either sticks or it doesn't.'

'How eloquent. A statement of religious ecstasy, near enough, in terms of dyeyard philosophy,' Gelis said. 'So I shall assure Bel that the Pope and Godscalc have your complete and unqualified support. And will you light a candle tomorrow?' She looked him in the eyes, a thing to beware of. The stone this time sailed past his ear.

Tomorrow. Tomorrow they would reach the southernmost port of their journey. Tomorrow they would arrive at the mouth of the Gambia and confront the *Fortado*. Or not. Tomorrow the horses ought to be exercised, and the provisions checked, and the arms oiled and prepared, and the slaves supplied and given such directions as might help them. Four were leaving, and two were desirous of sailing with them upriver. 'Tomorrow?' said Nicholas.

'Your Saint's Day. You hadn't forgotten?'

He had forgotten. Deliberately forgotten. He became slowly conscious that she was sitting gazing at him, her hand arrested on its way to the bowl. She said in a voice of horror, '*Katelina died on that day?*'

It startled him, that he had allowed the cast of his thinking to show. He said, 'No, Gelis. No. Other things happened.'

'And not pleasant ones,' she said. 'I can't say I'm sorry.'

'No. I am sorry enough for both of us.' In Lagos, he had tried to initiate this conversation, and perhaps would again, but this was not the time. 'It's late,' he said, but she was still seated, with that shrewd, considering stare. It struck him that their relationship was like that of two disputing men, one young and one older. Even in the grip of such an obsession, her mind had a cold, clear quality which surpassed, for example, anything the boy Diniz had shown. A mathematical mind, like young Tilde.

As if she had again guessed his thoughts Gelis remarked, 'How old are you then? Twenty-four?'

He shrugged without answering, as the ship kicked. A strong cross-current: where would they be? He saw his lapse of attention strike and sting her.

'And rich once more, and going to be richer. And powerful. But none of that matters to you as much as the way it happens. You worship duplicity for its own sake. You've grown up alone, because it suits you. You don't have to discuss your real plans with anybody. Last night we ran on a reef. It's probably the only event since we left Lagos that you haven't personally set in train. No wonder Godscalc is sick of you.'

Nicholas leaned forward and picked up two oyster shells and a date. 'No God is absent save Chance. What makes you think I didn't plan the reef episode too?' He bit the end of the date and then put it all into his mouth.

'The way you struck Filipe,' Gelis said. 'You lost your temper. How childish.'

'I wanted a matching pair,' Nicholas said, displaying a shell in each hand. The half-healed pits of her bite crossed one palm; the cuts of the hour-glass the other. He said, 'I take it, then, that despite the evident dangers, you have spurned my passionate pleading and intend to stay with the ship? Bel *will* be surprised.'

'Arrive in Ethiopia,' Gelis said, 'if you really wish to ruin all Bel's predictions. What are you aiming for?' The oyster shells, like two blinkers, filled the cavities of either eye, and the date stone stuck in his teeth, primed and canted.

'That,' he said; and spat; and heard her exclamation as the stone landed. There was a hiss and a stink of hot oil. He uncovered his eyes and found himself, rather pleased, in total darkness. He had managed to extinguish the lamp. 'I thought I could do it,' he said.

The wick reeked. He could hear her breathing; she sneezed. He got up and pulled back the curtain to let in air, and some light from the deck, and also to show the way out. She accepted, he supposed, that it was not only a joke, but a form of dismissal. As she rose, he looked to see how much she minded.

He expected contempt. He wouldn't have objected, this time, to contempt mixed with a tinge of amusement. He saw, as she went, only her habitual indifference beneath which lay something else that, as always, he could only guess at.

He went off to deal with Filipe.

Chapter 20

NEXT MORNING, obedient to whatever prompting, Father Godscalc held a special mass for the *San Niccolò*, entering perilous waters, as was in any case seemly for a ship of her name on that day.

In Venice, the first week in December would have brought cold high tides and raw air, and Margot would be opening the shutters of the Casa di Niccolò upon banks of grey mist through which boat would pass ghostly boat, as Julius travelled to the Rialto to balance ducat against groat and écu, and to count his reserves. This week in Murano, friends would warm their hands at the winter-long glowing furnaces of Marietta Barovier, who might tease her timid protégé the Florentine into raising a glass to a Venetian Pope.

In Bruges, ice might have filmed the canals, requiring Cristoffels to warm the pumps in the dyeyard, and Tilde and Catherine de Charetty to light the fire in their office as they paid out their wages and pored over their ledgers, and worried about the future of the Medici agents, now that the old man Cosimo, *pater patriae*, was dead.

And on two distant islands, the wheels of the sugarcane mills would be turning fast in the rain. On Madeira Gregorio, anxious, resentful, determined, would toil at his desk, and perpetually plod the muddy track between Ponta do Sol and Funchal; while on the other . . . The King of Cyprus would now be twenty-five years old and tired, no doubt, of his stolen mistress and petulant, perhaps, because David de Salmeton was no longer there; or even regretting, briefly, the banishment of his once-cherished Nikko. Zacco's mother would want her son to marry. His queen might already be chosen. The King of Cyprus would not, this St Nicholas Day, need to think of Famagusta.

And on the Guinea coast, one man celebrated his twenty-fourth Feast in tropical heat, and high expectation, and enough foreboding to make the blood race, and obliterate all the abominations of the past. On the *San Niccolò*, the caulking-pitch spat and sizzled in the shimmering radiance while below, the horses drooped, listless. Dolphins shouldered aside the warm sea, and sometimes the vast back of a whale rose and dipped, while sea birds perpetually swirled and swooped and perched on the caravel's rails and spars. And across the water the sounds of Africa reached the ship as well as the smells: an outburst of faint, rapid drumming would strike the ear from among the tall trees behind the green of the mangroves, although no huts could be seen, and there might be nothing on the beaches but the delicate white plumes of the egrets.

In time, the drumming became intermittent and faint, and as the final hours of the approach to the Gambia went by, there came to those on the *San Niccolò* another experience: the sensation of being watched; a conviction that the distant trees held more than wildlife; that the movements among the dunes were not always those of birds. And finally men became visible, gazing intently from the shore or paddling their canoes through the winding shallows until, as if by consensus, there came the moment when they came darting out to the ship and, rocking, encircled her.

Ten years before, poison arrows from these same canoes had greeted all foreigners. Now Loppe said, 'I will go to them. It is safe,' and slipping down the side stepped into the nearest, sitting hunkered in the deep wooden cavity.

Anything Loppe wished to do, Nicholas allowed. He couldn't keep perfectly still, but paced idly back and forth until from the boat the massive shoulders rose, the white teeth gleamed, the face turned, and Loppe was running up the ladder and back, with a basket of fish and the news for which he had taken the risk. 'They say a fine blue ship came down a day and a night ago and stopped at the island by the Gambia estuary. They say she bought all that traders could sell, and did not turn back, but turned into and sailed up the river, seeking more goods and gold. They say the under-Kings Gnumi Mansa and Bati Mansa will receive them and us, if we mean to follow, for these lords rule over parts of the region, and both are greedy. They say we should trust them only if we have many presents.'

'The same Kings!' Diniz said. 'The same Kings the caravels met! Gnumi Mansa is a Christian, isn't he, Nicholas? And Bati held a great congress for Diogo Gomes, far up the river. How they will welcome the padre!'

'We hope so,' said Nicholas. 'But time has passed since Gnumi was dipped by an abbot, and I doubt if Bati was ever brought to the fold of the Faithful. We can only hope that if they possess any venom, they expend it on the *Fortado*. For, my braves, it seems she is not sailing home: she is ahead of us.'

There was no need to underline the implications of that, and no time, then, to explore them. Ahead, within the vast lake of its estuary, lay the mouth of the Gambia, cumbered with shoals and flats and a tidal stream of two knots on the ebb which posed problems seldom found in the Middle Sea, and would test, very soon, the kind of crew the *San Niccolò* had made for herself. Let them enter the Gambia. There would be time enough after to plan.

Jorge awaited slack water, and launched the caravel boldly into its passage. With a lookout at the masthead and two in the bows; with the lead splashing and splashing and the ship answering keenly as a veteran to her helm, the caravel threaded her way from hazard to hazard. The master had been to the Gambia outfall before. He had the measure of its famous swamp of an island, barely one mile by three, and knew to sail its length to the preferred anchorage in the sandy mud of its eastern end. He moved cautiously, watching for masts.

The *Fortado* was not there, nor was there sign of any vessel other than the upturned canoes on the beach. There was no evident danger, but much emerging inconvenience: a lack of any one of the services that Arguim and Senagana had possessed: no store of timber or rope; no provision for meal or for water. There was scant welcome as well: the few blacks they'd seen had vanished by the time Jorge took his small party ashore, tying up to the drunken jetty some exasperated ship's carpenter had knocked together and left. Beyond was beaten sand and bushes and trees, and a few mud-brick huts, and a row of crooked boughs upholding tattered straw awnings over nothing but pressed and mat-patterned sand.

Jorge reported an hour later to Nicholas. 'There's nothing left. Doria bought what they had, and took all the provisions and even the water. The traders had a little gold to sell, but not much. They're sullen: Doria bullied them, and told them we would be worse, and had almost nothing to give them, which is near enough the truth: we must save what we have for the Kings. I don't want to careen here. There's an island we can get to tomorrow, where we'll have peace to look at our patches.'

Nicholas said, 'Did Doria say where he was going?'

'No. Just that he wanted to trade up the river. It is nine days' sail, as we know, to the rapids. Of course, they say he means to land there and go further. They say he seeks the source of the gold.'

'What did they think of that?' Nicholas said.

'They laughed,' Jorge said. 'They always do. Don't you hear the drums? Long before any ship can arrive, all seven hundred miles of the river know what is happening.'

'Then,' said Nicholas, 'there is no particular reason for stealth. All right. I assume it's safe to stay here at anchor tonight, and move on in the morning. Unless the padre wants to reconnoitre the settlement?'

'I should go ashore,' Godscalc said. 'There may be men of faith, left by other expeditions.'

'It is possible,' said Jorge da Silves. 'Father, it is for you to say.'

'Happy?' said Nicholas to Bel of Cuthilgurdy.

'There were tortoises on the beach,' Diniz said. 'And I saw a silk-cotton tree with an ape in it.'

'So you see,' continued Nicholas to Bel of Cuthilgurdy, 'the whole expedition has been worth while.'

The next afternoon (the island having proved deficient in grace), the caravel turned her back on the ocean and set her course upstream and into the interior, stopping only to deliver four of her slaves to the river-bank. The Mandinguas departed unbaptised, and with a frail enough prospect of ever reaching their homes. Godscalc took leave of them miserably and they embraced him; and wept on parting with Bel and with Loppe, watched without pleasure by Jorge da Silves.

Instead of more than a score of slaves he had two, but at least they were of high quality, and one of them, the bearded and articulate Saloum, even offered himself as a pilot, for he had used the waterway of the Gambia, he said, many times.

And indeed, as the river unfolded its steaming, tortuous course, full of currents and shallows and freakish suckings and surges of tide, Saloum proved their most precious possession. He it was who, repairs and careening over, guided them from point to point on the banks, enabling Father Godscalc to attempt to land at this village or that, so that he could see what religion, if any, the inhabitants followed, and talk to them with Loppe or Saloum as his interpreter. There was no immediate hurry, Nicholas said.

For Diniz there was no hurry: it was a time of rapture. The shining, slow-moving river, three miles wide, moved beneath him, obeying its own motion and that of the moon, while the seamen deployed all their skills to harness the uneven wind and turn back and forth among the sandbanks and islands and streams, between one low, leafy green bank and the other.

Strange birds soared over their mastheads and disappeared in blurs of scarlet and green, dun and rose-colour into the dense margins of bushes and trees, from which came a wicked chorus of noise, a screaming and twittering, mixed with the hoots and cries of unknown animals; while by night the frogs and cicadas performed a different chorus.

Impelled by the special enthusiasm of Diniz as well as the padre, the *San Niccolò* on the second day turned off to sail between the towering mangrove bushes of some ample creek which led forty miles or more, Saloum said, to the south; and, anchoring finally, sent her boats to penetrate even further.

From that expedition Father Godscalc returned with a manner which hourly became weightier and more silent, while Diniz ran up on deck, wet and bitten and glowing, to talk until he was exhausted of the wonders of the swamps – he had seen the man-eating lizards, monster upon monster, asleep in the shallows. He had seen apes, great baboons, carrying their children lovingly on their backs. He had been put to sit with a lot of people under a tree while Godscalc talked to them, helped by Loppe, and had been given beans and millet in bowls and offered two black girls to sleep with. The black women had hair like braided wool, and wore cotton shifts woven in strips by their menfolk, and three of them had circles of gold on their arms, but Loppe wouldn't translate any questions about them. He had tasted a gourd of palm wine.

'So I see,' Nicholas said. To Loppe, apart, he said, 'What happened?'

'The people are uneasy,' Loppe said. 'In some villages they ran away. In others they allowed the padre to speak because we gave them presents, but were glad when we left. It is not the leper-white skin or the caravels: they have seen traders before. Their holy men have told them that Father Godscalc is a sorcerer who will cast a spell on their millet, and cut the hair of young girls for his mattress, and who has incurred the hatred of trees.'

'The hatred of . . .?'

'It is a belief.'

Nicholas could be stolid as well. He said, 'But they are subjects of Gnumi Mansa?'

'I fear,' Loppe said, 'that Gnumi Mansa's Portuguese falcons may have died, and the houses built by his Portuguese mason abandoned, and his faith in six years has likewise melted away. The reproaches of a genuine priest would injure his dignity here at home, and harm his reputation abroad with his sponsors. He was baptised, as I remember, after Prince Henry.'

Nicholas said, 'You are saying that it would suit Gnumi to believe that Godscalc is an impostor? And that since he isn't, we may all be . . . what? Prevented from seeing him? Or killed so that we don't carry tales?'

'Either is possible,' Loppe said. 'The *Fortado* perhaps will advise him.'

Carefully, they were allowing the *Fortado* to lead. It laid them open to traps but possessed, meanwhile, other advantages.

'Doria and Crackbene, carrying out the orders of the Vatachino and Simon,' said Nicholas. 'I think I can guess what they will advise.'

'Can you?' said Loppe. 'They haven't turned. They're still trading.'

'All right,' Nicholas said. 'If all they want is a cargo, they'll go to the two Kings and Cantor and turn, having primed Gnumi Mansa to slaughter us. Do you think that will happen?'

'It may,' said Loppe. 'It may not. Saloum will count in our favour. On the other hand, your first theory is probably right. They'll load and wait at the falls beyond Cantor. Then they'll try to track where we go when we land. In which case we'll survive until then.'

'Some of us,' Nicholas said. 'They don't need Father Godscalc. And whomever they do want to preserve, this King may have other notions. Where is Gnumi Mansa to be found? Do you know?

'I can guess,' Loppe said. 'He came to meet Doria at the river-bank at Tendeba: we should reach it tomorrow. He moves about his domain with two hundred warriors and his wives; he won't be far away. Those are his *almadias*, his canoes, along the river-bank.'

Nicholas had seen them. Gliding in and out of the shallows, never approaching the ship; a chain of swift, shallow troughs with their double line of upright, wing-capped, white-shirted Negroes with their short-shafted paddles; wholly unrelated to the eager mercantile canoes of the coast, heaped with meal bags and kola nuts. Nicholas said, 'What will happen?'

'You will be sent for,' said Loppe. 'And you go.' He added no warnings. So far up the river, there was little to be done, they both knew, if the Kings took against them.

That night, the *San Niccolò* lay at anchor off the muddy banks of the river with their singing, croaking, rustling life, and the thirty-one men and two women on board passed the hours sometimes in sleep; sometimes listening to the cries of night birds and the sudden gurgle and swish of cloven water, or the low voice of Filipe, turning the hour-glass, and the mutter of Melchiorre, responding. Misted with wings, the great lanterns bloomed in the darkness, oiling the running waters with gold and touching the sleeping figures on deck, and blotted out, for fleeting seconds, by the leafy membranes of bats, silent as the watchers who waited unseen on either side, their shallow boats deep in the reeds. And just above the threshold of silence, there vibrated the throb of conversing drums.

Nicholas spent the night with the crew in the open, his pallet laid in the quiet of the after-deck. Twice Jorge crossed to kneel and talk in a murmur. The first time, it proved to be nothing of consequence. When next he paused by his bedside Nicholas made room for him to sit on the mattress while he pulled himself up in the half-dark, embracing the large sheeted hump of his knees.

None slept completely bare with women on board, but both of them were stripped to the waist, so that Nicholas could see the white seams of old wounds furrowing the other man's sinewy torso, and guess from Jorge's curious gaze how much of his own chequered past could be read from his naked shoulders and arms, his ribs and belly and breast. Jorge said surprisingly, 'You should appear thus to the King. You are going, this time, ashore?'

'I should rather appear thus to his wives,' Nicholas said, utilising one dimple with caution. 'Of course I shall go, as you will, if we're invited to meet Gnumi Mansa. I should like to leave behind the boy and the priest, but short of force I don't think I can contrive it. We shall have to ensure their well-being by other means.'

'But the priest must see the King!' da Silves said. He lowered his voice. 'Or else why are we here?'

'I've told you. I'll do what I can,' Nicholas said. 'But I've got to repeat. He and the boy are in more danger from the *Fortado* than you or I are.'

'More danger than your servant?' da Silves said.

It was clear enough whom he meant. Nicholas said, 'Lopez is not my servant,' and then wished that he hadn't.

'No. Forgive me. But if Lopez who is not your servant is in little danger, it is because the *Fortado* thinks him valuable. Lopez knows the source of the gold. He is going to lead you into Wangara. That is why you let him squander your cargo of slaves.'

'Wangara. Is that why you are here?' Nicholas said.

The half-lit face with its glimmering eyes seemed to change. They were very close, their voices low. 'You gave an undertaking to my King, and to me. You promised souls and gold for the Order.'

Nicholas remained, with some effort, where he was. A challenge over souls and gold he had expected. Now he perceived they were also talking about Loppe and Diniz and presumably even (remembering Ochoa's merriment) certain rumours from Cyprus and Trebizond. Making enormous adjustments, Nicholas picked his way towards safer ground. 'Jorge, what Lopez knows hardly matters. Say you do find the way to Wangara. You'll never induce the tribe who live there to show where the gold lies, or where they take it to barter.'

'And that is your answer?' Jorge said. 'What do these animals do with their gold? What would the Church do by comparison? You would hardly have to touch them – one blast of your cannon would persuade them.'

'I expect it would,' Nicholas said. 'And then what? Another blast for the middlemen of the silent trade? They don't know themselves where the gold comes from, and they certainly won't step aside while we track it down and usurp their business. So do we kill them all too?'

'You talk in extremes,' said Jorge da Silves. 'Did you murder your potential rivals when you sought to share in an alum monopoly, corner the Turkish supply of raw silk, control the royal Cypriot sugar estates? Some of them, perhaps; but not all. Do you know, sometimes I have a bad dream about you. Sometimes I think you and your Lopez want to track down the Wangara gold for yourselves, not for Portugal.'

There was a silence. From the invisible bank came the plash of an idling paddle and, further off, the pealing cries of a hyena, answered by a rush of cackling sound. The drums pattered. Nicholas changed his position. He said, 'If you are here for the Wangara mines, then you may as well go home.'

'You do want them!' said Jorge. His eyes gleamed.

Nicholas said, 'Every white man on the Guinea coast wants them. Doria for the Vatachino. Gomes, when he came here, for Prince Henry. You. And me. Of course I want them, but I'm not going to get them; I'm not going to try. Mention them to Gnumi Mansa or Bati Mansa and they'll kill us, as they would Doria and Crackbene. They'd slaughter anyone they thought would betray them, including Lopez, which is why neither you nor I will ever ask him whether or not he knows the way.'

'I look at you, and still I cannot be sure,' the master said. 'You want gold. It seems to me sometimes that you are interested in nothing but gold. You insisted on promoting Lázaro, and it is useless.'

'Vicente is a good trainer,' said Nicholas.

'Oh, yes. But now the ship has half his attention. The ship should be your concern, too.'

'I am sorry,' said Nicholas, 'Of course it should. I must have seemed a very poor comrade.' He paused. 'Over the gold. I am hurt that you doubt me, but it's easily tested. When we leave the caravel at the end of the Gambia, you will be with me. I am not going to Wangara, but I mean to buy gold on our route to the east, at the caravan posts where the middlemen bring it. Lopez will take us to these.'

'If,' Jorge said, 'he has not already gone to Wangara with Raffaelo Doria and Crackbene. He is not your servant, you say.'

'No,' said Nicholas. 'But he is still my friend, as you are, and friends do not betray one another. I am thirsty. Will you give me a drink from your flask?'

Their hands touched as he received it; he drank, and rubbed his eyes as if weary, and presently the Portuguese spoke to him softly and, rising, went away. Bel of Cuthilgurdy came up from below and lowered herself where he had been. 'Oh Christ no,' Nicholas said.

'I woke,' she said. 'I thought ye were going to marry him. Will he go for the Wangara gold on his own?'

'No,' said Nicholas. She had her head in a towel again.

'Unless he bribes Lopez or follows Lopez and you. Will Doria go on his own?'

'No. He's waiting for Lopez and me,' Nicholas said. 'That's why the Vatachino have sent him.' He resettled himself, crossing his legs like a Turk, his hands light at his ankles. The air seemed freer already.

'And you're not going to Wangara, you say.'

'You heard me say it,' he said.

'Oh, aye,' she said and, leaning forward, smacked a fly off his chest and pitched it aside. She said, 'And tomorrow. Ye thought the priest and the lad might be expendable. D'you mean to protect them?'

'Yes, I do,' Nicholas said. 'Till death us do ... No. That came from some of my other marriages.'

'Um,' she said. 'But will ye manage to save them, d'you think? You're namely for guile, but maybe it's less a talent for tactics, and more a kind of instinct of nature like the beasts have. Whiles it works, and whiles it burns the skin off your elbow.'

'Elbow? You've been listening to Godscalc,' he said. 'I think it should be all right. The *Fortado* will have showered Gnumi Mansa with gifts, but we have some other credentials. Having freed the slaves, for example.'

'Well, it'll prove your poor business sense,' said Bel of Cuthilgurdy. 'Which might be an asset in its way. But will ye get thanks for it? I thought the King was in there selling rival blacks with the best of them.'

'He didn't sell Saloum,' Nicholas said. 'I haven't wanted to disappoint the padre by telling him, but when we bought Saloum, we set free a marabout.'

'I once had them all round a hat,' said Bel of Cuthilgurdy. 'But they got tashed very quickly.'

The dough-like face remained, as ever, unchanging, and his sense of ease, as ever, increased. He said, on impulse, 'You do this for me. Why not for Gelis?'

'You're easy,' she said. 'And maybe ye get frightened more often. And don't flatter yourself. If you make mistakes, we all suffer.' And getting up, she hitched her clothes and walked off below.

Chapter 21

THE FOLLOWING DAY, Nicholas made no mistakes that he knew of. As the *San Niccolò* sailed the thirty tortuous miles to her next anchorage, the canoes that haunted the shores slowly grew bolder; and by the time she reached the place called Tendeba, they had silently surrounded the ship. Then Loppe, dressed in white as they were, went to the rail and spoke to the oarsmen.

Nicholas heard his voice as he stood back with da Silves, waiting. A beautiful voice, deep and gentle in speech; high as a woman's when curving and soaring in counterpoint. A man whose musicality could encompass the Byzantine ritual of Trebizond and the purity of Gregorian chant, learned in the high Alpine snows of the passes. But a man who did not sing here, in the country he came from.

Loppe had tried one dialect and then another, and was understood. The sun, a few hours past its zenith, lit the white caps and shirts of the King's messengers, and struck flashes from the sharpened iron that lay ready in every canoe. Loppe turned and said, 'The lord Gnumi Mansa hears that there are guests in the river, and offers them hospitality. He will receive twelve men, none of them armed, but they may bring what presents they wish. They must also bring an interpreter.'

'Tell him that we are honoured,' said Nicholas. 'We shall obey his every wish, and shall come when he desires.'

Godscalc had a portable altar. He carried it ashore an hour later in its box, along with pyx and vestments, chalice and censer and incense in the soft leather bag he had brought from Bruges to Venice, from Venice to Ancona, from Ancona to Lagos and south. When he met the priests of Prester John, he would set his crucifix beside theirs. Standing beside Bel he said, 'You say Saloum is a Mohammedan. I am sad.'

And Bel said, 'If he wasn't, you'd get no hearing at all, and

Senhor Jorge would feed you to the big lizards. I wish I was coming with you.'

He was glad that she wasn't. The two women stayed on board, and the two or three crewmen that were sick, and sixteen able men, including the boy Filipe and Melchiorre and Manoli, two of the three expert seamen from the *Ciaretti*. Bel and Gelis would be safe.

For himself, Godscalc was not afraid; only anxious in case of failure. The silent rowers who took them ashore did not speak; they landed among thick, stubborn mangroves and followed a path rich in mud to a grassy clearing as wide as a park, beyond which, on rising ground, he saw the straw roofs and smoke of a village. Diniz said, 'There was a snake; they say they can swallow a goat. Did you see the snake on the path? Did you see the red and green birds? Look at that tree!'

The tree was immense: the kind he now knew was called a Baobab; perhaps twenty feet in circumference, and set in the centre of the broad meadow, with its shadow, a great pool of darkness, lying beneath it. Then he saw that the shadow was tenanted.

Some three hundred warriors, their arms glittering, stood in a crescent beneath it, and in the centre, upon a carpet, sat a single black figure of Oriental obesity encased – thick arms, rounded shoulders, immense thighs – in some twenty yards of flowered Florentine silk of the kind exported by the Medici in Bruges at five to six ducats a yard. On the King's head was a crown of white ostrich feathers, and his ears, arms, neck and ankles were hooped and studded and bangled with gold. Behind him stood a group of chieftains in coloured gowns of a less expensive style, and to one side, manacled to a stake, lay a leopard.

Nicholas said, 'My lord,' and stepped forward. He bowed, without kneeling. Loppe, behind him, repeated the phrase, and a greeting in Mandingua. The King, ignoring Loppe and the two black men at his back, gazed in silence first at Nicholas, and then at Godscalc and Diniz; and then set himself to scrutinise the six seamen, beginning with Jorge da Silves, who bowed also. The King's eyes returned to Nicholas. He spoke.

The words sounded angry: made more so by the jet of saliva that shot from a vacant socket between the King's purple lips. His eyes, compressed by fat, seemed to glare, and as he spoke he scrabbled within the fringe of grey beard at his jaw as if his fingers were stinging or palsied. Loppe, listening, turned back to Nicholas.

'My lord King says he thinks the white men must believe him rich, that they appear begging at his door so frequently. He says he has nothing to sell, but will offer them a gourd of wine, since he is a great lord. First, he wishes to ask if it is true that they travel with a sorcerer.'

'I am no sorcerer,' said Father Godscalc in anger, striding forward. From under the tree, light as wind, there came a muted rustle, and assagais and arrow-tips twinkled. Nicholas looked at Loppe. Father Godscalc thumped his box on the ground, unlatched its sides, and standing to his full monolithic height repeated, 'I am no sorcerer. I am a man of God, from the same Church as the abbot of Soto de Cassa who came here two years ago to instruct you in the Christian faith, and who baptised you under its laws. Why do you use the name Gnumi Mansa when all the world knows you swore to worship none but God the Father, in token of which you bear the great name of the dead Infante Henry, whom you called brother?'

He had promised Nicholas he would not become angry, but it was impossible. Jorge at least knew that it was impossible. He saw Nicholas and Loppe glance at each other again; then Loppe began to translate.

It was extremely brief – so brief that he had hardly finished when the King shouted a question to which Loppe replied at length, without translating. The King, like Godscalc, knew when names were being omitted. The King, it was apparent, was even angrier than Godscalc at being deceived. He stood, continuing to exclaim; and the rustle behind him became an array of sloped spears and stretched bows. The King waved a fist at Loppe, and Loppe turned again to Nicholas.

'He heard the names of the abbot and Prince Henry. He knows therefore the padre is a genuine priest who may carry back tales of his backsliding. He continues to pretend therefore that he is a sorcerer. Father Godscalc, will you permit Saloum to speak? Our lives are lost otherwise.'

'He would kill a priest?' Godscalc said.

'No. He would let the leopard kill a priest,' Loppe said softly. 'And then he would make sure none escaped with the tale. Those on board the ship, too.'

He had to allow it. He had no idea how a marabout, a Muslim holy man whom – God in heaven – he had spent a week trying to convert to Christianity could save the lives of a boatload of men and women of the opposite faith. It was with amazement therefore that he saw the short Mandingua Saloum step forward with his fellow slave Ahmad – clever, polyglot Saloum with his curling black beard – and by merely naming himself and his companion, cause the vast, feathered figure before him to fling out his arms, and the twinkle of weapons to shiver and halt.

The King's narrowed eyes studied the three black men before him, and he asked a question. It was directed at Loppe, but

Saloum answered. He answered at length, during which a murmur passed through the armed men standing waiting. Then the King asked a last question, and was answered. For a long moment he stood, then, lifting his hands, he clapped them loudly. From somewhere behind, a horn wailed. Drums began to beat. The King tossed his head with its white feathers and, advancing, stopped before Nicholas, taking his hand and then releasing it. He snapped his fingers and spoke.

'Gnumi Mansa says *Peace, peace,*' Loppe said. 'Repeat it and bow.'

The King moved on, and stood before Godscalc, repeating the ceremony. Then the King clapped his hands once again, and this time a man came forward and laid before him a box. Once, it had been identical with that of Godscalc. Now the leather cover was frayed and furred over with fungus and the contents, when it was opened, were tarnished and sickly and crumbling from two years of insects and rot. The King spoke.

'He has kept your God for you,' Loppe said. 'He wishes you to eat your God with him, and will have fresh blood brought, since the old blood has dried.' And bending solemnly, he received from the King and held out a shallow worm-eaten receptacle in which still reposed the furred scum of wafers.

'Tell him,' said Father Godscalc, 'that before God I commend his safe keeping of such articles, and will willingly celebrate the mysteries with him presently, using the box and the wine I have brought. Meanwhile, will he introduce me to the other Christian men of his following?'

They began to walk together among the chiefs and Godscalc, listening to the King and to Loppe, took the hand of smiling black men called Jacob and Nuño, who cracked their finger-bones at him and offered him all their houses and the houses of their grandfathers for his sole use. He was aware, as he smiled and blessed these black recipients of the evangelical doctrine, that many more of both sexes were pouring into the grassy space, both from its confines of high trees and bushes and from the village on top of the rise, and forming a circle were moving round the Baobab, ululating and clapping their hands, while others brought mats so that all the meeting-place under the tree became floored.

Then, accompanying the King back to his carpet, Godscalc saw that the horse left by Nicholas on the shore was now being led into the arena by Lázaro, the splendour of its harness disguising the state of its lubberly legs. And behind it, conducted by Vicente and carried on the stout shoulders of Vito, Fernão and Luis, the strongest of all Jorge's men, was the mighty roll of flax canvas which contained, Godscalc knew, the fabric of a tent which would offer shade the equal of another Baobab tree to its new owner.

It looked in fair condition for an object brought two thousand miles for this purpose. The King, already erect and rustling forward at the sight of the horse, exclaimed and chortled with pleasure when the pavilion was spread and explained to him. Then Nicholas presented him with his spectacles.

When the platters of food began to arrive, Gnumi Mansa would have them taken nowhere else but the new tent where, lenses glinting, he sat in state with his chiefs, flanked by Saloum, Loppe and Ahmad, Nicholas and Jorge, and the other seven white men from the ship. Godscalc did his duty as well as he could, thrusting his hands into bowls of rice and maize and stiff breads, of improbable fish and melting fruits and unwieldy meats including, he suspected, the component parts of several dogs; and duly exclaiming with rapture over a dish of cooked elephant. His fingers, his robe and his chin all became unavoidably greasy and his throat ached as he conversed as well as any man could against the uproar of the King's feasting subjects outside.

The liquor, when it came, was all the more welcome, although it proved to be no juice of the grape but the yeasty stuff Diniz had already described, made from the sap of the palm tree, and with the appearance and flavour of whey. He was mildly thankful, draining his gourd, that along with fresh wafers he would be able to provide a flask or two of something more seemly for the Mass he was to hold, it had been agreed, tomorrow morning.

Nicholas, settling beside him said, 'Diniz was right. It's strong wine, Father.'

'I had already decided,' said Godscalc. 'Not at all suitable for the altar, although I shall have to draw on your stocks to give a sip to the numbers of communicants that our Muslim friend seems to have conjured up from this community of raging recidivists.'

He stopped, wiped his lips, and continued. 'I still cannot understand how such a thing came about. One moment, the King was fit, I swear, to kill the lot of us; and the next, Saloum the marabout had not only pleaded our cause, but exhorted the company to manifest its adherence to the Christian tenet.' He knuckled his chest and repeated, 'Manifest.'

'Saloum owes his freedom to you,' Nicholas said. 'He and the King both recognise it.'

'But his beliefs!' Godscalc said. 'Were I saved fifty times over, I could not have repaid my rescuer by damning the souls of my flock; by ordering them to embrace heresy, for so the Christian religion must appear to him.'

'It happened: why worry?' Nicholas said. 'Gnumi Mansa –'

'Henry,' said Godscalc. He kept his eyes open.

'Henry Mansa wants the good opinion of the Portuguese and only needed to be reassured that you weren't shocked by his respect for Saloum, or by any small disarray in his Christian practices. They've even brought out some goods to barter – a piece of civet and some half-dozen skins, and a sack of malaguetta in the pod. The visit is a success.' He stirred, as if about to get up and leave, but was prevented by the appearance of a young, brightly robed woman with pleated hair who stooped smiling before them with a dish of wild dates.

Godscalc found two or three and let her pass; the girl was one of a dozen, all charmingly dressed and gold-adorned, whose sole task had been to serve the King and his guests. Godscalc stared at the dates in his palm and spoke to the man beside him with sluggish bitterness. 'Why do you lie to me? I have been spared out of gratitude. I am allowed to say Mass out of gratitude, and commercial expediency. And the marabout feels no embarrassment because none of it is genuine. They are no longer Christians, and when I have gone, they will revert to whatever state they have lived in since the abbot departed. Tell me I am wrong!'

'Perhaps. Perhaps not. Loppe would know,' Nicholas said, 'if you think it worth asking him. I'd prefer Jorge, I must tell you, to keep his illusions. Whatever the truth, you can't do anything about it except agonise, and you might as well agonise over what can be helped. Look at this.'

He was pointing, Godscalc thought, to the black girl who had returned, all shining eyes and teeth and heavy gold bangles, and was now kneeling before them. Then he saw that she was offering coloured comfits, heaped in a willow basket made in Madeira.

'The *Fortado* has been here,' Nicholas said. 'They informed the King that you and Diniz your companion were secret enemies of the white men's Church who, if allowed to survive, would send thunderbolts to destroy his crops and burn his cities and dry up his rivers. They told him to leave the rest of your party untouched, but that the white lords would reward him if he destroyed you. Saloum saved you twice over. He told them you were a true priest, and persuaded them not to kill you for it. Now will you upset all he has done?'

Godscalc couldn't answer at first. He felt very tired. Now the shadow of the vast tree was dimming the roof of the tent, and outside the Mandingua voices seemed to have grown louder and shriller, half drowning the cries of the first of the night-flying birds. He could hear music: the wailing of some sort of horn; the sound of plucked and sawn strings; the drubbing, in increasing volume, of many different drums. There was a hollow tingle of bells. The skirts of the tent were folded back and Gnumi Mansa . . . Henry . . . returning bespectacled and staggering from the well-beaten place of common withdrawal was settling himself afresh and calling for Nicholas. Nicholas, who had avoided using his name.

Godscalc said, 'Did you choose to punish me because I believe in something? Or because of what I know?'

Nicholas viewed him. His face, gleaming fawn under his hat, was fretted, Godscalc saw, by the loops and rings of brown hair stuck to fresh, dimpled cheeks whose innocence seemed as always in harmony with the large open eyes, their whites and irises so distinct that they seemed to reflect heaven and earth in their soft, rounded expanse. Innocence echoed by the full, relaxed lips and profound voice. Innocence belied only a little by the curious, fastidious nose, and the set, perhaps merely stoical, of the chin and the jaw. Innocence wholly belied by long acquaintance, which taught that the features so assembled were the outer manifestation and cloak of a man few people knew – perhaps none.

Nicholas said, 'I brought you here because I needed a ship. It's nothing to do with me if you can't do your job.'

When the priest went to sleep, the King showed, despite himself, a certain relief. The box of decaying wafers, still prominently displayed on the carpet, was discreetly scuffed to one side and a number of elderly men robed in white could be observed making themselves at home at the back of the tent where the horse had also been tethered. Against its throat and below its fine gilded headstall hung a minute purse of red leather which had not been there before.

Nicholas sat between the King and Jorge da Silves in what appeared to be a great pressure of flesh, some of it belonging to the official party and some occasioned by the unexpected accommodation in their midst of the magnificent young women who had feasted them and who, now the platters had gone, still jumped up from time to time to refill the gourds. Jumped up and reinserted themselves in their places in a manner that turned Diniz crimson, Nicholas saw, and was already creating an awareness among the older men: the cheerful, hard-drinking Luis; the handsome helmsman Fernão; the lively red-headed Vito and even the austere Vicente himself.

The King, he saw, was aware of it and so were his chieftains. They seemed to be laughing. The palm wine appeared yet again, and he took two gourds and gave them both to Jorge. The drumming surged. Loppe, on the King's other side, paused in his translation and looked at him.

Smiling, Nicholas spoke in Flemish, not Portuguese. 'What is happening?'

It was a game they had played before. Loppe spoke to the King and to Nicholas, the words in Flemish slipped in between. 'The men and women outside are going to perform for you. The men will leap and fight, and when the fires are lit, the women will dance, clothed and half-clothed. They are graceful.'

'And the women here in the tent?' Nicholas said. Their shoulders were bare, and their arms, and their slender ankles and feet. He could feel their breath on his neck, and once, a tongue.

'All the women here are the King's wives. You are his guests until dawn, so he will offer experience of them as his feast-gift.' Loppe was smiling too, with rare affection and mischief.

Nicholas said, 'What do we do?' He felt hollow. He brought his brain on guard with some suddenness, like a sentry caught napping.

Loppe said, 'It is your choice. He will have made provision for all of you. He will be complimented if those of rank among you requisition the favours of his favourite wives. Not to do so might seem a slight, unless a man is clearly incapable. The padre is asleep.'

'And our Knight of the Order, or as soon as I can arrange it,' said Nicholas. A shocking pang ran through him and remained somewhere, throbbing.

'Leave him to me,' Loppe said.

'I don't know if I should,' Nicholas answered. 'Loppe, are you sure? It seems . . .'

'He has many more,' Loppe said. 'More than he can satisfy. This will keep them contented. These young women are mostly with child, and hence barred to him and restless. The occasion can produce nothing but good: the King will appoint you his brothers.'

Nicholas smiled at the King and felt the smile spread idiotically. The subject under ostensible discussion was unicorn's horn. He said in Flemish, 'What did Doria do?'

'He wasn't asked,' Loppe replied. 'He put altogether too many questions about the source of the gold. What you see before you, Niccolino, is virgin territory.'

'In a manner of speaking,' Nicholas said. When the wine came round again, he refused it.

Before the dancing began, when the tent had been removed and the carpets spread again in the low, golden light under the tree, he made his excuse and, getting up, wandered from place to place until he had spoken to all the five crewmen from the *San Niccolò*. They had to know what to expect; they too had to make their choice; they had to be warned what would be acceptable. He came last to Vicente and Lázaro.

Vicente heard him in silence, but his gaze travelled to where his Portuguese master Jorge was sitting, his shoulder supported, his eyes already half closed. Nicholas said, 'You are right, it won't please him. But it may be that he never realises that it has happened – unless, of course, he is told. On the other hand, you can abstain. It would make a better example for Lázaro.' And he smiled at the boy.

Lázaro said, 'I am thirteen.' He was looking at Vicente.

It was true. He was the same age as Filipe, although with something of a man's build already, and a deftness and strength that already justified the seaman's post he'd been given. Beneath the powerful harness of Vicente, there had been no more gratuitous horseplay on board.

On land, one would have expected the same. Vicente said casually, 'You are too young,' and then frowned as the boy reddened from his brow to the edge of his doublet.

The boy said, 'I can. If you do, then I do.' Then, as the *comito* hesitated, at a loss, he cried in his strange, husky voice, 'Do you want me to prove it?'

· Of the three possible resolutions, Nicholas picked the least injurious. He said, 'Are you going, Vicente? Then here's a stout fellow who, I'm sure, ought to be allowed to make one of these ladies happy as well. Only remember. Wait until you are asked, and behave with courtesy. The lives of your mates may depend on it.'

Nicholas made his way back to the close-packed, sweet, sweating humanity at the King's side, and was pulled down. He had walked straight past Diniz, who was more than thirteen, and a gentleman, and glacial with Scottish-Portuguese dignity. Nicholas had passed, and Diniz had melted as he passed, and then dissolved as Nicholas dropped an eyelid. The drumming, already loud, began to roll faster.

Many times, reliving that night, he pondered the vividness of it, and wondered what drugs might have induced it. The burning colours (from what impossible dyes?) worn by the dancers as, winding down the slope from the village, they stamped and swayed round the grassy arena before Gnumi Mansa. The hunkered knot of musicians on the King's right, their unseeing eyes on the performers, their hands and sticks resonating on curious hides with a rhythm that stirred forgotten memories: water striking on armour in battle; a storm of rain driving its tattoo across a great army encampment; the distant beat and roar of a fire consuming a house and a business.

The impact of sound, and the awesome impact of sight. The vast roseate bowl of the African sky as the sun sank in the Ocean of Darkness and, behind the frieze of darkening bush, a strip of satiny water barred by the slender topmast of the *San Niccolò*, bright as a needle, her pennant stirred by the light river airs. And here beside him, under the tree, the circles burning red as two lamps on either side of the King's spreading black nose.

The men fought, and the women danced, their feet rising and falling, their hands flailing, their heads low, their rumps in the air. The men retired and in the firelight under the indigo sky the women danced in circles, in rows, their hands twisting and clapping, their cries flying up to the brilliant stars, while the drums beat and beat. And from the watching, clapping crowds, first one woman and then another would slip out and join them, and then a man, and another man, the red light glistening on their eyes and their teeth and on the gold on their arms. Someone tugged Nicholas.

Already a group of the King's wives had joined the performers, one or two alone, one or two with a white man drawn by the hand. The girl who fetched him to his feet was the one who had pressed behind him in the tent, whose tongue had touched his ear and his neck and whose arching foot had played by his thigh. She was small, with lustrous eyes and a proud neck and inquisitive fingers pliant as candlewick. There was another girl, a little taller, who rose and came with her. He let them lead him into the dancing, heavy with the effort of present restraint; dizzy with the cavernous ache of a well-made, well-practised body long denied its habitual deliverance.

He had no idea how to copy their dancing, nor did it matter. The drumbeat throbbed through his veins; before and behind, the limbs and bodies of men and women pressed against him; he found the smaller girl leaping at his flank, his hand caught round her waist. Round his own waist were the arms of the other girl. His doublet was open, and his shirt. The fires flared; their shadows streamed and leaped over the grass; the noise of the drums drowned all speech and deadened all thought. He saw Vito, flushed, dishevelled, freeing the black, fulsome breasts of a girl perhaps four months with child, who laughed up at him as he sucked and caressed her. He glimpsed Fernão in the flickering dark, already halfway up the slope with a girl at his hip and another, laughing, carried in his stout shirt-sleeved arms. He saw Vicente, and what Vicente was doing.

He realised that abstinence was not only impossible, but that without warning he had reached a state of overwhelming necessity.

He could not speak. Unthinking, without effort it seemed, he found himself standing in the darkness under the trees, a girl's spread hands on his buttocks, his clothes swiftly wrested apart so that he could continue and conclude a function he did not remember beginning.

The relief – the shameful parallel could hardly be avoided – brought him to his knees. Then he realised that two girls had taken part, one promoting, one acting; and that both were close to him now, their arms wound about him, their fingers exploring his body while they giggled and chattered and laughed. And then a third joined them, wearing nothing now but her golden ornaments, although he recognised her face from the tent.

She laughed at him, and then, leaning over, opened his mouth and thrust her own tongue inside, while the other girls caressed them both, shrieking a little and sometimes slapping one another. The boneless creature with whom he had (definitively) coupled stroked his cheek and leaned back, her dark face enraptured; her body palpably keyed to the condition within which he also was suspended: pleased and soothed, alert and sharply receptive. He laughed at her softly and taking her fingers, kissed them. Upon which the others fell upon him, shrieking and biting and, pulling him up, ran him through the trees and up the slope to the great central guest-hut of the village.

It was not empty, but darkness concealed those who rolled on the straw with which it was strewn, and whose cries and creakings were audible. It seemed of little importance in the magnificent war in which he found himself; when a fourth girl joined him, hot as ginger, he laughed aloud and with a cheerful, a maniac zest charged into battle.

His life, oddly fashioned, had had little to do with bought love and none with orgiastic indulgence. Before the teaching years, the years of his training at the hands of aristocrat, princess, courtesan, he had discovered his own form of joy in the barns and attics and hedgerows of Bruges, with maids who had no expectations of marriage and who knew how to avoid trouble. He and they had made love, you might say, carelessly and freely as animals, except that animals were not moved by such exercise to affection, to compassion, to the benison of glorious laughter.

Since he was eighteen, he hadn't bedded a woman with laughter. He realised it just before dawn, and the girl beneath him – the third, the fourth, for they had changed, he well knew, all through the night – caressed him with her toes and her fingers and dried his damp eyes with her lips. And then, agile and cruel, witty and eager and inexorable, had brought in her reinforcements, and challenged his vigour again.

Gelis van Borselen, wakeful through the long night, watched the long troughs approach at first light with their sated, silent men. Her arms spread on the rail, she let pale Vicente go by, and tipsy Luis and fiery, half-quenched Vito. She saw Fernão miss his step, sleepily, on the ladder. She observed the child Lázaro plod on board, with his hectic face and brilliant, glittering eyes. She saw Godscalc confused, Jorge dazed, Diniz conscientious, and finally Nicholas, stepping from canoe to ladder with confidence, and from ladder to deck with positive triumph. Then he saw her, and clutched unexpectedly at the rail.

She began to laugh. When Bel of Cuthilgurdy strode to her side Gelis seized her for support and laughed harder. She said, 'Niccolino! What have they done to you?'

And Nicholas, rueful, happy, exhausted, broke into laughter as helpless as her own and said, 'Broken me. Don't laugh. My God, don't laugh. I don't think I can walk.'

'Would you like me to carry you?' said Gelis. 'What do you have in your hand?'

He looked down at the object. It was frail and white and peculiar. It was a bone.

'An aphrodisiac?' suggested Bel with some sourness.

He made a sound like an underground spring, examining it. 'It could be. I shan't pretend I should have refused it. But no. It was a present.'

'For services rendered?' It was Gelis.

He said, 'They thanked me in other ways.' His eyes, dark round the rims, shone pale and childishly bright in the dawn. He said, 'It was a present for you. A cat bone. It's hollow.'

She took it. He reeked of bed and women and happiness. It was a bone, and both ends were sealed. She opened one, and dust ran out into her palm. Yellow dust. She stopped it quickly and looked at him.

'For you,' Nicholas said. 'Unless you would like anything else.'

'How did you guess?' Gelis said. 'Come to my cabin.'

'Oh, my God,' Nicholas said; and, pushing himself off the rail, patted her on the shoulder as he passed and ruffled her hair with unforced, unthinking bonhomie. She heard him hit the wall as he wandered into his chamber. She was still standing looking after him when Bel moved her out of the way.

Chapter 22

IT WAS GODSCALC who, to universal stupefaction, declared that they must next call on the King Bati Mansa, four days' sail further on up the river.

He knew, of course, what had happened. So much was obvious during the interminable Mass held in the clearing before their departure and attended by all the ship's complement able to walk, as well as by eight hundred Mandinguas and Henry Mansa, wearing his spectacles.

The King smiled all through the service and so did his pretty young wives, who also wriggled and whispered. Saloum and the robed elders were absent but the leopard attended, and Jorge da Silves whose hooded glare showed much the same ferocity. The seven culprits stood with the rest, smelling remarkably of brackish water and weed, while Father Godscalc spoke, but not too loudly, and held his missal to protect his eyes from the excruciating white to which his vestments had been bleached. Nicholas hung his head.

His punishment occurred later, on board, when the decks had been cleared of apes, parakeets and three warthogs, assorted cages of poultry and a goat, together with a generous cargo of legless provender and some merchandise. Then, when Tendeba had vanished, and the ship was negotiating the first of the several difficult bends in the next thirty-mile stage of her voyage, Father Godscalc summoned Nicholas to his chamber.

The bulkhead muffled the words of the ensuing tirade more than the crew would have liked, but it was apparent that Nicholas had little to say, and that the little was soon swept aside. When he emerged after twenty minutes, looking serious, those on deck had had sufficient warning to scatter and busy themselves, and took care not to look round when he climbed aft and strolled to talk to the helmsman. Bel of Cuthilgurdy banged on the door he had left and opening it, pushed it shut with her shoulder. Then she crossed to Godscalc's table and dumped down a basket. In it was a flask, a cup which she filled, and a dish containing a comb of wild honey.

He was seated, his knees apart, his crucifix in his hands. 'To sweeten my temper,' he said. His large-boned face with its wiry black hair was sallow.

'The only thing wrong with your temper,' said Bel of Cuthilgurdy, 'is that ye should have lost it with that one long ago. Ye let him play with you. Ye let him play with you because you're convinced he's a prodigy. He's twenty years younger than you are.'

'I am aware of it,' Godscalc said. 'And has taken no vows.' He paused. He said, 'He knows I envy him.' He stopped again, and said, 'My only hope is that I think – sometimes I know – that he envies me.'

There was a silence. Bel said, 'None the less, ye had the right of it, surely. There were youngsters to think of. And fornication is not a general rule of the Church, even though it seemed natural enough to the King, and he may take more kindly to the Trinity for finding us so heartily equipped with good taste. Forbye, ye couldna have stopped it, even if ye'd had a heid for their drink.'

He groaned, and she pushed the cup of herbs towards him until he lifted it and drank and then set it down and covered his face. She wondered if he had seen Diniz that morning, and assessed his state of sparkling, expansive delight. She wondered if he had noted Lázaro's manner greeting Filipe: not conceited or scathing but comradely, like that of the other seamen; like a man with nothing to prove. She wondered if he had heard the obscenity with which Filipe had rebuffed his former idol. She understood, as well as Godscalc, the terrible dilemma inseparable from any man's dealings with Nicholas. She said, 'How did he take it?'

'He was respectful,' Godscalc said. 'And made no excuses. So now I find myself making them for him. It was a travesty of a mission: his part, if you like, was at least honest.'

'But ye hope for more from Bati Mansa the pagan? Father,' said Bel, 'ye can't need me to remind you. This particular man may loathe Christians. The *Fortado* will have put him against us. And if ye mean to take another party on land, you'll have to peg down the crew who missed the rut at Tendeba, or they'll storm ashore and surprise the King's wives whether they're tendered or not. Is it worth it?'

'Nicholas has agreed,' Godscalc said. 'And Jorge da Silves.'

'No doubt. And that ends it?' said Bel.

'No,' said Godscalc. 'I have decided, and that ends it. And this time, I want you and the demoiselle to come with us. Unless she is too shaken.'

Bel reflected. She said, 'No. Ye have to remember she's not your sheltered flower, and has van Borselen cousins. Paul's a devil already, and Charles showed his prowess well enough at Louvain before he died at thirteen. Nothing much can shock Gelis.'

She stopped too late: he was already looking at her with dismay and clutching his glum medicinal cup. She regretted, in her practical fashion, that she hadn't simply brought him another flask of palm wine.

Godscalc of Cologne was a priest who did not understand women, whereas Nicholas of nowhere in particular was a banker who did. His hilarious reception by Gelis had been fully appreciated for exactly what it was. For a space – a timeless portion of a strange African dawn – Nicholas had just been a man, to be teased and tolerated and even liked for his weaknesses. Of course, he had not come near her since, and she had not laughed with or at him.

In general, the escapade at Tendeba didn't prove as divisive as the wise among them might have feared. Although his elders from the *Ciaretti* might chaff red-haired Vito, neither Melchiorre the second mate nor his fellow seaman Manoli resented his luck. The two helmsmen were content to jeer at Fernão's account of his conquests while Vicente, the short-tempered *comito*, was neither laughed at nor envied. Diniz, in between cherishing his three remaining lean horses, preserved – hugged to himself – a well-bred Scotto-Portuguese reticence. He did, however, regard Nicholas with a new light in his eye.

The only unrest noted by Bel, aiding Godscalc with the sick men below, was provoked by the genial (and clinically improbable) recitals of Luis, which his fellow seamen both demanded and heard in a mood of lubricious jealousy. And above deck, observed by Gelis herself, there hung a constraint which, even through the vivid terrors and delights of the voyage, could be traced to the master, and to his relations with Nicholas and the three Negroes, but more especially with Lopez.

It was understandable, and vander Poele recognised it, she perceived. As a consequence, or so she thought, he passed little time in the company of Lopez in the days after Tendeba. On the other hand, the conversations he did hold with Lopez were so superficial, so markedly impersonal, that Gelis refined and revised her conclusion. It was not Jorge da Silves but the Negro himself who was vander Poele's prime and almost exclusive concern.

They sailed for three days and passed three nights at anchor without molestation, but in increasing heat. For the first part of the voyage, the canoes of Gnumi Mansa accompanied them, paddled by shouting, laughing young men. Word of their harmlessness seemed to have restored the usual traffic of the river: troughs of varying sizes passed and repassed, sometimes laden with provender; sometimes bearing a group of chattering women and children with their bundles.

The trees, the green, dripping tunnels of choked and mysterious creeks, the looming mangroves, their roots slippered with oysters, began to thin and pale as the estuarine flush fell behind them. Instead, on either side was bush and rolling savannah studded by cabins, and they saw ape-watch towers stamped like runes on the red of the sunset; stamped like runes, or the windmills of Flanders.

On the second morning, they viewed their first elephants: a group of grey beasts in the shallows, each as wide as a siege-engine and as high as the ship, and spraying water upon themselves from the tail suspended under their eyes. The following day, Saloum pointed over the water to the boulder-like heads and piggish ears of submerged water-horses: he said they could upset a canoe, and that oarsmen warned them off by rapping their boats with their blades.

Navigation of the narrowing river, with its bends and its shoals and its islands, kept them sufficiently occupied; and the evening landings for food and fodder, through mud and gnats and lurking dangers from beast and from man, taught them to depend on each other. At Cantor, more than one hundred and forty miles from the mouth of the Gambia, one of the sick seamen died, and they went ashore, a solemn and united company, to bury him.

The market of Cantor was as far up this river as Diogo Gomes had travelled; here he had obtained gold, and here he had been told of the caravan routes to the Sahara and to the east which in season met on this spot. The settlement still existed, and the traders, but there were no Christians among them to share in the service, nor any who wished to listen to Godscalc, and the sheds and warehouses were empty, swept clean as elsewhere by the *Fortado*.

'She is upriver,' said Loppe, on their return to the ship. 'Two days from here, at the place of the baboons, is how they describe it. They say they distrust her, and believe she will employ any force or ruse to find out and carry back the secret of the gold.'

Twenty miles beyond, gossip also informed them, the King Bati Mansa might currently be found. And two days' sail beyond that was the rock barrier and the falls beyond which neither caravel could penetrate, and the way (three hundred leagues to the east, rumour insisted) to the kingdom of the lord they called Preste João.

'So here are the choices,' Nicholas said, perched on the after-deck with twenty-seven fit men and two women around him. 'We may leave the ship here, with a guard, and set out east on foot, avoiding the King and the *Fortado*. Or we may continue to sail to where Bati Mansa lies between us and Doria, trusting to the *Fortado*'s ill reputation and our success with Gnumi Mansa to encourage the King to make us welcome. Or thirdly, we may sail past Bati Mansa without putting his goodwill to the test and proceed as far upriver as we can.'

Loppe's voice, responding, clashed with that of Jorge da Silves. Remarkably, they both said the same thing. The master spoke first, and Loppe elaborated.

'We should sail to Bati Mansa. It isn't true that Ethiopia is so near. To set out so early on foot would waste our time and our energy. Also, Senhor da Silves and Father Godscalc must be permitted to take the cross to this King, who may protect us from Doria. Threats were made at the Senagana with good cause. Doria has pride, and we tricked and shamed him with the gold and the *Ghost*.'

'We have cannon,' Nicholas said. 'And he has a full cargo. Will he risk an attack at suicidal close quarters, with nothing to gain?'

'That was,' said Gelis van Borselen, 'the received wisdom on the *Ghost*, as I remember. Just before Signor Doria turned his guns on us. He seems to be touchy.'

'Forbye, if he's full and finished his business, why is he waiting?' said Bel of Cuthilgurdy.

'To see where we go,' said the master. 'Or so I believe.'

'In which case,' Nicholas said, 'he's unlikely to harm us. He may even mean to sit where he is, and waylay us when we come back. So what do we do? We've heard nothing from Bati Mansa but surely, like Gnumi, he wants to court Portugal. I think as Lopez does – we should keep to the water. We have arms. We can reply if we're threatened by Bati. By the same token, we can deal with the *Fortado* if we have to. She may not fire. We might even manage to persuade her to leave.'

'How?' said Diniz.

'There are ways,' Nicholas said. 'We could invite the crew to listen to Luis. And if they don't go, we've still made provision. We disembark the horses. Our special boats can be carried. Once past the rock at the falls, we can take to the water again and outstrip anyone who wants to follow us. And when the Gambia peters out, we can make a portage to the Joliba, and the great lake everyone speaks of which leads to the east. Does that seem reasonable?'

'Not,' said Gelis, 'if you pass Ethiopia on the way. Who says it's more than three hundred leagues off?'

'I do,' said Saloum, his bearded face solemn. 'It is much more. Beyond a great river. Beyond the great lake. This I swear you.'

'There by Lent,' said Gelis to Nicholas. 'What do you wager? Lent by the River of Gems and the Fountain of Youth and the Copts.'

'I never wager on certainties,' Nicholas said.

It was a short meeting, and they might as well never have held it. That night, the drumming was loud and peculiarly insistent and the next day, when they crept round the deep bend of the river, clogged with treacherous islands, they found they were without escort or company. The casual water traffic had ceased, and they were alone but for the long, lazy shapes, fifteen feet long, of the giant lizards that watched from the banks. When, twice, they had to bring round the boats and tow the ship by the head, Jorge placed among the rowers four men with crossbows and hackbuts who kept their eyes partly on the water and partly on either bank. They had brought on deck all their arms, lightly covered with sailcloth, and the cannon were already in place, although blanketed too. As yet, they wore no armour.

There was a great deal of noise. The first holms they passed were full of the chatter and screams of baboons, and the fields and villages were a cacophony of birds attracted by the aftermath of the harvest. Clouds of chaff drifted over the ship, light as moths, lighter than the sand of the open sea: the spacious, salt-scoured, safe open sea. They heard elephants trumpeting, and hunting beasts roar.

By early afternoon they knew they were close to the massive island, six miles long and more than two miles across, which occupied that part of the river where Bati Mansa currently was holding his court. The river on either side, Saloum said, was at least a hundred yards wide but narrowed by drying mud-channels. Midway along the north side of the island was an anchorage. He would not trust the caravel anywhere else, Saloum said, overnight.

'We shall see,' said Jorge da Silves. 'And on which bank do you expect the King to be settled?'

'On either,' Saloum said cheerfully. 'Or on the island. It is in the hands of . . . of . . .'

'The Lord God,' said Lopez gravely. 'Or of Bati Mansa, if my sight serves me well. Or are these breakers ahead?'

It might have been surfing waves over rocks. It might have been the froth beneath a line of felled and jostling timber, but it was not. On either side of the island ahead the river was blocked by a flotilla of war-canoes. They lay in the afternoon haze, glimmering white from the dress of the oarsmen and suffused with the sparkle of metal. Vicente said, 'Senhor Jorge? Do we fire?'

'No!' said Godscalc.

'Not yet,' Nicholas said. 'I see a canoe coming this way. Bring the *Niccolò* round. Let them parley.'

'Poison arrows?' said Vicente.

'Perhaps,' Nicholas said. 'But I think they would have shot them already. I shall speak to them, with Lopez.'

No one disputed the privilege. The canoe approached, and it was seen that its double line of black, white-capped oarsmen were without weapons and smiling, and stood knee-deep in gifts, ranging from a pack of fine hyena hides to a great elephant tooth that took four men to heft up to the *Niccolò*. Then the two dozen men came on board themselves, shy and eager and anxious to reply to Loppe's questions. The King Bati Mansa had heard that the esteemed Portuguese lords wished to trade in his region, and would lead them to safe anchorage, and invite their presence at his palace on the island.

'Palace?' said Gelis.

'Something with a roof to it,' said Bel. 'And guards outside, to keep off the lions. Same as everywhere.'

'Has he any wives?' piped Filipe, adding, in Portuguese, a number of brazen specifics.

He was going ashore. Twenty-three of them were, since this time good management seemed to suggest a large landing-party. Of the nine who remained on the *San Niccolò*, Vicente was chosen to hold the command, with Melchiorre to act as his deputy. It meant that at worst they could sail, since two helmsmen were also aboard: the same solid family men who had preferred not to go on shore at Tendeba. To work the ship they had a couple of seamen, weak but recovering, and two more – Luis and Lázaro – who were altogether too healthy for shore-leave. And last of all, they had Lopez.

It had not been part of the plan. As chief interpreter, if nothing else, he had been a constituent of every mission. It was Jorge da Silves who proposed otherwise. Lopez should be left to stand by Vicente, who spoke no Mandingua. On land, they could employ the other blacks, who had made such an impression on Gnumi.

Nicholas had hesitated. When Lopez, without hesitating, had politely demurred, the master developed such vehemence that Nicholas, intervening quickly, gave way. Saloum and Ahmad would manage.

The island was low-lying and smelt of the river. Stepping ashore with Bel at her side, Gelis saw nothing but a village of hovels, poorer than Cantor, where the river-folk came to exchange produce. She stood with Godscalc and Diniz while one of the long escorting canoes landed its emissaries. Around her she counted fifteen men from the *Niccolò*, including Fernão and Vito and young Filipe, and ahead of them, Jorge da Silves and Nicholas with the former slaves. The canoeists, landed, walked ahead and signed to them to follow. They were still smiling and weaponless, and set up a cheerful chant as they went, clapping their hands and occasionally leaping. When she walked, the ground swayed up and down.

Godscalc said, 'It is God's blessing. God is with us.' Jorge da Silves crossed himself but vander Poele didn't. He was looking about at the trees and the bushes and his face was ruddy with heat. So was that of Diniz. Both were wearing shirt, doublet, hose, cap and cloak.

Gelis said, 'Let me guess. He's carrying the forecastle mortar, and you've got the balls in your jacket?'

'More or less,' Diniz said. His gaze, rapt and intent, was on Nicholas.

Both women saw it. 'Ye'll not wean him now,' said Bel dryly.

It was a long walk. After half an hour in the heat they were stopped and led to a place in the shade where refreshments had been prepared. They were given fruit and juice and bread baked in the sun. Three of their escort went off hunting and came back with some birds. Saloum, who had gone with them, returned laughing and sat to deliver a broken-tongued bulletin. 'We shall reach the palace in another half-hour. They prepare a feast for us. They say the King is a great man, and generous, and loves horses beyond anything.'

'Hell and damnation,' said Diniz. 'Don't we have another tent?'

'We could give him a warthog,' said Nicholas. 'Do you think we could get them to hurry? I don't want to come back this way in the dark.'

In the end, the place they came to, although far inside the island, was not unlike Gnumi Mansa's riverside clearing, except that there was no village near it, nor any provision for water or ovens. The forest about it was thicker, and instead of a great central Baobab there stood a man-made hut without walls: a low henge of vertical tree-trunks, upon whose bare crooked forks rested a mighty domed roof made of millet-stalks. The airy arena below, sufficient for the congress of two hundred people, was currently being enjoyed by a small flock of goats. Otherwise, entering, they found it quite empty.

Nicholas walked round it once, with Saloum. He said, 'Ask them. Where is the King?' Before he fully reached the end of the sentence, he stopped and turned. Apart from Saloum and Ahmad, there were only white faces inside the pillars. No flashing smiles and white caps. No black, assiduous figures racing up to inform, to reassure. The grass before the hut was quite empty. The escort had gone. There was no one for Saloum to ask.

There was someone. There was a voice declaiming outside; a sonorous voice, employing superb Italian.

'I very much fear,' said Raffaelo Doria, strolling heavily across from the trees, 'that the lord Bati Mansa is unavailable. Perhaps I may be allowed to entertain you instead? Demoiselle. Mistress Bel. Senhor Vasquez. How very happy I am to catch up with you.'

He wore a half-suit of armour, and there were fifteen armed men in mail at his back. Bel of Cuthilgurdy dropped a slight curtsey and Gelis, when prodded, did likewise. Dear oh dear, thought Mistress Bel. Dear oh dear, *shellfish*.

No one spoke. Jorge looked like a killer snake faced with another. Nicholas, his face bland as a pat of butter, said, 'Signor Doria, you may always be sure of entertaining us. And, of course, may be further assured we shall cause you no trouble. Senhor da Silves, gentlemen, *no trouble, d'you hear?*'

The last words, spoken as quietly as the first, were in Portuguese; and as he said them he walked slowly forward, blocking Bel's view. She realised why he was blocking her view, and felt queasy.

'That is wise,' said Doria. 'The ladies may sit. There are mats. Did you receive some refreshments? I have sent for more. Messer Niccolò, you will remove your cloak very slowly and unbuckle and drop whatever weapons you carry below it. Senhor da Silves the same; and then all the rest of you. Then they will be collected, and you will be searched. As you see, there are fifteen crossbows trained upon you.'

Nicholas said, 'No, padre.'

'But yes,' said Godscalc, walking up to Doria and dumping a box before him. Bel wondered, not for the first time, why he had chosen the Church, and not made use of his build, his ability, his muddled belligerence to serve as a happy warrior in some freebooting troop. And Doria, with his firm, meaty face and machicolated teeth, looked less the Caesar than the hard-headed trader he probably was. But the sword at his side was real enough.

Godscalc opened the box. 'Perhaps you wish to search that for arms? I came here to celebrate Mass before the black heathen. Why are you, a Christian, preventing it?'

'Why did your friends, supposedly Christian, fire on the *Fortado*?' said Doria. 'And from the stolen ship of my dead cousin? Why did you cheat and lie at the Senagana, employing even your ladies to rob us of trade? I brought you here; there is no question of Mass – the King has his own mumbo-jumbo and would not listen. I brought you here because I wished to express my disappointment. And you will agree that I have not been unduly cautious. You come oddly prepared for the sacrament.'

'I knew nothing of this,' said Father Godscalc. The hidden arms, rattling down, formed a buckled pile at the feet of every man from the *Niccolò* with the exception of Saloum and Ahmad. Nicholas, if not bearing the forecastle mortar, had been fortified with a small Turkish bow and a quiver and a very handy short sword, all now in an untidy heap slightly behind him. Three of Doria's searchers began to move forward.

'Goats,' said Nicholas shortly, in Flemish.

Behind him, plump on the floor beside Gelis, Bel stared at his back. Behind him, the previous occupants of the compound, uneasily cornered, sniffed the foreign smells and eyed the butchers' knives on the ground. The leader, a great beast with curled horns, suddenly squealed at the top of his voice, leaped straight into the roof, and then bolted. Gelis withdrew her pin. The rest followed.

Dust rose. The heaps of arms tumbled with the vibration. Bel braced herself for attack: for the clash of swords and the thud of arrows as Nicholas and the rest snatched their weapons.

They did not snatch their weapons. Nothing happened because Doria's crossbowmen stood firm, their bows already stretched, their barbs levelled. A charge by Nicholas, whatever its outcome, would have cost the lives of some of his party. And Nicholas had preferred not to make it.

The three soldiers, stepping forward, resumed their uplift of arms. Hemp was brought, in great coils. The seamen were tied hand and foot. Nothing had happened, except that Doria's men, now cackling, had been given a fright. Nothing, except that Gelis, she saw, now had two knives inside her chemise and a quiver lodged between that and her tunic. And the object she was thrusting towards Bel was a bow.

As it chanced, Bel had already come well provided with helpful objects matched to her contours and headgear. Reassembled, she settled back in a sitting position. 'Och, och,' she remarked. 'It near gars ye wish that they'd try for a rape. What next, d'ye think?'

What came next, irrelevantly, was a supper, brought in baskets and spread on the floor for their captors. Perhaps they were hungry. They took it in turns, Bel observed, to eat and stand guard: two in front and the rest spaced outside round the pillars. Doria, reclining at ease, invited Nicholas to share his meal, sitting opposite, and then thought to make room for the ladies, and finally for Godscalc and Jorge and Diniz. He wanted, she thought, to humiliate Jorge in particular. Doria's men kept peering at Gelis, who smiled back at them from time to time. Bel hoped she knew what she was doing. She could hear Filipe, whining.

She stirred a finger in a few dishes but felt no compulsion to eat.

She envied the rest of the party, including Filipe, who had not been invited – who, indeed, would have been a puzzle to feed since the seamen had been left, tied and stripped to the waist, where the goats had been. There was, as before, nothing to be done; nothing, yet, that was worth risking lives for. Outside, shadows crawled on the brilliant grass, black as predators, and above the trees, the first pallid stars were just visible. Nothing quite yet.

Doria's crew still wore their jacks and their helmets. Beside them, the *Niccolò*'s men looked like peasants: bare of head, and reduced – even the priest – to gaping shirts over their hose. No one had suggested that the ladies should disrobe, which was as well. Which was, Bel understood, what Nicholas had intended.

She let her gaze dwell on him, and then wander over Diniz. The lad had filled out better than you would have expected. She could imagine, without looking further than the two of them, what King Gnumi's wives had also imagined. She glanced at Gelis, and had the impression that Gelis had recently directed her gaze somewhere else. She had the further impression that Jorge da Silves had seen it and was scowling. On the other hand, he had been scowling ever since they arrived, either upon Nicholas or upon Saloum and Ahmad.

Two lamps had been brought, warming the underside of the corn roof to chestnut. Outside, something screamed in the bushes. Inside, Nicholas, dabbling in rice, was placidly clarifying the situation. He said to Doria, 'So you bribed the King to stay away?'

'It wasn't difficult,' Doria said, a bone between his ringed hands. 'We had, through your kind intervention, this large bale of weapons to offer him. He has a great deal of hunting to do, and has told his young men that they may amuse themselves as they like in his absence. They don't like gold robbers or spies.'

'They can't afford to harm us,' Nicholas said. 'Whatever you tell them.' He sounded quite calm. Diniz sat like a man under orders, and da Silves like a man rebelling against them. Father Godscalc, his eyes lifted, might have been praying or chewing.

'I'm afraid they'll get the blame, none the less,' Doria said. Gelis drew in her breath. The two lamps burned in the silence. Outside, it was black.

Nicholas said, 'Were your orders to exterminate us? It seems a little unpolished for the Vatachino. What you promised the others I don't know.' Underlit, his eyes might have been pursed with laughter. It was a face fixed in the mould of frivolity. Bel had seen others like it, some of them dead.

'I always make the same promise,' said Doria. 'To bring back the largest profit they have ever known. As a result, I am rich.'

'What did Simon de St Pol ask you to do?' Diniz said.

Godscalc turned his head. Gelis didn't move. Raffaelo Doria looked at the boy. He said, 'I never discuss who my clients are.'

'We know who they are,' Diniz said. 'The Lomellini, the Vatachino and St Pol. What did St Pol ask you to do?'

'Why?' said Doria. Reclining on one elbow, he had nibbled half down the bone.

'He was my father's partner. He sold his half of the business to the Vatachino. He wants my half.'

'And so he might want your death, you think? And perhaps Messer Niccolò, as his business rival – as everyone's business rival – is also feeling vulnerable?'

'I generally do,' Nicholas said. He stopped kneading and sat back to study the Genoese. He said, 'I don't think you have orders to kill us. I think you've decided to do it from pique. You'll blame the Mandinguas. And if that doesn't stick, you'll blame your patrons. Would I be right?'

'You flatter my patrons,' said Doria. He put down the bone and, drawing a kerchief, wiped his hands slowly. 'Some wine? You may drink it with confidence. You are one of the two persons who are going to survive this little adventure.'

'What? What, you scoundrel?' said Godscalc. Diniz gripped his arm, but he was staring.

'Who is the other person?' Nicholas said. His voice had flattened.

'Ask Saloum,' Doria said. 'Is that what you call him? Or his Negro companion. They conducted you here, to get you away from the ship.'

'*Away from the ship!*' It was Jorge da Silves.

'Oh, the *San Niccolò*, I am sure, is in perfect order,' Doria said. 'A little emptier, perhaps, than you left her. As you must have expected, your other dark gentleman, your travelled gentleman, your Lopez has joined us.'

Chapter 23

THE CICADAS SHRILLED in the invisible grass. A bird flew over the guest-hut, complaining. Somewhere, as always, drums were beating.

A pulse was ticking, too, above the damp lawn of the shirt Nicholas was wearing. He said, 'No.'

'Go to the ship,' Doria said. 'You will find your Lopez has gone.'

'You have taken him,' Nicholas said. He hadn't moved, but he seemed to have solidified, sitting hunched opposite Doria. His brow was striped with sweat released from the crooks and curls of his hair.

'I warned you,' ejaculated Jorge da Silves. 'Blackamoors, unbaptised and dyed in sin as black as their skins.'

'Be quiet,' said Nicholas. 'Saloum!'

Bound and prone beneath the threat of the crossbows, the men of his crew and the two slaves could hardly be seen in the dark. Saloum shifted his head. 'If Lopez has gone, he has been captured.'

'He elected to stay on the *Niccolò*,' said Jorge da Silves.

'It was your suggestion,' said Nicholas. 'So who has taken him? Has Crackbene? Where is Loppe?' The early name came by chance, Bel guessed, out of an unusual distraction.

'I told you,' said Doria. 'Lopez was loyal but you offered him nothing. I promised him he should have half of whatever the secret of Wangara was worth. He is with my people now, waiting to lead me there. And to make sure that he does, you are coming.'

'No,' said Nicholas again.

Godscalc looked at him. The look was full of alarm, as if a bear trained to caper had suddenly snarled. Gelis spoke under her breath and stretched out her hand. Slowly, Bel slipped the bow into it. Nicholas said, 'He will not take you to Wangara, whether I am there or not.'

'You would kill him first, or see that he was killed? I assumed as much. I assumed he had told you the secret,' said Raffaelo Doria. 'That is why you are coming. One of you might deceive me, but not both.'

Nicholas moved. It seemed to Bel that in the next moment she would see him hurl himself forward at Doria; it would have been, she thought, the first unpremeditated attack he had ever been seen to make. Doria, in fact, was expecting it: he was sitting back with his unsheathed sword in his hands, waiting to use it, while a glitter came from the line of raised bows all round the cabin.

Instead, quicker even than Nicholas, Godscalc jumped to his feet, stamping hard on the hand Nicholas had spread beside him as leverage and thrusting him, deliberately or not, to one side. 'How dare you!' Godscalc said to Doria. 'How dare you prate of gold, and threaten good men! If these poor people, the miners, wish to protect their livelihood, neither you nor we have any right to wrest its source from them. Neither would Lopez, I am sure, dream of doing such a thing, for himself or for us or for you. What is more –'

'He is giving us time,' murmured Gelis in Flemish. Her face contorted with fright, she pulled herself back from the supper circle and sat studiously shivering. 'Why?' Bel put her arm round her. Behind them, she thought she heard rustling. Doria was toying with his sword.

'– what is more, if you lose all chance of redemption by perpetrating what you seem to have in mind, you will suffer for it on this earth as well. *The pillars will fall about you, as strong men pull down your false edifice.* And do not think you can blame the Mandinguas. Men will come. They will find crossbow bolts in our bodies.' In his vehemence, he had delivered part of his harangue in Flemish, as Nicholas had already done.

'They may even find lead balls from new handguns,' Doria said. 'For it seems that some vile trader has recently armed the Mandinguas. Bati Mansa will hang, and Gnumi Mansa will take over his territory. What could be neater?'

He rose to his feet and stood breathing strongly, a little grease on his chin, his naked swordpoint teasing the priest's matted chest. Godscalc clenched his fists. Nicholas, sitting limply, appeared to be looking up at them both. In fact, Bel observed, his gaze was focused prayerfully rather above them. She heard herself make a sound, and Gelis looked at her. Raffaelo Doria scratched with the point of his sword, lightly, and then turned the blade towards Nicholas.

'I think it is time. Get up. Walk out. And we'll have no more Flemish.'

'All of us,' Nicholas said. It was between a plea and a statement.

'You. Of your own will, or not. They have their orders not to kill you. You might find yourself with one arm.'

Doria's men ringed the hut, rope in their hands. The seamen from the *San Niccolò* and the two slaves lay in the corner. 'The women?' said Nicholas. He got up suddenly, unfolding the neat-jointed, powerful frame, so at odds with the comedian's face. Godscalc watched him, visibly anguished. Diniz stood as well, but quietly, as a young brother might. All through the voyage they had been at odds, these three. Only now, her mind busy, did Bel see confirmed the truth of it. And the dawning horror on the face of Jorge da Silves.

'Everyone will stay,' said Doria. 'Everyone but you. Out. And no Flemish.'

'No,' Nicholas agreed. Side by side with Doria, he walked to the edge of the hut, about to leave; about to abandon them all. At the very last he turned, the light from the two lamps bright on his unconcerned face. He said caressingly, 'Date stones.'

Doria took it, perhaps, for an obscenity. Gelis lifted her fist. The nearest lamp shot spinning over the carpet and overturning into the dirt floor, extinguished itself. Sprawling full length, she got a grip of the other and smothered it. Darkness fell in two stages. Doria's sword flashed, and the swords of his men, their bows useless. Where Nicholas had been was the paler black of outdoors, and the sound of his voice, and the sound of Diniz, replying, taken up by many voices.

Bel, rising, found herself buffeted by many bodies, some mailed and some not. The space under the millet was filled with shouting and the thudding of feet; with the clash of steel and the smack of flesh meeting flesh; with grunts of endeavour and anger. Someone screamed. Someone fell. She felt her arm grasped and realised that she was being dragged running out of the hut along with Gelis: Godscalc's voice in her ear said, 'Stay there.' She slid on the grass, and saw his big shape in the faint starlight, running back to the hut. She heard Diniz shouting somewhere and voices replying: gasping voices from outside the hut where figures struggled, some dimly sparkling with mail, others shirted.

The crew. The crew somehow were free, and slowly pushing Doria's men inside the building. The clash of arms became muffled. She heard the voice of Nicholas, calling names, and being answered. Then she saw, a blur in the darkness, that between the encircling pillars every figure was white: the building was ringed by linked men as by chain. Then Nicholas shouted.

'Heave!' he yelled.

Afterwards, Bel thought she had heard the panting groans of endeavour, the stamping feet, the first creaking and grinding, the startled screams of apprehension. At the time, she was aware of little but the immense shock of the crash: of the rumbling roar of thirty trees tumbling and bouncing and blundering against one another; of a forest felled, and slamming all that once stood or lay under it. The pillars, pulled inwards, collapsed. And upon them descended their cap; fell, with an encompassing thud, the mighty tiered roundel of millet, with Doria's men pinned down beneath it.

Silence followed. Bel panted. Not far away, several men started to cough; and the same sound, but fainter and mixed with muffled shouting and moans, began to emerge from under the dome of the roof. Sharply, the roof itself broke into sound, became a buzzing, squealing, rustling city of frantic wildlife. Birds whirred. Something swarmed over the tail of Bel's skirt, and she heard Gelis exclaim.

Bel of Cuthilgurdy sat up and, groping within the arsenal of her shift, pulled out a tinder-box and made a torch of her kerchief.

Gelis was standing beside her. Diniz, a stick in either hand, was running howling towards her through rushing streams of brown rats. Behind him, a pair of feet were advancing which she took to belong to da Silves, behind that were many more legs and feet whose upper parts were wholly concealed by a deep, powdery cloud of dirty saffron which arched over the clearing and rose into the indigo air until it expired in faint columns of verdigris.

The legs were running forward, bringing their owners out of the blanket of chaff, and the coughing and wheezing, now tremendous, had become charged with whoops of what appeared to be excitement and triumph – indeed, both emotions were plain on the battered faces that now emerged into the clear. The rodents proceeded to vanish.

Diniz said, 'They meant to do that to us. Did you see? They'd weakened all of the pillars, and connected them with the rope. Saloum saved us. Saloum and Nicholas. Saloum had a knife in his hair. He freed the crew and they dragged the soldiers inside. Oh glory be, did you *see*?'

'Is anyone hurt?' Gelis said.

'Oh yes,' said Diniz madly, 'but we're all out. Here he is. Here's Nicholas. It was Godscalc who warned us, you know.'

'And Gelis who put out the lamps,' Nicholas said. 'Three to be carried: Diniz, go and help Jorge. Saloum says every man needs a torch. We form a column, the wounded in the centre, Saloum in front and Ahmad in the rear: they both know the way back to the ship. What weapons do we have?'

What they had concealed or picked up were distributed. Da Silves said, 'The men under the roof?'

'They can breathe,' Nicholas said. 'They'll cut their way out in time. I want to get to the anchorage.'

'Why leave it to chance?' said Jorge da Silves, and lifted his torch.

A vast hand closed on his arm. 'What?' said Godscalc. 'Are you no better than the Genoese brute inside there? Throw that torch and I'll have your head off your neck – you and any other who tries it.'

No one set fire to the thatch. No one knew, either, the condition of the men under it: how many might have taken the weight of the rim; how many lay with limbs snapped below the tumbling trunks. A fate meant for themselves, and devised, as Nicholas had already said, wholly from injured vanity.

They would be released by the morning, or sooner. They would be alive, all or most of Doria's men. Alive and beaten and vicious, and free by the morning, or sooner. Trudging in the midst of the hastening column, Bel found herself shivering. Then she found Filipe beside her, teeth chattering, and asked him to hold her hand tightly.

They couldn't hurry enough to suit Nicholas. The journey from the ship had taken an hour, even omitting their rest-time. Now, returning, Nicholas allowed them no rest, but despite his merciless harrying the uneven ground and the darkness and their weariness made them slow. Twice, they were stalked by glowing green eyes, and were made to chant, and bang sticks, and wave their flaring brands. Halfway there, hoarse with goading, Nicholas fetched Ahmad to the head of the troop beside Jorge and, taking Saloum, set off at a lope into the darkness. Diniz, attempting to follow, was turned back by a voice sharp as a blow. He obeyed. The wounded had to be guarded.

What they would find ahead, no one knew. The crew talked, in gasps, among themselves. That old Genoese bastard, he was lying. The black, Lopez, was a reasonable fellow. He'd never cross sides. And if he didn't want to, how could a few sailors capture him? Vicente was on board, with the cannon, the handguns, the crossbows. If, of course, he hadn't turned about and sailed off to safety.

Silence followed that, for a while.

Jorge da Silves, applied to, said that if any man sailed off and stranded him, he'd have his liver. And if the black had gone, there were other interpreters. The fellow Saloum knew his way about.

The fellow Saloum, said someone, sotto voce, had led them all, hadn't he, right into this trap? The fellow Saloum was likely working for the *Fortado*, and would knock young Niccolino on the head first go off, and drag him back to the Genoese. If the Genoese hadn't got killed by the roof, which he deserved. The master had had the right idea: burn them to cinders. Talking of Nicholas, the general tone was a blend of kindliness, admiration, and a judicious awareness of the prejudices of Jorge da Silves and his cronies.

A little later, they fell to reminding one another about King Bati's men in the canoes. Scores of heathen blackamoors waiting about in canoes, fully armed with the *Fortado*'s consignment. Filipe called out a phrase he knew fitted blackamoors, and Fernão cuffed him. Godscalc said, 'We have no alternative. These murderous men are behind us. We must go on, and pray to God, and trust to our patron. If vander Poele has taken Saloum, then he has no doubts of his loyalty.'

'I should think,' Gelis said, 'that is probably true.'

At midnight, Ahmad spoke stiltedly. 'We shall soon be in sight of the anchorage. Does my lord wish to put out the brands?'

'No,' said da Silves. 'The main party will stay here, the brands lit. You will lead me in the dark to the anchorage. I trust you, but I have a knife, you understand?'

The Mandingua smiled and nodded, and then saw the knife and nodded again, but uncertainly. Godscalc said, 'Will you signal?'

'One whistle for *Come*,' da Silves said. 'If you hear two, hide yourselves. I shall find you if I can.'

This time, no one spoke. They sat or lay where they had stood. The wounded men, one with a smashed leg, the others with split ribs and a bloody, half-severed hand, groaned and whimpered. The burning wood crackled. The voice of the bush began to make itself heard again: the shrilling insects, the twitter and screeching of birds, the bark of a jackal and the belly-grumble of an irritated animal, drowsy with food. Their torches eddied and flinched in strange currents, and streamed sideways as something heavy passed overhead: an ape, the flame bright in his eye. A high, thin sound came from the darkness ahead. It was not repeated.

'The whistle!' said Diniz. He jumped to his feet. So did Gelis.

'Or a bird,' said someone on the ground. 'A damned bird. Or a lure.'

'Well, we'll never know, will we?' said Diniz. 'Unless we try.'

You could be jumping with fear, thought Bel of Cuthilgurdy, and still be struck to the soul by the great, jocund stars that shone now upon them, and the clarity of the high-sailing moon against which the stems and fronds of the trees were like fine Lucca velvet on silver. The water beyond ran thin rippled satin.

She could hear the Gambia flowing. She could hear no other sound: not the splash of paddles nor the hum of men's voices. Certainly not the boom or crackle of gunfire. With the rest, she beat out her torch, and padded forward into the moonlight.

The stretch of river opening before them was empty. It unreeled its emptiness as they pushed past the last trees and walked through the trampled dust of the trading-place and stood on the strand of the island, off which the *San Niccolò*, their pretty caravel, should have awaited them.

There was nothing there. Nothing in the anchorage, and nothing across the broad silvered expanse of the river, visible to the opposite shore. Then Gelis said, 'The boats. The special boats from the *Niccolò*.'

She had keen sight. The two boats, once towed at the rear of the *Niccolò*, lay upside down on the same strip of shore they were standing on, but far off down the river: so far that in the luminous glow from the sky they might have been river-horses, crouched and lowering. As they squinted, the distant figure of Jorge da Silves detached itself from the shadows and the solitary, mournful pipe of his whistle reached them again; in summons, not in warning. Ahmad stood beside him.

The boats had been destroyed. It was the first thing they saw, running over the mud. Buckled, battered and split, these portable barges would never carry them to the upper Gambia, and from the Joliba east to the River of Jewels. It had been done by many hatchets. Godscalc said, 'But where is the ship?' And Jorge da Silves pointed.

The swampy islet was yet further downstream by some distance, and the *Niccolò* had driven on it with some force, spinning round so that her bow had run high on the slime and the rest of her was tilted over, a third among bushes and the remainder still in her natural element. She glimmered, fragile as tortoiseshell in the misty, rippling light which touched, now and then, one or other of her three intact masts.

Nothing else stirred. She had come there by no error of navigation: her cable must have been cut; perhaps she had even been driven there. Godscalc said, 'The men? What sign of the men?'

'None,' said Jorge da Silves. Then he said, 'Someone is coming.'

They looked behind, expecting Doria. Then, as da Silves didn't turn, they followed his gaze to the caravel. A bark canoe had put off and was approaching; black as flotsam and poled by one man. They heard the splash as his blade touched the water, first on one side and then on the other. They didn't speak. He came nearer. They saw, bit by bit, that he was European, and bare-headed, and wearing a torn, open shirt black with bloodstains. They saw it was Nicholas.

Jorge da Silves began shouting, and Vito and Fernão and half the others. Bel didn't call. She'd put Ahmad and two of the crew to piling up firewood, and before the bark touched the mud, the stack was alight, and their shadows were running behind them. Nicholas lowered his oar, hesitated, and stepped heavily into the water, while others ran the boat up. Diniz ran up to him, but Jorge da Silves stayed, and Godscalc, and Gelis. Gelis had made no effort to help with the bonfire.

Nicholas stood and looked at Father Godscalc. He said, 'I have lost Melchiorre.'

His voice turned Bel cold. Diniz halted. Godscalc stepped forward and took Nicholas by the arm, drawing him to stand on the mud. His feet were bare and cut, but the blood on his shirt was not his own. Godscalc said, 'You saved everyone else.'

'No,' said Nicholas. 'I have lost Melchiorre. Will you search the beach? Who is fit? Diniz this way, with a brand, and you, Vito, go there.' His voice lost momentum. He added, 'Saloum is still on board.'

'And Lopez?' said Jorge da Silves. 'Shall we look for him, too?'

'I have looked already,' said Nicholas.

'Then come and sit by the fire,' Godscalc said. The wounded lay there already, and the others moved about nervously, looking at each other and at Jorge and Nicholas. Two fireflies far down each beach were the search parties, in quick counter-motion. Behind, the bush loomed and threatened.

Jorge da Silves said, 'Well, talk, man! Sit if you must, but for God's sake, tell us what happened! I have men here to think of.'

Godscalc lifted a large arm and pushed. Jorge staggered, and snatched at his scabbard. Gelis said, 'Listen.'

From far away, Diniz was calling. Nicholas woke from his trance. He was running before the rest started.

They had found Melchiorre. Melchiorre the Florentine second mate; the good, competent seaman who had sailed with Nicholas on the *Ciaretti*. He lay where the river had cast him, with a hackbut hole drilled through his back. Nicholas knelt by his head; Godscalc joined him, and Bel gave them light. The man gasped. Nicholas slipped a hand under his neck and, when the priest nodded, moved him a little, the soaked hair rolling into his hand.

Melchiorre opened his eyes. 'My lord, I'm sorry,' he said.

'It was my fault,' Nicholas said. 'Was it Bati's men?'

'Mostly. They have him.'

'Lopez?'

Melchiorre shut his eyes and opened them. He said, 'The *Fortado* has gone. Downstream. With Crackbene. The pinnace eastwards. With Lopez.'

'Don't talk,' Nicholas said.

Godscalc leaned forward, hands busy. 'I need my box from the ship.'

'I'll get it,' said Bel.

'No,' said Nicholas. He was easing Melchiorre free of his rags. 'Someone else.'

Godscalc stopped and looked up. He said, 'You've lost them all. You've lost them all, Nicholas?'

'No,' Nicholas said with great patience. 'They are all on the ship.'

They were, all of them, still on the *San Niccolò*. Estêvão was yet at the helm, cut down perhaps while trying to save her. The other helmsman had fallen defending him. The sick men had both been beheaded: one below, one by the hatch of the hold, a bloody knife in his hand. Vicente stood on the forecastle – stood, because arrows piercing his chest and his belly had transfixed him to the foremast. And below where his open eyes stared lay the heavy body of Luis, his whoring ended, his last story told, and his hand gripping the dead hand of Lázaro who lay, a slow-match quenched in blood at his side.

Bel found them when, flouting authority, she and Gelis arrived, with da Silves. Saloum helped her aboard. The blood, the splinters, the gougings were proof enough that Vicente's men had fought for their lives, but there were no enemy wounded or dead lying anywhere. They had been removed, along with all that a native would value.

The cabins and chests had been ransacked. The holds were empty, but for some barrels of water and pig lard. And the pens and stalls were deserted as well. All the livestock had gone, and the three precious horses, saved with such pains to carry them on the rest of their journey. All that remained were some random objects, dropped in haste or overlooked in their places of stowage, Godscalc's travelling box being among them. And, apart from her boats, the ship and her gear had been spared.

'They were Muslims like you,' Gelis said.

'Muslims,' said Saloum. 'But not like me.'

She said, 'This we know, for you saved us. You are wise. What are we to do? Melchiorre is alive. He says Lopez went with them.'

'They took Lopez,' said Saloum. 'The Genoese took him by force.'

'How do you know?' She was filthy; her face had the soiled sheen of soapstone.

'He expected it. He told me. He left a mark in the cabin.'

'Show me,' she said. Bel followed. It was a strange mark: cabalistic; drawn on the bulkhead in what was certainly blood. Gelis said, 'Does that mean you can track him?' Bel stared at her.

Saloum said, 'I am not meant to answer.'

'Wait,' said Gelis. The lamps had been stolen, but there was a makeshift fire in the sandbox: its light, flaring, showed her his face. She said, 'What do you mean? You may have a chance, by this sign, to trace Lopez. Why should you tell no one else?'

'In case they fall into danger,' said Saloum. 'Lopez is concerned for his friend. For this Nicholas.'

Bel said, 'Never mind danger to yon one. If there's a way to track Lopez, you do it. Come, lass. The physics are needed.'

Jorge punted them back to the shore. From the ship, the bonfire looked small, Godscalc tiny. Melchiorre had been brought and set with the other three wounded. An insect appeared on the strand: a log boat from some fisher village village with their own men carrying it. Bel said, 'What d'ye think, Senhor da Silves? Yon's a tragedy. Maybe it's a sign we should turn.'

He dug the oar in. 'Maybe you should,' he said. 'The ship will repair. Gnumi Mansa is friendly. He'd give her a berth and watch over her. You could sail back to him and then wait for us.'

'You are going on in spite of what's happened?' Gelis said. 'If Doria's alive, he'll surely follow us. And if he's dead, the *Fortado* couldn't rest, could it, until we're all put away?'

'No. Not at all. Havers,' said Bel, 'you've forgotten the gold. Never mind us: they'll come and mop us up afterwards. But first, they've got what they wanted: someone – Lopez – to lead a team to Wangara. If Doria's alive, he's not daft. He won't go back to his ship. He won't waste effort on us. He'll march upriver straight off, and join the gold-hunting party with Lopez.'

'Which,' said Gelis, with animation, 'might do us some good. If we keep to our own journey east, we might miss them.' She tilted her head. 'How reassuring. Is that your idea, Senhor Jorge?'

'My idea,' said Jorge da Silves, 'is to trace Doria's gold-hunting party and kill them. I think you will find Messer Niccolò of the same mind.'

'Before Ethiopia,' said Gelis.

'Before they have time, quite simply, to turn on us.'

'And Lopez?' said Bel. Gelis was smiling.

Da Silves was not. 'They will kill him,' he said. 'There can be no other outcome. But first, he will lead them and us to the mines.

And now we know, thanks to the demoiselle, that Saloum can track him. You are quick, senhorinha.'

'Too damned quick,' muttered Bel. She stared at the bonfire. They were close enough to see Nicholas. He was talking.

Gelis had seen him as well. 'Nonsense,' she said. 'Look at him. You know he won't let Lopez escape, or the gold, or Doria. The senhor is right. I'll wager your comb to my kerchief that we'll be on the gold-hunters' heels before dawn, and until we've come at Wangara, Prester John and the padre can whistle.'

She broke off. She said, 'Do you realise that that's all we *can* wager? We have no means of support, and hardly a garment between us?'

'And I the same,' said da Silves. 'But we are not destitute. We have the fruits of the wild. We have some means to purchase necessities. We have all these fine barrels of fat.'

'Pig lard,' said Gelis. 'For Muslims. You couldn't give it away.'

'Neither you could. Fancy,' said Bel. 'So what, would you say, have we hidden there?' It pleased her to see Gelis jump.

They had arrived. Da Silves put down his paddle. Men came running to pull them aground. 'In the lard? Cowrie shells,' he replied. 'Thousands and thousands of cowrie shells. So that if we do come across gold, we can buy it.'

He smiled bleakly and made ready to land. He had said nothing of his seven murdered men. He hadn't mentioned Vicente. He had shown no passion over the fate of the ship. He had been attacked and mortified by Raffaelo Doria, for which he wanted revenge. He also wished to stop him from finding Wangara.

Bel stared at da Silves, and then, looking more closely, was struck by other signs she had missed: the hollow eyes, the lines of weariness, the genuine pain. For him, this was a pilgrimage. He had wanted the slaves brought to grace: it had been he who had urged Father Godscalc to carry the Cross to Bati Mansa. If he coveted gold, it was only partly for himself: it was chiefly for the Order of Christ and his masters. She wished that she liked him.

Then she stepped carefully ashore and carried the box to Godscalc and Melchiorre, taking Gelis pointedly with her. She slowed, passing Nicholas, in order to listen; but his senses appeared to have returned to him. He was regulating, in a voice she found unusually grating, the party which was to refloat and man the *San Niccolò* and appointing (as of right) the group which, with Saloum's help, would find a suitable boat and proceed with him into the interior.

Chapter 24

IN ELECTING TO GO upriver with Nicholas, it seemed very likely to Godscalc and to Bel that they were choosing death, and violent death, of the kind they had seen for the first time at close quarters today. To Diniz, already blooded, it appeared merely a glorious extension of the adventure to which Nicholas had introduced him. To Gelis, the added danger, the change of purpose, meant nothing.

They had all four been given the opportunity to turn and sail back to Gnumi Mansa on the rehabilitated *San Niccolò*. Halfway through the operation to refloat her, which lasted nearly till daybreak, Nicholas had come back to the fire on the beach along with Diniz and Godscalc, and had put to them all, with indifference, the question of their future.

Gelis had been asleep, lulled by the warmth of the fire and the knowledge that sentries had been posted. Waking suddenly she saw that Bel, too, had recoiled from the three grotesque, firelit faces suspended above them. Nicholas let himself down, his hose ripped, his shirt tattered. 'It's us. It's all right,' he said. 'Doria's gone, and if Bati's men were going to attack us by night, they'd have done so. But I want to get away before morning. What do you want to do? If you wish to come with me, you can. Or you can wait for four months on the *Niccolò*. I'm not sending her north to risk losing her.'

'No, why should you?' said Gelis. 'How do you know Doria has gone?' Her gown, although weak at the seams, was reasonably intact, and her hair had kept most of its pleating. Her muscles had stiffened.

'Ahmad went back to the hut,' Diniz said. 'He reads footprints. Can you imagine it? Doria just abandoned his dead and disabled. Ahmad says six survivors have gone off downriver as if to board the *Fortado*, and four, including Doria, went east. We think they've gone to join the pinnace with Lopez, and get ahead as fast as they can to the gold mines. Nicholas says they'll sail day and night, but Lopez will try to delay them.'

'How trusting of Nicholas,' said Gelis. 'But even so, can a bark canoe catch a pinnace? Doria has a long start.'

'I know. We had to refloat the ship,' Nicholas said. 'We'll catch Doria on land, I should think. Do you want to go or stay?'

Bel cleared her throat. She said, 'It isna a matter of Ethiopia any more, is that right? The gold mines come first.'

'Lopez comes first,' Nicholas said. 'And speed is everything. Anyone sick will have to be left until later. I'd prefer to take a fast party myself, but as a group we're safer together.'

'Until we catch up with Doria,' Gelis said. 'How many men will he have? Since we seem to be embroiled in your war?'

Tonight, nothing really came near provoking him. He said, 'Melchiorre saw three men in the pinnace. By now, Doria will have added himself and three more.'

'And Lopez,' Gelis said. 'Eight. And your party?'

'So far thirteen,' Nicholas said. 'Jorge of course, and seven crewmen, including Filipe. Saloum will come with me, and Vito and Manoli; and Diniz I think has decided. The padre is still consulting his conscience.'

'Two-thirds of your strength. I should have guessed,' Gelis said. 'Leaving an altruistic eight on the *Niccolò*, either too sick or too high-minded for gold-hunting. Plus, you are suggesting, Bel and myself?'

Nicholas said, 'Our caravel has no cargo to rob, and if you stayed, Gnumi Mansa would attempt to protect you. The *Fortado* is full, so, unlike us, Doria has had to leave the bulk of his seamen to guard it. Both ships could sail if they had to.'

'If no one comes back,' Godscalc said. It was the first time he had spoken. He had probably been making his opinions known, Gelis thought, all the time he and Nicholas were shifting the *Niccolò*.

'Padre?' said Bel. 'Are ye for going?'

'I have been invited,' said Godscalc. 'It has been made clear that I shall find no Christians, since no Christians have ever come here. And that, should I pause to offer my doctrine to the princes of Guinea, I shall be left behind.' Brawny, filthy, half-naked, he spoke with precision.

'Until we find Lopez,' said Nicholas.

'And Doria,' said Godscalc. 'I assume you will now kill Doria; unless he pre-empts you. But eight against fourteen, he can have little hope.'

'Fourteen? You are coming?' said Nicholas. 'And the ladies?'

'Answer first,' Gelis said. 'What will you do to Doria?'

'In detail?' said Nicholas. 'It rather depends on what he has done to Lopez.'

'So we're coming,' said Bel. 'Sixteen against eight. Against seven, if we're lucky. And all the heathens and wild beasts of Africa.'

'Good. I have to go,' Nicholas said. 'We have a canoe. We should leave in an hour. Listen to Diniz. He will give you your orders.'

They launched the great hollow bark an hour later, and scrambled aboard, all sixteen of them, with their puny provisions. They were five hours behind Raffaelo Doria. The torch at their bow illumined the dark, ripping water and the backs and snouts of the river-horses, awake and moving about to their grazing. Behind, the *Niccolò* fretted and swerved, not yet ready to leave, her reflected flares swirling below her. A group of men stood on her forecastle, their arms waving, their farewells reaching thinly over the water. Every plank, every seam of the *Niccolò* was familiar. Eight weeks ago, to gunfire and trumpets, she had set out on her virginal voyage from Lagos. Godscalc said, 'Let us pray. We need God's help, and God's forgiveness. Let us make supplication for the *Niccolò*.'

'And the *Ghost*,' remarked Nicholas. 'Pray that she's beating up to Madeira by now.'

Afterwards, it seemed insane to those who survived that they decided that night to proceed east, instead of boarding the *Niccolò* and simply sailing her home without Nicholas. Except that, of course, Jorge would never have abandoned his quest – to find not just gold, but the permanent source of the gold. And to both Diniz and Godscalc, it would have been cowardice.

The three days they spent in the canoe represented their first taste of real deprivation. They had water, and, choosing their landings with caution, were able to bribe food from unwilling people. Saloum showed them how to cook it on board, and which fish they could trust. Saloum taught the seamen how to propel the boat standing or sitting, and navigated for them until he grew too tired, and had to take rest.

He only slept through the day, and then by snatches, while the others worked in relays, attempting to carry out what he had taught them. By the second night they were all very weary, partly from ceaseless travelling and partly from fear, and strain, and the sudden winds which brought chill to the night, and battered them

with baking dust through the day. The canoe leaked, and had to be
baled. Bel and Gelis and Filipe spelled one another in that, because
Filipe had no knack for the paddle, and by that time Nicholas and
Godscalc and Diniz were helping the others. They had not yet seen
any sign of the pinnace.

One man had begun to vomit by then, the kind of bile they had
all seen before. Bel helped him as much as she could. While they
had not suffered themselves on the voyage, they had witnessed
others die at close quarters: from bites, stings, bad food,
unexplained fevers. There was little privacy either: simply two
open ends, and a long tattered hood made of matting which turned
the central part of the boat into a tunnel. In that they hung cloths,
and used buckets.

Nicholas appeared not to sleep. No one questioned their speed.
It was understood that the party ahead must be caught: if they
gained too much of a lead, they might vanish. Unless Lopez really
left marks. Diniz said, once, 'How do we know that we haven't
passed them?'

And Nicholas, poling, his eyes ahead in the dark, had said,
'Because they're too few for an ambush. Also, Lopez knows only
one route, and that runs from the end of the river. They have to go
there, and try to outstrip us.'

He was proved right at the rocks, which blocked the river and
ended their voyage. There, Saloum bought information. 'Lord? A
Portuguese ship's boat with a sail came here yesterday. Its people
landed; the boat was dragged to the bushes and hidden.'

'Burn it,' said Nicholas. 'Where did they go? Do they know how
many there were?'

'Eight,' Saloum said. 'And they passed north-east, to a place
called Tambacounda.'

'A trap?' said Jorge da Silves.

'No,' said Saloum. 'There is, drawn on a tree, the special sign
that I told you of.'

They left the sick seaman there, at a village, and paid for his
care. He clung to Bel, parting, and she kissed him. Then she went
out and mounted the donkey they had bought for her. There were
only six, for a party of fifteen. Godscalc said, 'You shame me, the
comfort you brought him.' But all that day, riding, she found
herself blowing her nose.

The transition from water to land was disturbing, and not only
because of its dangers. On the Gambia they had yearned for dry
land, and although the ground heaved beneath their feet when they
trod it, they had revelled in the extravagance of their brief excursions; the vivid growth, the strange beasts, the beautiful birds, the

presence of human beings outside the claustrophobic community of a ship. And yet the ship had been there, a retreat and a harbour. Until the last time.

Here, they had only themselves to rely on – the eagerness of Diniz, the instinct of Nicholas, the knowledge of Saloum, the watchfulness of Jorge da Silves. They learned quickly which were the real perils and what precautions might be attempted against them, while accepting there was never total protection. They learned to recognise when they were being spied on, and to keep their weapons concealed and their manner unthreatening.

Children dogged them, just out of sight. Reports were passed on by drums, and by the youths they glimpsed hunting, or herding, or gathering berries or fuel. Before every nightfall, Saloum would try to discover the tracks – of humans, of goats – that might lead to a village, and they would listen for curs barking, or the cry of a cock, and sniff the air for fresh dung and woodsmoke.

Then if they found a place, Saloum would approach it with gifts, always wary because of Doria. But Doria's party – small, swift, well supplied with food and clothes from the *Fortado* – had no women to care for, and no need to waste time either placating villagers or rousing them against other white men. Doria's group had been seen, Saloum reported – no one moved in this country unnoticed – but were avoiding the villages, and had not been molested.

Sometimes Saloum was successful. Then the villages would agree to admit them, and they would sleep in the compound, or on the dirt floor of a hut, crowded with wondering watchers. If he was not, they built fires of their own, and dug and cooked sweet white roots, and seethed maize and beans to go with them.

Sometimes the village they found would be already deserted, and the people hidden, and too afraid to be coaxed. Once Jorge tried to occupy such a spot and was summarily commanded to get out of it by the soft voice of Nicholas. Some of the crew agreed with Jorge, but changed their minds quickly. A community ousted by devils might well come back with poison-tipped arrows. The argument, although short, cost them time, and darkness fell before they reached other shelter. That night, neither Jorge nor Nicholas was popular.

At Tambacounda there was no sign of Doria, but evidence that he had called there in passing, and that the approach of a second white party was suspect, however disarming Saloum's appeal for admission.

This was not a remote village inhabited by the timid, but a settlement of many huts, and a thorn wall with a gate behind which the villagers massed, spears in hand, while the headman was sent for. He arrived after some time, accompanied by a tall black man of a different race, wearing straw at his ankles and hung with clattering charms. The headman was frightened and angry, and wished to impound the donkeys and drive the white strangers off. Saloum conversed with them placidly, while fondling a small bag of cowries.

The shells were found sufficient. The barriers were opened. Two cocks were bought and sacrificed, and Nicholas deployed his crossbows to help bring down game for a feast which they ate out of bowls on the warm beaten earth of the compound. There were plenty of children but no luxuries here: no nubile wives, no silk robes from the Medici. After the palm wine had gone round Nicholas went to sit with the drummers and make tunes on a reed pipe and sing, and made the others hop and sing as he did. Manoli trod on a snake; the music faltered at the sound of his scream and then continued, although the grandmothers bent over him, chattering, and crowded about as he was lifted into a hut.

Nicholas cut into the place of the bite and sucked and spat as the blood streamed, as did Godscalc. Every district had its own hopeless remedy. Godscalc plastered on what the crones brought, and bound the blackening foot while Manoli whimpered. He shook his head as he rose.

Nicholas said, 'Stay with him. I must go back, or they will think it's bad luck.' And back he went, playing and singing, but returning to Manoli's side every so often. Just before dawn, the man died. He had been with Nicholas since the *Ciaretti*. After a few hours' sleep, they went on.

The terrain was not in itself physically difficult. It was Sahel country in December: undulating plains of yellow grass, sometimes shoulder-high; velvety wastes of crazed mud; a dotting of trees, sometimes green, sometimes skeletal. It was not physically difficult except for the sun. Away from the river, the heat had increased by a third, although by night it was cooler sometimes than was comfortable. But they dare not travel at night.

They covered themselves against sunburn. Godscalc and Bel anointed great angry rashes and chafe-marks. Nicholas bartered their frayed cloaks and sweat-sundered garments for cotton and coarse thread and thorn-needles and, instead of wearing chemises and hose, the men thrust their heads through cloaks formed of joined sheeting, and made themselves voluminous breeches caught at waist and at calf with rush-string. For boots and caps, they had skins.

Bel kept her stout, frayed garment longest of all, and wore her cloak as a veil from the sun. Gelis, abandoning the useless fine cloth of her mourning, grimly requisitioned two squares of coarse cotton, one to wrap as a skirt and the other, slit for her head, to drape her upper body and arms like a kerchief. What was left, made a Muslim-style headcloth. They spoke little to one another. They were too tired, and saved their strength for survival. But wherever they went, they cast about for the red marks of Lopez and followed them as Jorge followed the planets. The donkeys stumbled.

They were a day behind, Saloum said. It revived the seamen, but however they hurried, the day never seemed to be made up. Saloum, being black, could not look as worn as they did, but his eyes had sunk, and his hair and beard dulled. At the end of a week, they seemed no nearer their quarry and another man had fallen ill. Lying roofless that night, Godscalc said, 'How long must this continue? We are not overtaking. Doria will find the mines, and Lopez will be killed, and these poor men are dying for nothing.'

'Doria is not near the mines,' Saloum said.

Jorge da Silves had overheard him. With heat and low diet the lean face had become leaner, the folds deeper, the eyes brighter still. 'Not near them?' said Jorge.

'Not yet,' Saloum said. 'It takes time.'

Jorge said, 'How do you know? Do you know where the mines are? If I thought you knew where they were, and hadn't told us, I would pitch you into that ant-hill.'

'Be quiet,' Nicholas said. 'You'll rouse the others. Of course he doesn't know where they are. He's helping us follow Lopez.'

'And of course, that's all you want,' Jorge said. 'Not the gold. You're worried about the good health of Lopez.'

'And you are not?' Nicholas said.

It was later, when Jorge had fallen asleep, that Godscalc crossed and sat beside Nicholas. He said, 'What did Saloum mean? Do you know? Is Lopez misleading Doria?'

'I shouldn't wonder,' said Nicholas. He lay on his face.

'But Lopez knows you are following,' Godscalc said. 'Isn't he leading you to the mines?'

'Jorge certainly hopes so,' said Nicholas. 'I can't tell you anything, except that it's vital to hurry.'

'You will kill us on the way,' Godscalc said.

Nicholas rested his head on his hands. 'We're dead anyway, without Lopez to lead us.'

Three days after that, they came to the river. On its banks was a settlement larger than any they had yet come across; one surrounded by harvested meadows and cattle with upcurving horns, and whose thatched huts were shaded by silk-cotton and Baobab trees and defended by fences and matting. They dismounted and waited outside, as they always did, while Saloum conferred at the barrier. He eventually passed inside, taking Nicholas with him.

Seated motionless in the dust, Gelis said, 'You know what this river is? It's the Senagana.'

They all knew. She had no need to say it. It was the Senagana, the river at the mouth of which, three weeks before, she had been heartily embraced by King Zughalin. 'So we appear,' she added, 'to be travelling in circles.' She was in pain, for the same reason that had led her once to bite Nicholas in the hand. It pleased her to deal with it all without mentioning it.

Diniz had learned when not to reply. He slumped, his back to a tree. Perhaps tonight there would be a hut. The headman was a person of consequence: the chief of Boundon reserved some of his wives here. It was unlikely that he would behave like Gnumi Mansa. Even if he did, few of them could take advantage of it. Diniz remembered Nicholas at Tendeba and the display of cheerful simplicity so unlike anything he had seen in him before or since. It had seemed to be genuine.

And now Nicholas and Saloum were in there, reduced to begging for food and shelter for thirteen. That was their whole number now: Jorge with his four handpicked seamen and that fool Filipe; Nicholas with Saloum and Vito and himself; and the padre and the two stupid women. For the rest, their Christmas Mass had been a funeral service.

It was almost true that they were travelling in circles. They had followed Lopez north-east until they had actually intersected the Senagana. Had it been navigable, and had some prophet warned them, they might have saved all these last weeks of travail.

Gelis had intended to say so, until she saw Nicholas return, and watched Godscalc lift himself to his feet, waiting for him.

Like them all, the priest had lost weight, and the big frame beneath the crumpled cotton was blotched and lumpy with bites and abrasions and his boots patched with blood. He hadn't shaved for ten days. All the men were the same, and most of them grumbled but bore it. The lure of the gold was enough. In Godscalc's case there was no lure, Gelis saw, only a growing despair, watching the feverish race: Jorge competing with Nicholas in how much speed might be made; Jorge resenting the younger man's nominal dominance, all the more as it became apparent that it was actual dominance – that Nicholas possessed somewhere the kind of rare sense that told him how to lead.

She had not, herself, expected that. In the political battles of Bruges she had studied the unattractive qualities that made for plebeian success; extreme ambition being the foremost. She had looked to find it in Nicholas, as well as the common attributes of the soldier: physical stamina, physical boldness, a convenient coarseness of feeling. These, she thought, were all there, but present also was something inborn that advised him in his dealings with people.

On the voyage, he had got his own way with guile. Now he gave orders. No one, placed as they were, could disobey him, but his objectives were not necessarily theirs, and the result could have been gloom and resentment. He had worked to make sure it was not. He endured the same hardships, and worse. He excelled Jorge in concise exposition, so that they knew what they were doing, and why. He taught Filipe the use of a crossbow and took lessons from Vito in butchering. He gave each man his due, and when rest was imperative, he contrived the best of comfort and food he could manage. He supported Bel and Godscalc in their doctoring, and talked them through and over each death. He did it all, as she knew, because he wanted to get to the gold.

Now he walked over to Godscalc and said, 'We can spend the night here. Doria came, but passed over the river. Saloum has gone to see where.' His white surtout was smeared with tree-climbing, and Bel had sewn him a brimmed goatskin hat with hanging strings on it. His beard and moustache had come in daffodil-yellow, and already the dimples were covered.

Godscalc said, 'I was afraid they had escaped us by water. Was Lopez still with them?'

'And Doria,' Nicholas said. 'And six bearers with all their spare clothes and food. Or so we gather. Saloum isn't sure of the dialect.' He paused and said, 'I'm not sitting down, because I have to go and catch fish.'

Gelis said, 'He's done enough. I'll come with you. Have you a net, or have you come for my hair?' Under the headcloth it hung in long, plaited rats' tails.

Nicholas picked up the end of the longest. 'No, but come. We'll put a slug on it and hold you head downwards. Or . . .' He looked at Godscalc.

'Do you want to?' said Godscalc.

They knew, of course, about women. She felt her pallid cheeks flush, and then was angry, but chiefly with herself. She said, 'Thank you. I want to.'

She had to wait, but briefly, while Nicholas marshalled the rest of his party and saw them into the hands of the headman to be allotted places to sleep and to eat. The people here were not afraid: the compound shook to the thud of the pestles as the women pounded the grain-vats and tittered; children ran among goats and poultry and girls paused to stare on their way to fetch water, languidly skeining cloth into a headpad and placing great yellow gourds on their crowns. They bore themselve like empresses.

Jorge was absent, no doubt for the usual reasons, so Vito and Diniz took charge. Nicholas supervised for a while. When he came back to Gelis, he carried two pails, slung on either end of a yoke over his shoulder. There was another for her. He said, 'We don't need equipment. We've been invited to help in the fishing. I throw out the fish and you catch them.'

She said, 'How will you know what they are saying?' The ground was soft. She had left her skin shoes with Bel and her toughened feet pressed down the grasses.

He said, 'You shouldn't do that; remember Manoli. We'll manage. I could interpret St Augustine to a deaf and dumb Jalofo by now.'

Ahead she could hear the sound of the river, and splashing. She said, 'What would you do if anything happened to Saloum?'

He said, 'Follow the signs. But it would be difficult.'

She glanced round at him then. 'We are only really safe, aren't we, because he is a marabout?'

'He commands respect,' Nicholas said. 'Although few of these people are orthodox in their beliefs. But yes, they don't attack us because he is black, and a marabout, and may have greater magic than theirs, and we freed him.' He was looking ahead through the trees. He said, without any change in his voice, 'To no avail, it would seem.'

The unseen river ran still, overlaid with the hiss of the cicadas. In a bough overhead something hooted, to be distantly answered from the massive canopy of birdsong that twittered and chirruped and sang below a reddening sky. Drums pattered emptily in the distance, or throbbed closer at hand; and somewhere not too far ahead was a murmur of voices unevenly pulsing together, with a single voice filling the spaces. The fish were being apostrophised.

The man staggering towards Nicholas and Gelis contributed nothing to the general noise because his mouth was smashed in, and his nose broken, and his black skin glistening through a moving river of blood. It was Saloum, alone.

Gelis ran forward. Nicholas reached the marabout before her, and was already grasping his body as the Mandingua dropped to his knees. The blood from his face had spurted over his garments and the blotches were soaking together. He sank back on his heels and Nicholas, holding him, ran a hand lightly over the rest of him. He said, 'Only his face. What happened, Saloum?' Gelis pulled off her headcloth and knelt.

'I hit him,' said Jorge da Silves, and walked up to them all from the trees.

Cloth in hand, Gelis stayed where she was. Nicholas relinquished Saloum and stood up. 'I was going to kill him,' said Jorge. 'Until I remembered we had nobody else.' He had a club in one hand, and his nostrils above the black beard were blanched. He said, 'I found him drawing the symbol.'

'Where?' Nicholas said.

'At the river. He was going to cross to the opposite bank. He has drawn them all,' Jorge said.

'How do you know?' Nicholas said. He had a knife at his waist but hadn't touched it. His voice and eyes, resting on the Portuguese, were both quiet.

'He has the carmine, there in his garments. The paint was wet.'

'But all of them?' Nicholas said. Beside Gelis, Saloum rose to his feet. He had wiped his face with her cloth and held it, smeared with blood, under the fringe of his beard. She rose too, and stood between him and Jorge.

'All of them. I told him,' said Saloum. His lips, swollen and fissured, would hardly move. He was swallowing blood. 'I am sorry,' he said.

'You . . .?' said Jorge, and took a step forward. His neck and face were suffused.

'No,' said Nicholas, and, catching the club, twisted it from the other man's grasp. He flung it away. 'Don't. It's bad, but he isn't an enemy.'

'He isn't?' Jorge said. 'Where is Doria? Where is your so-called friend Lopez? We are not following in the footsteps of either. We are being sent to our deaths by their ally, this traitor.'

'Perhaps,' Nicholas said. 'Although I don't think so. I suggest we ask him. If he can speak.'

'He needs water,' said Gelis. 'If you take him back, the others will kill him.'

'They will do,' Jorge said, 'what I will do, when I have picked up my club again. Beat him until he tells us the way to the mines. And then force him to lead us in shackles.'

The sky flared with the last of the sunset; soon they would be in darkness and outside the compound. A swirl of smoke rose from the banks of the river where torches and fires would be lit. They could find no refuge from curiosity there. In the last of the light, she saw that Saloum's whole attention, mind and soul, was on Nicholas. And in the eyes of Nicholas was an expression she had never seen: one of desolation that came close to anguish. He said, 'I must speak apart to

Saloum. There will be a hut where he could hide in the village. Gelis?'

She looked at Jorge.

'Will you take him, Gelis?' Nicholas said.

She understood, without words. He said, referring to Jorge, 'I won't harm him.'

He was lying, if one took it too literally. She had hardly started to move when Nicholas drew back a fist and struck the Portuguese such a blow that he fell senseless. Gelis didn't wait to see more. She said, 'Come!' to Saloum, but could not make him hurry as, walking stoically beside her, he accompanied her back to her hut in the village.

An hour later Nicholas came, and Bel and Gelis admitted him. The single torch showed him Saloum, his clothes fresh, his face swollen and salved. Nicholas crossed and sat Turkish-style facing the three of them. Saloum bowed his head. Gelis said, 'He has deceived us.'

'I guessed,' Nicholas said. 'I gave Lopez the slaves, but I didn't impose any promise. The mines are a secret. He kept it.'

'He arranged with Saloum to lead you away. You were not to follow him. You were to be led to the caravan terminus, where you would find gold enough.' It was Gelis.

'That is so?' Nicholas said. He was looking at Saloum.

'That is so,' Saloum answered, through stiff and whistling lips. His gaze, clear as Godscalc's, rested on Nicholas. 'He has taken Doria to his death, but he will not lure you on the same path. He said what you said. He made you no promises. He told you he would do as he chose when the time came.'

'But how will he escape?' Nicholas said. 'It is death to show strangers the gold. If the miners don't, Doria will kill him.'

Saloum's gaze didn't alter. He said, 'I am to tell you that you must forgive him.'

'You were to tell me?' Nicholas said.

And Saloum said, 'He thought you would find out, but hoped it would be too late, as it is. He wished you to know that the source of the gold is a secret that he would not betray, even to you, whom he loves. He has not taken the Genoese there, and would not take you. They have gone to the place of silent trading.'

'Where they will be killed?' Nicholas said. 'But so will Lopez. Saloum, so will Lopez.'

'You cannot help him,' said Saloum. 'He does not want to be helped. And you could not get there in time.'

The silence this time was a long one. Then Nicholas said, 'So what does he want?'

Saloum rose and, stepping across, took the place of submission before Nicholas. He said, 'Out of love, he would have you go to the terminus. I will take you. It is where the caravans come; it is on the way to your great Prester John; it will bring you, he says, what your heart and your soul both have need of. It is far, but we shall set out tomorrow. It is called Timbuktu.'

Gelis listened, and Bel beside her said nothing. Nicholas said, 'Jorge will not go.' A dimple appeared, out of his distraction. 'I should have to gag him.'

He was gagged already, Gelis suspected, and bound as well, in some corner known to Nicholas. Saloum said, 'Perhaps I could persuade him?'

Nicholas frowned. 'Why not?' Gelis asked. 'Saloum persuaded me. Send him over to tell Jorge the truth. Saloum doesn't know the source of the gold, but can take us to where we can buy it. Isn't that so?'

'That is true,' Saloum said. 'By all I hold sacred.'

'Then send Saloum over,' said Gelis. 'Get them reconciled. You can't keep Jorge tied up for ever. Let them talk on their own, if they want to. Then you can free Jorge and announce changed plans tomorrow. How long a journey is it to this depot?'

'To Timbuktu?' said Saloum painfully. 'From here, senhorinha, three to four weeks at the most.'

'Did you know that?' Gelis said.

'No,' said Nicholas.

'And if we had gone direct?'

Saloum answered. 'Senhorinha, I have brought you the easiest way, if the slowest. It was what I was told.'

She said nothing. Nicholas left, taking Saloum, and no one returned. Diniz came, bringing gazelle meat and palm wine and maize cakes, but didn't stay long; even his bright black eyes had deep circles beneath them. Gelis wondered where he would call next. Since no one appeared, they lay on their straw without speaking, and presently Bel's gentle snore filled the air. Gelis lay for a while, and then slept.

They were awakened by movement and voices, then by shouting, and the clatter of loading. Someone rapped on a post of their cabin, and Gelis took Bel's cloak and pushed back the matting. Nicholas stood there, the sky lightening behind him. He said, 'Jorge has gone on without us, and so have five crewmen and Diniz. I have to follow. I'll take Vito with me.'

'Diniz has left you for *Jorge*!' said Gelis. 'Why? Where are they going?'

'To the silent market,' said Nicholas. 'They know how to get there. Damn them, they've stolen the donkeys.'

'Saloum went with them?' she said.

'No. I kept him with me to prevent it. But he had already given Jorge all the directions.'

'He wanted Jorge dead,' Gelis said.

'Oh, yes,' said Nicholas. 'Do you want to beat him for it?'

Chapter 25

THE VILLAGE OWNED a single camel, which Nicholas bought
for a sackload of cowrie shells. He mounted with unthinking ease, as if he had done it many times before, and had
to lean to help Vito behind him. Godscalc watched, hastily dressed, with Gelis and Bel at his side. They were all that
remained, but for Saloum. Gelis went to Saloum and said, 'Are
you satisfied?'

Yesterday, he had been in pain. Now he looked ill. He said, in
his stumbling Portuguese, 'Senhorinha, they were crazy for gold.
They would have stopped at nothing to learn where the market
was. Your lord also said he could not tie up the senhor for ever.'

Gelis said, 'It is not the senhor who concerns us. It is the boy
Diniz, and the lord Niccolò who has now gone to retrieve him.
You have told him the way?'

'Yes, senhorinha,' said Saloum.

'Then take us the same way,' said Gelis. 'We have weapons.
However slow we may be, we can surely help somehow. Then take
us on to your caravanserai, where the camel-trains come from the
desert. You must be useful for something.'

They didn't speak on that morning's journey. Tied like puddings,
their worldly goods paraded before them, borne on the heads of six
men from the village. Saloum chose the way, and Godscalc and Bel
walked behind Gelis.

At mid-morning, with the land shimmering yellow before them,
they made a halt on a patch of harsh grass below the dusty leaves of
a group of acacias. Godscalc said, 'Spare them all a thought. The
boy Filipe is with them.'

'He needn't have been,' Gelis said.

'That is harsh,' Godscalc said. 'But Diniz need not have gone,
either.'

'It was for his mother,' said Bel.

'And perhaps he was encouraged,' said Gelis. 'It would suit many people if Diniz didn't return.'

'You think,' said Godscalc, 'that Nicholas has gone to kill him? With Vito as witness?'

'I didn't say so,' said Gelis. Saloum was praying, his brow touching the ground, his torn and swollen face darkened with pressure. She was not sorry for what he was suffering. Unrefreshed, they got up and went on.

They saw the camel first, and then the red hair of Vito, and only later that there was someone lying prone in the shade, with Nicholas on one knee beside him. Vito greeted them with joy and relief. 'It's the padre! The lot of them!'

'Be quiet,' Nicholas said. The man lying beneath him looked round.

It was Diniz, his face hollow with pain. 'You shouldn't,' he said. 'You shouldn't have come.'

'But how useful that they have,' Nicholas said. 'Forward the doctors. We are not making too much noise at present, because Jorge's men think that they've left Diniz to die, and we'd like them to go on thinking it.'

'Where, my hinny?' said Bel. She knelt, her own face paler than usual.

'A crossbow bolt in the shoulder, and a lot of good blood leaked away. A falling-out among thieves.'

'Thieves!' croaked Diniz. 'They're madmen! They've gone crazy for gold!'

'They talked,' said Nicholas, 'of going back and torturing Saloum, it appears. They thought he'd misled them, and they believed he really did know the way to the mines.'

'I did mislead them,' said Saloum. 'The silent market is not where I told them.'

Diniz wriggled in Godscalc's arms. He was breathless. 'Well,' he said, 'they know where it is now. They caught a man and began to force him to tell them. That's when I told them to stop, and the little bastard – and Filipe shot me.'

'You'll get your reward,' Godscalc said. 'Although it may not feel like it at the moment. Nicholas, will Jorge be in danger?'

Nicholas was looking at Saloum. 'You misled me, too,' he said. 'You knew . . .'

'I knew you were not only concerned for the boy. But I chose to give you the boy,' said Saloum. 'Had I not, you would have missed him.'

'And now?' Nicholas said.

'Oh, now, if you wish,' said Saloum, 'I shall take you to the silent market. I have kept my promise. You are too late for Doria and Lopez. If you wish to rescue these Portuguese murderers, I leave the matter to Allah.'

The silent trade known to the Carthaginians had many places of concourse, but all of them depended, as did this one, on rivers. The salt came by boat, grey-white slabs scribbled over with charms, and still corded in packs as when it crossed the Sahara. The gold came from Wangara, brought on foot over many days' travelling. The salt was left, and the signal fires lit, and in time the gold would be found placed beside it. Then the invisible bartering would begin.

Jorge da Silves never reached it. The hunched, naked clusters of vultures caused Saloum to stop, a glance of warning at Nicholas, and the trudging procession came to a halt, the porters dropping their loads, the camel resting, that carried Bel and Diniz. The object, when they found it, might have been some half-eaten kill of the wild, but was not. The death had been merciful. Jorge, the acolyte of the Order of Christ, had been killed by the soft leaden ball of a hackbut.

'His own men,' Diniz remarked, having forced the information from Godscalc, returning.

'Yes. He must have protested, in the end, as you did. It is in his favour,' said Godscalc, and adjusted his harness with hands still bleeding and soiled from the burial. 'There are only five of them left.'

'Will they ambush us?' Diniz said. He was burning with fever.

'They don't know we're coming,' Nicholas said, coming up. 'How is Bel?'

'Shellfish,' she said, her ravaged face smiling grotesquely.

'You *will* indulge,' he said, and smiled back at her. There were mountains on the horizon. He had no means of hurrying now, with his sick to carry, and the five renegades already far off and mounted. And as Saloum said, they were too late for Lopez. He said to Godscalc, 'Decide. Do we go on?'

'The gold is not worth it?' said Godscalc. Then he said, 'I am sorry.'

'No. My postulatum was almost as objectionable. Are these five men worth it?' said Nicholas. But he knew what Godscalc was going to answer. And he would have kept on, himself, no matter what the rest did.

It was Saloum who ended the matter. 'Lord, there is no choice. In such heat, these people cannot walk back. It is not the gold that will save them, it is the river.'

They didn't reach it that day, or the next, for between the Senagana and the silent market was a valley, and hills. Events blurred in the memory; reduced this, the first white man's march past the Gambia, to the daily routine of the Calabrian peasant: the perpetual grubbing for food – the prize of a small flock of guinea-fowl – the forage for wood for the nightly bonfire; the watch for arrows, or animals. The stoicism of Diniz; and the growing evidence that Bel, their anchor, was succumbing to the hateful ailment she had so often nursed.

Gelis walked by the camel, and wiped Bel's brow, and fed her the milk that, wherever they were, Nicholas found. There was no shortage of water. Half the drama of the bald, infertile landscape was contained in the steep, tree-filled chasms and dwindling waterfalls. But it was not a country for crops, or for people, and the pyramid cities of termites were all that seemed to thrive in it.

Three of their porters ran off. The camel bore, without complaint, what extra burdens it might, and obeyed Nicholas, who talked to it in Greek and sometimes called it Chennaa. The loss was of small consequence, except that the harder work had to be shared. They passed some meagre settlements, but met with shut doors rather than the bold curiosity of the past, and the asses' hoofmarks in the dust told them why.

They paid desperate prices for goats' milk and dried meat and millet, and crossed a valley and plodded up broken slopes which made the camel complain, but called no sound from Bel. Diniz watched her. Eventually, he said, 'Nicholas? She is too weak to be jolted. If I walk, you could carry her.'

Nicholas let him walk, with Godscalc's help, for a while, and rode the animal in his place, the bundles about him and Bel, swathed in his arms, stained with vomit and blood. He hissed and crooned as he rode, and controlled the steady pace of the beast with a little stick he had made. She said once, 'Who was Chennaa?' and Gelis, watching, saw his face touched with a smile. He said, 'A love I once had.'

Then, in a while, he made Diniz mount once again and gave Bel to Gelis to care for, while he and Godscalc turned a mat into a shape between harness and a stretcher so that they could take her on foot. Carrying her, Gelis noticed, he crooned and hissed the same way, and sometimes sang under his breath. Once, she thought she heard a whisper from Bel, joining in. They came to the mountains.

That night, even Diniz was silent, but Saloum said, 'Do not fear. It is cool. Over there, cattle graze; there are people. We have only to climb. Tomorrow,' he said, 'you will see it.'

They saw it sooner than they had feared for, late that day, collecting dusty earth-nuts and berries and roots, Vito found two of their stolen donkeys, quietly grazing in a sparse copse of trees. One had a deep slash crowded with flies on one shoulder. There was no sign of the other three beasts, or of Jorge's five men who had taken them.

'I should say there has been a fight on the plain, near the market,' said Saloum. 'These animals have been chased back to the hills, and some days ago. That is not the wound of an assagai, or an axe, or an arrow.'

'They met Doria's men down there?' Nicholas said. He didn't expect Saloum to agree. He didn't expect Lopez really (he convinced himself) to have led Doria over these hills to the market.

Saloum said, 'Doria's men would not be alive. The salt traders kill every stranger, and so do the men from Wangara. It is how the secret is kept.'

The next morning, they passed through a cornfield and up rising ground where brilliant flowers grew among rivulets. The path wound about rocks and climbed higher, enclosing them in chasms of stone. Saloum walked, and Vito and Godscalc dismounted, allowing Gelis, who was lighter, to ride. For a while Nicholas also walked by the camel, with Bel and Diniz strapped above him in silence. Then he said, 'Give me that poor ass for a moment,' and, lifting himself to its back, rode off and left them. The donkey's hooves echoed ahead, where the track twisted and plunged through a gulley.

They all heard him halt. Gelis looked at Godscalc, then trotted after. She had anticipated some blockage, a barrier, but as it descended the path became suddenly broader; became a ledge; became a plateau stark in the sun, which blazed from the south-east ahead of her.

Nicholas sat in the opening, the reins on his knee, looking outwards. He had seldom ridden in Bruges. If he had, Gelis thought, he would have looked like this, stolidly equestrian on the ridge of the wall, except that the sky would have been paler, and there would have been a windmill beside him. There was wind, now, where he had stopped. It fluttered the cloth at his shoulder, which was otherwise still. Gelis dismounted, and walked her mount down beside him. He said, 'There it is.'

She saw, again, what had been given her from the deck of a caravel, which was a vision of space. The manuscript of the sky, stained with blue, franked by the seal of the African sun. Below it, a horizon so far that the haze of distance made it uncertain, a haze which lay not over the Ocean of Darkness but an ocean of light, of a fertile land of golden grain and green grass and the terracotta of alluvial soil, sprinkled with the deeper green of great trees and freckled with cattle. And through the plain ran a broad silver highway, rimmed on its far side by hills and edged by miniature townships, neat as constellations of straw.

She wished to ask what the highway was, but could not. Saloum's footstep, careful, courteous, sounded behind them. He said, 'It is the Joliba, senhorinha. The great river you know of. It flows east, no man knows where. The caravanserai you seek is fourteen days from here, close to its banks.'

'And the silent market?' Nicholas said.

Saloum came to his side. The donkey shifted. 'It is there,' Saloum said. 'On the stretch of river you see, over the plain.'

No one spoke. Then Nicholas said, 'I see no fires.'

And Saloum said, 'No, my lord. The trade will be done.'

It was done. They descended the slopes. When next day they moved over the shining, flowery grass it was evident that there was no one there on the banks of the Joliba, although on their journey they saw that the soil of the meadow had been roughly churned here and there, and pitted by uneven footmarks, and the agitated small prints of donkeys. Of the five men who had probably died, there were no bodies visible, and in the rich soil, no trace of spilled blood.

The river-bank consisted of fine, ruddy shingle smoothed by the water, so that they could see where cattle had stood, and the slots of a leopard, and the scuff of hurrying rats. Further up, the grit was dry and tumbled and littered with what had been left when the water shrank. Further up still, it was mixed with grass, and on one spot they found a great heap of wood ash, half blown about and quite cold, with some chicken bones lying, and the kind of detritus a group of men left when eating and waiting together.

When they walked down the shingle again, at a different place, they could see where several canoes had been hauled to the bank, and some mooring posts sunk, with bits of Baobab rope still wound about them. Then, much further up, Vito found the trading-station itself.

It had been set up on a stretch of hard ground, reinforced in some places by boulders. As on the Gambia, the booths had been placed in a line, and the sockets and mat-prints still showed although the thatched roofs and uprights had gone. One of the mats was still in place, with the oblong imprint of the salt slabs plainly visible. Two of the places were blackened and Vito, kneeling, picked up a piece of charred cloth. 'Look!' he said. 'They don't often sell cloth. Why should they burn it?'

Those who could walk were hastening towards him, Godscalc keeping with Nicholas, and Gelis passing Saloum. Saloum said, to Nicholas rather than Vito, 'If they cannot agree, if the trader cheats, if the tribesmen are angered or fearful, sometimes they will burn the dealers' merchandise and take back their gold and go home.'

'So they thought they were being deceived?' Nicholas said. 'Or saw that strangers were coming, and blamed the traders?'

'Maybe,' Saloum said. 'Or perhaps the hollows scooped for the gold were thought to be unreasonably deep. The traders can sometimes be obstinate.' He was speaking monotonously, his Portuguese worse than usual.

'Where are the hollows?' said Gelis. She looked for Vito, who was still on his knees. 'Oh, I see. One, of course, by each booth.' She walked up. 'Why . . .!'

'. . . There is something still in them. Move her away,' Nicholas said.

There were only six of them filled; but after all Doria had only had seven men to begin with, counting Lopez, and had probably lost more men and bearers than they had. Much of the flesh of the heads had been eaten, but some of the hair still remained, and you could tell which skin had been white, and which black. Doria's eye-socket had an earring dropped into it. Nicholas couldn't say which of the blacks had been Loppe. If there had been a body, he could have told from the hands.

Vito was retching, but Gelis had not gone away. She said, 'This was why he brought them here. That was what Saloum said, wasn't it? This was why Lopez brought them here, and didn't want you to follow. He knew this would happen.'

She looked at Nicholas. He hadn't lifted his eyes. She said, 'He knew that if Doria brought you together, one of you would tell him the secret of Wangara.'

'I didn't know it,' said Nicholas. Across the grass, Diniz had got up and was coming forward, shambling a little.

'We had better bury them,' Nicholas said.

'Don't you hear me?' she said. 'He saved Wangara, and the men from Wangara have killed him.'

It was to be noticed that, from then onwards, few of the six who were left disputed with Nicholas, and the standing of Saloum, too, was secure. If Nicholas gave it much thought, which uniquely for him he did not, he would have discerned well enough the chief reason. He had not exploited his friendship with Lopez. Lopez had received from him the unconditional gift of the slaves and, faced with a conflict of loyalties, had reconciled some of them here, and shown himself ready to die for them. And Saloum had been faithful to both.

Nicholas gave the subject no particular thought, since he was busy. His party had to ride for a little. But once past the falls – a stretch of rocks and rapids and currents so fast that a craft could shoot twenty-five miles in three hours – the Joliba turned itself into his highway. A log boat fifty feet long had been purchased, with men to manage it, and the sale of the asses and of Chennaa – of his camel – had bought them a bountiful load of provisions, without recourse to his porcelain shell-coins. The heat, though at times disagreeable, was ten degrees less here by day than they had suffered, and by night was cool and fresh as a spring dusk in Flanders.

The river, half a mile wide, flowed to the north-east, where they were going. Vito, nimble and bright as a marmoset, had manufactured extra rigging and canopies and made them beds and partitions within the roomy, hooded interior. The paddles splashed, and the skins of goats' milk and water swayed overhead, and from the long cooking-trough there floated back the warm smell of partridge roasting in Kalita butter, or the bubbling of a fine piece of perch, or pieces of fresh beef cut up among rice. Borne on the smooth breast of the Joliba, Bel and Diniz began to recover.

Godscalc no longer demanded to take his box ashore and carry the Cross to the princes of Guinea. It was not that the shores were unsafe, as were those they had found on the Gambia. Here, children played on the straw-littered strands, and women beat out their washing beside the twisting blue smoke of the earth-ovens, and herds of cattle, of camels, flocks of goats, lines of ponderous sheep picked their way through the scrub of the landscape. He saw men weaving cloth in the freshness of sundown: their looms like tangles of thorn by the waterside, their cotton as white as the egrets. That was before the bull-frogs took up their song, and the water-horses bellowed and splashed in the shallows, and the birds filled the air with their cries, wheeling like ash against a conflagration of sky and of river.

No, he didn't refrain from going ashore because he was afraid, or because the need for haste wouldn't allow it. There was no need for haste now. He abstained from the exercise of his mission because he had seen confirmed what he did not wish to believe: that he, a white man and a stranger, could not deliver his message to a simple people so alien. They heard him with fright. And even if they had received him with love and peace and full understanding, they were bound not to follow him, unless their King followed him too. His was not a mission to his fellow men, who must be heedless as those screaming baboons. It was a message only for Zughalin and Gnumi Mansa and Bati Mansa and those other great lords such as Prester John, to whom he was an envoy, a person to pamper or kill.

But perhaps, most of all, he sat here with his faith locked within him because the people of these shores, he had been told, were practising Muslims, and that was Saloum's creed. Once, he had despised Saloum for leading a priest to Gnumi Mansa. Now, he understood that he had saved all their lives.

He had asked Saloum what Timbuktu was like, but had learned only what he already guessed: that it was a place of trans-shipment; a terminus where the camels, ten thousand perhaps in a train, could rest and feed and take water while the goods they had brought from the desert were moved to the yards of the dealers, and from there to the boats by which they would be dispersed when the floods would allow. A place of seasonal haggling, and gold. *What your heart and your soul both have need of*, Lopez had incomprehensibly said.

He supposed Nicholas still needed gold, although he hadn't said so: the journey had to be paid for, and the *Ghost* might not have arrived. Diniz, his shoulder still bound but dry and without inflammation, sometimes talked about that, and the surprise his mother would get when she found he had made her so rich, and how good Gregorio was, and what a fine job he and Jaime would make of the estate in Madeira now they could buy in more land. And how furious Simon would be, wherever he was, and the man David from the Vatachino. Diniz wished that everyone knew what had happened to Raffaelo Doria. He wished the same could happen to all the men still on the *Fortado*, including Michael Crackbene.

'I don't think you mean that,' said Godscalc, but knew well, of course, that he did.

Vito also spoke with satisfaction about the fate of Doria, who had wanted to kill them all under that hut. He was less comfortable with what had happened to Jorge da Silves, who had been the ship's master until he had decided to make his own way to the gold. It sometimes worried Vito to think that the traders who killed the signor's men might be in this place Timbuktu, and angry with Signor Niccolò for being white, and of the same party that frightened the Wangara men into burning their goods.

Godscalc, who had had the same thoughts, said that he hoped that Saloum, whom they had freed, might protect them; and that the traders liked spectacles. If the place seemed too rough, they would simply pass it and proceed on their way.

'To Ethiopia,' Vito said, with a pleased, freckled smile. Although in awe of Nicholas, he had sailed with him all the way from Ancona and possessed for him an uncomplicated admiration, as well as a belief in all his works. Only now and then, when he saw a black lion motionless on the strand or a group of monsters with long marbled necks in a bush, he would speak of how he would shock all the oar-makers in Venice, but that they would never believe him. And he rambled on sometimes, too, about Melchiorre, who was the best fellow he knew, and likely to be recovering well on the *San Niccolò*, assuming that that King and his wives hadn't exhausted him.

'Perhaps,' said Gelis, 'we are all finding time to be homesick.'

'Are you?' Godscalc said.

'I have no home to be sick for,' she said.

He had never heard her speak before with self-pity. He thought perhaps she was frightened, for last night the river had been joined by another, and this morning both had gone, to be replaced by a sea: by a lake that stretched from one side of the sky to the other, interrupted by shallows and islands, by outcrops upon which cabins perched, and fishermen mended their nets, and women waded in rice, or pushed out their boats and went visiting from this islet to that.

'It is only the season,' he said. 'Saloum says January is the time for the flood. We shall find the river again.' That morning they had travelled through grass: a meadow of tall, rustling reeds below which water glinted. Driven by poles, the bark had sheared its way through them, leaving behind it a trail bright as mercury. They crossed other trails, seeing no one, but hearing the crackle of reeds all about them. Next, they had floated through acres of lilies, white and lilac and yellow. Godscalc said, 'Are you sorry you came?'

In the shade, she had pulled off her headcloth. Her hair was bleached by the sun, the plaits smooth, although the threads of it curled at her temples. Her face, fined into hollows, was thin-skinned and brown, and so were her arms below the crumpled, bleached stuff of her cape. She said, 'No. I promised myself that I would.'

'And are you then glad?' Godscalc said. 'What have you learned?'

'About Katelina?' she said. Her eyes gleamed.

Nicholas was far ahead, in the bows, in the sun. 'About this young man,' Godscalc said, 'who meant her no harm.'

'That is the refrain Diniz sings me,' she said. 'Did you not ask yourself, before you came here, how many would die because of Nicholas? Is it an excuse you would permit, that sometimes it happens by accident?'

If she were less clever, he supposed, she would be happier. And those around her as well. He said, 'But at least you accept, then, that your sister's death was an accident? For if you do, your duty must be forgiveness. Does he not grieve, do you suppose? Does he not grieve for his friend at this moment?'

'You trust him,' she said.

He wondered what to say, for she was waiting, amused, for a lie. One could never trust Nicholas, not entirely. Nicholas himself had told Lopez not to trust him, and Lopez had not. It made no difference, in the end. Nicholas had made his way to the silent market for gold. Doria and Lopez and Jorge had taken the risks. It was not because of bad planning that the gold had not been there.

But that was nonsense. Godscalc said, 'I trust him in the things he believes in, which are not, in my view, to be despised. Ask Mistress Bel.'

'Yes,' said Gelis. 'He is afraid of her. So, are we close?'

'I think,' said Father Godscalc, 'that we have come two-thirds of the way.'

The last two hundred miles were not difficult, which Nicholas found irritating, being a person who derived satisfaction from problems. He was not unaware of the murmur of gossip under the hood, and took it as evidence that his charges were rested and fed and recovering. He exchanged pleasantries with them all – which he could hardly avoid, even with fifty feet of timber to roam through – and they always ate under the hood, especially when the gnats hummed and whined in the evening. They had always been apt to afflict him but, shrouded as they all were in cotton, he did well enough.

In any case, once they found the river again, they were able to move much more swiftly. Sooner than he expected, he began to see dunes on the left bank, and although there were still patches of green, and the right bank was florid as ever, there was no doubt that they had come far north as well as far to the east, and very soon now would be touching the desert.

It was cooler again, and he slept better. That was to say, he never slept a great deal, but latterly had found the knack of resting elude him. Now he fell once or twice into thorough slumber, from which he awoke with a headache. The only person who noticed was Bel, who spent her days peacefully under the hood, reduced in size and in colour but not in spirit. 'What's the matter?' she said. She had cultivated the company of the chicken the crew kept for good luck, and it sat on her lap, making messes.

'Too much sunshine,' he said. 'We are having lungfish. Vito caught one.'

'Are you sure?' said Bel.

'Yes,' said Nicholas. 'Well, he says so.' He moved away, training his mind on other things. The flood. The flood they said reached Timbuktu during January, and carried the river, or a channel of it, up to the depot. If there was a wharf, there would be a picket of animals. He could get one for Bel. The men and Gelis could probably walk, depending on distance. Depending on distance, they would need packmules for the goods. The upshot was he had better leave them on board and go with Saloum first of all, to look about and call on the headman, who was said to be a Tuareg and unpopular.

Nevertheless, they might qualify for some sort of shelter until he worked out how long they would be staying. How much gold there was, or wasn't, and how long a wait it would mean to acquire it. He wondered if it was February yet, and was amazed to find that he had lost track of the calendar. It occurred to him that the stores ought to be checked ready for disembarking, and he went off to see Vito and Diniz. They were excited, and therefore talkative, which he found painful.

He realised what was happening. There was nothing he could do about it.

The arrangements seemed to take a long time to make, and he went outside again, where it was fresher. He saw the shore was sandier, although there were bushes. He saw a great silk-cotton tree upholding a snowdrift of slumbering ospreys. He saw some birds from the crane-wheel in Bruges. He began writing things down.

That night, he dreamed he was in a boat. He probably was, for Loppe was rowing. The first time they met, he was swimming. He tried to remember his face, but could only remember how black it was. Black, with a nose as long as a Nubian's, and black fingers turning the ledger. *The sugarcane has done well. Of course it has. But what will you do with no hands?*

Someone said, 'Nicholas?' and he woke.

The hired boatmen knew, too, that they were getting close to the terminus and a dispute began, which Saloum had to interpret. They wanted money to take them back home. They wanted the boat, perhaps. Nicholas got hold of Diniz and they agreed terms, with a small show of force. If they got the gold, they might have to store it. If they got a lot of gold, he might split the party and send Diniz back to the *Niccolò*, although he didn't want to mention that yet. Assuming Godscalc was bent on Ethiopia. Assuming Ethiopia wasn't where he was beginning to suspect it was. He wondered what to do about Gelis, and then thought he could leave that to Bel and to Godscalc. He remembered that he'd written down none of his plans for the *Ghost*. He thought he had better lie down, but not yet.

He said to Godscalc, 'I want to take Saloum ashore and then come back for you. If I don't, tell the men to row out. I've paid them to wait, and they're due more if they do what I've asked them.' Soon, they all went to sleep, and so did he.

The trouble was Raffaelo Doria, and the child he had snared for his bed in the *Ghost*. Except that the name of the ship was the *Doria*, which meant Raffaelo could claim her, unless a black boy could be found to cut his head off. Then old Jordan claimed her instead, and laughed, and hit Nicholas in the face, and took Marian away. Sent Marian away, so that she died of starvation in Cyprus, and her son was killed in a tournament. Although he was so young. He was too young, far too young for a tournament.

Someone said, 'It's all right. He's dreaming.'

Diniz. Then the voice of Gelis said, 'Really?'

'Wake up, Nicholas,' Diniz said. 'We've arrived.'

The water had reached far up to the terminus, but there was no view of the place, only dunes behind the ramshackle buildings of the wharf. Under a few dusty trees, everyone including the curs seemed to be sleeping, and the empty boats rocked in the heat, reeking of stale nut oil and ordure and fish. Everything stank.

There was a last-minute quarrel, once they had wakened people and hired mules and a couple of porters, because Diniz announced he was coming. It was not expedient. Nicholas couldn't remember why it wasn't expedient, except that Saloum said so. He wondered if it was Saloum, in the first place, who had suggested they go first together. He left Diniz behind, scarlet and fuming, with Godscalc and the women and Vito. He was himself worried, for they couldn't manage without him. He couldn't manage, either, without them. He had to get the gold back to the Gambia.

The ride was not long, which was fortunate. He had an impression of gaining a rise and seeing a sheet of water before him with the walls of the chief's house beyond it, made of whitened mud bricks and not brushwood. He thought that this was certainly wise, in a place where goods were stored in the compound. He had heard that the caravans lodged to the north, in sandy plains outside the depot.

He found he and Saloum had arrived at a pair of vast timber gates, studded with iron. One of their porters banged on it, and a voice enquired who they were. It spoke in Arabic. Saloum replied, 'It is the marabout Saloum ibn Hani.' He spoke in Arabic, too.

The gates opened. There were armed men inside, with caps and

white shirts and trousers, and slippers on their feet. They were
black. Saloum said, 'Send word. Quickly.' No one asked who
Nicholas was. They rode through.

Because of the buildings there was shade, which was a relief, but
chilled the sweat on the skin. Nicholas shivered, and opened his
eyes. Buildings. That was what was strange. He was riding through
the dark of a street, with buildings rising high on either side of
him, and lanes running to right and to left, also lined with houses
of two or three storeys. Ornate dwellings, with doorsteps and
windows; and a glimpse of green courtyards, and curious pyramids
stuck over with quills. A square opened out, and another.

There were few people about, with the sun at its height, but
those he saw paid them little attention. They seemed well dressed,
their garments spotless, their heads covered. They were all black.
A carnival, he realised. Was it Lent? Was it February? They
passed San Marco. Not San Marco: it was smaller, and had a wall,
and gardens, and its towers were red and white and had no mosaic.
If it was San Marco, he would be in a boat, and not riding a mule
rather badly. In Venice, the streets were not made of sand. They
came to a palace.

Here, there were people awake. They ran to take the mules, and
lead the porters away. Saloum let them, and Nicholas didn't
complain. It was hard enough to dismount, although someone
helped him. They walked up steps between pillars. He thought at
first it was going to be like Trebizond, and he would meet the
Emperor, and someone would take him to the baths. He thought
they might do him some good.

Then he saw that the portico opening ahead of him was more like
a pavilion in Castile or Granada, as travellers described them. He
had seen something like it in Málaga, but not so magnificent. The
floor was of marble, a little untidy with sand, and above the masts
. . . above a harbour full of unmoving columns there rose arches of
fragile white stucco-work. He had never had a sugar-cook who could
create a masterpiece of that order, or finish it before it had melted.

Between the columns, now he looked, he could see men in robes,
some watching, some moving slowly. He thought he saw a woman
among them, although she was veiled. Saloum turned from a quick
conversation. Speaking, he hid his mouth, Nicholas noticed, to
catch the spit from the gaps in his teeth. Saloum said, 'The
governor was to have received you, my lord Niccolò, but that has
been put off until later. A house is being prepared.'

'You speak Arabic,' Nicholas said. It surprised him that Saloum
hadn't tried it before. He found he fell into it himself very well, as
he should.

Saloum said, ignoring this, 'I shall take you to the court of the judges. It would be better for you to rest there. Or Umar will take you. He belongs there.'

'Umar?' said Nicholas.

'Myself. Umar ibn Muhammad al-Kaburi,' said Loppe.

Chapter 26

THE PRESENCE OF Loppe was in no way surprising to Nicholas who had, after all, been conversing with him under somewhat obscure circumstances for several days. Huddled shivering upon a cedarwood bed in a large, darkened room, Nicholas was content that Loppe's face, its features satisfactorily reassembled, appeared from time to time among the many other black and brown faces which accompanied him from the palace of pillars to the house where he now lay. He talked to them all, but especially to Loppe, whose alternative names escaped his memory. He had always disliked even calling him Lopez.

He heard other conversations, but did not take part in them. The first might even have been a dream. It began with the violent opening of both leaves of the door of his room. Through half-open lids he saw the servant behind it stagger back, and two others jump. Loppe, who had been sitting beside him, stood up in his white robe and cap.

It was Father Godscalc who came in, bringing the same cold voice and high anger he had shown the other day in the boat outside Murano, but now very wild in appearance, with curling black and grey face-hair tangled amongst the long hair that fell back from his brow, and his cotton cape and pantaloons filthy. After his first hasty steps to the bed, made in silence, he appeared to swing round and address Loppe. 'So! It is true!'

'That I am alive? You might say so, Father. I asked Saloum ibn Hani to beg you to wait until I had seen to Ser Niccolò's comfort.'

'He has marsh-fever. As he had in the Abruzzi. In Trebizond. I thought you called him Nicholas,' Godscalc said. 'You might as well call him Nicholas, now you have become a trickster, as he is.'

'He intended to stop here. I know what sickness he has. He is being treated for it. I shall explain to you shortly,' said Loppe. When he restrained himself, his voice became deeply musical, like a chant.

'Will you,' said Godscalc. It was not a question. 'You'll tell us how you came to stay behind on the *Niccolò*, but were the only man to escape. How you led Raffaelo Doria to the Joliba so that the Wangara miners could kill him and his men – and again, you were the only man to escape. How you ensured that Nicholas would follow, believing you were in danger, and instructed Saloum to gull Jorge da Silves and send him and his men to their deaths. Did you mean Diniz to go with Jorge and die? Did you mean us all to die except Nicholas?'

Nicholas heard his own name. The servants seemed to have left the room, including the one who had been fanning him. The bed linen was heavy and wet, but his body was weightless. Loppe said, 'It is a perilous journey to Timbuktu. The most capricious danger is greed.'

'And you think Nicholas free of it?' Godscalc said. 'Diniz was not.'

Loppe said, 'I am glad the boy survived.'

'Are you. And who are you,' Godscalc said, 'to tempt men to sin and then punish them for it?'

'Did they need tempting?' said Loppe. 'I led Doria away from Wangara. If he had gone there, you would have followed. You would all have been killed. And I, too.'

Godscalc said, 'But you did not tell us your plan.'

'No,' said Loppe.

The conversation stopped. Nicholas drifted towards another dream. Loppe spoke again, slowly. 'Perhaps he can hear me. It is only right if he does. Nicholas came to Africa for the secret of Wangara. It was the only way to keep him from it.'

'At the cost of how many souls?' Godscalc said. 'And will he stop now?'

'Look about you,' said Loppe. Or perhaps, since it didn't make much sense, he didn't say it, but it was merely part of the next dream. The next nightmare.

There was a lot of shouting in that, but Nicholas didn't recognise either Loppe's voice or Godscalc's and wondered if Jordan had found him again. His teeth drummed through his head, sticks on skins, sticks on ivory, shell upon shell. Instead of shouting, he spoke with his teeth, but no one listened.

Gelis said, 'I am frightened.'

No one answered her. They were in Timbuktu, and had spent their first night there. Now it was early morning and she and Bel, Father Godscalc and Diniz found themselves in a courtyard, about to ride out from the house of two storeys to which the tall Negro stranger had brought them. The tall Negro who, frighteningly in the half-light, proved to be no stranger at all, but Lopez in life again.

Arriving weary and late, they had found the transformation hard to assimilate. Last night, they had barely noticed where they were staying, being concerned only with Nicholas, who had been conveyed there already, and was sleeping. Lopez had seen them settled and then returned to the sickroom. The building, they gathered, was borrowed, and Lopez, but for tonight, lived elsewhere. There was no sign of Saloum, but many servants were at hand, attentive and smiling. None of them spoke a familiar tongue.

It was not surprising. They were in limbo. They were in the legendary entrepôt where, in due season, the salt from the Sahara was transferred from camel to boat and made its way up the Joliba to the silent place where it was replaced by gold. They were in Timbuktu, and Nicholas had successfully brought them there.

Last night they had been exhausted. Today they awoke to the reality of Loppe's living presence; of his transformation from Negro slave to a man named Umar ibn Muhammad al-Kaburi who, captured and sold to the Portuguese, had not lied when he said he had no father or mother, brother or sisters or wife, but who had not confided in them his identity. And who had let them mourn him for dead.

They were disturbed because the deception was too great for them to trust him. They had heard Godscalc's account of his interview. Diniz, confused and angry, had tried to resume that confrontation, but Godscalc had stopped him. Whatever had caused Loppe's – Umar's – actions, the key lay with Nicholas and nothing more should be done until Nicholas was able to speak.

Meanwhile, Godscalc found himself avoiding the man he had known for so long, and Gelis maintained a pointed van Borselen silence. Only Bel, perhaps recalling the slave-laden *Niccolò*, spoke to Loppe-Umar naturally – indeed much as she had talked to her chicken. His eyes showed his gratitude.

For the rest, the former Lopez accepted it all as if well prepared for their censure and puzzlement. Only the condition of Nicholas had clearly startled and worried him: he clung to the sickroom, they saw, as if willing Nicholas to awake. But Nicholas, burning with fever, had retreated currently into a separate world and could not recognise his former companions, much less communicate usefully with them.

Last night Diniz, too, had lingered frustrated at his bedside, but had learned nothing from Nicholas, and less than nothing from his physician. The man was a Negro.

'From Kabura,' Umar-Lopez had answered, when fiercely questioned. 'Of my own race, many of whom live in this quarter. He is a master of medicine, as fully qualified as your friend Abul Ismail of the Mameluke army. Would I offer Nicholas less?' He had paused, and seemed to brace himself to make an effort. 'You are about to say that, but for me, his journey here would not have been so impetuous, or so damaging. It is true. I am sorry.'

'Nicholas didn't have marsh-fever in Cyprus,' Diniz said. 'On that occasion, he gave himself other punishments. He is going to be very angry, I think, when he understands you are not dead, or a dream.'

'I am sure of it,' said Umar-Lopez. After a moment he said, 'It is unusual, to interpret even so much of how Nicholas thinks. But of course, you are of his blood. Of his colour.'

'Colour? What has that to do with it? I saw him lose Katelina van Borselen,' said Diniz.

Now it was morning and their host – their captor? – had indicated that he did not wish to leave the building today, or have them leave. Pressed, he delivered a blunter reply. 'It is customary,' Lopez said, 'for guests of Timbuktu to remain indoors until summoned by the governor, the Timbuktu-Koy, to his residence. When Nicholas is well, you will go.'

'I do not wish to wait,' Godscalc said. 'I propose to ride round Timbuktu this morning, either with you, or without you. Vito can sit beside Nicholas.'

He didn't expect Umar-Lopez to agree, but he did. He had not, therefore, total power over their movements. No less than the others, Godscalc was concerned over Nicholas, but it was necessary to go out and take bearings. Held indoors, they were dependent wholly on Lopez. Now, however brief the tour he allowed, they would at least see where they were and, when Nicholas woke, move towards independence if necessary. It was imperative to believe that Nicholas would recover, and soon.

Godscalc and Diniz, Gelis and Bel made their journey through Timbuktu mounted on small Arab horses and veiled, robed and gowned in the style of the country. The ride was to be short, and unobtrusive. 'Or?' Diniz said. His arm was paining him.

'Or you cannot stay in Timbuktu,' had said Umar-Lopez regretfully.

In the semi-dark of the previous evening, they had registered little. Now, all was unexpected and new. Emerging from the yard, their horses stepped out upon sand between high walls of coated mud-bricks, shaded by trees and heaped with creepers and flowers. The lane they had entered surprisingly led to another, and another.

They reached a fine open space, strung with awnings and shaded
by trees, which proved to be a market of produce, rather larger
than might have been expected, and displaying a bounty of both
river and pasture. There were heaps of rice and millet and
tamarinds, piles of kola nuts, sacks of Baobab flour, calabashes of
honey and wax and soft cheeses. There were dates and fresh and
smoked fish, goatskins of milk, and stout yellow gourds of sweet
juices.

Goats bleated, and tied chickens flapped, while vats of palm oil
sizzled and smoked and children skipped about, shouting. The
sellers and buyers were of every colour from chestnut to black, and
many were naked. They sang and chattered and laughed. It was a
place of enchanting gaiety.

'They are of different tribes,' said Umar-Lopez, 'and come
daily. You will hear Songhai, Tamashagh and even classical Arabic.
There is another market, for pots and baskets and bowls from the
craft-shops.'

'The dealers are there?' Diniz said. They moved away from the
market.

'No,' said Umar. 'In Timbuktu, the merchants deal from their
houses. We are reaching that quarter now.'

'That quarter?' said Diniz. He was tolerant, until the street
turned. It widened. There were mansions planted on either side,
some of them walled and enclosed, others confronting the street
with immense, glittering doors, their flanking walls fretted with
openwork. The road between them was marbled with light.

'This is a *town*!' Diniz exclaimed.

Umar-Lopez looked at him. 'Oh, yes,' he said.

There were people here, too; many of them. Some walked, black
and naked and smiling, with bundles on head or at hip, or driving
goats, or sheep, or a cow. Some rode on mule or donkey or camel
and were enveloped in clothes; booted men robed like the nomadic
traders of Arguim and masked by the double blue headcloth, so
that only the measuring eyes could be seen. There were men in
coats and dark turbans, who might be brown-skinned or black,
hairless or bearded or wearing moustaches. There were men,
brown-skinned or black, in white gowns and swathed heads who
walked soberly, a cane or a scroll in their fingers.

There were groups of black-eyed women in veils, followed by
servants who were wholly black, and neither women nor men.
There were black servants of both sexes or none escorting black
women who were not only young and unveiled, but without any
garments whatever. One such cortège came into view as they
watched: unclothed men and girls passing with long-limbed

indolent strides, heads high and polished skin gleaming, the lady distinguished from her retinue by her slenderness; by the gold earrings and armlets she wore; and the gold chain with its red leather locket fixed between breasts like ripe figs.

Diniz had seen such a necklet before. Umar-Lopez was wearing one at the throat of his robe. He looked again at the girl, to make sure.

He realised that the same Umar-Lopez was continuing gravely to speak. 'You see the Tuareg before you, who cover their faces. Berbers. Bozo fishermen from the Joliba. From beyond the river, the men and women with marked faces, and those with gold through the lip. The men of the jurisprudence, the scholars, are those wearing white.' He had kept his voice solemn.

The men of the jurisprudence, not incurious about the small group of riders, would sometimes smile at Umar, and bow. Three or four times, a man turned with a startled expression and then, hastening over, greeted him with a torrent of Arabic, to which Umar would reply smiling, but briefly. 'They are not all surprised to see you,' Godscalc observed.

'I have been here some days,' said Umar-Lopez. They knew that by now. Once free of Doria, he had sped on his way at three times their own laborious pace, borrowing horses; making his sure way from village to village; being transported by the fleetest of boats.

Diniz thought of Nicholas, carrying Bel in his arms. He said, 'How long have you been away from your home?'

'For ten years,' said Lopez. Said Umar.

'And you have not tried to come back until now?'

'A slave cannot travel,' said Umar. 'Nicholas and Marian de Charetty set me free, and I have tried to repay them. This is a merchant quarter, as you see. The house where you stay is in another such. The dealer who lives in your house is away, and his family have moved to another they have. They have left you some of their servants.'

'Slaves,' Gelis said. The houses were of mud-brick, rough-cast over, or of limestone, covered with clay. The clay must have been imported, and the limestone. There were quarries, she had heard, in the desert. The walls sloped, and bore peculiar ornaments: chimney-like buttresses and attachments like pyramids. In the distance she could see a great, blurred building large enough to kennel a sphinx. It was stuck with thorns like a porcupine. There was a minaret by it.

'Slaves? Yes,' said Umar-Lopez.

'And eunuchs,' Gelis said. 'That is a mosque.'

'We have passed several,' said Umar-Lopez. 'But that is the

oldest. It is a university also, and around it are the houses of the
savants and teachers. I should have taught there, had I not been
captured. There are many schools. You will wish to see them one
day.' He was speaking to Godscalc.

Godscalc said, 'Your name is Umar ibn Muhammad al-Kaburi.
You were reared as a Muslim?'

'Forgive me,' said Loppe. Below the white cap, his eyes were as
clear as a black and white drawing.

'You were never the Christian you pretended to be?'

'I was baptised,' said Umar-Lopez.

'You broke faith with your teachers, and are now forsworn, or so
I suppose it, a second time. Those are not the acts of a scholar,'
said Godscalc.

'I do not excuse myself,' said Umar-Lopez. 'Save to say that I
did not seek my own benefit. There is the house of the imam of
this region, who is also a judge. It is the profession of my father
and grandfather: I know what justice consists of. We have reached
the northern boundary, as you see. Beyond is the *abaradiou*, the
pools and the pastures where the camel trains rest at the end of
their journey. The main *azalai*, the salt caravan, arrives here in
May, but there are others between.'

'I see soldiers,' said Godscalc.

'There is a post here,' said Umar. 'The main garrison buildings
are by the palace. Timbuktu has few defences, but the commander,
when he is here, keeps good order. We should start on our way
back.'

'By the *palace*?' said Gelis. 'Is that Egyptian as well?'

Umar smiled at her. He said, 'No. It is Andalusian. You have
found a strange caravan terminus, have you not? Fifteen hundred
miles from the sea: a station, a fulcrum. One arm points to the
desert, the other south to the swamp, the river, the steaming
rainforests of the cannibal blacks. To my forefathers.'

Her gaze did not challenge. 'How many people live here?'

'Forty thousand,' he said. 'You are in a city the same size as
Florence, the same size as Bruges. Bigger than Genoa or Cologne;
twice the size of Pavia or Lübeck. A melting city built upon gold.'

'Melting?' she said.

Umar said, 'You have not been here in the rain. Mud-bricks
dissolve; rough-cast crumbles. Limestone here has a life of a
hundred years, not much more. The marble, the pillars, the stucco
are for today, not tomorrow. Tomorrow, we build them again. We
should go back to Nicholas.'

'Did he know?' Gelis said.

'Of the nature of Timbuktu?' Umar-Lopez said. 'I did not tell him.'

On the way back they passed another great mosque, but Umar would not allow them to pause, or later to glimpse more than a gleam between palms of the exquisite building he had called Andalusian. They smelled flowers, and heard water, and caught sight of gardens. Godscalc said, 'You are in a great hurry.'

'I am concerned about Nicholas,' Umar said. He was looking ahead. Before them, they saw, was the trampled parade ground, the high walls and flat roofs of the city garrison. 'I am sorry,' said Umar.

'Why?' said Godscalc, and then stopped, for he, too, saw the cavalry flooding out of the gates and spreading out to encompass them.

What took them all by the throat was the suddenness of it, and the silence. One moment their path was clear; the next it was blocked, before and behind, by a circle of blank, faceless horsemen, their heads wrapped in the blue cloth of the Tuareg. No one spoke. The garrison horses, tightly held, stamped and fidgeted. Every rider was armed: their swords rattled. One man began to ride forward.

Umar said something under his breath. The word was Flemish. Diniz said, 'Who?'

'The commander of the garrison,' Umar said. 'He has heard, and come back into town.'

'Heard what?' said Godscalc.

'That Christians are here,' Umar said. 'Conceal your faces. Leave this to me.'

They could do nothing else. Gelis and Bel bent their heads, their faces covered. Godscalc and Diniz, armed with their pitiful Arabic, watched the commander rein in and speak.

The man wore the same clothes as his soldiers, but his gazelle shield and bow and sword were heavily encrusted with gold, and his lower veil had been loosed from the beak of his nose, baring a thick black moustache and russet skin pitted with scars. Round his shoulders lay gold chain thick as a cable. He said in Maghsharen Arabic, 'You seem amazed. Would Akil ag Malwal neglect to share the joy of the *umma* at the return of a son of the city? Greetings, Umar.'

'Greetings, my lord Akil,' Umar said. 'No, I was certain you would not neglect it. You are well?'

'Assuredly. And these are your wives, and this your eunuch. He is singularly well provided with hair. And the young man has the colouring of a *bidan* from the Maghgreb. Your secretary, your servant perhaps? Or a friend for your pillow?'

The man reached out towards Diniz and touched his cheek with the butt of his whip. Diniz glared, his fists tight on his reins.

Umar spoke in his voice of untrustworthy honey. 'Being absent, lord, you could not share in my gladness at the Timbuktu-Koy's message of welcome to me and my companions. They are worthy souls: a party of traders and map-makers, travelling east. They have paused to rest, and to scatter joy, gifts and alms in the halls of the Timbuktu-Koy. He will tell you.'

'I go to him now,' said the commander. 'Your women are traders? Praise be to Allah. I go to him now to learn his wishes about your companions —'

'I have told you,' said Umar. His voice was deeper by several degrees than the other's.

'But of course, except that the Koy has not yet granted them audience, as I understand. They cannot therefore be said to have been accepted. Deception is possible. You yourself may have been deceived. And meanwhile, they roam the streets and may infect and corrupt our poor people. You see my dilemma?'

'I see, perhaps,' said Umar, 'good reason for us to hasten back to our lodging. I confess my mistake. I gave way to my pride in my city. As it happens, our ride has been short and no one, to my knowledge, has found his faith weaker because of it. However, we shall retire. We shall await the Timbuktu-Koy's summons.'

'You may await it here,' said Akil ag Malwal with a nod of his head. The armed circle opened about them, leaving a path to the gates of the command post. 'It is a temporary expedient, of course. You led the Genoese dogs to their punishment, and your companions may be equally innocent. But their leader, I am told, is a man intent on Wangara gold. His Portuguese vanguard gave battle to our own Timbuktu traders.'

Diniz flushed. Umar-Lopez said, 'They did, and died. Their leader, a Flemish lord, had no designs on Wangara. Some of his following disobeyed, and, as you say, have received the ultimate punishment. The Flemish lord has lodged no complaint, and the Timbuktu-Koy has been apprised of the matter. If, therefore, that is all, we should prefer to return to our lodgings.'

'Then you shall,' said the Tuareg captain with a smile. 'No one, knowing your worth, would doubt your good intentions. But it is I who must answer for it if harm still befalls. The Flemish lord has made no complaint, perhaps because he intended evil, and still means to practise it. He is the leader, he is responsible. I have sent to have him arrested for questioning. We shall go to his house together. You and your companions may stay, and the Flemish lord will ride with us back to our prison. It is a comfortable one.'

'Arrest him?' said Umar. 'He is sick. That is why the audience has not been held.'

'We have reasonable doctors,' said the commander. 'I advise you not to concern yourself.'

'*I will concern myself!*' Diniz said, and rode forward. There was a sudden whine of drawn swords. Godscalc and Gelis crowded upon Diniz, and Godscalc seized his reins. The words had been in Portuguese, but his face was translation enough.

'My colleague is young and hasty,' Umar remarked, 'and forgets in which town he is guest. I, of course, bow to your wisdom, but my learned confrères might demur. Saloum ibn Hani the marabout was freed from slavery by this very Fleming and, judging him honest, led him and his party to this place. The Timbuktu-Koy knows of this. It might also please him to know that, in difficult times, my lord Akil made no hasty decisions, and moreover supplied these men with an interpreter.'

'Yourself? Well, so be it,' said the commander Akil. 'Stay with them. Relate to them what I have said. I am not an inclement man. Their lord shall have the best of the prison.'

They returned by the way they had come, except that this time they had a corps of two hundred armed horsemen escorting them. There were no bystanders, now, who cared to call out to Umar: the alleys were clear as if scoured by a ramrod. They entered the narrow lane between walls where their lodging was.

Diniz bit his lip. Against such force, they were helpless. Vito would be there, but unarmed. The physician, an Arab, was useless, and Nicholas, crazed or oblivious, could defend neither himself nor them. Bel, whom he had thought beyond speech, said, 'Umar? What can we do?'

'Pretend,' Umar said. His eyes elsewhere, he spoke flatly.

Gelis flung back her veil and said, 'Look!'

The gates to their courtyard stood open, and a crowd had gathered, attracted by some spectacle. The wall hid what it was. Godscalc said, with anxiety, 'Mary Mother of God!' and tried to hurry.

The commander Akil was not in the same haste. He held up his hand and his cavalcade slowed, Godscalc and his companions with it. They drew level with the crowd, which fell back. Then they moved up to the gates and saw what was happening.

Nicholas, manhandled or safe, was not there. The yard between the gates and their house was full of soldiers. Different soldiers. Soldiers who were clearly not Akil's, for their noses and mouths were not covered. They were not Tuaregs, but Sanhaja Berbers on foot, and carrying swords. They occupied the forecourt, a throng rather than a drilled squadron, but with an alertness about them that made of them a unity. They held spears and knives also, but

not aggressively: more in the manner of guards, and they made no
effort to close the gates before Akil.

Akil ag Malwal entered and halted, and his troops, flanking him,
trotted so far and stopped. The groups of men looked at one another.

'Greetings,' said someone. It was one of the men in the courtyard,
a swarthy, powerful man swathed in wool. 'The Timbuktu-Koy
sends us to commend your assiduity. He has placed these incomers
under his hand. I am to thank you, and say he is protected.'

'Then Allah be praised,' said Akil ag Malwal. 'If you will step
aside, I shall see for myself. I have some men inside, I believe.'

'Alas,' said the man who had spoken. 'I was forced to expel
them, since I have orders to admit none but the Flemish lord's
party. The Flemish lord is to stay.'

A sound hung in the air which might have been a growl from
two hundred Tuareg throats. The men in the courtyard were not a
third of that number. Bel began to cough, and Gelis, leaning, put
an arm around her and cried out to the captain. 'My lord! I do not
know what you fear, but she is ill.'

Her meaning, like that of Diniz, was plain enough. Her face,
unveiled and stricken, looked wonderful. There was a general
murmur, perhaps of pleasure. The commander Akil displayed
none. For a moment he sat without speaking. Then, with an abrupt
gesture, he threw a command to his men. Their horses stirred, and
began to retreat to the gates.

Umar said, 'I am grateful. May many blessings ensue.' The
commander ignored him and, turning, rode out.

The gates closed. Umar bent from the saddle and spoke to the
Timbuktu-Koy's captain. Diniz dashed for the inner courtyard
and dismounted, followed by Godscalc and the women. No one
stopped them. By the time Umar joined them, they had already
reached the main part of the house. Vito came running to meet
them, his face yellow.

Umar said, '*What?*' He was breathing quickly.

'Those bastards!' Vito said. 'They wanted to take Messer Niccolò
off! You left me no weapons, you know you left me nothing to
defend him with? And then the governor's men came in and
stopped them. I thought they'd killed you all at the least.'

'No,' said Umar. 'But Ser Niccolò? Is he worse?'

'He is not better,' said the physician, entering decorously. 'But
he suffered less, perhaps, in his delusions than you did in reality. It
would be as well, however, if he were not moved again. Tonight
may be crucial.'

'Tonight,' Umar said, 'you shall have weapons, and I shall
watch with the rest at the gate. Although now we should be safe.'

Godscalc said, 'It was our fault, for demanding to go. It might have helped had you told us the dangers.'

'I did not know Akil was back,' Umar said. 'He would have heard, and tried to come for you anyway. It would not have happened if your audience had taken place. Will you sit with Nicholas? There should be someone there through the night.'

'Of course,' Godscalc said.

'And here's Gelis,' said Bel. 'She'll spell you.'

Godscalc drew breath to object, and then paused. After a long time he said, 'Yes. Let her sit with him. Unless she is frightened.'

'Not of that,' Gelis said.

It was doubtful whether, in fact, Nicholas in his delusions had suffered less. He had very little recollection of being dragged out of bed, or of the clash of factions which resulted in his being restored to it, after a vertiginous period during which people kept trying to rouse him with questions. Since he could neither understand them nor parry them, it was as well, in a way, that his answers were confined to quite different enigmas which vexed him.

What transpired was a rambling dissertation of little interest to Tuaregs or Berbers, especially since it was conducted in French. His everyday language might be Flemish, but in time of distress it was the tongue of his mother he spoke. He spoke it all through the night when first Godscalc, and then Gelis, sat at his side. Towards morning, the fever broke once again into drenching sweats, and Gelis called the physician, and gave him her place at the bedside.

When he invited her to return, she found the sheets and mattress renewed, and Nicholas, sponged and freshened and folded into a dry cotton bedgown, laid back flat as a doll on his pillows. The doctor said, 'It is the end, you understand, the end of the fever? There will be much sleep, and to drink, and eat sparingly. Now it is safe: you can leave him.' He patted her shoulder. 'You are tired.'

He looked tired himself. The lamp flickered, competing with the light of dawn around the edge of the window. She said, 'Soon,' and smiled, and, thanking him, ushered him out. Then, crossing the room, she stood by the shutters and opened them.

A cock crew, the sort of sound you heard anywhere, and a child cried. A camel swayed down the lane, a boy on its back flicking his stick, first on one side, then on the other. On the roof of the house opposite, a vulture was sitting. Nicholas said in a doubtful voice, 'I am sorry. Who is it?'

She turned, and came back to the lamplight. Against the light, with her hair unbound, she must have seemed strange. She sat on the bed-edge and looked at him. Through the night, as never before, she had had leisure to study him. Wringing out the cloths for his neck and his brow, freeing the hair from his eyes, supporting his head to offer him water, she had measured his shape, his size and his weight; formed an opinion of the capable hands; considered the traits which had produced the broad, straight lines on his brow, the sunny lines by the eyes and the others, dimples at present, which one day would deepen and alter his face.

It was altered already, by the deprivation of the last weeks, as well as by illness. He was not old enough to reflect strain as Godscalc did, whose large frame appeared hollow, and whose joints became knobs. Nicholas emerged from adversity concentrated in essence, like a nestling firmed into maturity. It was misleading. Listening to him, as she had listened all night, she did not think he had ever been immature, or a nestling. She did not want to talk to him now.

He had recognised her. He said, 'Have you been here all night?'

'And Father Godscalc. It was Bel's idea,' she said.

'Was it interesting?' he said.

She didn't pretend to misunderstand. 'Yes,' she said.

He said nothing, but kept his eyes open. 'Go to sleep,' she said shortly.

He said, 'I thought you wanted to tell me what secrets I gave away.'

'Nothing I didn't guess,' Gelis said. She blew out the lamp and rose from his bedside.

'Nothing? My good God,' he said. His eyes were still open.

'Or very little. I knew you had a child by Katelina,' she said. 'The son that Simon thinks is his. Godscalc knows.'

'Godscalc and Tobie,' he said. 'Tobie, my doctor. My other doctor. One of my other doctors. If you tell Simon it's mine, he will kill it.'

'It? I thought it was a son. You don't want Katelina's son?' she said.

His eyes were pale grey, with hairline pleats of darker grey round the iris. He said, but not immediately, 'I prefer a quiet life.'

Elsewhere in the house, people were rousing. She heard voices, and footsteps. The night was over, and there had been no attack. She observed, 'You nearly had a very unquiet life yesterday morning. The governor and the garrison commander were fighting over you.'

He said, 'I remember being sick over someone. Who won?'

'Umar,' she said.

'Umar,' he repeated. She saw that, for the moment, he was too deadened by weakness to think. He said, 'I don't even know where I am.'

'Timbuktu,' she said.

'And who is Umar?' he asked. His voice was fractured; he had been hoarse for some hours, but hardly seemed to be aware of it. She hesitated.

The door had opened so quietly that she hadn't heard it. Lopez was standing just inside. Lopez. Umar. He remained standing until Nicholas noticed him. Neither spoke. Gelis held her breath.

Unable this time to dissemble, the invalid on the mattress lay still, except for his altering face. His instinctive emotion, Gelis thought, had been fear.

The silence stretched. Then Nicholas dragged himself up on one elbow. 'Now I remember,' he said. His pale skin was livid.

'Leave, please,' said Umar, without looking round.

She had no need to stay. She knew what Nicholas felt about Lopez. She knew what Nicholas felt about a great many people, but especially about Katelina.

She hadn't needed the ravings of Nicholas to tell her that Katelina's body and hers were alike. Alike, of course, except that hers was intact, while Katelina's had enjoyed lover, husband, maternity. Except that she was alive, and Katelina was dead. She didn't want to hear what happened between Nicholas and a man who only made believe to be dead.

As she opened the door, she saw Umar walk forward in his spotless robe and white cap, and abruptly drop to his knees like a servant. She heard Nicholas speak. Nicholas said, '*How dare you. How dare you do what you have done.*'

The violence of it stayed in her mind as she left. She could not imagine feeling such rage, had Katelina come back.

Chapter 27

THE EFFECT OF THE collision between Nicholas and Lopez was unexpected. Instead of being thrown back into fever Nicholas stayed, entrenched and determined, on the high ground to which temper had propelled him, and the vitality he had lost came flooding back.

The same might have been said of Lopez. The explosion over, the familiar figure, broad and black and reserved, emerged as if from limbo to speak and act once again as he had always done. As if, with Nicholas there, he need have no fear of misrepresentation, even if he had neither approval nor support. Even Diniz, with his vaunted insight, could not fully understand what had happened, and Gelis, when unobserved, wore an expression of doubt. Bel said, 'What is it sin-eaters do?'

'Never mind,' Godscalc answered. Recently, they had spent some time together, but neither had spoken of, or to, Gelis.

On the afternoon of that same day, Nicholas had asked them all to come to his room and delivered a statement in a low, restored voice. Propped up by pillows, he had denounced Loppe as the murderer in spirit, if not in fact, of Doria and his men, and Jorge da Silves and his. As Godscalc had not done, he also recounted Loppe's reasons.

'To me, the grounds for killing these men were insufficient,' he ended. 'By his lights, they were not. In any case, you might say, it happened; it is over; and, now the motive has been removed, it will not happen again. The deaths that occurred on the ship and on the journey would have taken place anyway. We might have fared a great deal worse had we not been given Saloum, who is absent because ... Umar ... wished us to understand that Saloum deserved none of the blame. Umar did not see fit to advise us of the character of Timbuktu, or of his standing here, because he was committed to deceiving us about Wangara. The secret of Wangara being safe, he is willing to rejoin us now, and to guide us through the trade we have come to effect, and to help us on the next stage of our journey, if we want him. I don't know whether I do. You are here to make your voice known. Have I been fair?' He looked, unsmiling, at Umar, who had been Loppe.

'No,' said Umar. 'But it is your language, and your standards, and your company.'

'Then make your own case,' Nicholas said. 'You are, I hear, a jurist.'

'I should not presume,' Umar said. He, too, looked sombre.

Diniz said, 'We've come a long way. We need help. We couldn't even go back.' He thought. 'He provided this house, and looked after Nicholas, and protected us from that bastard Akil. But will he let us buy gold?'

'Yes,' said Umar. 'This is a legitimate market. It is the silent trade and the mines you are debarred from. As has been said, I have no reason to deceive or hinder you now.'

His gaze, as he spoke, was on Godscalc. He had made no plea; said nothing of all he had done for them in the past in Cyprus, in Trebizond – even, so Godscalc had been told, on the homecoming entry to Venice. Godscalc knew, from personal experience or hearsay, more than anyone present but Nicholas about Umar ibn Muhammad al-Kahuri, linguist, colleague, protector, singer of Gregorian chants.

The thought led to another. Godscalc said slowly, 'The next stage of our journey?' Umar looked away.

Nicholas said, 'I promised I'd take you to Prester John. Perhaps you don't want to go.'

Gelis said, 'Father?'

Godscalc looked at her. She said, 'God himself would not ask it. Surely it is enough to have reached as far as we have.'

'Child,' said Bel. 'They're talking of the way to the East. That's always been what the game was about and, being men, they're not for rushing to change it until it's changed for them. So we need help. So we need help whether we go on or go back. So yes, I agree to accept Umar's offer. So does Diniz, you've heard. So, once she gets her senses in order, will Gelis. I don't know what way the padre will vote, but that's a majority. Umar, what will it cost you?'

He said, 'No more than I am willing to pay. Nicholas has not voted yet.'

'I don't need to,' said Nicholas, reopening his eyes. 'You have a majority. Welcome, Umar, Timbuktu agent of the Casa Niccolò, Venice. Father, will you stay behind, please?'

They all rose. Godscalc said, 'I could come back in an hour.'

'Don't you want to get it over with?' Nicholas said. The others left. Godscalc reseated himself and set his hands on his knees.

Nicholas said, 'Who else have you shown them to?'

Godscalc said nothing, in a cloud of belligerence. Had he been a lesser man he would have cursed.

Nicholas said, 'You knew I would write down my orders. I did it before. Who else have you shown them to? Gelis?'

'No,' Godscalc said. 'If you see a change in Gelis, it is not due to that. You know she sat with you last night?'

'At Bel's suggestion,' Nicholas said. 'What did I say?'

'The truth,' Godscalc said. 'It is not a bad thing to have out in the open. I cannot tell you whether Gelis is less your enemy than she was: you took her by surprise, I should guess, and she has much to consider. I showed your notes to Bel, not to Gelis. She won't talk of your plans.'

'Except, no doubt, to me. I could have wished you had waited,' said Nicholas.

'For your nurses to find them? Or Lopez? You addressed the packet to me,' Godscalc said. 'And I haven't shown it to Diniz. That, I take it, is what you really want to find out.'

'You don't approve,' Nicholas said.

Godscalc thought. He said, 'Surprisingly, I think that I do. It would be easier if we knew what was happening at home.'

Remote though he seemed, Nicholas laughed. He said, 'Bring in your brushes and write these words in gold on that wall. Or read the minds of Simon and David de Salmeton for me.'

A day later, he left his bed and moved restlessly through the house, and Gelis avoided him. Two days later, he rose at sunrise and, dressed in a robe Umar had brought him, walked into the courtyard where the others awaited him with the horses. He walked steadily, because they were watching him. It was too soon, perhaps, but he was no longer prepared to tolerate the perpetual confinement, the perpetual guard.

Approached, the governor had agreed to receive Niccolò vander Poele of Venice and his party of traders in formal audience at the Ma' Dughu, the palace of the Timbuktu-Koy on the western edge of the city that morning. It was time, and more than time.

They rode there enclosed by their retinue: Diniz in figured silk and draped hat, Godscalc in fine priestly wool and the women veiled in thin tissues. They had ceased, now, to be surprised that such things could be procured. They knew, because Nicholas had demanded to know, the essential facts about Timbuktu, which for centuries had been no more than an oasis above the flood-plain of the Joliba, where merchandise from the north might be transferred from camel to boat, and bartered for the produce of rainforest and river. The trade in salt and gold had come later, and forced the Tuaregs who engaged in it to seek a secure place for their stores, and for the caravanserais where merchants and dealers could stay. So the city was founded, and for 350 years had grown and flourished.

In isolation. A man from Bruges or Venice or Lisbon, each with its flourishing hinterland, could only wonder that such a thing could be possible: that a crossroads occupied by a dozen races on the edge of the desert could become a centre of wealth; and although never a city-state, could contrive to rule its own destiny.

Nominally, Timbuktu had had several overlords, and once had belonged to the kingdom of Mali. Few princes troubled to visit it often. When Mali weakened, the Tuaregs had seized control once again, but for thirty years had been content to rove the Sahel and the Sahara, leaving the day-to-day labour of ruling to the present excellent Timbuktu-Koy, who paid himself a third of the tax levied from rich traders. The other two-thirds were the privilege of the garrison lord and his army.

They had met this man, the Tuareg Lord Akil. The Timbuktu-Koy, said Umar, was an old man, Muhammed ben Idir, who had been clever enough over many years to keep control of the city, and prevent Akil from interfering on his sudden descents. The Koy's son and natural successor was a young man with a young man's impatience who, it could only be hoped, would prove as cunning. They would be offered food and drink after the audience, and might partake, even the ladies. In Timbuktu, Umar said, the segregation of women (except for business) was not insisted on.

The Ma' Dughu was the palace seen once by Nicholas in his fever. Now, mounting the steps between the palms and the acacias, he knew it was not a dream of his, but of the great King of Mali who, proceeding to Mecca with a fortune of gold sufficient to destabilise the entire Egyptian market, had brought back with him from Cairo the architect Al-Tuwaihnin who had caused a new mosque and a new Alhambra to rise in the desert, its materials brought stone by stone on camelback from the north.

Over the hundred years that had passed, the sun and the climate had distorted the dream. The marble steps of the Ma' Dughu were broken and warm to the foot, and while the snowy air from the Sierra Nevada was blowing cool through the halls of Granada, the dust of the harmattan blasted the fine onyx pillars in Timbuktu, and scoured the carvings and stucco-work in its corridors, so that the bands of Koranic writing were half-erased by dust and by light. Light pounced like a lion through the vaults and arcades of the Ma' Dughu and hung shimmering over courtyards sprawling with flowers where the pools were half full of sand, and creepers drooped from the tiles.

Only the hall of ceremony was cool, for trees shaded its walls, and deeply carved doors admitted the emissaries of Venice and Portugal from the leafy dusk of a garden.

Inside was another dusk, made of gold. Gelis drew in her breath, and even Nicholas stopped for a moment, so that Umar, leading them, checked and looked back. Then they moved between silent men into the chamber, sixty feet long, that the architect Al-Tuwaihnin had built a hundred years before for the King of Mali, and which his master's successors had been pleased to adorn with the wealth of their city.

The carved ceiling might once have been painted, but it was the soiled gold of its leaf-work that glimmered down on them now, matched by the darkened gold of the plates on the wall, within which candles burned, revealing the hung skins and cracked tiles behind them. Gold touched the running bands of calligraphy – austere Cufic, and sensuous cursive – which, blemished and stuttering, proclaimed *Allah alone is Conqueror* along every wall.

But the massy blaze which drew the eye to the end of the room came from the dais, draped in silks, upon which stood a gold chair occupied by a bearded man, half Negro, half Berber, wearing a great golden headdress and jewelled robe and surrounded by gold-accoutred soldiers, and by younger, unarmed men who might have been his sons. Behind the chair stood two children, black and naked, each stirring the air with a great, long-stemmed plume of white ostrich feathers, and beside it lay three beautiful hounds, wearing bells and collars of gold.

In the hand of Muhammed ben Idir, Timbuktu-Koy, governing prince of the city, reposed a sceptre of the weight of ten pounds of pure gold, and beside him stood tables laden with articles of his treasury: bowls and ewers and plates, cups and vases, all of the same metal. To one side lay a saddle, studded with rubies, and a set of horse-harness, also worked, and recently, in brilliant gold. The styles suggested smiths from every quarter of Europe and the East, and the glow of it was like the glow in the clouds over Murano. Umar led the way forward.

But for a space in the centre, the chamber was full. All were men: dark-skinned Negroes or Berbers seated in silence on cushions; some of them dressed and turbaned in white, some in turbans of extravagant silks and sumptuous coats of the kind Nicholas had been given. They looked at the Europeans as they passed as they might have looked at a consignment of salt.

Envoys and those making supplication approached the Timbuktu-Koy on their faces, and pouring dust over their heads. Nicholas walked forward and knelt, his neck bowed. At his side, Umar prostrated himself and then stood. The Timbuktu-Koy addressed him in Arabic, and Umar answered. At a sign, Nicholas rose, and bore the Governor's peering scrutiny with resolute calmness. The Koy was an old man, and in his lined face could be seen both the broad bones of the Negro, and the liquid eyes and prominent nose of the Sanhaja Berber. Muhammed ben Idir had ruled Timbuktu for many years.

'Approach him,' said Umar. 'You may cause your gifts to be brought in.'

Already, walking up to the dais, Nicholas had taken note that Akil was there, the enemy who had tried to seize them three days ago. Beside him was a group of his henchmen, but none of them seemed to bear arms. He looked, without seeming to look, at the merchant princes, and wondered which of them, if any, were among those who had intercepted Jorge da Silves' men at the silent trading, and had come back disappointed because the Wangara natives had killed Doria and fled with their gold.

The wealthy patricians sat together by household, their kinship obvious in the colour and cast of their faces, in a place where the tilt of an eye or the quality of a tuft of hair declared everything. The parochial leaders, the scholars, the marabouts, the judges held together as well, in mellow patches of white. He saw Saloum among them. The dark-skinned man nearest the dais must, he thought, be the Katib Musa, the religious leader and imam of the Sankore Mosque. Umar had impressed the name on him, he didn't know why. Heat and heavy scents eddied about him; his head swam for a moment, and then steadied. The servants entered, bearing his gifts to the Koy.

Nicholas had lost virtually all the goods he possessed on the Gambia. To placate the Timbuktu-Koy he had nothing to offer but a single small box saved, with three larger, from a hidden bulwark of the *San Niccolò*, and a felt satchel, much worn and stained, containing a heavy object given him that morning by Umar. He knew what was in it. When he remonstrated, Umar had only said, 'It is just.'

To a ruler, the offerings were insultingly small. The soldiers around Akil looked at one another and smiled. Nicholas took the satchel and, approaching the dais, held it up in both hands to the old man. One of the sons lifted it; a stout olive-skinned youth a little older than Diniz but younger than himself. He held it with distaste, as if about to cast it on the ground.

The imam said, 'My lord, wait.' He turned to Nicholas. 'It has travelled far, your packet. What is its nature?'

'It is a manuscript,' Nicholas said.

'Ah!' said the imam. 'And, if it is permitted to ask, in what tongue?'

'It is written in the Arabic language,' said Nicholas, 'but is of great age. It would delight me if the Timbuktu-Koy himself would receive it.'

'My lord Umar is about to present it on your behalf,' the imam said. 'Lord, the trader Niccolò gives you a book. Your son will open the cords.'

The youth had big hands, not overclean, and even as he ripped open the ties the half-rotted material gave way so that the object within would have fallen, had the Timbuktu-Koy not caught it and laid it on his knees. It consisted of many sheets of thick vellum, covered with elegant writing in several colours. The last time Nicholas had seen it was in his cargo at Kerasous. He had been told a dealer had bought it in Venice. He hadn't known until now that the dealer was acting for Loppe.

The youth Umar said, 'You give short measure! Where is the cover? The jewels? The boards?'

'No, no,' said his father. 'Here is surely something of worth. Katib Musa?'

The imam joined him quietly on the dais. He said, 'I have never seen this, although I have heard of it. It is a scribe's copy, a Greek scribe who was familiar with Arabic. It is a copy made ready for translation, but perhaps never transcribed. Would I be right?' He looked at Nicholas.

Nicholas said, 'It came from Baghdad to the Empire of Trebizond, before it fell.'

'It will be the jewel of my lord's library,' said the Katib Musa.

'And this?' said the Timbuktu-Koy in his courteous way, indicating the box that still remained.

Nicholas opened it. The two pairs of lenses glimmered from their silk beds, and struck with light the frowning faces of the Timbuktu-Koy and his heir. Nicholas said, 'If my lord will permit,' and, lifting a frame, set the box down and, in turn, mounted the dais. He said, 'Give me leave,' and touched the Koy's face and retreated.

The Timbuktu-Koy, puzzled, turned his head, and where his eyes had been, there flashed circles like mirrors. Throughout the hall, men drew in their breath. The imam Musa said, 'My lord, the Venetian has given you sight. Lower your eyes to the book.'

The great turbaned head bent, heavy on its aged stem. A horn-tipped finger touched the page, and then travelled down it. Muhammed ben Idir said, 'I am reading the words of Abu Abdallah ben Abderrahim of Granada, and my heart is filled with joy. How can such a treasure as this come from Trebizond?'

'Through trading,' Nicholas said. 'And a trader has brought it back. I would stay in your city, and exchange my wealth for your wealth, so that all may prosper. Do I have your permission?'

The old man lifted the spectacles from his nose and looked at them closely. His hand shook. He said, 'You have come for gold. How will you pay?'

'I am fortunate,' Nicholas said. 'I have many shells.' He spoke with confidence. He had not so many, but the Timbuktu-Koy didn't know that.

'And manuscripts?' said the old man.

'Certainly. They will be sent for, as soon as my lord makes his wishes known,' Nicholas said.

'But you have no more of these,' said Muhammed ben Idir, touching the heavy rims under his hand.

'That,' said Nicholas, 'is what I have brought to offer for gold. But first, I should have to see the extent and quality, forgive me, of your supplies. Gold is not hard to find, but few of the princes of Europe have ornaments such as these. They are made in secret, and are bought by great men, so that others may know they are great. Also, they buy so that their scribes can read and copy and paint, and the words of holy men may be multiplied.'

'I see,' said the Timbuktu-Koy. 'I am attracted by your proposition. But the city owns many traders, and on a matter as vital as this, I must seek their advice. I would have approach the lord Akil ag Malwal, the lord And-Agh-Muhammed al-Kabir, the sons of Muhammed Aqit and the imam Katib Musa. What say you? We, by tradition, trade across the great desert with the peoples of the north. Here is a trader who comes to us from the west, from the sea. Behind him may come many more. He wishes gold. What is your answer?'

The men he called were those most richly dressed, except for the imam, and the Tuareg And-Agh-Muhammed al-Kabir was as aged as himself. It was he who said, 'I trade with Florence and Venice. I do not wish to lose my trade to strangers from Portugal. Let them pick up the dross from the coast.' Round his neck, on a mismatched chain made of gold, he was wearing a short silver whistle.

'It is my thought,' said Akil the commander. He had sound teeth, often displayed.

'I agree,' said a young man of the Aqit family. 'But we pay at present whatever the Venetians or Florentines ask. Would they not offer more, if they knew they had rivals?'

'What!' said Akil the commander. 'Would you place wealth above the souls of your fellows? These men are infidels, and that man is their priest. But for Umar, they would have extorted from us the secret source of the gold, and returned with mighty hordes to wrest it from us. You know this.'

'Forgive me, but I, Umar, do not know this,' said Umar-Lopez. 'There were Europeans so desirous, but they are dead.'

'Certainly,' said And-Agh-Muhammed, and, lifting the chain from his neck, tossed both it and its appendage to the ground. 'Most of them are dead: my own family killed them.'

'Most?' said Nicholas. In place of carpets, the floor had been strewn with fine leopard skins. Jorge's whistle glinted through dusty fur, the words *San Niccolò* plain on its side.

The old man looked at him. 'Were they of moment? One escaped, a young boy.'

'They were of no moment,' Nicholas said.

Umar glanced at him, and away. He said, 'The lord Niccolò had no wish but to trade with you. He will tell you whether or not hordes will follow him. I do not think it likely.'

'Umar is right,' Nicholas said. 'The journey from the sea has cost many lives, and few if any will want to follow us. I tell you this as a Fleming and a Venetian, although my ship and part of my cargo are owed to Portugal. I have no wish to destroy whatever bargains you have made with other nations. Nor do we wish to do more than honour your faith. It is not our purpose to subvert your peoples.'

'Indeed?' said the imam Katib Musa. 'It is not the news I have heard from the Gambia. Your holy man has not confined himself to addressing those of his own faith.'

Godscalc lifted his head. Shaved, his chin showed corpse-grey below the tan on his cheeks. Umar said, 'He has remonstrated, as you have, with witch doctors, and with as little success. It is true, he competes for the souls of the heathen. Do you fear the power of his preaching?' He was smiling.

The imam smiled in return: at him, and then at the chaplain. 'I respect him,' he said, 'but I do not fear him. Until he learns our language, perhaps.'

'Then, as to the gold?' the old man enquired.

It was the man of the Aqit family this time who replied. 'My lord knows that there is a little in store. In three weeks or four, the salt caravan will arrive, and its goods pass to the market. In four weeks after that, the gold for which it has been exchanged will come back. There will be a great deal. I have no objection to the white traders paying for part of it.'

'Nor I,' said the Timbuktu-Koy. He, too, was smiling. The smile faded. 'It does not please you, I see.'

'Did I hesitate?' Nicholas said. 'Only because then we cannot leave in the spring, but must beg your indulgence to establish our party here until autumn. If such a thing can be done, you see me happy.'

'Naturally it can be done,' the Timbuktu-Koy said. 'Yes, my lord Akil? Agreed, my lord And-Agh and those of Aqit? Katib Musa?'

'You have my agreement,' said the Katib Musa. 'Although it seems to me that, did you desire it, you could take the gold that is here and sail before the rains come. But rumour says that you have plans to journey east?'

'We are strangers, and curious,' Nicholas said, 'but we mean no harm to anyone. As to the gold, we do not know whether to wait for the greater portion or not, but consider it wise, having come so far, not to hasten home unless we hear of a reason. And positioned where we are, that is unlikely.'

'Positioned where you are?' said one of the young men of the Aqits. 'Are we off the edge of the world? A caravan takes only six months to come and go from the Maghgreb. A message can travel from Fez to Timbuktu in two months. If you have an agent, you will have news from him.'

Nicholas stood very still. 'Yes, I have an agent,' he said. 'A man in Madeira. If he writes, can I reply?'

The older man answered. 'You may reply,' said And-Agh-Muhammed, 'but it is unlikely that the answer will reach him. From the south to the north are many hazards. Lord, are these matters settled? I wish to make water.'

'They are settled,' said the Timbuktu-Koy. 'We propose to retire. We thank the imam and judges, and invite our guests and fellow-merchants to join us.'

'I'll come with you,' Nicholas said to And-Agh-Muhammed in a comradely way. 'If you'll show me the custom. Where are the ladies?'

'They have gone to the harem,' Umar said. 'And-Agh-Muhammed will take you when you are both ready. I am glad that you have what you wanted.'

Nicholas stood still. 'You meant the book for someone. Who?'

'The imam,' Umar said. 'He knows, and does not regret it. Nicholas, it is a time for rejoicing.'

'Now it is,' Nicholas said. 'And you have made it so.'

Gelis van Borselen, it had to be said, had withdrawn from the chamber under protest: it was with a great deal of displeasure that she found herself, with Bel, in another courtyard while the vital conference was still under way, and before she knew what was happening to Nicholas.

'He'll be fine,' had said Bel obtusely. 'Wabbit but fine. He's got over these fevers before.' Gelis, scowling, had marched after the large black men who had obstinately diverted them.

The courtyard they finally reached was in fact delightful, and the corridors of lustreware *azulejos* that led to it were better swept than the rest, and carried the word *Baraka*, divine grace, repeated over and over, for that, explained the hostess who welcomed them, was the motto, the soul of the city.

There seemed to be many hostesses. That is, the rooms adjoining the courtyard were full of women, from young children to crones bundled in veiling. All but the latter were nude, and most were beautiful. Among them was the young Negress who had so taken Diniz, the first day they had moved through the city.

The girl had stopped to speak to a man. It was one of those men who had led them here. With a start, Gelis saw there were many men present. She made a discovery. She said, 'Bel, they're eunuchs.'

'Right,' said Bel.

'So we're in a harem,' Gelis said doubtfully.

'Right,' said Bel again. 'And they want ye to take off your gown.'

'Why?' said Gelis.

'So that you'll be comfortable,' said Bel of Cuthilgurdy. 'And I don't see why not, you've a nice shape to ye. I'm exempt. They let ye off if you're old or you're married.'

'But they're Muslims,' Gelis said. 'Muslims go about veiled, except to their fathers and husbands.'

'The great thing about Islam,' Bel remarked, 'is that it's adaptable. It got so flexible in Malian days that all the girls stayed the way they were born, including the King's own unmarried daughters. Ye could say the Maghsharen are a little less lax, but they're fairly easy. People say it makes for civilised conduct. If there's cake on the plate all the time, ye don't feel the urge to devour it. Are ye going to strip?'

'How do you know all this?' Gelis said. Someone was lifting the veil from her hair. She remembered the Senagana and the King's wives plucking at Nicholas, and wanted to laugh. She remembered what she had learned about Nicholas and didn't want to laugh after all. They were unfastening her gown.

'Umar told me,' Bel said. 'It's all right. The women don't unless asked, and the men canna. They want to know if you'd like a steam bath. They've got a few jets to work.'

All the fountains were rusted, Gelis had noticed. She said, 'I'll
go in if you do.'

Nudity had never concerned her. The waters were scented and
warm; she emerged from them refreshed, and let them lead her
into the garden, where the silken awnings floated yellow as honey,
and divans had been set among the rioting flowers and beside the
long, lilied pool with its impotent sprays. She lay on her side, her
hair coiled like wax over her shoulders, and let her fingers fall
among flowers. A child wafted a fan, and she shivered with
pleasure.

They were all as she was, except for those who, like Bel, had
bathed fully dressed and now lay damp and idle under the silk.
One of the young Negresses, smiling, said, 'Here are sweetmeats,
and men. Praise Allah, that life should be wondrous.'

Gelis looked where she pointed. Slaves had entered, bearing
platters enough for a feast. And it was true, there were men,
standing in light, lustrous silks under the honeycomb arch at the
end of the pool. Men, fully dressed, were drifting into the
courtyard. Turbaned men, old men and young, with black skins
and brown. Men with caps and white skins glazed by the sun,
among whom were Diniz, and Godscalc, and Nicholas vander
Poele. Not eunuchs, but men. Gelis said, 'You knew this would
happen.'

'Maybe,' said Bel of Cuthilgurdy. 'He's a cantankerous, argle-
barglous young man, but sometimes he's afraid. He may as well see
there is nothing to be afraid of. Or is your belly so precious, that
ye would like my wet cloak to conceal it?'

'No,' said Gelis. But the scents pulsed from her skin as if her
heart were a pestle compounding them.

Diniz noticed her first. To begin with, Nicholas saw only the
Negresses, lithe as eels on the cushions, their voices merry as
raindrops on bronze. Then he thought he saw, long-limbed and
languid and pale, the luminous form of Primaflora as he had seen
her, white against black, in the noseless woman's palace in Cyprus;
after she had seduced and betrayed him, over and over. Primaflora,
his wife, whom he had taken to save Katelina and who, perhaps,
could not therefore be blamed.

Then he saw it was not his wife – his second, his temporary
wife – or Katelina; and that Katelina's sister was not like Katelina
at all.

She hadn't moved. The Byzantine eyes, drawn in black, were
fully upon him. He guessed that she had had no warning, and was
touched suddenly by her courage. He obeyed an instinct and,

instead of turning aside, made her a gesture of ordinary courtesy. The merchants showed no surprise, but, talking together, moved about the court and freely mingled with the women, sharing their couches as the bowls of food were brought round. Musicians came, and the sound of pipes and horn and drum and single-string fiddle began to weave behind the chatter.

The Timbuktu-Koy took Nicholas to where his wives and daughters were seated, and Nicholas behaved as he should. Beside him Father Godscalc said in Flemish, 'They should not have done that.' He looked heated.

'Gelis? said Nicholas. 'She chose, I imagine, to conform to the custom. Bel is robed.'

'Bel is a dangerous woman,' said Father Godscalc. He paused. He said, 'These are high-born women. But if they offer a slave, it would not be a sin in this place to take her. You cannot obey every rule of the Church.'

'I know it is a long time since Tendeba,' Nicholas said.

'Then take your eyes from her,' said Godscalc.

He spoke roughly. Nicholas looked at him. He said, 'Gelis? I am in no state to deflower her. I am only looking at an object of beauty, not yet soiled, not yet defaced, not yet neglected. I wish I had never brought her.'

'You wanted her to know the truth,' Godscalc said.

'And does she know it?' said Nicholas.

'Do you know it yourself?' Godscalc said. 'She knows your nightmares. I think sometimes she shares them. But turn your gaze from her, Nicholas. You got a child on her sister.'

'She is not Katelina,' Nicholas said. It was not the answer it appeared to be: he had forgotten Godscalc was there. The discovery filled his mind, and his body, too, began to acknowledge it. He felt giddy.

Godscalc rose. He said, 'Nicholas, come away. You are unwell. Your hosts can be in no doubt about it.' He caught Umar's eye.

Umar said, 'No harm has been done: perhaps good. Let him withdraw: there will be other meetings. Diniz can stay and bring the ladies home.'

'You trust Diniz?' said Godscalc. He gave a half-smile.

'Wholly. He thinks of Bel as his aunt, and Gelis, I fancy, as an inconvenient and difficult cousin. Which is not to say –'

'– that his jaw hasn't dropped,' said Nicholas unexpectedly, if blearily. 'Umar? If you're taking me home, you'd better do it.'

Chapter 28

'HOW MUCH IS A little?' said Diniz the next day. They were in a chamber of their own residence, discussing their audience. 'They said they had some gold in store. We could go now. We could get back home now.'

'And spend it,' said Nicholas. His colour was back, and his grasp. He always recovered quickly, once the weakness caused by the high fever had left him. He said, 'Don't you trust Gregorio? He has leave to borrow everything you need for your business, once the Bank's affairs have been settled. The *Ghost* carried enough to do that.'

'If she got home,' Gelis said. Today she was properly clothed, if more lightly than usual. It was a statement. In his turn Nicholas, who had shunned her after the night of delirium, was treating her now with all the pleasant informality he used towards Diniz and Umar, which was another statement. Bel, watching, had sometimes had to escape from the room.

Godscalc said nothing. The point at issue, he knew very well, was whether or not they were going to Ethiopia, and hence miss the spring sailing. Diniz wanted to go home rich to his mother, and pay out Simon, and start becoming a Nicholas. Gelis wanted Nicholas to go home, he thought: he was not quite sure why. On the other hand, Nicholas had given him a promise, and had made it possible to keep it, by ensuring that the Timbuktu-Koy would let them stay.

Umar said, 'A little, by the Koy's standards, means a reasonable consignment of gold. But if you stay until the autumn, there will be much more. And the *Fortado* will have gone.'

Godscalc had forgotten the *Fortado*, with Mick Crackbene on board, waiting patiently at the mouth of the Gambia. He wondered if the child Tati was there, or had been got rid of, or had even gone with Doria, poor creature, and died. He said, 'They don't know Doria and the others are dead.'

'They will,' Umar said. 'They will hear Raffaelo Doria lost his life, and that there is no secret map of the gold mines to wait for. And then they will leave.'

'When?' said Nicholas. 'We took nearly two months to come here.'

'Filipe will tell him,' said Bel.

They looked at her. Then Nicholas said, 'Of course. The boy who escaped from the slaughter of Jorge's other wretched gold-hunters. But he would try to follow us. Or go back to the *Niccolò*.'

'Would he?' said Bel.

'No. You're right. He mightn't,' Nicholas said. He looked at her thoughtfully. 'So when might the news reach the *Fortado*, if he ran very hard? Perhaps within the next week? Umar, would the drums take the news quicker than that?'

'Not in detail,' Umar said. 'Crackbene would not sail until he was sure.'

'Could he sail?' Diniz said. 'How many men has he left?'

'Nine. Just one more than the *Niccolò*. Yes, he could sail,' Nicholas said. 'He could be in Madeira by the last days of April.'

'Handing over his cargo to Simon,' said Diniz, shifting irritably. 'I think we should go.'

'I think we are discussing this far too early,' Nicholas said. 'We have at least two weeks in hand before the river starts to dry back. If the *Fortado* is going to leave, we might as well give her time to do it. And I should like to see the salt caravan coming in. Because of us, the Wangara gold wasn't sold last time. If there is enough salt to make it worth while, the next market might bring gold well worth waiting for.'

'You mean we don't buy it direct?' Diniz said.

Nicholas gazed at him. Gelis said, 'Not unless you want And-Agh-Muhammed to wear your whistle too. In any case, I doubt if the Wangara gold-miners want spectacles.'

'You have shell-money,' Umar said. 'But the demoiselle is right. You need the goodwill of the merchants: you must not steal their primary trade. This will make the gold dearer to buy, although it will still bring you great profit. Do you have enough money, or spectacles?'

'Yes,' said Diniz. 'If we took away the existing gold now, and sent back the *San Niccolò* with a cargo.'

'But then,' Umar said, 'you could not go to Ethiopia.'

It was like a dance, Godscalc thought: each of the innocent proposals represented a hidden interest; no one acting from purely unselfish motives except himself and, he thought, Bel. Nicholas said, 'I haven't forgotten Ethiopia. That is why I have said, let us wait two weeks until the caravan comes. Then we shall talk again.'

There followed a curious two weeks. The sun blazed; the city seethed with activity; and no one now slept even at noon at Kabara its port, for the linking pool and canal were already shrinking, and soon the river would fall, and all the easy trading would cease.

The rains that formed the Joliba fell from February to July upon the distant hills at its source and took a year to creep along its full length. By July the height of the flood had reached the low-lying land two hundred miles before Timbuktu and turned it into the single vast lake they had crossed, weakening and slowing the surge so that Kabara did not enjoy true high water till January. Then from April to July, the river diminished to its lowest, most difficult level. So the harvests by the Joliba took their season from the flux of the river, and so did the gold-mining, confined to the space between January and May, between the fall and rise of the flood. By summer, the city would pant and crumble in silence.

Umar was prepared to talk of these things, and Godscalc listened. The rift between Umar and Nicholas had ended, and the friendship between them, always positive, seemed heightened by the past contemplation of loss.

It was more difficult to persuade Umar to talk about Prester John, and when he did so, the news always seemed to be bad. The travellers who crossed the desert to Cairo spoke of the way to Ethiopia as a hopeless journey through waterless sands or, further south, of dripping, shuddering rainforests full of animals and of heathens who ate human flesh. Beyond that were terrible mountains, terrible even for travellers, and impassable for a Christian army.

'Is that what you fear?' Godscalc said to Umar, when for the second time he had heard such a tale. 'Yet you knew I had sworn to find my way there if possible. I have undertaken to you and the Koy not to parade my faith, or attempt to obtain converts here. Those heathens you speak of are the ones I must see. And if, as you say, the way is too hard, then I shall bring back notice of that, and you will be spared visits from others less amenable. I think I am being fair.'

'You are never less than fair,' had said Umar gently. 'If you wish to go, none will stop you.'

They had seen the gold. It lay with other goods behind locked doors in the large storeyed warehouses where the resident merchants had their homes, and where the traders came to stay and to buy. The central courtyards were full of roaring camels, and scavenging birds jostled about on the roof-tops. There was, as Umar had said, a reasonable amount. There was enough to make a return trip to Lagos worth while, if they wanted to make it. They entered into the first preliminary talks that might, in time, lead to a bargain; and, before he left, Nicholas sometimes mended their pumps.

It amused Gelis, Godscalc saw, this eternal preoccupation of Nicholas's with the practical. The rusting machinery of the palace gave him pain, and he arranged twice to go there, and spent a contented few hours in some courtyard. He was not excluded from the public part of the harem, although Gelis had never returned. The day after their audience, the Timbuktu-Koy had sent young girl slaves to serve Diniz and Nicholas.

They were older than Tati had been, and experienced. Nicholas did what Godscalc had given him leave to do, and the priest hardly knew whether to be glad or sorry. He was sorry that Diniz, too, should find restraint impossible, but he kept silent. They were neither of them promiscuous, and the governor had had his reasons. If Bel and Gelis also noticed, they had said nothing to him.

Umar had thought he was referring to it when, walking in the street with him one day, Godscalc mentioned slaves. They were talking Flemish and could not be understood, but even so, Umar slowed a little before he spoke. 'They are both young men, Father; and without wives.'

'You're over-tolerant,' Godscalc said. 'You are not old, and celibate so far as I know. But that was not what I meant. I questioned your logic. You accept slavery here, despite all that occurred on the *Niccolò*?'

'You think we exploit them?' said Umar.

'I think, from what I have seen, that you treat them as the Portuguese do,' Godscalc said. 'In a wealthy community, they are needed as servants, and seem happy and comfortable in that role. They wash, they market, they cook, they carry burdens, they bring water. They tend gardens and plant herbs and run errands. We said on the *Niccolò* that the lives of such slaves were pleasanter than they would have been with their families, except that they are not hired by their own choice, and have lost their homes and their dignity. And the more they are needed, the greater their value in money, and so the trade is debased.'

He had spoken with vehemence, but Umar showed no offence. They were stopped, twice, by acquaintances before he replied. Then he said, 'I told you that you were free to go to Prester John's land, but if I am not eager, then this is the reason. Yes, the slaves here are happy, although some masters are more just, as in every country, than are others. They come to the city from the lands round about. Some were brought in or were captured, but many came from choice, and most of these were idol-worshippers from the forest, who are now of my faith. Also, at present the city is orderly: it cannot itself be plundered of people. Hence the situation is very different from the coast, where tribe despoils tribe, and the traders pass up and down every hour, collecting their booty. It could become like that here, if the Christians come.'

'Or even if the Mamelukes come,' Godscalc said.

'Yes,' said Umar. 'You might find black faces in strange places then. I think I see Nicholas over there. I am glad you asked me. I should perhaps tell you that it was not intended that I should be celibate. My family have chosen a wife. Her name is Zuhra.'

Godscalc halted in his surprise. He said, 'You are happy?' He wondered if Nicholas knew.

Umar smiled. 'It is my duty. Of course.'

'Then you plan to stay here?' He realised too late that it was an uncivilised question.

'I think,' said Umar, 'that Europe will manage without me.'

Gelis, too, became familiar with the narrow lanes of the city: the sludge walls and soft, rounded corners where the rains had dissolved the grey rough-cast and left melting, half-repaired shapes of booths and houses and workshops, shrines and markets and mosques. The secret of baking mud-bricks and using mortar had come, it was said, from the masons of the towns of Dia and Djenne, two hundred and fifty miles to the south-west; but there was clay to be had at Djenne, whereas the villages along the Joliba made their bricks from mud mixed with gravel and dung, so that families lived through the rains in homes made of half-liquid ordure.

In Timbuktu there were mud-and-straw huts on the outskirts, but the wealthy could afford to import something more permanent. Many of the merchants' houses were built of clay-covered stone as was the Andalusian mosque, although the rest seemed to cling to the primitive fashion, rising tall as monuments made of cuneiform blocks and webbed with shadows cast by the rods men scaled like flies to repair them. The exception was the Grand Mosque they called Jingerebir, built in the style of the palace and likewise mismanaged, so that water for the ablutions had to be brought from outside.

Nicholas had not been allowed there, but the pieces of its irrigation system had somehow found their way to his lodging, so that whenever Gelis entered the courtyard, she burned her ankles on fragments of metal. Then, apologising, he would remove them into the shade and resume what he had been doing, which was sometimes nothing to do with metal at all, but an idle pastime such as carving a *farmuk*, with which he entertained the hordes of black children from the slaves' quarters.

Gelis had seen one before: he had sent a toy like it from Florence when Tilde de Charetty was a child, and she had tried to force Tilde de Charetty to give it to her. It was only a split wooden ball that rode up and down on a string, although he could make it do much more than that. She stayed sometimes with the children, watching him with it. Watching him. He was always careful to talk to her, and once remarked on her new robe. She wondered what sort of compliments he paid to his little black girl, who went about wearing nothing at all.

She had a new robe because she and Bel had been visited by a man with bales of cloth made in Florence. The man said his employer had some from Syria, too. The regular Barbary galleys left Pisa in April and unloaded at Tunis, Algiers and Oran before going to Almería and Málaga in July or later. The goods they brought came south over the al-Sahra with the next camel-train. They would know when it came.

Gelis and Bel bought what he had, and even found someone to sew it. Directed to a wide portico covered with straw, they had discovered a group of white-shirted men seated cross-legged beneath it, their black heads stooped over their needles. To one side, an old man read aloud, a great book in his hands.

He was robed, and had a pair of Murano spectacles clipped on his nose. Gelis said, 'So how did that come about? Maybe the price of the girl?'

'Do ye want to take her place?' Bel of Cuthilgurdy enquired. 'If ye don't, dinna mention it. The folie love of lichory is doing well enough in this city without you. There have been, I understand, some advance negotiations in the matter of gold: a case of making wee, tempting pre-emptions while the prices are high. If ye look over the wall at the Sankore, ye'll see the scholars all walking about bumping into each other.'

'In return for what?' Gelis had said.

'Oh, the same,' Bel had answered. 'Gold or such-like. The doctors and imams here are all merchants. Ye remember what Father Godscalc was saying. It's like Bishop Kennedy of St Andrews. If you can read the Good Book and count the holy angels of paradise, you might as well get into business.'

Gelis remembered. She remembered Godscalc's expression on returning from his first excursion into that part of the city they had so far heard of and discredited, because the pursuit of learning for its own sake, the ability to set up schools and attract great men of letters, the purchase of writing materials, the hiring of scribes and the formation of great collections of books were the privilege of a few princes in Europe whose courts scholars were proud to attend. Centres of high education did not occur on the edge of the Sahara.

Of course, Muslim teaching had come early to Africa with the traders — even before Timbuktu itself had been founded. Under the Mali empire there had grown a tradition of learning. In Timbuktu, the first teachers, they said, had been black; and from Umar's own family in Kabura, by the Joliba flood-plain. Tuareg settlers grew rich, and joined the ranks of traders and scholars, to whom in turn the ruler gave lavish concessions. Pilgrims came to dead scholars' tombs, and students arrived from the south. The city became endowed with *Baraka*, divine grace. The word was written — they had seen it — in the palace. It was also thus, they had heard, in Granada.

They had been told there was a university within the arcades of the mosque of Sankore, the disciple of Cairo and Damascus. They had been told of pupils sponsored by merchants who, becoming distinguished pedants themselves, set up their classes in the courts of their houses and taught logic and rhetoric, grammar and history, prosody and astronomy so long as there was light.

Moving astonished through the city they had heard the calls to prayer, but also the rhythms of chanting, the drone of the solitary voice interspersed with responses, to the accompaniment of drumbeats and piping. Some of the choruses were formed of the shrill voices of children reciting the Koran as they exchanged their native Mandingua for stumbling Arabic. Others had not been young at all.

Godscalc had come back from his first visit to such men in silence, and then had talked for two hours. Bel said, 'And what did Nicholas make of them?'

'Was Nicholas there?' Gelis had said.

'Yes,' said Godscalc. 'It was Nicholas who found out the professors were traders. He stayed behind to look at some goods.' His voice was sour. It conveyed a disappointment that Gelis saw reflected more sorely in Umar. Umar had thrown open the casements of Timbuktu's spiritual wealth, and Nicholas had responded, as ever, to the dulcet call of personal profit.

Bel said, 'What do you expect? With what he has on his shoulders, he doesna want to sit down and speir whether Moses lived before Homer.'

'I see that,' Gelis said. 'He prefers to sit down and mend pumps. Pumps don't argue.'

The next day, she found a teacher who would instruct her in Arabic, and thereafter visited him daily. The lesson lasted an hour, and she spent it poring over a washed wooden tablet, learning to recite the *Fatiha* alongside thirty-two black *pequeninos*, none of them aged over six. She felt ill with excitement.

The salt caravan arrived just before March. Diniz heard of it first, and burst in among them, his face blazing. Nicholas was carving a puzzle. He said, 'Well, you know what will happen. The merchants go to deal, and the camels unload in the appropriate storehouses. Then they return to the *abaradiou* to rest and wait with their drovers. Until the storehouses are full, we do nothing.'

'We could go and look,' Diniz said.

'We could,' Nicholas said. 'The traders would assume us to be rivals.'

'Jorge's whistle,' remarked Bel. It had become a team-word for doom-laden tactics. It didn't stop Diniz from borrowing robes and, convincingly turbaned, trotting a mule to the north of the city and going to see for himself.

It was not one of the largest caravans: not the ten-thousand-beast *azalai* of May, but there were more than a thousand animals in it, swaying in with slabs of salt on each flank, and the drovers trudging between them. The smell, the groans of the camels, the shrill cries of the men from the haze of sand that surrounded them were as thrilling as if every animal had been loaded with gold.

And they were. They virtually were. He would have stayed longer, except that his looks and his youth attracted attention. He let the traders dismount, and walk to meet their fellows ahead of him. He was setting off quietly home when he was stopped by a hand on his reins.

It belonged to a soldier whose blue headcloth concealed all but the bridge of his nose and his eyes – not one of the bodyguard of the Timbuktu-Koy, but a man of the Tuareg chief Akil ag Malwal. There were four of them, and their master rode up before them, his knives at his knee, his gazelle shield slung behind by his quiver.

The commander Akil said, 'So modest, lord! One would think – we are honoured – that you wished to be taken for one of us. May I assist you?' His moustached and pitted face was unveiled.

There was no interpreter, but the man had used simple Arabic. Aided by anger, Diniz scraped together what fragments he had. He said, 'When one trades, one wears the dress of a trader. I am here only for pleasure. I wished to see a sight unique in the world.'

Akil replied with elaborate courtesy. 'I hear you, but alas, my poor brain cannot distinguish your words. Is your master, who speaks Tamashagh, not here to interpret?'

'I am my own master,' said Diniz. 'My lord Niccolò, if you seek him, is at his lodging.'

'No doubt. It was Umar ibn Muhammad I spoke of,' said Akil blandly. 'But now, as I recall, he claimed to have no control over you either. The girl pleases you?'

Diniz stared.

'I sent you a girl, and another to the lord Niccolò. The Timbuktu-Koy requested it. He has many daughters to protect, and soldiers' whores make good slaves. But I detain you. I have a packet for you, addressed to the lord Niccolò. Perhaps you will convey it to him, with my compliments? It came with the caravan.'

'With . . . A missive from the north, for the lord Niccolò?' Diniz said. He began by speaking quickly, and slowed. A soldier was unpacking a satchel.

The parcel he took out was thick, and rolled many times in waxed cloth, and then sewn. It was addressed, in unknown writing, to Niccolò. The commander, God rot him, took and held it. 'You were expecting some goods? Jewels, perhaps? There is a tax due.'

'These are only letters,' Diniz said. It was obvious.

'I do not doubt you are right,' said Akil ag Malwal. 'But it is easy to prove. Open it.'

There was nothing Diniz could do. Akil could read. With what languages would he be familiar? None, surely, but for Arabic in its various dialects. He would not know Portuguese, or Spanish or Tuscan, but there might be scholars in the Sankore who had lived in Europe. The only safe language to hope for was Flemish.

The packet was untied and fell open. The contents ran to many pages, written over and crossed. The language was Flemish.

Diniz Vasquez belonged to a family intimately connected with Bruges, and from childhood had been taught that tongue among others. He read the first words and felt the blood leave his stomach. The commander Akil said, 'Why did I doubt it? There is nothing here but a letter. It contains good news, I trust. Your sisters have had sons in your absence, your property flourishes, your lord has granted you many and valuable offices? I see by your face it is good news. I send you homeward rejoicing. May Allah bless you.'

'May God shorten your life,' Diniz said. He said it in Flemish.

Nicholas was not there when, breathing hoarsely, Diniz strode into the house, and neither were Godscalc and the women. A message had come from Umar ibn Muhammad, supplicating their presence at his betrothal feast. The house of Umar's cousins, where he lived, was to the north, in the quarter he had just left. Diniz remounted and fled there.

He hadn't changed his attire. He was made aware of it as soon as he was admitted through the great doors and led through corridors to the courtyard, hung with silks and lit with sweet fuming lamps, where Umar's remote, vestigial family were holding festival in honour of his betrothal.

Umar himself came out to greet him, tall and shining and black and dressed in crimson damask collared with gold. He said, 'I am so happy. They said you had gone, and I was concerned for you.'

Diniz said, 'I am sorry.'

His voice, it seemed, was enough. Lopez – Umar – said, 'You have news. It is bad?'

'Nothing to disturb you,' said Diniz. 'A letter for Nicholas. I am sorry. I meant only that I should have come sooner.'

'What letter?' said Umar. 'Wait. I shall call Nicholas.'

'No!' Diniz said, but too late. He stood under the arch, looking upon shifting colours and flowers and light, and listening to music and laughter. Nicholas said, 'What is it?' Umar was behind him, and Godscalc and Gelis.

Diniz said, 'I have a letter for you from Gregorio. It came with the caravan.'

'You have read it?' Nicholas said.

For once, he was too desperate to be frightened of Nicholas. Diniz said, 'Akil made me open it, but couldn't make out the Flemish.'

'But you did. Who is dead?' Nicholas said.

'No one. No one's dead,' said Diniz in anguish. 'Nicholas, we've lost the *Ghost* and everything in her.'

As if rubbed with a slicker, the face of Nicholas became smooth: smooth as a mud wall in rain. Then he said, 'I understand. Well, nothing we can do now will change it, and there is something here much more important. You see the exquisite young lady over there? She is Zuhra, Umar's future wife. Come. Come quickly.'

Umar said, 'Nicholas!' in distress, and then fell silent. Nicholas put his hand on his shoulder. 'There will be time later,' he said.

The girl was exquisite. Her ears and neck were circled with gold; her robe was the colour of soap films. Black and shining and slender, she had the same stout-boned face as Umar, the straight nose and large eyes and pretty lips that were part Arab, part Negro, part Berber. If not a full cousin, she was of his house, it was certain. Diniz kissed her, as was the custom, and made himself known to those relatives he had already met, and to those who were strangers. He ate, and drank, and clapped in time to the drums, and watched the performers, and listened silently with the rest when the marabout came to sit in the flower-filled spray and tell them his stories. He saw the strain on Godscalc's face, and Nicholas smiling.

Gelis said, 'Does it mean nothing? The end of his Bank, the ruin of Diniz and his mother, perhaps?'

'He is acting,' Godscalc said. 'And he loves Umar.'

'You would think –' said Gelis, and stopped.

'If you do, you don't know Nicholas,' Godscalc said. 'It is Umar you must be sorry for.'

Late that night, having read Gregorio's letter to the end, Nicholas brought them all to his chamber – Gelis and Bel, Godscalc and Diniz, and told them what was in it. He had thrown off his robe and sat on the sill in his shirt, for tonight the great drop into coolness had not occurred, and it was breathlessly hot. Outside in the courtyard the moon silvered the palms and caught the spray of the fountain, while moths pattered against the night veils that protected the unshuttered windows and doors. It was very quiet, and he showed, now, the marks of his illness.

He said, 'If there's any blame, it is mine. I knew the risks when I sent the gold north with Ochoa, and I should do it again – it was the only chance that we had. It isn't entirely clear, even yet, what has happened: I can only tell you what Gregorio says. The *Ghost* arrived in Madeira and was met by a team of experts who identified her as the roundship stolen from Ceuta, and had her seized and impounded. The Lomellini also took part.'

'When?' said Godscalc.

'At the end of December. That is the date of this letter. Gregorio says he hasn't protested, since he doesn't want a link between me and Ceuta, or between the *San Niccolò* and illegal trading. He has, however, suggested an enquiry into the early history of the *Ghost* to establish its proper ownership. If it takes place, and if I am there to answer it, we may possibly win. It wouldn't be hard for a good lawyer to prove that neither Simon nor Jordan his father can claim her.'

'What are you saying?' said Gelis. 'The ship is nothing; all that counts is the gold. They surely can't lay claim to that?'

'There is no gold,' Nicholas said.

Diniz was silent. Bel looked at him, and away. Gelis pushed back her veils and a coil of hair fell unpinned. With sudden irritation she dragged it all free. Nicholas said, 'When the *Ghost* arrived in Madeira, she carried no cargo. The Lomellini signed papers to that effect, and so did the customs searchers who boarded her. Ochoa confirmed it. He said she had been unable to trade, being unlicensed, and had therefore been sent back home empty. Gregorio tried to get hold of Ochoa, but found that he'd been spirited away from the island, together with all the seamen he had sailed with. He also tried to quiz a Portuguese patrol vessel about some tale of a clash between the Lomellini's *Fortado* and a roundship of uncertain colouring. The master avoided him. He got nothing either, out of a Portuguese from the Senagana.'

'So who has it?' said Godscalc. 'Someone who can pay for silence, it seems. So you can rule out Ochoa.'

'Can you?' said Gelis. 'Aren't there two separate things: the loss of the gold, and the rivalry of the *San Niccolò* and the *Fortado*? The silence may be to protect the *Fortado*, not the thief of the gold. That could still be Ochoa.'

'It is a possibility,' Nicholas said. 'He might have landed it somewhere beforehand. He might even have done it for our sakes: it may be lying somewhere waiting to be uplifted for us when he thinks that it's safe. So let's hope he doesn't die. Or it may not be Ochoa at all: the Lomellini may have done away with it, and bribed Ochoa to lie. The Lomellini backed, of course, by David de Salmeton.' A dimple appeared. 'Sharp justice. We kill Doria, and the Vatachino get all our gold.'

'Simon,' Diniz said. He had spoken hardly at all, so great was his despair. 'Simon doesn't know the Vatachino are in league with the Genoese?'

'With the Lomellini? No,' Nicholas said. 'Unless he has found out. Why? You think the Lomellini may have done this, and Simon has taken his share?'

'If he has, I'll kill him,' Diniz said. He said it quite calmly. He added, 'So we go home now. There's no alternative, is there?'

Nicholas didn't answer. Godscalc looked at him.

Diniz said, 'We must. The gold we've got will save the Bank for a little. It may not be enough to do me much good. But we could send back the *Niccolò*. We could borrow enough to load up the *Niccolò* and send her back in the autumn for more. And meanwhile –'

'Meanwhile we could kill your uncle,' said Nicholas. 'Or Ochoa. Or David de Salmeton or somebody. You have a very strong case.'

'How soon can we leave?' Gelis said. 'The channels are drying. You have the gold spoken for. You need a boat, and a crew, and bearers for the stretch between the two rivers.' She paused. 'Bel? We'd take it gently.'

'Oh yes,' said Bel. 'My outside hears ye, but my inside's none too sure. And Nicholas there has a wabbit look to him yet.'

'Thank you,' said Nicholas. Two words only.

'What?' said Diniz. Fear and anger had turned his face old.

'We didn't consult him,' said Gelis. In the lamplight, her eyes were enormous.

'Yes, I like to be consulted,' said Nicholas. He rose stiffly and wandered over the room. Godscalc looked up from his stool. 'Don't you?' Nicholas said.

For a forceful man, Godscalc sat still, and spoke without emphasis. 'No. My path in life is not yours. This is your decision.'

'But you are staying,' said Nicholas.

'Yes,' said the priest.

'To go east?'

'If I am spared.'

'And you're not going to persuade us to stay?'

'No,' said Godscalc. 'I would preserve you from a vendetta. I should not preserve you from saving all those who depend on the Bank. It is your choice.'

'I am glad you think so,' said Nicholas. He had left his purse on a coffer. Now he turned and, opening it, took out a key and used it to unlock the coffer itself. When he straightened, he held a packet of papers. Some of them looked familiar.

'Well?' said Diniz.

Nicholas laid them in his lap. 'When I fell ill, I made notes for Father Godscalc. Now I have amended them. They will tell you all that should be done when you get to Madeira; what you should say to Gregorio and how the gold should be used. It will also tell Gregorio what to do about Bruges and about Venice. If you leave now, the *San Niccolò* could take the ladies to Lagos by June, and be reloaded and ready to leave by October. By mid-December she should be back in the Gambia. We shall board her there.'

'*We?*' It was Gelis.

It was a weary clown's face that smiled: the ridiculous eyes, the raised brows, the two appalling dimples. 'Father Godscalc and I,' Nicholas said.

Godscalc jumped up. 'No.'

'You're not *staying?*' said Diniz. 'Nicholas, you fool, you're not staying? Why are you staying?'

Nicholas was smiling at Godscalc. 'To go to Ethiopia,' he said.

'And, of course, to take possession of the new season's Wangara gold.'

Chapter 29

I F, IN HEALTH, Nicholas had a skill, it was to get his own way without confrontation. That night it failed him, largely through tiredness, and his friends and opponents, seeing their advantage, pursued it. He must go, and defend his right to the ship, and prosecute the recovery of its cargo. He must go to escort the women. He must go to redeem his damaged Bank, with the help of Gregorio and Julius and Cristoffels. For if he went to Ethiopia, he might never come back.

At one point, reasonable though he tried to be, his temper began to grow short. 'And if Father Godscalc doesn't return? You note you are all leaving him, too?'

And – 'I don't want you,' Godscalc had said, his face lined with conflicting emotions. 'I thought that I did, but I don't.'

'What a pity,' said Nicholas. 'Because you've got me, whether you want me or not.'

He said it again when Bel, groaning, had persuaded Diniz to escort her to her bed and Gelis, too, had slipped from her place. He said it to Godscalc, his head in his hands, sitting on the stool Godscalc had occupied while the priest paced up and down. Godscalc answered him harshly.

'You don't believe in it. Maybe once you wanted to go, to find the magic mirror, the River of Gems, the priest-king all the world yearns to know about. But now you know as I do that we are barely a quarter of the way to that country. That no one goes there, not because they lack courage but because the way is almost impassable. And that when men do arrive, even Christians, they are captured and held.'

'You have heard? How?' Nicholas said. He had lifted his head.

'Not through Umar,' said Godscalc dryly. 'I have spoken to others. There are travellers, monks who have lived at the court of Prester John for thirty years. They are well treated, it is said. But they never come back.'

Nicholas said, 'You have tried to release me from my promise to go there. Why then keep to your own? The waste would be greater by far.'

'No,' said Godscalc. 'I don't think so.'

There was a long silence, broken by Nicholas. He said, 'You want to show it cannot be done.' Then, when Godscalc did not speak, he said, 'But you can do that, and come back. I will bring you back.'

Gelis saw Godscalc leave. Sitting motionless by the fountain she did not expect to be noticed, and the priest had already passed her when he stopped and turned slowly, speaking her name. She rose. He cleared his throat and said, 'You are waiting?'

She said, 'I wondered . . .' Below his hood, his face was in shadow.

'No,' he said. 'I have not persuaded him. Did you think that you might?'

She said, 'He must be tired.'

'He is not sleeping,' Godscalc said. 'And there is no one with him.' He sounded curt. But for that, she would have thought he had been weeping.

She made her presence known by rapping on the post of his door. She said, 'Nicholas.'

His voice said, 'Gelis.' He had begun to answer, she thought, from his pillow, but had risen to finish the word. When she entered he had pulled himself up on the coverlet, his back to the wall. His shirt had been unfastened but not yet pulled off.

She said, 'I didn't mean to disturb you. I wondered if you wanted something to drink. My nursing instincts.' She sat on the edge of the bed.

His smile was so slight that it didn't rouse either dimple. 'You haven't any,' he said. 'You've come to cut off my hair.'

'I have,' she contradicted. 'Nursing instincts. You've forgotten.'

'I like forgetting,' Nicholas said. 'That is what I am going to be famous for: not remembering. Africa has given me a clean sheet, and I like it. Don't you like clean sheets?'

'Until December,' she said. 'You only have until the *San Niccolò* leaves in December. So why not face it all now?'

'Because,' said Nicholas, 'there are certain advantages. This way, Diniz will do all the dirty work. He might even kill Simon.'

'You want that,' said Gelis.

His eyes, like those of Godscalc, were set in black shadow, but of their own making. 'Did I say so?' he said.

'No. But you won't do it yourself. You'll never harm Simon yourself, only his business. And Jordan can scar your face if he wishes, you won't strike him back. I didn't understand,' Gelis said, 'until you told me.'

'It isn't a fever that kills,' remarked Nicholas, after an interval. 'Or not directly. There is a difficulty about all this being known. Arigho . . . the child Henry is being reared as Simon's heir.'

'Difficulty!' Gelis said, and then quietened. She said, 'Arigho? Is that what you call him?'

'His name is Henry,' Nicholas said. 'I don't call him anything. I can't acknowledge him. Simon married Katelina in the belief that the coming child was his own. The trouble was . . . The trouble is . . .'

'That Simon is your own father,' said Gelis. 'And Katelina found out. So that, in biblical terms, you led her to have carnal relations unknowing with a man and his son, and to bear a child to the younger, which she passed off as the son of the elder. And because she found that she loved you, it killed her.'

'Yes,' said Nicholas, again eventually. 'Now you know why it's appealing to stay in Africa.'

Gelis looked at him. It was, perhaps, one of the reasons why he was staying in Africa. It was not the only one. She said, 'But suppose the imposition of the child wasn't planned, although at first Katelina thought it was. Suppose you didn't mean it as an act of private retribution against Simon because he refused to acknowledge you. If in fact you are wrong and Simon is right, you have committed no sin, except one of stupidity. Unless, that is, you really want Diniz to kill Simon for you. That would be monstrous.'

'He won't kill Simon,' said Nicholas. 'Simon might try to kill him. I've warned Gregorio. As a family, we leave something to be desired.'

'What do you desire?' Gelis said. She moved the lamp slowly to illumine his face. His eyes were heavy, and his skin moist in the heat. Her hair, still unloosed, fell forward a little.

'You,' he said. 'Was that what you wanted to hear?'

'It was polite, certainly,' she said. 'Then why not come to Lagos?'

His lids had closed. He smiled. He said, 'There is no privacy on a caravel.'

'Then,' Gelis said, 'I shall have to stay, shall I not, in Timbuktu?'

His eyes opened then, but their expression was one of guarded amusement. He said, 'I want to be there when you break the good news to Bel.' Then he said, 'You can't mean it?' He had lifted his head from the wall.

'I always meant to,' she said. 'Diniz and Bel owe a duty to Lucia, but I don't. I want to stay. I've begun learning Arabic.'

His gaze searched her face. He hardly listened to what she was saying. He said, 'You do mean it. Why?'

'You said you desired me,' she said. 'You half meant it.'

'Men often do,' he said. He had all his wits about him now, she saw. He said, 'You would like to tease me? It isn't much your style. You were ready enough to go home an hour ago.'

'Then I thought you were going as well. Would you like a drink?' Gelis said. She rose from the bed. 'I should like to tease you.'

'All the way to Ethiopia? Without Bel?'

'I should stay behind while you did that. Umar would see to my household. I've found some milk. I've found something else. Oh!' She turned round. 'Fermented spirits? Nicholas!'

'Bring it,' he said. 'Take some yourself, if you want it. It was invented for moments like these.' His hand was steady, taking it from her, although she made sure that her fingers touched his. When he only sipped, she knew she had lost him.

She said, 'So you are too old to be teased. When you find Prester John, perhaps you should bathe in the Fountain of Youth. I shall wait for you.'

'Do. You might have to suckle me,' Nicholas said. 'So what is it? You want to be the first to know if we die?'

'More or less,' Gelis said. 'That is, when you die, someone has to take home the gold.'

'And that is why you let your hair loose,' Nicholas said. He set his cup down. Gelis smiled, and moved up to collect it. He stretched one arm to prevent her, and then, lifting the other, imprisoned her suddenly. She gasped and stumbled, half to sit on the bed and half over him. He took her by the arms and sat her primly upright confronting him. She felt his hand touch the back of her hair, and for a moment thought he was going to draw her to him. Then she saw his face, which was thoughtful.

Her own, she hoped, was impassive. She hadn't resisted. 'Well?' she said. 'I think you may have left it too late, but whatever you have in mind, I still propose to remain.'

His hands steadied her and then lowered, leaving her sitting there. He said, 'I wondered. But thank God . . .' He stopped.

'What?' she said. Without her knowing it, her breathing had halted.

He said, 'You don't know how to seduce. Never do it. Never, never do it, do you hear?'

She could have done many things, including striking him. She was stopped by the look on his face. She said, 'If you let me stay, I shall be as Umar to you. Nothing more.'

'Let you stay?' he said. 'How could I prevent you? By force?'

She rose slowly, thinking of the stricken joy in Godscalc's face, seen in the courtyard. Of Umar's anguish, and the painful relief in the face of Diniz, given his congé. She said, 'Force? Nicholas, a man seldom needs to apply force who is himself a master of the art of seduction. If you want me to go, you'll get rid of me. If you don't, I shall stay. Which?'

'Ask Godscalc,' he said. 'Then do what you want. I shan't stop you. Your death will be on your head, not mine. You may have crumpled it somewhat, but I have a clean sheet.'

Godscalc, of course, was obdurate, for many reasons, in insisting that she should go. When argument failed, he enlisted Bel, and was astonished to find her less positive.

'Oh, you have the right of it: she's a lassie, and virtuous, and virtuous people in hatrent are to be pitied. Forbye, they'll be leaving her alone in strange company. But if she goes back, will it heal, this great skaith she has suffered, or will it fester with her all her life? Her feeling for him is changing.'

'I wondered,' he said. 'She learned more, for sure, than he wanted, the night of his fever. Maybe it has been for the good. Bel, will you stay with her?'

'No,' said Bel. 'It is not easy to leave. You'll never know, friend of mine, how it slays my soul to have to leave, but anything I could do has been done. Now she has her own way to make. I will answer for it to the few folk she has left.'

Godscalc had held the small woman by the shoulder. 'Bel? Are you kin to Gelis?'

The formless, boneless, powdery face had lifted to his, and then smiled. 'You don't need to share a blood-tie to love someone, or admire them, or pity them. I'd have taken that one into my house even though she hated the whole of mankind, as she does.'

To Diniz, the defection of Gelis was, first a surprise, and then a rebuff. At some cost to himself, with a small party and only Saloum to guide him, he had been prepared to convey and protect two weak women all the way back to the Gambia.

Now Gelis was staying, and it made him uneasy. Four months of proximity had not drawn Gelis and Nicholas close. He didn't see why she should want to protract it. He wouldn't admit that he was hurt because she would be with Nicholas, and not himself. Diniz, going home with their gold, was consumed with both joy and anxiety, but the joy was not what it had been, when he had believed Nicholas was coming home too.

They left in the first week of March, with Saloum to guide them and Vito to give them his stout, unlettered energy. Already Vito was talking of the men they were going to rejoin on the *Niccolò*: of Melchiorre, if he had recovered – and of course, being a Florentine, surely he would. Of Fernão and the other five seamen, and even Ahmad, if he was still with them. But most of all, he talked about Venice, and the mist, and the cool nights, and the water. Of them all, Vito was happiest to be going home.

They left from Kabara, and Nicholas stood in the shimmering heat with the rest, watching fifty feet of canopied canoe being poled into a river which, brimming when they arrived, was now shallow, rock-strewn and foaming. On board was eighty tons' weight of arms, provisions and cargo, including locked chests containing five hundred pounds of gold worth sixty thousand ducats. And a valiant, rough-tongued small woman; and Diniz his cousin.

Gelis was dry-eyed, but Godscalc was not. He said, 'When shall we see them again?'

'Tonight,' said Nicholas. 'If they don't row any better than that. Come on. We have to go back and wait for the gold.'

From six they had become three – or four, if you counted Umar who, as if to compensate for their loss, unloosed now the constraints on his friendship. At first, visiting now and then, he put forward with diffidence his proposal for this feast, or that visit. By the end of the first week, the scope of his suggestions had widened.

They began to see feats of riding and spear-throwing and wrestling, and Nicholas, for a wager, once or twice even took part in them. They attended a marriage-banquet (not Umar's) in a great amphitheatre hollowed out of the grit with terraced gardens tumbling down to a pool.

Gelis was found a teacher of classical Arabic who laid before her a field of beauty and wisdom through which she breathlessly wandered. Wisdom, too, was what great teachers purveyed, outside whose houses the slippers of Nicholas would lie unregarded sometimes from first light to last.

Godscalc, accompanying him, saw that Umar was unsurprised, and berated himself for his lack of insight. He had seen the treasures Nicholas had brought with him from Trezibond: the manuscripts he had bought, such as the one Umar had later possessed. Nicholas always knew what was valuable. Having a busy, inquisitive mind, he had taught himself Greek to that end, and some Arabic, and learned something, obviously, of ancient scholarship. Until now Godscalc had had no idea of the extent of his learning.

He realised that Nicholas had been privy, as he had not, to the talk of the Emperor's philosophers; that in Venice he had listened to Bessarion, and to the priesthood in Cyprus; that on his travels alone he had used his connections to join, for a night or two, the company in more than one private studio school. He had never heard Nicholas dispute any subject in his own field and now grew cold, wondering what he really felt – had all along felt about this broken-backed mission; this illusion that, single-handed, Godscalc would bring Christ to the end of the world, and embrace the Church that lay over the mountains. At nights he lay awake, anxious.

His conscience began to trouble him, too, on his own behalf. His fingers itched to touch the vellum he saw in the hands of the Timbuktu-Koy's scribes; to pick up a brush and indulge in the luxury he had forbidden himself, because it brought him too much delight. He groaned when taken first to a place where books were copied and lent – a bookseller's as thronged, as invigorating, as that of Vespasiano da Bisticci in Florence, although situated under heavy arcades of clay, with the beat of drums perpetually throbbing.

He felt here a hunger for books as great as he had heard to be the hunger for salt, when a man rotting and lost in the rainforest would eat his own arm for the life in it. He saw his first library in the home of the imam, and trod in silence through its chains of rooms, lined with crumbling wood shelves, upon which rested copies of the Chemail of Termedi, the Djana of Essoyouti, the Risala of Abou-Zaid of Kairwan, the Hariri, the Hamadani. He counted two thousand volumes in all.

Returning, he described it to Nicholas. 'Some damp, some covered with mould, some eaten by insects. The roofs leak, and the air itself weeps, they say, when the summer rains come. How can they be protected? There are books there that I swear have never been read since they were written: that are unique in the world.'

'Umar showed me,' said Nicholas. 'The Qadi's library is the same. The city is an emporium of knowledge, Greek and Arabic and Hebrew, and unless it is copied it will dissolve as the city dissolves every summer. But it can't be renewed.'

'How would you protect it?' said Godscalc.

He spoke without thinking; and only realised his mistake when Nicholas replied coolly, 'Do you really want me to tell you?'

Gelis, encouraged by the gentle invitation of Zuhra, ventured to return to the harem at the palace. The attraction, as the deadly heat grew and grew, was the fresh, scented opulence of the baths, now efficiently operational at the expense of her ankles. She said, lying back in their waters, 'You have so many learned men. Why are there none to care for the city?'

Zuhra, naked, was like an ebony houri from Paradise, with minute pointed breasts and a spine shaped like a lyre. She had just attained her fifteenth birthday. She said, 'Because they talk of the meaning of life and only slaves care for pumps.' She broke off. 'I have spoken unwisely. Your lover is a great man, and powerful. He is as big as my Umar.'

Gelis swallowed water, and returned to the surface coughing. It was not worth correcting. She said, 'Umar will make a fine husband. You were young when he was captured?'

'Yes. No one else,' Zuhra said, 'has a husband who has travelled so far, and has such powerful friends, and speaks languages. And I shall be his first wife. I shall give him twenty sons: he will hardly need to take others. Does your lover have wives?'

'Two,' Gelis said. She was beginning to enjoy herself.

'Ah!' said Zuhra wisely, but her eyes had grown very large. 'And you, for his pleasure? He is a strong man, like Umar. And how many sons does he have?'

'I'm sorry, I have misled you,' said Gelis. 'He has had two wives, but one is dead, and he is unmarried at present. He has no legitimate sons.'

'So!' Zuhra said. 'He is old, like Umar, and is hoping to breed some on you. You are fat, and white, and are like the cows of plenty my father has always favoured, who drop their calves in due season, and make milk, and are fruitful. Why are you laughing?'

'Because I like you,' said Gelis, and got herself out of the water, still laughing.

'Well, you *are* fat and white by her standards,' Nicholas said, when she described the scene at supper that evening. 'Why do I never get invited to the baths? I ought to qualify, *minus potentes*, as your mechanical lover.'

'I shall ask Umar to warn her that you're not,' said Gelis. 'Just then, it seemed a pity to spoil it. As for the baths –'

'I didn't mean it,' said Nicholas.

'Of course you did,' Gelis said. 'I know the rattle of a rutting goat when I hear it. The baths are forbidden. You may, if you are invited, come to one of the entertainments that follow. There's one tomorrow. Umar will bring you.'

'It doesn't sound very licentious,' Nicholas said.

She said, 'Then perhaps it needs some attention, like the pumps. If you put your mind to it, you may evolve another Tendeba.'

'The comparison,' said Nicholas, 'leaves something to be desired. If it's a glutton-feast, I might come. Shall I take a puzzle?'

'You've made another one?' she said. They sat on the same side of a trestle set up in his chamber, and a black eunuch was serving them. Another stood by the door. Godscalc was not there, but she was well protected if she wanted to be. Equally, she could have dismissed them both, and no one would have cared. It was a liberal society, that of Timbuktu.

Nicholas had been watching her. He said, 'Yes. It's over there. You have to tilt the box so that the ball is steered round the traps.'

'It looks easy,' she said.

'It is,' he said, 'until you play it in spectacles. What makes you nervous? The girls? They don't come when you're here.'

'I know,' she said. 'I wondered what Diniz had done with his of-fering.'

'Sent her back to Akil,' he said. 'I've kept mine. She spies on us all, and it's useful.'

'But she doesn't know Flemish,' said Gelis. 'Why should Akil spy on us?'

'Because we might upset the balance of power,' Nicholas said. He was fishing for bits of duck with his fingers. 'Akil's got the authority, and the army, but they don't want to stay here: they move about; they're nomads and brigands. The old man stays and rules, and reluctantly gives up what is owed Akil in tax money. He probably cheats, and in return Akil occasionally descends on the city and tries to shake out more profits, which the old man resists.'

'The Timbuktu-Koy,' Gelis said.

'Yes. The Timbuktu-Koy does nothing, as is plentifully obvious, about irrigation, or building, or stock-breeding, or food storage or the simplest measures of defence. But he makes sure the city's trade is run well, and the imams are respected, and the schools flourish. If he didn't, Timbuktu wouldn't make money. If he did it alone, without Akil, he'd probably be tempted to skim off too much for his own use and wreck it. So while these two are at odds, the traders actually flourish. The imposts are not too high, and there's some sort of order.'

'So how do we threaten it?' said Gelis. She forgot to keep her voice even. 'Damn you! You've finished the duck.'

'Look, I've left all the rice. We don't, at the moment. We might, if we attract other traders with ships. We might, if we were to help the Koy in some way that increased his power. Re-establishing his domestic water system so that you can dance around in the nude isn't going to upset Akil too much, unless he sees you.'

She said, 'It didn't impress you overmuch.' Now that the days were so hot, the nights, too, were warmer than was sometimes comfortable.

He said, 'You weren't dancing. I waited and waited. Anyway, I was already intellectually enslaved. I should have spoken to you before about what you did on that island. The goats and the lamps.'

'I thought,' she said, 'you took obedience for granted. I the ball, and you the master's hand on the box.'

The eunuch had come with a basin and napkins. His head bent, Nicholas slowly wiped his hands clean. Then he laid his fist on the table. It had a knife upright in it. The eunuch looked at her, and then moved quietly away. Nicholas picked up her hand where it lay and put the knife into it. She let it stand in her grasp. He took his hand away.

He said, 'I take you for granted as much as it is prudent for any person to do so. I trust you as far as is sensible. I enjoy your company as far as it is allowable. I will banter with you and expect you to banter with me just so far and no further. I have confided in you, by accident, more than was wise but probably not enough to make any difference. I shall not do it again.'

His eyes were grey, and pale, and perfectly steady. He said, 'It is hot, and we are often alone. You have two weapons, one of which is that knife. I expect you, sometime, to use one, but I don't want you to use the other.'

She said, 'I remember. You don't want me to cut off your hair. But you gave me the knife.'

'I know,' he said. 'That is what I am trying to tell you. I gave you the knife. I have no cause for complaint. I expect you to use it.'

'I thought I had used it,' she said. 'I thought you had felt it for four months. I thought you knew it had blunted.'

There was a drop of blood on the table. He said, 'It has bitten you,' in a wry voice. Then, differently: 'No. I am sorry, let me take it from you.' He drew the knife from her fingers and, laying it down, looked at the small cut in her palm.

He said, 'Too much rhetoric altogether. It's time I left Timbuktu. You will take the gold to Gregorio?'

She said, 'You have still to receive it. You have still to leave. You have still to come back.'

There was a silence. She said, 'So you will come to the harem tomorrow? I might dance.'

'So might I,' he said, and got up, and smiled.

He went, next day, to the feast at the palace harem, held when the increasing heat of the day had yielded to the passive warmth of the night. He was a good guest, and a natural entertainer: the invitation brought many more. Gelis, among her own increasing numbers of friends, watched him carolling along with the singers, inventing

stories when the marabouts required it, making music, making
verse, talking. He told long jokes in Arabic which made people cry
with laughter. Twice, he made her laugh, although she stopped
quickly. Zuhra said, 'I like your man.'

It was a good-humoured, easy society. Sometimes the feast
lasted through the night and into the next day, and men and
women slept in the shade, while the pastilles of incense were
renewed, and the fountains refreshed, and the baskets prepared
with fresh pastries and sweets, honey-cakes and wheaten biscuits,
kous-kous and pigeons and mutton.

Nevertheless, it had nothing like the cruel, indolent lubricity of a
Trebizond. When the banquet was over, men returned to their
affairs, and the slippers of Nicholas lay again outside this school or
that library, and Gelis found Godscalc again with the camel-drov-
ers, or in some book-store, or sitting at home, drawing and drawing.
Not manuscripts, as he might have wanted, but maps.

The last time she discovered him so, it was the end of March.
She said, 'The gold has not come yet.'

He had lifted his head. The heat did not suit him: his big face
was blotched and his hair, tangled and thinned, had grown grizzled.
He said, 'Gelis, I will stay till it does.'

'But you are preparing,' she said. He was making a rutter, a map
that contained all the information he could glean about the roads
east. It seemed either overwritten or blank.

He smiled. 'It is not what you would expect, is it? But guides
die. One must have something. And of course, one must prepare.
It is a long way, they tell me.'

She said, 'Is Nicholas helping?'

And Godscalc said, 'Oh, yes. He has made every practical provision you could think of. As soon as the gold comes in, and has been
bought, and has been made secure, we shall leave.'

'But he doesn't want to,' said Gelis.

'Of course he doesn't want to,' said Godscalc with calmness.
'Why don't you stop him? You probably could.'

'I might,' Gelis said. 'But I wonder what good it would do?
Without him, your chances are lessened. Without you, he would
have to stay here until autumn anyway. There seems quite a lot for
him to do. He might not go back to Europe at all.'

Godscalc's gaze came up and met hers. He said, 'Surely not.
Too much rests on it. You remember Gregorio's letter.'

She remembered every word of Gregorio's letter, because she
had been present every time they had discussed it, before Diniz
had left. She knew the Vasquez business was failing; that Lucia,
learning that her son Diniz had abandoned her to sail off to

Guinea, had taken ship for Madeira and, bursting in upon Jaime and Gregorio, had been thrown into fits of screaming by the news that Simon her brother had sold his half of the business and gone off to Scotland, and she was a pauper. It was why Bel had gone.

She knew that Martin, the agent of the Vatachino, had appeared in Bruges, and that some crisis in trade was approaching from which the Charetty manager was trying to shield the two girls. She knew that Julius, with whom once, at a very young age, she had thought herself in love, had sent a long and sombre report of the Bank's doings in Venice, although she had not been shown the figures. She knew there was what Nicholas thought was a piece of good news: there was a new Pope, and he was a Venetian.

When Diniz left, she in her turn had given Nicholas every opportunity to think and talk about Gregorio's news; about the gold and its future. She had enough van Borselen blood to understand about trade, and she could ask intelligent questions. Another man, she thought with annoyance, would have enjoyed it, but very soon Nicholas diverted the talk and presently Godscalc also, she saw, ceased to mention Europe himself and discouraged her when she opened the subject.

It was clear enough why. Nicholas, these last weeks, was steeling himself for the forthcoming expedition by not thinking beyond it. And Godscalc was brutally held to his cause, which hoped for the strong arm of Nicholas in the future, but which also needed it now. Gelis said, to the air, 'Would anyone like to take a small wager?'

It was then April, and unpleasantly hot, and dangerously close to the rains. Far off on the Gambia, sick and weary and thankful, a boatload of people strained their eyes to see the masts of a ship, but long before the mangroves gave them their view, they heard voices shouting in Florentine and Portuguese, and saw shooting towards them a primitive boat, in which rocked the familiar persons of Melchiorre and Fernão, with other remembered faces cheering behind. And around them flocked the boats of King Gnumi Mansa.

The drums had done their work well. Diniz and Bel, Vito and Saloum had the welcome they deserved, and the crew of the *Niccolò*, weeping, saw their fellows again.

Three-quarters-way through April, the *Niccolò* left with five hundred pounds of pure gold for the north, sailing out to the sea past the empty wharf where the *Fortado* had once lain in wait for her. But Raffaelo Doria was dead, and the drums had carried the news long since to Crackbene, who had recognised that it was time to take his cargo home, and reap the rewards of patience and loyalty.

He had two months' start. So it was that the *Fortado* arrived in Madeira before anyone, with the news that Diniz Vasquez had perished. For on board was Filipe, who had shot him.

Chapter 30

TWO DAYS AFTER Gelis made her wager, the Wangara gold reached Timbuktu.

Unlike Diniz, Nicholas failed to rush to meet the camels as they lurched in from the wharf at Kabara, although he guessed what was happening. Since first light, he had been in the first-floor storerooms of the Qadi And-Agh-Muhammed, which were empty of gold but contained many books, some of which he wanted to study merely for the quality of their illustrations and the pigments they used. Their sources, being similar to those for his dyes, told him sometimes as much as the text about their age and their origin. He enjoyed patiently tracing the clues, and the words made him think, and kept other thoughts out.

When he heard the tambours rap in the streets, he thought of the other drumming he had heard in the night, signalling something of moment. And then the distant shouting outside had erupted into the yard of the caravanserai where he sat. After a while, he went out on the long, wooden balcony and looked down upon turmoil.

Solid in the midst of the running feet, the throwing open of great doors, the scurrying of servants and clerks stood the turbaned person of the old Tuareg, his son al-Mukhtar at his side. He looked up and saw Nicholas. 'Hah! Is there gold coming, do you think, or has some mother-defiler spoiled the silent trade for a second time?'

'How should I know?' Nicholas said. 'I suppose those men who are not blind will see the panniers coming, full or empty. Or those who were blind will see the panniers empty and know that they are thieves and debtors.'

'You speak of these trifles?' the merchant said. He lifted a string from his waist and waved the glittering thing at the end of it. 'I hold you a thief and a liar. You said I would see. I see your face on the balcony, but I do not see my book. I would rather see my book.'

'Then,' said Nicholas, 'you need two pairs of spectacles. I shall think about it, when I have seen whether you have gold or not.' He waited, smiling, while the old man roared with laughter, plucking his turban and flinging his arms in the air.

It meant – that conversation – that the gold had arrived, and that his pact was remembered and honoured. It meant that he was as wealthy, or wealthier than he had been on the day he came back from Cyprus, provided the *San Niccolò* returned with her cargo. Provided the gold stayed secure until he returned from the mountains. Provided he returned from the mountains.

He did not go home immediately, but waited until the calls for prayer had ceased, and walked quietly through a city virtually silent except for the chatter of captive monkeys and the bad-tempered groan of camels tied in the shade. The rise and fall of murmuring voices warned him, in this lane or that, to give way to a group prone in prayer. When he passed the wall of the Grand Mosque, the Jingerebir, the sound from the thousands behind was like the resonance of a beehive, firm and steady and confident as the voices you heard, too, in San Marco. He arrived home, and opened the door of his chamber, still thinking, and found Umar standing there.

In Latin dress, Umar had always had a presence. He had more than that in the white garments and cap of the justiciar, pure against his black silken skin; moulding the power of his shoulders and body and arms. His face was as it had always been from the day he dived into the harbour at Sluys, and Nicholas first came face to face with him. He stood as if he had been waiting for some time.

Nicholas said, 'You're not at the mosque?'

'No,' said Umar. 'They are thanking Allah for the safe acquisition of the gold.'

'I see. Sit down,' said Nicholas. He kept all sign of irritation out of his voice. 'Sit down, Umar, and let me sit down too. You know I need the gold?'

'Of course,' Umar said. 'Or you wouldn't have come. You need this gold, yes. But you don't need to leave now it's here. You don't need to find Prester John and come back with more. There are no rivers of gems. There is no miraculous mirror. You know that.'

'There is Father Godscalc,' said Nicholas. 'I gave him a promise. I gave you a promise.'

Umar said, 'I didn't put you at risk of your life.'

'I thought you did,' Nicholas said. 'Not, of course, over the slaves; but afterwards. It didn't strike you, apparently, that you were the person I was concerned about. You believed I was determined to find the mines at Wangara, and you misdirected me accordingly. It doesn't matter. Except that now you think my whole object is to tap the wealth of Ethiopia, and you would like to misdirect me again, by telling me it doesn't exist. That is not why I am going.'

Umar always sat well, his head up, his back straight, his hands now clasped in his lap. They were clasped so tightly his nails glittered pink-white. He said, 'So how do I stop you?'

Nicholas tilted his head. 'Several ways. Kill Father Godscalc.'

'Do you think I am joking?' said Umar. He raised his hands and lowered them slowly as fists on his knees. 'Why should I do this? Why should I come here, knowing what you will say? Do you think I do not know you? You make promises, extravagant promises, in the hope of obliterating what you think are your mistakes. I did not, I do not deserve the promise you gave me. Now I know it, now I can tell you. You owe nothing either to the padre. He is a good man: his cause is good; he depends on you. But your own nature pushed you into making an undertaking that was senseless. Nicholas, you have a place in this world. Men will lose more if you die than they will ever gain if Father Godscalc reaches Ethiopia.'

Ending, he had leaned forward a little, his back rigid, his hands outspread on his thighs, Nicholas saw, to stop them trembling. Nicholas uprooted himself from his seat and took two strides away, and then made himself turn. He put both hands in his belt. 'Two groats up on the écu?' he said.

'That,' said Loppe. Umar. 'Money management, yes. Management of estates: I ran Kouklia, but you designed it. Management of a people, if one were to find a man wise enough to take you as his counsellor. Let me tell Father Godscalc. Let me tell him you must not go.'

'Have you done that already?' said Nicholas. He had spent the day in the grip of fear, and apprehension, and joy. Now he felt only pain.

'No,' said Umar. 'He will say yes. He is half ready to say it already. If you withdraw, he will accept it.'

'And go alone to his death,' Nicholas said. 'So that no Christians will come to or from Ethiopia.'

Umar rose too. The trembling had stopped. Nicholas looked him in the face, and saw what he had done. Umar said, 'I am sorry. I see that of course you must go, and that it would not be right for anyone of my kind to stop you. But if you will allow – although I am not of your faith, and although I can give you no Christian safe conduct – if you will allow, I myself will come and guide you.'

Then Nicholas said, 'No! No, I am sorry,' and took a step forward, gripping Umar's arm with his hand. Beneath his fingers, the flesh felt like wood. He said again, 'No, I was unfair.'

He dropped his hand. He said, 'I'm going with Godscalc; I must go. I understand, I think, what you're saying. You may be right; I accept it. Another time, perhaps it could be different. But not this time. I must go. And of course, you mustn't come with us. If you thought I had a place, yours is even more clear. Your place is here, with your people.'

'It makes no difference,' Umar said. 'If you go, then so do I.'

'No,' said Nicholas. They stood facing one another and Umar's face looked, he thought, hollow and weary, as if it had been the face of his own father or grandfather. He wondered if his own looked the same, and was swept with disgust.

He could think of nothing to add. Umar said, 'How do you think you can stop me?' Then he turned, and walked out of the house.

The gold was in the house by next day, thirteen camel-loads – four thousand pounds of it, enclosed in iron boxes with many locks which had once contained books, before they rotted. The next night, the Timbuktu-Koy gave a great banquet in the palace, so that all might rejoice over the safe return of the traders with their chief expedition safely accomplished. There would be more gold, diverted this time through Djenne, or other gathering-places. The white traders who had come from the sea had taken much of this load. But in return they had cowries, and promises, and whether the promises came to anything or not, they owned the twinkling moons, bright as diamonds, which none in Timbuktu had ever seen before, much less possessed, and which the greatest kings of the world would still gaze on in wonder. They had spectacles.

Umar did not come, as he usually did, to lead Godscalc and Gelis and Nicholas to the palace with the pomp of his full family retinue, and they made their way with their own servants, mounted for dignity's sake, and attired in brilliant light silks. Gelis, unveiled, had dressed her hair in Italian style, winding it with the pearls she still had, and it shone like wheat, and hung before her ears like barley-husks. In return for his gifts, the Timbuktu-Koy had not been niggardly, and her arms clicked with heavy, smooth bracelets. Godscalc, too, had left behind his white gown and wore a caftan of silk, with a cap of the same colour on the pruned and tamed bulk of his hair.

Nicholas had tried, also, to choose a brocade worthy of the occasion, and his servant had wound and pinned a scarf of silk round his hair, and laid on his shoulders the necklace the Timbuktu-Koy had given him. Hung from it was a grey hollow object which he understood to be a unicorn's horn, and efficacious against almost everything. A week ago, he would have joked about it. Now, riding to the palace, he said nothing.

It had been a curious day. For the first time, clouds had hidden the sun, and by afternoon, the sky was livid and splashed with flickering light, which seemed to stream to the low yellow horizon. Sometimes, above the cheerful din of the streets, a low growl would be heard, as if a pride of lions were stalking the firmament. It was breathlessly hot: a few weeks hence, the sun would hold the city at the height of its thrall. Gelis looked up and said, 'You will need to go soon.'

Since the gold had arrived, they had not spoken of what was to come. There had been enough to do, signing documents, making formal depositions, taking physical charge of the great weight of metal. At least, shod in iron, it wouldn't be simple to steal. And Umar would see it was safe.

He hadn't seen Umar since yesterday. He wondered if Umar had spoken to Godscalc, and whether that accounted for the priest's heavy silence. That, or the inescapable reminder that mankind thought that gold was important. Or perhaps simply an accumulation of doubt over an adventure which had always seemed faintly unreal, and which now seemed quite plainly foolhardy.

They would see Umar at the palace. Nicholas hoped, with fervour, that the disagreement was dismissed and forgotten, and that Umar had abandoned his madness. If not, Nicholas wondered how he would prevent the other from coming, short of hurting him. He would probably have to hurt him.

Gelis said, 'For a rich man, you look very bleak. It may not rain after all. How lucky that you mended the fountains.'

Tonight, the whole of the palace had been opened, with all its chambers, courtyards and pools, all its flat roofs and its balconies. Lamplit flowers, sickly with scent, poured and clambered over the pillars, and incense smoked in the pavilions where tasselled cushions were heaped on the benches. The cloths which hung from the walls were magenta and purple and gold, and occasionally sewn from the skins of spotted cats of the hunting variety. The floor-tiles had been swept, although grass grew in petty wisps where the cracks were. The sound of water, in spray and in movement, could be heard everywhere.

'Now they have a water engineer,' Gelis said, 'all they need is a really good manager. Why doesn't Umar take it in hand?'

'Why don't you?' Nicholas said. 'It will give you something to do.' He had been given a cup, and was sipping from it.

'I told you,' she said. 'I've begun learning Arabic. That's fermented.'

'I know. Would you like some?'

He found himself under close scrutiny. She said, 'Oh, dear. That's why you were so quiet on the journey?'

'I don't think so,' he said. 'Drink, I'm told, usually makes me rather noisy. Are you sure you wouldn't like some?'

'No,' she said. 'I'm not celebrating. You don't look as if you're celebrating either. I suppose I don't blame you. Do you have to go?'

He said, 'I've only just come.'

'To the Fountain of Youth.'

'Just another irrigation job,' Nicholas said. He was slightly taken aback to discover quite how much he had had to drink. He said, 'I'm not worried. Not about that. Let's go and find some sheep's eyes.'

'Then about what?' she said. They were standing in one of the corridors and all the other revellers had passed them by.

It seemed likely she would find out. He said, 'Umar and I disagreed. I shall find him, and all will be well.'

'Will it?' she said. 'I don't know all that many people who can tackle Umar sober and alter his mind. What about? Ethiopia?'

'No,' he said. He saw Zuhra walking towards them with her frizzled hair grooved and pleated, and gold earrings the size of thick golden buckets suspended on either side of her headband. He deduced that Zuhra's family had dressed her for today: she wore a long tunic made of silks and all the rest of her bracelets, which presumably represented her dowry. In spite of it all, she looked lovely. He felt embarrassment for Umar, and then resentment, and then the pain he had felt before.

Umar was not with his future wife, or at least not the Umar who had been Loppe. Walking beside Zuhra was the youth of the same name, the Timbuktu-Koy's son. He was pestering her. At the same moment, Zuhra saw Nicholas. Her face stiffened.

It occurred to Nicholas that it was no pleasure, being extremely rich. He took a single, cowardly step to one side. Gelis said, 'That's Muhammed ben Idir's son. Damn him, look what he's doing!' She looked round. 'You're not going to let him?'

Nicholas, now four paces away, said, 'He'll stop now.' Behind him, the corridor led to a garden pavilion and freedom.

Umar ben Muhammed ben Idir, who had been caressing the neck of the future wife of his namesake, looked up and grinned. His face, big-nosed and teak-coloured, was more Tuareg than Negroid in character, and he had the Tuareg's bad teeth. He called, in Arabic, 'Is she not a pretty monkey? Will her big, stupid husband know what to do with her, after ten years with white women who cannot tell whether it is a little dog or a man in their bed? Do you not think we should teach her some secrets?'

'You know Arabic,' Nicholas said sadly to Gelis. He stopped retreating and prepared to advance. Before he could move, Zuhra tore herself from her tormentor's grasp and, tramping up, stood before Nicholas. Her earrings clanked and jangled, and she looked furious. Behind her, the Koy's son looked astonished. Nicholas said, 'You'll give yourself a headache.' Gelis suddenly giggled.

Zuhra said, 'You will not take him.'

'Holy Mary!' said Nicholas.

'Wrong culture,' said Gelis.

'Do you have peace? Nothing but peace,' said Nicholas rapidly. He began to walk backwards and bumped into a pillar. He was in a chamber full of pillars, with a white vaulted ceiling made of honeycombed stucco, and a basin in the middle which he had never managed to mend. It led to a court with a pool. He said, 'Gelis, take her away.'

'Why?' said Gelis.

'Indeed, why?' said the other Umar. 'This is my father's house.'

'And in it,' Nicholas said, 'are . . .' He backed down the steps to the courtyard. 'Many fountains.'

'You will not take him away,' said Zuhra again, following. 'Who are you to erase Umar's name from the tablet of life? To make his sons fatherless, and myself a young, grieving widow with no shares in your Bank? Take some other man to save your life this time.'

'You aren't even married to him yet,' Nicholas said. He spoke crossly, and hurriedly. The Koy's Umar had also followed and was standing beside him, one arm round Zuhra's shoulders. She shook it off, and the Koy's son slapped her, smiling.

Gelis said, 'Stop that! Why don't you stop him?'

Nicholas said, 'Zuhra, come here. See here, you. Hearken, O Lord. Forgive us if we offend, but the lady's well-being has been confided in me by her future husband, to whom we now propose to – Gelis. Don't.'

She put down the foot she had raised. She said in Flemish, 'You didn't mind when I did it to David de Salmeton.'

'No, I didn't, but you weren't in his father's house at the time.' He turned to see the Koy's son reach again, viciously, for Zuhra. Her earrings jangled.

Nicholas said, 'Oh, Christ God, she'll probably drown.' Nevertheless, with resignation, he caught the girl by the arm, whirled her close and, running, jumped with her into the pool. On the way down, she hit him three times.

He awoke coughing up water in quite a different place: a pleasant chamber containing cushions and chests, on one of which sat Gelis, still haphazardly laughing while trying to console Zuhra, who stood weeping. She was naked again, and a large, sweet-mannered eunuch was engaged in drying her off. Although dripping wet, Nicholas himself was still fully clothed. He sat, absently choking, and looked about him.

'The harem,' Gelis said. 'The only place we could find to take you. How drunk were you? Are you?'

'Are,' he said. 'I don't know. It was a new sort of drink. What happened to the Koy's Umar?'

'Father came and took him away. Very concerned in case you had come to some harm. We said it was all a complete accident, and Zuhra's earrings knocked you out as you fell. Why did you fall?'

'So that someone would bring me into the harem,' he said. He weighed up the situation, coughing again. 'I had to speak to Zuhra.'

'Well, you can speak to her,' Gelis said. 'In front of me.'

The eunuch had gone. The girl his friend was going to marry sat enveloped in homely cotton, her earrings discarded, her knotted hair tight as a newly bathed child's, her swollen eyes fixed on Nicholas. She said, 'He is mine now. It is not just. You have your woman. Take your woman to Ethiopia.'

Nicholas rose and, slopping across the warm marble, knelt before Zuhra. 'She doesn't want to go, Zuhra,' he said. 'And I don't want her. I don't want anyone except the priest I am going with. I have told Umar this. He has misled you.'

'You call him a liar?' she said. Her fists coiled.

'What are you saying?' Gelis asked. She was not laughing now. Instead, she sat down beside Zuhra and touched her shoulder while she spoke again to Nicholas. 'Do I understand that you thought of asking Umar to guide you to Ethiopia?'

Nicholas looked at her, and back to the girl. He said, 'He offered to do it. Of course, I refused.'

'He offered!' said the girl. 'When he is about to take his first wife?'

'From courtesy,' Nicholas said. 'Zuhra, he is that rare man who counts no cost if he thinks he can help a friend. The offer came from his heart, and took no account of his longing to stay, or his marriage. He will do as much and more for you in your years together. He made the offer, and I refused it. That is all. You need have no fear. He is not going to leave you.'

'But if you had said yes?' Zuhra said.

'Then,' Nicholas said, 'I should not be his friend, as I am. Have no fear.'

She looked at him. Her lip trembled. She said, 'He is a very fine man.'

'I know that,' Nicholas said.

'He has land in a country that has its own salt mines,' she said.

'He is a very great man,' Nicholas said. 'Zuhra, you must keep your eunuch with you until you are married. The son of the Timbuktu-Koy may be jealous.'

'That oaf!' Zuhra said. She rose. The eunuch had returned, a fresh robe over his arm. Her earrings clanked from his finger. She said, 'I have known that oaf since he had no more manhood to him than the end of my finger. If he does what I do not care for, I strike him. You felt my fist?'

'No,' Nicholas said. 'I was felled by either a spade or a sling-shot, the tomb of all bravery. Nevertheless, I don't intend to complain. I shall merely keep well clear of your Umar. Your fresh gown has arrived. Perhaps I should drip somewhere else?'

'I know where to take him,' Gelis said.

It was a small chamber, with several mattresses and no windows. There was no one else in it. Gelis disposed herself calmly on the floor, and Nicholas stood with his back to the door and looked down on her. She said, 'She hardly hit you at all.'

'No,' he said.

'So all that performance was simply to get rid of the Koy's son.'

'And you,' he said.

'And me,' she said after a pause. 'And be taken somewhere where you could pacify her. Was that true? Did you try to force Umar to take you to Ethiopia?'

'No,' he said.

'She thought you did.'

'I told her the truth. Umar offered. I didn't tell her that Umar wouldn't take a refusal.'

There was a silence. She said, 'If it's like that, then why is he marrying her?'

'Because it isn't like that,' he said. 'Or not the way you're thinking. He asked me not to go. When I wouldn't, he threatened to come as a means of changing my mind. Of course I shall stop him.'

'So he doesn't mean it,' she said.

He stirred. 'Oh, he means it,' he said. 'He is as interested to keep me here as you seem to be. What did you put in the ewer?'

She was so adept, her eyes didn't change. She said, 'A new kind of drink. As you called it.'

'I enjoyed it,' he said. 'But since you couldn't keep me asleep for a week, presumably you had another outcome in mind. This room? Are you going to disrobe?'

She said, 'You are the one who is wet.'

He said, 'I see,' and crossed and sat on a cushion quite near her. The damp spread through the silk and reminded him of something. He smiled.

'What?' she said quickly.

'I was thinking of Lagos. I thought you wanted to get rid of me and take home the gold?'

She folded her skirt primly and looked up. She was twenty years old, and above middle height, with the kind of firm, solemn face you saw in altar paintings, usually suspended above childish, blunt-fingered hands holding a psalter. There were hairline creases under her eyes, not sufficiently used to be called laughter lines. Because of too little nourishment and too much heat in the five months' pilgrimage he had inflicted on her, her breasts were still bud-like and young, and hardly disturbed the cloth of her gown, although they were distinct in his memory: curved and white as a lily, without the blue veins that would come as they pouted and swelled. Her waist was a twist of gristle, as Katelina's once had been, and she had longer legs than Katelina. The place between them, too, was fair and not dark.

He stood where he was and said, 'No, I'm wrong. You do want me to go. But first you want me to stand here and feel this.'

'Yes,' she said. Her colour, he thought, had risen a little.

He said, 'If I had been the worse for what you gave me, I might have done something about it. You would have screamed, I suppose.'

'No,' she said. It was obvious now that she had flushed. Her eyes were like aquamarines. She said, 'Next day, you could not have borne it.'

'And would have gone off to Ethiopia, agonising. Not a bad scheme.' He moved forward, his head to one side, engaged in unfastening the clasp of his mantle. He dropped it. Beneath, he was still wearing his robe. The dampness of it on his skin was a luxury. Then he lowered himself to the cushions: close, but not quite close enough to touch her. He said, 'What makes you think that, next day, I'd regret it?'

She smiled, but the hair-creases below each eye hardly deepened. The changes in her were so slight that, had he been further off, they would have been invisible: a low pulse near her throat; a quick breath. She said, 'Wouldn't you?'

He drew up his knees, and studied the toe of her slipper. He said, 'If you didn't want me, you wouldn't be able to give me much pleasure. A virgin unmoved makes an unsatisfactory victim of lust. Didn't Bel tell you?'

Now the colour in her face had pooled and heightened. She said, 'Hardly. Although I have heard of failure. A poor experience might even have sent you off all the sooner. I'm glad all your other women were eager.' She bit off the word.

Nicholas squeezed his eyes shut, and after a while, opened them. He said, 'Oh, stop. Let us both stop. She's dead. Gelis, Gelis, this is a terrible way to mourn her. If you want me, I'll take you, whatever it does to me later. And of course I was lying: you could never be, or give, anything but delight. But you mustn't offer yourself out of revenge.'

He could hear her breathing. She lifted a hand, as if unsure where to place it. He took it in his own. He said, 'The moment of truth. A thumb, and four agile fingers. The possibilities are infinite.'

His mind was determined on calm. It was his blood which sent the pulse through his fingers to hers. He could not stop it, and he saw her recognise it for what it was. The Byzantine eyes smiled. She said, 'Take me, then. Take me the way you took Katelina.'

He dragged his hand away, and stood up; then, more slowly, picked up and threw over one shoulder his wet, crumpled mantle.

'I took her under a waterfall, as I remember,' he said. 'But we've done that part, and I'd rather not get wet again. I thought I'd go now. Will you ask Umar to bring you home?'

'The Timbuktu-Koy will be angry,' she said. When he opened the door, noise and light streamed into the room.

'He will be ashamed,' Nicholas said. 'His son behaved badly. But in time, when the old man has gone, there will be no one else to protect Timbuktu against Akil.' He stopped and said, 'I am sorry. I hate this. You should have filled me with drink, and it would be over with.'

'It is over,' she said. He could not see her face. 'Isn't it?'

'Is it?' he said. 'Then you are lucky.'

He didn't look for Umar before he left, or for Godscalc, or for Zuhra, or any of the gentle, austere, witty friends he had made in the last weeks. Friends of the mind, whose attentions made it unnecessary to pamper the body. Until tonight.

He walked to his quiet house through crowded African lanes, and ensconced himself behind veils in his chamber, his drying clothes cast aside, his flesh oiled with sweat in the heat. He lay open-eyed, listening to the lions grumbling in the ether, and watching the light from the summer storm flicker over his walls. Much later, he heard the sudden rush of rain falling. He imagined the palace, with its flowers drenched and its lamps all put out, and the carnival rising to its glorious, animal pitch, with young bodies weaving and dancing in the tepid, bountiful rain. His door opened.

He thought it was Godscalc. Then he thought it must be Akil's girl, although he had dismissed her because she had revived the old, the constant, the inconvenient hunger. When rain-splashed flesh slid against his, he flung out an arm.

It met warm, unbound hair: European hair. He drew a breath, and a palm was laid on his mouth. 'I am not here,' said Gelis; and touched him with a thumb and four fingers without possessing, without surely possessing an inkling of what she had unleashed.

Chapter 31

ITT WAS APRIL RAIN which visited Timbuktu in the course of that night: warm and irregular, evaporating almost as soon as it touched the hot earth, the drifting sand, the baked clay carapaces of airless, intimate chambers.

The April rain fell, too, on Madeira, but in token of a moist and sluggish retreat: the mild, wet season was ending, and flowers were springing again from the bottomless tilth: orchids and lilies, brooms and buttercups, the carpets of white and gold immortals and rose-coloured groundsel; the new green of cane plants and vines Gregorio sometimes thought, if you thrust a toe into the soil here, a foot would grow, and a calf and a knee. Only he, lying hearing the rain, was solitary and sterile.

Towards the end of the month, he rode, as he often did, to the sea cliff at Câmara de Lobos and gazed south. Four months ago he had looked and seen the great ragged sails of the roundship *Ghost*, beating her laborious way into home waters, and had ridden to Funchal to meet her, with the results he had tried to send to Nicholas.

The roundship had arrived empty, because – so they said – her master had been entitled to deliver, but not to buy merchandise. Gregorio didn't believe it. No one, familiar with the way Nicholas worked, would take that for anything but a stratagem. But if it was, where was the money they were desperately waiting for?

No word came, from the *Ghost*'s master Ochoa, or Nicholas. The ship, positively identified as the *Doria* by a dozen experts sent by de Ribérac, had been first impounded, and then dispatched with its whole crew to Lisbon. Ochoa had never set foot on shore and Gregorio, daily fearing a charge against Nicholas, had not dared to insist on boarding and seeing him. When the *Ghost* sailed, and the experts left, and no one had accused Nicholas of anything, Gregorio felt illogically convinced that something was finally wrong. At that point, he had sent off his message.

He had no idea whether Nicholas had received it; or if he was alive. They said the *San Niccolò* had touched at the Canary Islands; had called at Arguim; had unloaded horses at the Senagana. After that, she had turned south. No one seemed to know who had sailed with her, although reports spoke of a priest and white women.

Gregorio knew the *Niccolò* had carried Bel of Cuthilgurdy, and that Gelis, expecting to join her, had instead embarked with the men on the *Ghost*. He couldn't understand, even yet, why she had done it, or how Nicholas had come to allow her. For a time, with each Portuguese vessel that came, Gregorio looked to find her a passenger. Then had come the *Ghost*, with nothing and no one.

So, today, he sat his horse on the cliff and held himself harshly in hand when, far towards the south-western horizon, there appeared, small and clear, the three masts of a ship rigged with triangular sails: sails that could only belong to a caravel, winning its way skilfully north against oncoming winds.

He waited until he saw her paintwork, which was blue, and not black. Then he rode to Funchal, but with dignity, for he had some calls to make, and there was no need to appear anxious or excited. Even though, on a long voyage, ships suffered damage, and sometimes altered their colour. Even though this might be the *San Niccolò*, and the battle to shore up the *quinta* might be over.

It was not, of course, the *San Niccolò*, but her rival. Weighted down to the load-line with pepper and elephants' teeth, dyes and gums, ostrich feathers and civet and a few modest packets of gold, the *Fortado* sailed into the harbour at Funchal six months almost to the day after she had left it; and, hearing her triumphant cannon, the colonists poured down to meet her, led by Zarco, the captain, and by Urbano and Baptista Lomellini and their families.

It was only when they stood on the wharf that they noticed how clumsily she lowered her sails and moved to her anchorage. And then, that her flags were flying at half-mast. Gregorio, waiting behind the welcoming throng, heard the news the customs vessel brought back.

'The ship has brought in a fortune. The Lomellini and the Scotsman are rich. But only ten men have returned, whereas they sailed with twenty-five. The sailing-master is there. But Raffaelo Doria is dead.'

'God's mercy! How?'

'Killed by natives. And eaten, most likely.' Everyone except Gregorio crossed himself.

He knew by now who the sailing-master was: everyone did. But Nicholas had left without learning that the *Fortado* had hired Michael Crackbene. Crackbene, who had once been employed by Raffaelo's kinsman Pagano Doria. Crackbene, who had helped kidnap Diniz from Cyprus, and whom Nicholas had punished for it in Sanlúcar. Punished, and stupidly freed. *He who spares his enemy*, ran the saying, *dies at his hand*. And now here was Crackbene, but where was Nicholas?

It was the Lomellini who supplied the answer: the Lomellini who invited Gregorio to their merchants' residence in Funchal to celebrate their good fortune for, of course, the Lomellini acted for the Duchess of Burgundy and her secretary Sir João Vasquez in Bruges, and knew all about Master Gregorio of Asti.

Over the past six months, Urbano and Baptista Lomellini had shown a kindly sympathy towards Gregorio's trials at the Vasquez plantation – a sympathy he received without gratitude, since the estate wouldn't be split if the Lomellini hadn't let Simon sell them half of it.

It helped to know they'd cheated Simon as well. They hadn't mentioned to Simon that the Vatachino had a share in their venture. They hadn't mentioned that the voyage of the *Fortado*, if successful, would not only benefit him, but would fill the coffers of his greatest competitor.

Gregorio would have enjoyed personally enlightening Simon de St Pol about that, but the bastard hadn't chosen to come to Madeira. His sister Lucia had arrived, yelling and screaming, but he hadn't wanted to tell her. It was bad enough making excuses for the desertion of Diniz. Then he'd had to tell her what Simon had done to the company. He'd had to get a sick-nurse to calm her, and had seen her sail back to Lagos with both exasperation and pity.

None of this, he discovered, appeared to affect the pleasure the Lomellini took in his society. Business was business, and friendly rivalry need not (it seemed) upset personal relationships. He was reminded of other Genoese with similar attitudes. With the Genoese, it paid to be vigilant.

The reception was a lavish one, as was to be expected, but to his surprise he had hardly entered the room when his host Urbano seized him. 'My friend. Signor Gregorio. I have something to tell you before it becomes public knowledge. Come into my office.'

Gregorio stood still. He had not brought Jaime with him. He had no one with him but his groom. He said, 'It is bad news.'

'Come in. Sit down,' said the Genoese; and placing him on a board stool, sat opposite. He said, 'Yes. It is bad news. It is from the *Fortado*. I shall break it swiftly. Diniz Vasquez is dead, killed in a dispute over gold. I have told you first, because you manage his business. I cannot tell you how sorry I am for you, and for his poor mother, widowed so recently.'

'How did it happen?' said Gregorio. 'On the *San Niccolò*? Did the *San Niccolò* arrive in the Gambia?'

'She arrived, but met with the greatest misfortune: an attack, it seems, by murdering natives which left her boats smashed, her seaman mostly injured or dead and her cargo carried off. A tragedy. You have my profound condolences.'

'There were women on board,' Gregorio said. 'And, of course, Niccolò vander Poele who led the voyage.'

'They survived. Let me pour you some wine. It is shocking news. There are implications also, of course. We shall think of these, you and I, some time soon, for I must leave you to see to my guests. But no, the ladies and vander Poele survived, and so did the boy Diniz, at that stage. It was later, when travelling to the goldfields, that the boy lost his life. And Jorge da Silves, the master. You will hear the details. I have asked Master Crackbene to relate them to you. Ah yes, here he is.'

The door had started to open. Urbano Lomellini rose, distress firmly fixed on his face. Presumably, he knew perfectly well what lay between Crackbene and Nicholas. Presumably he judged that, in such a case, it had lost its significance. Probably he was right. Gregorio thanked Lomellini and stood watching as he walked to the door and passed the man standing there. Then Gregorio allowed himself to look at Crackbene.

Last autumn, haled from prison in Castile, the sailing-master, although battered, had still been recognisable as the large and powerful man who had joined the service of Nicholas after Trebizond. Now as he entered the room, placing his feet like a man long at sea, Gregorio saw the change in Michael Crackbene: his fair hair whitened and thinned, his skin patched like a leper's, his whole frame shrunken and light. He looked as other seamen did, coming back from the Senagana and Arguim: his sight pitched to some horizon, his body worn out with flux and fever and stress.

Gregorio thought of the women, and cursed Nicholas under his breath, and himself. He said, 'What happened?'

The blue, Scandinavian eyes gazed at him with little expression. With the same erratic gait, Crackbene walked slowly over the room to the wash-stand, from which he lifted the ewer of water, and stood, as if judging its weight. Then he poured a little into the basin, and set both palms downwards into the liquid. 'We had a successful voyage,' he said.

Gregorio looked at the back of his neck. He said, 'I suppose it was hard, bringing her home with only ten of you. But you chose to go.'

'Nine, really,' Crackbene said. 'The boy was useless. Yes, I chose to go. I was offered the post.'

'And you could take your revenge,' Gregorio said.

'You think so?' said Crackbene. He had a curious accent, part Flemish, part northern. He had never been anyone's man but his own. He said, 'I didn't deserve the thrashing vander Poele gave me. But he got me out of jail. The Genoese would have liked us both killed. I'd rather have sailed with vander Poele than Doria. Or I thought so then.'

'But not now? Why?'

'Because I don't like what he did,' Crackbene said. He turned, and taking a towel from the stand, dried his hands slowly, rolling the soft linen over each of his big-jointed fingers. He said, 'Vander Poele killed the Portuguese boy. And murdered da Silves.' He looked up.

'What Portuguese boy?' said Gregorio stupidly.

The big man threw the towel down. 'Diniz Vasquez. The youngster I brought back from Cyprus. The lad ran back to vander Poele, sailed with him, and then fell out with him over gold. You heard how the *Niccolò* was attacked?'

'Yes,' said Gregorio.

'Well, vander Poele left a small crew on board, and he and the rest set off by canoe and by land for the gold marts. Only Jorge da Silves and a few others had grown a bit tired, it seemed, of my lord Niccolò's high-handed ways and thought they'd feel safer with the gold in their own hands. He followed, and killed them.'

'You saw it?'

'I heard it from someone who saw it.'

'And you believe it?'

'You don't?' Crackbene said.

'Never,' Gregorio said. 'A quarrel with da Silves, perhaps: men get greedy; there might have been a struggle. But the boy, never. You'd be spreading a lie, if you say so.'

The big man shrugged. 'It isn't my lie.' He spoke without venom and almost without interest. Gregorio believed him. Crackbene had brought the *Fortado* home, and he was half-dead of it.

Gregorio said, 'I have a cup of wine I don't want.' And when Crackbene had taken it, Gregorio added, 'So where is he? Vander Poele? And the ladies?'

The other man emptied the cup. He sat down, nursing it, and looked at Gregorio as if for the first time. 'You don't know how good that was. Vander Poele took the two women up-country with him. The dame and the van Borselen girl. The old woman was ill. They all got as far as the place where Doria was murdered, near the Joliba. I wouldn't have blamed vander Poele, mind you, if he had killed that bastard Doria, but the Berbers got there before him. I don't know if he went on any further. The *San Niccolò* was to wait in the river until the third week in April, and then come home. If she does, she'll be here in a month or just over. If there are enough left to sail her.'

'Where were they going?' said Gregorio.

'The vander Poele party? To look for more gold, I was told. And to visit Ethiopia, if it seemed to be easy. There's a place on the way there where the caravans come down through the Sahara.'

'I know. They take messages. I've tried to send one,' Gregorio said. 'To say the *Ghost* arrived empty.'

'I heard. Well, he deserved that,' said Crackbene. 'Not but what it was ingenious. They gave the *Fortado* a spot of trouble, that ship, and it wasn't all Ochoa's idea. I have to give him that. Nicholas vander Poele is nobody's fool.'

He sounded admiring. Gregorio said, 'How was he ingenious?'

Crackbene lifted his lids with an effort. 'What?'

'You said Nicholas had been too ingenious, and deserved what happened to the *Ghost*.'

'They impounded her,' Crackbene said. His eyes had opened.

'I know. But you wouldn't expect her to be empty.'

'I don't know,' Crackbene said. 'She hadn't a licence to trade. Not even the caravels always bring back a cargo. We were lucky, but your *San Niccolò* ended up in the Gambia with nothing. And if those who killed Doria decide to do the same to your party, that's what your caravel will turn up with this summer.'

'The same as the *Ghost*,' Gregorio said.

'Yes. Christ, I'd better go back before I start sleeping.'

'Yes. I suppose,' Gregorio said, 'you don't owe us anything. I could wish this nonsense didn't go further about Diniz. You can't believe Nicholas brought about the lad's death. And the mother will hear.'

'Signor,' said Crackbene. 'Her son is dead. If vander Poele returns, he can vindicate himself. If he doesn't return, does it matter? He has no family.'

'He has friends,' Gregorio said.

Later, in the *quinta*'s house with Jaime and his wife, Gregorio ceased talking and said, 'One should break the news to Lucia de St Pol. Her son is dead, and there is no money, and none to come, very likely. Should I go?'

'To Lagos?' the factor said. He picked up a toy and examined it absently. The resentment he had shown at the arrival of some Flemish-Italian lawyer had long since gone. For six months, he had led, with Gregorio as partner, the life of a good manager, and had been given all the support there could be, without money.

He said, 'Goro, what good would it do? The *Fortado* is sailing to Lagos, and the Lomellini will go with her. They'll break the news to the mother. And besides, her brother is now a rich man. But you do not wish to be there when she begs Simon de St Pol to give her money?'

There was a silence, during which the Senhora Inês rose and retrieved the small toy from her husband's restless fingers.

Gregorio said, 'No. But you are thinking as I am. If there is no money to come, the lady Lucia may be best advised to sell what is left to the Lomellini, and hope that they might be generous. One could not influence her against that.'

'No,' said the factor. If that happened, he could find work nowhere else. He didn't say so.

'But of course,' said Gregorio, 'so far as we know, the *San Niccolò* will come back. She may have a cargo. Whatever the lady Lucia wishes to do, we must persuade her to wait until that happens. Or stay out of her reach, for she cannot sign papers without us. Yes. I will not go to Lagos.'

'Vander Poele will come back,' said Jaime's wife unexpectedly. 'In four weeks, or five, you will see him. What is the Land of the Blacks, to a young man, strong as he is? And you say he has his priest at his side, and his friend Lopez to help and protect him. What need a man fear, so long as he has friends?'

In Timbuktu, Gelis van Borselen lived in outward harmony with herself, the city and its inhabitants.

She had a new home. The morning after the storm, Umar had called on her and, sitting quietly before her, said, 'I have spoken to Nicholas. He has not changed. He will go with the padre to Prester John.'

It was strange that when she received the news, it should be from Umar. The disappointment was so great that she couldn't conceal it. At first, she turned her head away, and then did not. Umar said, 'I am sorry,' and she realised he had guessed.

He could not have known. Just before dawn, Nicholas had carried her back to her chamber and resisted her, but not willingly, when she tried to keep him there. She had not had to use artifice, virgin though she no longer was. Dear God, dear God, she had not had to pretend. The ache in her body this morning was not there because she had been misused or ravished. It was there because he was not.

Umar. Of course Umar would guess, if anyone did. She said, 'I see. But you are not going with him? You mustn't.'

'No,' he said. 'I was foolish.'

After a while she said, 'Did he send you to tell me?'

'No,' said Umar. 'But in delicate matters, the mind sometimes requires warning, or else the heart speaks. He is concerned for you. I have said I know of an establishment. Small; without great stables or compound, but large enough for your servants and friends. I shall take responsibility for the gold, until he comes back.'

'And if he doesn't?' she said.

'Then, this autumn, I shall take you and it to the Gambia,' Umar said. 'They will send back the *San Niccolò*. But, despite what you have said, you and he will be on board. And Godscalc, if Allah is willing.'

Later that day, Nicholas came and told her he had determined to leave. He spoke tranquilly, but his eyes were heavy and bright as a drunkard's. He said, as Umar had done, 'I am sorry.'

Once, she might have said, 'There will be compensations.' Or, 'What little girls will you take with you this time?' She said, 'I understand. I have had a night of teaching.'

'Too long a night,' he said, and touched her wet cheek with his fingers.

He dropped them immediately. Even so, the blood flooded her face, and ran beating again through her body. She saw him respond, and try not to respond, and succeed. She said, 'No. Never too long.'

'But not to be repeated,' he said. 'Now you have –' He broke off.

'Failed?' she suggested.

He didn't answer.

She said, 'Nothing is as simple as that.'

'No. You gave me solace,' he said. 'You meant to do that, too, I think. It doesn't matter what else you gave me. Unless . . .'

'What?' They were sitting two yards apart, in her chamber.

'Unless you know,' he said. 'Unless you received it as well. There is broken cullet, and crystal. You don't throw away crystal.'

'No,' said Gelis. 'It breaks easily enough, of its own accord.' She kept her eyes on his face. 'What are you trying to say? That we should continue as lovers?'

'That would be . . . No,' Nicholas said.

'Then what?' she asked. The ache had turned into something

much worse. She said, 'We want each other. We have a priest. Is that what you are hoping I'll say?'

'Oh, dear heaven,' he said. 'Over Katelina's dead body?'

'You didn't say,' she said, 'if you thought of her last night.'

He made to move, and then didn't, his eyes fixed on her face. He said, 'Do you think if I had, I could have . . .' He broke off again. He said, 'I didn't ask you that question.'

'You asked me one about cullet and crystal. It was the same one,' she said. 'Do I want a lover? If I take one, it will be you and no other. Do I want marriage? Not to you. My sister gave birth to your son. And yes, I thought of Katelina when I came to your room. It began with cullet.'

'And now?' he said.

'Now you are going to Ethiopia, and there is time to reflect.' She shifted, easing her shoulders. 'We have exchanged a gift, that is all, that neither of us quite intended. Put it down to the heat of the furnace.'

She remembered the words, standing on the wharf at Kabara to see him leave with Father Godscalc, in his trough-canoe crowded with bearers. She did not weep, and he did not touch her, although he was silent, for Nicholas.

She had given him a present, if of a curious kind. In place of self-hatred, self-doubt; in place of distrust, an abiding puzzlement, combined with an emotion which now could not be shown, far less released, for fear it might destroy his resolution to leave her.

She knew what it was, for it lived with her, too, every night. One could not call it love. The name for it was longing.

Because he had not sailed on the *San Niccolò*, Nicholas was a long way from arriving in Madeira that spring. At the time Jaime's wife made her confident prediction, he and Godscalc were travelling eastwards along the great river which had changed its name from the Joliba to the Gher Nigheren. Rock-strewn and powerful, it sometimes allowed them to travel precariously on its waters, but more often required them to unload their belongings yet again, and place them on the heads of their porters, and follow them on camelback, if they were lucky, or more often on foot.

The porters were grudging and surly. All the fishing huts on the river were occupied by Songhai Muslims, who were unaccustomed to any other colour in mankind but red-brown and black, and who knew nothing of other beliefs except those of the medicine man. Father Godscalc had found no use, yet, for his portable altar except as a bulwark of his own faith.

A good-hearted, outgoing man who got on well with soldiers,

and had fought in a few wars of his own, Godscalc found the journey an ordeal – not just because of the dangers and the discomfort, which soon became extreme – but because he knew it meant nothing to Nicholas.

Nicholas was here for Godscalc's protection. He had not tried to pretend that he longed to see Prester John, or open the way for a Crusade of the Church. In order to reach Timbuktu, he had been willing to accept this as part of his duty. Perhaps, had there been no other profit, he would have felt some requirement, on his own account, to pursue the River of Jewels, to track down the other treasures of legend.

But long before now, they had heard enough first-hand reports to understand that they were risking their lives for an aim that could never be realised. Even for a troop of well-provisioned men, travelling with the consent of the tribes of the country, the journey from Timbuktu to Ethiopia was impossible in the six months they had given themselves, and was probably so on any terms. All they could do was attempt it and die, or attempt it and bring back their account of the failure.

They had to follow the bend of the river to Gao, the black Songhai capital. From there, as the Gher Nigheren plunged south, they must strike east and south, exchanging rocks and bushes for the steaming terrain of the wetlands. There, as here, men would be afraid of them, and their guides would be ignorant and avaricious, and speak no language they knew.

When, for the first of many times, their porters deserted them, and they had to bribe their way into a village, Godscalc had said, over the fire, 'What have I done? I should never have brought you.'

'You had no choice,' Nicholas said. 'I don't mind you bringing me. If you said, "I should never have come," that's a different matter. Come on. You were going to draw maps. Where's the cross-staff?' Then after a moment, 'What would it be worth if it were easy? I'll give you something hard to do. Sit down here, throw a stick on the fire, and convert me.'

They had always respected one another. On that journey was born something that was to last as long as they both lived, and do them both harm. For Godscalc, who had glimpsed the real danger, was too blinded by false hopes to scotch it.

This time, as May drew to a close, Gregorio of Asti kept no vigils on the peaks of Madeira, and did not pause on the cliff between Ponta do Sol and Funchal. He was afraid to see the *San Niccolò* coming.

Crackbene and the *Fortado* had gone, and news of that magnificent cargo would have spread very soon to the money markets in Bruges, and then Florence and Venice. So would the news that the *San Niccolò* too was on her way – perhaps also triumphant, and laden with gold and fabulous gifts from the Negus Prester John, but perhaps not. Already the rumours were spreading. The Vasquez boy had died. Who else of the land party had survived? Or, as on the *Fortado*, was there no one at all except a few seamen left on board a ship which, in this case, was empty?

By now, Simon de St Pol would know he was rich, and might have had the grace to travel to Lagos and comfort his doubly-bereaved sister. No word had reached Gregorio from there.

By now, Urbano and Baptista Lomellini had had the promised discussion with Gregorio, in which they had made a reasonable offer for the *quinta* at Ponta do Sol, and had asked him to convey it to Diniz' sorrowing mother. Gregorio had not passed it on.

He had heard nothing directly from the Vatachino, and was glad of it. David de Salmeton had left Madeira for Bruges in the autumn, although his hand, Gregorio knew, lay behind the concerted manoeuvre to have the *Ghost* waylaid on arrival and identified.

His hand, too, lay behind the trouble that had erupted at Bruges. Gregorio heard only hints of it, and longed to be there, and occasionally wished that Julius could have remained in Bruges, instead of Cristoffels. But the Bank was more important than Bruges, and had first call on the best man. So Nicholas had ruled, with absolute and understandable finality.

Nicholas could not have foreseen, all the same, that the Vatachino would continue to expand as they had done, opening offices, recruiting clerks, venturing into more and more fields as if their coffers were suddenly inexhaustible.

Nicholas had recognised them, of course, as his rivals in Guinea. Even before he learned of their stake in the *Fortado*, he had suspected that the Vatachino wanted him to go to Guinea with Diniz, and find the gold, the mines, the wealth of the Negus. And then, when he and Diniz failed to come back, the gold, the ship, the Vasquez business would be easy to take.

Half the Vatachino plan had succeeded. Of the two ships, the roundship had gone. Diniz was dead, and his *quinta* defenceless. The *Fortado* had brought back a full cargo, by whatever means. For the rest, the *San Niccolò* had to find her way home from the Gambia, and Nicholas himself had not been heard of since he reached what they called the Great River.

But then, when had Nicholas not been able to extricate himself from the worst situations? Crackbene had patently not told all he knew, but even in his voice there had been respect for Nicholas and a kind of confidence, despite what he had said of the dangers. Nicholas always came back.

By the end of May, Gregorio was still comforting himself with such thoughts when a ship came in from Lisbon, carrying passengers.

He had been up in the mountains when it arrived. Normally, his was the paperwork, the planning, the visits to Funchal, the sending of orders and the leasing of cargo space on the ships that plied between Madeira and Portugal. The *quinta* had been kept in repair as much as was possible, so that the main house still looked trim and well cared for, and the yard was mended and swept, the stables watertight, the mills in good order, the cabins of all their workers solid and decently thatched. He had used his workers to do it, for now, with the St Pol estate gone, there were too many of them. Too many to house and feed and support, with all their increasing families, with so little coming in.

He had done, too, what he could about that, leasing out the free time in his mills, using ground hitherto wasted to plant the herbs and roots that grew so freely in the rich soil, to eke out their food. And he had laid out some money on poor ground high on the slopes which came cheap because it had to be terraced – a job requiring many people – and irrigation channels had to be led.

With the warm, rainless season approaching, there was need for haste, and Jaime spent his days with his men and their wives, hauling stones and laying them in neat ridges, and passing the nights with them as well, beside their rough withy shelters, singing and talking round the cooking-pots and sleeping under the stars.

Gregorio, riding up one day alongside the cook's daily mule-load of food-panniers, had dismounted and tied up his horse, unbuttoned his doublet and, taking his place at Jaime's side, had worked with him till the sun set. Then he had sat on the bare earth in his shirt and hose and, taking someone's fiddle, struck up a tune Margot used to sing to, when she presided over the Ca' Niccolò and they had friends to sup.

It would be a year, soon, since he had seen her. She knew now he was in Madeira: he had received three dog-eared packets, the first arriving in March. He was not a person who would seek consolation elsewhere for what he missed, and he knew she was the same. They each withstood the separation, but he knew that he had the better part of it, even though Nicholas hadn't chosen to take him to Guinea. He slept well and even happily that night, rolled up in a blanket with the smell of pine and juniper and fresh earth in his nostrils. Then next day, he rode alone down to the *quinta*.

He knew something had happened as soon as he came near the yard. First he heard the dogs barking. Then he saw two of the women servants standing in the yard as if at a loss, with strange boxes and baggage strewn on the ground about them. From the stables, usually quiet, there came the sound of horses trampling and men's voices raised angrily, cursing. He had left no men. All the men were up in the mountains. He ignored the stables and walked towards the front door as it was flung open.

Jaime's wife stood in the opening, her face pale within its neat voile, her hands clasped below her plain girdle. She said, 'Has Jaime come with you?'

Gregorio said gently, 'He will come later. I will deal with it. Inês?'

'*Deal with it?* What a welcome!' said an amused voice behind her.

It came from an angel. It came from the most beautiful man in the world: blue-eyed, golden-haired, and dressed in pale, elegant, thickly jewelled damask. He stood in Jaime's hall, exuding some remote, sensuous perfume, and one long-fingered hand rested on the shining gold head of a wonderful man-child, perhaps four years of age.

The man said, 'Henry? Do we wish to be *dealt with*? Surely not. Surely not by the little man who once – I am right? – tried his hand at swordsmanship with your father. Meester Gregorio, you may enter. You may tell this good woman that, since I have leave from the owners, I am entitled to spend this night and, indeed, as many more as I wish on these premises until the poor, sad *San Niccolò* stumbles into Funchal.

'Henry, this is Gregorio of Asti, of the profession which, like vultures on carrion, feeds off the unfortunate of this earth: he is a lawyer. Meester Gregorio, as your scars may remind you, I am Simon de St Pol of Kilmirren, uncle of the late Diniz Vasquez and this (Stand straight, my son. Breeding requires courtesy, even in unusual places) – this is my son and heir, Henry.'

Chapter 32

A s if conjured up by catastrophe, the *San Niccolò* sailed into Funchal two days later, and Simon de St Pol proposed a party to take horse to meet her.

The time between had been awesomely terrible. Feared, expected, prepared for during all the long voyage from Venice, the lord Simon had issued his smooth, written challenge and then failed to remain to meet Nicholas. He had stood aside, permitting the encounter between Lucia and Nicholas; allowing Diniz to be traced; abandoning Gelis to unimaginable danger – and had taken no action, except for the one which would ruin his sister and nephew. He had sold his half of the company to the firm Lomellini, and retired to safety in Scotland.

And now, wealthy with the profits from the *Fortado*, he had returned, endured the screams, the entreaties, the tedious reproaches of his sister, and obtained her permission, without overmuch trouble, to sell the remaining Ponta do Sol estate to the brothers Lomellini, before or after he had avenged the family honour.

He had clearly accepted, without question or even surprise, that Diniz was dead, and that Nicholas – *Claes* – vander Poele was responsible. He showed no sign of mourning. He gave his first attention, arriving in Funchal, to the matter of greater importance. He had interviewed the brothers Lomellini, and the sale of the Vasquez estate was concluded.

The factor and his wife had no legal right to remain at the *quinta* where they had spent all their lives, beyond what hours or days the Lomellini (or Simon, their self-appointed agent) might allow them. Gregorio had no place there, nor had any of the men and women who, all unknowing, were still on the mountain, toiling for love of Jaime and their late lord and his son, the lad Diniz.

Whatever hopes Nicholas might have had of Madeira, Simon

had eradicated them, along with the hopes of his sister. And now he was prepared to stand to his challenge. The first thing Nicholas would see, arriving ragged and spent, with the *Ghost* lost, Diniz dead, the Madeira business destroyed, would be Simon de St Pol on the quay, his sword unsheathed in his hand, and his beautiful son at his side.

Gregorio was not a man trained in chivalry, but he knew right from wrong, and spoke up for it; he possessed the scar Simon had spoken of to prove it. He drew on his lawyer's training. He placed before Simon, or attempted to, the arguments he knew Nicholas would have brought to the meeting which Simon had avoided.

He spoke to stone. Simon had no doubts about how his wife Katelina had died, and who had killed his sister's husband Tristão, and who now had caused the debauchment and death of Diniz Vasquez. And however wild such a theory might be, it was based on a set of unfortunate facts. Around Nicholas lay the dead of his family; the fruits, anyone could say, of his vengeance. Anyone, that is, who knew (as Gregorio knew) that Nicholas was the son of Simon's first wife. Anyone who believed (as Simon did) that Nicholas would commit any crime, in order to be accepted as heir, and legitimate.

Gregorio tried to shatter the stone. He said, 'He doesn't care. Nicholas doesn't care any longer. Why should he kill any one of your family? And it can be proved he nursed your wife, he didn't harm her. Diniz will –' And he had stopped.

'But Diniz is dead,' had said Simon, with his angelic smile. 'And even when he was alive, so I hear, he was unable to convert Katelina's sister. I don't suppose Gelis will return. Unless she is quick with a knife. Quicker than Nicholas.'

And at length Gregorio had said bitterly, 'Then don't you fear for the child? If Nicholas is the cold-blooded murderer you imply, will Henry be safe?'

'My dear Meester Gregorio,' Simon had said. 'I don't mean to take Henry on board the *San Niccolò*. You and I and some of my servants will go. A posse of soldiers, already promised by Captain Zarco. But I propose to leave the child at the *quinta* until the lists have been set up. Then he will come to Funchal to see how his father bears arms. Gentleman against churl: it is not wholly suitable, but Zarco insisted. You know he has given me leave to execute the sentence against Claes myself?'

'What sentence?' said Gregorio. 'For what crime? He hasn't even arrived yet.'

'For the death of Diniz,' Simon said. 'The *San Niccolò* will bring enough witnesses. And if that isn't enough, we have the boy's account. The boy who stood there and watched it.'

'What boy?' said Gregorio.

'One of the *grumetes*,' said Simon with patience. 'Does it matter? A poor, frightened lad when I saw him last on the *Fortado*. His name was Filipe.'

'Was it?' said Gregorio slowly. 'Then you have accepted the word of a liar, my lord. A thief and a liar. And I shall tell the captain so.'

'You may if you wish,' Simon said. 'But of course, it will not affect trial by combat, which is what, in my magnanimity, I am offering. It may even last a little longer than once it did: Claes might know one end of a sword from the other. But of course, the outcome is not in doubt, as everyone present will see, including the child. I mean the child to be there. I should like Claes to look Henry de St Pol in the face. I should like Henry to see his head fall.'

Waiting on the wharf at Funchal, Gregorio watched the *San Niccolò* sail slowly up from the south, and his gut twisted within him.

He had done all he could to reverse what Simon had done. He had visited Zarco, pleaded with the Lomellini, made depositions. He had laid information as to the character of the boy Filipe, all to no effect. He had not slept for two nights. And now he stood with Simon and Urbano Lomellini and a pack of soldiers, waiting to embark on the pinnace that would lead the *San Niccolò* in. And then board her. And then take Nicholas off to his death.

And yet he watched her come with an aching pride, for she had won home; the lovely caravel which had left Lagos so bravely. And she was making a brave homecoming too: her flags flying, her cannon saluting the town. Far off, there carried the sound of a trumpet. And the flags that were flying were those of celebration: none was at half-mast. So Nicholas was alive and here, to face whatever awaited him.

Her sails came down and, as she took to her oars, Simon led his party into the pinnace to meet her. The vessels slowly converged, and they all saw the real state of the *San Niccolò*.

She was still painted black. They had bought paint, Gregorio guessed, at Arguim or Grand Canary, and it had been brushed over the great patches and scars in her planking, but roughly, as if there had been few men and little time for the operation. The way her sails had come down spoke, too, of a working crew as sparse as that of the *Fortado*; and, like her enemy, she lumbered, sluggish with weed.

The rest of her was a patchwork: the cannons half gone; the rails mended with different woods – but the oars were new, and some of her spars pristine and gleaming. She was trailing two boats, one a stout skiff of the kind they used on Grand Canary and the other hacked out of some garish timber, and half full of water.

There were men running about on the deck. Gregorio glimpsed the oarsmen, but no one came to the side but a thin, dark man robed in expensive blue damask. The *Niccolò* let down her anchor. A moment later, the companion ladder came down, and the pinnace made fast to her side.

Simon stood, preparing to advance to the steps. Gregorio, rising in the same moment, said, 'I beg your pardon,' and, using both elbows, plunged on to the ladder instead. When Simon snatched at his doublet, he kicked. Then he clambered as fast as he could to the top.

The man in damask was Melchiorre, the Florentine who had sailed on the *Ciaretti*. He looked ghastly, but his face was blazing with happiness. He said, 'Signor Gregorio!' and held out his arms.

Gregorio seized him. He said, 'I've got a man behind, Simon, who wants to have Nicholas arrested and killed. Tell Nicholas quickly. Tell him to get away. Help me delay them.'

'I thought you might do something like that,' said Simon's voice sweetly behind him. 'There is another boat waiting behind, just in case. Do you know you kicked me just now? What a great athlete you are, to be sure.'

He had already drawn back his arm. Gregorio tried to avoid it, but the caravel swayed, and he stumbled. Another hand caught Simon's fist and held it. Gregorio saw who it was.

Simon did not. Simon saw a young man, thinned by privation, but still hard-muscled and tough, and enveloped in the same strange blue damask robe as the man at the head of the companionway. He wore a twist of the identical stuff as a hat, and beneath it his eyes were deep-set, and black as a Negro's. He said, 'Goro. Are you all right?'

'Now I am,' Gregorio said. His sight was suddenly blurred.

'Nicholas isn't here,' said the young man. 'But he's all right. He's all right.'

'And who are you?' said Simon de St Pol, and tore his hand free. It didn't come easily. The score of a nail showed suddenly red on his wrist as he laid his palm on the hilt of his sword.

The young man made no effort to draw his, although he was wearing one. He glanced at Gregorio, and then, his expression changing, back to Simon de St Pol. The young man said, 'Who am I? A man who admired you for upholding the family honour, but now does not.'

'Because of Claes?' Simon said. The soldiers, climbing aboard, had begun to spread through the ship. They were armed. His eyes followed them, and returned to the young man. 'Whatever Claes has said, it's a lie. He is no kin of mine. If he were, I should do this no differently. He has spilled blood, and must pay for it.'

'Claes? *Nicholas?*' the young man said. 'I was speaking of the way you treated your sister. You found her widowed, and sold off your half of the partnership, you cowardly, self-seeking, conceited goat.'

He had spoken quite softly. Gregorio heard, and Urbano Lomellini beside him. Simon looked as if he had not heard. His sword, sliding out of its sheath, seemed to come very slowly. He said, 'I don't think I caught what you said.' The sword rose. Gregorio shivered.

The young man said, 'And would you kill me for it if you had? Even though it was true? Even though I *am* your kin, uncle?' He waited, ignoring the arrested swordpoint, submitting with dispassionate calm to the scrutiny – dangerous, uncertain, shocked – of the swordsman.

Simon said, 'Diniz!'

'Yes,' said Diniz Vasquez. He pushed his uncle's sword down with one finger. He had made no move at all towards his own. He said, 'Nicholas isn't here. He thought he would wait until the autumn, as there was too much gold for one ship to carry. If there is nothing else, perhaps you would call your soldiers off? We are rather busy, and Bel might object.'

'She's here?' Gregorio said. His voice was hoarse. 'And Gelis? Godscalc?'

'They waited,' said the young man, without looking round. Simon of Kilmirren was sheathing his sword.

Urbano Lomellini said, 'Excuse me. Who is this?'

It was Gregorio's moment. He stepped forward. 'This,' he said, 'is Diniz Vasquez, owner of the Vasquez plantation at Ponta do Sol which, against all informed advice, his uncle has just tried to sell to you. I am afraid, as Senhor Diniz' lawyer, I shall have to initiate some serious claims for redress.'

Lomellini opened his mouth. 'They said you were dead,' Simon said.

'Did they?' said Diniz. 'Well, I was left for dead at one point, but Nicholas saved me. Who said I was dead?' His voice sharpened. 'And who gave you leave to – Have you sold the *quinta*?'

'To me,' said Urbano Lomellini. 'He said –'

'Claes attacked you,' Simon said quickly. 'You wouldn't know. You were close to death. Filipe saw it.'

'Filipe *saw* it?' said Diniz. 'Filipe shot me.'

There was a silence. 'You're protecting Claes,' Simon said. 'Even now. That was why I broke up the partnership. Your infatuation for –'

'His name is Nicholas,' Diniz said. 'And admiration is different from infatuation. I'm not surprised Filipe thought I was dead. I should have died if Nicholas hadn't followed and found me. I had let him down: he had no call to, but he did. If you don't believe me, Vito there tracked me down with him. And if you don't believe either of us, ask Bel. She helped treat the wound. Is that proof enough?'

'So no crime has been committed,' said Lomellini. 'How fortunate that vander Poele was not here, or we might have found fraud compounded with murder.'

He was looking at Diniz. Diniz said, 'You asked who I was.'

'I am Urbano Lomellini, Senhor Diniz, merchant of this island, and a wiser and less trusting man than I was a few minutes ago. I hope, in our dealings, we shall not be harsh with one another.'

'Of the *Fortado*?' Diniz said. 'The family with the stake in the *Fortado*? Did she arrive?'

'A month ago,' Gregorio said. He felt weak with anticipation.

'With her cargo?'

'With a very fine cargo,' said Gregorio. 'The family Lomellini and my lord Simon have profited greatly.'

'And, one assumes, the Vatachino,' said Diniz.

The face of Urbano Lomellini returned his gaze stolidly. Simon said, 'The Vatachino?' with irritation.

The eyes of Diniz, moving round, rested on Gregorio's face, and one of them flickered. He said, 'In view of their majority stake in the *Fortado*. In view of the shares Signor Urbano allowed the Vatachino to have. Three-quarters, I believe, of all the Lomellini holding in the *Fortado*'s excellent cargo? The success of the voyage must have delighted David de Salmeton.'

Simon said, 'This is not, of course, true?' He spoke to Lomellini, who hesitated.

'I am afraid it is,' Gregorio said. 'It is another matter you may wish to take up with Signor Urbano on shore. Meanwhile –'

'Wait,' said Urbano Lomellini harshly. He was deeply flushed. 'Wait. The Vatachino are rivals of the Banco di Niccolò as well. You knew – Nicholas vander Poele knew they helped finance the *Fortado*. So how did Raffaelo Doria meet his death?'

'Killed by traders,' said a comfortable Scots voice from behind them.

Bel of Cuthilgurdy, emerged from the cabin, toiled towards them. She wore the uniform robe of blue damask wrapped round something much less than her former rotundity. Nevertheless the smile under the fresh linen headcloth was wider, trained on Gregorio, than it had ever been, and the eyes above the hollow cheeks and blotched skin sparkled naughtily. If she saw Simon, her gaze slid calmly past him.

She said, 'They're having a terrible job with the chests, getting them unlocked and put by for the searchers. Diniz, I think ye'll need to give them a hand; all that gold's a fair scunner. Did ye tell them how much we were suing them for?'

No one spoke. Diniz said, 'I haven't had time. They were just asking about Raffaelo Doria.'

'Well, I'm glad they realise,' Bel said. 'D'ye like the robes? It was the best I could do: we got the bolts off a man in the Canary. I'm glad they realise what Doria and his men did to us. Luring us to our deaths, pretending to be King Bati's natives. Attacking the *San Niccolò* in the river, and killing every last man except Melchiorre there, before persuading the blacks to ransack her. There'll be a great cause to be pleaded for that, with costs and compensation. Diniz, ye ought to come, if these gentlemen will excuse us.'

'Bel!' said Simon de St Pol. To do him justice, he had composed himself. His shoulders straight, his face rather pale, he looked no older than the handsome man who nearly five years before had married Katelina van Borselen. He said, 'You forget what you're saying. Any nonsense like this will harm Lucia.'

Bel turned. 'I don't see how,' she said. 'Ye said you and she had separate businesses. That was when ye sold your half of the partnership. So I don't see how she'll be harmed by anything a St Pol has to forfeit. Forbye,' she said thoughtfully, 'if it damages you, it'll also gie a wee flecht to the Vatachino. Now. Doesna that make ye feel better?'

Simon said, 'I find all this hard to believe. Claes – vander Poele is not on board?' One of the soldiers shook his head. They had gathered at the ladder to wait for him.

'Then,' said Simon, 'I suppose Signor Urbano and I should – should leave for the moment.' He paused, clearly confronting for the first time the practicalities of what was now threatening him. He said, 'Do I take it that it is your intention, all of you, to stay at the *quinta*?'

Gregorio looked at Diniz, and smiled. He said, 'I hope so. Although there is rather less space than I'd wish for. Perhaps, if you have friends in Funchal who could accommodate you . . .?'

Simon's eyes were on Bel. He said, 'You would throw the boy out?'

'The boy?' she said. The glint in her eyes had quite vanished.

'Henry is with me,' said Simon. 'I brought him. I rather wished vander Poele to set eyes on him. Now, of course, it must wait.'

'Your son Henry?' said Diniz. Bel's eyes went to his face.

Gregorio said curtly, 'What do you wish to do? You are his father. He has a nursemaid.' He had, a girl of seventeen with long, opulent hair.

'Leave him,' said Bel. 'A child of four will make nothing of some fancy household in Funchal. Leave him. He knows me a little. Then I hope ye'll settle your business and go. Scotland must be fair longing to welcome ye back.'

Gregorio stayed, and watched with the others as the pinnace left, with the rest of the party on board.

Diniz said, 'Dear Gregorio.' He looked pale. 'Come and meet Vito and Melchiorre and the others again, and look at what we've brought. We have a lot to tell you.'

The essence, perhaps, was related in that moment. The detail had to wait until the next day when, in his bureau at Quinta do Sol, Gregorio listened to Diniz and Bel, refreshed by their first night's rest on land.

By then, he knew what the *Ghost* had carried. He had heard how, coming north, the *San Niccolò* had called at all the places Ochoa might have visited. Nowhere had they heard even a rumour of the three mule-loads of gold, the cargo of gums and spices and dyes which had been transferred to the roundship at the Senagana.

At the Senagana itself, they had found only one Portuguese who had been at the post when the two ships were there. He said the *San Niccolò* had stuck in the estuary, and the *Ghost* had taken her cargo to lighten her. Once over the sandbar, the *Niccolò* had taken it back.

'Crackbene knew they didn't,' Gregorio said. 'He knew Nicholas had pulled off some trick, although he wouldn't admit it. And Ochoa's mouth had been shut by some bribe. So who has it? Who bribed them?'

'Someone who waylaid the *Ghost* on her way north,' Diniz said. 'We tried to find out who. Every ship has to put into port at some stage. We asked in every harbour for a list of the ships passing through at that time, but they were all routine, and harmless. Whoever did this was rich. If he could bribe Ochoa, he could bribe some sweating, half-crazed harbour official.'

Diniz paused. 'If you hadn't sent your message, we couldn't

have done even that. We shouldn't have known that had happened. And they probably counted, anyway, on our never returning.'

'Especially,' Gregorio said, 'if the Vatachino had a hand in it. But now we know what the *Ghost* had on board. Isn't it time to make the theft public? You would have a powerful ally. If it's the *San Niccolò*'s cargo, a quarter of it belongs to King Alfonso.'

The blue damask in which Bel was encased stirred. She said, 'Do you want to link the *San Niccolò* and the *Ghost*?'

The men looked at one another.

'Also,' she said, 'there's a faint glimmer – a wee glisk of a chance, is there not, that yon Ochoa has packed it off somewhere? And if we find it, we keep it, and don't even lose a quarter to the excellent monarch of Portugal? I'd recommend ye do nothing until the ownership of the *Ghost* has been proved. Nothing but hunt for it, that's to say.'

'She's right,' Diniz said. Looking at him, Gregorio wondered again what school Nicholas had sent him to, that produced this toughened, confident man. Diniz said, 'We'll need that gold, if the rest of our plans don't succeed. But meanwhile there's quite enough to buy the land you want for the *quinta*, and solve the worst of the problems at Venice. And I have to go to Bruges.'

'I thought –' Gregorio said. From what they said, it had seemed all their troubles were over.

'Instructions,' Diniz said, smiling. 'Twenty-five pages of them, written in letters of iron by Nicholas. I told you, we found no gold on the Joliba, and all we could bring was the moderate amount they had in store in the city. However, it pays to exaggerate.'

'But there is more coming?' Gregorio said. 'Nicholas is setting out with the rest in the autumn?'

'That is what we are saying,' said Diniz. The smile had gone, so that the lines of strain and privation could be seen again. Whatever the school had been, Crackbene also had known it.

'But it isn't true?' said Gregorio sharply. They had talked of Nicholas; of Godscalc's work with King Gnumi; of the large, busy city they had discovered on the edge of the desert, into which Gelis had settled without apparent discomfort. He had deduced, without much time to consider it, that Nicholas had made his peace with the girl, and was glad. So long as it didn't go further. With Nicholas, one never knew. It worried him, that Gelis had stayed.

It worried him, also, that Loppe had brought them to Timbuktu so indirectly, concealing his interest, and leading Raffaelo Doria, there was no doubt, to his death. Most of all, it worried him that there might be some doubt about Nicholas. Not because of the gold, but in terms of his safety. He realised that silence had fallen. Behind several doors, a child was screaming in temper.

Bel said, 'There will be a fortune in gold. We saw the salt come in, and Nicholas has arranged to buy most of what it fetches. So far as the world is concerned, he is waiting for it in Timbuktu, and will take it to Cantor to board the *Niccolò* in December. If he doesn't do it, Gelis will. That's why she stayed.'

'Why shouldn't he do it?' Gregorio asked.

'Because he has gone to keep his promise to Godscalc. He and the padre have gone to try and reach Prester John,' Diniz said. 'They know now it's all but impossible. They know it's further than anyone thought, and ten times as difficult, but they've gone. I don't see that either of them will live to come back.'

The door opened then. Gregorio paid no attention, his eyes fixed on the other man. It was Bel who said, 'Well, well: and who needs a trumpet with Henry de St Pol in the house? What ails my little man now?'

Children, to Gregorio, were an unknown country. He had supposed, over the last couple of days, that all behaved as this one did; and especially a child born of such a man as Simon de St Pol and such a wilful young woman as Katelina. A lover of beauty, he found himself distracted, yet again, by the child's glorious hair, curling and yellow as corn; the open, dense blue of the eyes, the perfect lips, the carnation of the round, silken cheeks. In one of them was a dimple.

He said, 'What is it, Henry?' and then remembered, belatedly, who Diniz was, and that the two had not so far encountered each other. He said, 'Henry, this is Diniz, your cousin.'

The screeching stopped. The blue eyes narrowed. 'No,' said Henry. 'That's a man. That's his mother. His mother is Bel, my aunt Lucia's servant. I have a nice coat. I have a sword and a dagger and a horse and three dogs. That man is dirty, and so is his mother.'

Below the suntan, Diniz had become very pale. Gregorio knelt. He said, 'Haven't you seen how the sun makes people brown? They're wearing the only clothes they could bring back from Guinea. They've been to Guinea, where the black people live.'

'I want my dinner,' said Henry.

'It isn't time yet, my hinny,' said Bel gently. 'Inês told you.' The mouth opened, became square.

Diniz stirred. He said, 'The girl should – where is the girl?'

'In Funchal,' said Bel placidly. 'Simon sent for something he wanted. It doesna matter. We shall manage perfectly well.'

Gregorio thought of Agnès, the capable Frenchwoman who had spoken lovingly of this her nursling in St Omer. Lovingly of the boy, and of Katelina his mother. He rose. He said, 'Has the child no one else?'

Bel looked at him. 'He has his father,' she said. 'Simon wishes the boy to grow up a man. He is training him himself.'

They were speaking over his head. The child walked over to Bel, and kicked her as hard as he could in the shins. 'I want my dinner,' he said. Then he screamed.

Diniz, gripping both arms, had lifted the boy off the floor and held him suspended. The childish boots flailed in the air. The child in its rage had turned scarlet, and whooping cries left its lips.

'Don't,' said Bel. Gregorio was holding her, and there was blood on the Canary blue damask. 'Don't. You won't cure it that way.'

'How will you cure it?' Diniz said. 'Except by starting again, with a different father?'

Bel said, 'No.' Removing herself from Gregorio's arm, she shuffled forward. She said, 'No. Put him down. Henry, hurting people won't get you your dinner. Your father has to stay in Funchal, to make the ducats to buy you all these coats. He'll be back. Soon, you'll have dinner together. Now, when Inês is ready, you can eat with her. Come. She has toys you haven't seen yet.'

They went, the woman limping, the child sullen and frightened, hand in hand. Gregorio said, 'She's a saint, that unlikely small woman, but I think it's too late. There goes a man born to the mould of his father.'

Diniz sat. He said, 'He has his looks, too.' He paused. He said, 'I meant to ask you about something else. Do you – did you know that Nicholas was born to Simon's first wife? And used to believe himself to be Simon's son?'

'You've heard that?' Gregorio said. 'It's true that he maintained it, but there's no proof that he is. Simon and his wife were living apart when Nicholas was born. The woman is dead, and Simon refused to have anything to do with the child. I gather Nicholas never importuned him over it, but always hoped for some kindness. Instead Simon took against him, as you see. A wretched business.' He paused. 'Does it worry you?'

There was a long silence. Diniz said, 'If it were true, Nicholas and I would be cousins.'

'Yes,' said Gregorio. 'In any case he is a good friend. I know he is proud of you, although he wouldn't have told you himself. A remarkable man.'

He got up quickly. 'Diniz? You're more tired than you know. That's enough. Go and rest. We can go over the papers tomorrow.'

Diniz rose to his feet, with an effort. Gregorio walked with him to the door, also anxious. At the threshold, Gregorio said, 'What are the chances? A terrible journey, you say. What are the chances he will come back from Ethiopia?'

'I don't know,' Diniz said. 'I don't know what to hope for.'

Chapter 33

BECAUSE NONE OF THEM could see the whole, none of them (except Nicholas, who was not there) could admire the felicities of the plan which immediately began to unfold itself, touching lands lying between Scotland and the Levant, Flanders and the deserts of Africa.

Gelis van Borselen, who had seen those twenty-five written pages, knew part of it, and had time to consider it, and even elaborate on it, during that part of her life she was about to spend in an Andalusian city in Africa, in her well-staffed house, with no one from her past to visit her but Umar.

It was not a habit of hers to be lonely. Taken to Scotland, to Brussels, to Geneva; to any of those places where her father had business: she set herself to acquire interests and friends, or at least acquaintances. Had he lived a little longer, Florence van Borselen would have come to rely on her way of acquiring trade secrets; the guileless questions she had found a young woman could ask, and have answered.

She had been useful to her uncle, the seigneur of Veere, and had listened, patient if not much impressed, to Wolfaert her cousin, who held a Scottish earldom because of the Scottish princess he had married. She knew all about the family of St Pol of Kilmirren in Scotland, and the unpleasant grandfather Jordan who bore a French title and lived at Ribérac, and advised the French King on finances. She knew about the philandering Simon, and why her pregnant, stupid, dead sister Katelina had married him. She had guessed more than half of Nicholas's story before he had proclaimed the truth in his fever that night. She had found out what Nicholas was capable of, and had trained herself to act and think as he did.

It was disconcerting, therefore, to find that, four weeks after his departure, she had still failed to implement fully the disciplined programme she had set for herself. When she should have been learning Arabic, she called on Zuhra, whose marriage contract with Umar was now final. The girl's affairs didn't much interest Gelis, but Zuhra was the only innocent in Timbuktu who assumed, without a second thought, that Nicholas had been her lover.

It was worth reminding herself of the fact, since an affair of even one night should not be forgotten. It was part of one's history. Katelina had not wished to stay a virgin, and neither had she. One required a catholic viewpoint.

It was because of the wider, worldly stand-point that she deferred her visits to the Qadi's library, in order to assemble her thoughts on the scheme Nicholas had prepared for Bel and Diniz and Gregorio.

He had specified the exact cargo of the *Ghost,* and had jotted down a long, orderly list of the many ways in which it could have been stolen, together with recommendations for tracing it.

He had examined the case of the impounded ship itself, and proposed that Gregorio now set on foot the moves that would vindicate his ownership, remove the injunction, and restore either the ship or the insurance money. He recommended that Astorre, the captain of his mercenary army, should be traced, and Tobie his physician, now fighting in Albania with Skanderbeg, since both could describe the ship's early history.

He proposed Gregorio should sue the *Fortado*, especially if Melchiorre had survived to give evidence. He thought it likely that my lord Simon and the Lomellini brothers would fall out, once Simon found the Vatachino had shared in the *Fortado*. This might make it easier for Diniz, with Gregorio's help, to expand the Ponta do Sol property. He had said precisely how much of the gold should be spent to that end, and how much in Bruges and Venice. He had recommended that, having established Jaime in Madeira, Diniz should consider whether his mother wished to remain in the Vasquez home in Lagos or return nearer her relatives. Nicholas suggested that Diniz take her to Bruges, where she could stay meantime in the house of João Vasquez, and close to the van Borselen family.

'Why?' Gelis had said, when Nicholas had been physically present, seated among them, reading from the papers.

He had looked up. 'Your sister married Lucia's brother.'

'But she's dead. And the child isn't there. That's why I went to Lagos. Simon doesn't let the child come to Bruges. You would think he was frightened of something.'

'I can't think what,' Nicholas had said; and went on reading.

So Lucia and Diniz were meant to go to Bruges, while Gregorio stayed to complete his work on Madeira and see the *San Niccolò* restored and turned round with a fresh cargo. And the rest of the money was to be dispensed in Venice, but the notes had not said how. Or not the parts she had seen. Perhaps he guessed that she was not quite disinterested.

The plans were all provident, careful. They had to be. It would have been different, had the *Ghost*'s cargo also survived. And, of course, there was no saying that the *San Niccolò* itself would arrive. It might be lying now on the bed of the Gambia. It was lack of news that made her so restless.

The news staggered in. First, from downriver. The two mad white men had been attacked by idol-worshipping black men, who had killed their guide and threatened their encampment with spears, but the party had driven them off, and had been seen making for Gao.

Then news from the Gambia. The white boy who escaped from the Joliba had returned to the blue ship on the Gambia, and that ship had set sail. The time, from the account, must have been mid-February. So the *Fortado* had gone off, with Filipe.

In May, three months after Bel and Diniz had gone, Gelis heard that the other white party of madmen from Timbuktu – with one mad white woman – had arrived on the Gambia, boarded the black ship with King Gnumi, and left. The *San Niccolò* was on her way home.

On hearing the news, she hurried over to Umar's house, where she could share her delight with him and his wife of five weeks. Zuhra slipped out, halfway through the excitement, to vomit briefly outside. She came back smiling, and all her aunts and cousins laughed and patted her. She was fifteen, and pregnant by Umar her husband. Gelis went home, and settled down at last to her studies.

There was only one further report from the east, from a caravan coming through from Takedda with copper. They had come across cowrie shells which had originally been bartered by two white men for food, and skins for their feet and a night's shelter from the rains. The rains, as everyone knew, were unhealthy in that region, which was why wise men kept to the north. But then, wise men went to Cairo or Mecca, not south through the swamps and the forests that led to the mountains.

Saloum, who returned in June from the Gambia, came to see her, and talked about it as he sat on her cushions. 'You will forgive me. He is your holy man. But I thought him a man of doubts, your Father Godscalc. I would not have thought him so brave for his faith.'

'You were brave for yours,' Gelis said.

'But I am sure of Paradise,' Saloum said. 'That is, is it not, why Muslims are supposed to be strong? But I have seen a man do more than his best, just from fear of fear.'

'Or from love,' Gelis said.

'Or from fear of not being loved. Man's heart is a thing made of sand. You know there is unrest on the river?'

'Unrest?' Gelis said.

'Your friends chose the right time to go home, and the right ally. King Gnumi had looked after your ship. He told me there will be trouble.'

'Between the two Kings?' Gelis said. 'Because of what happened to us?'

'That! No,' Saloum said. 'That was no more, forgive me, than a crossing of spears during an elephant hunt. This is war.'

'In the east too?' Gelis asked.

'Everywhere.'

'But not Timbuktu.'

'Timbuktu? One can plunder it, but one must possess it to make use of its commerce, and this requires more than a sudden raid by hot-tempered neighbours, or by the drunken youths from this village or that, shaking their assagais. It requires a ruler,' said Saloum. 'A man of power, with an army behind him.'

'There can be few of these,' Gelis said, 'stronger than Akil or Muhammed ben Idir.'

'Few. Luckily few,' Saloum said; and went on to praise the white woman, and Diniz.

By then, the great heat had begun, and the regular rainstorms, of which the first had been so freakish and so memorable. The drifted sand steamed in the streets, but there were days when the sky was bright blue, instead of the dust-coloured grey of harmattan-time, and when it produced no rain at all. Nor, when it did, was it the kind of torrent that fell further south, and turned obscure tracks into sinks of waist-gripping mud, and formed pools of thick teeming water, they said, which could cause a man to die through one drop on his skin.

Gelis roved the city during these weeks, and on one of these walks, met the Italian.

She assumed, that is, that he was a native Italian because she heard his voice first. She was kneeling on a piece of open ground at the time, poking with a stick at a bank of sand, the usual large moulded seat upon which house-owners sat to take air. In this case the house behind it was ruined, and the rains had caused the bank to open and slip, revealing the debris that had lain under it. The brilliance of a glaze had attracted her attention; the stick was in case of scorpions, and her two servants stood patiently behind her, along with the deep circle of men, women and children that gathered good-humouredly wherever she was.

The voice said, 'You have found some tiles, madonna? They are very old. I have a few in my shop.'

The Italian was perfect, like Umar's, but it was not Umar's voice. She looked up.

It was a Berber. Or no, it was a bearded man of the Maghgreb with bold, high-coloured features closer to those of a Tunisian Arab. He wore a magnificent turban, and his boots, under her nose, were of embroidered crimson kid under a robe of – she would have sworn – Lucca velvet.

She straightened. She said, 'We have not met before,' in Italian. All the circle beamed and murmured with pleasure.

The man said, 'No. I have been with my brothers in Tlemcen. I came back with the spring *azalai*.'

She had seen it: the biggest caravan from the north. It had been fifteen miles long. She said, 'You are a trader? With the Italians?'

He said, 'Would the madonna care to see the silks I have brought? My humble house is nearby, and my wife would be honoured to offer refreshment. My name, as all around you will tell you, is Abderrahman ibn Said, and I am a merchant of Timbuktu. And you are madonna Gelissa from the King of Portugal's ship, about whom everyone in this city has told me. Pray come. If the tiles intrigue you, my boy will stay and dig for you. He will bring what he finds.'

She accepted. In his large, well-furnished house, she met his wife and his family: 'This is the madonna from Lagos who is a friend of Umar ibn Muhammad al-Kaburi, and of Saloum ibn Hani and many others.' Then, as they sat on cushions fingering sweetmeats and supping sherbet: 'This is the lady who likes to see how the maize grows, and the rice, and the sorghum, and who ponders our storehouses and likes to watch which irrigation channels silt up, and how bricks are made, and baskets woven, and leather cured. This is a lady of many talents.'

'I am curious,' Gelis said. 'I am fortunate, to have time to spend in your city.' Neither of them had mentioned her fortune in gold.

'You prefer, as I do, practical matters. And, of course, matters of history. You were right. The tiles were precious, even broken. You also read?' said the Arab. He hadn't mentioned Nicholas, either.

She said, without answering, 'I should be interested to see the silks you spoke of. One brought cloth to my house, perhaps from these very stockrooms in your absence. Someone buys them for you in Europe?'

'Ah yes,' said the man. A little ape jumped on his lap, and he tickled its chin. 'A man called Benedetto Dei. He travels on the Cyprus galley this year, but I hope to tempt him to Timbuktu when next the fleet comes to Barbary, or passes with alum for Flanders.'

He set the ape aside. 'But all is upset now, after the death of the old man. Cosimo de' Medici, father of Florence. A loss, a terrible loss. The son is proving a hard man on his managers; Tommaso, who thought to have all his own way, is in despair. You come from Bruges. You can imagine.' Somewhere, someone was milking a goat.

'*Tommaso Portinari?*' said Gelis. It was the sort of naïvety she used to deplore in Diniz Vasquez. She shut her lips quickly.

'Of course. We are all Medici agents,' said ibn Said. 'I and my brothers; Benedetto Dei; Tommaso Portinari, who, of course, also manages the office in Bruges. We all import from the firm of Medici, and execute orders. You will realise, therefore, that the silk is of the first quality.'

She examined the silks. She expressed a wish to see all his imports. She said, 'Forgive me if I have not understood you. You do not purchase these goods direct from their source, but you receive them from the Medici agents and then resell, paying commission to the Medici?'

'That is so,' he said. If he felt surprise, he was far too subtle to show it.

She said, 'I know salt coming over the Sahara can increase its price by four times, and no doubt the profit is high, too, on other goods.'

'The expenses are high,' said ibn Said. 'The double journey takes four or five months – six, if the camels are to be rested. You know, perhaps, the cost of a camel, yet they cannot survive this expedition more than a very few times. And men are hired and die, or are waylaid by parties of robbers. There are few waterholes, and the way hidden by sandstorms. One mistake in the desert, and whole caravans can and do perish. The sands are half made of bone.'

'So, soon men will bring it by sea?' Gelis said.

His eyes were large and dark as the pool of the harbour at Sluys. 'Did you find it easy to do so?' he said. 'And as you have found, although men and camels like water, silk does not.'

'I see that,' she said. 'I wondered if you knew what price such fabric sells for in Flanders. Especially fabric with the flaw which, as you see, runs through this cloth; or with the faults in the cropping you see there. The licence fee for selling such cloth should not be too demanding.'

'Madonna. you interest me.' said Abderrahman ibn Said, merchant and agent. 'Let us sit down and talk.'

Gelis did not, in the normal exchanges with Umar's household, find it absolutely necessary to discuss her visits to the households of merchants, although she found that Umar, too, had begun to offer some of his European experience, tactfully, to the city fathers. If he sought a public appointment, he failed to receive it. The Timbuktu-Koy, in poor health, seemed little interested and his son deaf to advice. She noticed, for ibn Said told her, how the Koy's taxes had abruptly increased, and how much profit had been peeled from the latest caravan.

'It is not wholly wise,' had said ibn Said, in his meaningful way. 'Merchants stay in Timbuktu because it is profitable. But there are other towns.'

'Gao?' she had said. They had formed a habit of meeting, always in the presence of his family. He found her advice of value and even of profit; she did not object when some not insubstantial gift came her way. You might almost say they had entered a partnership.

'Gao? No,' he had said. 'The Songhai are rather too powerful. Although, of course, it is a place of importance, where the trade leaves for Egypt and Tripoli. Your lord Niccolò will pass through Gao and Kano.'

'I believe he has passed through Kano,' she said – she could not resist saying.

The Arab had kept silence. Then he said, 'I salute, of course, the hardihood of your friends. Had they chosen to go to Egypt, it would not have been difficult. The desert routes, despite their dangers, are known. Through Air, he could have proceeded by the old pilgrim highway to Azawa, Ghat, Murzak, Aujila, Siwa to Cairo. There are salt caravans which pass from Air to Bilma and back and are so common that the peaks near Bilma – do you know? – sing to warn when the camels are coming. But south of Kano . . . There you leave the land fit for camels, the land of Muslims, and enter the rainforests which have few tracks, and are the province of pagans. I have known only one man who has ever tried to go to Ethiopia from Timbuktu, and he did not come back.'

He paused. 'You wait, madonna. How long will you wait?'

'Until October,' Gelis had said. 'I have to go from Timbuktu in October, or the caravel which expects us will leave.'

'It is July,' had said the Arab thoughtfully. 'If your friends have not turned by now, they will never come back in time.'

By August, Gregorio was in Lagos for the second time. The first time, he had merely paused there, to deliver Diniz and Bel to the ecstatic Lucia de Vasquez before sailing with Melchiorre north to Lisbon. There he had made his accounting with the King of Portugal, and sold the *San Niccolò*'s cargo.

He would like to have taken the bullion to Flanders, but there was no time. The price he got in Lisbon was good enough – all Europe was screaming for gold – and by horse and by ship, a bill of exchange could travel faster than a box on a galley. He knew how much to send to Bruges, and how much to Venice. He knew there was no time to waste.

He would have liked, also, to have bought the caravel, but there was not enough money for that. He hired her for another year, and the King made the terms easy, and also the loan arrangements which would permit him to buy his next cargo. So he had lost little in the markets, after all.

When it was all finished, he spent a night at Sintra with Diogo Gomes, who enjoyed the news of Madeira, but listened to what Melchiorre had to tell with hunger in his eyes. At the end he had said, 'And vander Poele – he is still in Timbuktu?'

'Until the autumn,' Gregorio said. 'You will hear the adventure from his own lips when he comes back next spring. And meantime, you must come south and call on young Diniz. You have a fine young Portuguese explorer there.'

For the sake of the market – why else? – the expedition to Ethiopia was not to be mentioned. The King, of course, had wanted news, but Gregorio had merely replied that the distance seemed greater than was at first thought, and the journey impracticable. The King had not demurred, any more than he had expressed dramatic regret at the loss of Jorge da Silves, potential Knight of the Order of Christ. Gregorio had not said how he died. And the King, with the gold in his lap, was not overmuch distressed by either occurrence.

Gregorio spent some time with other lawyers, establishing his Bank's intention to challenge the ownership of the empty roundship now called the *Ghost*, and also their proposal to take to court the joint owners of the caravel *Fortado* for her actions in the river Gambia and elsewhere. He met the lawyers for the Vatachino, but neither David de Salmeton nor Martin was there. He said nothing to anyone of that fact that the *Ghost* had carried a cargo, and no one, even Diogo Gomes, even seemed to have considered the possibility.

Everyone else who might know anything had gone. Simon de St Pol had long since passed through Lisbon on his way from Madeira, returning, it was concluded, to Scotland or France. Michael

Crackbene and the boy Filipe had vanished, but that was not surprising, given the coming case against the *Fortado*.

Even less surprisingly, there was no trace of Ochoa de Marchena and his crew. There seemed no doubt, by now, that if Ochoa had purloined the gold, it had not been to keep it safely for Nicholas. The *Ghost* herself lay in dry dock, and Gregorio was not permitted to view her.

The next time he left Madeira, it was to co-ordinate the refitting of the *San Niccolò* at Lagos, and to complete the arrangements for her cargo. He took the same house as before, empty this time of Nicholas and Godscalc and Jorge da Silves.

And of Loppe. He could not get used to calling him Umar, as Diniz did. He could not get used, either, to what Diniz had told him about Loppe. About the slaves, first of all. And then about how he had joined Raffaelo Doria, and led him to his death. To preserve the secret of Wangara, Diniz had said.

Gregorio had refrained from asking the questions which plagued him. Had Loppe promised to lead Nicholas to Wangara if Nicholas indulged him over the slaves? Or had he only promised to act as his guide, knowing what Nicholas would expect, but determined to baulk him? If Doria had not been there, would Loppe have had to decide between Wangara and Nicholas?

These were matters Gregorio would discuss with Godscalc, perhaps, but not with young Diniz, and especially not since he had discovered Diniz knew who Nicholas was, or was not. Since that one, unexpected exchange, Gregorio had found Diniz mute on the subject of Nicholas. Mute and anxious.

Gregorio had only called once on Lucia de St Pol e Vasquez, and then on his return voyage, when she should have recovered from the shock and delight of her son's return, and the considerable pleasure of discovering that the Vasquez estate had a little money again, and might have more. He had also had no wish to find Simon de St Pol living there, with his obstreperous child.

Simon he now knew had not even stopped to see his sister on his way north. The child had stayed, he discovered, and then had been sent for.

'How should I know where Henry has gone?' Lucia said. 'They sent a nurse for him, and an elaborate escort. You would think he was the vicomte already.' Bereavement — even mistaken bereavement — had made her a little stouter, although the golden hair was still perfectly coifed and her morning gown and linen immaculate. There were lines round her mouth.

She added, 'I suppose you met the child? Then you know. An ogre. I told Bel, really, not to trouble.'

'Bel?' said Gregorio. She was the real reason why he had called. He hadn't seen her.

'Bel insisted on joining the party travelling with Henry. First to Ribérac, and then somewhere else.'

'To Ribérac? To his grandfather Jordan?'

'I told her Simon would be furious,' Lucia said. 'He's training Henry to be the first champion jouster in napkins. You know all this madness was for Henry? Simon sold the estate and invested in the *Fortado* to make money for Henry? The idea of losing it in some sort of court case, I tell you, is driving him mad.'

'I'm sorry,' Gregorio said.

'No! Don't be,' said Lucia with elegant spite. 'A dynasty founded by that child? I think they should present Henry to the van Borselen family. They wanted him. They sent the girl Gelis.'

'You think he'd make a good merchant?' said Gregorio. His smile felt artificial, even to him.

'I don't think he'd make a good anything,' Lucia said. 'He's too like his father.'

At the end, she said, 'And so, when does the *San Niccolò* sail for the gold?'

'In October,' Gregorio said. 'With a new master, and a good clerk, and a pilot who can make use of our charts. She'll arrive in Cantor in December, and bring Gelis and Godscalc and Nicholas back. I can't go with her: I must go to Bruges.'

'I don't want Diniz to go,' Lucia said. 'He is not to go back to Guinea.'

'I know he thought of it. If you like,' Gregorio said, 'I could take him to Bruges. I need help. Jaime will do very well in Madeira without us.'

He wondered if she would object. Bruges was connected with Nicholas. A year ago, she had been convinced that Nicholas was trying to kill all her family. Presumably, he thought, she had observed that Diniz and Gelis had survived, and that the person most worth despising was Simon. He waited.

'Perhaps I could come to Bruges too,' Lucia said.

Gregorio clung to the smile. It was what his orders required. He had hoped, truth to tell, to sidestep this particular order. 'Why . . .' he said. 'Why, of course.'

In the second week of September, when Zuhra was five months pregnant but hardly showed it, Umar invited himself to the house he had taken for Gelis van Borselen and, leaving his shoes in the garden, followed her servant into the largest chamber, where she sat surrounded by carpets. It had been coarse cloth, *chigguiya*, last

time. He came and knelt smiling before her. He said, 'You know
we don't make anything in this city. We buy from one man, and
sell to another.'

'You make books,' she said, looking up. In the heat, she dressed
mostly as Zuhra did, in a single garment of cotton, with one of
coloured silk to wear over it in public. In private, in the steam
baths and pools and lounging-rooms of other women she often
went bare, he knew from Zuhra, and probably did so here, too. She
had made for herself a way of living in an environment as different
as Europe had been for him. He knew how much fortitude it
needed – and even more how much energy, how much understanding, and how much intelligence. He could not understand why,
with all that, she had not left Nicholas alone.

They never spoke of him. They spoke a lot of Timbuktu, and all
that concerned it. She saw it not just as an exchange mart, a centre
of peace, of learning, of wisdom, of retreat, of happiness, although
she recognised all these things. She wanted to give it more: a
wealth of its own. Even though the carpets around her were poorly
woven and inadequately dyed, she contemplated them, frowning,
to see how they could be made better.

Umar said, 'Gelis. We make books and copy them. Is that not
enough?'

'No,' she said. 'Books can walk. If Akil demands more than his
third for the army, if a caravan fails to arrive, or the Joliba floods at
the wrong season, then books can leave Timbuktu and make their
home anywhere. Wealthy scholars find it easy to leave. But artisans
who supply swords and slippers and good dyed cloth can survive
on little, and will stay, and so will the heart of the city.'

'I think perhaps,' said Umar slowly, 'you are becoming at home
in this place. Do you want to go back?'

She looked at him. To be truthful, her eyes always made him
uneasy by their paleness, and the unexpected lines of brown lashes,
all of it framed by the pallid, wheat-coloured hair. She appeared as
if coated with sugar; while within, something quite different was
rooted.

She said, 'Do I want to go back? I dream of nothing else.'

'Very well,' he said.

He had no need to say more. She looked up. 'Ah. You have come
to tell me there is no news, and that there are therefore decisions to
be made. I am sorry, Umar. I should have guessed. Come in. Let
us leave this, and talk.'

She was brave, of course, and had considered the possibility that
she might have to set out for the Gambia on her own. She would
have to leave Timbuktu in three weeks at the most, to make the

long journey back along the course of the Joliba, and then down to the Gambia with the gold. 'I shall come to Cantor,' Umar said. 'And the Timbuktu-Koy has promised a boat and many men, strongly armed, from his own bodyguard. The *San Niccolò*, which will be waiting, will have her own artillery and far more than her usual complement.'

'I know,' Gelis said.

Of course she, too, had read all those meticulous pages. Once before, in Trebizond, Umar had read such a list of directives, when sure that Nicholas was not going to return.

Umar said, 'There is still time. They are late, but the *Niccolò* can wait for a little. Not for long, but a little. The unrest may even have helped. If Godscalc found the path doubly barred, he might have had to turn back the sooner. Then all that would hamper them would be the rains.'

Gelis said, 'You never thought they could get there.'

'No,' Umar said. 'Nor did they. Father Godscalc had determined to try it for the sake of his faith, and to save others. And Nicholas went to protect him.'

'And not for the River of Gems?' Gelis said. Her smile drew the sting, or appeared to.

'He needed the gold for his Bank,' Umar said. 'And now he has it. Who knows what desires he has now? What drew him, or what will bring him back?'

Gelis said, 'I think he is dead.' And looking at those bleak, Baltic eyes, he saw that she had spoken, for once, her true mind.

On the lower Joliba, which men called the river of rivers, Gher Nigheren, the villagers paid some lip-service to Allah, and slightly more to the holy man who came and killed chickens and foretold the size of the maize crop next year. They had, however, learned that Allah, or his servants, liked to know when true Believers met their death, so that words might be said over them by men with their heads bound in cloth and a leather parcel hung round their necks and the necks of their horses. Therefore they sent word up the river when bearers arrived carrying the remains of two men who were certainly Tuareg in some part of their blood, going by their colour, and the shapes of their noses.

Not that either their colour or the original shapes of their noses could clearly be distinguished, as they had been found in the forest, where the hyenas had certainly had a look at them; and where, before that, they had been systematically attacked by both spear and axe, and perhaps by arrows, since the limbs of the older man were both discoloured and distended in places. But that might

have been because the bones in both his upper and lower arms
had been broken, and most of the bones of his fingers.

The younger man displayed, too, the gouges and hack-wounds
of recent battle, but also the signs of older injuries, and with them
an extremity of exhaustion which suggested other causes. That one
lay without sound or movement, but the older Maghgrebian, when
first brought in, muttered a little.

Dead and dying, the unfortunate men had no money and no
possessions and, indeed, might not have been identified as Tuareg
except that it was a Friday, and someone from upriver came into
the mosque, where the bodies had been laid out to keep them out
of the rain, although the walls had begun to dissolve, and the straw
of the roof had seen better days.

But it could be seen, of course, that the community's intentions
were good, and messages had been sent off straight away, and
straight away answered. They were ordered to carry the two
corpses immediately towards Timbuktu, from which city great
(and generous) men were setting out already to meet them.

A man and a woman couldn't travel as quickly as drumbeats.
Umar brought men and camels and – in eternal hope – a physician;
he and Gelis raced with them down the side of the shallow, rock-
strewn, inimical river until they heard the sounds of chanting and
horns, and saw the drift of men and women and children strolling
cheerfully towards them, with a herd of goats, a hump-backed ox,
and two litters.

Umar swung himself down, ignoring the greetings, the people
pressing around him, laughing and singing. He used his shoulders
to push through the crowd to the litters. A goat stood astride one.

Gelis got down more slowly, and didn't come forward as Umar
drew back the first rain-sodden blanket.

Beneath it was what had been the vigorous bulk of Godscalc of
Cologne. The eyes in the misshapen face were intact, and were
open. Umar looked down. Godscalc said, 'He is not dead.'

His eyes had not changed, nor his lips moved. The words, in
Flemish, were nothing but breath. Umar said, 'I hear you. Dear
friend, I have you under my hand, and I thank your God and
mine.' Then, answering some pleading in the open eyes, he turned
to the other.

He knew, by then, that Gelis had run forward and had knelt
beside Godscalc and that the physician, too, had forced his way
through. He kept his back to the girl, and unfolded the cloth,
soaked with blood, that lay over Nicholas. He heard the doctor's
voice, speaking gently to Godscalc, and then felt Gelis behind him.
Her eyes were turned away. She said, 'Tell me.'

Umar looked down, unspeaking. He touched the cold skin.

There seemed nothing familiar about the bloodless face, turned to one side, its saucer eyes closed and pushed about by blackened pillows of flesh, scored with white contusions, so that the eyelashes stuck out at unnatural angles. Half his face was raw and marbled, like meat on a stall, and his swollen lips were stuck fast together. Nicholas could not have spoken, even if the bloody mess of his body was an illusion; even if he had been alive. Then Umar saw a shadow move, small as a mite on the torn flesh of the neck, and then a bead of fresh blood.

He said, 'He is alive, but . . .' He stopped, for the physician pushed him aside. Umar rose.

Gelis said, 'But?'

The doctor said, 'I can do nothing here. We must take them back quickly. The camel-litters are steady.'

'But?' said Gelis again. Her skin was so pale it looked dead.

'But?' said the physician testily. 'But I do not know if either will survive the journey. As it is, this one should not be alive.'

He was referring to Nicholas. Umar thought, as he stepped forward to take the weight of the strapping, how many people had said that of Nicholas, through all his brief life. And he wondered whether it was by their wish or his own, that this had happened. Some of the hostility Nicholas generated had been his own fault, but not all. It was a heavy burden for a man to carry unless he were very sure of himself, and Umar doubted whether Nicholas had ever been as sure as he seemed. That was – that had been – his saving grace.

Chapter 34

SEPTEMBER CAME TO an end, and no long procession of bearers left the Metropolis of Negroland to journey south-west to the sea with the possessions of Nicholas vander Poele, Gelis van Borselen and Father Godscalc of Cologne, accompanied by four thousand pounds' weight of pure gold.

In Timbuktu itself, whose name was currently on the lips of every banker in Europe, all time seemed to have stopped. None spoke of the day, or the month, or the season now slipping away, in case all else were to slip away with it. Death remained an everyday guest, not quite present, but not out of sight, or out of mind.

In the quarter of the imams, the scholars, the ancient mosque of Sankore, the Timbuktu-Koy had made free a house where men of medicine could watch over the ill-advised Europeans whose arrival had promised so much – which still might mean so much – to the future of the city. Brought there so close to death that it seemed impossible that either should live, the holy man and the Venetian Fleming seized the vigorous fancy of the city.

Gelis, leaving to visit them, would find gathering about her on the way a flock of concerned and affectionate people, bronzed and black, Negroid and aquiline, naked or veiled, tattooed, painted, hung with bucket-earrings of gold, or with lips turned down to their bosoms, their hair lush or crimped or shaved or piled on top of their heads. 'Do they live? Poor lords, everyone knows what pagans will do when they think they are threatened.'

Always, she went to Godscalc first for, broken, desolate, he kept some thread between himself and the living, and sometimes he talked. None of them understood how he, the elder, the unworldly, had struggled to surmount what had happened while Nicholas lay, day after day, unresponding.

Unless it was deliberate. Umar thought so. Umar never left the chamber in which they both lay. As she did, he pieced together what had happened: the agony of the journey, where land, beast and man had been against them. Godscalc spoke again and again of the valour of Nicholas, early beaten down in Godscalc's defence and refusing to stop. Until, in the end, Godscalc himself had begged to abandon what he had come for, and had led the way back, to be waylaid by frenzied, terrified men who thought them devils, monsters, leprous magicians who would conjure their wells to be dry, their wives barren, and who had beaten them, and left them for dead.

They had had no means of defence. The night before, suspecting danger, their bearers had fled, taking all the little they had. Afterwards, Godscalc had waked to find himself sunk in the forest floor, his broken hand enfolded in that of Nicholas in a gesture of comfort and – he felt – friendship, but not in expectation of meeting again in this world. Then, he had thought Nicholas dead.

Dry-eyed, Gelis listened. Godscalc began to recover. But not Nicholas.

In October, Umar said, 'Demoiselle. Gelis . . .'

And she had stopped him. 'I am in no mind to leave them.'

He had looked at her gravely: this black, gentle, serious man whose attachment to Nicholas she had seen, at last, for the tremendous and terrible thing that it was. He said, 'It is for you to decide. The gold is needed. Nicholas founded a bank, and thereby took upon himself the welfare of many people. If it does not reach the *San Niccolò* now, it will be too late. Whether he lives or not, this was part of his plan.'

'He would want the gold to go,' Gelis said.

'He would want you and Father Godscalc to go with it,' Umar said. 'The padre could travel. He must go. If what has happened means anything, he must tell the world of it.'

Gelis said, 'You want me to leave.'

'No,' said Umar. 'If Nicholas lives, and if you choose, from pity or friendship, to stay with him, no one would dissuade you except, perhaps, Nicholas himself, if he knew. In your own world, it might be different.'

He paused. He said, 'I have ascribed to you friendship and pity, but I do not know your heart. Forgive me, I am of a different race. I must also say therefore that if you wished him punished he has atoned, as few men have ever atoned, to the point of death and maybe beyond. If that was your sole aim, then I beg you to leave him.'

'In our own world, it might be different?' she repeated.

'There is your dead sister,' he said. 'There is his father. His grandfather. The battle for money and power to keep his independence, to defy and defeat them. In all that, you are his natural antagonist. You may be so no longer, but you are still part of the war he is fighting. It does not promise peace.'

'You think he should stay here?' said Gelis.

'He has no choice, for the moment,' said Umar. 'If he recovers, as you know, he is his own man. He will decide.'

'But too late for this ship,' Gelis said.

'Take this ship. If he – if he wishes to follow,' Umar said, 'I shall carry him myself to the coast. I shall find some means – a Portuguese vessel – to send him home. There will be only one season lost. And if you do not know your mind now, you will know it by then.'

It should not have disturbed her. She was afraid sometimes that Bel understood her. So perhaps did this man. Then she remembered, and interpreted, the hesitation. She said, 'You don't think he will recover.'

'They say he might,' Umar said. 'They say he can. Do you know who is his heir?'

The gold. She searched his face, but it showed only fatigue and distress. She said, 'His partners, so I suppose; apart from the claims of the Bank. He has no family. No –' She halted.

He said, 'No recognised family. In death, it might be different. In death he might receive what he always wanted.'

He said no more. For a moment, she felt too sickened to speak. Then she said, 'Simon hates him.'

'It is a great deal of gold,' Umar said. 'For an inheritance such as that, would Simon not proclaim Nicholas as his son, having Henry to succeed him, and being free of Nicholas for ever? If it has struck me, it must have occurred to Nicholas too.'

'I think,' Gelis said, 'that Nicholas values life more than you think. I think he likes fighting more than you think. I think you are speaking of a weak man, and that he is not.'

'I am glad you think so,' Umar said. 'So you will stay? Or you will go?'

She said, 'I will come to see him tomorrow, and decide.'

But she had already decided. She sat beside Nicholas the following day, and left whenever the doctors came to examine the bones they had rebroken and set; renew the ointments; change the nature of the liquids with which they hoped to nourish his body; ask him soft, patient questions to which he gave no reply.

Alone, she did not talk to him. She sat paralysed when, once, the abyss of his gaze opened, and he looked straight into her eyes.

She expected perplexity. She saw the reverse: full awareness. Then his eyes closed abruptly again.

Later, she called at Umar's house, and told him that she meant to leave with Father Godscalc, and the gold. She did not tell him why.

The city of Bruges in November was damp, cold and wet, like the rest of Flanders. Diniz Vasquez, arriving there straight from the interior of Africa, promptly fell prey to the worst cold in Europe, which he treated by wearing two shirts, a pourpoint, a doublet, a large hat and a thick velvet cloak lined with marten. He had never been happier in his life.

He didn't mind that his mother had insisted on coming. She was in the Vasquez house, and he saw little of her. He didn't mind that Gregorio, having taken him there, stayed two weeks and left to go back to Lisbon. Gregorio was expecting the return of the *San Niccolò* with a breathtaking cargo of gold, and Gelis, and Godscalc, and Nicholas. He, Diniz, had wanted to go back to Guinea on the *Niccolò*, but now he was glad that he hadn't. He had been a child when he had last been in Bruges. Bruges had changed. Bruges was full of girls.

Bruges was a rich, civilised city with well-maintained roads and canals, and proper administration and defences. It was inhabited by gentlemen, by prosperous traders, by busy, industrious crafts-men, and was one of the three great money markets of the world. Its streets and waterways were lined by handsome stone houses, comfortably furnished, where he could sit eating eggs and collops and shred-pie and talk about millet and sweet roots and Baobab juice with a great cup of good wine in his hand. And about serpents with a hundred teeth and four legs (which was true) and about the way gold was found in the nests of ants as big as cats (which was not strictly true, but which everyone took for gospel in any case).

It was a pity he had not been to Ethiopia (the younger ladies were thankful he hadn't tried) but it had been found to be too far away. He felt guilty, knowing that Nicholas and Godscalc were attempting that very journey, but he had been told not to mention it. In any case, no one seemed concerned. He had been to the end of the world. He was a hero.

He was invited to the Princenhof, where the Duke wanted to see him and commend his service with his sons Antony and young Baudouin in Ceuta, and enquire closely about his experiences in Guinea. He met Ernoul de Lalaing again. He had a private audience, somewhat fraught, with the Duchess Isabella, sister to the late Prince Henry of Portugal, who consequently knew as much as he did about trade, and whose secretary was his uncle. Briefed beforehand by Gregorio, he said, he hoped, no more than he should.

Others were anxious to hear of his experiences. He was invited
to all the clubs: the White Bear gave him a feast; and Anselm
Adorne arranged a gathering of friends at the Hôtel Jerusalem
from which the Lomellini alone begged to excuse themselves.
Louis de Bruges, seigneur de Gruuthuse, entertained him, and so
did the Hanse merchants and the English, led by their Master and
Governor William.

Diniz Vasquez was not an innocent: he knew very well that every
man in Bruges – in all trading Europe – would be affected in one
way or another by what Nicholas had done. He was being invited
for his own sake, but also because he was young, and might let fall
something that Gregorio wouldn't.

The serious work in Bruges was being done by Gregorio who,
during the two weeks of his stay, was invited out even more than
was Diniz, but who chose very carefully where he went. The
Duke, the Duke's controller, the Scots at the Metteneye hostel,
Adorne himself, and the Spanish merchants all received his attention, and he spent perhaps longest of all with Tommaso Portinari.
Sometimes he took Diniz with him.

Always, Gregorio spent some time each day with Diniz, explaining what he was doing. In some ways, it was the most exciting part
of the homecoming: those sessions with Gregorio and Jannekin
Bonkle, the friend of Nicholas who, appointed by Gregorio, ran
the Bruges bureau of the Banco di Niccolò.

Gregorio lived on the office premises, as did Bonkle, and
sometimes Diniz made a bed for himself beside them so that,
whatever the argument was, he could stay and engage in it. The
bureau was hardly palatial: two rooms leased from the Charetty
mansion and warehouse in Spangnaerts Street which Gregorio
ought to know well, having worked there for Marian de Charetty.

Venetian merchants called there, from the families of the Corner
or the Bembo. Sometimes Cristoffels, the Charetty manager, would
slip in of an evening and join them, and once or twice the older
Charetty girl came with him, and took a cup of wine, and asked questions.

One of the first things Diniz had had to do, along with Gregorio,
was to have a formal supper with the Charetty girls, and answer
their queries about Nicholas. It was what you would expect, since
Nicholas had been husband to their late mother – although from
what Diniz had heard, neither girl had approved of the marriage.

It astonished Diniz, all the same, to find that their very pertinent
questions were directed to the intentions of Nicholas *vis-à-vis*
trade, rather than to the adventures he wished to relate to them.
Tilde, the elder, put him through an inquisition as thorough as the

one he had faced at the White Bear, and made one or two points he found hard to parry.

Emerging, he found himself unexpectedly sorry for Tilde and Catherine. They were astute enough, for young girls, but the business wasn't what it should be for its size. He hoped, if the gold came, and if Nicholas was giving them any, that he would devote some thought to the Charetty company. Cristoffels was excellent, as a notary. But he hadn't personally worked among dyes.

By November, they had taken the straps from his limbs, and Nicholas was presuming to walk. His progress was slow, but quite measurable. He had excellent physicians.

He knew, of course, that Gelis and Godscalc had gone, and the gold with them. He had not been in his senses at the time, although he could recall their faces in short, vivid flashes which seemed to indicate that he had not been wholly unconscious. Once they were out of reach, he had found himself awake most of the time. It had been a doubtful blessing. The one constant, for so long as he could remember, was pain.

He had no other complaints. His bed was soft. Day and night, the sweat was smoothed from his skin; the torrid air was perpetually stirred by black, solemn children with fans. When he began to awake, and experience the full, awful weight of what had happened, there had appeared a sequence of quiet, respectful youths bearing books, who had bowed, seated themselves on the ground, and proceeded to read.

The early days of his recovery were shaped, distorted, made hectically lyrical by sweet voices reading in Arabic. The words, flowing on, drew him into no deep current of thought, but described light romances, heroic adventures, mystical odysseys. He found them soporific.

Then, expecting them one day, he had opened his eyes to the dry voice of the imam Katib Musa. 'It pleases my lord, to listen to stories for children?'

By then he could move his head, and his arms. Nicholas said, 'I cannot praise them sufficiently. They have been charmingly, tirelessly read.'

'They are our youngest scholars,' said Katib Musa. 'Unfortunately, it is no longer safe to send them. Here are some books, perhaps more suitable for a grown man.'

He was strong enough, now, to hold another man's gaze. 'Why is it no longer safe?' Nicholas said.

The imam made a small gesture. He was of middle years, and not imposing, but possessed a cold, still authority. 'You know this city. When the power of the Timbuktu-Koy is low, then that of Akil ag Malwal shows itself. The commander is at the gates, with his army. He knows you have paid your tax to the Koy, and will try to wrest most of it from him.'

Nicholas said, 'But the Timbuktu-Koy, also, has a bodyguard.'

'He had one,' said the imam. 'But, alas, it is on the Gambia at this moment, protecting your friends and your gold. Forgive me. There is nothing you can do. But it seemed to me that the time had come to distance yourself from children's stories.'

Umar had tried to smooth it away. 'It is Akil's way. It is no fault of yours. There is always some excuse to enter the city and claim more of its wealth than he merits. It is how the city is run.'

'It should not be so,' Nicholas said, and read the books, thinking. When he could walk, he went to the imam, and to the Timbuktu-Koy, and to the house of And-Agh-Muhammed, and asked questions. And because he could not walk far, very often the scholars who heard of his questions came to visit him, and talked, and brought books from which they read portions. And these were not children's books.

By then, he had confronted the central problem of his present life, and obtained from Umar an account of the departure of Gelis and Godscalc. He knew why Godscalc had gone, and was glad. He ought to have been able to guess – he, who was so good at guessing – why Gelis had not stayed, but there were too many imponderables. He asked Umar.

Umar said, 'She did not give her reasons. I can only tell you that she took long thought before she decided to go. She may have thought it best to part. She may have wanted to draw you after her. She may have thought you would not survive, and she could serve you best by completing your task. I could not read her mind.'

He had paused. 'All that is sure is that your task is complete. Father Godscalc has returned with the maps and news of Ethiopia which will save others from dying. And your Bank is preserved, and the Charetty company, and the Vasquez. You are free to do as you please.'

'Tell that to my body,' Nicholas had answered, smiling. His face, nearly healed, still felt stiff, and the blond beard, left to grow, hid his dimples. It didn't matter. Here, he had no need of guile.

Umar said, 'I could hardly make my way to your house, there have been so many meetings today. They wish to sink a well, and make some proper storage for millet, but no one can decide how it should be done.'

In February of the year 1466, the caravel *San Niccolò* completed

She saw dark, long-lashed eyes resting on hers, belonging to a man of middle height with loose dark hair, and fine jewels, and two beautiful hands, one of them stretched gracefully to gather one of her own, and raise it to his lips.

'Unless you have been warned to avoid me?' said David de Salmeton.

In Timbuktu, the Feast of St Nicholas came and went, such a celebration having no place in the Muslim calendar. If Nicholas felt rather more than a year older, he didn't say so. He had, in any case, other things to occupy his attention.

In January, Umar's first child was born. It was a son. By March, Zuhra was pregnant again. Nicholas felt only delight on Umar's behalf. He himself had no yearnings as yet: his body had been too abused, too broken. If he did, he knew that some gentle child would find her way to his bed, not from Akil this time. He was not sure what he would do. He was not sure how he wanted to order his life, except that he needed to know more.

Now he could walk, he spent half his time with the imams; with the teachers, the thinkers of the Sankore Mosque; the judges who passed on their learning; the scholars attached to the other great mosques, the Sidi Yahya al-Tadulsi, the Jingerebir.

Latterly, the imams had allowed him to enter the Sankore, 120 feet long, eighty feet wide, with its five naves and forest of masts. Of columns. Of slender columns, like those of a caravel. He had been admitted, dressed as he always was now, in the loose robes that men found comfortable, with his hair bound with a scarf, rakishly knotted.

Afterwards, he would talk about what he had heard, and even dispute it, but never with heat, and the habit of orderly, dispassionate appraisal was one he gladly acquired. He spoke and thought in Arabic, and could make himself understood in Mandingua and some of the other vernaculars. He had almost forgotten his French, his Flemish, his Tuscan.

There were exceptions. Abstract thought, for him, could never occupy all his mind when there were also practical things he could do. The deficiencies of the city were well known to him, and some of them could be simply repaired. Going about it, he was taken aback, now and then, to find that some problems had already been touched on, and even attacked. Umar had not told him that Gelis had been active in Timbuktu during the six months he had been absent. It raised, again, the question of why she had left. For a while, Nicholas returned quietly to his teachers, to think about it.

About that time, he was called upon by the cloth merchant

Abderrahman ibn Said, of whom he had heard, and who, breaking into unexpected Italian, seemed to be offering him a consultative partnership in his business. They talked of other things: the disruption of trade caused by the Songhai and their perpetual raids; the greed of Akil; the iniquity of high taxes. Ibn Said gave the impression that he was accustomed to receiving advice. Nicholas spent some time with him and saw him out, smiling. Gelis, again. And Tommaso Portinari, by God.

Having no official position, all that he did required the sanction of the Timbuktu-Koy or, latterly, as the old man grew feeble, of his son, whose name was the same as Umar's. A heavy youth of limited intelligence, the Koy's heir made few objections, unless the proposed improvement threatened to cost more than he thought worth his while. Matters were helped by the fact that Umar himself — Loppe — was now teaching, and held a post of some little power. And even without the Koy's experienced, if erratic, hand on the helm, the city was still being centrally run, from the magnificent palace of the Ma' Dughu.

Visiting the Koy, Nicholas was conscious, even in weakness, of the pleasure — the virtue — he received from its sweet columns and shining tiles and carved arches, its painted ceilings and grilles, from its pools and fountains and the heady, strange pot-pourri of its inward life: the camels tied in its yards, the petted apes, the bright birds, the extravagant leopard skins strewn in its chambers; the sounds that mingled the voice of the jungle, the rainforest, the savannah with the clear, miraculous voice of high learning.

He felt in no sense superior. He knew that not only Umar but many of the thoughtful, witty men whose conversation he sought had passed many years in the world outside the Land of the Blacks; they, as well as he, knew the singularity of what they and their forerunners had created.

He walked therefore with an open heart as well as an open mind, and accepted all that was offered his senses: the beating drums, the braying African horns mingled with the ululation of Arabic voices; the clank of gold, crude and solid as iron, hung upon naked, slender black bodies; the chanting voice of the storyteller and the singing voice of the imam, reciting the Koran. As the season changed and, once more, coolness returned to the night, Nicholas rested by scented fires in the Koy's flowery courts and watched unfold, beguiled, the spontaneous expression of many kinds of happiness, from the clapping hands, the rhythmic, light-hearted dancing of the young to the gentle ambulation of the Negro philosophers in their spotless white turbans and robes, agreeably discoursing, or exchanging verses, or drifting to repose in some bower to take their ease, and refresh themselves, body and spirit.

It was what Timbuktu offered. Umar had known. Umar, through Saloum, had wanted to draw Nicholas here. Nicholas remembered his words. *It will bring you what your heart and your soul both have need of.*

Umar had meant Timbuktu. He had called it *the terminus.*

Chapter 35

BY THE TIME the rainy season had come, Nicholas knew that it was true, and that he was indeed free.

Wisps of information always reached Timbuktu from the caravans. Sometimes several copies of the same packet would arrive; sometimes only part of one would get through. The most reliable were those addressed to ibn Said, although these were narrow in scope, and referred almost entirely to the doings of Tommaso Portinari, manager of the Bruges branch of the Medici bankers, and counsellor to Duke Philip of Flanders and Burgundy.

From these, Nicholas heard that Duke Philip still lived, although his heir's wife had died, and there was a scramble afoot to replace her. Tommaso thought the new bride would be English. Tommaso knew all about that because France, too, wanted English marriages, now it looked as if the Yorkist King was going to be permanent. Tommaso did some work on the side for the King of France. Or appeared to. France and Burgundy were virtually at war, and Tommaso could be useful to both sides.

He sent, as usual, some bales of casually packed silks with a large invoice attached. 'The lady was struck by these terms. By the Medici terms,' said ibn Said absently. At the time, Nicholas, amused, gave him some advice.

The next caravan after that brought to Nicholas, better than silk, the news he had silently longed for. The *San Niccolò* was at anchor in Lisbon. Godscalc and Gelis were safe, and his gold. So he could do as he wished.

He was mobile now, too. When the river would allow it, he visited some of the places he had passed full of fever on that first journey from the Gambia. He found his way to Djenne, and looked at bricks, among other things. He rode out to quarries. He talked to planters and fishermen. When his Feast Day began to approach again, he brought Umar to sit by his fire and said, 'Tell me about the Songhai.'

By leave of the Koy, he had continued to reside in the house to which he and Godscalc had been taken. It was close to the schools, and he could pay for it. One of his earliest anxieties had been that he might be living on charity, or at Umar's expense. Umar had reassured him. When the *San Niccolò* left, part of her gold and part of her cargo had remained, to support Nicholas. 'For life, should you wish,' Umar had concluded, smiling.

The unbroken gravity of his European days had left Umar now: in his own home he sat writing and crooning, his infant son sprawled on his lap; in a week or two, in December, his next child would be born. Among his own, he was loved and respected. Visiting Nicholas, he bent on him the same friendly, considering gaze he always used, and answered his question.

'Long ago, the Songhai came from the south and settled in villages all down the Great River for a thousand miles, where they made a living as farmers and fishermen. They looked like me' – he smiled again – 'although perhaps not quite so big. Then, six hundred years ago, they were conquered by Muslims, the Lemta Tuareg from the north, who made Gao, where you have been, into their capital.

'And they prospered, so that the King of Mali became envious and one of his generals conquered Gao, and then Timbuktu. As a result, all the Songhai kingdom became part of Mali until in time Mali weakened, and others rushed in. In the case of Timbuktu, the Malians were driven out by Akil, the commander of the Maghsharen Tuaregs, as you know.'

'Who allowed a Timbuktu-Koy to rule, at a price,' Nicholas said.

'Of course. And now, a new, gifted leader has appeared in the Lemta dynasty of the Songhai, who seeks to recover what the Songhai kingdom has lost, and add more. Where he is fighting, it is dangerous to travel, and as you have found, there are some here in the city who fear he will take advantage of the divided authority to pounce. But, Nicholas,' Umar said, 'have you not heard this from the Timbuktu-Koy or his son?'

'Who carries news in Timbuktu? The storks?' Nicholas said.

'Yes, the Koy's son called me to the palace this morning. The city is frightened, and has lost confidence in Akil and his garrison, who descend at tax-time and drink fermented liquor, and break open warehouses and sometimes help themselves to maidens who complain that they were not willing. The Koy's son wishes to know how a city of the north would defend itself.'

'And you said?' Umar asked. He wore the bland expression that Nicholas enjoyed most.

'The same as I said to the commander Akil, who called me in yesterday and asked the same question. There are things that can be done. If they wish, I shall help them. But Timbuktu is not Djenne. It has no natural defences. A higher wall will deter an ill-equipped enemy. A larger garrison, well armed and provided with food and water, could sustain a short siege. But do you wish a large garrison? There has been trouble already. Attack may not come, or may be intermittent. Even Astorre and his soldiers would find such heat, such idleness tiresome, however well they were exercised and diverted. And these are nomads, unaccustomed to staying long anywhere.'

'*Akil* consulted you?' Umar said.

'You might call it that,' Nicholas said. 'He sent a troop of horse to bring me, whether I wanted or not, and informed me that if I wished to continue to live and spy in idleness, I should work for my permit. They have some old hackbuts, but no knowledge of how to make balls.'

'I am sorry,' said Umar. His expression had changed. 'You should have told me.'

'I have told you,' said Nicholas, 'but not so that you will take any action. They wish to preserve the trading metropolis that is the source of their wealth. It is worth preserving. So is your greater heritage. Katib Musa has not begged me to show him how to use a crossbow in defence of the *ulama*, but he does not need to. Of course I shall help, but there is not a great deal that can be done.'

'Without you,' Umar said, 'nothing could be done at all. I shall complain to the Koy on your behalf.'

'No,' said Nicholas. 'It is the enmity between these two that will admit the Songhai. Let me stay uncommitted. Let me do what I can for them both. Umar, what am I learning for, if not for such as this?'

There was a silence. Then Umar said, 'It has been my prayer that you would find something more at the end of your search. Oh yes, if the city is threatened, I am not too proud to ask you how it should be defended, so long as you think it of worth. If it should be better run, and it pleases you to devise how to enhance it, every man here is your slave. So long as, in the end, there is something for you that you would not otherwise have had.'

Nicholas said, 'You know the school, and the teachers. You know what I have had. Do you want me to tell you what it means to me?'

'I know what it means to you,' said Umar slowly. 'And so do

your teachers. One has only to watch. But only you know what use you will make of the powers it gives you.'

'That is true,' Nicholas said. 'And as a teacher, you will know that one does not offer a gift, and then require an accounting.'

'I think perhaps,' Umar said after a moment, 'that is –'

'Unfair?' said Nicholas quickly. 'It was. I am sorry. You hoped I would begin to discover what I wanted to do with my life. You hoped I would find a confidant, since you think I need one. But Umar, what confidant did you ever allow yourself before you came home? Until that moment, whom would you trust, whom would you burden with your hopes and your doubts and your fears, and still call yourself a grown man?'

There was a long silence. Then Umar said, 'Nicholas, it is not always a mark of weakness to lay a burden on someone else, so long as they can bear it. I might have put my faith in you, but you were not yet a grown man.'

It was the cruellest thing he had ever said. Nicholas answered at once. 'Do you think I should disagree with that? No, it is not a mark of weakness, having found the right person, to ask help of them. But it also depends on the nature of the burden.'

'You are wrong,' Umar said. 'That is vanity speaking still. Nothing matters but what you are. You yourself.'

'And you think I had better find out,' Nicholas said. 'Well, you are probably right. Self-knowledge is not sold on the Rialto. And if it were, few people would buy.'

After that, Nicholas was patient and did nothing to offend Umar, or his other friends, or those who ruled the city. As he had offered, he used the cooler months at the start of the year of 1467 to strengthen the defences of the city, and when Akil, restless once again, collected his garrison and, with well-oiled hackbuts, galloped off to cause trouble elsewhere, Nicholas took the Koy's bodyguard under his wardship and initiated a month of hard, brutal, competitive sports. At the end of it, five men had been killed, twelve injured, and fifty had joined from the city, with more begging to come. And he was fit again.

Little news came over the Sahara but not, he thought, because of any action of Umar's to prevent it. What did come was either painfully specific – ibn Said's brother in Tlemcen had had another son – or painfully general – the English had forbidden all trade with Flanders, and so Bruges was suffering. The old Duke of Burgundy's son, like the son of their Koy, was afraid of no one, and fighting every day in some cause or another, mostly in France.

It added point to the news when the old man, the Timbuktu-Koy, actually died, and the new Koy, his son Umar, dispensed with the counsel of Nicholas and took over control of the Koy's force himself. Umar's second son was by then two months old, and named Umar Niccolò in honour of Nicholas rather than his Christian Feast Day. Umar spoke of Godscalc at the time, although not for long.

There had been no news, of course, of the priest or of Bel or of Diniz, since the report that all three had arrived safely in Portugal. Unbidden, there came to the mind of Nicholas, now and then, the recollection of his twenty-five pages of instructions. He knew the gold had reached Lisbon, where it would be converted into transferable funds. He had no doubts that Gregorio and Julius would have disposed of it as he wanted, resuming all that he had begun in Venice and Bruges, Cyprus and Alexandria and Scotland. They should by now have an agent in Scotland.

He had heard nothing, of course, of the legal action he had asked Gregorio to take, concerning both the *Ghost* and the *Fortado*. Again, he assumed Gregorio would do the best that he could: tracing Crackbene, finding Ochoa, bringing Tobie back (if he would come), and Astorre. And with such a cushion of gold, the two complaints hardly mattered. He really believed that they hardly mattered. Simon and the Vatachino could do as they pleased. And Henry was out of his hands. Henry was only safe when out of his hands.

He had heard nothing, and in this place would never hear anything, of Gelis van Borselen. More than a year ago, she had decided to leave, and having done that, there was no reason for her to send him a message. If she had, he would have received it by now, through ibn Said.

He himself sent no letters north, but had reason to believe that the caravans sometimes carried short dispatches from Umar. He understood that they conveyed the information that he, Nicholas, was well, and were intended largely – perhaps solely – to prevent any unnecessary expedition to find him. By the time he, Nicholas, had realised what was happening, it was not important enough even to mention.

In that month of February, while the port was still open, there came news of outbreaks of fighting upriver, where the Mandinguas of Mali were confined by the Songhai in the north, and the Fulani of Futa on the west. There had been some gold on its way, which was lost, and men from several tribes killed.

Abderrahman ibn Said, when Nicholas next saw him, was undisturbed. 'Some years it happens. There are many peoples of different tribes, different persuasions. In good times, they fight as the Songhai do, because they are vigorous, and yearning for power.

When the flood is late, or the locusts have come, then they must fight even more, or else starve.'

'We were fortunate,' Nicholas said, 'to make the journey twice from the Gambia?'

'You were cared for by Allah,' said ibn Said. 'The first time, you brought yourselves only, without merchandise, and how many died? The second time, the Koy's bodyguard protected your freight. It could never happen again. The present Koy would never risk it again. And another time, Gnumi Mansa may not turn Christian for you. He might find it too dangerous.'

Nicholas looked at the worldly, impassive brown-black eyes. He said, 'You are saying that there will never be trade between Timbuktu and the coast? It is impossible?'

'Impossible as trade between Timbuktu and Prester John,' said ibn Said. 'If you wish to leave Timbuktu, the only sure way is the desert.'

That night, sitting cross-legged in the forecourt of the house of And-Agh-Muhammed al-Kabir and his sons, Nicholas found relief, as he always did, in the measured voices of his fellow guests reading from the books they had brought, and in the careful unfolding and examination of some momentous topic, with many voices contributing, including his own. He knew every man there as a friend: his spectacles flashed on noses black and ruddy and nut-brown, flat and aquiline.

One of them, a son-in-law of the host, raised his head and said, 'I hear Akil has raided a village and captured a caravan to the east. Soon he will come for his taxes.'

'He will be disappointed,' said another. 'The Songhai, the Fulani have half the goods this time.'

Nicholas said, 'Does the Koy know?' and someone laid a soothing hand on his shoulder. 'He has been told. Rest. Thanks to you, Timbuktu has never been stronger.'

Afterwards, he remembered hesitating, leaving the house of the Qadi. But it was late, and as quiet as it ever was, for a city filled with humans and animals. The wind thrashed in the palm trees; the air was hazy with sand. Behind some locked courtyard he could hear the wail of a single-string fiddle, and on the outer edge of his hearing, drums beat. He paused at the gates of the Ma' Dughu and then walked on, because the Koy's bodyguard had been warned, and he, the outsider, should not stand on one side or the other, but should balance them.

He had chosen to sleep on the roof of his house, and the smoke wakened him. At first, he took the conflagration above him to be that of dawn: against a fierce, crimson sky darkened by sand all below him seemed black – the pillars of Andalusia, the pilasters of Memphis, the blind Arab walls and square houses of this strangest of cities. Then he saw that houses were burning, and what beat in the sky was the glow from the flames. Then the great gongs began to sound, and the horns that he had got Muhammed ben Idir to command in every corner of the city, and Nicholas ran down to the street as he was, calling his servants.

The fires had begun near the northern gate and all those who lived in the quarter, but for the officials, were trying to escape. He could hardly get through the lanes for the throng running against him, their children in their arms, their goats, their cows following. Others, like himself, had seized brooms from their racks and were forcing their way to the danger; he called to them, making sure they remembered the scheme. Some to the fire; some to the pools, the canal, the wells, the fountains, the buckets. Brought up in Bruges, he had always known what to do in a fire. Unless it was destroying his own business and home. Unless his father had started it.

Umar said, 'Where is it?'

Of course, Umar would be there. His house was not in danger. From the roof, as if Donatello had been there, outlining it for him, Nicholas had memorised the course of the fire. One main source; two subsidiary ones. Not the palace. Not the three mosques – or not so far. But the shops and houses nearest the north gate where a drunken army might descend for food and drink and girls and – being short of money and temper – might kick over a brazier, fling a brand in a disapproving householder's face or even, less carelessly, decide to see just how efficient the young Koy and his army might be, and how easy it might be to frighten them.

Running, Nicholas gave Umar his orders, and saw Umar leave. Still running, he came up to the first of the great houses and saw their servants doing what they had been taught to do: to drench, to dowse, to dig. Then he came to the seat of the blaze, and a dozen men with him, flinching back from roaring, wind-smashed tatters of fire and gush upon gush of hot sand, flung frying upon beast and man.

The straw huts of the outskirts had caught the first sparks and stood burning like haystacks, with no one still living inside. The houses of pressed mud or mud-brick had fared better, but most were thatched, and full of matting and blankets and rugs, as well as people. It was still possible to drag children out: to gather up the frightened and hurt as they staggered into the streets and rush them to safety, sheltered from the tearing wind with its ash and sand, its sizzling sparks, its burning gobbets of straw and nooses of whirling Baobab rope.

Some of the people Nicholas carried that night were known to him; some tried to smile. One woman, when he touched her, had a smile which didn't change, and the heat of her arms seared his hands. By then, the fire had reached the large houses.

If ever Nicholas had wondered what he would choose, he learned to know that night. He, who had seen his father in Bruges cast into the fire the ledgers that contained all his hopes, that night in Timbuktu broke through door after blistered door, their metal patterns red-hot and spitting and smoking, and, ignoring the burning books, the priceless, curling scrolls, the smoking vellum, rescued the people. Not the scholars, who were quick to comprehend, and fit, and able to act, but the others: the households of servants and their families; the grooms asleep behind the plunging mules in the stables; the elderly, lost and bewildered in smoke darkened rooms. And gradually, as the streets and houses were cleared, the flames began to hesitate at the ditches and to shrink under the onslaught of water. White steam became mixed with the smoke, and the hissing of water with the crackling growl of the fire. It was being contained.

Nicholas had suffered all this before, long ago, on a hill-top fortress in Cyprus. Then, the blaze had been intentionally started. He knew, as if he had been told, what kind of part Akil had played in all this: half deliberate, half experimental. As his work slackened and he could think, it became clear to Nicholas that it would not be possible to bring the commander to book; that the Koy was not strong enough to deal with the crisis this would evoke. As the fire had been contained, so must be its repercussions. As he worked, Nicholas began to talk to the people about him.

It was over by dawn. By dawn, a quarter of the city had gone, but the rest had been saved. By dawn, Nicholas in the Ma' Dughu, with the Katib Musa and the members of all the great houses, had drawn the commander Akil ag Malwal before the young Koy and with determined voices had defined the mistake, reduced the disaster to an event which would not happen again, and for which there were both remedies and compensation. No one there was in any condition to say more, nor should more have been said.

They dispersed, having arranged to meet in due course. But meantime, no retribution would be wreaked. The breach had been closed, at the expense of twenty lives and a suburb destroyed.

'But it will happen again,' Umar said, in the house of crying babies and frightened wife to which he had taken Nicholas to bathe his blisters and rest. Even with the shutters fast closed, the acrid smoke crept into the room, so that he ended the words with a cough. His hands and face, too, were grey with scorching.

Nicholas said, 'They managed well. They will do better if it happens again. And there is time to rebuild before the rains. How could Akil be so stupid? Their trade disrupted, their precious books lost, and the young Koy ready to be provoked by every challenge.' He broke off. 'Oh, Christ God, the books.'

'Do you wish you had saved them?' said Umar. He stood, his face masked in the creams Zuhra had smoothed on his skin, his burned hands hanging loose. He was not looking at Nicholas.

It was the tone that made Nicholas look up. Seated on the low bed, his head bent, his hands dropped between his knees, he had been thinking of the two libraries he had seen and known, their contents now ashes. Now, his senses quickened, he listened to Umar's voice. He said, 'You would have put them first? Before ordinary people?'

'I *have* put them first,' Umar said. 'The jurists, the scholars, the libraries. Is that not why I came back? Of course, I thought, they cannot always be saved. Of course, disasters occur. Teachers are killed, schools destroyed, books unhappily burned. But properly nurtured, the tradition of learning continues.'

He broke off. He said, 'If, that is, one is not forced to make the choice that you made tonight. When such a thing happens, one man cannot be expected to save both people and books.'

'Umar?' Nicholas said. He rose, but without coming closer. He said, 'Do you think I don't know why you have done what you have?'

Umar faced him. There was nothing comic about the daubs of white on his brow and cheekbones and nose, on either side of which his eyes shone, black and white. He looked fierce, like a witch doctor himself.

He said, 'I brought with me the greatest magician in Europe, but what I dreamed is impossible. It is too soon; there is too much against us; it is the waste of a life.'

'You have decided,' said Nicholas. He felt pain, but was too weary to consider where it came from. He said, 'You had so many motives, Umar. You wanted Father Godscalc to see the plight of the slaves, and how that traffic might worsen. You wanted us both to find that the way to Ethiopia was impossible, the tribes far from conversion. You wanted me to find the gold that would free me from responsibilities, and yet not find its source. You wanted us to discover the futility of founding stations in the interior, of attempting trade between the coast and this place. You wanted my help, but you wanted Timbuktu to remain untouched, sacrosanct, a shrine of learning, a repository of the world's wisdom, forever fuelled by its trade, but safe from the Christian armies of Europe.'

He stopped. 'I saw that. You must have realised it. I agreed. I stayed.'

'Yes,' said Umar. He raised his hands and held Nicholas at arms' length, a blistered palm on each shoulder. 'As we once said, we did not confide in each other; but you stayed. Why, Nicholas?' His hands tightened, then dropped.

Nicholas sat. He didn't say, 'For your sake,' for that was not what Umar wished him to say, and it was not really true. He said, 'I thought I told you. I agreed with what you were trying to do.'

Umar sat also, but not close. He said, 'You saw what I wished for the city.'

'And what you wanted for me,' Nicholas said. 'You have large ambitions, Umar. You wished to save the magician, as well. A shrine of learning, a repository of wisdom, safe from the corruption of Europe. You have brought me here to be shriven. I am willing to think you have succeeded.'

'No!' said Umar, and rose. A child cried out somewhere, and he moderated his voice. He had begun to pace back and forth. He said, 'I have begun to see that I was wrong. Tonight, I knew it. Timbuktu is no more a haven to you than Trebizond, or Urbino, or the studios of the Florentines would be. Timbuktu is threatened like others with dangers, and yet is as a child among others, a child which will be none the better, Nicholas, if its guardian is wise, and sensitive to the awfulness of his burden.'

He turned, and a tear had melted the cream on one cheek and ran white down to his mouth. He said, 'Timbuktu requires a guardian of its own kind, who is strong, and lives for the day, and does not torture himself over the choice between a book and a woman. I was wrong,' Umar repeated. 'You should not be here. You should go home.'

'Because of one fire?' Nicholas said. 'Because of Akil? Because of the Songhai? I, who have dealt, for God's sake, with Marietta of Patras?'

'Stop,' said Umar.

Nicholas stopped. He said, at length, 'You would send me back? You think it would be better than this?'

'I have changed my mind,' Umar said.

'Then,' said Nicholas, 'would you come with me? With Zuhra, the children?'

'This is my home,' Umar said.

Nicholas got up. 'Then to hell with you, Umar,' he said. 'You tell me to my face how you tricked me, used me, manipulated my life the way you believed it should go. You didn't discuss it with me because – what was the phrase – I wasn't yet a grown man. You are not discussing it now. I hear an announcement, that's all. *I have made a mistake. I am sorry. Goodbye.*'

'No,' said Umar. The track of the single tear showed, but no others.

'Yes!' said Nicholas. 'And I, too, see no need to discuss it.' He walked to the door, and thrust it ajar. 'You chose to bring me,' he said. 'Now I choose to stay. Go to your own room and sleep. I want some rest without you.'

He expected Umar to argue. Instead, the other man hesitated, and then bowed his head and walked out. Even in misery he looked magnificent.

Nicholas sat. After a while, he found he had covered his face.

The next day, at the Timbuktu-Koy's palace, Nicholas expounded his plans for the rebuilding of the burned quarter of the city, and for an elaborate project, to be completed before the first rains, to bring water under pressure to those parts most at risk from future fires. He had some books, with diagrams in them, and had made more drawings himself. At the back of his mind were a number of talks he had had over the years with the best engineer he ever knew, John le Grant. He had, on occasion, wished John were with him, and then immediately cancelled the wish.

The Qadi, the Katib Musa, the judges lacked John's skill, but were familiar with ancient sciences, and could bring their intelligence to bear on a problem. The discussion lasted some time, until the Koy grew restless and closed the session. There was to be a public execution of the men who had started the fire. Akil, defiant and sallow, had nevertheless agreed. The Koy was eager to attend it. You could see Akil noting the eagerness.

Umar had attended the meeting and, as he left, fell into step beside Nicholas. They had not spoken that day. Umar said, 'You had no sleep.'

He had had no sleep, and no energy left to confront Umar. Nicholas said, 'It seemed best to force an agreement while the fire was in everyone's minds.'

'Yes,' Umar said. 'They forget easily. Your scheme.'

'Yes?' Nicholas said.

Umar said, 'It is complicated. It is more complicated than the wheels which run the fountains.'

'But I shall be here to operate it,' Nicholas said.

'And after you?' Umar said.

'I shall teach. I shall leave notes. Once,' Nicholas said, 'you were happy to leave it so. Why despair now?' They had arrived at his house. He waited. 'Umar? Do you want to come in?'

He tried, exasperated, to put a real invitation into his voice. But to his relief, Umar shook his head and walked on.

The following night, Nicholas was roused from his sleep gently by anxious, frightened servants. The commander Akil ag Malwal had entered the gates with his troops, and now stood at the door. It was a matter of taxes.

It was a matter, very obviously, of Tuareg reasoning. In the absence of Akil, Nicholas had ingratiated himself with the Timbuktu-Koy. He had strengthened the bodyguard. He had set forth plans for fortifications and safety, as if such a fire could ever happen again. Meanwhile, the commander Akil himself had experienced a sharp drop in income. Being currently at a disadvantage with the Koy, he proposed to extort what he could from the Christian.

Diplomacy was not Akil's way. Entering, he came to the point. Men had remarked that the city's guest, the Flemish trader, had paid some minor tax on that part of the gold and ship's goods he had by him, but yet had engaged in no subsequent trading. Did he intend to continue bringing his ship's merchandise to Timbuktu? Did he intend to take part in the Sahara trade? Or did he intend to remain as a perpetual resident of the city to which he had come, therefore, under false pretences?

Nicholas had asked the commander to sit and take sherbet, and had seated himself, wrapped in a loose mantle. He had deliberately left his head bare, which was an insult. He resented being awakened.

Nicholas said, 'I am utterly at fault. I confess the Timbuktu-Koy has failed to renew the permission his father extended during his life and I, humble as I am, have not ventured to ask it. I now see, from what you say, that it would be refused. I am not trading. I desire only the privilege of living in your great city and perhaps serving it. At my own expense. At my own expense, I must insist to you.'

'The Timbuktu-Koy is not his father,' Akil said. 'He takes advice from his men of religion. They may suggest that it is evil to harbour a non-believer. That such a man may be here to subvert both Timbuktu and the Faith.'

Nicholas poured, with grace, from the ewer. He said, 'Did I harm you last night? Have I ever harmed the city with any action of mine?'

Akil sipped. He said, 'It is my conviction, of course, that you have not. But you have gold. You are richer than most of those who rightly live in the city. One could say that you are holding your hand; that soon you will use your gold as the other white traders do, to corrupt and delude. I feel the Timbuktu-Koy does not fully understand this.'

'And it is your duty to explain it to him,' Nicholas said. 'Unless
I set your mind at rest? What would set your mind at rest?'

'I do not wish,' Akil said, 'to constrain you to leave, although I
would say, in the privacy of this room, that it would be wiser for
you to do so, and best for the city. Indeed, if you were to leave,
there would be no difficulty. Failing that, I should like some
earnest of your resolve not to interfere.'

'Would the Timbuktu-Koy feel so strongly?' Nicholas said.

'I do not know. No doubt, in due course, you will ask him,' Akil
said. 'In the meantime, I have asked my men to enter your
storeroom and remove half of all the gold and the goods that they
find there. If the Timbuktu-Koy finds me over-zealous, he will no
doubt tell me. It will be between him and me.'

'It seems to me,' Nicholas said, 'that this is entirely between you
and me, my lord Akil. Suppose I say that I have no objection to
your taking this tax, and that I shall not complain to the
Timbuktu-Koy?'

'I should commend your wisdom,' said Akil. He said it after a
moment.

'Although,' said Nicholas, 'I am unclear on one point. If I
decide to leave, will it be returned to me?'

The black moustache moved in a smile. 'Your soul has lived
before, in the person of a sage. The tax pertains to all the days you
have spent here, and cannot be rescinded. But if you leave, you
may take with you freely all the goods and gold you have left.'

'You are generous,' Nicholas said.

His first trouble, next day, was soothing the passions of the men
who called on him, indignant, enraged by the news of the theft.
His second trouble was Umar, who did not come. In the evening,
when Nicholas knew the children would be asleep, he called on
him. Zuhra met him on the threshold; seventeen, lovely, her
breasts swollen with milk. She said, 'We have heard.' Her eyes were
anxious.

'I know,' Nicholas said. 'I blame Umar, of course. I am fiercely
critical of you, and am ashamed of Muhammed, and renounce
Umar Niccolò as my name-child. Zuhra, I am here to put it all
right. There is nothing to fear.'

She dropped her eyes and leading him in, drew her veil down and
over her shoulders for the first time he remembered in her own house.
When she had left them alone, he spoke to Umar. 'You expected it.'

'I didn't provoke it,' Umar said.

'No. But you knew I could become the catalyst in the war
between these two men. The excuse for division.'

'They would find another,' Umar said.

'But in the meantime, as you did not tell me, loss and indignity, at the very least, might lie ahead of me. You thought, if you told me, I would think it just another deceit.'

'I am sorry,' Umar said. 'I shall make good your losses.'

'There is no need,' Nicholas said. 'I am not staying. They have frightened me away.'

Umar's hands tightened. He did not answer.

'No, you don't believe that.' Nicholas said. 'I could take one side or the other, and perhaps make it successful. But it is the balance of power, isn't it, that has brought peace to the city, and my presence which is going to disrupt it? And anything I can do will fall apart after my death, because you are right: you cannot perpetuate a civilisation ahead of its time unless those around are civilised also. I have decided to go.'

'And do what?' Umar said. His hands remained doubled.

'Zuhra veiled herself just now,' Nicholas said. 'Perhaps I envy you. Perhaps that is the lesson I learned here, not what the doctors were teaching me.'

'It was not — it was not my purpose,' Umar said. His face, puzzled, had lost some of its strain.

'No, you had another purpose,' Nicholas said. 'I am aware of that, too. But you are happy? Not just from duty?'

'Not just from duty. Here, it is not difficult to be happy in marriage. Zuhra is young. There are no great requirements laid on her. We cannot disappoint each other.'

'A warning,' said Nicholas.

'I should not presume,' Umar said. 'You mean to leave? When will you leave? It is March. The May *azalai* is largest and safest, and should protect you from the ill-will of — anyone.'

'You think I should go through the Sahara?' Nicholas said. He smiled, and Umar smiled a little in return.

'Yes. it is never safe; but for one man, it is better than the long trip to the Gambia and then, perhaps, the wait of six months for a ship. A caravan leaves, and in two or three months, you would be in Barbary; in Bruges or Venice before the end of the year. We shall ask ibn Said. His brother might come to Taghaza to meet us.'

'Taghaza? Us?' Nicholas said.

'The city of salt. The desert post where the salt you see comes from. Of course, I shall go with you,' said Umar. 'To Taghaza, but not beyond. It is my terminus, Nicholas, but not yours.'

Chapter 36

IN JANUARY OF THE same year, 1467, the Albanian patriot Skanderbeg died, and much of his army and many of those attached to him were dispersed. In May, the personable manager of the most aristocratic bank in Venice returned from a profitable evening at some ship-owner's supper to find his private parlour pre-empted by a squat, balding man he had not seen for over five years.

He had been warned as he entered the house. '*What?*' had said Julius. '*Who?*'

'Tobias Beventini of Grado,' said Margot, in the forbearing way that most annoyed him. 'Niccolò's physician. He's finished his work in Albania. He heard he was wanted to testify. He thought Niccolò would be here.'

'Tobie!' said Julius. He dropped off his cloak, which had gold-work all down the edges. 'I haven't seen Tobie since we came home from Trebizond. Girls. Piss, drink and girls, Tobie used to be interested in. I thought he'd given up Niccolò.'

'Hasn't everyone?' Margot said. They rubbed along well enough, he and Margot, but at times, he wished Gregorio had come and collected her.

'He'll come home,' Julius said. He didn't entirely believe it. Despite all the curious dispatches from Bruges, he sometimes found it hard to imagine how the former Claes was surviving in Guinea. At other times, he was inclined to the view that, surrounded by nubile natives and heat, no healthy young man of that history would ever want to see Europe again.

Meanwhile his gold had arrived, and Julius was dispensing it. Rather successfully, too, if somewhat hampered by strictures from Bruges. Julius had run the Banco di Niccolò in Venice for almost three years: longer than Gregorio had. Now that they were all rich, he didn't need Gregorio to keep writing from Bruges. He had the instructions Niccolò had written down, and was obeying them. It did no harm to add a little style to the Bank and its manager. It gave the Serenissima confidence.

The impact on Tobias Beventini, physician, was different. 'Holy Mary Mother of God!' he exclaimed when Julius walked in 'Grass time has come, and the silly sheep with it. I thought I'd come to a whorehouse, till Margot corrected me. So have you spent all the money?'

Julius had never allowed himself to be greatly ruffled by Tobie. He said, 'The money you made for us with Skanderbeg? Yes. I bought a button with it. Where's Astorre?'

'Coming later. Margot says Nicholas has solved the world bullion problem single-handed, but is probably dead.'

'She keeps saying that,' Julius said. 'She knows perfectly well we've had word of him.'

'But not from him. And Father Godscalc is crippled?' When Tobie felt indignant, the bald part of his cranium turned pink. Now he had reached thirty-seven, the halo of fine, colourless hair had receded and there were purses under his round, pale blue eyes. His face, with its rosebud mouth and small nose, was otherwise sensationally smooth.

'He's all right,' Julius said. 'Living with Gregorio and the others in Spangnaerts Street. Wouldn't give a Jacques de Lalaing much of a run in the lists, but he can do all a chaplain usually does. The Pope has praised him and fixed him up with a benefice.'

'I thought the Pope was a Venetian?' Tobie said. He scratched under his cuirass, which was dented. The matted wool he wore underneath smelled strongly of ointment and horse. 'And Nicholas was financed by Portugal?'

'Not now,' Julius said. 'He bought the caravel from the Portuguese, and he's paid all that was due them. By the time he comes back, no one will know as much about the African trade as Nicholas will. And he'll have Loppe there, his very own agent. You know the blacks think Loppe is a lawyer? I don't know why I spent all those years in Bologna. I've wasted my chances.'

'From the sound of it,' the doctor said, 'you need all the lawyers you can get. A shipload of gold disappears and you can't even trace the ship's master? The ownership of the *Ribérac* herself is still in dispute three years after Jordan stole her? The claim against — what's her name? — the *Fortado* is still unsettled and the Genoese and the Vatachino are getting away with murder, because no one can find Michael Crackbene?

'By God,' said Tobias Beventini, getting angrier. 'I don't know what golden cloud you think you're sitting on, but I tell you, it wouldn't have stopped me hunting down all those bastards and making them pay for it all. Godscalc broken. Nicholas stuck somewhere sick on this river. What has it done to that stupid girl? And what about Diniz? Has old man Jordan got him again?'

Margot had come in while they were speaking. Julius gave her a cool look, which she returned with a half-lifted eyebrow. He would have preferred to tell Tobie all that news himself. In time. And not all at once. And not from Gregorio's point of view.

Margot sat down beside Tobie. She said, 'You'd quite like Gelis van Borselen. They all had a bad time, but she's well enough. Lucia de St Pol took her with her to Scotland, and I suspect she'll end up at Court like her sister.'

'Why Scotland?' said Tobie. His nose twitched. Julius remembered how his nose twitched.

'Not for any of the reasons you're thinking of,' Margot said. 'The van Borselens are related by marriage to the monarchs of Scotland. Gelis didn't have any money. And David de Salmeton was taking a very great interest in her.'

'What?' said Tobie. He sat up, and a belch of horse emerged from three different gaps in his cuirass.

'Really, Tobie,' said Margot. 'You must go off and get yourself clean. I know all about David de Salmeton, and I've seen what Martin his partner can do. I gather Gelis knows even more. The interest wasn't reciprocated.'

'De Salmeton goes to *Scotland*?' Julius said. He hadn't heard that item of gossip. Because, obviously, Gregorio hadn't told him. Gregorio had been to Venice once, briefly, and had divided his time between the business and Margot, which suited Julius. He had left Margot because he was coming back.

Margot said, 'He's not in Scotland at the moment, with Tommaso Portinari throwing his weight about in Bruges.' She turned to Tobie. 'Remember Tommaso?' Julius wondered if she had a soft spot for Tobie.

Tobie's short pink mouth widened, as if he had a soft spot for Margot. 'Finger-rings. I always said he would kill to get control of the Bruges Medici. How's he enjoying it?'

Margot laughed. She was a handsome woman, if over-opinionated. 'Remember Controller Bladelin's palace in the Naaldcn Straate? Tommaso's bought it. For the Medici. For visiting officials. For himself to entertain in. He's one of the Duke's counsellors now, did you know that? And a diplomat. He's one of the envoys arranging the English marriage for the Duke's heir. If it happens, there'll be enough velvet on order to keep the Medici in profit for years. And the rest of Bruges. Diniz is ecstatic at the mere thought of it.'

'You mean Gregorio,' Tobie said. 'But tell me first. What happened to Diniz?'

Margot laughed again. She said, 'How do you remember him? A frightened boy, swept from Cyprus by the hated Jordan? You will be surprised. He works for the Charetty company.'

'The . . .?' said Tobie. He stopped.

'As their deputy manager. In Spangnaerts Street, but with special reference to the dyeshop. Why are you laughing?'

'At Nicholas,' Tobie said. 'Nicholas the glorious, the devious bastard. Oh, where in God's name is he? It's a feast, it's meat and drink, it's the greatest game in the world, but it isn't the same without Nicholas.'

The message came two days later, on a Barbary ship. Nothing for the Banco di Niccolò was ever delayed in Venice now. Handed ashore, it was taken by runner direct to the Bank, where Julius seized it. He flung open the doors to the chamber (the painted, the tapestried, the elegant chamber) where Tobie was talking to Margot.

Julius said, 'He's coming. Nicholas. He's crossing the Sahara next month. He should be on the coast by September at the latest. We have to send the *Ciaretti* to Oran.'

He couldn't see himself, his face flushed, his eyes shining, but he saw the reflection of it, had he known, in Tobie's face, and in that of Margot. Margot cried out, and ran forward. Somehow, he found himself hugging her. She kissed him, and they both turned to Tobie. Tobie, his face scarlet, said, 'I want to be kissed,' and she hugged him as well. She was crying.

Tobie said, 'Let me see it. Not you, woman, men first; you get the wine and the cups. Let me see. What does he say?'

'It isn't from him,' Julius said. 'Or at least, it isn't his writing. There. Just the instruction, the bastard, as if it will be easy. September. She'll have to sail in July. Where *is* the *Ciaretti*?'

'It doesn't matter,' Margot said, jug in hand. 'My heavens, you've got enough ships. The *Adorno*, the *Niccolò* – you can get one of them ready.'

'And I shall sail with her,' said Julius. He emptied his cup, tossed and caught it.

'No, you won't,' Margot said. 'You'll be in Scotland with Bonkle by then, and Gregorio will be here. And over my dead body is Gregorio going to Barbary. No, my sweet men. This ship may have to wait in Oran a long time, and if she has to stay all autumn and winter, then she'll do so. The ship herself will be his welcome. The rest can wait.'

'Maybe,' said Tobie.

*

The May *azalai* did not come. The sun burned; the temperature began to rise daily. After waiting all month, Nicholas began to assemble a caravan of his own.

It wasn't easy. Now the worst of the summer heat was upon them, and no camel-trains would arrive until autumn. He spent some time talking to agents; persuading those with heavy stocks or a willingness to run into debt to add their camels and drovers to his. It need not be too expensive, he explained. There were always caravans going north from Arawan, and he would join his force to theirs, and share costs. He only realised afterwards that when they agreed, it was because Umar also had spoken to them.

All the same, he had to use most of his reserves to hire his own camels and six men to drive and defend them: eight hundred ducats to take himself and his provisions and the few objects he had selected on the long journey north. It was two thousand miles to Oran. It was five hundred miles to the salt mines at Taghaza, where Umar would leave him.

The eventual caravan, it began to appear, would amount to some two hundred and fifty loaded camels, of which six would be his. There would be rather more than that number of people.

So small a company demanded experienced men. The dealers, drovers and guard who made up its larger part were mostly veterans of the double trans-Saharan journey. There were not many of them. No one tried the two-way crossing more than once in twelve months, or, indeed, more than five times in a lifetime. But Umar was only going to Taghaza and back, and Nicholas was crossing once only. The camel-station at Arawan was four days away, and a guide had been selected to take them there.

Nicholas had, in the end, only formal farewells to make, since it had long been known he was leaving. He was given a feast in the Ma' Dughu, which the commander Akil also attended. The Koy made his gratitude known, but also made it known, behind his hand, that Europeans belonged on the coast, and it was time that this man returned there. The sultan Akil was amiability itself, in his regard for what the lord Niccolò had done, for the benefits he had initiated, for the wisdom of his decision to leave. The evening was long, and exhausting.

The farewells of the scholars had been different. He possessed already a cargo of books; it was his main burden. Every teacher had a parcel for him: of some exquisite original, or of a manuscript carefully copied. The imams, the judges, the Qadi reminded him in grave, exquisite Arabic, of his mistakes and of his achievements in that order, and of all they had spoken of doing together. The talk developed, as of habit; each visit extended far beyond the time he had planned. He conversed unsleeping with his friends in all those last days, as a man facing the desert drinks water. But it was not water he drank.

He took his leave of his servants, and of those many men and women of every kind who had become friends, and he distributed gifts to the utmost of his means, and received them in turn. One of the many graces of this strange society was its attention to gifts; his own had been made for the most part by his own hands, and were mainly for children. For the scholars he had prepared works of another kind. Last of all, he went to make his peace with Zuhra.

She stopped his speech with her hand. 'I know. I, too, would have him refrain from this journey. But how would he think of himself, did he stay? How would we live, Umar and I, if between us lay this thing that I had stopped him doing? It is only to Taghaza. It is nothing.'

'It is not nothing,' Nicholas said. 'Zuhra, I am a child of Umar's strength as much as your children are. I would not exist but for him. And you are for him what he has been to me. I know he feels he must come, and I cannot stop him. But his force comes only from you, and he will return to renew it. He will return.'

He was not sure. He had to seem sure.

He spent the last night alone, walking the lanes of the city, and finding one lamp lit, in the gateway of the imam, the Katib Musa. As he hesitated, the porter's voice spoke. 'Lord. The Katib is asleep. He asked, if you passed, that you would enter, and sit in his library.'

He sat until dawn, with the books under his hands, and his cheek on them. Then he rose, silent and stiff, and went for the last time to his house.

There are few wells in the Sahara, and the journey between them depends on navigation as exact and as strict as that employed by a captain at sea, venturing out of sight of his port, and into waters unknown. In time of clear skies, the Sahara caravan makes its way as the birds do, and the captains: by the sun and the stars, and by whatever landmarks the sand may have left. But the winds blow, and dunes shift, and the marks left by one caravan are obliterated before the next comes. And so men will wander, and perish.

The guide Umar had chosen for Nicholas was a Mesufa Tuareg, and blind. For two days, walking or riding, he turned the white jelly of his sightless eyes to the light and the wind, and opened his palpitating black nostrils to the report of the dead, scentless sand which was neither scentless nor dead, but by some finesse of aroma proclaimed its composition and place. At each mile's end, he filled his hands with the stuff and, rubbing, passed it through his brown fingers. Then he smiled, and said, 'Arawan.'

'Umar,' Nicholas said. 'I hope you know what you're doing.'

To begin with, they spoke very little. With the rest, they walked through the first night and part of the day, halting rarely. Sleep was brief, and taken by day. During the worst of the heat, they lay with the camels under the white, shimmering sky, and ate, and rested.

Their drovers made tents of their mantles, but Umar's hands erected the light, makeshift awning that sheltered Nicholas and himself, and arranged the cloths, coated by Zuhra with mercuric paste, which they wore against the sting and bite of the pests of the desert. Then, mounting while the sun still glared upon them, they rode until dark, each man his own tent, alone under his own cone of shelter. The chanting, the chatter stopped then, and even the goats became silent.

The nights were marginally cooler. Then the riders revived, and dismounted, and unlashed the bullock-skins of warm water, and drank, and filled the leather bags at their sides. And the camels had their one meal of the day, from the fodder they carried themselves.

The company was congenial enough, and consisted of men and women and children, for there were families going to Arawan. As the heat became less, they grew lively. Every hour, the ropes on the loads needed adjusting: a camel would kick and bite and, roaring, disrupt the procession; the goats would stray; a dispute would break out over some trifle. At such times, the caravan carried its own clamour with it, like a long, narrow household perpetually singing, arguing, quarrelling, cackling. They hardly stopped for food, except during the enforced sleep through the heat, but passed between them gourds of maize and sour milk or rough bread. The fresh food had spoiled by the second day.

On the second day, the blind man came to them both and said, 'Lord? You have been generous.' He spoke to Nicholas, but his eyes were on Umar, the katib, the man of learning.

Nicholas said, 'You have need of something?' He kept his voice low, like the other's.

The man said, 'It might please my lord to know that many horsemen have passed this way to Arawan recently. Not today. Perhaps three days ago.'

Nicholas said, 'Someone told you?' The pale, shining sands were everywhere pristine.

'My nose,' said the man. 'The manure has been covered while fresh. It is unusual.'

'It's Akil,' said Umar, when they were alone. 'Not the commander himself, he was at the banquet. He must have sent his troops on. Arawan is a Maghsharen settlement.' They sat within their makeshift tent, their clothes soaking. A camel groaned and someone, irritated by their voices, coughed and spat. It was time for sleeping.

Nicholas said, 'Would Akil's men dare to attack us?'

Umar was repairing the thong of a slipper. The needle slipped in and out, as it had done when, manager of a large household, he still contrived to keep his master's garments in order. In Cyprus, in Trebizond.

He said, without looking up, 'He would perhaps tell them to hold our six camels. Let the others go on, and then send us off alone on some pretext. We should be reported murdered by wandering bandits.'

'You think he wants that?' Nicholas said.

'I think he knows the Koy wouldn't mind. Akil has shared the power with the Koy for thirty years. I think he doesn't want competition from Europeans and Christians traversing the Sahara. He wants to trade with them at the coast, on his terms. Now,' Umar said, 'you are going to ask me why I didn't think of that, before I brought you to Guinea.'

'You didn't know. I'm going to ask you something else. Must we stop at Arawan?'

Umar put down his needle. His thread had broken. 'I'm sorry,' he said.

'I'm not. Answer the question,' said Nicholas.

'We could avoid Arawan,' Umar said. 'But the rest of this caravan won't. Some are staying there. The others only came this way to pick up protection. It's late in the season. Two or three hundred camels are rather few against troops of armed Berbers.'

'Six would move quickly,' said Nicholas.

'Until the nomads observe them,' said Umar. 'And it means only six camels to carry food, fodder and water, our belongings and us, if we tire. It leaves no margin for sandstorms or straying or accidents. And lastly, if we don't get to the water at Arawan, there are exactly two hundred miles between the first well after that and the next one.' He had rethreaded his needle. He said, 'I think we should avoid Arawan.'

A large smile overcame Nicholas: he felt his beard creaking inside his dimples. He said, 'You're just trying to get us both killed. Let's go and talk to the rest. Perhaps there are a few others who don't fancy Akil.'

In the end, fifty camels separated from the rest and chose to carry on to the north without calling at the Arawan post of the

Maghsharen Tuareg. They left within half a day of its gates, carrying with them (for a price) all the surplus water the remaining travellers could spare and also the guide, who received, and counted, a hundred gold mithqals for his services. Then they set off, rather fast, for the nearest oasis.

Later, Nicholas realised that Umar had been afraid that Akil would damage the springs. In fact, the Maghsharen had not been so prescient. It was the winds of the previous week that had silted them up, so that when their camels raced towards the green of the palms, there was no broad sheet of water to see; only stretches of mud, with pools of sluggish water lying between them. There was enough, perhaps, for the camels. There was not enough for fifty camels and forty men with a waterless journey before them.

The chief merchant turned to Umar. 'Katib. We must take what there is, and turn back to Arawan.'

'You must turn back,' Umar said. 'We shall go on. But, from your kindness, allow our beasts to water first, and let us share out what drinking water there is. Your journey will be shorter than ours. Also, there is the guide.'

'Take him. We know the way back,' said the merchant. He looked relieved. He had agreed to come in the first place, Nicholas thought, only to show respect for the katib. The merchant said, 'Will all your men wish to continue?'

Two of them didn't. It left four, and himself and Umar to deal with six camels. He paid for some goats, and took what food could be spared. It was mostly millet, and kola nuts. He didn't comment on that. He said. 'Do we need all these camels?'

'Yes,' said Umar. They set off that night.

Now there was silence, for worried men did not talk for too long, especially as the night deepened and walking became automatic; the feet of men and camels travelling up and down the long, curving dunes, leaving them ploughed but unplanted behind them.

Above, the stars hung, enormous and glittering. Nicholas knew their names now: the names he'd learned on his first, ecstatic voyage; the names Diogo Gomes had used; the names in the books he had left behind, in the city where he had just spent part of a lifetime. The drovers had other names for them as well. Some were cheerfully obscene. Some were beautiful.

Beauty was what surrounded them now. It had been there from the beginning, but made indistinct by the host of people about them. Now they were but seven pepper-seeds upon an ocean which stretched, white as curds, to the rim of the universe; specks as remote as those he had watched from a sea-spattered cliff-top in Europe. And as the sun rose, disclosing the scalloped forms of the dunes, and sank, a vast glory at night, Nicholas experienced the liberation he had not so far been vouchsafed in his life: an emotion of awe and of thankfulness that he had felt nowhere else.

He said little that day or the next, but walked, and sat alone swaying for hour after hour on his beast, the two sticks of his tent in his fists, his shadowed eyes blind, while his mind began to make sense of many things. Whatever it was he had found, it was not the Sea of Obscurity. It was light, and self-knowledge, and peace.

On the third day, Umar roused him. 'I have taken a decision.'

The world returned. Nicholas said, 'Never mind your decision. What is this place, your desert?'

Umar smiled, 'A place to go, when one has feasted with wise men, as you have. Do you want to hear of the problems of the flesh, instead of the soul? We cannot reach the wells by Taodeni as we wanted. Our water is low, and the guide, the *takshif*, says he smells a storm coming. Therefore we are travelling towards the wells of Bir al Ksaib instead.'

'We'll reach water much quicker that way?' Nicholas said. For two days, he hadn't felt hungry. Now he did.

'Three days sooner. Perhaps two and a half. It may make all the difference.'

'But it's out of our way. So it will take longer to reach Taghaza afterwards?'

'It will add two days to the overall journey,' Umar said. 'But the storm may add many more. We shall need to be prepared, that is all, and in good heart. We are eating. Come and talk to the men.'

The sandstorm, when it came, was the first, but not the worst. During it, nothing could be done but sit cocooned in its path while it belaboured the back and tore and whipped and stung its way through to the flesh, so that every man's body was heavy with sand, and the eyes, the mouth, the ears became choked with it. The camels stamped: ropes broke and burdens went swinging; the objects of most vital necessity – their water-skins, the carcasses of the goats they had had to kill – required constant and desperate protection.

When it was over they were exhausted, and had lost two days' travel. And all about them, the slopes, the valleys, the outcrops of fine sculptured sand had radically altered. They were where they had been, but the desert had reformed about them. Then the *takshif*, silent throughout, stirred and rose to his feet. 'Katib?'

'Yes?' said Umar.

'I will guide you by the shift of the sun, and the wind. In a little, the sand will speak louder. But it is speaking already. Tell your men not to fear, and be strong.'

The men were strong, and also experienced. Nicholas thought that, given the choice, they preferred the natural perils of the desert to the black camps, the sudden attacks of the winter. Now, they were unlikely to be troubled by brigands, and were beyond Akil's power.

Success depended on how long it would take to reach Bir al Ksaib, and on their strength, and that of the camels. All the desert was strewn with the bones of long-dead camels, and often those of the men who accompanied them. The sands round Timbuktu were threaded with ivory rib-cages, and it had been the same at the oasis and Arawan. Their owners had died within sight of water, as if joy itself had stopped their tired hearts.

They walked and rode for three days before the next storm, and after that, walked more than they rode, to save the camels, for whom there was little food left. They killed a camel the day after the storm, and cut up and dried its flesh in the sun, seething some of it in the liquid wrung from its own stomach and bladder. The rest they poured into their empty water-skins. One of the drovers fell sick and had to be carried. The desert contained, in tidy piles, the discarded loads from both camels.

Umar had counted the days, as well as Nicholas. The second night after the storm, Umar said, 'If we had gone to Taodeni instead, we should be there.'

It was not really the case. The sandstorms would have held them up just the same. But it was true that their food was nearly finished and their water so reduced that they were perpetually parched. Umar said, 'Do you wish me to bring out the *goro?*'

He was speaking of kola nuts. Nicholas had seen them. The size of a chestnut and expensive, the most efficacious were white. Chewed, they dispelled in time all sense of hunger and weariness. They were the means Nicholas had used to bring Godscalc back from Ethiopia. They took their own toll. Nicholas said, 'Soon, perhaps. But not yet.'

Soon, Nicholas began to dream of the pools in the Ma' Dughu, and of the river that ran past his gardens in Kouklia. When Umar shook him awake, he laughed creakily, and told him that he was thinking of the water-wheel at Bruges, and what he had done to it.

That was the day the sick man went crazy, and Nicholas thought perhaps he himself was affected as well, because there on the dancing, quivering sand was a lake, with palm trees about it, and animals drinking.

'They tell you it is the sport of demons,' Umar said. 'But it is a trick of the light. There is such a place. But it is not there, on the sand.' Umar had become thin and sunken of eye, as they all were, but he had shown no emotion except when the thread broke. At home, Nicholas knew, Zuhra was already carrying their third child. It would be born before Umar returned. Nicholas didn't need to be told what Umar was doing for him.

Then the blind man came again, as they rested at noon, and said, 'Katib, I smell a storm. There is one camel I see you have favoured. Give it to me, and I will take it to Bir al Ksaib and bring you back water. I can outrun the wind.'

'Tell it to everyone,' Umar said. 'We shall all decide.'

They let him go, for the trust they felt in him. Under clear skies, he explained, the strongest might just reach the well in two days. Travelling hampered by storms, none could do it. By waiting for him, man and beast would harbour their powers. They would have four camels left, for six people. When he came back, there would be five between seven. And if there were others for hiring, he would bring them. But the Bir al Ksaib was just a pool.

They watched him out of sight, and then prepared as well as they could for the day, and the night, and the storm. But first, the sick man died, and they gave him a mantle of sand.

The storm came, and they lived through it for two lightless days, and into the dawn of a third. Their food and drink, which was almost nothing, had been apportioned to last precisely four days.

They had the camels, slumped bickering and groaning beside them. These had little urine to yield, and could give no more blood and still walk. If the *takshif* didn't come back, it would be necessary to ride them, or to kill and eat them and walk. It would be necessary, but not likely to be very successful.

Nicholas had stopped being hungry, and thought he would vomit if he had to eat camel again. Umar said Nicholas would be surprised what he could do, given a little discomfort.

They joked when they could. They sat together, five men, and talked sometimes, but talking was painful. Nicholas dreamed a great deal. In some of his dreams, he was with Godscalc, bleeding, retching, striving to climb down some impossible gully. In some he was in Famagusta, where others were starving and he was in a kind of pain that was worse. He was always in pain, waking or dreaming. They all were.

'Well?' Nicholas said on the fourth morning. 'I wager you a piece of camel against a big layer-pasty that he's missed the way and gone on to Marrakesh. A really big layer-pasty, the kind with duck and pigeon and goose and whole eggs in it. And a girl, all covered with sugar.'

'That's disgusting,' said Umar. 'You're thinking of your stomach again. If you must think of something tasty, why not mutton? Or remember the Koy's last feast, when he tried to serve lion?'

'Lion suet,' Nicholas said. 'Lion suet is good for the ears. Bel was always trying to melt it. Do you hear anything?'

Sometimes, they forgot to listen. Sometimes, their eyes burning and swollen, they couldn't see. One of the men said, '*My lord!*' He lurched to his feet.

Nicholas sat with his back to the sun, and didn't turn. He sat opposite Umar, and let Umar's face tell him what was happening behind him.

Umar said, 'Which camel are you going to eat? You're not damned well going to cheat and eat the fresh ones. I want to see you eat something that stinks as much as you do.'

His face quivered, then steadied. Nicholas took both his hands and held them tightly. Then he got up, for the three others were standing embracing each other and calling, and when he went forward, they put their arms round his shoulders too, and then Umar's.

'Allah!' said Nicholas crossly. 'But you are a hard race to kill, you great bullocks from Guinea. What is a poor trader to do, who led you out here to die so that he could eat all the camels?'

They laughed as if they were drunk. They laughed, and croaked, and kissed one another and him, for the *takshif* was riding towards them, with three mounted men and five camels.

Chapter 37

THE WATER OF Bir al Ksaib was brackish and warm, and better than wine. There was food there. They rested for three days, and took fresh camels, and completed their journey to Taghaza.

It was not easy. It was further than the way they had come, and the winds were still blowing. But they had strong mounts, and willing men to go with them, and a new guide. The blind *takshif* would have come, and their drovers, but Nicholas gave them great presents and turned them back. He tried to turn back Umar too, but failed. 'You didn't keep your wager,' Umar said. 'If you won't eat the camel, then you have to supply me with the pie.'

There wasn't much likelihood of finding a layer-pasty in Taghaza, but Nicholas was willing to try. Umar, with his bright intelligence and generous nature, was the golden thread which permeated the whole Olympian experience; Umar as a whole man of his own race at last, and able at last to make affirmation of what he felt and believed.

They had always communicated, Umar and he, in a practical sense. The planning of the future of Timbuktu was only an extension, in a way, of the planning of the plantations at Kouklia. But Umar was also a man widely read and well taught, who had used the years of isolation and exile to ponder in silence. In the schools of Timbuktu, he and Umar had both spoken, and been heard, and continued in private the entrancing deliberations in which they had taken part. Their relationship changed, but their discussions, except for once, had remained general.

On the long transit to Taghaza, walking under the Andalusian vaults of the stars, there was time to talk again now and then – and a need. The clarity of the desert demanded something as rare; demanded truth, vision, honesty of those who walked in it. But it was less possible, now, to divorce their thinking from what they now knew of each other. And when Umar, with hesitation, began one day to speak of his forebears and family, and then, slowly, of his capture and the years that came after, Nicholas was aware that he had finally been given the gift that the other had always withheld.

'Should I regret it?' Umar said. 'It humbled me. I had thought myself learned, of illustrious race, one of the chosen. Had I not been captured, I might have travelled as far, but in Muslim countries, and treated always with respect. As it was, I was made to learn many things, and came to understand more than one religion. We have talked of all this. You challenged Father Godscalc to defend his beliefs, and reinforce yours, but I should guess that you were careful not to disturb him. He needs what he has.'

'You had no crutch,' Nicholas said.

'Yes, I had,' Umar said. 'The one I have tried to give you. Understanding, and vision, and peace with oneself. You have to win that war, Nicholas, before you can win any other.'

'But you would not let me stay,' Nicholas said.

'I should not be so bad a friend,' Umar answered. 'It is enough to have had what we had. Your departure is the last proof of its worth.'

In return, Nicholas had opened some of his heart. Not more: he could never do that. Never, in any talk that they had, did he speak directly of Gelis and the hopes that he had, or the deepest and most terrible fears. As for his past, Famagusta was still too near, and too deadly. But his wife – his first marriage – that, suddenly he found he could talk of; and the careless ridiculous pleasures of boyhood in the Charetty dyeyard, with Marian de Charetty's despotic benevolence making everything secure.

'And then you grew, and she loved you.' said Umar. After a moment, he said, 'I did not mean to hurt you. But she gave you so much: you cannot regret it. You must not blame yourself. They are very close, the love of a mistress and the love of a mother. She had both to give, and you needed both.'

It was strange to receive that absolution from Umar, and no one else. As those days drew to an end, Nicholas was conscious of a great relief, as great as the bond he felt with Umar, and a thankfulness as cleansing as the light and peace of the desert. He thought, whatever came, he would be prepared for it.

For the last week of the journey, when the storms seemed to have ceased, and their provisions were fair, and there was only the heat of Hell itself to contend with, the new drovers, too, expressed their relief in the form of languid horseplay and contentious gambling, and burst frequently into long, ululating song as they rode or they walked. The peace of the desert disappeared.

Nicholas said, 'Can we do as well as that?' and, heaving a load of peppery air into his lungs, launched into a ditty from Bruges blasphemous enough to earn him a thunderbolt.

Umar joined in. Umar said, 'I know one worse than that,' and produced it. They sang a third one together. At the end, Umar said, 'You did that in fifths.'

'I know. You've too big a range for me,' Nicholas said. He thought it was obvious. At the next halt, they tried a few more, and then had to stop because their voices had cracked. The next day they continued.

The day after that, walking in front of him, Umar unexpectedly drew breath and sang, alone, the beautiful 'Deprecamur te, Domine' that he had sung once before, in the icy snows of the Alps.

He was parched, but the splendour of the great voice was only dimmed. He ended, and the last note sank into the heat, and the camels plodded beside them.

Nicholas said, 'Now teach me to sing the Koran like that.'

Umar turned his head and considered him. 'It is to one God,' Umar said. 'Listen.' And he began to sing, very carefully.

Nicholas knew what he sang. Standing troubled in Trebizond, outside the church of the Chrysokephalos, he had tried not to listen to this, the great Akathistos Kontakion, intoned by many voices. He had never heard it since. After a moment, not to seem graceless, he joined his voice to his friend's.

It was plainsong, its refrains repeated over and over with the subtlest variations. He didn't notice when Umar ceased to sing, but became aware of his voice stealing in, softly, to merge into a later refrain. Nicholas stopped.

His fellow singer, slowing his pace, fell back to his side. 'I thought so,' Umar said. 'You have a gift being wasted. It goes with numeracy.'

'What does?' said Nicholas. Despite himself, he spoke with reserve.

'You heard that music only once? Let me find something you don't know.' Umar half sang the start of an introit, and when Nicholas shook his head, went on singing, beckoning him to join in. It was too high, again. Nicholas tried fifths, was dissatisfied, and began to experiment. He stopped when he found Umar, laughing, shaking him by the shoulder. 'My voice has gone, and it is time to make camp. You know that is called a descant?'

'No. Yes, I do. I don't want this,' said Nicholas.

The camels had stopped, and so had they. 'Then you need not have it,' said Umar, his eyes attentive. 'Or not in that form.

Anyway, the drovers are becoming impatient. Tomorrow, nothing but coarseness.'

After that they did sing together quite a lot, but always bawdy pieces, or love songs, or drinking songs; and as the moment's aberration receded, he and Umar settled to talking again, and the last days were long. When, standing in a peony dawn, Nicholas saw a diamond wink in the wastes far ahead, he did not break into the silence with the news that the journey was over.

'Taghaza,' said their guide, who was not blind. 'The arsehole of the world, believe me, but where would all you filthy rich people get your money from, but for places like this? Nothing to see but the salt mines, and the depot, and the places where the camel-drivers and muleteers wait about to rob honest people. If you want mules, I have a cousin who's reasonable.'

'That,' said Nicholas, 'is unexpected.'

It was the end of the peace. By the time they stopped next, Taghaza had grown to the size of a diamond brooch on the sand dunes; a handful of crystal, crushed beneath someone's heel. When, finally, they halted to share their last meal, its walls were plainly in sight, and its gates could be seen to be open. Specks emerged: specks which became a troop of armed Tuareg on camels, followed by a stream of running black figures. Nicholas rose.

'They think you have gold,' said the guide. 'Or food. Millet, they hope for. They have a few salty wells, but there is no food grown in Taghaza, and no living soul for twenty days in any direction. If no one brings them in food, then they starve.'

'They look energetic enough,' Nicholas said. The riders were almost upon them. They were screaming, and waving their swords.

'These men are mounted, lord. They can get away when they wish. They are the Mesufa Tuareg who own Taghaza. The blacks are the miners who live here. My lord should wave back in greeting.'

'This is a welcome?' Nicholas said.

The black, naked figures were still running. Passing them, the camels arrived and, skidding, were made to stand in a circle, while their riders still shouted. The leader, blue-turbaned, commanded his camel to kneel, and descended. Another did likewise: a portly middle-aged Arab, dressed in the style of the Maghreb.

Nicholas said, 'Christ! I know who he is.'

'Be quiet,' said Umar, but smiling. The fat man walked over to Umar and Nicholas, stopped, and flung out his arms.

He cried, 'Lords! May Allah be praised! You have arrived! You ask who I am? Lords, I am Jilali, humble brother of your servant Abderrahman ibn Said, here only to welcome and serve you. You will eat at my house! Good liquor, and rice and fine camel flesh! And then you shall show me what you have brought.'

'Layer-pasty,' said Umar, but in a murmur. 'Nicholas? You promised me layer-pasty?'

Then and in the day that followed, they saw all they wished of Taghaza, place of salt and gold and starvation.

The greatest buildings in it were the bullion warehouses and the caravanserai, and the patched-up walls which surrounded it for security. The other erections were low, for salt collapses under its own weight, and all the dwellings and mosques in Taghaza were formed of salt-bricks, and the flat roofs were covered with camel-skins.

So Taghaza sparkled and glittered and blazed, set upon its acres of empty white sand. And year after year, the caravans arrived and departed, bringing gold and carrying salt to the south for the Negroland people who craved it. And the other caravans came from the north, and took the gold away, and brought back silk for Timbuktu, and pestles and cooking-pots and food for the miners, and sometimes cloth for their tents.

The day they arrived, Nicholas had first set eyes on the tents, thick as cysts, clustered round the black lips of the underground salt mines. And emerging from the caverns at dusk, an ant-crawl of Negroes, each with a basket of slabs on his head. It was not gold which was found in the nests of ants as big as cats; it was salt.

'It is a sight worth seeing once,' had said the brother of ibn Said cheerfully that evening, pushing steaming bowls under their noses. Jilali was pleased: Nicholas had brought him a fine gift of civet. 'But there is no need to return: we who deal here are happy to act for you. There are troubles. You were asked for a toll on the way? The Sanhaja like to charge a ducat per camel: bare-faced robbery. And the slaves you have seen. None but the blacks can work in this heat, but they last only two years. The wind is excessive; the wind blinds them. You are enjoying the drink?'

Nicholas spoke, in the face of Umar's silence. 'It is remarkable. I have tasted fermented millet before, but not this.'

'Rice,' said Jilali ibn Said. 'It is good after a long journey such as yours, even if you have to resume it tomorrow. And it puts energy into the miners. It makes them happy, so that they will go and cut the difficult salt, for the white always fetches the best price. You know your Timbuktu merchant will buy five hundred slabs at a time? And if he stores double that, and waits for the price to increase, he can make such a profit! I have known one man make a thousand gold mithqals a season. You brought no gold yourselves?'

'The katib is not trading,' said Nicholas. 'And no, I have none but gold for the journey.'

'I happened to see,' said Jilali. 'But books, that is excellent. Forgive me, but my lord could have brought more books had he not packed so much of small value. The weaving in Timbuktu is naïve, and the carvings remind me of those made by children.'

'They were made by children,' Nicholas said. 'I am desolate to suggest it, but with such a journey behind and before, the katib and I find ourselves in great need of sleep. Would it offend you and your household if we retired?'

'How could you think it?' said the merchant. 'It is the rice wine. And tomorrow we must set forth, for the caravan departs, as I have said. You know I can take you only so far as Sijilmasa?'

'You have said,' Nicholas said.

'But my brother Mustapha will guide you from there. Sijilmasa is a metropolis! It will amaze you! And travelling there, by the grace of Allah, I shall have three good weeks or four in my lord's company. Such an honour!'

The chamber they were given to sleep in was unlit and full of men snoring, but Umar spoke Flemish to Nicholas. 'Such an honour!' he murmured from the next pallet.

Nicholas groaned. 'Come with me!'

Umar laughed a little, to show he understood. Here at Taghaza was where he turned back. He could not do so at once: there was as yet no caravan travelling south, so he must wait till one gathered. Meanwhile, the camels could rest. All the camels Nicholas possessed were now Umar's and, sold at home, would bring him the worth of a hundred slabs of salt each. Being well enough off, Umar had protested, but only at first. To continue at once to Sijilmasa was beyond the beasts, worn as they were. It was bad enough that Nicholas had to do it.

'No. I'm glad,' Nicholas replied, when he said so. 'It's best to be quick. I wish I could see you leaving as soon as you're ready. There are so few going south.'

'To Timbuktu,' Umar said. 'But if I can't find a caravan going there, I'll get one soon enough for Walata. Send me word from Oran.'

'And you, too,' Nicholas said. 'About everything. Will it be another Zuhra?'

'There can only be one,' said Umar, a smile in his voice. 'So where shall I send this word? Where are you going?'

'I don't know yet,' Nicholas said.

There was quietness. 'I thought you did,' Umar said.

'That, yes,' Nicholas said. 'I think I want a stake in the world.

The kind of stake that you have. If I couldn't have it in Timbuktu, then I must find somewhere else to begin.'

'You have begun,' Umar said.

'There is no cradle under my roof,' Nicholas said. 'I want the teachers sprung of your line to help instruct the poor fools sprung of mine. I mean to match you, child for child. I think I have become patriarchal in your desert.'

'I think it began long before that, ' Umar said. 'You had another and better teacher in worse adversity.' He broke off.

'Godscalc?' Nicholas said. 'Different, not better. I challenged him to try and convert me.'

'To what?' said Umar.

'To anything,' Nicholas said. 'No. I don't mean that. But the way to Ethiopia, with the best teacher, didn't do for me what you have done.'

'Yet,' said Umar, 'you are troubled for me, when I turn to Mecca at sunset, and yet raise my voice in praise from the Christian Eucharist. I should like you to trust me in some things. There are many forms of perfection. You and I, we try to attain them. You know how I have failed.'

'You speak to me of failure?' Nicholas said.

'Is that not what we have been speaking of all along?'

'Yes,' said Nicholas. 'I know. I will remember. And this place? You brought me here to see Taghaza, too.'

'I should have spared you, I think,' Umar said. 'One small race exploiting another: there is no solution. But remember this when you are trading.'

'Trading?' Nicholas said. 'You make it sound like the filthiest occupation on earth. Is it?'

'Yes,' said Umar. 'And no. It depends on the trader.'

They parted next day. Umar rode outside the walls with the caravan, and kept pace for a little by Nicholas. Then he leaned over and touched him, and left. Nicholas watched him go.

Umar didn't look back. He rode directly to Taghaza, where the diamond huts were set sparkling among the empty black holes of the mine-shafts. He sang under his breath as he went.

Nicholas heard it, as he walked in the opposite direction. His beast plodded beside him; the caravan was full of chatter so that his voice, fitting itself into the plainsong, was no more remarked on than Umar's, for both were half in the mind.

Nicholas wove no descant around it, for the descant stands off from the song. He sang each second line, and Umar's voice, disembodied, alternated with his, and became one with it in the refrains. At the last, the distant voice was only an echo. Then

Umar went through the gates, still without looking back, and the singing was gone.

Sijilmasa *was* a metropolis: a teeming green crossroads at the edge of the desert from which the caravans set out south, for the gold. Under the palm trees of Sijilmasa were fruit and flowers, eggs and cheeses, milk and dates and sweet water, and also every vice that money could buy, because it was wealthy – the Tuareg capital of a vast river-watered oasis. Under the palm trees of Sijilmasa, Nicholas lost Jilali ibn Said, and the desert.

He was sorrier than he had expected to part with Jilali. He had grown used to the clamour of his voice and the pressing intimacy of his manner. It concealed a shrewd brain, a lively eye, and great courage. Whatever the hardship, Jilali ibn Said had surmounted it with immense noise and equal efficiency; the sight of his solid body and florid features was enough to make the most recalcitrant muleteer quail.

He waved aside expressions of thanks, shaking Nicholas by the hand over and over, and kissing him frequently on the cheeks. 'Were it another season, I could have taken you to my home at Tlemcen! But here is Mustapha, my young brother, who will accompany you. Unless you will not reconsider, and remain for a while? The houses of pleasure are all remarkable. There is nothing you cannot have. And in three weeks, the date harvest will begin. Ah! Sijilmasa when the fat, fresh, luscious dates come to the table!'

Nicholas refused, but with gratitude. After the desert, the onslaught of noise and colour, not to mention the sudden accession of food, made him feel giddy. He also felt a trifle lost, because the caravan family he had lived with so long had dispersed, albeit with protestations of undying affection.

The new convoy was shorter, and led by Jilali's plump bearded brother. With some prodding, it managed to leave Sijilmasa in under three days. Mustapha, as it proved, had all Jilali's enthusiasm, if not quite his efficiency. He also had many friends. They stopped a great deal, pacing up the lush river valley with its ardent hills. In due course, Mustapha hurried them across wastes of stone and swathes of soft, coloured sand; he had more friends in the villages tucked behind rocks, or in unexpected clumps of palm trees: he was energetic and talkative even when ascending the massif, the plateau that would take them to Tlemcen. There, as they camped, Nicholas said, 'It is nearly the end of September.'

'You will be in Oran by October,' Mustapha said. 'But you will stay with me in Tlemcen first? Oh, the wonders of Tlemcen! You have never seen such a palace, such a mosque. As great as Granada, as Córdoba, with their pillars and pools, their filigree and their cedarwood, their arches like icicles, carved into hollows like honeycombs. I tell you –'

'I can imagine,' said Nicholas. 'But alas, I should hasten to Oran. I may have to wait long for a ship.'

Mustapha ibn Said plucked his beard. He said, 'They call if they have a cargo, but not often. It depends where my lord wishes to go. Is my lord going to Fleming-land?'

'Flanders? Anywhere,' Nicholas said. 'Flanders, Florence, Venice, Ragusa. I shall take the first ship that comes.'

He didn't know when he had reached that decision: to make no decision. To leave his destination to fate.

It was October when they came to Oran, and plodded through the great landward gates and into the caravanserai near them. Mustapha paid the caravan dues and found a place for their beasts and their goods and said, 'I have friends who run a good tavern. If they have room, it will be better than this. And not expensive, even if you have to stay through the winter. Come and see them. Or perhaps you are tired?'

'A little,' said Nicholas. 'Please go and see your friends, Mustapha. We can talk when you return.'

He was tired, but not more than they all were. It was the sight of the city itself that had oppressed him. The forest of minarets within the stout walls; the descending clutter of innumerable houses; the clamour of people. He had braced himself for it at Tlemcen, and he wished to prepare for it now, before plunging into it.

Besides, it was the end of a journey. The end of a very great journey, such as he had never undertaken before, in any land. He had left Venice on a summer's day three years ago, beset by angry enemies. He had sailed as an army would sail, to seize its objectives. He had proposed to confront his doubting family, and force them to swallow their accusations. He had meant to hunt down Crackbene, who had opposed him; discover his ship; find the boy Diniz; compel the Vatachino to fear him as a rival. And find gold to pay for his Bank.

And he had not thought, at all, of what that would do to the people around him. Many were dead. All were altered. Most of all, late and laggard, himself.

He did not think he would change again. He carried with him now, below all the turbulence, the quietness Umar had found for him; Umar and the desert. When he was alone, as now, sitting in silence, he had only to reach for it.

He was so far lost in his thoughts that he didn't at once hear the voice of Mustapha, calling up from the yard to his balcony. 'Lord! They have rooms! You may stay as long as it pleases you! And there is one ship in the harbour.'

Nicholas rose to his feet. 'Going where?'

'No one knows. It lies there, gathering weed. My friends have sent to the wharf to seek news of the patron's intentions. It is a galley. My friends have written its name.'

He held up a paper. Nicholas ran down the steps. In the humid air, his skin felt slippery, as if it had been oiled. He took the paper.

Mustapha's friends were not scribes, but they had managed to letter the name of the ship. They had seen it often enough. She had been at anchor in Oran since September.

Nicholas managed to read it as well. He read it twice, while Mustapha watched him. Then he read it a third time, or appeared to.

The galley that lay in the harbour was his own. The name of the lone, steadfast ship was the *Ciaretti*.

The tavern used by the crew of the *Ciaretti* was on the quayside, and a good deal more lax about liquor than the one belonging to Mustapha's friends. When word went round that someone was enquiring about the *Ciaretti*, the crew did what they usually did, and deputed the two least drunk to row out to the ship and inform the officers.

So it came about that, when Nicholas pushed his way down to the port, two men in Venetian dress had already landed and were hastening uphill towards him. They saw each other at the same time. He stopped, and the men from the *Ciaretti* faltered.

They saw a tall man in a striped cloak stained with travelling, his head and shoulders bound in a white corded headcloth. Beneath the cloak was a gown of thick cotton, from the girdle of which hung a heavy, curved sword, and, on the opposite side, a leather purse ornamented in sticky, frayed silk. His sandals, too, were much mended, although once elaborate. Within the Egyptian cloth was a lean face, broad at the cheekbones and brow but hollow elsewhere, and in two tints of brown, as if a beard had been recently shaved.

The face slowly broke into a smile, producing two dents black as caverns. 'Melchiorre?' Nicholas said.

Melchiorre Cataneo of Florence jogged unevenly upwards towards him and, reaching him, found himself in an embrace he might or might not have initiated. Nicholas said, 'You are well?' and Melchiorre hesitated, and then gave a choking laugh, looking behind him.

'You are speaking in Arabic,' said Tobias of Beventini, physician, climbing rather more carefully. 'God's Dines, have ye turned? The Pope'll murder you.' His nose was pink.

'*Tobie?*' said Nicholas. He added, more clearly, 'But you were always seasick.' It came out in Flemish.

'I nearly didn't come,' Tobie said. He put his hands on the striped shoulders and held them, but not over-tightly. His thumbs moved about. He said, 'Come down to the ship. We can't all stand and weep in the street. You didn't expect us.'

'It was a really pleasant surprise,' Nicholas said. It came out in Arabic again. He couldn't make jokes and deal with the shock also. His mind filled with the fragments of a hundred queries, but there was only one now that mattered. Or perhaps two. He said, 'Godscalc, Tobie?'

'In Bruges with young Vasquez. He's all right,' Tobie said. 'Everyone's all right. The Bank's all right. What about Loppe? Nicholas?'

'Umar,' said Nicholas. 'He's staying. He's well. I left him two months ago. So what cargo do you have?'

He had asked the question of Melchiorre who glanced in a dazed way at Tobie.

Tobie's round blue eyes had revived. Tobie said, 'Majolica, mercury, sheepskins, and bales of Perpignan and Languedoc cloth. We can sell them anywhere. Where do you want to go? There's no one in Lagos. Gregorio should be in Venice by now. Julius was leaving Venice for Scotland, unless he's waited to see you.'

'I don't think I should disappoint Julius,' Nicholas said. 'Melchiorre? Could you take me to Venice?'

'Anywhere,' Melchiorre said. He was smiling and weeping again. He said, 'I can't believe you're here. We thought the message might be a hoax.'

'Don't be too sure it isn't,' said Nicholas nonsensically, in some language or other. In silent Arabic, he was collecting his thoughts. He hadn't summoned them. If the *Ciaretti* had been here for a month, then someone else must have sent off the instruction before he himself left Timbuktu. Before he had decided to leave. Umar. Umar.

The street was packed. People bumped into them as they talked, and the noise was deafening. There would be two hundred men on the *Ciaretti*. Tobie said, 'The boat is just over there.' It was his professional voice.

Nicholas set aside all he was thinking, and his Arabic. He viewed Tobie. He said calmly, 'I don't suppose for a minute that you know how the écu is doing?'

'Of course I do,' Tobie said, instantly relieved. 'Julius has these silver-gilt carrier-pigeons he sends us from Venice every day. You're going to like being rich. We all like it. You don't even need to go back and do it all over again. Are you tired of eating old camel? We have a layer-pasty on board.'

'Lead me to it,' Nicholas said.

Chapter 38

I T WAS JULIUS and not Gregorio who greeted the magnifico, the owner of the Banco di Niccolò, when the *Ciaretti* appeared through the mists of winter in the San Marco basin; Julius and a host which included the highest officers of the Republic of Venice. And the *Ciaretti*, aware that she was expected, rowed in, pennants streaming to the sound of drum and trumpet and flute, with every man dressed in silk, and Nicholas standing obediently on the deck of the forecastle.

This time, the Rialto had emptied, and the staff of the Ca' Niccolò had not lingered around their own doors but had come to the square in a brilliant and uniform body. And instead of the modest two-oar *barchetta*, a stupendous gilded *bissona* rowed by twelve men carried Julius and his senior colleagues to where the galley dropped anchor.

Nicholas was watching it approach. '*Non est vivere extra Venetiis.* You did warn me.'

'He does love it. Don't spoil it,' said Tobie. 'He really did work miracles with nothing before the gold came.' He saw Margot in the boat, which was a good thing. He wondered again where Gregorio was. He wished he knew what Nicholas was going to do from one minute to the next.

Julius rushed on board, and then remembered to help Margot up the steps. He was wearing more ribbons than she was. He said 'Hey!' and stood, his good-looking face red, before his former minion. He said, 'You were always exploring something, you bastard. Usually in a chemise.'

'There's gold everywhere,' Nicholas said and pummelled the other man scientifically on the back. 'Julius, you're flabby.'

'Solemn, and rich, and soon to be fat,' said Margot obscurely. There was a glint in her eye. She gave Nicholas a sudden fierce hug, and smiled blinking at Tobie. 'We thought perhaps you had all decided to stay.'

'I'm not flabby. You're as thin as a pike. Mind you, you got off a lot better than Godscalc,' Julius said. 'Or so they say. You know he can't hold a pen? Or walk very well. You were mad to try and get to Prester John. My God, you didn't need jewels on top of all the gold you sent home.'

'I was looking for the Fountain of Youth,' Nicholas said. 'Where is Gregorio?'

'Bruges. He had to stay in Bruges because of the Wedding,' Julius said. 'That's why I'm here instead of getting to Scotland. Diniz is in Bruges as well. You'll never guess what he's doing.'

'Tobie told me. Whose wedding?' said Nicholas.

Margot looked at him. She said, 'Duke Charles with the English King's sister. Did you know Duke Philip died? His son Charles needs an heir for Flanders and Burgundy. Hence a wedding next spring, and a lot of lavish expenditure. Your lady Gelis van Borselen is going to miss it.'

Nicholas smiled. 'I don't think she would appreciate hearing you call her my lady. But she turned out to be a remarkable traveller. Tobie tells me she's in Scotland.'

'She was. She came back to Bruges for the winter. She's due to go back to her Scottish princess in May. But you'll see her. You'll be going to Bruges soon.'

'Not,' said Julius, 'if I have anything to do with it. Nicholas, look at that landing-stage. Look at the money on it. They're all in your pocket. You've been where no one else has been. You've sent back more gold than anyone has ever seen in one load. You're in the good books of the Pope, and your Bank is becoming one of the pillars of Venice. There they all are, standing waiting to welcome you and put you among the privileged in their Golden Book, I shouldn't wonder. And you talk of going to Bruges!'

'I didn't. I'm not going to Bruges,' said Nicholas mildly.

He turned out to be speaking the truth: Nicholas didn't leave Venice. Indeed, he hardly left the Bank premises.

The Ca' Niccolò with Nicholas in it was very different from the same establishment under Julius, quite apart from the somewhat moody departure of Julius from the middle floor to the top. Margot wondered if Julius had really expected Nicholas to leave the master chamber to him, and decided that he probably had. To Julius, it was just a freakish talent for opportunism that had taken Nicholas so far beyond his station; in other ways he was still the Charetty apprentice.

Apart from the fact that he was now twenty-six, the Nicholas of today was not even like the Nicholas of three years ago, never mind eight. Three years ago, he had been in the city all day, interviewing, discussing, prosecuting his business. He had given a feast, and been entertained in all the great houses.

This time, aside from his official reception by the Doge, and another at the Collegio, the only appointment he kept outside his house was one at the Camaldolite monastery on the island of San Michele, to which he went unaccompanied. For the rest, everyone who wished to see him, or he wished to see, came to the Ca' Niccolò.

During the ghostly grey days of December, there arrived a procession of eager gentlemen who would pass from the mezzanine office of Julius to the big chamber with its bed and its desk which Nicholas had again made his own, there to resume the fascinating exchanges about cloth and carpets and rope-walks which had been interrupted by the hiatus three years before.

These he would entertain with great courtesy, but never keep long. Others, like Marietta Barovier from Murano, he would keep for a short while at his desk, and then lead through to the long central chamber whose front balcony overlooked the canal, there to talk and take some light refreshment.

Sometimes Tobie found himself asked to attend, and sometimes not. He became increasingly puzzled. After the visit of the extraordinary female glassmaker, Tobie invited himself to Margot's room to discuss it.

He knew he was welcome, if only because she was weary of Julius and shared his misdoubting affection for Nicholas. She rose from her sewing to pour him some wine and, sitting, said, 'They would have a lot to talk about. Barovier supplies the glass for the spectacles the Florentine makes. You know he's taken on an assistant, and they've quadrupled the business? And now that the Strozzi sons have been allowed back from exile, they can help more directly.'

'She was talking about mosque lamps,' Tobie said. 'And table fountains. And alum. It seems Venice needs a lot of alum now the glass business is growing. You knew that the first big trading deal Nicholas ever made was to do with an alum monopoly?'

'I remember all the secrecy,' Margot said. 'It's a powder, isn't it? They dig it up in Turkey and Rome, and dyers and glassmakers need it. I thought the Medici had the Roman rights. Or don't they, now Cosimo's dead?'

'It's shaky,' said Tobie. 'Cardinal Bessarion has a lot of say in it now, I believe. Friend of Julius and Godscalc.' He watched Margot thinking.

She said, 'And of course, there isn't a Medici branch now in

Venice, since Martelli died. Tobie? Are we wrong? Nicholas is in business again?'

It was what had mystified them both about Nicholas. He conducted business all right, but all the initiative came from outside. He had begun nothing new, only enhanced what was already there, or what Julius had begun to restore.

In fact, it was all that was necessary. Built on its new, secure base, the Bank could hardly avoid increasing its wealth on its loans business alone; and with the bought-back *Adorno*, they had three ships in the water making profits. Julius handled the day-to-day routine trade. And the rest of the time, Nicholas could spend as he chose. He spent it in his room. They didn't know how he spent it.

Tobie said, 'He didn't rise to it. I think Marietta was disappointed as well. That is, he was calm and practical and agreeable and sketched her some rather nice drawings of table fountains with the suggestion that she get someone to make them. Nicholas! Who used to throw off schemes like a Catherine wheel!'

'Julius appreciates the change,' Margot said. 'Smitten with awe, his staff are working twice as hard as before, while Julius is still free to go to all the best suppers. Privately, Julius thinks Nicholas has come back beaten in spirit, like Godscalc. Or he's sick.'

'He's recovered now,' Tobie said.

Margot looked at him. 'He talks to you.'

'About medical books. I've never heard how he got over the Sahara. All I know about the Ethiopia attempt is what you've told me of Godscalc's account. When I met him in Oran, Nicholas looked the way he looked after Famagusta. I told him.'

'And?' Margot said.

'He said Famagusta was only a rehearsal,' Tobie said. 'But that's all he said.'

The most frequent callers, after the merchants, were the geographers, the sailing-masters and the makers of maps. The first to come was Alvise da Ca' da Mosto with two friends, one of whom was the Ancona cartographer Gratioso Benincasa, who was making a map of Timbuktu. After they had gone, Tobie said, 'You weren't very helpful.'

'Wasn't I?' Nicholas said. He had filled out a little, but not much, and was still wearing the loose, quilted garments Margot had had made for him against the season's seeping cold.

'I gather Ca' da Mosto was generous enough with his advice,' Tobie said.

'He's a Venetian. Benincasa makes maps for anybody.'

Julius, this time, had joined them. 'The Genoese?' he said. 'You think he's making maps for the Vatachino?'

'He's making this map for the former Milanese envoy Prosper Schiaffino de Camulio de' Medici,' Nicholas said. 'Remember him?'

Julius stopped drumming his fingers. 'He represented the Genoese in your alum deal. Nicholas. They threw him out of Genoa in February, and the Medici wouldn't have him in Florence. He plots.'

'So why does he want a map of Guinea?' Nicholas said. 'You work it out.'

'The Vatachino likes plotters,' said Tobie. 'I see the dangers. All the same. You aren't going to let all this information go for nothing? Godscalc has sent all he knows to Bessarion.'

'Then no doubt they'll commission a rutter in Rome,' Nicholas said.

'But not in Venice? You went to San Michele,' said Julius. 'Was that not about maps?'

'I had a book for the abbot,' said Nicholas. 'And I wanted to commission copies of others. As for maps, I'm not particularly interested in helping the Genoese.'

'Or anyone else?' Tobie had said. 'You don't really want anyone to go where you've been. Why is that?'

'They have troubles enough,' Nicholas said. 'We have all the money we need. We'd only be helping our rivals.'

'And the Church's mission?' Tobie said. 'Or don't you mind their rivals?'

'As much as you do,' Nicholas said.

It began to exasperate Julius. Now Tobie had come, Julius had expected Nicholas to march off to Bruges and set in motion a splendid watertight case which would enable them to recover the *Ghost*. He had further expected him to spend money in Lisbon, and even go there, to pursue both the *Ghost* and the case against the *Fortado*.

Failing both these things, Julius had offered to do the work for him, but Nicholas had refused. Nicholas complained enough about the Genoese and the Vatachino, and yet he wouldn't seize the chance to attack when he had it.

'He's had enough travelling,' Tobie said. 'Give him time.'

The Feast of St Nicholas and the Feast of Christmas had both passed with due celebration, organised wholly by Julius, on a scale enjoyed by the staff and admired by its clients. Epiphany came and went. Julius reported to Nicholas all that was happening.

The market in Bruges was still depressed because of the quarrel with Scotland: Bonkle had gone to Scotland to find out what was happening. The ducal wedding had been postponed until June.

When it came, it should profit both Gregorio and Diniz. Under Diniz, the Charetty company had rallied.

Nearer home, the Bank's mercenary troops under Captain Astorre were still in Albania, helping to hold Scutari and Croia against the Turkish invader. Recently, Astorre had been joined by the rest of his army from Cyprus. Now, that is, that there was no place for his army in Cyprus.

There was no need to go into details over that. All the news about Cyprus had been rushed to Nicholas by the Venetians. By, to be precise, Caterino Zeno, Venetian merchant (of alum) and his exquisite lady the Trapezuntine princess Violante, who had called to see their dear and respected young friend, and congratulate him on his amazing venture. It was perhaps a mark of what Margot felt about Violante of Naxos that she admitted them both to the Ca' Niccolò. When Nicholas smiled at her, receiving them, Margot had felt deservedly guilty.

Rumour, which was generally right, said that Nicholas had been the lover of two if not three of the remarkable princesses of Naxos, while remaining on cordial terms with their husbands. On this occasion, all the civilities over, Caterino had introduced the subject of Cyprus.

'What was happening when you left? The Vatachino had been given the dyeworks, and the unfortunate Zorzi expelled (you know his Bruges business failed?). And then – of course, your fees would be affected – King Zacco's increased tribute to Cairo made it impossible for him to pay the army, or the dues for the sugar estates, yours and ours.

'We all wished, my dear Niccolò,' said Signor Caterino Zeno with a smile, 'that during your stay on the island, you had been a little less hard on the Mamelukes. However. No one has attempted to slay you, I believe, on this visit? And I have to tell you that conditions in Cyprus are improving. And will improve more.'

Margot watched him watch Nicholas. The Venetian sugar estates were the largest in Cyprus, next to those run by the Banco di Niccolò. As Zeno had said, no dues had come from either since the King ran out of money. She knew Nicholas had received nothing from his private farms either.

Nicholas said, 'I'm glad to hear it. Who will benefit?'

'Oh, everyone,' had said Zeno expansively. 'The whole of Venice. Every Venetian with interests on the island. If you lose the royal estates, there will be others for you, I am sure. After King Zacco is married.'

'You think so?' Nicholas said. 'I heard he hoped for a Queen from either Naples or Rome.'

'Tattle,' said Zeno. 'When a man is young and unmarried and has need of legitimate heirs, such talk will go round. No. He has chosen a Venetian bride.'

'Not someone I know? Not a kinswoman of your own?' Nicholas asked. His voice was awe-struck.

'Are we not honoured? And you have met her. You remember Catherine?' Violante of Naxos enquired. 'My sister's daughter? I am to be the aunt of a Queen. I feel aged.'

'In no respect, except perhaps when compared in age with a child,' Nicholas said. 'Can she be marriageable?'

'She is thirteen,' said the merchant. 'We expect womanhood in a matter of months. And meantime the papers are signed. King Zacco of Cyprus became a son of Venice by proxy this morning. A pretty sight. All the other children were there. Our young Pietro as well. Violante and I were lamenting. Had he not been born a boy, Zacco's eye might have fallen on him.'

Both dimples appeared. 'Don't despair,' said Nicholas, smiling.

On the way to their boat, Violante detained him. Perhaps she knew Margot was near; perhaps she didn't. 'Deprivation suits you,' she said. 'But where is the sweet young ox that once I favoured? I hear you live the life of a monk. I hear you do not even console the motherly Margot.'

'Have I made a mistake?' Nicholas said. 'I didn't know that consolation was what I was supposed to be dispensing. I must have let you down badly.'

She was beautiful, and clever, and no more visibly engaged than he was. 'You and Zacco,' she said. 'I am told he remembers you still. He has put aside your Primaflora long ago. You must not let this new marriage affect you. It is good for Venice.'

There was a note of something that might have been wistfulness in her voice. Nicholas said, 'Poor Zacco. Doesn't he deserve something a little closer to his own tastes? I thought your husband, by the way, looked rather poorly. Do take care of him.'

Violante of Naxos flicked him on the cheek and, laughing, walked to the edge of the wharf.

'Bitch,' said Margot.

'I thought you were there,' Nicholas said. 'Do you want me to console you?'

'Not if you want to stay here,' Margot said. 'What do you think all that will mean?'

'At a guess? The Venetian families get the royal sugar franchise. Cyprus becomes a Venetian fortress, with Zacco its puppet. Cairo loses its tribute, and is therefore keener to trade with people like me. And John le Grant is out of a job. He might do rather well in Alexandria. Shall I suggest it to Julius?'

'You're the head of the Bank,' Margot said.

'No. They are. Gregorio and Julius. I,' Nicholas said, 'am the evil genius who whispers from time to time in their ears, but prefers to be absent.'

But he hadn't been absent.

Then February came, and one morning, at dawn, a messenger at the door of the Ca' Niccolò. At first the porter refused to let him in, but when the man presented a paper, the porter opened the door. Margot, in her bedgown, said, 'What?'

'For my lord Niccolò,' said the porter. 'This man has been paid to bring such a message whenever it comes, and to deliver it personally.'

'Come with me,' Margot said.

Afterwards, she thought that Nicholas had heard the disturbance; or perhaps he had been sleeping lightly. At any rate, she had hardly knocked before the door opened. Nicholas looked from her to the man, who held out the packet he carried.

'Wait,' said Nicholas. 'Margot, will you excuse me?'

There was a lamp already lit by his desk. He took the packet over, and lifted scissors and snipped all the threads. The seal had told her nothing, except that it was made from poor wax. Then Nicholas turned and came back.

He really observed her then, she thought, for the first time, and caught her by the wrist, saying, 'It's all right.' Then he turned to the messenger. 'This is what I was expecting. You received your wage?'

'Every week, my lord,' said the man.

'Good. Then our arrangement has come to an end. But you have been watchful. I appreciate it. Let me close the transaction with this.'

She couldn't see how many gold coins there were in his palm, but she heard the man's gasp. He coloured, and tried to kiss the hand that had given them to him. Then he backed off and ran.

'Well?' said Nicholas to Margot, standing still in the doorway. 'What news was it, do you think?'

Something told her. Something identified the reason for all the weeks of waiting, the curious withdrawal, the reluctance to move. She said, 'I think it is good news of the one person you have been waiting to hear from. I think it is to say that Loppe – that Umar is safely home.'

He kissed her then; a kiss of pure affection and relief and a number of other emotions she could not then name. He said, 'I don't need consolation any more, and if you do, it's going to take the form of strong liquor. Margot, go and wake Tobie and Julius. I don't want to sit here alone, not even with you. And then I have to make plans.'

'You're going?' she said. 'Now you can move, you are going? Where?'

'Where else but Bruges?' Nicholas said.

Bruges in spring was the homecoming gift Nicholas had refused for three months to allow himself. When he left Venice, he took Margot with him, with the extremely ready permission of Julius. She was a quiet companion, and the journey, though hard, was not painful. No sweet singing voice disturbed the snows of the Alps, but the same voice was still lifted in song, if in a different land, and there were three children now to hear it, including a daughter.

The spirit of Marian de Charetty remained, but as a dear and benevolent presence, and no longer the source it had once been of self-reproach and of anguish. Marian his wife slept near Dijon. Six years ago, her two orphaned daughters in Bruges had forbidden him to enter the Charetty house. Since then, Tilde had met him in Venice, and he had tried to make her into a friend. She and Catherine her sister had permitted Gregorio to use part of their house for the Banco di Niccolò, and any lingering doubts, Nicholas suspected, would have been swept away by their new guide and manager, Diniz Vasquez. And Godscalc was with them.

Nicholas had heard from Gregorio, and from Diniz. Hasty letters received just before he left Venice, they expressed incoherent joy at his return. Godscalc had added a great sprawling line with a joke in it.

He had received other letters – from his fellow merchants, from the city fathers, from the boys he had grown up with. He was a burgher of Bruges; he had been seen to do the town honour: there would be a reception almost as great as the one he had been given in Venice. He was prepared for it; crowds did not disturb him now. He had not barred himself from society out of fear, only from a need to establish, in peace, what had happened to him. He knew what he wanted, but until Umar was safe, he would not snatch it.

He had received no letter from Gelis van Borselen, and looked for none. Whatever had to be said, good or bad, had to be spoken. She knew he was home, and could guess he would come, sometime, to Bruges.

If she did not want to see him, she had only to leave early for Scotland. She had not left. And if she had not done so immediately, he thought she would wait for him now.

He had forgotten how green and wooded the countryside was, and the noise of the birds, and the density of the colours: the chestnut of ploughing horses; the crimson caps, the russet tunics, the dark leather aprons of the men in the villages; the ruddy cheeks and muslin-wrapped heads of the women; the scarlet and gold of poppy and buttercup in the hedgerows. And on every side, the blinding flash of sunlight on water, brighter than diamonds.

Then the brown walls of Bruges stood before him, the windmills turning above; the tunnelled, towered portico open; the drawbridge down over the canal; and a crowd on the far side. Among them he saw silk and velvet, banners and trumpets. In the centre was the Black Lion of Flanders, the great standard of Bruges.

Nicholas brought his cavalcade to a halt, and rode forward alone. Understanding, he did not feel either a fool, or contemptuous.

From the town issued a group of three échevins and three laymen. He didn't look at the échevins, for the other three were Gregorio, Diniz and Tilde. Beside him, Margot was weeping.

Then the leading official stepped forward, and to a flourish of trumpets, bid welcome home to his town the Knight Nicholas vander Poele, honourable burgher of Bruges.

Chapter 39

BEFORE HE SET OUT for Bruges, Nicholas had in mind that, by some subtle arrangement, his first words there to Gelis would be spoken in private. On the other hand, it was always possible that she would choose (as she did) to come face to face with him before others, and on an occasion as public as the reception given for him by the Lord Louis de Gruuthuse.

Considering Gelis, Nicholas took into account (he took everything into account) that it was two and a half years since they met. The only intimacy between them had been the physical bond of one night, and in her only sight of him since, he had been a senseless invalid, in a worse state than Godscalc.

He himself had not realised, until the faces of Diniz and the other two warned him, that his own colleagues had come to the Gand gate apprehensive of what they would see. They had heard he was safe: he had sent them messages; he was obviously capable still of journeying over the Alps. If they were so relieved to see him properly gowned and largely unchanged, then presumably others had shared their misgivings. It was not until he saw Godscalc that he understood the whole cause.

By then, he had replied to the speeches and received the scroll with the burgomaster's name on it, and led his small cavalcade through all the familiar streets to the tall, elaborate house he now shared with the Charetty. The citizens of Bruges did not line the way, although the most curious had come as far as the bridge and plenty of others glanced over their shoulders as the banners and trumpets trooped past. He saw a few rascals he knew, and a few old friends, and one or two very old enemies. He didn't embarrass any of them by stopping to speak.

Diniz was, he thought, disappointed; but Gregorio, flushed with emotion, explained over the noise of the hooves. 'I'm amazed they managed the trumpets – they're punch-drunk with ceremonies. The old Duke's funeral, the new Duke's entry, the Chapter of the Golden Fleece, the Easter processions, and now this bloody Wedding, twice postponed. Are you really well?'

His eyes kept travelling beyond Nicholas. Nicholas said, 'If you stopped yelling in my ear, you could drop back and ride beside her. Margot, tell him we're all really well, and you've agreed to marry me.'

Both now scarlet, Gregorio and his splendid Margot changed their order of riding. Tilde said, 'They should marry.'

She looked well, too; twenty-one years old, with her brown hair long and burnished under her cap and her lightly furred cloak falling from straight shoulders. She was smiling into space.

Diniz said, 'Everyone should.' He was smiling into space, too. Then they both turned and spoke to Nicholas at once.

At Spangnaerts Street, their town escort departed and Diniz, by magic, disposed of the servants and soldiers they had brought with them. In the yard were all the dyeyard workers from Henninc downwards, and the office workers led by Cristoffels. And Catherine, Tilde's young sister, crying a little. And a tall, bent man in a priest's robe with a crutch under one arm who held out the claw of a bird and said, 'Now I am content.'

'And I, also,' said Nicholas. 'But there is still room for improvement.'

That day he spent among them all, as was right. The barrels of wine were broken open and the platters of food came steaming through from the kitchen, accompanied by the cooks themselves, and the whispering kitchen boys in relays. And as the hours wore on, others came – not of the greater sort, but small clients and craftsmen who would not figure at the town's board, but who had known the Charetty family long enough. Among them was Colard Mansion, scribe and painter.

'My dear! The Baptist, angelic and meagre! And sober, on your day of rejoicing?'

'It's a lie. I'm as drunk as you are. Did you get my letters?' said Nicholas.

'What letters?' said Colard. 'Yes, I got them. Never mind farting business. You should see what vander Goes and I have done for the Wedding. You heard about the Wedding? We had to get it all ready for May, and now it's not till nearly July. The twelve bloody labours of Hercules – I am serious. Ships, and trees. A lion. A leopard. A unicorn. A whale. A camel – you ought to know all about camels. Anything that can take a tube up its arse and pee wine. Come and see it all. I'll get Governor William to come.'

'Will you?' said Nicholas. Godscalc was out of hearing.

'Yes. How much money have you got?' said Colard Mansion.

'Enough for half of what you're thinking of,' Nicholas said.

'You're a mean bastard,' said Colard, without rancour. 'You're a mean, sober bastard who likes to see other men drunk.'

Nicholas went to Godscalc's room that night, after he had spent time with Tilde and Catherine and Diniz, and had told Gregorio not to wait, since he was too tired to see him tonight.

Godscalc smiled when Nicholas reported that to him. The priest was not in bed but, wrapped in a robe, was resting in a chair with a back, his feet propped on a stool. He said, 'If you hadn't brought Margot, he would be a sorrowful man. *Are you tired?*'

'Not for this,' Nicholas said. 'Are you in pain?'

'A little,' said the big man. 'But I have my life. I am glad you have yours.'

'It was given me,' Nicholas said. 'I should like to do something in return. I have something to show you.'

He had brought all the books with him, apart from those he had left at San Michele, and several Tobie had kept. The crates were too heavy to bring up, but he had filled a satchel with the best, and now he put them on the table at Godscalc's side. The priest touched them with the heels of his hands and then, applying his wrists, lifted one down to his lap and pushed the boards open. After a while he looked up.

'You knew what to choose. I have never seen this before. Once I could have copied it for you.'

'I know. I don't want it copied,' Nicholas said. 'I want it printed, and I want you to help me do it.'

'In Venice?' Godscalc asked. He was gazing at a page.

'No, here. Colard will translate. And Tobie will help, when he comes. You'll see, we have a great many medical treatises, and Tobie is looking for more. There's room to annotate them. Even to publish our own. If you would be interested.'

'Some of these are from the Sankore libraries. You were planning this then?' Godscalc said.

'I had time,' Nicholas said.

He left an hour after that, for although he was not tired, Godscalc was. Towards the end, it came to Nicholas that Godscalc wished to talk of the journey that had crippled him; that one of his greatest deprivations had been the absence of a soul other than Diniz to share it with. And Nicholas in return had described something of what he had found in the city, and Umar had shown him. Something only, for it was too rich in some ways to share. And in other ways, too private.

'It is strange,' Godscalc said. 'Once I believed I could help you, and longed for you to come, so that I could try. And now you are the rock.'

'None of us can claim to be that,' Nicholas said. 'Our weaknesses are different, that is all.'

The next day, came the celebration, and Gelis.

The home of Louis de Gruuthuse, Knight of the Golden Fleece, lieutenant-general of Holland, Zeeland and Frisia, famous jouster, famous bibliophile, counsellor of Duke Charles and leader of the Burgundian armies, was a red-brick palace on two canals, surrounded by gardens. Nicholas and his entourage reached it by way of the Bourse and the length of the marketplace, and this time attracted quite a lot of attention, as even his pages were jewelled.

For himself, there was very little of his draped hat or brief doublet where mere cloth could be seen. His horse-harness was of gold, and so was the staff of his standard. Invisible assets, in Venice and Bruges, were no assets at all; gems were what the town and the seigneur de Gruuthuse expected. Accepting the parade as the duty it was, Nicholas felt less elation – less of anything – than he had the day before at his entry. The unaccustomed freedom from skirts slightly disturbed him.

Eight years ago, he had entered this house, an impertinent apprentice called Claes who had married his widowed employer. Then, he and Marian had been insignificant guests among hundreds; the occasion a requiem for a monarch of Scotland.

This time, Marian's daughters walked behind him, with Gregorio his deputy and Diniz Vasquez the Charetty manager. This time, Louis de Gruuthuse himself stood in the tiled hall to greet him, his van Borselen wife at his side. Then they went up the grand stairs to his reception.

The hall with its ceiling-high fireplace was full of men and women Nicholas knew. The officers of the town. The Duke's Controller, and the uncle of Diniz. Some of the young men he had grown up with – Anselm Sersanders, but not Lorenzo di Strozzi, now in Naples, or Jannekin Bonkle, now his agent in Scotland. The merchants the Charetty did business with. The foreign colony: men he knew from the Hanse; Spaniards whose cousins he had met in Valencia. Some with Portuguese interests, including a cool Genoese trader called Gilles whose second name was of course Lomellini. Venetian friends, including a Bembo; but not Marco Corner, whose child was trysted to Zacco of Cyprus.

Representing Florence, Tommaso Portinari, fine-featured, black-haired and gorgeous, who spread out hands whose rings this time were genuine and kissed him on both cheeks, exclaiming,

'Dear Nicholas! Such good fortune! I have been trading in that area myself – you will have heard. You and I have so much to talk about. I shall send my secretary to bring you to supper. You know where I am? The old Bladelin building?'

'Tommaso,' Nicholas said. 'Everyone knows where you are.'

The Genoese, represented by one named Doria and by the person of Genoese birth who had become, by descent, an aristocrat also of Bruges. Anselm Adorne said, 'Margriet wept when she heard you were safe, and I swallowed a lump, I confess. Godscalc has told us something of what happened. You are a noble man, Nicholas.'

'Persistent, rather,' said Nicholas. 'You have been kind to Catherine and Tilde. I have to thank you for that, among other things.'

'Come and see us,' said Margriet, and held her cheek to be kissed.

He would, in time. He had married Marian in the Adornes' church of Jerusalem. Here, in this room, Nicholas had stood beside Marian and listened to the voice of Simon de St Pol shouting at him in public. Here in this room he had learned for the first time that Katelina was pregnant, and that, rather than tell him, she had married Simon and passed the child off as his. Henry. Henry was not here, or Simon. Or Katelina.

A voice he knew said, 'It has all been too much. The excitement. The unaccustomed weight of the jewels. What on earth, my dear sir, is the extraordinary chain you are wearing? Some man-eating order of chivalry?'

Nicholas emerged from his thoughts. Before him, last to present themselves, was the van Borselen family of Veere. The noble lord Henry, after whom his own son was named. Wolfaert, son of Henry and cousin of Gelis and Katelina. And Gelis herself.

He saw her; registered the elaborate veil, the jewelled collar, the pale, precisely drawn eyes before he dragged his own to the seated man who had spoken. Massive in magnificent velvet, it was Jordan, vicomte de Ribérac, Simon's father.

How old would Jordan be now? Sixty, at least. The scar Nicholas himself bore on his cheek was thin and white now; it was more than eight years since Jordan's ring had incised it. It was four years since, under the most terrible of pretexts, Jordan had abducted his young grandson Diniz, from Cyprus. Yet he was not greatly changed: the bulk as impressive; the jowls clean-shaven and heavy, the eyes bold.

Nicholas said, 'My badge? It is the Knightly Order of Cyprus. They gave it me for not stealing anything. Have you decided to give up the *Ghost*? It would delight us.'

'My dear, the natives have sharpened your wits. I am amused. But let me turn to something even more unexpected. This is the first view I have had of my grandson. Come here, Diniz.'

'Of course, Grandfather,' said Diniz. He stepped forward; moderate in height, deeply tanned, the well-made doublet displaying the slender waist and deep chest of a soldier. He said, 'They may not have told you that I have been in Bruges for two years? I must express regret that we are to take you to law, but one must uphold justice.'

'If one can recognise it, of course. And this *we* of yours, child? You have ascended the throne? You should have told me.'

'Diniz and I are to be in association, monseigneur,' Nicholas said. 'Since he is to take to wife Tilde de Charetty, one of my step-daughters. Here she is. You may wish to give them your blessing.'

That morning, Diniz had come to Nicholas and asked his permission to marry. It had not been a surprise, and he had given it. Lucia, absent in Scotland, had no power to prevent the betrothal. Jordan's only power was the denial of money, and Diniz had plenty of that. There would be no public recriminations either; not here and now, in the palace of Louis de Gruuthuse, with the boy's uncle, the Duchess's secretary, present.

Senhor João, having overheard, was already hurrying over. Tilde grasped her gown, her eyes brilliant, and, running to Nicholas, kissed him. Guests began to gather around them. Nicholas said, 'Diniz, I'm sorry. But it seemed an appropriate place.' Diniz laughed at him, and took Tilde by the hand. They disappeared into the circle.

'Charming,' said Jordan de Ribérac. 'Nicholas, I do congratulate you, provident child. I thought she had fixed on that tiresome fool Julius. That would never have done. And now, with the groom in your pocket, you acquire the Charetty business as simply as if your step-daughter had died. I am right? The girl has agreed to a merger?'

'If my shareholders approve,' Nicholas said. 'I could offer you special family rates? And you could give them the *Ghost* as a wedding present.'

The sharp eyes, looking up, searched his face. The man's complexion had hardly altered; the plump hands on the head of his cane were restfully folded. Jordan said, 'You have been learning. How?'

'By example,' Nicholas said, and bowed, and turned his attention elsewhere. Gelis had joined the circle about Diniz and Tilde. She was smiling at them, which surprised him. Soon after, they were all called to table, and he saw that Jordan had gone.

He supposed afterwards that it was all by design: that Gelis had wished to watch from a distance, and had known her place would be far from his at the board, or perhaps even arranged for it to be so. The world knew that she, a lone woman, had stayed behind in Guinea when Diniz left, even if the priest had been left behind also. The world knew that Nicholas had returned, but not to Bruges. The present distance between them preserved the illusion, perhaps the reality, that there was nothing between them. She had been right to arrange their first encounter in public. Perhaps there would be no other.

On the other hand, the dreaded meeting with Jordan was over. Nothing had happened. He had been surveyed, and had been able to hit back, for once. And Jordan, he learned, was on his way out of the city. There were speeches at the meal, and a great deal of wine drunk, and healths of Diniz and Tilde much invoked. It pleased him to share the day with them. Someone ought to enjoy it.

It was usual, at the end, for the host and hostess to escort the principal guest to their doors, and for the company to disperse. The cavalcade assembled; the grooms held the flambeaux aloft; the fine blue flag with its cross-hilted sword flew above Nicholas as he mounted. The pristine veil at his stirrup belonged to his hostess.

Marguerite van Borselen said, 'I hope you are not really tired. Monseigneur was attempting to attract your attention. When the others have gone, we should be charmed if you would remain and take wine with us. Gelis will show you where to come.'

He felt the blood leave his heart. 'Of course,' Nicholas said.

He might have expected that, steel-willed as she was, she would have obtained the complicity of her family for this first meeting. That she would be present, modestly reticent, at the drowsy gathering before the great fire, after which Nicholas rose to leave. That, offering to escort him below, she should suggest that they pause in the library.

Eight years ago, the mansion Gruuthuse had consisted of one single wing. Since then, it had grown and was growing still. Scaffolding rose against the night sky, stark as ape-watchers' ladders, and from the windows could be seen puddled mud where the bricklayers had worked. Hods lay idle about it, but no sleeping lizards, their jaws ready to snap. And the ghosts in the glinting water were swans, and the water itself ran black and clear, with no forest of reeds through which a boat could pass, creaking and rustling, while the egrets stood like plumes in the water.

Gelis said, 'This is the library. Come and see.'

He had glimpsed it once before. Into his mind came a narrow, beautiful room with thirteen dormer windows, through which the indigo night sky looked down upon tiered ranks of shelves, twelve on each side. And at the end of the long, shining river of parquet, silver candelabra glowed on a table.

With extraordinary violence Nicholas said, '*No!*'

'What?' she said. 'Nicholas, what?' Then, in her usual voice, 'It is not like the Qadi's, or Katib Musa's. Come in. It's quite different.'

And then he saw that she was right, and it was not like any room he had been in before, and especially not one of the kind he had imagined, which he had never seen in his life. He walked in, therefore, saying, 'The Qadi's library is half gone. There was a fire.'

She stood still. 'A fire? How?'

'Begun by Akil's men. It will be all right now. I showed them what to do. And Umar is there. He got home. You heard.'

'Yes, I heard,' she said. 'I know he helped you over the desert. Three children now?'

'The last a daughter.' In the candlelight, he saw her face soften. She had changed, as he had. The wind had printed fine lines on her brow, and her skin would never again have the pure, fine grain of the child. Her eyes seemed bigger, as the flesh now clung close to the bone, and her lips had a tuck at each corner, as he had seen them when she first sat with the smallest black children, penning her lessons. Her hair, straight but not straight, like satin touched by the teazle, had returned from streaked silver to oat colour, and the fronds of her lashes were brown. She had pulled out a book and was gazing at it. Godscalc had done that.

Nicholas said abruptly, 'Do you have peace?' He said it in Arabic.

She looked up, her lashes aghast like a doll's. When she answered, it was in harsh Arabic, and not with the called-for response. 'No,' she said. 'I don't know who I am. Bel has gone. I can only find the person I was when speaking to Godscalc, or Diniz. Or you. I hoped, you. But you have put it behind you.' Her knuckles were white on the book.

He drew the book from her. 'No,' he said. 'I carry it with me.'

'How?' she said. It was what Jordan had said.

'I had teachers,' he said. 'And books, like these. And the desert. Mostly the desert.'

'But you didn't want to stay?'

'Oh, I did,' Nicholas said.

'But the gold drew you back?' She sounded fierce.

'No. I was driven out,' Nicholas said. 'Paradise lost. Or not even that, really. I was doing them harm.'

'How could you?' she said.

'I think we should look at books,' he said. 'If that is what I'm here for. You know I brought a lot back?'

'How could you do them harm?' she repeated. She sat on a stool, suddenly, like a child in her fine clothes. 'You said yourself that you helped them.'

Nicholas looked down at her, and didn't answer at once. Then he said, 'I know what I've left. I am not going back. No one can help them yet, except themselves. Umar accepts it as well.'

'So he took you there for nothing?' Gelis said.

'You may judge it so,' Nicholas said. 'We laid his country open to rape, and he allowed it to teach us some truths, and in the end, protected it from us. None of us can be the same. What clods would we be if we were? Your mould is broken: you are afraid, but you have a chance few people have, to make a new one. What you see of me is his handiwork. Diniz will make a good man. Bel brought her own goodness with her, and increased it.'

'And Godscalc?' Gelis said. She stopped. 'No. That isn't fair. Heaven knows, that isn't your fault, or Umar's.'

'No,' Nicholas said. 'You have it wrong. It's not the men of passionate faith for whom martyrdom is a glory. Godscalc has made good his vows, whereas all his life he feared to fall short of them. The hands are his sacrifice. And he and Colard Mansion are going to drive each other crazy. Gelis, I came back for you.'

He said it in Flemish. He said it deliberately, while he stood and she sat; while they were speaking, and he had not even touched her, so that she would know he had come intending to say it.

Everything in the house now was quiet. 'Why?' she said.

'Because there has been time to reflect. Do you remember?'

'Yes,' she said.

He looked at the book. *La Danse aux Aveugles* was the title. It was only a title. He said, 'We made each other a gift. You said that you would take me, if you took any lover. You said – and I said – that there could be no prospect of marriage. I have a question to ask you. According to you, I asked it before.'

'What?' she said. There were shadows under her eyes.

He said, 'The night we spent together. I know why you came to my room. Did you feel the same when you left it?'

Her gaze was so open, he could see the candle flame in it. When he moved, the light from his jewels travelled over her. She said, 'I thought you could tell.'

He moved his lips, as if he were smiling. 'You think I was conscious of anything that night but what was happening? But I thought about it while I was away. I didn't believe we'd come back. And when we did, and I woke, you had gone. I wondered why you had left.'

'To make you follow me,' Gelis said. 'Umar wanted me to go, rather than hurt you. He thought then that you ought to stay; that coming home would only plunge you into perpetual misery. He wanted peace for you.'

'I have peace. I have followed you,' Nicholas said. 'I am here, if you want me.'

She said, 'Even though I haven't answered your question?'

'You have,' he said. 'What revenge would there be in having me follow you, unless it was to refuse me once I came? And you haven't.'

'Not yet,' she said.

He said, 'Listen.'

She had flushed. 'What?' she said.

'Your breathing,' said Nicholas. 'And mine. Gelis, I want to touch you, and I don't like this library. Must I go home?'

She sat without speaking. The jewels flared at her throat. He remembered the pool in the palace, and the tendril that was her young body, and the child-like buds of her breasts. He thought it would be hard to go home, but he didn't move.

She said, 'What would it be, but animal pleasure? You should want more than that. So, I suppose, some day shall I.'

'If you know who you are,' Nicholas said. 'But with me, you will. You said it yourself. I am like Godscalc and Diniz, the other half of your life. The other half of your mould. I don't even ask that you try to complete mine.'

She rose. It was late. There were lamps here and there on the staircase: the doorkeeper was awake, and no doubt there were servants and pages. But he was a guest of the house, and had only been holding converse in a library. It would be easy enough to make an exit.

Gelis said, 'There is a way into the new wing they are building. My room is near there. I am afraid it has books in it.' Now she stood, he could see her skirts trembling.

Nicholas said, 'If someone sees?'

'I am a van Borselen,' Gelis said. 'In the wrong bed, I am invisible.' Her voice came from the door.

He opened his eyes, and walked after her, quickly and quietly, through many corridors. 'I wish,' he said, 'that I had been born a van Borselen. Which door? Go in. I'll wait to see if it's all right, and follow.'

He did wait, but no one had seen them. He saw, while he waited, the moon hanging yellow as cheese over the roof-tops, and heard a distant bell, and a dog bark, and a solitary horse ambling by somewhere. From the church of Our Lady came a rumour of plainsong. His body had begun to take charge. He felt sick.

When he opened the door, Gelis's room was in darkness. Taken with his present cataclysmic absence of peace, it was enough to make his throat close. He had told her himself how to hurt him.

Then he moved, and touched a European woman's long hair, which led his palms down to a smooth neck, and two naked breasts, and a supple waist with a gown half unfastened below it.

He said, 'That's no way to undress,' in an uneven way. And then didn't say very much more, for his own finery was receiving its quittance from eight methodical fingers and two sundering thumbs.

Chapter 40

SCHOOLED BY THE DESERT, Nicholas had learned the lesson if not the habit of moderation. It was not likely – indeed, it was impossible – that he could be temperate in any room with Gelis van Borselen, but at least he could so manage this time that he stayed with her only an hour, and did not allow a night-long sequence of the kind they had shared once before.

That night had come about for many reasons, the best of which still existed. It was a precipitate and sensual union; she had seen that clearly enough. It was perhaps unusual in those terms: close in age but unequal in experience, they possessed a physical match he had rarely, if ever, found before. It was a matter perhaps of simple energy, or of empathy, or even of a kind of imagination he had not suspected. He experienced in her an extreme of joy, and knew, accomplished as he was in this at least, that he had brought her the same.

The best of reasons was not that, it was what they had spoken of: an act of more than bodily fusion. Apart, they were indelibly marked by the year-long travail they had lived through together, and what they had also borne on their own. He carried, for life, the imprint of his journey with Godscalc, and of the two years that followed. She, in turn, had in his absence faced and conquered an alien city, and had single-handed fought her way back to the Gambia with Godscalc, sick and suffering, and brought him successfully home.

Even now, it was not perhaps enough to make the union they should have had, but for Katelina. Tonight he had said nothing of the future; had not wanted to speak; nor had she. She had not wanted to disengage either, holding him with a kind of ferocity before suddenly letting him go.

He had said, 'Gelis? It's your cousin's house. We don't know what we want ourselves yet.'

And she had risen as she was, and lit the lamp and, taking a brush, drawn it slowly down the length of her hair. She was different from Katelina. And everywhere, she was fair.

He said, 'Come to Spangnaerts Street tomorrow, and see Godscalc. We can talk.' He was half dressed.

The brush moved slowly down. She said, 'I have to go to Scotland next month.' The long strands lay between her breasts, and outside them. She held the ends of her hair in one hand.

Nicholas said, 'Don't make it difficult.'

'Why not?' said Gelis. She was still brushing when he opened the door, and held it, and went out.

It was not so late, and he should, perhaps, have expected that Godscalc's lamp would be lit when he returned, and that Gregorio would still be sitting by the priest's bed, relating all that had happened. They had heard him at the gate, and greeted him, smiling, when he joined them. Godscalc said, 'You have had a great reception, I hear. You deserve what you have had.'

There was a benignity in his smile, and in Gregorio's. Nicholas wondered, not for the first time, what sixth sense men possessed that enabled them to detect this particular activity even when, as now, its level was markedly wanting. He supposed they guessed who his partner had been.

Godscalc had so far talked little of Gelis, beyond praising her devotion on the voyage. There had been no pastoral admonitions. Gelis and Nicholas were being trusted to reach their own decisions uninfluenced. That there were decisions to be made must have been obvious.

Nicholas said, 'The Gruuthuse family did me great honour. I think perhaps I have found a niche for Astorre and the army, from what I hear of Duke Charles. And I saw Gelis. She is returning to Scotland.'

'Before the Duke's wedding. The postponement has thrown everything out,' Godscalc said. 'Gelis seems to enjoy the young Scottish princess's household. Wolfaert's niece. The girl is only sixteen, and already married a year.'

'And we are to have a wedding here?' Gregorio said. 'Diniz has returned to his chaste bed at his uncle's, but not before he and Tilde told us all. I am glad you agreed.'

'It was a difficult decision,' Nicholas said. He let himself down on a stool and, leaning back on the wall, stretched his legs. 'They don't want to marry until Lucia comes. They've sent to tell her.'

'Is that wise?' Godscalc said. Since Nicholas came, he had been smiling most of the time.

'She was coming anyway,' Gregorio said. 'For the ducal wedding.

The Vasquez connection. All the Scots who trade in Flanders are coming. I've also written to the Vatachino and Simon. But you don't want to talk business.'

'Yes, I do,' Nicholas said. 'Tomorrow, perhaps. I want to hear what you've done in Madeira; and what Simon said when he saw Diniz was alive, and he had to hand back half the business. And what he did when he found he was sharing the profits of the *Fortado* with David de Salmeton. I wish I'd been there.'

'It was quite a satisfying experience,' Gregorio said. 'He is, I fear, a vain, naughty man. And his son Henry, I can tell you, is his unpleasant mirror.'

Nicholas remained leaning back, without blinking. Godscalc said, 'Children grow up. This Henry is young. Why don't you make Nicholas wretched with the rest of the news? Tell him about the two ships.'

'Simon's son was in Madeira?' Nicholas said. 'Why?'

'To see you executed, principally,' Gregorio said. 'As a treat. The child should have been put down at birth. He cut Bel's shins to ribbons when she wouldn't do what he demanded. And angelic, withal. All the wonderful looks of his father.'

'Bel took him north,' Godscalc said. 'He is only a child. The problem, as I understand it, is that ownership of the *Ghost* may be harder to prove than we thought. Even with Tobie and ourselves to swear to what happened. Jordan says he gave Simon the ship, and you killed his factor and stole it in Trebizond. Everybody else who knew the true facts is dead.'

'How awkward,' Nicholas said.

'You don't want to know. It's late,' Gregorio said. 'We'll fight it, of course. But the other difficulty is the lost cargo. You see, even if we won our claim for the ship, we still couldn't admit she'd been trading. There is no way we can claim the lost gold if we found it. And as for the *Fortado* . . .'

'Spare him the *Fortado*,' Godscalc said. 'At least – you might as well know that absolutely no uninterested spectator will depone that the *Fortado's* crew slighted your ship or your men on the Gambia. The survivors all swear the crimes were committed by natives. Have we spoiled your day for you?' His smile was not really a smile.

Nicholas said, 'I think it's spoiled for Gregorio rather than for me: he's the man whose work is being frustrated. I don't know if I mind.'

Gregorio sat up. He said, 'That's tonight. You'll feel differently tomorrow.'

'I'm not sure,' Nicholas said. 'I've felt much the same about it

ever since I came back. But if you think you can get anywhere, go
on with it.'

'You don't *want* the *Ghost*?' Gregorio said.

'I should quite like it. I don't need it. There are other things to
be done. The Charetty business to be properly integrated. The
Bank. I think,' Nicholas said, 'we have perhaps paid too much
attention to Simon.'

Gregorio said, 'This is new.'

'Then let it keep until tomorrow. Or later today. Shouldn't you
be in bed?'

These days, Gregorio needed little persuading. He left. Nicholas
remained, sitting over the brazier, the poker in his hands. He said,
without looking at Godscalc, 'I gave Tobie a paper to give or send
to you. Did he?'

'What was in it?' said the priest.

'A deposition,' Nicholas said. 'Signed by Katelina in Cyprus. A
statement that Henry de St Pol is my son.'

'It has not reached me,' Godscalc said. 'But if it does, what do
you want? You cannot claim the child, Nicholas.'

'No. I know that.'

'Then shall I destroy it?'

'No!' said Nicholas. 'That was not why I spoke.'

Godscalc looked at him. He said, 'You may have other children.
What then?'

'You know the truth,' Nicholas said, 'and can swear to it. And
Tobie. And my wife, if I have one. I should like the paper to be
kept. Not for myself, but for the boy, in case he needs to claim
me.'

He saw Godscalc consider his words. The priest said, 'In case,
you are saying, Simon were to turn against the boy? Or in case
Simon died destitute?'

'Both are possible. And against the day, too, when both Simon
and I shall be dead. I have something to leave now,' said Nicholas.
He rose. 'But there is no need for Gregorio to know who the child
is, and be sorry. I've alarmed him enough, without that.' He
paused at the door. 'Sleep well. Gelis is coming to see you tomorrow.'

'Indeed!' said Father Godscalc with gentle irony. 'Today, life is
full of surprises.'

It was a short night. The first call Nicholas made in the morning
was to the house of João Vasquez, to ratify the betrothal between
his step-daughter and Diniz. The marriage already had João's blessing: Diniz had assured him of that yesterday morning. There

would be no dispute, Nicholas knew, over the conditions. He hoped he would be forgiven for announcing it so precipitately. Seeing Jordan, he had suddenly felt impelled to have the union made unassailably public.

Now, he was relieved to find himself welcomed by the family into which Simon's sister had married. None of Simon's accusations seemed to have taken root here; or if they had ever been entertained, Diniz had dispelled them. When Tristão his father had died, it was at the hand of another assassin.

He would be meeting the Duchess's secretary again, when the Duke and Duchess received him in due course at the Princenhof. As they had wished to question and entertain Diniz, so the nobles and merchants of Bruges wished, with far deeper purpose, to assess the older man who, with no evident guidance or patronage, appeared to be making such arbitrary business alliances – with the Venetians, with the Portuguese, with (but it had come to nothing, thank God) even the Pope.

Nicholas knew what lay behind the invitations which, by herald or secretary or porter, poured each day into the Charetty–Niccolò mansion. He had a bank, and connections. He was too powerful, now, to be left to do as he pleased.

None of that was overtly referred to in the house of João Vasquez, but even so, Nicholas found himself surprised twice.

On the first occasion, Nicholas himself had brought up the name of the caravel *Fortado,* whose joint shareholders he was taking to court. Diniz was with him.

'I know of this,' João had said. 'I think Raffaelo Doria was a man not to be trusted, and I am prepared to believe that he did as you say. If it can be proved, it is right that the shareholders who employed him should be penalised. The fact that one of them is Simon my brother-in-law should have no effect on this marriage. The king of Portugal has his due from the cargo, and that is all that interests my country. Further, I take it that your own challenge expects restitution in ducats? You have no desire to possess the *Fortado* yourself?'

'I have no wish for another caravel,' Nicholas said.

'That is as well,' said João Vasquez, 'since I have to tell you that the *Fortado* no longer exists. She came to grief between Madeira and England, when charged by me with a cargo of sugar.' He paused. 'I fail to remember, Diniz, if I told you I had taken the ship when she ended her Guinea trip? The patron and the insurers, of course, have had some cause for distress. She was heavily insured.'

No one spoke. 'With whom?' Nicholas said.

'Let me see. A Genoese called Jacques Doria, I believe. And the patron was Alfonse Martinez. The name is very similar to another one hears. I trust they are of the same family.'

'Uncle!' said Diniz.

'Unless you think that unchristian?' said João Vasquez.

The other matter was different. The final matter raised in that quiet panelled room with its small, high windows forced to a close something that should have been closed long ago, and arose so suddenly it took Nicholas unawares.

They were talking of consanguinity: a marital link between Tilde's aunt and the first wife of Diniz' uncle which, they had already agreed, was too remote to impede the coming marriage. 'Unless,' added João Vasquez, 'undue emphasis comes to be laid on it publicly because of the closer connection. Diniz tells me, Ser Niccolò, that you are yourself related to the first wife of Simon de St Pol.'

Diniz said, 'Senhor!' He had flushed.

His uncle looked at him, and then at Nicholas. He said, 'I am sorry, Diniz. You told me in confidence, but there is no one here but ourselves. It is of importance to the marriage.'

'It doesn't matter,' Nicholas said. 'Anyone who wished could find it out. Sophie de Fleury was my mother.'

'That is the lady of whom we speak? The first wife of Simon my brother-in-law? And your father?'

'I told you –' said Diniz. He stood up.

'You told me,' said João Vasquez, 'that this gentleman, regarded – forgive me – as illegitimate, might not be so; might in fact be the legitimate son of Simon and his wife. If that were to be publicly proved, it would constitute a second and much stronger link. We should then require, I believe, a dispensation before you could marry.'

He looked from Nicholas up to his nephew. He was a soft-spoken man, black-haired as his brother had been, but with the extra bloom, the extra craft of the courtier. 'Sit down, Diniz,' he said. 'As you see, Ser Niccolò is not disturbed. We shall reach conclusions perfectly well, and nothing need be said of it outside this room unless we wish it. Ser Niccolò: is it probable that you will in time pursue this contention of yours, and that you will succeed?'

In the desert, what mattered was friendship, not consanguinity. Friendship; and truth, where it could be spoken without causing harm. Nicholas said, 'If there ever was such a claim, I do not mean to renew it. Regard me as the natural son of Sophie de Fleury. If I require a family, or a cousin, I shall choose one.' And he sent a smile, full of reassurance, to Diniz.

He made the rest of the encounter as brief as he could, but, on leaving, could not prevent Diniz walking with him towards the gate in the garden, or giving voice to his tumbling apologies. Eventually Nicholas stopped and turned. 'I didn't bind you to silence over my mother. Many people know who she was. I hope Tilde does, and that if she doesn't, you'll tell her. What I believe or believed about my father can be forgotten about.'

'Not by me,' Diniz said. 'I saw your son in Madeira.'

They were in a small orchard. There was no one else there. Nicholas said, 'That is not something you should ever say.'

'I know,' Diniz said. 'You don't need to speak. I guessed. Gregorio doesn't know. I won't tell anyone else. I realised in Famagusta. Simon himself doesn't know, does he? He brought the boy to Madeira to watch you die at his hand. Nicholas!'

'I'm sorry,' Nicholas said. 'I'm not going to admit to any of that. Henry is Simon's son.'

'I know. He has to be,' Diniz said. 'I suppose you've given him up. I suppose there's nothing you can do about it; I see that. But Nicholas – he is the image of Simon.'

'Then he must be Simon's son,' Nicholas said. 'Goodbye, Diniz.'

Nicholas left without looking back, but conscious that the boy was standing still, staring after him. Now it was over, he experienced a great relief, of the kind he had felt in the presence of Umar. He had already decided to rid himself of this burden, and now it was done.

He remembered, then, that Gelis was coming, and thought that, for once, self-abnegation was about to receive its reward.

She came in the evening, as he hoped she would. The time between, he occupied with his own business: with Gregorio and his staff in the Banco di Niccolò, studying the ledgers and reading the reports sent back by Julius. He saw, through Margot's eyes, the change in Gregorio: the assurance of Venice added to the personal labour, the heart-felt pioneering of Madeira, coupled with a burning sense of injustice. Gregorio would not readily allow the Lomellini, the Vatachino or Simon de St Pol to escape their deserts.

After that, Nicholas had gone to the Charetty, and talked to Cristoffels and let Tilde and Catherine show him what they had done. Tilde, large-eyed and blushing, had held him back at the end, his hand in both of hers. 'You like him, too?'

And he had put back her hair and held her face with his hands: the face that would never be as bright as Marian's, but which had Marian's eyes, and her brother's terrible nose, and all his own childhood locked somewhere inside it, and said, 'I like him. And

Felix and your mother would have loved him. All you need to do is love him as well.'

When Gelis came, he was away at the dyeworks, sitting on a bench among the familiar vats, trying to hold a serious conversation about orchella while being side-tracked by all the jokes and gossip and laughter that you got from men you had known since you were ten. He had given up, in the end, and ordered a barrel of ale and they were all drinking it when the servant came running. He was required at Spangnaerts Street to welcome a guest.

It was Gelis van Borselen, of course, who could diagnose a man in liquor whether she was lying unclothed by a pool among Negroes or dressed from breast to hem in meticulous velvet, with a fine, bulbous hat on her head. Her hair, which he had cause to know was well brushed, was out of sight, wrapped round her head. She said, 'Fermented liquor again?'

'They keep slipping it into my cup,' Nicholas said, 'in the hope that I'll ravish them.'

'I'm sure,' she said, 'that Henninc has been trying hard for a very long time. I want to see Godscalc.'

'He's here,' Nicholas said. 'You'll have to help me up the stairs.'

He was a little drunk and thankful for it, for, once in Godscalc's room, whatever they planned, Timbuktu enclosed them. Godscalc and Gelis knew it almost as he did; and hungered to talk. The common irritations: the sand, the wind, the heat, the insects. The exotica they had described to others so often: the apes, the parrots, the river-horses, the lions, the elephants.

The people they had not described. Once, in Venice, Julius had mentioned a blackamoor he had acquired for his boat and Nicholas, frozen, had asked what tribe he belonged to, and had seen the uncomprehending expression in the other man's face. All that, he and Godscalc and Gelis shared as, for a shorter time, had Diniz and Bel.

They asked him about Umar, and he told them a little, and a little more of the journey to Taghaza. He fell into dispute with Gelis over the fortifications he had left; and again, over where the canal should be. He criticised the type of wool she had proposed for the weaving-shops. Godscalc said, 'If you are going to quarrel, could you do it somewhere else? I have a headache.'

She was instantly full of remorse. The remorse was as spurious as the headache. Nicholas said, 'May I see you home?'

'I don't know,' said Gelis van Borselen. 'Can you walk?'

He could walk. He walked her to where she was sleeping, which was not the Gruuthuse palace, he discovered, but the van Borselen house, where Wolfaert stayed when in Bruges. It was empty, but for two servants.

At the door he said, 'What do you want of me?'

'A night,' she said.

There was a door at the back. He let himself in, and left by the same way in the morning; and it was like Tendeba, but all enacted in a dream, with one strong, pliant girl. One girl, with the myriad allurements of Tendeba. He tried to tell her, but she laid her palm over his lips, and her body on his, and under it, and between. The morning light showed her spent, and still smiling. He said, 'Gelis. We shall make a child if we go on like this. What do you want?'

'What I am taking from you,' she said. 'I can protect myself. I shall bleed through and after Easter, which will give us both a respite. Is that too womanly for you?'

'And after Easter?' he said.

'We shall have three weeks before I go back to Scotland.'

He said, 'You are going back?'

'Oh, yes,' she said. 'Unless I cannot do without you.'

'Or I cannot do without you?' Nicholas said. And laughed suddenly, for he knew what she was going to say.

'What has that to do with it?' Gelis said.

Nicholas supposed, if Godscalc suspected before, that he must be sure now of what was happening. He himself had never needed much sleep, but the nightly toll left him sometimes light-headed. He stood in his office and leafed through the reports from Julius in Venice; from le Grant in Alexandria; from Valencia; the orders for dyestuffs for the Wedding; and thought mostly of the previous night, and the next one.

She was ingenious in arranging where to meet. The van Borselen house only twice. The next time, at Veere, where he required to go, as was right, to talk to those Scottish merchants who had objected so strongly to the increased market tolls that they had broken off trading in Bruges. He took with him some letters from Bonkle.

She had a boat at Veere, and proved to him, as she had promised, that she could sail. There was room for two of them, and a small sail which took them to a beach which remained deserted all afternoon. Later, he came to his senses and apologised, aware that he had allowed her no respite. Yet she had shown nothing but a powerful compliance. She said, 'If I don't want you, I'll tell you. Gregorio says he saw Katelina's son and disliked him. Does that pain you?'

'Yes,' he said. He felt her naked weight shift on his arm, and looked reflectively upwards. The sky was pale, and the sand lay where it was, without rising. All around them was water.

'You might win him back,' she said. 'Now he has brothers.'

Nicholas looked at her.

Gelis said, 'Didn't you know? A fertile kitchen-maid and now, they say, a well-born maiden whom Simon may have to marry. They say that possessing one child often leads to the siring of others. Simon will have a family.'

'I don't grudge him it,' Nicholas said.

'You envy Umar,' she said in a soft voice.

'I am happy for him,' he said. 'I am also patient.'

She moved a little. Then, rising, she came to stand over him, bare feet apart, damp hair streaking her breasts in the sunlight. 'How patient?' she said, and let herself slowly down. 'This much? Or this? Or will you let me do this, and do nothing?'

'No,' he said; and closed her laughing mouth, and took up his licence to union once again.

At Easter, they parted, she to take her woman's retreat, as she had warned him, and he to take his share in the ceremonies. She had mocked him over his first reaction to her news. 'You were disappointed! You were hoping to discover me pregnant and help-less?'

He said, 'I should like you, yes, to be able to make your decision. I shouldn't want to oppress you with an unwanted marriage or children. It's as well.' In less than four weeks, if she kept to her plan, she would be gone. He wouldn't allow himself to say more than he had. He wouldn't allow himself to say, 'Am I to be only your lover for life? Don't we fit, mind to mind as we do body to body? Or do you still hate and want me at once, because of Katelina?'

The rest of the time, of course, they were in fierce opposition. Even while they were sleeping apart, she would find her way into the Charetty counting-house and browse with Diniz and Tilde through the ledgers, and then burst in on him or on Gregorio later with some violent stricture. 'Do you know what you are lending the town, for their costumes? Why are you not fighting to keep importing the alum you want? What are these terrible fountains? They don't work!'

None of Nicholas's friends knew what to make of it. Gregorio, talking quietly to Godscalc, would say, 'They are exhausting one another. He came back with a strength she hasn't been able, yet, to disturb. But she will destroy herself, if she doesn't make up her mind soon.'

'Margot's assessment?' Godscalc had said. 'I think you are both right, but I also think there is nothing you can do. Gelis is torn between loyalty to her sister and something else. It may be mere fleshly pleasure. In which case, it will fade.'

'Leaving Nicholas where?' Gregorio said.

And Godscalc had said, 'I shall speak to her, Goro. But not yet.'

As if to justify his decision to wait, the weeks after Easter seemed to show Nicholas less beset, and something less inflammatory about his resumed connection with Gelis. However discreet they might be, the occasions were always created: the hunting excursion, the expedition to sail or to shoot which always left them alone, out of Bruges. She had returned to the house of Louis de Gruuthuse, and there, too, one could guess, she had company in her chamber. But between, Nicholas behaved as would any wealthy head of an empire: he conducted his business and visited his fellow merchants, including Tommaso Portinari, manager of the Bruges branch of the Medici of Florence. On that occasion, he took Diniz with him.

Once, an ambitious, struggling deputy, Tommaso Portinari had despised the apprentice Claes and the circle of young men in which he had found himself trapped. Handsome, poor, dependent on the patronage of his family and, over them, of the Medici, he had struggled to be where he now was: not a twelve-year-old junior, but the undisputed controller of the Bruges business; a trusted counsellor of the new Duke; a monopoly supplier of silk; a near-monopoly supplier of alum; a diplomat whose secret letters were welcomed in France, Milan, England. A wealthy, unmarried man of forty-three, whose home was the Hof Bladelin in Naalden Straate, the great turreted house where the treasurer of the Golden Fleece used to hold his receptions at carnival-time.

Tommaso had seen Katelina van Borselen there, the year she had married St Pol. The year the Charetty dyeworks had gone on fire. It pleased him to welcome Claes – Nicholas – now, and the young Vasquez nephew. Tommaso walked across the tiles of his parlour and held out both adorned hands, saying, 'My dear Nicholas, how I have longed to have time for a talk with you. And Diniz, who has become as close to me as his uncle. What will you find tolerable, do you think? A piece of fine sugar candy? My kitchen knows I have a sweet tooth.'

'I shouldn't mind a piece of fat mutton,' Nicholas said, 'rolled up with ground maize and an eyeball. Tomà, it's me. Bought any ostriches lately?'

'I – It's been so long,' said Portinari. At first sight, because he wore no jewels, Nicholas looked the same, except that his face was somehow more hollow, and his eyes amazingly direct. Then you recognised the quality of the hat, and the sleeveless tunic, and the gown over it. Tommaso said quickly, 'We are all so thankful that you came safely back.'

'Are you?' said Nicholas, following his gaze. 'I got the silk off ibn Said in Timbuktu – which reminds me, I've got to settle his debt to you. You may not much like having me back. You're being a damned fool over the alum.'

'I beg your pardon?' Tommaso said. A servant had come into the room. He sent him off, snapping an order.

'Freely granted,' said Nicholas. 'The Pope's got a lot of good alum, and you want to sell it for him, with no competition and at a fine, high old price.'

'The money goes to the Church,' Tommaso said. 'The Duke has agreed to ban all other alum. Why did you go to Ethiopia if you don't support the Christian Church? Or, forgive me, try to go. You failed to get there, I hear.'

'I ran out of candy,' Nicholas said. 'The Duke can agree till he's Ethiopian black in the face, but the merchants will go on taking Turkish alum as well. Myself included.'

It had been a shock. Nevertheless, Tommaso Portinari had met self-made fellows before, with no notion of how to conduct meetings. Wine arrived, and a tray of well-sugared pastries. Portinari said, 'I do sympathise, of course, with your mixed allegiances. To deal in Timbuktu at all, you had to conform to Muslim beliefs. You must have many Muslim friends now.'

'Well, the ibn Said brothers,' Nicholas said. 'Do you still use Benedetto Dei as well? Or is he a Christian?'

'Of course he . . . Benedetto Dei does not live in Timbuktu,' Tommaso said. 'Although he is calling there. He went with the *Ferrandina* to Rhodes and Constantinople last year, and she was expected in Marseilles this spring. He may travel south from the Barbary coast. Is it a difficult journey?'

'Not if you like camels,' Nicholas said. 'And while I remember, here is your commission from Abderrahman ibn Said. He says it should be correct.'

It was a draft on the Banco di Niccolò. Tommaso said, 'I am glad to have it. It must have been difficult, carrying gold such a distance in safety.'

'I brought books instead,' Nicholas said. 'I wanted to ask you. The coastal route, as you've heard, is impossible. Do you think there is room for us both in the Sahara?'

Tommaso stared at him. 'You are considering a Barbary trade?'

'I have enough ships,' Nicholas said. 'Or shall have, when my litigation is over. I find I rather like going to law. What a pity you've let Dei go without revising his contracts. Never mind. How are your brothers?'

Walking back to Spangnaerts Street, Diniz said, 'That was disgusting.' He was still red with laughter.

'I know,' Nicholas said. 'He was always easy to tease. He can command, and he can fawn, but he can never be anyone's equal. Take it as a terrible warning.'

'Did you mean it?' Diniz said. They had reached the Charetty–Niccolò yard. 'You won't take the caravel route, but you might join the trade through the Sahara?'

'I don't know yet,' Nicholas said. It was a reply Diniz was becoming tired of.

'But you'll buy Turkish alum?' Diniz persisted. 'Bessarion and the others won't like it.'

'I shall have to,' Nicholas said. 'Look. Come into my room. Not the counting-house. I had a visitor yesterday.'

Diniz had been in this parlour before. It was smaller than the great chamber in Venice, and inconvenient, and rather impersonal. He sat down while Nicholas hitched himself on the high stool at his desk. The desk was covered with drawings.

Nicholas said, 'Do you remember Bartolomeo Zorzi? You will do. He came to offer me a great opportunity. The rights to sell papal alum in Venice and the whole of the region beside it. The Curia and the Medici have fallen out, and the Pope is inclined to seek other agents. Zorzi is one of the most skilled, but is bankrupt. He needs capital to buy basic stocks, and if I will provide it, I shall share in the profit. What do you think?'

Elbows on desk, he played with a pen and, lifting it, held it level between his two hands. It was a quill, of the kind they filled with gold dust in Wangara. Diniz said, 'He was manager of the dyeworks in Cyprus. You apprenticed me under him. He encouraged me when I wanted to kill you, and let me escape, knowing I would end in Famagusta, and you and Katelina would come. He killed Katelina, in a way.'

Nicholas said, 'Yes. The Vatachino expelled him from the dyeworks and he set up here in Bruges, and then failed. This offers a fortune. He doesn't like either me or the Vatachino, but he would ask me first, because of his brother.'

'And you said?' Diniz asked. And then flushed and said, 'I'm sorry.'

'No. I might have been hard-headed enough to agree, but I wasn't. I rather think I told him what to do with his alum. I shall have to buy it, to a degree – everyone will. But I shall make it up, as I've said, with its Muslim equivalent. You approve?'

'Yes,' said Diniz. 'I had forgotten.'

'What?'

'That it was you who placed me in the dyeworks in Cyprus. To humiliate me, everyone thought.'

'Well, that was a damned failure, too,' Nicholas said. 'Look at you.'

Diniz said, 'So you meant me to come here.'

Nicholas laid down the quill and left the stool. He said, 'Only if you wanted to. It was your own choice.'

'And Tilde?' Diniz said.

Nicholas didn't answer.

Diniz said, 'I should like to think that you meant that as well. I hope you did. I've been afraid that perhaps it was not what you wanted.'

'It was what I wanted,' Nicholas said. 'Just occasionally, something comes right. You were going to have half the Ochoa gold for your marriage. Now *there's* a challenge. If you find it, you can keep it, provided they don't hang you first. Go and tell Tilde. You wouldn't think it, but I have some work to do.'

Then May came, and the time for Gelis to leave.

Chapter 41

YOU WOULD SAY THAT, when everyone else was celebrating in the streets, a private life would be easy, but in these last weeks Nicholas had not found it so.

It was, of course, the first spring of the Duke's accession, and although he had already made his restless, moody, thorough entry into his town of Bruges (as he had done or was about to do in his other towns throughout Flanders and Burgundy), Charles returned to it in May. So Bruges found itself occupied by the Court, and witnessing the three-day gathering of the eleventh Chapter of the Duke's Golden Fleece Order, and the Holy Blood procession on top, with every street filled with banners and choirs and platforms with actors and singers.

As once at St Omer, Gregorio saw parade before him the thirteen Knights in their collars and robes, Henry van Borselen and Louis de Gruuthuse among them. And Diniz, soldier of Ceuta, met again the Duke's half-brother Antony, and spoke to Simon de Lalaing, remnant of the flower of chivalry. The Duke himself received Nicholas at the Princenhof, and questioned him about his adventures. His interest seemed to be part commercial, part religious and part romantic: Nicholas did his best to conform.

Charles, by the grace of God Duke of Burgundy, Lothier, Brabant and Limbourg and Count of Flanders, Holland and Zeeland, was less comely, Nicholas thought, than the late Timbuktu-Koy and, he suspected, not as shrewd. The Chapter of the Fleece, with boyish hilarity, had reprimanded the Duke for his reckless yearning for battle, and, with Arthurian gallantry, he had admitted it.

As to the possession of mistresses and wives, Duke Charles couldn't even rank with King Gnumi. The Duke's first two wives were dead, and the one he was about to marry was a well-used maiden, they said, who had given birth to at least one live child, stupid girl. But an English alliance was necessary, and the King's sister was the only royal bride then on offer.

After the audience had dragged to its end, it was made known to Nicholas that the Duke expected him to attend the bridal celebrations. 'As the ape,' Nicholas said, describing the complete scene to Gelis. 'I come on between the dwarves and the unicorn. I've become the Guinea Minstrel of Burgundy. Why won't you take your clothes off?'

'Because I can't,' Gelis said. 'As at Easter. Nicholas, I'm sorry. I'm as sorry as you are.'

'*Christ!*' said Nicholas, and gave a half-laugh. 'No, you can't be as sorry as I am.'

It was the last night he and Gelis had together before her ship sailed for Scotland, and they spent it in the Charetty–Niccolò mansion, where Tilde had kept her a chamber. The reason was genuine enough: the houses of Gruuthuse and Borselen were full of knights and their retinues. The excuse by that time hardly mattered. Before the household was fully abed, Gelis came to his room.

He had known he would pass the night awake, but not seated in stillness at a window, with Gelis in her chemise, white as his, at his knee, her head and arms laid in his lap. She said, 'You would make a very good ape.'

'I have been practising,' Nicholas said.

Her head moved under his hand. In the moonlight, he could see the curve of her cheek, and her lashes, and the profile of her nose. It was red. 'You're not a plaything. Don't pretend you could be,' she said. 'Anyway, you've reached perfection. You don't need to practise.'

'I enjoy it,' he said. His throat ached. He said, 'I wanted more. Tonight. Or even always.'

'I know,' Gelis said.

He waited, as he had learned to wait, and gazed out of the window. The stars were different. It was hard even to discover the stars, because of the glow of the city. Hung on the sky, he could see the ghosts of coquettish gables, and the round glass eyes of casements, and a branch of lilac blossom, swaying in lamplight. He thought of space, and slowly everything quietened, even his cheated senses.

Gelis said, 'Sometimes, I am afraid of your patience. If I said – I still don't know; wait for me twenty-five years? What would you do?'

'Express astonishment,' Nicholas said. 'Anyone who can act as you do doesn't need twenty-five years to decide whom to marry. I've seen you shoot to kill with a crossbow. This should be easier.'

He felt her cheek move as she smiled, but she didn't change her position. She said, 'We are discussing marriage?'

He said, 'I thought we had managed to come round to it at last. You said, I think, that if you didn't want me, you'd tell me. You also said. . .' He didn't finish.

'That I was going to Scotland, unless I couldn't manage without you. You know this Princess Mary in Scotland?' Gelis said. She lifted her head. The place where it had lain felt damp and rather cold.

Nicholas said, 'You've been serving her. She's seventeen, and the Scottish King's older sister, and has married into a family who have rather a questionable grip on her brother's kingdom just now. They say King James wept at her wedding.' He recited it. Gelis was sitting apart on the floor, her hands on her knees. She wasn't looking at him.

'Thomas Boyd,' she remarked. 'Boyd is the name of the family who are trying to dominate Scotland. King James is sixteen, and his brother, the one who stayed in Bruges, is three years younger. Bishop Kennedy, who would have helped them resist this, is dead.'

'And you want to advise them?' Nicholas said. 'Canals and carpet-weaving, and how to get their fountains in order?' She had spent endless hours rearranging the table fountains he had had made in Venice.

Gelis said, 'Mary's husband is to go away in July. Thomas Boyd. He's to go to Denmark to arrange a royal marriage. She could be pregnant.'

'I understand all that,' Nicholas said. 'Gelis. Would you sit on a chair, and let me look at your face? It's a nice face, and I feel I shan't be seeing it for very much longer.'

He stayed quiet. After a moment, without otherwise moving, she turned her face to him. Then he said, 'Wait,' and rose.

The brazier glowed by the bed. He lit a lamp from a taper and, bringing it back, stood it on the table beside them. She didn't protest. After a moment, he sat down again.

He said, 'At least, if you are weeping, it hasn't been easy. I can say goodbye, Gelis, if I must. We exhaust one another. We quarrel. The bond we have from what we found on the journey may come to mean less. And you cannot forgive me, or forget.'

It seemed better that he should say it. She kept her eyes fixed on him throughout; pale blue eyes liquid with tears. Before he finished, her eyes on him still, she gave a short, barking sob, followed by others. Then she gulped and silenced herself. Her face was still contorted.

Nicholas said, 'Oh, no, Gelis!' and made to kneel with her.

'No,' she said. 'I'm sorry. It's . . . I don't know what it is. I need a handkerchief.'

He gave her one, and she used it. He said, 'It's the time of the month; I should know. I always get –'

'You always get hurt then,' she finished. Her face, roughly dried, was patched and pink, and her eyes were deep-set and enormous. She sniffed, and rose to her feet. The front of her chemise was soaked. He could see the pink and dark-pink of her breasts, as if through buttered silk. He found he was very tired.

Gelis said, 'Now I shall sit at your desk, and you will stay where you are, and I shall say to you what has to be said. Do you know that Godscalc spoke to me tonight?'

She had reached his desk by now, on its dais, and was perched where he usually sat. She picked up the quill he had picked up when Diniz came.

'About us?' he said. He had shut the casement and turned, so that he could face her.

'About you,' she said. 'He said that, whatever I felt, you had a destiny that must be fulfilled, and that nothing petty should stand in the way. He said he felt you had found the way you were looking for, and wanted a partner. He said that he was not surprised that your choice had fallen on me, for I was in all things your complement.'

'That at least is true,' Nicholas said. 'Here and there, we have proved it.'

'Don't!' she said. 'Nicholas, don't. He said that you would accept me, without question, if I offered myself. He said the responsibility was mine, to bring you what was sound, and not what was secretly blighted. He said if I had any doubts about this at all, I should leave you for ever.'

Nicholas said, 'What it is to have friends. I carried him . . .' He shut off the words, and his eyes, with his palms.

She said, 'Oh, Nicholas. Nicholas.'

He took his hands down. He said, 'Tell me, then. Gelis, I won't blame you, or harm you, or think ill of you. After all – did I tell you? – I love you. As it happens, I have said that to nobody else.'

She looked at him. She said, 'I am going to Scotland. I have a duty. I want to fulfil it. I am afraid, too, of exactly the things you have mentioned. We may be natural mates, but not partners. What we have gone through together may run through our fingers. You have found a way of thinking, and I might destroy it. We need to separate for a while.'

He drew a long breath, and held it. Then he said, 'Not outright rejection? Look. I am sitting prepared for it.' His head swam.

'No,' she said. 'No, my idiot Nicholas, no. But a space of six weeks to consider. I am going to Scotland. You will hear my answer from Lucia.'

'Lucia?' he said. He thought of Lucia: the perfect hair, the screams in the bedroom in Lagos.

'She is travelling to Bruges for the Wedding. If I stay to lead my own life, she will tell you.'

'And if not?' he said.

'Then,' she said, 'I shall be on the same ship.'

She left presently: the shortest night but one they had ever spent together. The next day he went to Sluys to see the Scottish ship sail, and Godscalc, riding awkwardly on an old mule, accompanied him. Gelis was already there, surrounded by her van Borselen family. She kissed him chastely goodbye, and commanded her page, as she went, to deliver to him a leave-taking parcel. A gift, she said, in token of the many small kindnesses she had received from him.

Long after the ship had moved out, he saw her face as she said it, the deep-set eyes wide, the lips pinched and curled at the corners.

When he was home, he opened the parcel. It was a working model, in wood and metal, of a table fountain. It solved the Baroviers' three problems of linkage. He could hear, now, the critical van Borselen voice, and his own belated, tolerant answers. Godscalc said, 'What is that?'

'A reproach,' Nicholas said. 'But a clever one.'

Those who knew Nicholas, and suspected what had happened, treated him each according to their natures in the six weeks that followed. Tobias Beventini his physician arrived, accompanied by Captain Astorre, the head of his mercenary army. Tobie, having summed up the communal health problem of the double company, threw himself into the hilarious revival of friendships, interspersed with long sessions with Father Godscalc, spent partly on manipulating his hands, and partly on arguing about medical literature. From Godscalc, he learned all he needed to know about Nicholas and, as a result, left Nicholas to himself.

Astorre, to whom Nicholas was a mascot, slapped him on the back, asked a couple of questions (purely anatomical) about the Empire of the Blacks, and demanded to be taken to the seigneur of Gruuthuse, seeing that he had the right sort of men for the seigneur's cannon.

Julius arrived three weeks later, disinclined to be apologetic about having left the Bank to itself in order to attend the Duke of Burgundy's wedding. He said if Tobie came, he didn't see why he should miss all the fun. He wanted to know if it were true that Tilde de Charetty was going to marry the Portuguese boy, and the Charetty and the Bank were to merge? He wanted to know why Nicholas hadn't come back to Venice.

Gregorio, acting as a one-man Bruges reception committee, assured Julius that he would see Nicholas soon, and that they had all found it hard to plan, because of the upheaval caused by the Wedding. 'I can see that,' Julius said. 'Every street being repaved and scaffolding everywhere else. All the same. Is Nicholas doing any work? The *Ghost*. The *Fortado*. The missing gold. Nothing done about anything. I don't know how you've found it in Bruges, but in Venice he just walked through the day as if it didn't much matter. Of course, the Bank does run itself, in a way.'

'What more do you want?' Gregorio said. But, of course, it was true in Bruges as well. Gregorio had tried to set up enquiries and meetings, but so far nothing had come of them, because Nicholas largely ignored them. Nicholas worked, but not as he once had.

During this period Nicholas worked mainly, truth to tell, on the contrivances for the Duke of Burgundy's wedding.

It began with a project so properly his that he hardly needed a cry for help from the town's master carpenter to engage on it. From that followed other requests, tentative, plaintive or actively frenzied. Accustomed to the sufferings inflicted on all the Guilds and city technicians by the normal celebrations of a Bruges year, Nicholas had missed the Duke's father's funeral and was not born when the Duke's parents had married at Sluys. He had had no idea until now of what was actually entailed in a royal wedding involving two weeks of festivities, six banquets, and a joust every day in the marketplace. When he found out, he went to the master of ceremonies and said, mildly, 'Use me.'

When he was not there to greet Julius, and had not entered the Charetty–Niccolò doors for two days, Julius lost his temper. 'Where is he?'

They were eating in the Charetty common-room, because it was bigger. The premises, once enough for Catherine and Cristoffels and Tilde, had already overflowed in the form of sheds into the gardens Tobie said, 'How should I know? Ask Gregorio. With the blacksmiths designing the waterworks, or the carpenters producing the show-pieces. At the Fox with Goeghebuer and the masons. Getting tents out of the sail-makers, or tapestries out of the weavers. On the streets putting up booths, or up a ladder painting something elaborate with Hennekaert or Coustain or Hugo or Colard.'

'The bastard!' said Julius enviously. 'He'll be pissed from morning to night. I remember.'

'You remember him at eighteen,' said Gregorio dryly.

Nicholas had not been drunk since the work started, which had been quite a feat, considering the company he kept. He felt he owed them his best: guilds were guilds, and but for the emergency he would never have been allowed to meddle. As it was, he was working side by side, day and night, with the best and most ingenious craftsmen there were. Hence, when he did actually arrive in the middle of the meal, Julius, viewing him critically, saw a kind of vitality which had been lacking in Venice, even if coupled with a disappointing sobriety.

Julius got up and, walking to Nicholas, greeted him with a slap on his back, which was dirty. 'Well, thank God you've put the hermit behind you. What have you found to waste your time on now? And you've packed the lady friend off, so they tell me. That was a damn fool escapade. Stick to the Mabelie type.'

Even to Julius, the silence was startling. Then Nicholas began, quite genuinely, to laugh. 'Welcome back, Julius,' he said. 'Give me a Mabelie, and I'll stick to her. Do you know what else you've missed? Remember the bath you and I floated to Damme? I've just floated another from Brussels.'

'Another bath?' said Julius, sitting down, cheered.

'No. What do you think of a timber banqueting-hall seventy feet wide by a hundred and forty feet long by sixty feet high, with five double windows fourteen feet high, and two gables? Horses bolted and women gave birth as we passed.'

'But you did it.'

'I did it. It is here.'

'And what else?' Julius said.

'Come and see,' Nicholas answered, smiling.

It would have been better if he had had Nicholas to himself, but Gregorio wanted to go, and then Diniz – the boy, the foreign boy who had somehow got round Tilde. It was too late, Julius assumed, to do anything constructive about that; but he was extremely glad (as, after all, he had said) that Nicholas had stopped making a fool of himself over the van Borselen girl, who had no money, and who had chased him all the way to Africa on the pretext that he was murdering his rivals in business.

Well, she'd had a change of heart, from what he heard. And having made the most of it for six weeks, Nicholas had shown her what he really thought by throwing her out. That was the interpretation Julius had heard. He had tried to pump Father Godscalc about it, and Father Godscalc had dropped off to sleep.

The work Nicholas was doing proved to be all over Bruges: they'd tented the streets near the marketplace where the lists were going up, and near the Princenhof where the Duke would give the banquets for his bride. Some of the guilds were still trying to work in their houses, but wagons kept coming in from Dijon and Lille with harness and tapestries and furnishings to be fixed: all movement in the centre of Bruges was reduced to a compressed and bad-tempered crawl.

The mechanics were in a warehouse near the Princenhof, remarkable for its size, the number of people in it, and the sheer volume of imprecations filling the air. The sound of hammering was interspersed with curious noises which turned out to be a group of mermaids, squeezed out from neighbouring premises, who were attempting a chorus.

'Bloody awful lyrics,' said Nicholas equably. 'They're to sit in the whale. All that is the labours of Hercules. Don't go near them; they broke their mountain, and they're all blaming Theseus. That's the fire-eating dragon, and that's a man with a spit, toasting the birds that were meant to fly out of the griffon. That's a copy of the tower of Gorcum, and that's a goat playing the flute. There is also a consort of wolves, apes and boars. They're terrible too, but I'm working on them. Now come and see this. Mind the dwarves.'

They passed a unicorn, a singing lion, and a leopard with a daisy in its hand. Gregorio lingered.

'A marguerite. Her name's Margaret,' Nicholas said, ducking. An acrobat hurtled over his head, calling to him in English. Everyone knew Nicholas, and he knew everybody by name. Julius recognised some of the names. Andries. Pieter. Adrien. Joos. They passed some imaginative dispensers of wine, human and bestial. They passed Colard Mansion, up some scaffolding painting a giant, and Hugo vander Goes, on his knees before a row of wet escutcheons. He gave a roar as Nicholas passed, and Nicholas joined him in amiable chorus. *'Fourteen puking sols a day for all this!'*

'Is that all he gets paid?' Julius said.

'I hope so,' Nicholas said. 'It's going to come out of our taxes. You know Canon Scalkin?'

Clearly, Gregorio and Diniz were familiar with the man smiling before them. Long ago, Julius had met the canon of St Peter, maker of miracles. There was one standing in front of him now: a pair of candelabra. Or rather, a pair of towering castles perched upon flowery slopes and backed by seven immense mirrors. Round the slopes spiralled a path, slowly moving, up which rode or walked the effigies of men and women and animals. From each creation extended eight arms ablaze with wax tapers.

The figures moved; a windmill appeared; a dragon leaped, and then vanished. Diniz said, 'How is it done?'

'Ask your friend,' said Canon Scalkin. 'Without the seigneur vander Poele, all would have been lost. It is done from within, by a man. By, you understand, different men. It is a thankless task. Come and see. Nicholas, open the door.'

Later, it seemed to Julius that Nicholas really did not expect what he saw when, moving round to the back of the object, he gripped a projection and turned it. By then, they were all gathered round him. Nicholas opened the door, and stood back.

Within, naked but for his drawers, was a fair-skinned man of powerful build, his legs and arms still forcing onwards the mechanism, his head purposefully down.

The canon said, 'Michael? You may halt now.' The man stopped. The man turned his head. And Julius found he was staring at Michael Crackbene.

The shipmaster of the *Fortado* was not looking at him, or at Diniz, or Gregorio. It was Nicholas who eventually spoke. 'You knew I was here?'

'Of course,' said Crackbene, and returned him an odd, crooked smile. 'I thought we might have something to say to one another: you and I, and a young man I happen to know.'

'Perhaps you would care to come back to my house with me. Canon Jehan,' Nicholas said, 'this is an old shipmate of mine. Would it much interfere with your work if I stole him?'

'Not at all! Not at all!' said the canon. 'My dear Nicholas, what we owe you!'

They left, past the spouting archers, the dribbling pelican, the John the Baptist dispensing showers of experimental water. Julius suddenly shivered.

'I know,' Nicholas said at his side. His other arm was engaged with that of Mick Crackbene. 'John the Baptist is hell for the bladder.'

They wasted no time on the journey, hurrying the seaman back to the house and quickly into the room private to Nicholas. Once there, Gregorio went and fetched Tobie and Godscalc. Both, like Julius, had known Crackbene in Trebizond. Tobie had been there in Cyprus when Crackbene had made off with the *Doria*, now called the *Ghost*. With all of them present, they had a chance of hearing the truth.

Crackbene waited until the six were sitting about him. A stolid man, he did not at once speak and Nicholas, rising, brought him wine, and then gave it to Diniz to serve. Diniz, his eyes cold, kept glancing at Crackbene. It was Gregorio who began. 'Three years ago, you said to me in Madeira that you wished you had sailed with Nicholas, instead of with Doria. But you wouldn't speak out for

Nicholas because you thought he had killed Diniz. Am I right?'

'I owe you something,' said Crackbene to Nicholas. His face, after the Gambia, had remained lined, although the heavy frame had recovered. He said, 'I told your fellow, Gregorio, that bringing home the *Doria* with the boy on it was nothing to do with me. It was a contract with de Ribérac, and the blame lies with him. You'd no call to take me into the ring at Sanlúcar as you did, but you got me out of prison, and you put me ashore, which was more than Doria would have done. Doria went far too far in what he did on the Gambia. I had no part in it. But I heard from his own men what had happened, and the boy knows as well. Filipe.'

'You know where he is?' Nicholas said. He had shown, throughout, no extraordinary excitement.

'He was on the ship with me. When we left, I got him work. Far away from the Vatachino and the rest, I can tell you. I knew they wouldn't trust me to keep quiet.' He broke off. 'Truth to tell, I was hoping you'd bring your case against them, and win it. But you haven't.'

Gregorio said, 'We had only Melchiorre's account of what happened to the ship, and those of the survivors for what happened on land. It was hardly enough.' He paused. 'You meant to meet us. Does this mean you would testify?'

Michael Crackbene, sailing-master, heaved a great sigh. He said, 'I can't go on hiding for ever. They'll find me, one of them. De Salmeton, or the Lomellini, or St Pol. Even Anselm Adorne had shares in the *Fortado*. I'm not safe anywhere, nor is Filipe. Protect us, and we'll testify.'

'Adorne!' Nicholas said.

Crackbene looked up. 'Why? A few shares, not like the others. He's into most kinds of trade.'

'It doesn't matter,' Nicholas said. 'Of course we'll protect you. You'll stay here, with Filipe. No more candelabra. And let's have this law suit over and done with. That is, you would testify also to the *Doria*'s origins? We have to admit she is the *Ghost*, but we also hope to explain that she was a prize, and belonged to us in the first place. And since she was empty, we can't face charges of piracy.'

'Yes,' said Crackbene; and smiled for the first time. 'I was sorry to hear that, considering what she carried when she left the Senagana. I dare say Ochoa de Marchena could tell you a story.'

'If we knew where he was,' Nicholas said.

No one spoke. Diniz, flask in hand, lifted Crackbene's half-empty cup and filled it again. He said, 'I wish I knew, because I've been offered half of it as a gift on my marriage. I'm being married quite soon.'

Crackbene looked up at him. He said, 'She's a lucky girl.'

'And I'm my own man now,' Diniz said. He sat down, his eyes still on the other's.

Crackbene said, 'Ochoa might know. There was a rumour. Someone said he was in Alexandria. He'd be scared, of course. Scared as I was, for other reasons.'

'Do you think he took it?' Gregorio said.

Crackbene pursed his lips. 'Maybe. Maybe he'd got tired of the sea, but I don't think so. And you can't do that kind of thing and keep sailing. I think someone took it, and paid him to say nothing.'

'Who?' Nicholas said.

'Someone who knew it was coming. Someone with a ship able to keep out of the usual ports. Someone who got quite rich – not marvellously so, as I remember – but quite comfortably rich after it happened. I don't know.'

'Neither do I,' Nicholas said. 'But thank you for telling us. You won't suffer by it. I have a few ships and need masters. All we have to do is settle these cases. Gregorio? Soon?'

'Soon, if I had my way,' said Gregorio. 'But not as soon as you'd like. I've taken this up with the magistrates. It seemed to me it would suit us to have this settled in Bruges, with your reputation as it is, Nicholas, and no one much enamoured of France. They're willing to allow us to put it to arbitration, but to do that, they need someone representing the Lomellini as well, and the Vatachino, and Simon de St Pol on his own behalf and on his father's. And two of the three are not here.'

'Which two?' Julius said.

Gregorio looked at him. 'The Lomellini are willing to be represented by their kinsman in Bruges, Senhor Gilles. St Pol and David de Salmeton are at present in Scotland. However, I heard today they are returning in time for the Wedding. Nicholas? Simon is coming to Bruges with his sister. The date I have is the third week in June. As soon as they come, we can start the proceedings.'

'Christ!' said Julius. His own face smiling, he looked round the others. Crackbene smiled in return.

Julius said, 'Well? What's wrong with that?'

'Nothing,' said Nicholas. 'We'd all been longing to know when Simon was coming to Bruges. And now we have a date. I think we should celebrate.'

Gregorio cleared his throat. He said, 'We certainly have something to celebrate.'

'Well, come on!' Julius said. 'Another flask! It's not so long to wait. And when he comes, I suggest we all go down to Damme to meet him.'

'Yes. We probably should,' Nicholas said.

Chapter 42

ONCE, ON A SUNLIT September day nine years before, three young men in a bath had sailed along the canal from the port of Sluys to the port of Damme, and set in train all that was happening today.

One of the young men, Felix, was dead. One, Julius, the ambitious notarial secretary, was now a major shareholder in a bank, and a competent manager, and reasonably wealthy. One had become the founder-owner of what promised to be the richest business in Europe, and was the first man on earth to lead an expedition up the River of Gold, and find his way to Timbuktu from the west. Claes, they had called him when he was eighteen. Now his name was Nicholas vander Poele, Knight of the Sword.

All his friends went to Damme with Nicholas on the day the Scottish ship was due to arrive. She was to sail into Sluys, and her passengers were to take boat for Damme, where horses for Bruges would await them. These were the Scots merchants come for the English–Burgundy wedding. They included Simon de St Pol and Lucia his sister. They included David de Salmeton of the Vatachino trading and brokerage company. Nicholas did not expect them to include anyone else who concerned him.

He had known, from the start, that the others would insist on accompanying him. Julius, because he was Julius. Gregorio and Tobie, Godscalc and Diniz because they knew what they knew, and wanted to protect him from Julius. Nicholas thought, with a shaft of amusement, that he would probably have found it less trying with Julius blundering about on his own. She wouldn't come. There was no point in pretending that she would.

The day was cloudy and warm. The city officers waiting under their banners were not unlike those waiting nine years ago, except that their dress left something to be desired. With the English

bride due in four days, every last ruby was already sewn on somewhere else.

There were a few Scots in attendance among them. The Bonkles,
waiting to welcome their John. Metteneye, who ran the Scots
hostel, and Stephen Angus, their agent. No churchmen: Bishop
Kennedy was dead, and John de Kinloch was not here. Two
members of the van Borselen family: Paul the bastard, and Wolfaert
his father, to greet Lucia, who had served his Scots wife. And, of
course, João Vasquez, the brother of Lucia's late husband.

And someone else. Anselm Adorne, with his elegant clothes and
his fair, ascetic face, stood as he had stood all those years before
and said quietly, 'Nicholas? May I guess why you have been
avoiding me?'

Nicholas had called on him once, it was true, but not again.
Nicholas said, 'I thought it might be embarrassing.'

'Because of the *Fortado*?' Adorne said. 'I have many ventures,
Nicholas. If the men who ran it were knaves, then they should be
exposed. I deserve any loss I may suffer. Don't let it come between
us. Not now.'

'Very well,' Nicholas said, with a smile. With both dimples
deployed, rather absently. Nine years ago, he had ended flounder-
ing there in the water, and had been beaten for it. If he had been
standing on dry land, like this: if he had worn a fine, shady hat,
and an embroidered shirt, and a gold-trimmed pourpoint and
doublet; if his hose had been long and embroidered and silken, his
boots of kid, his sword buckled with jewels; would Katelina have
married him? And then, would he have met Gelis?

The barge was coming. They could never sail a ship up to
Damme. The luggage was transferred to lighters, and the
prestigious passengers came like this, on a grand barge. Not quite
as grand, he thought, vaguely, as the one Julius had bought him in
Venice. He scanned the people it carried.

Jannekin Bonkle, of the button eyes and large, florid face, to
whom he had confided certain business. Jannekin Bonkle, signalling
success, and clutching his hat, which the signal knocked off.

Lucia de St Pol, with the towering headdress over hair of
remorseless bright yellow, who sat extruding her chin as if she
would scour him with it. Lucia, displeased.

David de Salmeton. Oh, yes. David of the soft, dark coiffure and
charming face and long-lashed, perfect eyes; holding the silken
swathes of his hat with one white, fine-fingered hand and smiling
at him. Nicholas bowed.

Bel. Why had he not expected that? Bel of Cuthilgurdy, Lucia's
companion. Godscalc's companion. The dear, gallant person who

had come so far, and had brought Diniz back, and had cared for . . . had been good to a child no one wanted. She was gazing at Godscalc. Then she turned and flapped her hand at Nicholas, and he opened his arms over his head in rejoicing.

Bel, Bel. And accompanying her, the man who had caused all the wretchedness he had now overcome, and could put behind him. Beside Bel, Simon, his father. Simon who, of course, was not (he said) his father and should never be called so; who despised him, and had tried to destroy him, and who was now projecting upon him from his fair, wonderful, golden-haired, untouched person a smile of supreme mocking triumph. He couldn't know. He couldn't know – could he? – whom Nicholas had been hoping to meet, or measure his disappointment. Or perhaps, somehow, he'd guessed. It didn't matter. Nicholas returned the look without fear, or yearning or envy. It had all disappeared, now.

And that was all.

Except for one person.

She was here. She was sitting so quietly, so low, that Nicholas did not at first see her; only he felt he should not look away; he should look past Lucia's anger, David's amusement, Simon's contempt. He felt drawn to look, because the warmth of Bel was not the only warmth in the company. Gelis was there.

Julius said, 'She's come back! The van Borselen girl! Why's she come back?'

Nicholas hardly heard him. He felt someone grasp his arm tightly – Diniz, he afterwards thought – and then release it. He walked forward to the edge of the quay.

Simon said, 'Claes, as I live. Carefully dressed, so I see, by your servants. And Diniz, poor boy. It has all happened, hasn't it, as I suspected? Nicholas followed you. And now you are tied to a dyer's daughter, and he has the Churetty company.'

No one answered. David de Salmeton disembarked, bowing with a slight smile as he passed him. Jannekin bounced ashore, began to talk, and then was dragged off by Gregorio.

Lucia said, 'I am sensible of how much we owe you. However, I must tell you, I cannot forgive you for this.'

'I am sorry,' he said.

'Don't be,' said Bel. 'Is she not beautiful?'

She was beautiful. He had never thought to consider her so, and never cared. He watched Gelis step from the boat, bare-shouldered, her hair in the jewelled coif of a maiden, her body come to perfection within the folds of her gown, the muslin band, the collar of pearls. He gave her his hand as she stepped up beside him. He said, 'I thought it was going to take twenty-five years.'

'It probably will,' Gelis said. 'But I thought I should like to spend them with you.'

He kissed her hand, being unsure what else he might be permitted to do. Someone was trembling. He said, 'Does anyone know?'

The fine brows rose. 'You have changed your mind? Then I have to tell you, Meester Nicholas vander Poele, that I shall take you to law. I have told all these my friends that I am to marry you.'

'You have? Then there is no escape,' Nicholas said. 'I shall have to admit it to my friends as well. Tobie? Gregorio? Julius? Godscalc? Diniz?'

'He simply wishes to tell you,' Gelis said, 'that I made such a very amenable mistress that he has decided to promote me to wife.'

'Nicholas?' Julius said. 'Well, of course. I'm delighted. We all are. But what a damned funny place to propose.'

'I didn't propose,' Nicholas said. 'I accepted.'

It was wrong, since heaven had relented at last, that he should chafe because he never had her alone. First, the extempore intimation to her van Borselen relatives who expressed genuine pleasure, he thought, mixed with equally genuine relief. There, at least, he could stand on the wharf with his arm about her, and his fingers not so still as they appeared, so that her colour came and went, and she smiled. Then she had to go with her family, and he arranged to call, with due solemnity, on the seigneur of Veere.

He visited Louis de Bruges, seigneur of Gruuthuse, as well, and received his measured congratulations, and the excited regard of his wife. He wondered exactly how many people had found occasion to wander about the new wing of the Hôtel Gruuthuse at night.

He talked, perhaps most importantly and at greatest length, with Father Godscalc, alone in his chamber that evening. The priest lay in his chair, his feet propped, his twisted hands on a book. He said, 'I am glad for you.'

'It is against the laws of the Church,' Nicholas said. 'I thought you didn't want it.'

'Katelina and you were not married,' Godscalc answered. 'That was all that concerned me. And more important by far, the girl knows, and has forgiven you. Her struggle has been far greater than yours.'

'I know that,' he said. 'Her struggle sent her to Africa. Without that, she would have hated me still.'

'Did Umar know?' Godscalc said.

'Yes, he knew of it,' Nicholas said. 'It was one of the reasons he sent me home.'

'Sent you?'

'Oh, yes,' Nicholas said.

'And hence your provision for Henry. You and Gelis are agreed about children?' Godscalc said. 'You should have them, and soon.'

'It has been difficult avoiding them,' Nicholas said frankly.

He pulled a deprecatory face, and Godscalc laughed, and covered his hand with his own. 'So all Bruges is aware. The Duke should be as fortunate. So you wish to marry as soon as you may?'

'Sooner,' Nicholas said. 'But I suppose there are rules.'

'They can be stretched,' Godscalc said. 'If you have a friend who knows an amiable bishop.'

'You would help? Do you by any chance know how I love you?' Nicholas said.

'Perhaps you do,' Godscalc said. 'Sometimes love is very close to good planning. It can be whenever you want. Give her some days to prepare.'

'Then will you ask her?' Nicholas said. 'Otherwise she will find herself here tonight, in her travelling clothes, being made wife over your portable altar.'

'She might not mind that,' Godscalc said. 'But it is wise to consider her family. And Tilde and Catherine will, of course, wish for expensive new dresses. I don't think you can afford to get married.'

'That's all right,' Nicholas said. 'I'll save the price of a bishop, and get myself some priest who will do it for nothing. When?'

'And there is your case against St Pol and de Salmeton,' Godscalc said. 'You have to make allowance for that.'

'To hell with making allowance for that. When? When?' Nicholas said.

'Eleven or twelve days,' Godscalc answered.

Twelve days from that moment, having been betrothed at Sluys and married at Damme, the inappropriately attractive English princess called Margaret, aged twenty-two, made her ceremonial entry to Bruges as the third wife of Charles, Duke of Burgundy, dark-natured, autocratic, and nine years her elder.

On the same day, between noon and the jousting, Gelis van Borselen, twenty-three, was engaged to be taken in third marriage also by Nicholas vander Poele, knight and former apprentice, and twenty-seven years of age since the previous December. They were to be united in the palace of Gruuthuse, and the wedding Mass was to be sung in the church of Our Lady adjoining.

It would be brief. The churchmen and noble families of Bruges had much else to occupy them. After, they had made plans to go nowhere but Spangnaerts Street.

The scheme suited both the bride and the groom, who were each of a singular independence of mind, and anyway had, as was widely suspected, no momentous hymen to break. The union, as it were, was an old one.

That said, it was to their credit that, from the moment of their formal betrothal, they observed the proprieties. Godscalc, self-appointed impresario (with Gregorio), was sentimentally entertained by the unaccustomed restraint of the pair: Gelis magnificently housed in the Bruges home of Henry van Borselen; and Nicholas sleeping, or not sleeping, in the excellent Hof Charetty–Niccolò by himself.

Remembering the dusty, indolent, sweetly benevolent harem of the Ma' Dughu, Godscalc smiled. Considering everything, his two strong-minded children were behaving very well. As for their combined past, he knew that Nicholas had sent a message to Umar, through Portinari. It might take six months to reach him, but it would conclude, for Umar too, a long and sometimes troubled wait.

Nicholas and Gelis met in company, naturally enough, every day. Arrangements had to be made. It was not always easy, the English princess having arrived with her fleet at the town's port of Sluys, and the ducal court passing and repassing on its way to the various ceremonies. The future Duchess was to stay there a week. Nevertheless, Henry van Borselen set aside time, and over several days the papers were drawn up which protected Catherine de Charetty and the Bank, while making of Gelis a very rich woman.

She had brought Nicholas a dowry, lodged long ago through the Florentine Monte which took care of such payments. It was not inconsiderable, and she had protested against further settlements. Gregorio, Godscalc thought, would have let her have her way, but Nicholas had been immovable. It was fair. If this was why he had brought back his gold, then he deserved to use it as he wished. It had cost him enough.

The meetings at the Hôtel Vasquez were of a more difficult nature. It was hard for Lucia de St Pol to oppose a marriage between Gelis and Nicholas who had, after all, brought her brother's perfidy to light and had repaired it. He had also repaired the fortunes of Diniz.

Even so, Lucia possessed strong reservations. She did not enjoy the idea of her son being joined in marriage with a daughter of Marian de Charetty, and leading the life of a burgher instead of that of the landowning class he was born to. She explained her objections, and both Nicholas and Diniz were soothing. She could do nothing about it, save complain.

Godscalc guessed, having met many of her kind, that in time she would forgive them. It crossed his mind to wonder what the journey from Scotland had been like, with Lucia and her brother and David de Salmeton confined together in mutual discord. It made him not unhappy.

Simon, staying with the other Scots merchants at Metteneye's, had kept well clear, Godscalc saw, of his sister's family. He had, however, sent his lawyer to register his formal dissent to both unions. He wished to forbid Diniz his nephew to marry a trades-woman's daughter. And he wished to establish the strongest legal and religious objections to the marriage of Claes vander Poele to Gelis van Borselen, orphan sister of Katelina, his poor, deceased wife.

They had expected it. The Vasquez lawyer had already ratified all the papers for Diniz, and nothing his uncle could do would make any difference. Lucia, however resentful, was capable of weighing up the income offered by a small estate in Madeira and comparing it with the yields of the Charetty company, in association with Nicholas. She was far from aiding her brother.

As for the rest, there was only one way Simon could stop Nicholas marrying. Some of them knew what it was. Simon's lawyer, understandably, did not. He did what he could, but was amiably blocked from all quarters. To stop Nicholas marrying, Simon would have had to proclaim himself father to Nicholas. And in proceeding to marry, Nicholas in turn had surrendered that claim.

Godscalc was glad Nicholas had done with it; done with the contention even before this situation arose. For of course, there was no chance whatever that Simon would make such a proclama-tion.

Bel of Cuthilgurdy, who had been silent throughout, afterwards walked into the street with the priest, without holding his arm. Since Tobie came, Godscalc had been made to stop using his crutch, and depend on his limbs. Bel said, 'I hope Simon can afford the fee for his lawyer. You know he's hired him to get back the *Ghost*? What are the chances?'

Since Bel arrived, she had been twice to the Charetty–Niccolò house, and had spent a long time with himself, and with Diniz and Nicholas. She had sat with Tilde, mending a tablecloth.

Godscalc said, 'They keep postponing the hearing. Now Simon and de Salmeton have come, and won't agree to a date.'

'Why should that be?' she said. She stood, gazing upwards. On the street corner before them, a group of men on a platform were rehearsing the marriage of Alexander the Great and Cleopatra.

'I don't know,' Godscalc said. 'Nicholas is high in favour just now. They may be waiting for the Duke to leave Bruges. They may be trying to get hold of our witnesses.'

'Crackbene and Filipe?' Bel said.

Godscalc looked at her. 'How did you know?'

'Filipe came to see me. All happed up in a great hood, poor laddie, but I knew who it was. I havena told anybody. Alexander and Cleopatra,' said Bel reflectively. 'Who were their children, again?'

Godscalc looked down on the top of her head. He said, 'Crackbene seems to have befriended Filipe. Perhaps he was the right sort of man. A seaman, standing no nonsense.'

'I think so,' said Bel. 'I liked what I saw. Although Nicholas had it right, as he usually does. The lad who died had more in him. The lad Lázaro. But this one ran away, and lived to give evidence. Or will, I hope. Ye didna see Simon's boy Henry? He's seven now.'

'No,' said Godscalc. 'I heard you took him north.'

'Part of the way. I come across him now and then, though not if Simon can help it. I was telling Nicholas.'

'And Lucia thinks he's an ogre,' Godscalc said. 'Or so Gregorio says.'

'Yes. It's a pity,' Bel said. 'Another Simon in the making. I'll wager that lot couldn't rear children either.'

'What lot?' Godscalc said.

'Alexander and Cleopatra,' Bel said critically. 'Orgies. Sinister affections of the sensual appetite. Forbye, so far as I can see, they're both men.'

Once, on a sunlit day in September, Nicholas had been surrounded by friends, and had been one of them.

Now, on this dawning day of Sunday, the third day of July nine years later, he stood among friends but was not one of them; as Gelis stood among friends, and was alone.

It had not been as hard as he expected, these twelve days, to keep apart from Gelis van Borselen. Nicholas supposed that she, too, was taking stock of what had gone. He saw in her a certain stillness he had not been aware of before, as if she were coming to the end of a long journey, and were half afraid.

They were to wed that afternoon. The Duke had married that morning, leaving for Damme in the grey dawn at four, and returning after the ceremony to snatch some sleep in the Princenhof, while his wife, in her golden litter, her glittering crown, her surcoat and mantle of pale bridal gold heaped with ermine, set out with her retinue of English and Burgundians to make her dazzling state entry into Bruges.

As a van Borselen, Gelis rode with the retinue. As a merchant and burgher, Nicholas sat his horse knee to knee with a solid phalanx of velvet-dressed personages outside the Holy Cross port, waiting to greet and form a component of the procession

He felt, as he had felt arriving in Bruges, part of a continuity which had to be recognised, no matter how incongruous it might seem. Congruity, today, seemed a little uncertain. The skies above were smoking and curdling and dark, as if concealing a fire. There came, every now and then, a rumour of thunder, and a glimmer of light which made the horse beneath him move, its eye showing white.

Here on the ground, in the torrid warmth of July, there stood assembled the bourgeoisie of Bruges and the noblest blood of Flanders and Burgundy, cumbered with fine furs and expensive, deep velvet. Around every representative group stood sixty hot servants with torches. In the darkness of day they glowed like a burning forest of resinous pines; the dirt of their smoke spiralled to heaven.

During the Mass for the soul of Duke Philip, the lead in the church windows had melted, they said, from the heat of the massed, burning candles. Now, the thunder growled, the horses shifted, and Nicholas felt a sudden pity – for what, he didn't quite know. Perhaps for the small, gleaming, golden train coming towards him, headed by heralds and archers, and followed by the ladies of Margaret of York, mounted on snow-white hackneys or carried in chariots. Followed by Gelis, who saw all this as no being could who had never moved from Bruges or Venice or Florence. Who had never ventured beyond the Sea of Obscurity, and into the Land of the Blacks.

As a Venetian banker, he could have joined the contingent, swathed in vermilion velvet, which waited to lead the merchant colonies. The Florentines stood assembled to follow in black figured satin, led by Tommaso Portinari in the different colours of Duke Charles, whose adviser he was. The Spaniards had produced thirty-four merchants in violet damask; the Genoese numbered 108 and had brought St George with them, and the maiden he saved from the dragon. The Hanse were grey-furred; the Scots followed. Nicholas knew every face.

He had chosen to appear not as a merchant but as a burgher, and so was crammed with the group who stepped out from the Holy Cross port to offer wine and wax to Margaret of York, and beg her to be a gracious lady to their city. Above, from the turrets, musicians sang; and flowers floated into the still, sultry air; and doves, stark white against the black sky, rose in freedom and then, blenching, fled. Fled, because the heated skies, protesting, had opened. Rain, like a wall, fell upon the celebrating city of Bruges.

It put out all the torches. It uncurled the hair of the ladies and gallants, soaked their velvets, draggled their furs, made their costumes attractively transparent. It bounced from the ground in a haze of fine road-layer's mud, and plastered rose petals to the nose and the lash, and made the grand procession through the streets, which stopped at every street corner, into a hissing misery of pantomime smiles and applause tangible as the spray of two thousand involuntary sneezes. There were real sneezes as well.

There was no one there with whom he could laugh. He hadn't seen Gelis pass, for, after the prelates, the men of the town led the procession, followed by the suite of the Duke's half-brother Antony, plastered with forty thousand francs' worth of ruined livery covered with wet golden trees, which signified the theme of the tournament. Next, the musicians. Next, the Duchess. Next, the Knights of the Golden Fleece. Next, the ambassadors. And next, the foreign merchants. It pleased Nicholas to ride so far ahead of Tommaso Portinari.

In front of the Princenhof palace there stood a tableau of St George and St Andrew with two archers, one dispensing Beaune wine, and the other white Rhenish. Beyond them, on a tree, perched a pelican, from whose wounded bosom sprayed an efficient deposit of hippocras. Nicholas thought of John the Baptist and Julius, and wondered if happiness killed, or merely made you insensible.

Everyone went in to dinner. Gelis said, 'I thought we were supposed to be getting married? What did you do to the weather?'

'It's a left-over prayer from Taghaza,' Nicholas said. 'Gelis? Could we consummate our marriage now, and hold it later?'

'We have consummated it,' Gelis said.

'I can't remember,' Nicholas said. 'I think I've forgotten how to do it. What about – '

'What are you doing?' said Julius with exasperation. 'You know you're hours late? You know everyone's waiting? Come on. Or don't you want to be married?'

'Do we?' said Nicholas.

'Well, we'd better,' Gelis said. 'If you've forgotten, someone will have to remind you, or you will have a very odd life.'

The Hôtel Gruuthuse was very quiet, for the great officers were today at the Princenhof. Only Marguerite van Borselen had stayed behind, and a few other faces from the past, Anselm Adorne and his lady among them. The legal hand-fasting was mostly witnessed by his own people: Tobie and Julius, Gregorio and Margot, Astorre and Diniz, Tilde and Catherine, Cristoffels and Henninc and Bonkle.

Melchiorre and Vito were there, and unexpectedly Lucia de St Pol, her arm in that of Bel of Cuthilgurdy. At the last moment, Henry van Borselen came, with his son Wolfaert, to kiss the bride and leave, with whispered apologies. Then the Mass was heard, with Godscalc, shaved, steady, unrecognisable, conducting it.

Then it was over, and his life had changed for ever.

Nicholas embraced his wife. It was the first time, for two months, he had touched her. She said, 'I think you have remembered. What was all this about jousts?'

'That comes later,' he said. 'As from now, we rejoin the ducal wedding and proceed with due care to the marketplace. I've taken a house for us all. We watch them all hit one another. We retire to the Princenhof for the grand Wedding banquet – '

'Ours?' she said.

'No, the Duke's. It's better, and free. And then we go home to bed.'

'The Duke's?' she said.

'Well, you can if you like,' Nicholas said. 'But you'd have some competition. Why not stick with me?'

The rain slackened off for the jousting which, delayed by the entry and dinner, was not ready to start until six. The marketplace, lined with arcades and hung with silk and gold tapestries, was unrecognisable to anyone who hadn't been toiling to make them, while the painted portals at either end and the vast gilded fir in the middle reminded the lieges yet again of the theme of the spectacle. The Tournament of the Tree of Gold was about to begin.

Nicholas, who had leased a whole house for the price of eight camels, was willing to explain it to anybody. 'It happens all the time. Some princess of an unknown isle has proffered favour – '

'What sort of favour?' said Tobie.

'Has proffered top prices at the next wine auction to any knight who will deliver a certain giant, kept in captivity by a dwarf. That's the giant, that's the dwarf, and that's the golden tree the giant's chained to. The participants arrive at the St Christopher end, bang the golden hammer, and issue their spirited challenge.'

'Met by whom?' Gregorio said.

'Are you blind?' Julius said. 'All the challengers are being met by the Bastard Antony.'

'He's forty-seven,' Tobie said. 'I don't see him lasting the pace.'

'He's not bad,' Diniz said.

'Where is he?' Gelis asked.

An immense yellow pavilion rolled on to the lists, propelled by six sweating pages and followed by wild-eyed horses covered with purple velvet and bells. The tent opened, and the Bastard of Burgundy leaped from it, fully armed, on the back of a horse.

'You don't mind,' Nicholas said, 'if I don't actually watch this? I'm expecting some guests.'

Gregorio got up, and so did Diniz and Godscalc. Julius and Astorre and Tobie were already standing.

'Who?' said Gelis sharply.

'It doesn't matter,' Nicholas said. 'It's a sort of wedding present, in a way. A capitulation. An armistice, anyway. Shall we go?'

The door opened as he spoke. Simon de St Pol stood in the entrance. He said, 'I understand you had something to say to me. Some words of apology, might it be?'

'You never know,' Nicholas said. 'I kept a room below. I thought we might talk.'

'Talk?' Simon said. He looked amused, glancing at Gelis.

'Discuss something,' Nicholas said. 'I thought we might get out of the way the whole business of the *Ghost* and the *Fortado*.'

Gelis rose.

'Today? Now?' Simon said. 'What a very silly idea. A proper tribunal will be held in due course. I am quite willing to wait for it. At the moment, I rather think we are expected to celebrate the ducal nuptials. Yours, I prefer not to think of. I hope you will excuse me.'

'I don't mind,' Nicholas said. 'Would you like to take Crackbene's deposition with you? And the boy's? I have copies for Gilles Lomellini and de Salmeton. As a matter of fact, it could be settled in my favour immediately. Save some money, I thought.'

'Crackbene's?' Simon said. He had reopened the door.

'And Filipe, the boy's. They confirm the *Fortado* was selling arms to the black tribes, and attacked my crew and my ship in the Gambia. We all have something to say about the *Doria* as well. The *Ribérac*, I should say. Or the *Ghost*.'

'I don't want to hear,' Simon said. He said it slowly.

'Of course not,' said Nicholas. Outside, to the applause of the crowd, Adolf of Cleves and the Bastard of Burgundy were driving lances at each other. A giant sand-glass on the judge's tribune was half empty.

Nicholas said, 'Of course you don't want to miss all the excitement. I can talk it over quite easily with Lomellini and de Salmeton instead. They should be downstairs by now.'

Simon said, 'You asked them as well?' His gaze lingered on Gelis.

'My wife,' Nicholas said. 'You have met? Yes, I asked them as well. Perhaps you want to come, after all.'

'Why don't we all go?' Gelis said.

The others were waiting below. Summoning them, Nicholas had counted on this: that once they knew their partners were coming, they would prefer not to refuse. In any case, the Lomellini and the Vatachino were allies. Gilles Lomellini, acting for his cousins, rose formally when Nicholas entered the room, but David de Salmeton jumped up smiling and came towards Gelis with his two hands outstretched. 'The bride! My dear, you are blooming!'

In fact she wore the look, alert and somewhat censorious, that Nicholas always liked, and had always mistrusted. She said, 'It's the rain. Have you heard what Nicholas has done?'

'Apart from marrying you?' Smiling still, the long-lashed eyes were observing Simon de St Pol among the group who were entering the room. David de Salmeton said softly, 'What else has he done?'

'Found Michael Crackbene,' Nicholas said. 'Among other things. That's his written statement. Now tell me I don't own the *Ghost*.'

During the hour that they talked, they could have heard, through closed windows, the blare of the trumpets and clarions; the signal that the half-hour of the sand-glass had run; the pause to rearm; the further fanfares and tattoos that announced the next stage of the contest. Within, no one listened, for they were fighting with words.

Nicholas had never thought it would be easy. The *Ghost* had begun life as a ship of Jordan de Ribérac's purloined by Simon, but without Jordan no one could prove it. It had been sailed to Trebizond by Simon's agent and had been captured by the Turks, and had been recaptured and salvaged by Nicholas, who now claimed it as his own.

The court of Trebizond, where all that had happened, had gone. Tobie was there to speak to it, and Astorre, and Godscalc and Julius as well as himself. But he had no independent witness except one.

'Where is Crackbene?' said Simon de St Pol. 'Is this his writing? And if it is, what of it anyway? A man who will change his tune for a fee is worth nothing.'

'He is in Bruges,' Nicholas said. 'He will tell you how we tricked the Turks and brought the *Doria* home. I shall find for you, if I must, some of the merchants we saved.'

'What would they know? Only what you cared to tell them. The truth everyone knows,' Simon said, 'is that you killed Pagano

Doria and stole the ship. And stole it again, when it was in service against the Muslims in Ceuta.'

'And that's a lie,' Julius said. He had interrupted a great deal, not always successfully.

'It is a lie,' Godscalc said. 'I can tell you now that what Nicholas says is the truth.'

'How strange,' Simon said. 'One might almost say you had identical reasons for favouring Nicholas. A share in his wealthy Bank, could it be?'

'There is another fragment of evidence,' Nicholas said. 'I should rather not use it. But it's there. You may like to see it.'

'Written by another member of your Bank?' David de Salmeton said. 'My dear Nicholas, it is all rather incestuous.'

'You may think this even more so,' Nicholas said. 'I think it is rather brave. She wrote it out for me herself, and signed it. An account by Catherine de Charetty of how Pagano Doria died, and what happened afterwards.'

He didn't look at Godscalc, for Godscalc had brought it to him. The only help Catherine could give him, and the most painful for her. For she had sailed on the *Doria* to Trebizond, and had thought, to the end, that Pagano Doria loved her, and had made her his wife.

'Poor child,' said David de Salmeton. 'The sister, is she not, of your fiancée, Senhor Diniz? A brave lie indeed. But it is still true, is it not, that you purloined the *Doria* from Ceuta, and changed her name to the *Ghost*? It is also true that she attacked the *Fortado*, and engaged in illicit trade. I feel for you. I should like to be lenient on your wedding day, but I am afraid that I, too, see no evidence that would hold up in court.'

'One might, perhaps, point out some contradictions,' Nicholas said. 'I did take the *Doria* from Ceuta, but I took what was my own: that is not theft. I did deprive the garrison of her services, but on the other hand I was risking my life to find gold for the Church, and take a mission to Ethiopia. The King of Portugal found no fault with that, nor the Order of Christ, nor the Pope. And what illicit acts did she perform? Crackbene will tell you that she made no attack on the *Fortado* – he is quite positive, I find, on that score. And trading? She sold horses in Grand Canary and took supplies to the Cape Verde islands, after which she returned wholly empty. You have seen that verified for yourselves.'

'There is no case,' said Gilles Lomellini. 'I have listened. There is no evidence to prove you own the *Ghost*.'

'You think not?' Nicholas said. 'Then I shall have to concentrate, shall I not, on the case against the *Fortado*? And that, my dear sirs, is a different matter.'

It was. It depended, he knew, on the professions of Michael Crackbene and the boy. It depended on Melchiorre's evidence – but the very scars on his body would speak for Melchiorre. The other evidence had to come from themselves. But there were seven of them still alive and accessible who had been caught in Raffaelo Doria's trap in a hut on the Gambia, and among them was Gelis, and Bel.

He was aware, as he told the story, that Julius was silent at last, and so were all those who had not been there. Gelis, as she had all along, let him unfold the case in his own way. He ended by describing how Raffaelo Doria had died.

'He was greedy,' Nicholas said. 'So were some of my own men. Gold is a cruel master. But he was ready to kill, even women. I cannot let that pass. He is dead, but you, all three of you, stand responsible for what he did. And the selling of arms is a hanging matter.'

Gilles Lomellini said, 'I do not wish this brought to court.'

Simon flushed. 'What say do you have? Your cousins preferred secret partners. It is for me to say what we do.'

'It is for all of us to say,' said David de Salmeton. 'Messer Simon, you wish to go to law to justify your possession of the *Ghost*, and there I agree with you heartily. If the *Ghost* belongs to the charming Ser Niccolò, then the Vatachino must return his insurance money.'

'So we go to court,' Simon said.

'But,' said David de Salmeton, 'it is not, is it, merely a matter of money? I do not care for what I hear of Raffaelo Doria.'

'They can't prove it,' said Simon.

'But if they could?' de Salmeton said. His eyes were on Nicholas. He said, very softly, 'Messer Simon, I think someone would like you to take this to court. I would remind you that someone has already pointed out that the sale of arms to the natives of Guinea is punishable by death.' He held Nicholas still with his eyes.

Far off, trumpets brayed in a fanfare. A remote voice spoke; there was a roar of acclaim. Music struck up. Gelis was looking at him, her eyes pale and wide.

Nicholas said, 'I brought you here today to listen to you, and so that you could hear what I had to say. And so that, whatever conclusions we reached, they would still remain private to us, and capable of a private solution.'

'A *private* solution?' Simon said. He was frowning. Amid the vanity, the self-interest, perhaps he was coming to reason. Or perhaps not.

Nicholas said, 'The *Ghost* is mine, but I may not be able to prove it in court. The crimes of the *Fortado* are yours, and can be shown to be so. Give me the *Ghost* in free ownership, and I shall absolve you from the deeds of Raffaelo Doria, and forget that you ever sold arms.'

Julius sighed. David de Salmeton said, 'And the insurance money?'

'Repayable to me,' Nicholas said. 'Your partners in the *Fortado* will, I am sure, be persuaded to help you. Gregorio?'

Gregorio rose. The papers he laid on the table were already drawn up, and there were copies for each man.

Nicholas said, 'That is your statement accepting my account of the *Ghost*. And that is mine, absolving you from any harm the *Fortado* caused on that voyage. If you sign, you will hear nothing more.' He didn't add – it didn't matter – that the *Fortado* had sunk.

They signed. Both his cases against them were in fact without flaw. He wondered if Simon would ever realise it.

He should have felt elated, when it was over, and de Salmeton and Lomellini had gone, followed after a moment by Simon who had stopped as if he would speak, and then, with a curious laugh, had departed. He *was* elated, after a bit.

Julius said, 'What were you thinking of? You could have won both these suits!'

'No. He did as he should. It was a day for lenience,' Godscalc said.

'I thought so,' Nicholas said. 'Why has everyone gone? The lists are empty! Have they all killed one another?'

'Don't get excited,' said Tobie. 'They had to stop the tournament to make time for the banquet. If we hurry, we can get there before they start eating. Gelis, how do you like receiving a ship for your morning-gift?'

'It isn't morning yet,' said Nicholas complainingly.

'So she's got it without working for it. And my God,' Tobie said, 'it will be morning by the time they finish this banquet.'

It was three o'clock in the morning when the Duke's wedding feast came to an end, and his guests rose from their places in the great timber hall at the Princenhof, brought there and lovingly laid on his tennis court through the practical labours of Nicholas.

Painted and draped in white and blue wool, hung with tapestries and furnished with cloth-of-gold tablecloths, it had been transformed. Piled with gold in the centre was a buffet containing half the Duke's treasures; the effect, Nicholas thought, was much the same as the Timbuktu-Koy strove to attain. Among the singing, dancing, erupting artefacts had been a dromedary with a genuine black man on its back, dressed like a mountebank.

Gelis had watched it, and then turned. 'Couldn't you stop them doing that?' Beneath a barmican of veiling, her face was pale and her lids extraordinarily heavy: she looked like a piece of elegant sculpture encased for some procession in tinsel. Her ring was so new it caught all the light.

'His name's Jacob,' Nicholas said. 'He's a baptised Mandingua and quite pleased with himself, as it happens; he's never had so much food or attention. The other side of what Umar wanted to show us. The candelabra. What do you think of them?'

'Do you really want to know?' Gelis had said.

'No. And the verse? You did approve of the verse?'

'Of course I approved of the verse. It was the only time you stopped talking. Calm down,' Gelis had said. 'Don't let go all at once.' She sounded on edge.

It was good advice, he supposed. He further supposed that it was the sort of advice the bridegroom should be offering the bride, not the other way round. He had other things he was waiting to tell her. About the land and the pretty house he had bought, or Bonkle for him. About the plans for Spangnaerts Street. If she wished she could live with him in Cyprus. In Alexandria. In Damascus. In a single, small room, with a fountain playing outside. *I want the teachers sprung of your line to help instruct the poor fools sprung of mine. I mean to match you, child for child . . .*

It seemed that, once out of the hall, Tobie and Julius and Gregorio were waiting to escort them both home. Godscalc, less fit than the others, had ridden before them, with Tilde and her sister.

It was not far to go, and the sky above them was paling. They walked, and others walked with them, full of yawning and laughter, dropping aside at their doors with a final bawdy rejoinder. The Duke would be in bed soon, and so would he. They walked up Naalden Straate past the Hof Bladelin, and found themselves still attached to Tommaso Portinari, less than sober and profoundly desirous of company. After two ineffectual attempts to dispose of him, Julius and Tobie took him over, and walked him along to Spangnaerts Street between them.

Bel and Diniz had already gone. She had kissed Nicholas, and he had hugged her in return. In his arms she felt plump again now, and not at all the quiet, suffering woman he had carried to the Joliba. And Diniz, surprisingly, had kissed him as well; a cousinly kiss, full of affection. There was, Nicholas dimly reflected, a lot of affection about him. He was not really standing alone, nor was Gelis. They had been apart for eight weeks.

He began to want, very much, to be with Gelis; and smiled at her. She raised her hand; there was a glint from her ring. The silver stuff of her gown in the half-light looked like a mermaid, a

mirage. He put his arm round her shoulders, and found he was
shaking. He removed it. 'Oh, Jesus!' he said. 'Don't let go all at
once. When we get to the house –'

'Marching orders?' she said. 'When we get to the house, I shall
go upstairs, and you will stay below and sing the lion's song three
times over. You remember the lion? Its song?'

'Shall I ever forget it?' he said. And proved it all along the last,
short street to his house.

> *Bien vienne la belle bergére:*
> *De qui la beauté et maniére . . .*

Julius joined him, and then Tommaso, and Tobie, ending before
his own gates.

> *C'est la source, c'est la miniére,*
> *De nostre force grande et fiére.*
> *C'est nostre paix et asseurance.*
> *Dieu louans de telle aliance,*
> *Crions, chantons, à lie chere,*
> *Bien vienne.*

Gelis went in.

'I have to sing it twice more,' Nicholas said, and began.

'Three times,' Tommaso said. They were trying to turn him
round.

'I've done it once,' Nicholas said. 'Oh, bring him in. Tobie, find
him somewhere to sleep. Father Godscalc?'

They were, at least, inside the door. Godscalc, still in his best
robes, said, 'Bring him in. What are you doing?'

'Singing under my breath,' Nicholas said. 'I have to do it once
more. Well, twice.'

Godscalc laughed. He said, 'You must wish you had less good a
memory. Nicholas. That was well done, today.'

'Which?' Nicholas said. 'The wedding, the Wedding, or the court
case that wasn't?'

'The court case that wasn't,' Godscalc said. 'You are a fine man
when you want to be, Nicholas. And tonight, you deserve your
reward.'

'I'm on the last verse,' Nicholas said. He was already elsewhere
in spirit. No, not in spirit.

Tommaso said, 'I owe you some money.' They had let him
down on the floor, which was clean.

'Never mind,' Nicholas said. 'Tell me tomorrow. Today. *Bien
vienne*, everybody. And its opposite.'

'For the message to Guinea,' said Tommaso Portinari. 'No need
to send it.'

Nicholas turned. He said, 'Oh, damnit, Tommaso. Hasn't it gone?'

'No need to send it,' said Tommaso again. 'Heard the news just this morning from Dei. Remember Dei? Going to Marseilles?'

'What news?' Nicholas said. He perched on the stairs. The others were lounging about. He felt, as yet, slightly puzzled, with only the merest thread of anxiety.

'About the rising,' said Tommaso Portinari. 'You know those damned tribes are always rising? Well, some big black king of some tribe called the Sunny –'

'Songhai,' Nicholas said. No one else spoke.

'– has marched into Timbuktu. Called in by the fool Timbuktu ruler to throw out somebody else. Hackle.'

'Akil,' said Godscalc softly. He came and knelt by the stairs.

'But ended by taking over Timbuktu for himself, and murdering most of the scholars. Some of them escaped to Walata. Hackle helped them. The rest couldn't ride camels.'

He sat, swaying slightly, and confused by the silence.

Nicholas said, 'You didn't send my message to Walata?'

'Ibn Said's all right,' Tommaso said. 'It's the other one, the one you sent the message to. That one is dead. And his wife. And all but one of his children.' He stopped swaying. 'I'm sorry. You liked him.'

'Umar?' Nicholas said.

'The one you call Umar. Loppe. The Negro you had. He's dead,' Tommaso said.

It was cold on the stairs. Tommaso had gone. Everyone had gone but Father Godscalc. Nicholas said, 'He said he was going to Walata. He needed the camels. But they couldn't have got out in time.'

Godscalc tightened his hand on his shoulder.

Nicholas said, 'I told you. He sent me home.'

After a while, Godscalc said, 'Go up to her.'

She had probably been in bed a long time. The silver stuff was properly folded: she must have dropped it at first; and then, when he didn't come, she had got out and smoothed it. Her hair was loose, and her breasts were bare where the sheet crossed them, and he could see the line of her body below. Her eyes were deep in shadow.

She had put the lamp out; he could smell warm oil, and the scent she liked to use best, and the smell of her skin. Of herself. The low light through the window was blue. He opened the casement.

She said, 'Who was below?' Her voice was hoarse.

He said, 'No one. Tommaso.'

It was light enough to see, vaguely, the colour of the small, speckled bricks on the opposite wall, and the grey and purple and green of the slates on all the roof-tops beyond, and the red of the pantiles and even, somewhere, a flashing light reflected from water. It was fresher than yesterday, with no thunder anywhere. No lions. *Bien vienne.*

She said, 'Come and sit.'

He would have to burden her with it. Of all people, she knew Umar; knew what he had done; what he was; what he meant. To be told was her due. He did not want, nor would she, words of comfort. He turned and, walking slowly, moved to the bed and sat on it.

She had turned the sheet down and lay, her fine hair spread about and around her. He let his eyes rest on her night-shadowed face, and wondered how tired she was, and how to tell her. He took her hands, which lay on her thighs, and were cold. She said, 'Nicholas? Look at my belly.'

His thoughts, already in pieces, made no sense of that. She hadn't smiled or made a luxurious movement, only surrendered her hands. He had not thought to look at her body from the moment he had brought himself to come in. He said, 'Why?'

'Because it is six weeks full of a child,' Gelis said.

There was no alteration in her position or face; only her voice was still hoarse. 'Ours?' he said, because it would have been strange to say nothing.

'Six weeks,' she repeated. She said it tersely, as if he had annoyed her.

Then he brought all his thoughts together, and looked at her body.

The changes, so early, were small, but plain to a lover. He sat still, until he could breathe. 'Whose?' he said. Even then, his mind did not travel.

She said, 'Guess. What would truly, truly, avenge Katelina and her son at long last?'

He gazed at her, and through her.

Godscalc's hand, resting broken in his. A man, coming out of the desert, leading five camels. The sound of a voice, raised in pure, heartfelt love and praise and selfless wonder at the joy and mystery of the world.

Nicholas raised his hand and struck her once, on the cheek, as he would have cuffed an ill-mannered pup. Then he rose, and walked to the door.

She raised her voice as he went, not quite shouting, but making sure that he heard. 'It's Simon's child, Nicholas. What shall I do with it? Kill it? Rear it? Tell Simon about it? Or let the world think it's yours? Tell me! Whatever you want, I shall do it!' He closed the door on her voice.

He had thought there was no one in this wing. He stood at some window, and only became aware after a while that a man was quietly waiting; had been there perhaps for a long time. He experienced a fear, like a physical pain, that it was Godscalc. It was Gregorio.

Nicholas said, 'Did you hear?'

'Yes,' said the lawyer.

After a while, Nicholas said, 'What do they say? *Allah alone is the conqueror.*'

Gregorio said, 'Will you let me deal with it?'

'*Deal* with it?' Nicholas said.

'Send her away. See that the child, discreetly born, is well fostered. Arrange for your marriage to end. There is a rumour of plague. She could leave Bruges tomorrow, and you also.'

Nicholas said, 'His name is Sunni Ali, King of the Songhai. How could you deal with it?'

Gregorio said, 'God forgive me . . . Nicholas, you cannot go back. All you knew in Timbuktu is dead and gone.'

'What else is there?' Nicholas said. *Zuhra had covered herself.*

'What you brought back,' said Gregorio. 'You will find it again.' His voice was filled with compassion. The first of many voices.

'Of course,' Nicholas said. 'Then you will deal with all this? Or no. I am quite capable of dealing with it myself. No divorce. I like being married. I seem to have some new business I ought to attend to in the north. Gelis can retire to her cousins at Veere. Let it appear a legitimate child. If Simon can rear one, so can I.'

Was it quick for the babies — for him? Or was it stab upon stab upon stab?

'She is too young to hate,' Gregorio said.

'But she does,' Nicholas said. 'Or she thinks that she does.'

'She doesn't know what the word means.'

A NOTE ABOUT THE AUTHOR

Dorothy Dunnett was born in Dunfermline, Scotland, in 1923.
She is the author of the Francis Crawford of Lymond novels, a historical
sequence set in the sixteenth century; seven mystery novels; *King Hereafter,*
an epic novel about Macbeth; *The Scottish Highlands,* a book of
photographs by David Paterson, for which she wrote the text in
collaboration with her husband, Alastair Dunnett; and three earlier
Niccolò novels. In 1992, Queen Elizabeth appointed her an Officer of the
Order of the British Empire. Mrs. Dunnett lives with
her husband in Edinburgh, Scotland.

A NOTE ON THE TYPE

The text of this book was set in a digitized version of Imprint,
a Monotype face originally cut in 1913 for the periodical of the same name.
It was modeled on Caslon, but has a larger x-height and different
italics, which harmonize better with the roman.

Composed in Great Britain
Printed and bound by The Haddon Craftsmen,
Scranton, Pennsylvania